Manda Scott is the internationally b...
Boudica series and the Rome ser...
Her 2018 Second World War thrill...
the McIlvanney Prize for Best Sco...
shortlisted for the Orange Prize, an...
and has been translated into over twenty languages. She teaches
contemporary shamanic practice, is host of the Accidental Gods
podcast and co-creator of the Thrutopia Masterclass. She lives with
her wife on a smallholding in the borderlands between England and
Wales. @mandascott

Praise for *Any Human Power*:

'Instantly immersive and compelling, rich and strange, human and
humane, and most of all inspiring... an extraordinary story'
Lee Child, author of the Jack Reacher series

'Manda Scott is an unmissable, visionary author and has created a
compelling political thriller that inspires belief in the possibility of a
better future. Born of dreams, *Any Human Power* is a dream read'
Adam Hamdy, author of *The Other Side of Night*

'There are many ways that we could create the better world that we
want. This bold and thrilling vision is one of them'
Anthea Lawson, author of *The Entangled Activist*

'A hugely entertaining read with compelling characters, elegant prose
and a story where we really want to find out what happens'
Fantasy Hive

'A polemical thriller like no other, an absorbing manifesto to change
the world. It constantly surprises. Manda Scott's characters play
havoc with your emotions, her narrative keeps you turning the
pages, and her ideas might just change your life'
Andrew Taylor, author of *The Shadows of London*

'*Any Human Power* has the feel of a book that's landed at just the right moment... Scott's imagination has brought forth a radical manifesto, a holistic ideal in which seeing oneself in relation to eternity matters just as much as housing or transport policies, and she's done it in a way that makes it seem as though it's only five minutes in the future'

Herald

'A taut political eco-thriller... I would recommend this to anyone who is a fan of Ursula Le Guin, speculative fiction in general or concerned about the current global situation'

British Fantasy Society

'An astonishing novel, at once powerfully contemporary and mythopoeic. Of its many achievements, the greatest is giving a sense that there is a way forward from our current predicament: the creative gift of hope'

Oliver Harris, author of *The Shame Archive*

'It's wonderful. One of the many amazing things about it is the way Scott writes from both right and left brain at once. Super-high-tech and ancient, intuitive wisdom seamlessly interwoven. The spiritual and political as one'

Dr Jenny Goodman, author of *Getting Healthy in Toxic Times*

'Hopeful, engaging, heartfelt, imaginative'

Rozie Apps, editor of *Permaculture Magazine*

'Descrying the thin path between populist rage and static social decay is the great problem of our times. Without lights like Manda Scott and her blessed book, we would certainly fall'

Glen Weyl, economist and co-author of *Radical Markets*

'Manda Scott will change your mind with this visionary novel'

Audrey Tang, free software developer,
politician and author of *Plurality*

MANDA SCOTT

ANY

HUMAN

POWER

Also by Manda Scott

Kellen Stewart
Hen's Teeth
Night Mares
Stronger Than Death

Boudica
Dreaming the Eagle
Dreaming the Bull
Dreaming the Hound
Dreaming the Serpent Spear

Inès Picaut
Into The Fire
A Treachery of Spies

Rome
The Emperor's Spy
The Coming of the King
The Eagle of the Twelfth
The Art of War

Stand-alone novels
No Good Deed
The Crystal Skull

Non-fiction
2012: Everything You Need to Know
about the Apocalypse

1 3 5 7 9 10 8 6 4 2

First published in 2024 by September Publishing
This paperback edition published by September in 2025

September, an imprint of Duckworth Books Ltd
1 Golden Court, Richmond, TW9 1EU, United Kingdom
www.septemberpublishing.org
www.duckworthbooks.co.uk

For bulk and special sales please contact
info@duckworthbooks.com

Typeset by RefineCatch Limited, www.refinecatch.com

Printed and bound in Great Britain by Clays Ltd

ISBN 9781914613692
Ebook ISBN 9781914613579

*We live in capitalism. Its power seems inescapable –
but then so did the divine right of kings. Any human
power can be resisted and changed by human beings.
Resistance and change often begin in art. Very often in
our art, the art of words.*

– Ursula K. Le Guin, Speech to the National Book
Awards, 2014

This book is dedicated to generations who lived before us and to those yet unborn, that the wisdom of both may inform the present.

Book One

— THE PROMISE —

Just because you die, doesn't mean you get to be wise.
— Chris Luttichau

PROLOGUE

February 2008

A grey midweek afternoon; raining, warm for the time of year.

The crow stoops straight out of the sun, spears into cloud and is lost for a while. It emerges into the kind of dreich drizzle that makes an umbrella seem like overkill, but still keeps the wipers moving intermittently on a stream of ambulances lining up outside the hospital below.

The hospital is the crow's target, specifically, a single occupancy room on the third floor with a west-facing window outside which stands an ash tree, skeletoned by winter and sagging under a week's weight of rain.

A final sweep brings the crow to rest in the tree's crown. From here it skip-hops down to a long branch that has grown parallel to the window ledge, close enough to see in to the solitary bed. The branch is a perfect diameter for a long sit: nine days and nine nights in winter weather. Nine, the number of Odin, and thrice three, the number of Bride, both of them deities of death, birth and battle.

Time is what we make of it, and this crow is the very embodiment of patience. Only slightly grumpy, it hunches its shoulders, sidles closer to the tree's trunk and settles in to wait.

Presently, a new occupant is brought into the room and installed in the bed: Alanna Penhaligon, sixty-two years old, grey-haired, and not known, if we're honest, for her patience.

CHAPTER ONE

Nine days later

'Lan?'

Finn tapped lightly on my arm. His gaze sought mine, which was odd enough for me to meet it.

'When you come home,' he said, 'can we—'

I thought I hadn't moved, but one eyebrow must have risen a hair's breadth because he bit off the rest of the sentence and his gaze skittered sideways to the ash beyond the window and the crow that waited there.

It was a patient crow. It had been waiting for days. I thought perhaps there was more than one and they were rotating in shifts, just as Finn was doing with his mother. He was very nearly fifteen by then, which was plenty old enough, apparently, for Maddie to leave him at my bedside, watching while I drifted off to a seashore, somewhere he'd never been . . .

It was a wild place, that shore, with rocks and fierce waves and—

Another tap, braver. 'Can we go to sit on the hill at dusk and watch the crows going to bed?'

Clever boy. He'd lived with me long enough to know that if I were given a choice of what to do with any free evening, I'd climb up to the hillside above the farm and sit for an hour or so watching the crows settle in for the night.

So, on every level, that was a smart question, not least because it wasn't remotely what he'd been going to ask before my blasted eyebrow twitched. He'd had his World of Warcraft face on, the slightly-not-here look that meant at least half of him was away killing Orcs in the digital landscapes of Azeroth.

I didn't think anyone else recognised that look. It was our secret.

4

Sixty-two-year-old grandmothers aren't supposed to play World of Warcraft. Teenagers are, although their mothers have a tendency to impose curfews and restrictions and would be aghast if they knew the ease with which both were circumvented.

Finn's mother in particular would have had screaming kittens if she'd known who was helping him do the circumventing, but he'd left home and moved in with Kate and me by then, working through the teenaged angst of a fatherless boy. We were in Suffolk and Maddie was in Scotland and he could have been dealing drugs or crashing motorbikes and she wouldn't have been any the wiser. Warcraft seemed a pretty tame option, all things considered.

I didn't introduce him to the game, I swear. It was just that when we needed a way to bond with the twelve-year-old who had called us out of the blue from Cambridge train station one evening late in October of 2005, it seemed useful to let him draw me deeper into his latest addiction.

He was brilliant and I was not, but as the years progressed, he stayed true to the partnership we built. We were never, therefore, in the top percentile, but good enough to join a solid ten-player team to fight in the player vs player battlegrounds and make the kinds of friendships that grow out of saving each other's (digital) lives.

We joined a guild called ReadyCheck and helped them organise server tournaments once a month where the best teams could slug it out for rankings on a clunky website that Finn set up to collate all the scores. And that was us: both addicted, both having fun, and definitely bonded.

And now my co-conspirator had his tournament look on. He'd been desperate to play since an Orc Warlock had vaporised him near the end of last month's final match. A month's a long time though. Things had changed. Crows, for instance, had come to sit in the tree outside—

'Lan?' He was still looking straight at me. I thought, in fact, he'd fixed his focus on the place between my brows, so it could seem as if he were making eye contact without actually having to do it, but even this was pretty good.

And because he was trying, and because the crow was not going to be patient forever, and because today was ... what it was, I nodded for water and when he supported my head with one hand and dribbled it off the spoon into my mouth with the other, I saved enough to let some words flow.

'Finn, my love, I'm dying. There is no coming home from here. You know this.'

I'd been right about the between-the-brows thing because now his gaze snapped tight to mine and the feeling was quite different. His face had gone blank, a shield covering a shatteration of feeling. Except, of course, it didn't cover anything.

'Hey.' I tapped his arm as he had tapped mine. 'We've been talking about this for months. It's fine. Dying happens to all of us. I just get to know when.'

Soon, obviously, but I didn't need to belabour things. Not when I could see the crow in the fat shine of a tear when before I'd had to move my arm to get the drip bag to swing clockwise about five degrees and hope to catch the reflection on the backswing. Or wait for the particular nurse who understood these things. Nancy. She had a mirror that made crow magic. She was off shift by now, which was sad. I didn't think there was time left to say good—

'What happens, Lan? When you die?' He was using words to draw me back to the room: always was a clever lad.

'No idea.'

'Lan, it's your *job*.'

Well, yes. And, ironically – one could even say arrogantly and stupidly – I really had thought I was up to speed with all the possibilities of this. What I had lately discovered was the ocean of difference separating a lifetime's academic exploration of existing and historical indigenous cultural beliefs concerning the metaphysics of death . . . and the actual lived (sorry) experience of it.

My thinking had become significantly more specific in the months since an oncology registrar who looked as if she'd had no sleep for weeks fixed her gaze on her notes and said I had multiple myeloma and while this wasn't amenable to surgery I could have chemo if I wanted (I didn't) but perhaps not to plan too far ahead. So, I'd had time to consider the implications with more personal interest than I'd ever done before, but there were still way more gaps than certainties.

I was fairly confident the shoreline that kept nudging into my awareness was the Between, the transition zone said to link the lands of life to the lands of death. The Tibetan Book of the Dead names this place as one of the six Bardos. Other cultures have other names, and we all have different landscapes. You might see it differently when your time comes: a forest leading into a meadow, maybe, or the boundary of a treeline high on a hill, a riverbank, a desert oasis: what matters is the edge-ness of this place, and that it calls to you.

I have always loved wild seas: there's something captivating about the sharpness of fierce, salted air, the feel of it whisking your hair and the way the sun shines across the water, so bright, so straight, like a roadway to the skies.

Without exception, everyone I'd ever spoken to had said to go towards the light. The sun was the brightest thing I'd ever seen and I could feel its pull more strongly with every passing heartbeat.

Everyone had said, too, that the people gathered there would be the ones I'd trust most to guide me on the next phase of the journey. I was waiting for Kate, but so far I'd only heard Robbie.

It made a kind of sense. He'd been dead for decades when she'd only beaten me to the finish line by a handful of months, so (perhaps? One of the bigger unknowns) he'd had more time to get to know the landscape on the other side of the line and knew his way back to the borderlands.

Also, we'd known each other longer, which may have counted for something. Robbie was the first deep, true friend of my adult life, the first person I came out to, and he to me; the first one I could talk to about the things that mattered. We met over a Bunsen burner in the biochemistry lab and each recognised a kindred spark in the other, for all that he was a bishop's son and I was a farmers' daughter. We were both only children, which had its own stigma in those days, and the rest was too near the surface for it not to flash like a Belisha beacon.

We became each other's shadows, talking, talking, talking, letting out all the words we'd held inside for what felt like forever. Everyone thought we were an item, so when some idiot drunk ran him over on Christmas Eve, the bishop invited me down to Taunton for the funeral early in the new year.

I took the train into what Robbie had always called Enemy Territory and I had always thought was an exaggeration. I was

Scottish and young and while he had said often enough that the English upper classes considered overt displays of emotion to be on a par with public sex, I hadn't understood – until I stood weeping among a host of black-garbed, stone-eyed Anglicans and felt their disdain burn acid on my soul.

Only his cousin was different: Connor, the Irish one, who was training to be a priest, but kept a low profile at the funeral because the Reformation wasn't that long ago in their scale of things, and a man displaying Papist affinities ranked lower than a woman displaying emotion. He had riotous black hair, longer than mine, and wore a black linen jacket that almost hid his collar. I was amazed they'd let him come.

We found each other in the shadows where their scorn couldn't reach, and so, at last, I had someone I could ask the question that burned inside. 'Where is he now? What happens next?'

'Oh, Lan . . .' Connor cradled me close. He was bigger than Robbie, a grand, wild oak of a man with a soft Galway voice. He smelled of woodsmoke and hot iron and the sheer strength of him held me whole. 'Do you want what my brethren would tell you? Or the bishop?'

I laughed snot onto his beautiful jacket. 'Hardly.'

'Good. Because if I know anything, it's that both sides have lost all sense of the truth somewhere in these past two thousand years.'

'Someone must know.' Indignation felt sharp and hot and good.

'I would like to think so. Just not anyone here.' Holding me out at arm's length, he thumbed the tears from my chin, then drew me in and planted a chaste kiss on the crown of my head. 'Maybe you could find out, eh? Go find the people who have the knowing and then bring it back to those who have forgotten. That would be a grand and lovely service to the world. A good remembrance for Robbie.'

I explored the idea, searching all its hidden angles and found none I didn't like. 'I could prove the bishop wrong.'

'You could publish whole papers proving him wrong.' When Connor grinned, I could see his cousin in him, and something older, like a wild Irish hero, come down from the hills. 'That would be bold.'

In the Ireland that suffered under the yoke of England, being 'bold' was seriously bad. When the Republic recovered itself, bold became exceptionally good.

I grinned back at him, feeling my face stretch with the strangeness of it. 'It would, wouldn't it?'

We skipped breakfast the next morning and shared a taxi to the train station. Connor headed west, for the ferry to Dún Laoghaire. I travelled straight back to Cambridge, where I ditched a medical degree for anthropology: the whole of my life's trajectory redirected by the power of death, and a five-minute conversation with a man whose voice had melted my bones.

I had my one big question – what happens next? – and spent the best part of the next four decades asking it of people who might reasonably be expected to provide an answer. Among the clutter of cultural overlays, they all said more or less the same three things:

First: those whom we had loved in life and who had loved us in return (unrequited crushes didn't count) would come to guide us from the lands of life to the lands of death;

Second: it mattered a great deal to make this crossing with full awareness of who and where we were. In their eyes, the Western habit of medicalising death was no saner than our habit of medicalising birth, and both were evidence of cultural insanity;

Third: it wasn't a good idea to hang around in the Between. Bad things happened if the dead didn't get on with being dead and instead hung around to tread on the toes of the living.

I did not plan to hang around: this, I will swear this on whatever you can find that we both hold sacred.

I planned to step consciously into death, and believed I knew how. I had, in fact, been practising every night for several decades on the instructions of my earliest teacher, a young Mongolian woman who had taught me that our dreams were a practice ground for being dead and anyone with sense would use the experience they offered to good effect.

Her name was Uuriintuya, which meant something like Shining Dawn, and I met her when I was a new postgrad, too young to know that real academics observed their subjects but didn't (absolutely did not, under pain of excommunication from the ivory tower) practise the things they so meticulously recorded.

With the optimism of youth, I'd managed to pull in some grant money for six months in the Mongolian Steppe, and then on the second day, embodying the noun too literally, I stumbled getting out of the Land Rover and broke my ankle.

Uuri was six years older than me in actual years, and several centuries in wisdom. She had dreamed both my coming and my fracture far enough in advance to have ordered a pair of Western-style crutches and some plaster of Paris, neither of which were a normal part of her healing repertoire.

She offered to fix me, and I accepted without asking what 'fix' actually meant, although, to be honest, if she'd spelled it out in words of one syllable I would not have understood.

When I considered them at all, I thought dreams were night-time neuronal twitches that gave rise to a Jungian jungle of hidden metaphors and were generally best ignored. In Uuri's world, by contrast, dreaming was a deliberate act undertaken to shift someone from the mundane world to the land of the gods, guides and spirits, in order to ask for help. It could be practised while awake or asleep and was as essential to life as eating and drinking. The children of her people learned the basics around the time they learned to talk.

This being the case, it took a while before she realised I couldn't remember my dreams. The moment when she did so was ... memorable.

When she calmed down enough for us to talk, she was genuinely aghast that I had survived into my early twenties without understanding – without practising nightly – the essential fact of life: to wit, that if I could remember my name and state while asleep (I am Alanna Penhaligon and I am asleep) then I could do the same when newly dead and thus make a swift crossing to the Lands of the Dead; this last being fundamental to the welfare not only of the dead person themselves, but for the whole of their community.

I didn't believe either that this was possible or necessary. We argued. I lost. As punishment (she called it education), she held me in a state of grit-eyed exhaustion for the next nine days, waking me whenever I fell asleep and making me tell her what I'd been dreaming.

When I had provided dreams colourful enough to keep her happy, she moved on to gaining awareness within the dream: look at your feet, look at your hand, look at the sun and the moon and the horses and the eagles and anything else that arises both in waking and in your dreams and ask yourself, 'Am I dreaming?'

If in doubt, write your name, look away and look back at it again. If you can still read it, you're either not dreaming or have been practising this a long, long time. No danger of this in my case; it took me a decade just to reliably remember my name. I am Alanna Penhaligon and I am asleep is fine when you're actually awake, but it's a lot harder than it sounds when you're not.

Anyway, in Uuri's theory, when you've got this nailed, you can begin to interact with a series of progressively more dangerous spirits, guides and gods with whom you can develop reciprocal relationships. The reciprocity is crucial, and there is a whole other curriculum that teaches what each god, guide or spirit values so you can offer the appropriate gift. I learned this on my third trip out, about a decade later, when she deemed me sufficiently adept to make use of it safely.

This first round of education spanned the length of time it took for a fractured talus to heal, plus extra for suppuration that I'm pretty sure wouldn't have happened if I'd been smarter. In the end, though, I had remembered my own name well enough through the length of one long night to find a guide of whom I could ask the question I had memorised, and to which I could not possibly have known the answer. The response I brought back into the waking world was proof that the whole thing hadn't been a fake.

None of this was reliable, or even necessarily repeatable, but good enough that Uuri deemed me safe to let loose back into the world. There were five-year-olds in her family more proficient, but they weren't expected to survive in a culture where the mere concept was career kryptonite.

I was and I did. The trip flipped some inner gate from not-knowing what real academics thought or said or did to not-caring, except I was careful who I spoke to thereafter, and even more careful who I chose as teachers (aka 'research subjects').

I taught the kids, too. Correction, I taught Kate about six months after we met, when it was clear she wouldn't either leave or have me sectioned, and then I taught Maddie when she was old enough to walk away if she didn't like it.

With her blessing, I tried to teach her children as they came along. Kirsten got it the best. Niall the least, Finn somewhere in between. I never found the right incentives. 'You'll be glad you can hold on to a clear sense of self when you're dying' doesn't have a whole lot of traction with the under-tens.

It's true, though. Lying on the hospital bed in Addenbrookes, Cambridge (the original one in East Anglia, England, not any of the copies around the world), in those last days with my tongue turned to boot leather and my joints filled with fire ants and every breath a labour, I could hear Uuri in my head, her voice dry as the skull of the Steppe eagle that spun on its thread over the fire. 'Every night you walk through the lands of the dream. If you can remember who you are from dusk until dawn, you will remember it, too, when the final night comes. Knowing who you are is what lets you walk clearly into the sun.'

So, with the dusk of this final night approaching, I walked along the wild sea's shore, watching the edge places where sea met land and land met sky and looked at my hands, my feet, the crow sitting high in a tree on the headland and kept on telling myself, I am Alanna Penhaligon and I am—

'Lan?'

What?

'Lan, don't go!'

Finn.

It was like a tightrope, my name: a thing to walk along from one high place to another and never mind the drop beneath. Never did like heights.

'Lan, you need to tell me about dying. What happens. What it's all about. Nobody else will.'

Not true. Maddie would do her best. We'd had a lot of conversations about death these past few months since she'd come down from Glasgow to take care of Finn. By December, she was pretty clear on the basics and she wasn't shy of broaching the topic with the medics who had a thousand euphemisms for passing over or passing on and jolted as if she'd stabbed them with a cattle prod when she cut through the mess and spoke the word 'death' aloud.

I was proud of her, truly. We'd done a good job of rearing her, Kate and me. She was—

'Lan, *please*.'

A rope walk. One step after another, inch by inch, back to this boy who holds my heart in his hand. Thing is, I'm not enjoying the whole physicality of living right now. Breathing hurts. My mouth is an ashcan and—

'*Lan!*' Ouch, that was sharp. He was never a sharp lad, Finn; too kind-hearted and decent. Should have called him Robbie, but it wasn't my say and Maddie wanted to honour his Irish ancestry, so—

I'm back. Let me focus a moment. One . . . two . . . three . . .

Finn's gaze pounced on mine, grab-holding me in the place where he was real. His eyes were deep brown, slow-moving, like a mountain river. I could have drowned in them then, but he wanted me present, so I focused instead on the rest of him, the bits that were less of Maddie and more of his father.

Eriq Karim was Moroccan and he may not have hung around long after the thrusts of fatherhood, but he gave Finn his beautiful, smoothly olive cheeks and his thick, blue-black hair drawn back in a high ponytail so that it seemed short from in front. His was a face made to soak in the sun, but it was the middle of winter, so he looked a bit sallow.

I love him so very much.

Hard to stare at him for long, though; staring hurt. And his face kept swinging in and out of focus in a way that left me feeling sick. I let my gaze drift past his face and shifted my arm to move the saline drip bag the few degrees necessary to see out of the window. The sun had moved. The crow had not.

It was a crow I had asked for help in that first dream walk with Uuri. She'd called it a Crow and I was pretty sure what waited outside my window was a Crow, too. Certainly, there was a sharpness to its gaze that helped me think.

I nodded for water and on its wetness asked, 'How long was I—?' I couldn't think of the word. Gone wasn't right. Nor dead.

'Away?' Finn offered. I nodded. Without checking his watch, he said, 'Nine minutes, six seconds, forty-fi—'

I tapped. He stopped. I smiled, and said, 'Still here.'

The Crow scattered in a falling tear. Cold fingers cramped on my arm. 'Don't leave me.'

'Everyone dies, Finn.'

'But what happens after?'

'Honestly, I don't know.' So many ideas. So many ways of distracting ourselves from this one question and the absence of its answer. 'I've left you my notebooks, did I tell you?'

Obviously not. Five full shelves in the library. 'All yours.'

'I won't understand them if you're not there.'

Ha! He wasn't much practised at flattery, but that was a valiant effort. Spitless, I mouthed, 'Nice try!'

'Lan . . .' He was crying harder now. 'Please don't go. I need you. Nobody else . . .'

Understood him. This was true. They tried, honestly they did; they just didn't always succeed. I wasn't sure I did, but I got closer than most. We were too alike, Finn and me. I had no idea how this happened when we didn't share any actual genetic material, but nurture had won out over nature, at least for us. It's one of the reasons he'd come to live with his crazy grandmothers in a slant-walled Tudor farmhouse with angry ghosts in the living room, instead of a perfectly nice cottage in the hills north of Glasgow with his perfectly sane mother. I didn't think he'd—

'Lan.' His fingers made dents in my arm, as if he could pin me to life by sheer physical force.

Something moved outside the window. Finn's gaze shifted right. A thousand crows reflected in his eyes.

One. There was just the one Crow. I could feel its presence like a promise of things to come, and behind it I could hear the sea. Someone was calling my name. Not Kate, yet. Robbie. '*Alaaaaana!*' The vowels echoed over the surf. Too many vowels. Maybe next life, I might have more consonants.

No drifting now. The Between was as real as Finn: more so. I could feel the sea, taste the salt spray on my cheek. Along the shoreline, I could see the incandescent sun. Its pull was undeniable.

'Finn, love. I'm going.'

Panic lit his eyes. He half-rose. 'I'll get Mum.'

I put my hand over his. 'There's not time.'

'Let me text her.' He thumbed out a single letter. They must have set up a code. Maddie was going to be late, but we'd said our goodbyes a dozen times those past few months, no need to belabour things now.

Finn's eyes didn't leave my face. Tears pooled along his lower lids. 'Lan.' His voice was thin.

Mine was surprisingly robust. 'Still here.'

'I don't want to live in a world with you not in it.'

'You'd better get used to the idea or—'

Blast. His face. His eyes.

'Finn . . .' My mouth was full of sawdust and this time it wasn't the fucked-up cells fucking up my metabolism that was robbing me of fluid, it was naked panic.

I created spit by sheer power of will. 'I'm not leaving you. Trust me. I have no idea what comes next, truly I don't. But if you need me, you can call. If it's at all possible, if it's in my power in any way, I'll come to you. I promise.'

I promise.

I promise?

Alanna Penhaligon, what have you done?

Yggdrasil stood stark outside the window. A Crow waited among its branches to guide me onward. And I had just uttered an oath. A vow. A *Promise*.

There was a dead hush in which the world halted in its turning, and the gods rested their labours to peer through the veil into the realms of mortal stupidity.

Far away on another shore, Robbie, faintly alarmed, said, 'Lan?'

We'd spent a lot of our time together, Finn and I, wading through the old myths, exploring the power of words. When I opened my eyes that last time, he smiled down at me. 'I am going to hold you to that,' he said.

I drowned in his gaze.

15

CHAPTER TWO

The sea was wild and beautiful. A million shifting shades shimmered through it, sharper than I had ever known. I was entranced. Siren voices tried to lure me back to the world I had left. I ignored them all.

Except for one. In the valleys between the waves and the keening wind, sharp words landed somewhere yet undefended, '. . . do *not* get to die without my being here. And if you'll have the grace to hang on about five more minutes. The twins are nearly . . .'

Maddie. You made it! I wasn't trying to leave without you, I just didn't want to make trouble.

Sorry.

Maddie was Finn's mother, Kate's daughter by Connor, who'd understood the value of a father who was around when we needed him, but not always on top of us.

Maddie was the first human being I had ever loved absolutely unconditionally. Adult relationships are always complicated, but I'd caught Maddie as she came into the world and between us, me and Kate, we'd—

Kate.

Kaaaaaaaate!

I'd really believed she'd be here by now; one of the upsides to dying was imagining the conversations we could have when we met again. Not the frustrating wool-world of her final eighteen months, but actual, honest-to-goodness words that meant the same thing to each of us. And hugs: I wanted to hold her, to be held, to feel the purpose in her strong sculptor's hands, to smell the scent of planed wood in her hair.

Kate, love, I am on my way, but our daughter is making a point and I need to gather what is left of my attention and wrench it one last time to the place I am leaving.

'. . . text. Two more minutes and you can go. We're not going to drag you back. You asked us not to. I'm hoping that's still what you want.'

I squeezed the hand wrapped in mine and Maddie squeezed back. A last goodbye. I love you, but I have to go now. It's fine. Truly. I wish I could tell you how fine it really is. Kate had the sketches ready for a piece that was going to show my ideas of the Between, so the whole world could know how fine, and—

Oh! The twins made it, too! Kirsten and Niall, Maddie's chalk-and-cheese firstborns. Kirsten was ash-blonde and willowy: her father's colouring, her mother's shape and style. Niall harked back to Connor, his grandfather, so his hair was as dark as mine, though the curls were much tighter.

He was a hand's breadth taller than his sister, his features were square rather than elfin, and he was fiercely vocal in his opinions, where she spoke rarely, without rancour and always to keep the peace. People thought they were not alike, and they were wrong. They thought as one mind, these two, and time spent apart pained them both.

Seven years older than Finn, they had lives of their own up in Scotland. I hadn't expected them to come all the way down to Suffolk but was really pleased they had. I tried to thank them. The best I could manage was another squeeze.

Maddie said, 'She says hello.'

'Hello, Lan.'

'Thank you for holding on.'

They spoke together and then separated. On one side, Kirsten looped her fingers through Finn's. On the other, Niall wrapped his arm round Maddie's waist. No sign of their father, but Torvald and his specialist Scandinavian vodkas had been the spectacular mistake of Maddie's youth. She had dumped him when she dumped the last bottle around the time the twins turned five, and he hadn't been seen since. Nobody was mourning his absence.

Finn's father was never a mistake, but Eriq was just as absent. Not that he didn't love Maddie, just that Glasgow was cold and wet, and the southern hemisphere was a better match for a boy who had worked his way out of a suq in the deep south of Morocco by dint of charm and juggling. He sent birthday and Christmas cards to the son

17

he'd never seen and threw in some cash for Maddie if he had some, which wasn't often.

And so, this was my family: all of them that were left.

Maddie leaned in and pressed her lips to my forehead. I barely felt her. I was no longer in my body but hovering over the bed. Looking down, I could see—

Is that me?

I'd had no idea I looked that rough: withered, bald, gaunt . . . sucked to a red-eyed husk. It was easy seen why Nancy had used her mirror to show me the crows but nothing else. I'd have died at the sight of me.

Now, though . . . a pulse of something pure folded out of the me that was hovering over the bed towards the me that was dying on it. For my own ears alone, I said, 'I love you', and meant it.

Well.

That was a distinctly odd sensation. There hadn't been a single moment of the past sixty-two years when I could have said this with any honesty, but things change when life loosens its hold.

This was the me-that-had-been. Too many vowels. Too fixated on patterns: patterns of numbers, patterns of language, patterns of story and thought and relating. Too thin, too tall, too sharp with those I cared for, not good enough at loving.

This was the body that had carried me through a whole life. It had done its best and that best hadn't been perfect, but it had been good enough and I was grateful.

Kissing my own brow goodbye, I tasted sour sweat and this last frisson of life unhinged me. I was no longer Lan. I was the echo of an idea around which the passions of my family spun ever faster as I took my leave.

Nancy joined the circle; crow-magic nurse-girl. She filled a gap in the swirl and the kaleidoscope spun anew.

I was entranced. Why did life not have this much . . . life?

It did, a dry voice observed. *You just chose not to notice it.*

'Crow?' I knew that voice. I'd known it since the first dreams with Uuri and definitely these last nine days. 'Is that kind?'

Perhaps not. But it's true.

No. There had – absolutely had – been moments with this much

18

depth and heart, and the miracle of this moment was that I could bring them into being again.

As clearly as if each was happening anew, I could see Maddie being born. And the twins. And Finn. Pain and joy and the feeling of helplessness and tears and can I hold her again? And her and him? And him? How do we bear it, when whole pieces of our hearts take form and walk out into the world?

I could taste each separate memory, roll it across my palate and down to my solar plexus, chase it with another and another and another: a fragment of a day by the loch, playing with shells in the sand; an evening sitting on the hill with my back to the hundred-year-old hawthorns, watching the sun go down; a Christmas dinner, littered with easy, unconscious fun, first one at the farm with Kate when . . .

Kate.

Do you remember the first glance across a train carriage? It was your hair that caught me first, a living fire half a head taller than anyone else, and then your hands: made for making. But then you smiled, and there was a spark of connection I hadn't felt in years. You'd never known it at all. A shrug of invitation, a choice to get off two stops early, just to walk together through the turnstile, the brush of a hand on the back of your arm and the electricity of it . . .

First late-night conversation, first coffee at the Chip off Byres Road, first sex, first row, first exhibition with me at your side instead of Ger . . . never mind.

. . . First night at the farm after Grandad died and talking through to dawn about whether to move south and all it might mean for your career and mine. My old alma mater, Bancroft Hall, was offering me the wardenship, which was beyond huge and you had so much more room to create a studio to . . .

Stop. The Crow tapped on the hollow dome of my thoughts. *Alanna, you need to cut these ties now.*

. . . First bed we bought together, first sex, first row, first thoughts about family. Was having Maddie not the best idea in the world? Your living sculpture, wrought with your whole body. Our magical, powerful, glorious, girl. First steps. First run. First time on the stage. First—

Alanna, of all people, you know better than this. If you care for those you are leaving, you will stop now.

First boyfriend. Why are you with a m—? OK, I didn't say that. I didn't even think it. I'm sure he's fine. Tall, blond, fitter than fit, looks like Thor crossed with Baldur, great sense of humour when he's had a drink or six. Actually, now I know him better, I'd say more Loki than Baldur. Please don't stay with him. Except you're pregnant. Twins. Right. We'll support you whatever—

Alanna! You must let go now. You do know this.

I did know.

What I discovered was that knowing and doing were not the same thing. I'd thought I was prepared, but now that I was here, I didn't want to sever the links to my family.

See it as a rite of passage.

Hmm. I did used to say we needed more rites of passage in our world, more challenges to push us beyond ourselves.

Right, then. I have always had the kind of mind that makes metaphors into shapes. You might hear music, or scent something intricate. I shape ideas into things. In this final test of my life, I took the ties of love and made of them knotted threads that I could unravel, one by one by one; all the knots of a lifetime teased apart and let go until memories streamed through my hands too fast to taste or touch or hear or feel. Their loss ripped something from me, but with their passing, I was lighter and in the edge place of the shoreline, lighter was stronger, and more solid.

I untied the last knot and released the two ends.

Back in the room, the swirl of feeling round the bed split apart in a spray of colour that was pure and bright and heartbreaking.

Maddie sank to her knees. The twins, stunned by the power of her grief, folded in to hold her between them. Finn's grief made its own black hole. I was too far gone to comfort him.

I was lightness itself, easily pulled away. A lurch, a hop and for a fractional moment, I was in the tree outside the window, looking crow-eyed at the human clutter on the bed. Then I was on the shore by the jewelled sea.

Just here.

Nowhere else.

I spread my arms and turned towards the white-bright sun.

CHAPTER THREE

'Hello?

'Kate? Are you there?'

She should have been. Whichever one went first had sworn to come back to guide the other into the Beyond: for decades, we had held this as an article of faith between us.

Except . . . No Kate. Not even any light.

A fog had descended, so dense I could barely see my hands until they were in front of my face. Shingle rolled under my feet. Off to my left, I could hear the hushed surge of the sea, muffled as by layers of padding.

'Kate?' I turned on my heel and called her name to all four directions: front and back, left and right. Nothing.

I had no idea what to do. I had genuinely believed I knew what was coming. We're born alone and we die alone, but I hadn't expected still to be alone here.

Desperate, I turned a slow circle on the shingle. The fog was growing heavier. Now, I couldn't even hear the sea.

Alanna?

The call came from my right. Giddy with relief, I turned to walk inland, and then, tentatively, testing the feel of it, I ran.

A breeze arose, shredding the fog in a broad swathe ahead of me to reveal the vast scale of the ash tree that had stood tall on the shoreline from the start. Only as I came close did I understand its size: five adults, arms outstretched, would have struggled to touch fingertips around its girth.

Not just a tree, then, but a Tree: Yggdrasil made manifest, Odin's World Tree with its branches reaching to the heavens and its three great roots anchored in the waters of the world. From its height stared down a Crow that looked achingly familiar.

With cautious hope, I said, 'I'm lost. Can you help?'

Indeed. I am here to offer assistance.

That voice! Uuri had always said we would recognise those who came to guide us, I had just imagined they would all be human. The Crow was not Kate, but it was at least a familiar presence.

'It's good to see you again.' My mind was clearer than it had been for months. My body was shedding decades. With the rediscovered flexibility of youth, I bowed in the way I'd seen Finn bow to his martial arts mentors, nose to knees. 'I need to find Kate. Can you show me where to go?'

There followed a moment's awkward silence, as if the Crow had bad news it did not know how to break. Its feet tightened on the branch. Clipped, it said, *You are dead.*

'I know.'

The newly dead – a slight stress on 'newly' – *have licence that does not apply at other times. You could, for instance, visit your family.*

'Five minutes ago, you told me to let go. You said it was a rite of passage. I do know that I need to move on.'

I suggested you let go of the anchors that bound you to life and you did. That was well done. Its feet cramped again.

'Are you humouring me?'

The Crow blinked. *Finn is alone. You made him a promise.*

'I know.' And then, with swooping panic, 'He can't be in trouble already, surely? I was with him just now. And Maddie's there. She won't let anything bad happen.'

Time moves differently between here and there. In the lands of his life, it is nearly midnight.

Fuck. 'Has he called for me and I didn't hear?'

He won't call. He is too proud, and too raw and it is too soon. Nonetheless, he needs you and if you wish to help, you must go back swiftly. I watched the Crow's feet clutch around the branch for the third time. If it had been human, it would have been terrible at poker.

I asked, 'What's wrong?'

I felt the small huff of a laugh: it had heard the thought about poker. *I would like for you to have at least a semblance of choice.*

'There is no choice. I promised Finn I would help him.'

Indeed. It sounded weary. I didn't care enough to ask it why.

'What do I need to do?'

It tipped its head. *If you will look at me?*

I looked up. We clashed, gaze to black and shining gaze. With no more warning than this, my solar plexus inverted, and I plunged up off the shoreline as if I'd just jumped out of the tree and there was nowhere to land. The speed! And with it, terror . . .

'Crow!'

I wanted to say I'd changed my mind, to scream it. I wanted to claw my way back to the safety of the shore and never leave it. I wanted . . .

I wanted to fly. I wanted to revel in the ripe flavours of rain and the bliss of a month-old rabbit carcass I could scent halfway up the hill. A different part of me wanted to slide down the wind to the farmhouse far, far below us, to explore the chunky flint and Tudor pantiles of its roof and their mosaic of moss and crannies from which a probing beak might winkle out spiders, centipedes, larvae of nameless, taste-filled life.

Yet another part pushed me (us?) to rise higher until I could see the landscape. Because we were here, at my home, a place I had thought never to see again, and certainly not from this angle. But here below us was the village of Blackthorn Rise, huddled down in the valley with its clutter of ancient cottages thronged around the mill and then around them the wheel of bigger houses no more than a couple of centuries old.

To the east, the land rose steeply – one of the few hills in the flat East Anglian landscape – and here, half a mile up from the village and a few hundred yards south along an unmetalled track, was Blackthorn Farm.

Once a Templar priory, the main buildings were arranged in a rectangle around a central yard. The farmhouse with its enticing so-old tiles held the whole north side. Ash Barn where Finn had his bedroom lay to the west, the Dutch barns to the south, and to the east, with the hill sloping up behind, was the Piggery where Kate had made her studio. I hadn't touched a single thing inside it since she'd died.

Stung by the memory, I spiralled higher until I could see beyond the dense mass of the Rookery to the smaller quadrangle of the old Dairy that had fallen out of use in my grandfather's time when the work was too much and the help too little.

The herd had been Red Polls with bloodlines going back to when the stud book started. Seeing them sent for slaughter had been the last straw that had driven my father away to Scotland. I don't think he'd planned to be away long, but he'd met my mother and she wasn't for moving and they'd settled at Chroit Dhubh, the Black Croft, which lay inland from Oban between Kilmore and Loch Nell.

My father had loathed the farm, and, perhaps because of this, I had loved it with every bone in my body. Coming south had been hard, for all that Blackthorn Farm had been the family home for too many generations to count.

From the farm, the land rose up to the east and fell away to the south. It was not flat in any plane except for fifteen of our sixty-three acres that lay a brisk five-minute walk due south, round the elbow of the Rookery (ten minutes if you were walking back up the hill carrying anything heavier than a letter), which were flat enough to make hay from, and this, in turn, made it a good enough place to build a dairy, although it was too far from the farm to haul milk back on a snow-stacked winter's morning.

The Templars hadn't been thinking about distance. They had carts, perhaps, or a lot more people to carry milk churns than were around in my grandparents' time. Whatever the reason, they'd crafted the Dairy in miniature image of the farm's quadrangle with a cottage in the north, and then a milking parlour, a hay barn and a stock barn holding the west, south and east respectively.

Matt and Jens were there now, the young couple who'd come as interns to give a helping hand when Kate first fell ill. Within the first month, they'd cleared the nettles and docks that had been driving me mad and had offered to 'take a look' at the derelict dairy cottage and see if it could be made habitable.

Another month later, they'd moved out of the downstairs rooms of Ash Barn and into a second-hand caravan they'd put on the far side of the Rookery, so they could more easily work on the cottage. And the milking parlour. And the barns. They had plans, and while

I'm pretty sure we didn't know the half of them, we didn't need to: they were family by then, and anything they did was fine.

The Dairy wasn't isolated from the farmhouse, exactly, but definitely a place apart. By accident or design it was both hidden by, and nestled in, the lee of the Rookery, the big, dark wood south and west of the farmhouse, that draped like a black blanket between us and the village. Kate had always said it was a last remnant of England's primordial forests and Connor hadn't disagreed, so maybe she was right.

Last of the landmarks that mattered were the blackthorns that gave their name to both village and farm. Intermingled with hawthorns and elder, these strung a thick hedge on either side of the track that wove south and east up the hill towards the farm's top boundary. The trees thinned out before the top of the rise, leaving the path to thread across the open moorland, then over the top and down towards the flat, mirrored sheen of Five Acre Deep, the poplar-fringed lake that had supplied water and fish to the farm since earliest times.

I was watching for the flickers of movement in the water when I heard the crunch of gravel back at the yard and, never mind the fish, I wanted to slide down the wind and see the farmhouse up close; I wanted to look in the windows and see Maddie in the kitchen, and whose was the new(ish) car in the yard? I wanted to look in through the windows of Ash Barn and see if the twins had lit the fire in the living room, and if Finn was upstairs in his bedroom, or working out in the studio that took up the rest of the top floor. I wanted, no I *needed* to—

—grip my strangely long and too-few toes around a branch of a tree that felt so *alive*. In my newly hollow bones, I could feel-hear the hum of connection among its roots, along miles of mycelial networks, between clumps of bacteria, ions of metals, rare earths, molecules and compounds and atoms. All my life I'd known we needed to reforge our connection to the web of life and I had to bloody die to see it in all its bright and shining wonder, to *taste* the life in it, to—

Alanna!

'*What?*' It came out as a croak, which shocked me back to human sensibilities. I didn't lose my sense of the web, but the awe was numbed a bit, and I was sorry.

Open your eyes.

'Why . . .? Oh! We *are* home!' We'd been flying. I'd thought it a dream.

Indeed. I was Crow and not-Crow, both. In the part of myself that was not Lan, I felt a hesitancy. *You remember you are dead?*

'I do.' The reality hadn't quite sunk in yet, but yes.

Being dead is a lot like dreaming.

'Right.' Uuri said that once. Many times, actually.

As you do in dreams, you need to make this place real. Build your memories and make them strong enough to hold us both.

'No rest for the wicked, eh?'

A Crow's patience is a tangible thing, I discovered, especially when it frays. I straightened up. 'Memories. I'm on it.'

I looked around. We were in the tree outside the place Kate and I had named Ash Barn. Not the most original name, but in our defence, a rather magnificent young ash had been growing through the caved-in roof when we'd first got there after my grandfather died.

We'd had more to worry about in the early years than a dilapidated barn. Sometime in the 60s, the farmhouse had been given Grade II listing, which meant it drank money the way ticks drink blood.

Our first winter there, we discovered that none of the windows fitted and the roof leaked and this was the easy bit. Negotiating with planning officers and bank managers required skills neither of us had ever developed and were not fast to acquire.

On top of this, we had to manage a farm that wasn't quite big enough to make us a living, nor yet small enough to let a few sheep wander around as four-footed lawnmowers.

We tried a dozen different options, but it was only when we found Matt and Jens that we got the right fit. I keep meaning to talk to Maddie about them, tell her she needs to draw up a new contract so they'll be secure and—

Alanna?

'Sorry.' Memories. Focus.

Ash Barn. The tree in its heart grew undisturbed for years until the day Finn showed up on the doorstep seeking asylum and we wanted to give him his own space but had no money to do it. Then, almost the same day, the gods of serendipity smiled on us. Kate sold a sculpture to some weird hedge-funded museum in the US for more money than we'd ever seen and the problem solved itself.

The barn was long and tall and narrow and the planning officer had developed a bit of a crush on Kate by then, so we got permission to turn the whole thing into accommodation.

Given the freedom to do what he wanted with the long top floor, Finn had made a bedroom at one end and the rest was variously a martial arts and yoga studio, giant cinema and sterile(ish) space where he could build circuit boards. Downstairs, we made a couple of bedrooms and a kitchen/living room that were kept for friends, scholars, artists and the twins whenever they came to visit.

Even so, I wish we'd kept the piece. *Kettled By The State* was Kate's last major work before she got lost in the fog of her own mind. I desperately regretted—

Your memories are sound. Now, we need to find Finn.

There was an urgency to the Crow's voice I hadn't heard before.

'Up,' I said. 'His bedroom's tucked under the gable at the north end.'

This time, I was ready for the plunging vertigo. We landed on the branches outside the dormer window that overlooked Finn's room.

No curtains were drawn. He was sitting at his desk, his silhouette stark against the glare of a screen and I recognised the blue-tiled rooftops of Stormwind, capital city of the Alliance faction in the fantasy world of Azeroth.

'You're gaming? When I've only just died? Finn, how could you?!'

My heart did not yearn for the game, but it ached for the partnership we'd had. Playing in the battlegrounds was like rock-climbing, or caving, or anything else where a partner holds your life in their hands. Battle-death may have been wrought only in pixels, but it felt real. Those who didn't play didn't get it, but then those who didn't climb cliff-faces never got it, either.

We'd got it, me and Finn. We'd played for those moments of synergy and flow that were headier than any drug.

But even as I thought this, he hurled his mouse against the wall and, thrusting himself to his feet, began to pace the short span of his room. The same black hole enveloped him as had done at my bedside, but in my Crow-sense state, I could see its jagged edges, plumb the bottomless spiral of its menace.

'Finn!'

Need drove me through the window without stopping to ask whether I could. One moment I was perched on a branch with the Crow, the next, I was standing so close to Finn that I could feel the heat of his body, smell his grief as a metallic sheen over the familiar burned-toast smell of his skin.

'Finn, it's me!'

I stopped being part-Crow and became wholly Lan, as human as I could be in my newly dead state. I wrapped my arms around him. They passed through. I tried again, but I had no substance. Nothing made contact.

'Finn!'

'FINN!'

Frantic, I looked around. The pen tray on his desk was crammed with colour and his diary lay open. I went for the biggest, thickest Sharpie. Surely to goodness, I could hold this? But no, my fingers slid straight through.

His guitar hung on the wall above his bed. I had the musical aptitude of a house brick, but I knew how to pluck a string. Or maybe blow through it, to make a noise?

Nothing. Finn hurled himself onto his bed and lay with his fingers looped behind his head, staring dry-eyed at the ceiling. His stillness was more terrifying than the pacing had been. This was how he went when he was planning, and just then, all his plans had fatal outcomes.

'Crow? Help me?'

The Crow gave a sympathetic twist to the space between us but didn't move.

'Blast you. This is not fair.' I stormed back out to the branch. 'You understand how bad this is?' He took it hard when Kate died, but I was always there to talk him out of it. 'If I can't get to him, he'll do something terminal and I can't even ring Maddie. Nothing works! You have to—'

Alanna? The voice was more rasping than resonant.

'*Yes!*' And then, more soberly, 'What?'

You can act, but it will have a cost.

'I don't care. I promised Finn I'd do whatever I could. So tell me what I can do.'

What do you remember of the void?

'The . . .? You mean Pakak's void?'

Surely not.

Pakak Nutaraq had a Bachelor's in biological sciences and a doctorate in environmental law. I met him first at the funeral of his great-uncle, who had been so powerful in life that nobody dared speak his name aloud.

Five years later, he had taken the old man's role and was on the way to overshadowing him. I watched him dance a polar bear away from a fresh seal carcass with only the power of his mind. I saw him draw in seals to the hunt and keep submarines at bay. I thought he was fearless and said so one night when the smoke rose thick and we were both tired.

His laugh took on tones I hadn't heard before. 'Nobody is fearless who has stood at the edge of the void.'

'The what?'

'Seriously?' He rolled over to catch my eye, to be sure I wasn't joking. I spread my hands. He sighed and stared into the fire and I thought he wasn't going to speak; this happened a lot.

Then, 'Don't go there, Lan. It's not a place for Westerners. It's not even a place for us. I don't think Nameless ever went there, except at the end, and he never came back. Best not even talk about it.'

I was going to challenge him, but the smoke moved and I saw his face and swallowed the words.

Now, because I was pretty sure the Crow could read my thoughts, I asked, 'That void?'

Yes. You must enter and split the timelines of Finn's life. When you have seen the paths that lead to his death, you can weave the one that does not.

Fuck. This was at the very edges of my understanding. Pakak may have refused to tell me more, but I had other teachers less reticent, or so I had thought.

Mostly, I'd been wrong. Nine other men, women and two-spirits

I had loved and trusted had given me the same shuttered look and told me not to dig any deeper lest I bury myself in a place from which there was no coming back.

Two others unbent enough to sketch the terror of a place outside space and time, a boundless emptiness in which the seeds of all potential were buried. Both were clear that nobody sane went anywhere near it.

Uuri was the one who trusted me enough to go deeper. We were both old by then, and we knew I was dying. She'd flown over for Kate's funeral, and stayed on for a week in the yurt Jens, Matt and Finn had put up for her on the flat bit of hay meadow below the Rookery.

I had joined her there as soon as I could reasonably escape. There may have been no wolves calling under the summer moon, or horses grazing up against the walls, but even so, it felt like another place in another land and we'd tied the door shut and let ourselves be somewhere else for a week.

On the last night, as the fire burned down, Uuri had hung the eagle skull above in the smoke, watched it spin for a while and then offered me a healing. I did think about it, but not for long: Kate was gone, and, already, I was looking forward to meeting her in the Beyond.

Saying no felt like another line crossed. We wept together in front of her fire, but it was a good weeping and when it was ending, she pulled me close, my back to her breasts, her knees pressing tight either side of my rib cage and her arms hugging me into the curve of her body.

After perhaps half an hour of silence, in this place of no wind the old, smoke-weathered eagle skull had spun once more and this time came to rest with its beak facing me. Uuri had asked it questions in a language I had never heard and, after some discussion, had said, 'We all make choices that change the flow of life. The void holds all the lines of all the choices of all the lives that have ever been lived or ever will be. With clear intent, and a powerful need, one who walks the void can see the branches of a life's tree, map out the possible futures. Sometimes this may save a life, or change it in ways that the world will welcome.'

She was warm and her hands had begun to find the sore places in my lungs and ease them to calm. I was half-asleep and not thinking clearly. 'Are you saying that if I went into the void, I could see what might happen if I had let you heal me?'

'No. We don't see our own futures, only those whose lives we touch.'

'What's the point then? Why go near somewhere that so obviously scares everyone rigid?'

'You can see the places you did not act in others' lives, and in the gaps between, you can find what you could yet do.' I felt her shrug. 'So I have been told. I have never tried. If you make a mistake in the void, you die and your soul is lost. I can see no reason to risk such a thing. Death is not an ending; you know this. Losing your soul is forever. Only someone with nothing to lose would risk it, and everyone has something to lose.'

'Uuri, why are you telling me this?' I was slurring by now, a long, long way through the sleep gates.

'The eagle turned its face to you. You saw it.'

'Yes, but—'

'Hush. You'll know when you need to know. The threads of love will weave your path. You will know.' She slid her hands over my liver and the last vestiges of pain flared into the smoke and it wasn't going to stop me dying, but it gave me sleep and when I woke, Uuri had gone and the time for talking was over and the time for dying had begun.

Now I was dead, and I knew just enough to know that I didn't know enough.

'If the living make a mistake in the void,' I said to the Crow, carefully, 'they die and their souls are lost. What happens if one already dead were to misstep?'

The same. We will cease to be.

'We?'

Both of us. I must come with you. Just as you are our anchor here, I will be your anchor in the void. You must always have an anchor. The Crow's eyes were depthless pools. Its feet were locked too tight to cramp. I'd never thought I'd feel pity for a crow.

I weighed the risk of oblivion against my promise to Finn and it was a feather against the whole of my heart. I said, 'I need to do this.'

Yes. It is why you are here. You must build a path across the void and then we shall split the timelines and see what can be done.

So.

The void is always half a thought away. Several people had told me this, even as they had warned me to keep well clear.

I turned all of my attention to the places I rarely looked, to the felt-sense between this world and all the others, between life and death, between the Between and the Beyond, and here in this liminal space was a doorway, an invitation. Push open, step through and—

We fell . . .

CHAPTER FOUR

We kept on falling.

We fell in an unlit emptiness: no up or down, no boundaries in any plane, no sight or sound, no taste or smell or texture.

We fell in an infinity of space without even the stars to light it: the kind of place where anyone could get lost forever.

Panic consumed me, but Uuri had given me rules enough to navigate: in the void, intention and the power of our need are everything. Oblivion comes when one of these falters.

Oblivion comes, in fact, on the heels of panic.

At core, there are only two emotions. One is fear. The other is love. The two cannot exist in the same heart at the same time. So I had been taught and so did I believe. (And still do.)

Finn was my heart's fire, the love of my soul.

I had known him from his first beginning. Building love against the panic and building the path of his life so that I could traverse the void were one and the same; all I had to do was reach back for yet more memories.

Spring 1993. Blackthorn blossomed in snowy clumps on leafless boughs and the taste of late frost scratched the air. Maddie had brought her new love to visit Kate and me and the electricity between them lit up the whole farm.

Eriq was the most beautiful man I had ever seen; cheekbones you could cut a deal on even while you drowned in his eyes and died happy with both.

His hair was the colour of molasses, curled tight to his head. He could juggle kitchen knives, fleece you at cards and play eight different musical instruments without bothering to practise. Who cared if he hadn't got two brass farthings to rub together and thought nine-to-five work was the provenance of wage slaves? The rhythm of his drumming was legendary and if he brought the same effortless sensitivity to sex, it must have been spectacular. Certainly, Mads was luminous on the morning of their first full day. They had made a child in the night. Nobody spoke of it, but we all knew, and were, each in our ways, enchanted.

Like all enchantments, it faded fast. Not quite with the dawn, but a month or so later, Eriq offered his sad, but firm, goodbyes and got on a plane back to Rio.

For a week, Maddie wept enough to fill the Clyde, then dried her eyes, took stock of her life and the new human growing within her, and, with the same bloody-mindedness that had let her quit the drink a few years before, she gave up coffee and chocolate. A week later, she gave up the acting she had loved at the Citizens Theatre in Glasgow, and took to directing instead, which was supposed to be less physically demanding. It was also evidently far less satisfying, but having the twins had taught her a lot and, this time around, she was going to be the best mother the world had ever known: she swore it was worth the trade-off.

Six months on, for much the same reasons, she abandoned the shared, three-to-a-room apartment in Anniesland and took the twins to join a community of wild-haired women who raised their children as a feral gang and schooled them at home in the Trossachs, outside Glasgow.

It was all very late millennial, with a particular flavour of hedonism and responsibility, radicalism and stoic Scots sense, that wrapped Finn in its care when her wee Black boy landed in the heart of their milky-white community with his mother's long, lush hair and his father's eyes and his ability to juggle languages and music and nice bone china without dropping it (mostly); to find patterns in drums and in numbers, and flash his fierce, bright smile that promised slumbering beasts deep inside that you wouldn't have wanted to waken lightly.

All of these combined got him through the hard parts where Scotland was perhaps not as multicultural as it liked to think, at least until adolescence, when the nastiness peaked and a particularly vicious assault one evening saw him pack a rucksack and get on a train for England.

Maddie had thought it was a passing phase and had bitten her tongue and kept his room unchanged. Kate and I were not sure if he'd come for a few weeks or a few months, but we had always said he was welcome, and were both touched and honoured that he had sought out the sanctuary of our care. I had been vaguely aware that at least part of the lure that drew him south was Mo Bakar, the Chinese-Malaysian woman with multiple black belts who had recently moved to the old mill down by the river. She had brought with her a dozen students from all around the world who paid for the privilege of living a semi-monastic life: one third of their time training, one third meditating and the final third in service to the community.

She didn't teach children, but she had made an exception for Finn when he came down for the summer holidays that year and offered to help set up her computer system in return for some training. He'd got his first belt before he'd had to go back up the road.

All this I had known in life. What I saw now was the moment when, caught in the drizzle, under sodium orange streetlights with four of them laying into him, he had thought he was going to kill or be killed and had wanted – needed – to know how to avoid both. Mo was the only one he trusted to teach him how to be safe.

Oh, Finn. I wish I'd known . . .

On this thought, the steady path I had built beneath my feet wavered. I dropped as through slow mud, not quite in free fall, but not remotely stable.

Alanna! Do not stop! The Crow's voice was high and tight.

Shaken, I drove myself back to the clear memory of Finn standing on the doorstep with his life packed on his back and a stubborn look on his face. The ground became more solid. I built the pathway from the sound of his voice in the kitchen in the evenings when I got home from college, the scent of his sweat when he came in from training, the shared secret of our gaming: I never did tell Kate. After she died, I thought she must have known and might be angry. I was hoping the dead did not give way to base human emotions. I still hoped so.

Another step, and another. Finn grew taller, stronger, fitter. Too, he grew paler as he aged, and mourned the fact that half the population thought he just had a terrifically good tan, while among those who knew the truth were some who hated him for being able to blend so readily with the mainstream. Which was ridiculous: anyone who spent more than twenty seconds in Finn's company knew he wasn't for blending with anyone, that he was going to carve his own path in this world. We just had to get him past this first night.

This night.

Now.

I stopped, having nowhere else to go.

Part of me was aware of Finn lying on his bed in Ash Barn, lost in rage and despair.

The greater part stood in the boundless, depthless void with the broad path of his life a shining ribbon behind, as if my footsteps had bled moonlight onto polished obsidian.

This same brilliant dark rose sheer in front of me, as a wall I could not pass: the blank slate on which Finn's future – his many, many different futures – waited to be written.

Pressure mounted behind my eyes, and indecision.

Without taking my attention from the wall, I said to the Crow, 'I don't know what to do.'

I shall show you. Watch and learn.

It sounded like all the teachers I had ever known. I stood balanced on the knife-edge of the moment with the moon puddled at my feet and Finn's life bright-garlanding my shoulders, and felt the Crow take over.

And, Oh. My. Goodness . . . *This* was how will was gathered.

With bottomless admiration, I sensed a stretch-reach that speared deep, deep, deep through all the realms of life and death, of myth and hope and possibility and wove them all into one single stable root.

At the same time, it stretched up and out wider and higher than the night sky, casting far into the emptiness of the everwhere and the neverwhen, gathering into the Crow – into *us* – the essence of possibility.

Stability and Possibility: either one alone would have failed, but with two there was an anchoring. We were not just balanced on the knife-edge of now, we were balancing there with the thermonuclear power of ten thousand new-born suns held in either hand. Drop one, and the rest would have vaporised all the worlds in all the times that could ever have been.

The Crow did not drop anything. Rather, it drew inside all this measureless potential until we were ablaze. When we could not possibly hold more, when spontaneous combustion felt like the only possible option, it reversed the flow and spat it out onto the perfect, unblemished wall in front of us.

It was a laser; we were. The power of ten thousand suns bent on this singular point of time and space.

Which shattered without sound.

I felt the ripples rock the universe.

'Crow . . .?'

Alanna! Watch. Listen. Learn. I beg of you, do not move or speak until I give you leave. We are here to watch. We must not interfere, else the oblivion you have been promised will be ours.

Fuck.

Right.

Balanced on the razor's edge, I watched the black wall in front of us undulate as any pool does when a rock has shattered its equilibrium.

Quite fast, it cleared and . . .

I was immoderately proud of my restraint because we were looking once again into Finn's bedroom, but this time every sense was magnified beyond anything I'd ever known.

When I had been alive, I had been able to see him.

When I was newly dead, I had Crow-sensed him, and, naïvely, had been startled by the clarity.

Now I could *see* him in a way that redefined the meaning of vision. I saw every hair of his head as if it were a forest and I the moth flitting between the trees. I tasted each tear, heard his breathing rasp, smelled his so-familiar breath. I tasted the salt of his snot, of his sweat, of his tears and wanted to weep with him.

The Crow was within me, holding a warning as loud as if it screamed. I did not reach out. I did not speak.

Instead, I watched as Finn reached the end of his planning, blinked once, levered his long legs off the bed and—

When did he grow so big? How did I not notice these past few months that his head nearly brushed the ceiling light. He needs to raise it up or he'll—

Alanna!

'I didn't move. I did *not*.'

Please. Just watch.

Finn opened the dormer window that gave him an unimpeded view out to the hill behind the piggery. A half-hearted breeze teased his hair from his face. He leaned far out, twisted round to face inwards and, in a move that looked distressingly well practised, hooked his fingers around the iron bracket of the old drainpipe high to his right and pulled himself up onto the window ledge. He'd been climbing rocks since before he left Scotland. A quick trip up to the roof was no challenge.

Three more moves, any one of which would have been fatal if the drain brackets had come loose, took him onto the ridge. Arms out, he walked the tightrope of its length.

I could feel his life's thread growing increasingly taut. Beside me, the Crow thrummed with anxiety. I did not move.

Finn stood a long moment behind the weathervane; just him and the outline of a running hare that his four-greats-grandfather had wrought in iron. Like a high diver, he swept his arms back and up . . . and leapt out into nowhere.

Finn!

I did not call aloud. But my heart broke when I heard his neck snap.

Crow did not give me time to grieve, or even to comment. A heartbeat later, we were back in the void, standing in front of the obsidian wall as the Crow once again drew the bow of its intent and let it loose.

The backwash of ten thousand suns evoked a ripple in the darkness and when it smoothed, we were back in Finn's room, with him on the bed making plans for his own demise, and me still startled by the clarity with which I could count his tears.

Second time around.

Finn blinked. He rose. His head nearly touched the light. I thought—

No. I didn't. I watched as he cleared his drum kit out of the way and opened the fire escape door that led down to the yard. He was moving softly, to not wake Niall, who was a notoriously light sleeper and had the room directly below. Nobody moved.

Down at ground level, Crow and I tracked just behind his left shoulder as he vaulted the gate from the yard and headed onto the old path that snaked up the slope between the blackthorns. He was navigating by memory through the shadow-dapples, knowing where to take a long stride over a rotting log, where to angle ten degrees left, and then further on, five degrees right and then straight again.

Emerging from the trees, he broke into a ground-eating run and loped up the short stretch of open hill beyond, and down the other side to Five Acre Deep.

He'd swum in there since he'd been old enough to float. In a moment's blind optimism, I thought perhaps he might strip off and swim under starlight, but I was the idiot who had told him about Virginia Woolf and so it was no great surprise to see him search the area for stones. We were in flint country: our stones were not heavy, but they were plentiful. Lacking pockets to fill, Woolf-style, he tied his sweatshirt tight at his waist and stuffed them down his front until he looked grotesquely pregnant.

Finn, please . . .

If you value life in any form, you will remain still.

'Fuck you.'

I did not move.

It was over faster than I'd feared, and we did not linger beyond the certainty of his death. When the endless black mirror-wall shimmered again, I was ready for Finn's bedroom and his blink into action.

Four more times we watched him die and by the last, I desperately wanted to find a way to communicate with Maddie, because while I could well imagine that he knew where we'd hidden the keys to the gun cupboard, I could not imagine at all how he had bypassed the fuse box so it wouldn't cut out when he doused himself with a hose, stood in the puddle and bit down on a newly bared mains cord.

The climbing rope over the weathervane was less creative, but just as fast; his slipknot was exemplary, and he got a good drop. It seemed more certain than the jump had done.

The knife had taken the most courage. He was never keen on the sight of blood. He went for a heart kill and didn't botch it. In honour of the guts this took, I did not look away.

In the wake of this last, the obsidian wall shimmered and did not clear as it had before, but rippled languidly, waiting.

I was ragged, gut-punched and heart-sore, but I had not moved, or spoken or done anything to upset the filaments of time as they spread out into the void. In a mountainous act of self-control, I did not speak now, but waited.

Well done.

The Crow stood beside me. Its voice seemed to come from the other side of eternity, wrung out with exhaustion.

I did not turn. I was watching Finn as he lay on his bed. We were back to the beginning again, except that nothing was moving: I could barely see him breathing.

'Do I understand we have some influence over which one of these happens? Because otherwise, that was torture for the sheer hell of it.'

You have influence over what might happen instead. My task was to bring you to this. Whatever happens now is up to you.

'Are you going to give me a clue?'

The Crow had many grades of laugh. This one was dry as holly leaves, blown through a winter's hedge, and very, very tired. *What else have we been doing?* Abruptly, it sobered. *You have seen futures that may arise if Finn is left unaided. What you have not seen – what you can never see – is what might occur if you intervene. He needs to know that your promise to him holds, that you care about him, that you may be dead, but are not gone. If he believes this, he may no longer feel the need to join you in death.*

CHAPTER FIVE

For the second time, I passed through Finn's window and made a circuit of the room. He lay on the bed exactly as he had done on all the previous occasions. The difference was that now, I had to do something.

I stopped in front of his computer and an idea itched at the back of my mind. I'd bought this for him soon after he moved to the farm. The rest of the family had been aghast at the expense, but I'd said he was learning to write code and needed a decent computer and each part of this had been true. I was not a coder, but I was a gamer. There had been times when the world on the screen had felt more alive to both of us than the world outside and just now, this aliveness called to me in ways other things did not.

Right then.

The operating system, the firmware, the software of the game . . . all of these were a spin of electrons, flows of information, binary gates opening and closing faster than any living mind could parse. There was more code in one combat module than took rockets to the moon, but it was all energy and I had just seen what could be done with a clear enough intent. I was, and remained, a pattern-matcher, and here were patterns whose outcomes I knew intimately. How hard could it be to warp them as the Crow had warped the web of time?

Hard, obviously.

But not impossible.

Merging with the operating system of Finn's PC was not unlike the step into the void. Success came no more swiftly, but I probed and pushed until I felt that same sense of pushing against an open door that had taken me into the void.

It wasn't any more stable, either, but I found I could slow down the oscillations enough to separate the streams of data. Then, it was like listening to music I knew by heart. I could conduct this; I had the power to change the pitch, the tempo, even the refrain, to my liking.

Having gained some control, my most urgent task was to draw Finn to the screen. His screen-saver was a score card from one of the first battlegrounds where he got the top damage score and I was top Healer. Making it bounce randomly off the walls of the screen had been one of his earliest coding projects and to call it clunky would be generous.

I was glad of this now, though, because clunky was easy to tweak. It didn't take much effort to turn up the colour saturation to make Finn's name and mine glow a shade more brightly. When I added in a chime, faintly, not enough to alarm him, but just enough . . .

Gently does it. Geeeeently . . .

Yes! He rose from the bed and did not head out of the window or to the fire escape, but came to stand at the desk, tilting his head to stare at the screen. None of this had happened in the timelines in which I'd seen him die.

I twitched the colours another degree brighter and bled in a different saturation of red. There was a jolt around me as Finn hit the space bar to clear the saver away, but I had just spent time spinning in the void; a jolt wasn't going to knock me off balance.

Warcraft had been humming in the background. It was a whole different melody played by a different orchestra, but I could sing this one in my sleep.

Finn's main character was a Rogue which, with a distressing lack of imagination, he had called Nifty. I never did persuade him that running your own name backwards wasn't original or wise. It was Nifty, therefore, who mounted up and headed for the target-practice range in the north of Stormwind city. Here, rows of practice dummies stood in a mediaeval courtyard where young Rogues (and Hunters, and Mages, and Paladins, and Warriors and all the other classes we never explored) could test out their capacity to inflict damage on the enemy.

Which was exactly what he did. Before long he was dancing and jumping and spinning and turning somersaults and stabbing, stabbing, stabbing with every ability he had.

I searched through the patterns for the signature spikes when the random number generators calculated his damage score. The RNGods were a gamer's greatest friend and deepest foe. If you pissed them off, you'd be stabbing your opponent with a rubber spork. If they smiled, though, and your strikes went critical . . .

I reached into the place where electrons spun and gates opened and tried to emulate Crow's capacity for focus. Deep in the beautiful, crashing symphony of the game, I found the sweet note that was Nifty the Rogue, leaned the right way, *pushed* and—

'Fuck me!'

'Findley Karim Penhaligon, your mother would skin me alive if she heard you.'

He waited for the cooldowns to reset and stabbed at the dummy again.

Focus, lean, push. Another critical strike sent the damage metres sky high.

'Bloody hell . . .'

He was hooked. For five adrenaline-soaked minutes, Nifty scored impossible numbers. If the target dummy had been an actual living Orc – which is to say, another youth stabbing keys in another bedroom somewhere else in the world – they would have been resurrecting in the graveyard. If we had been in the battlegrounds, we'd have been unstoppable.

And that, I thought, was not a bad idea.

The ReadyCheck guild was led by a Druid bear-tank called Hawck, a man with a Merseyside accent who had served in the military in a capacity he never talked about. He'd done three tours of duty in places hot and sandy that he was similarly careful not to name. I had a suspicion he had been good and had probably risen to the point where more people had been saluting him than vice versa.

They'd still booted him out in the end, of course. PTSD freaks out the flatheads: they don't know what to do with something that can't be fixed by shouting at it. On the few occasions he and I had spoken of this, he had said Warcraft kept him sane. And alive.

All this added up to make him a genuinely good battleground leader who famously never lost his cool. When he said, 'Chill, people. It's a game. Nobody actually died', it had serious credibility;

we all knew he'd held dying comrades in his arms. He was one of life's good guys and these past months he had been the only in-game friend who had known both that I was Finn's grandmother and that I was on my way out. If anyone outside the family could help now, it was him.

A part of me kept Nifty scoring squillions while the rest of me hunted for Hawck. I found him with the rest of our team as they were capping the last flag in Warsong Gulch, the earliest WoW battleground. They'd picked up a spare Rogue, but it wasn't hard to get rid of him when the game ended: people's connections dropped all the time.

Just as he was about to start looking for someone else, Hawck got a private Whisper, ostensibly from Nifty: **Need a Rogue?**

Seconds later, Nifty had a Whisper that seemed to come from Hawck: **U up 4 a game?**

There was a brief pause while Finn unleashed all his cooldowns on the target and saw another max crit from the RNGods, then: **Invite?**

And like that, we were in the team and queuing up for the battlegrounds.

The ten-player battlegrounds in Warcraft rotated through a number of different maps with a number of different win conditions, but they were all about protecting your own team and killing the bad guys while defending a base or capping a flag. None of it was rocket science; the skill came in knowing how your character's class synergised with the other nine on the team, and how the opposition was likely to act.

If you were playing random games with people you didn't know or who didn't know how to play together, it was dull, frustrating and barely worth the time.

Like any team sport, though, if you had a team who played together regularly, with players who knew their classes well enough to understand the synergy of Rogues with Priests and both with Mages; who could tell the difference between a Human Priest and a Troll one, or a Dwarf playing a Beast Mastery Hunter compared to a Night Elf Survival Hunter and both compared to an Orc Destruction

Warlock ... then you were playing multidimensional chess at a sprint.

Our team was multinational, multi-gendered and omnisexual. Hawck himself was gay and one way to get kicked out of the guild before you had time to type '/sorry' was to use this word as a pejorative either on the voice comms or in the text chat. The other fast-kick routes were to use 'girl' as a /spit and/or to disparage anyone's nationality.

We were home to an Israeli, a Greek, a Belgian, a Canadian, a married pair of Danes who had both made Gladiator rank the previous season, and a Scot. With me as a Healer-Priest, Finn on his Rogue and Hawck on his Druid able to run either as a feral damage-dealing cat, or bear-tank, we made the full ten.

Since I had 'stepped back for IRL reasons' they'd brought in a Healer-Priest in my place. It had taken Hawck three weeks of carefully combing the forums to find a woman who would fit with the team. He'd emailed me her record so I could approve it before he'd taken her on. Checking her out had cheered what had otherwise been a particularly taxing day.

Tonight, though, my mind was deathly clear, I was all up to speed and I really did know how to play my class. Thus, ReadyCheck became, in effect, an eleven-player team and we were unstoppable. We shattered the Horde team that had creamed us last time, capping three flags in under six minutes, and would have been faster if our Israeli Mage hadn't decided it would be fun to /dance with the flag in front of the enemy graveyard for a while, letting Nifty duel each of the Horde team as they resurrected one by one. He was right.

Within half a dozen games, we'd beaten the teams we usually lost to at least half the time, and found ourselves in a higher bracket, matched against people who did nothing but play all day and all night and kicked anyone from the roster who mistimed a single key-press.

On any normal night, teams like this would have made mincemeat of us. Tonight, their Healers were locked down in endless crowd control, Nifty slaughtered their Flag Carriers before they ever got out of our base and our team fights were one-sided massacres.

We rose up the ladder the way cream rises up new milk and it wasn't only Nifty who was killing everything: winning carried the entire team to a new place. Everyone was calling their abilities on time, using them intelligently, synergising the fights and pushing the tactics to their limits. This was how the best teams played.

In the beginning, the voice channel was full of whoops and shouts and virtual high fives. By the time we had beaten the professional teams who videoed their games and posted them on the net for lesser mortals to see how it was done – and then beaten them for the second, third and fourth time, there was a hollow, shocked silence.

At two minutes to midnight, Hawck called it a day. Charm – the replacement Healer-Priest – spoke into the comms as everyone was calling their goodnights. 'I can leave the team if you want.'

'Why would you do that?' You had to hear Hawck in the flesh to really appreciate his accent. Think John Lennon and drag it into the murkier banks of the Mersey.

'You said you were 1700 rating. I can play at that. I'm not a 2.4k player.' Charm's accent was French with deep southern overtones.

Hawck's was mellow as ever. 'You played as well as any of us,' he said. 'This was a special night. Don't necessarily expect it to happen again. And please don't leave the team. We need you.'

We Need You! stuttered out eight more times in the text chat.

Charm had a softly dangerous laugh. She typed **GG**, for Good Game, which was the traditional ReadyCheck sign-off, then **CU 2morrow**, and was gone.

The others peeled off, one by one. Finn had a finger on the ESC key, and I thought it was too soon. I was about to send a Whisper to Hawck, when he beat me to it. 'Nift, can you stay a moment?'

They were in Stormwind, in the Dwarvish zone, in a bar. Of course.

Hawck typed: **Drink?**

Aloud, Finn said, 'Sure.' In the real world, he poured himself water. The combination of his mother's history and Mo Bakar's teaching meant he drank little else.

They drank in companionable silence for a while. I had a sense of words being considered and cast aside. Eventually, Hawck said, 'Your grandmother died today, right?'

I could feel Finn's shock. He stood up, shoving the chair back. I had an image of him dead, and dead, a hundred different ways dead.

Hawck!

Fast, Hawck said, 'I felt her with you. She was spinning the crits on your damage and piling out heals, keeping you safe.'

Slowly, Finn sat again. 'Is that a thing? I mean, can it actually happen?'

'How else are you going to explain tonight? Charm's good, but she's not that good.'

Finn's shrug spoke a thousand words. Hawck couldn't see it, but he could feel it. He said, 'I've never told you about Pete.' Another pause. Another drink. 'We served together. The army's different now than it was. A bit. We were . . .' he fished for the word, 'close.'

'Lovers?' Finn offered. He was nearly fifteen. He had no more tact than I did.

You couldn't hear Hawck's frown any more than Finn's shrug, but we knew it was there, Finn and me.

'Right. His ride went over an IED. Six of them inside and there weren't enough body parts to put in a bag. No holding him while he died, no chance to say goodbye, no time to undo the small hurts that happen when you're in a hurry and it's too bloody hot, and there's stuff going bad and tempers are running short.' The silence was full of reflection. I was wrong, Finn had considerably more tact than me. He waited.

In time, Hawck said, 'There was a track called "Joan of Arc" from OMD. Long before your time so don't worry about who that is, but—'

'Orchestral Manoeuvres in the Dark.'

Hawck huffed a soft laugh. 'Do you know everything?'

'Alt-Tab Google and I can type faster than you can speak. So that was your track, the two of you?'

Now that Hawck had opened up, he's going for it. 'First dance, first kiss, first . . . everything. We played it till it wore grooves in our heads and we never got tired. The night he was killed, I got a nudge to turn on the radio, twiddled the dial through a thousand hissing, fizzing stations of shite until I hit on OMD and "Joan of Arc". I don't know what station it was. I don't know if it even existed beyond that one night, but it played that same track from the moment I cried myself to bed, till I got up at dawn the next day. No sleep, not a wink, and I swear to you, just the one track for six hours solid. Nothing else. So yes, I think it's a thing.'

There was another pause. In the game, Nifty got up, walked around the bar and sat down again. Finn said, 'Did you feel Lan tonight? I mean Starlyng.'

'It's OK, I know her name. She and I spoke a bit off-game these past weeks.' Hawck didn't say that we'd talked about Finn, or that I had asked him to keep an eye. 'And, yes, I felt her. She pulled me out of a Death Knight grip in that last game against the Method guys when it looked like we were going down. That was definitely her. Maybe a few other times.'

His voice shifted, as if he were calling into a distance. 'Thanks, Lan. We appreciate it.'

And, because I was still immersed in the symphony of this, a Whisper arose on both their screens.

    Starlyng: Ur Welcome.

Five seconds of blank silence followed.

Then, in the audio feed, Finn whispered, 'Lan?' His voice broke on the word. In his room, tears flooded his face. But he wasn't going to jump. I could feel the unmaking of that.

    Starlyng: I can't stay. Just remember
    the promise. You need me, I'll come.

'Stay. Please stay. We can just keep on playing . . .'

    Starlyng: Can't. That's not how it
    works. Places to go, things to do.
    But remember that I love you. Play
    well. Live well. Make me proud. GG

I broke out of the game, out of the machine, out of the room, out of the lands of the living. I had done my best and my dead heart was fractured.

As I left, I heard Hawck say, 'Finn, this is my mobile number. You need anything, anything at all, you call me, right?'

I was gone before the string of numbers was complete.

As I crashed back to the Between, the Crow whispered, *Well done*.

CHAPTER SIX

'I should be going now, shouldn't I?'

We were high in the Tree on the shore of the Between, both of us exhausted. Thickly, Crow said, *Do you want to?*

Did I? I looked around. The fog had begun to lift, at least around us. I could see the sea and a short length of shore in either direction. Inland, I could see a long, lean loch with a waterfall at its head, its shores stippled with gorse, silver birch, hawthorn, bracken. Still in Crow-sense, I could smell bog myrtle and heather and peaty water, all of them far sharper than I'd ever known in life. If the best memories of my childhood had been overlaid all on each other, if a Crow, or a god had imbued them with mythic dimensions and let me understand at last the inter-becoming of the world, this was the landscape they would have given me.

I was too tired to consider the implications of this, or even to think far down the line of Crow's question. We sat in silence, enjoying the sense of no danger. An osprey stooped onto the loch and came up with a fish. Something inside me warmed and softened: relaxed.

'I feel I ought to,' I said. 'Every single teacher I've ever learned from said that after death, we ought to head towards the light as a matter of urgency. Most of them were pretty clear that hanging around in the Between was a seriously bad idea. And I did make a deal with Kate. Whichever one of us crossed first swore to come back for the other. If it's possible, she'll be waiting.'

Even as I spoke, I heard a high, faint chime, like the song of a single star. Looking out along the shoreline the mist shimmered and thinned and – at last! – I could see the rising sun and the bridge that arced from the shore to its white-hot heart. A thread anchored in my solar plexus and slowly, gently reeled me in. I thought this must be what migrating birds feel at the change of the seasons, or salmon, pulled upriver to spawn.

'This is it.' I bowed to Crow. 'Are you allowed to come with me?'

I can certainly escort you as far as the boundary from here to there. The sun caught it, making liquid night of its plumage. Sparks of iridescent blues and deep, deep violet rippled from the back of its head to its tail. It spread its wings and, almost lazily, lifted into a thermal that had not been there moments before. *Shall we go?*

Thus did I find what it was to fly. As a Crow, I spread my wings and sought the wind-road in a way that felt both new and ancient-familiar. The air had textures to it, the currents colours that spoke to parts of my mind that flowered under this new knowing.

Following Crow, I soared higher and higher still until we could see the full length of the loch that lay inland of the shore, see the heights of the waterfall and the wide, wild river that fed it, count the silver birch and the wind-bent hawthorns, sweep over the circling kite that whistled at our passing.

The land was a map of my life; not all of it, but the parts that sang deep: here, the path I walked barefoot as a child because I didn't want to get my new shoes muddy, and hadn't reckoned on the tide of black slugs on the path; there the head-high bracken where I made a den and lay in it reading for days on end, and was safe; over there, the birch spinney where I taught Maddie how to lay a fire with damp wood and get it lit; thirty years later, she taught the twins and Finn the same.

This felt like a last goodbye and I took time to drink in the air, to revel in the aromatic mint-sap-sweet of bracken and bog myrtle, to glory in that one, crisp moment when the sun's light met the sea, and strewed liquid gold across the silvered water.

The chime sounded a second time, louder than the first. There were voices in its harmonies: Robbie, my mother, maybe my grandmother on my father's side that I'd never known, Pat, Christie and yes, *yes* . . . Kate.

I slid steeply sideways along a cleft in the wind, angling down and again down to the point where the sun's arc met the shore. There was a gateway here, marking the place where Between met Beyond; not exactly a physical barrier as we would understand the gate to a field, but a boundary nonetheless, of the kind I had pushed open to enter the void.

I thought it would be good to approach it in human shape and thinking made it so. Crow hopped up to the crown of a small apple tree that appeared just behind my shoulder. I caught the flash of movement and turned.

Our eyes met and its feet cramped on the bough. I said, 'Can you not come with me?'

At this time, I cannot leave the Between. It sounded sad.

'I'll miss you.'

It dipped its head. Its feet cramped tighter. I wanted to hug it, but how does a human hug a bird? Anyway, it was out of reach.

I turned back to study the sun-bridge. I could do so now. The light had dimmed to just the right side of brilliance, so that the arc it made stood clear against the pale morning sky, not quite solid, but I could easily imagine walking across.

For the first time, I could sense something of what lay beyond: a landscape wrought in the time before people were here, when gods walked free across the world, and here, walked on a wide, open grassland bounded on one side by a primaeval forest with trees so big they were the age of the earth. The leaves were on the turn and the air smelled of autumn and magic. On the other side, far away, was the glimmer of a primal ocean, so full of life that I could hear the whales singing. The whole place hummed with the power of land and stone and fire and storm that promised an eternity's worth of exploring. Unbidden, I took a step towards it.

The chime sounded again for the third and loudest time. Threes are always the numbers of gods and there were many voices in this tone, some I knew, some I only thought perhaps I knew, but as the note shimmered to quiet, I saw on the bridge the throng of those I had so far only heard: Robbie right at the front, my mother to one side, Pat nearby, and Christie: all the friends who'd really mattered. My father wasn't there and I didn't look for him: he drank almost as much as Torvald and life with him had not been kind.

In any case, I was searching for the one face that mattered, and not seeing, not seeing . . .

Lan.

As the syllable hit me, the air filled with the scent of scorched metal and planed wood, of Danish oil and beeswax and all the tools of making that I had known for over half my life.

'Kate!'

I whispered it, even as relief surged through every part of me, and love, and a sense of homecoming that drove me to my knees. Grabbing the trunk of Crow's apple tree, I pulled myself upright and made myself walk the last stretch to the boundary line, not run.

We met at the place where the sun-bridge touched the shore.

'Kate . . .'

I looked up: she had always been taller than me and now she was standing on the slight upcurve of the sun-bridge, which gave her extra height. The rising sun at her back cast her in a halo of honeyed light that left her face in shadow. Even this close, she was hazy, as if she had been crafted newly out of gauze, or morning mist. I could see through her to the god-wild lands beyond, but I knew her face, however indistinct: I could map the planes and curves.

I said, 'You look young again. Younger than when we met, even.'

Lan.

I heard her say my name, but it echoed in my heart, not in my mind in the way I heard Crow. She leaned over towards me, bent at the waist, as if over a fence. I tried to hug her and my arms passed through exactly as they had passed through Finn.

She knew who I was, though, which she hadn't in the last months of her life, except for a sliver of time right at the end. And as we'd promised, she was here to guide me on. All I had to do was push open the gate and walk through. I'd done it in the void, which was, I thought, a far harder place to negotiate. Something in me felt unbalanced, but who wouldn't be wary, facing this final rite of passage?

As I had in the void, I felt for the boundaries of this opening, leaned into it, stretched out one hand, lifted a foot . . . and slammed into a wall so utterly solid I could not pass through.

'Kate?' My voice had no sound.

The others had all come to join us, thronging the boundary, as insubstantial as Kate. Robbie's hand passed through my shoulder. I felt his grief as rain, misting my soul.

My mother ruffled my hair, or perhaps it was the wind that arose out of nowhere. She tried to smile, but there wasn't enough of her left to do it. Christie pressed in close: she never did have any sense of personal space. Pat stood back and nodded when I tried to meet his gaze. Others were there I couldn't name, but half-remembered, as if, long ago, they'd been strong in my dreams. They pressed their brows to mine, soft as wood ash and no more permanent.

'Kate! *Kate!*' I hurled myself at the barrier and bounced off it again, again, again.

Lan. Stop. Think.

The voice came from behind and above. I spun so fast that I stumbled, but it was much easier to look up into the apple tree than to keep trying to go forward. 'This is not a good time for riddles, Crow.' I sounded angry, when in fact I was terrified.

You made a promise.

Kate and I promised each other . . .

Not that. As you were dying, you offered an oath.

'To Finn, yes. You were there.'

A promise freely given is binding. Specifically, this oath binds you in the Between. You cannot leave here and move on until you are free of it. Either Finn dies or he absolves you. There is no other way.

Why had I not known this? Perhaps I had.

I turned back to Kate. 'Stay with me? Time is slippery here. It can't take that long. And you love Finn as much as I do.'

She was alone at the bridge, the throng had faded to mist. I saw her eyes close, watched her reach deep inside. The scent of beeswax and new wood became an almost physical river flowing from her to me. Within it were notes of newly sharpened pencil, of clean sheets and woodsmoke, of summer hay and autumn bonfires: all the things we'd cherished together. I felt her enfold me, as she so often had, drawing me close to the boundary.

I leaned in, and she leaned so far over, that if she'd had weight and mass, she'd have fallen. But she reached me, and I could smell her, the actual scent of her skin, feel the strength of her arms, the touch of skin on skin. She pressed her lips so very hard to mine. I barely felt them. Somewhere in the cathedrals of my mind was a promise of waiting, a sense of pride and sorrow mixed, and of infinite time.

And then she was gone.

INTERLOGUE 1

2008–2023

You think that the dead watch over you all the time, that whenever you pick your nose, or lose it with the kids and shout something you know you'll regret, we're hovering at attic height, being silently, ostentatiously (and hypocritically) censorious.

You think that as soon as we die, we're cleansed of all that made us human, every single prejudice and foible – except our capacity for judgement.

You think we stand outside time unless we choose to step into it and criticise the conduct of our former friends and family.

You think, in fact, that we are omnipresent, projected instances of your parents at their most psychotic.

You are wrong, obviously, but it's hardly your fault when your entire world is wrought from judgement and its fallout. It's the curse of modernity, and that's assuming modernity began around the time of the Roman invasion, if not several thousand years before.

So, let's clean the slate and start again. We who are not currently living do not nurture the same priorities as we did when we were flesh and blood. Our focus is far more on the love lines connecting us to you than, say, your incomes, your politics, your social status and your capacity to clamber up the greasy pole of your chosen profession, even if you chose it because you thought we'd approve.

All of these are irrelevancies raised as shields by the living to avoid the things that actually matter. Once you're dead, there is no avoiding anything that truly matters and you will regret every second of life that you wasted on this kind of trivia. Trust me on this.

Back to the point: we who are dead have our own journeys and travails. Yours are no more likely to attract our attention than they did when we were both alive. Which is to say that occasionally we find you riveting. Mostly, though, you are the radio we left on in the background and forgot to switch off. Unless we hear our names uttered in all the white noise, we barely notice you're there.

In the space between the start of my education and Kaitlyn's posting of the message that broke everything open, my name was clearly invoked three times. On each of these occasions, I paid close attention to the lives of my family. In between, I had other work to do.

The first distinct interaction took place on the night after Maddie's wedding.

It was the autumn equinox, six months to the day after my funeral. Maddie was six months pregnant, also to the day. Finn had always wanted a younger sister and Kaitlyn Karim Penhaligon was on the way. Eriq, it seemed, had come to see me off, and had stayed.

I was still heart-sore and bruised from the rebuff at the sun-bridge but the idea of the family growing helped the hurt places to hurt less and none of my grandchildren were showing any inclination towards parenthood.

Finn seemed fairly locked into aromantic asexuality, all his passion thrown at the mat and into the Arenas. Kirsten and Niall were quite the opposite: their Alba Rising community was predicated on interchangeable intimate relationships. But while their lovers were many and varied, nobody ever imagined any of them was more than a friend. They had each other for everything beyond the physicality of sex and both were politically disinclined to increase the population while the world burned around them; procreation, accidental or otherwise, was not on their radar.

All this being the case, when a heavily pregnant Maddie dreamed her way to the lochside, still wearing her crimson wedding dress and a crown of plaited corn stalks, I was genuinely delighted.

'Lan!' She ran up to me, girlish in her enthusiasm. 'You're looking younger.'

We hugged. She kissed me. All kinds of stuck things inside me became fluid in that moment. I said, 'You look like a goddess', and meant it.

I took her hand as I had when she was small and led her on a tour of my home, starting with the hawthorn tree I'd wrought from one of the smaller trees that had been here when I had been turned back from the shoreline and made the loch my home. I had needed a way to stay sane and making the tree had kept me occupied for a good while: each leaf, thorn and flower was built of memories, woven through with my new appreciation for the web of life.

It was excruciatingly painful – anything that reminded me of Kate hurt as if I were being flayed and salted – but I was learning a lot about myself and the life I had lived and why I had made certain choices: it wasn't all bad.

Anyway, Maddie was impressed by the tree, and enchanted when I introduced her to Hail, the hound that had materialised when I'd most needed company.

He was not my creation, though I'd definitely have brought him into being if I'd believed it was possible. Dark brindle with white flecks scattered about his head and forequarters, he was the kind of beast that ran at the heels of Cú Chulainn in the myth-wreathed Ireland of our ancestors. His withers came up to my waist and when I lay down, which I did a lot when grief drowned me in the early days, he came to lie close, leaning his head on my shoulder so that I had a sense of myself, and my place in this halfway world. He didn't speak and had given me no name. I called him Hail because I could, and because it fitted.

Maddie liked him even more than the tree, and the three of us sat on a long, low rock, at the lochside, looking out across the water. Maddie and I had done this in life; her memories of this place overlaid mine in many ways.

Presently, she said, 'Did you enjoy the wedding?'

They had mentioned my name twice, and Kate's. The sense of both together had evoked the usual mix of pain and joy, but that was not something I wanted to dump on Maddie.

I said, 'Thank you for playing Runrig. That was kind.'

Maddie cocked one brow. 'We like it.'

I laughed, which felt rare enough to be good. 'I'm dead, Mads, not senile. You don't have to pretend to share my musical tastes.'

'Cynic.' She picked up a pebble and skimmed it across the water. Six bounces: not bad. 'It's your music and we love you, so we love it, too. Grant us that much.'

'I bet you had to fight for it, though.' Niall had never been a fan, and Niall was the one who organised the music. Finn may have been the tech-wizard in all other fields, but when it came to music, Niall made everything happen. Runrig didn't have nearly enough activist fervour for his tastes.

Maddie grinned. 'Only a bit. It was my special day, after all. And I can play the I'm-pregnant-so-I-get-what-I-want card if I have to.'

She leaned back, and the swell of her abdomen leaned forward. I had Crow-sense in this place, even when I was in human form: if I listened hard, I could hear a second heartbeat, which made my own heart leap. But when I turned to Maddie, there was a judder to her jugular pulse and she was pressing her fingers together to stop herself from biting her nails and both of those were signs I'd learned to read long ago.

As gently as I knew how, I asked, 'What is it you want, Mads? Much as I'd love to believe you just came to hang out, it takes a lot of effort to dream this clearly, so I'm thinking there's something else?'

The grin faded. She chewed her lip. There was only one thing I could think of that would make her this nervous. 'Do you need to sell the farm and want to know if it's OK?'

It had been in the family for centuries, so no, it wasn't, but it was going to have to be. She hadn't got much money and Eriq had none at all. Needs must and all that, except . . . 'Why are you looking at me as if I've just dropped a dead rat in your coffee?'

'Why are you asking me daft questions? We can't sell the farm! The twins would kill me, except they'd have to go through Finn first and he's the one with the fancy-coloured karate belts.'

'Not karate. Shaolin Kung Fu. They're different.' I knew this, but I'd forgotten how much it mattered to Finn, how much I'd cared because he did. And now memory struck me, hard.

Broadsided, I closed my eyes against an avalanche of returning sensations: pride in Finn getting his first belts; pride in watching his relationship with Mo evolve; pride when he joined in her crack-of-dawn meditations, this boy who never got up when the clock was in single figures; pride when he joined the devotions of good works to the village; pride in watching him grow to be the stellar human being I'd always known he could be.

I was used to the acid-ache that came whenever I thought of Kate and the parting at the gate. This, though, was a whole new order of pain, like terminal frostbite or coming up too fast from a stupidly deep dive: needles of ice unstitched my skin and bathed my bones in lava.

Maddie was frowning down at her hands and so saw none of this. 'Anyway,' she asked, 'where would we go?'

I planted my elbows on my knees and my chin on my closed fists and let the stability of this give me the focus for her words. 'Glasgow would be obvious,' I said. 'It's where you all grew up, after all, and the twins already have a base there.'

More than a base, Alba Rising was pretty much an institution in its own right. In the days before house prices became impossibly high, a dozen of them had bought a crescent of terraced houses in Glasgow's Southside. More recently, they had commandeered the former tennis court nestled within the crescent's arc to be their community garden. They had roots in real bricks and mortar, and their turnover of members was low.

More than anything else, they had built a community of purpose and passion as much as of place; one that mixed Niall's desperate wish for Scotland's Independence with Kirsten's need to make the world a decent place for everyone living there. They had steady jobs, too: Niall in law, Kirsten in psychotherapy. Maddie could go back to the theatre; they'd welcome her with champagne and wild dancing. What's not to like?

Lots, evidently. Maddie tossed a pebble from hand to hand. 'No chance. Too cold, too grey, too . . . northern. Eriq'd go mad.'

'Are you telling me he didn't stay away because of me?'

'Why would he do that?'

'Mother-in-law from hell?'

She choked on a laugh. Gently, the way Crow spoke when I wasn't coping, she said, 'It's not all about you, Lan.'

'Then why is he staying now when he didn't before?'

'Besides this?' She looped her fingers across the promise of her daughter.

'If being a father was enough to keep him, he'd have stayed for Finn.'

'He didn't *know* what it was to be a father. Coming back was a shock. He realised he cares for Finn and me as much as he does for Max, and now Kaitlyn's on her way and—'

'Max?' I already knew the family had picked the name of my not-yet-born granddaughter. I was honoured, obviously: me and Kate melded together (nearly), but even if I hadn't known, I wasn't about to be side-tracked while Maddie struggled with the shadow that was Max. I nudged her. 'It's a dream. Nothing can hurt you. Tell me.'

It still took her a while, and then, 'Max,' she said, tightly, 'is the love of Eriq's life. Perhaps now it would be more fair to say the *other* love of his life. They were an item long before we met. I knew when I got pregnant with Finn that he'd already promised to go back to Brazil. I didn't think he'd stay this time, but,' her smile took on a wry edge, 'he doesn't want to turn up to the next family funeral and stand in front of a child he's never met hoping they're not about to call him Mr Karim.'

'Ouch!' This laugh scattered the pain, which was an interesting discovery. 'Did Finn do that?'

'Not quite. They settled on first names. It was close, though.'

That would have been worth seeing. I let it go. 'So, can you make the farm work?' I asked. 'Financially, I mean?'

Another pebble. Nine skips. I was a dream: she could have done twenty-nine if she had put her mind to it, a hundred, but she wasn't watching. All her attention was on me. 'Jens and Matt think they can get the farm to break even if they go full-on agro-ecological and start selling direct to the local area. They've finished the cottage and the barns are all waterproof. They've turned one into a milking parlour and they can double the size of the herd and still keep it manageable, apparently. They got organic certification while you were in hospital and now Matt's experimenting with keeping the calves on the cows and only milking once a day so it's a lot better all round. Jens is getting into the chemistry of cheese and yoghurt. You know what he's like. If there's a technical angle, he'll find a way to make it better.'

If I knew which god to thank for these two, I'd be leaving offerings with every turn of the moon. I said, 'You should write them a new contract and then—

'Already done. The Dairy is officially a community land trust. Kirsten worked out the frame and Niall did the legal stuff. You can relax. It's all good.'

Right. Brilliant. Perfect. 'But none of that will put food on the table or buy shoes for a growing daughter.'

Maddie kept her gaze elsewhere. 'Riq's set up a new business with Max.'

'In Brazil?'

'Don't look at me like that, it's still on the same planet and we've got good enough broadband: he says he can make it work from here as well as anywhere. He just needs . . .'

'Money.' Obviously.

I expected some pushback. Instead, Maddie plucked a blade of grass and wound it round her finger, and it seemed we had reached the nub of her being here. 'We found a box of sketchbooks in the attic.'

'And?'

'There's one from the sixties, before I was born. There's a sketch in it. A nude . . .'

'Of me.' *Woah*. Too much, too fast. Glasgow. October. Rain hosing the windows. A taste of toast and sex and finger-touches like fairy dust on my skin and Kate, suddenly serious, picking up a sketchbook and telling me sharply not to move. She was newly out of her marriage. We'd never spent a night together. This was the first time I'd seen what she could do with a pencil and a plain sheet of paper.

Pain crashed over me.

'Lan?' Of a sudden, Maddie was kneeling, holding my hands in hers, seeing distress and thinking it was her fault. Fast, she said, 'Suzi at the Lavenham Gallery thinks—'

'You can sell it, Mads. It's OK.' Talking helped, or I wanted it to. 'How much does she think it'll make?'

'Seventy. Maybe up to a hundred if they can get a bidding war going.'

Oh. Well. It was only a scribble on an A4 cartridge pad. And the wedding must have cleaned them out. Breathless, I said, 'Good.'

'Seventy grand and you're looking like you just swallowed a wasp?' She poked her elbow in my ribs. 'You're hopeless!'

'*How* much?'

'Well, it's . . . erotica.'

'Madeleine Penhaligon!'

'Sorry.' She was laughing, high and embarrassed, but then it was sex, and it was before she was born, and . . . Her gaze narrowed. 'You're really OK if we sell it?'

'Mads, I am more than OK. Take it as a wedding gift from me and Kate. If you've found that box, there will be others. Sell anything in there that will bring in some cash. Suzi's solid. She won't rob you and she'll know how to set up the sales . . . What? I thought it was a good thing?'

She was looking crushed and I didn't know why. Thinly, she said, 'It *is* good, but Riq's not going to believe I met you in a dream and he's really touchy about treading on your memory. He has two grandmothers still alive who'd flay him with a blunt blade if he dishonoured you.'

'Really?' I sat up straighter. 'Give him a hug from me. Tell him it's OK.'

'I will, but it won't cut it. Could you do the whole—' she wobbled her hands— 'computer thing and tell him yourself? He'd listen to you.' A sharpness in her gaze, then, 'Or do I have to learn to play Warcraft first?'

What? An ice-brick jammed in my throat. I loved my daughter beyond measure, but she had a fierce, wild temper and I had never learned how to weather her storms. She wasn't raging yet, but I could see why she might, and wouldn't have blamed her, either.

'Finn told you?'

'I'm his mother, of course he did.' She huffed a theatrical sigh. 'I'm not cross with you, Lan, completely not. If he's right, you saved

62

his life. And I get why you talked to him and not me or the twins: we weren't about to hurl ourselves off the roof. Or whatever.' Memories twisted shadows around her. She shivered them away. 'Can you, though? Riq knows what you did. He'll believe it if you can talk on the screen. We could get the game, honestly. I've always fancied making a gnome Warlock with purple hair.'

'Please don't, Finn would die of embarrassment.'

'Fuck off!' She cuffed the side of my head, but lightly, so I'd know she wasn't cross. 'Still, can you?'

'I can't, Mads. I'm so sorry.' I had tried. Trust me, I had tried. I had hurled myself at the trying for half a year after the sun-bridge had closed as a way to get past the pain of losing Kate.

Crow had been kind, but had left no room for doubt.

'That was a one-time event. Exceptional circumstances and all that. I was newly dead and desperate and . . .' And the new-deadness, coupled with the void-walk had given me a boost, the like of which could never be repeated, but we didn't need to go there. 'It's never going to happen again. I wish it was. You'll just have to be convincing.' I picked my own pebble and sent it skimming right across to the far side of the loch. It was invisible long before it landed on the far shore, but the flow of its flight gave me an idea.

'What if I told you something you didn't know before, would that work?'

'Depends what it is?'

'Did you ever find Kate's camera?' Saying her name hurt. Worth it, though.

Maddie frowned at me and the question, both. 'I don't think so.'

'It's in the Piggery. If you lift the hatch in the far right corner under her workbench, there's a place . . . not quite a cellar, more of a lightproof box. Unless someone's got there ahead of you, her Minolta's in there and I think the last film's still in it: a whole reel of pictures she took on Newmarket Heath right at the end, just before she began to lose . . .'

A thunderclap of memory, then, straight to my heart and I was drowning, drowning, drowning, lost in fire and freeze and when I could open my eyes and sit up, Maddie had gone, and I was alone by the loch with Hail leaning hard against my shoulder and Crow perched on the rock by my elbow, tapping its beak on the back of my hand with terrible care, as if I were glass and a crack might destroy me.

I did not disintegrate. I did not, either, go back to the memories that had spun me so far out. I did, however, pay closer attention to the family, enough to see that Eriq had been wholly convinced by the discovery of the camera and its treasure trove of undeveloped, unseen Katherine Penhaligon images. (Kate was by far the more famous. My taking her family name had been an obvious move and had saved a lot of time when Maddie was born and all we had to decide was a given name.)

The sketch (*First Love*) invoked a ferocious bidding war and ultimately sold for one hundred and seventy thousand pounds to the same hedge-funded museum whose foundation had bought *Kettled*.

Not bad for a sex-laden scribble. If I'd been alive, I'd have shredded it, burned it and flushed the ashes into the septic tank rather than let anyone see me in a way that was remotely identifiable. But dead . . . it was good to have something to give Maddie beyond the occasional nostalgic dream.

Other sketches in the book sold at the same auction. The photographs sold later, when they'd been developed and printed up by Dave Holland, who was one of the few Kate had shared her ideas with. The results were a worthy last testament to her life's work. She'd been experimenting with minimalism and a couple of the shots of a red deer stag walking out of the mist in Thetford forest looked as if the Wild Hunt had descended to herald the end of time: hunter and hunted in one shot, deadly and vulnerable, death and its quarry. Deer had been for Kate what crows had been for me and I was glad they'd appeared for her while she was still able to appreciate what they'd offered.

In aggregate, the sale brought in over a million pounds. Maddie put one third of the money in trust for her unborn child, split one third among her existing children and gave half of the remaining third to Eriq to kick-start his new company. She kept the final one sixth as spending money to keep the family afloat until she could start earning again.

Kaitlyn Karim Penhaligon was born at home at dusk on the winter solstice. I was there for this, too, though not strictly called; it was impossible not to care, not to want to help, to feel, in fact, utterly helpless.

I wasn't alone. For the first time since being turned back from the sun-bridge, I felt the presence of the Beyond. I couldn't see anyone, but as I sat in Crow form in the damson tree outside the kitchen, watching this new thread weave itself into the web of life, I felt the gathered throng of love and attention.

Kate was here for sure, and her mother, though we'd never met. I think, in fact, all the mothers of her line, and my mother and all the mothers of our line, and a whole host of people I didn't know, had gathered in something that felt like a cross between a giant rugby scrum and a party: the same kind of welcoming group that would gather at a death, but in reverse, helping the new life come into being, letting her know that it was worth the havoc of life and she'd be back with them soon enough: time is slippery on all sides of the divide.

She emerged into the world in a water bath in the kitchen, with Mo Bakar helping. I didn't quite follow how someone with an international skill in breaking bricks with their bare hands was going to be useful at a birth, except they were small, neat hands and Matt had already co-opted her for lambing help occasionally, so she had a bit of useful experience.

As it turned out, she was there to offer breathing exercises, which must have helped, because labour seemed to pass far faster than I ever remembered and when Kaitlyn arrived, she looked like Finn had done, but smaller and far darker, and her smile blazed like the sun.

I watched her grow with the same fiery pride I'd felt for her brothers and sister, but she knew me only by photographs and the occasional family tradition: she never called for me by name.

Finn, on the other hand, talked to me all the time, though the clearest explicit call came in the spring of 2018, when he first fell in love. With a girl. Colour me shocked.

Giullia was from Italy, or possibly Bulgaria, I wasn't paying real attention, and wasn't required to: Finn just wanted to share the joy of a new-found soulmate.

In exhaustive detail, I came to know that they had met in the final year of his PhD, when she'd joined Mo Bakar's martial arts group. She was already proficient in Wing Chun, which was close enough, apparently, to Mo's style of Shaolin Kung Fu for her to step straight in just below black belt. She was also a caver and a climber and, in her exquisite company, Finn rediscovered his love of sheer rock faces in the sun and in the dark. They didn't, though, breach the boundaries of physicality until the summer, when they threw themselves into the restoration of the Piggery, turning it into a martial arts training studio with extra bells and whistles.

It had been Kate's studio, so I wasn't entirely thrilled about this, but they needed space, and while the Piggery itself had barely been big enough for her, and certainly wasn't big enough to train a hundred sweaty fighters, it turned out that Jens had a degree in architecture and was not averse to using it on the farm (he was entirely averse to using it in a corporate setting).

The planners, having caved once, put up remarkably little resistance, and so, under his direction, they raised the Piggery up to two floors and extended on round the corner into the adjacent Dutch barns. The result was big enough not only for training gyms on both floors but on the ground floor they added a lecture theatre that could double as a seriously big office alongside a kitchen fit to feed the five thousand, while upstairs the second, smaller training gym was joined by eight en-suite bedrooms. Matt and Jens helped with the building work. A lot.

The first class Finn and Giullia taught together in the new studio was for Kaitlyn and all of her friends in the village, which was strategic genius on Giullia's part, because by then it was obvious to anyone who paid attention that the way to Finn's heart was through his younger sister. He may have had no particular interest in anyone of either sex except as worthy opponents, but any individual who could make Kaitlyn smile that wide at least had the combination to the safe in which he had locked his heart. They became lovers that night.

Giullia didn't like his gaming much, which wasn't ideal given that the hardcore gamers of the ReadyCheck guild had renamed themselves Team Memory after my death and had begun to train with dedicated fervour. By the time Finn steered Kaitlyn and her friends through their first grading, Team Memory were ranked fifth on the European ladder, with Twitch streams and online video tutorials pulling in enough money that none of them needed to work.

They *wanted* to work, though, and sometime during his undergraduate years, Finn had set up Grey Ghosts Ltd (the name grew out of GG, for Good Game: adulthood hadn't changed his addiction to acronyms), a grey-hat hacking company that discovered the holes in the flagship software of the social media giants and then sold them the fixes before anyone else found them.

They charged a premium, obviously, and while this may not sound the kind of socially beneficial action the rest of Finn's family would have admired, he could have sold the same data to the Russian or Saudi hacking labs for orders of magnitude more. On a scale where black hats earned serious money and their white counterparts earned small unshelled peanuts, grey was as good as it got.

All of this meant that my grandson was on his computer from lunchtime till three in the morning most days, but Giullia loved him, so it was all fine. Also, the sex, did he mention? She may have missed his company on the nights when he was laughing with his friends rather than having an early night with her, but she didn't mind being woken in the small hours when he'd just had a winning streak.

Leaving her sexual prowess aside, she was a demon on the mat, cooked like an angel, spoke five languages and dreamed in three . . . and she left him halfway through lockdown for a rower who had been capped for her college. They had been sexting for a year before she mentioned his existence to Finn. His name was Gregory and he didn't play computer games.

Thus, the third time I heard my name spoken with real fervour was in 2020, when Finn's heart was broken. For nearly a week he lay on his back on the bed in Ash Barn, thinking of ways he might end it all. He couldn't dream the way his mother could, and I still had no other way to connect, but I sat with him through those nights and I think he felt my presence.

Even if he hadn't, there wasn't any real risk of him dying: he had too much to live for by then, including Team Memory's inexorable rise up the World of Warcraft Arena ladder. He had a big match scheduled at the end of the week and he was never likely to miss that. His teammates – Charm, the Franco-Berber Healer-Priest, and Juke, the Israeli Mage – joked with him as if nothing had happened and by the end of the weekend, when they'd come out top, he was back at his desk and functioning again; heart-bruised, but essentially intact.

And that was it. Three more peaceful years until the March of 2023, when, three months after her fourteenth birthday, Kaitlyn sent her tweet. I wasn't called then, I was sent. And afterwards nothing was ever the same for the living or the dead.

Book Two

— THE POST —

You have to act as if it were possible to radically transform the world.
And you have to do it all the time.

— Angela Davis

CHAPTER SEVEN

I was at the lochside in the Between, trying to light a fire.

I had gathered tinder of lichens, old leaves and dried grasses, sharpened a flint with which to shave tendrils of wood from an alder branch, found and stacked dried branches of elder, hawthorn and ash, the three woods I had always held most sacred, and was endeavouring to cause fire to arise with only the power of my mind.

It was the kind of thing Crow approved of. It was constantly devising new tests to keep me sharp and while none of them had been easy, this was by far the most difficult. I had practised for what felt like months, but in the slippery time of the Between, could as easily have been days or decades. This morning, finally, had brought into being a spark, a flare, a faint wash of heat and smoke threading up to the clear autumn sky.

'Hey,' I sat back on my heels. 'We have fire.'

I was waiting for congratulations: Crow was very keen on positive reinforcement. But something like thunder grumbled low and hard enough to shake the ground and Hail, who had been sunning himself on a rock by the loch, jerked to his feet and stalked stiff-legged to stand at my side.

Crow flowed down off the hawthorn and took up a mirror-stance on the other side. Neither of them was what you'd call relaxed.

She is not ready, Crow said, tightly. Plainly, this was not addressed to me.

She's fine, so, said a deeply rolling voice from my right. *She's as ready as she'll ever be. You just need to trust her.*

'Hail? You can speak?' All this time and not a word. But his voice was enthralling: Irish, I thought, though it was hard to nail down:

71

even these few words had dips and valleys and slants I had never heard. It sounded ancient, mythic, even. I wanted to sit down with him and explore all that he knew.

Crow, though, was on the edge of panic: blinking too fast and crabbing from foot to foot.

Hail nodded his big, kind head. *Go, the two of you. I'll be here when you get back.*

'Crow? Go where?'

To the family. They have need of you.

'Really?' I scanned fast back through recent events to which I had paid almost no attention. A week ago, Finn's senior students had been graded for their black belts, which, it had turned out, was every bit as nerve-wracking as if he were grading himself, but he was competent and Mo had trained him well and they'd all passed: no dramas there.

Two days later, Maddie and Eriq had returned from a fortnight in a smart hotel up on the west coast, across from Skye. It wasn't the kind of place they could ever have afforded before, but surprising though it may sound – it certainly surprised the heck out of me – Maddie's dodgy investment in Eriq had paid off.

Fifteen years down the line, his long-distance business venture with Max had become the umbrella for a whole series of distributed micro-businesses: dairies, bakeries, mobile phone vendors that then flowed their profits into schools and local healthcare. The model had spread first across Brazil, then into the rest of the continent and was extending into Indonesia, East Africa and the Antipodes.

Eriq had married into a family of activists and Connor was a non-exec on the board, so it was all strictly non-profit, but that didn't mean he couldn't pay himself a decent wage as long as it wasn't more than thirty times the lowest hourly rate.

He'd always spent his money freely, it was just he'd never had very much of it. Now that he had plenty, Maddie was there to stop him throwing it around, but the holiday had been an exception, and then, on the way back down the road, they'd made a surprise visit to Kirsten and Niall as they turned thirty-seven.

Leaving aside the presence of the older generation, the twins' birthday had been as unremarkable as ever. Following family tradition, everyone else had chipped in some money and each twin had bought the other's gift on the grounds that nobody else had a clue what they might want.

Thus Kirsten had been signed up for Sophy Banks's 'Healthy Human Culture' online course so she could learn about micro-return paths and the healing of trauma, and Niall now had a shelfful of textbooks on degrowth and doughnut economics, neither of which had been invented when I was alive.

Nobody could pretend his reading habits were normal, but unless someone had taken umbrage at one of his political rants and bludgeoned him to death with a luminous green hardback, I couldn't see any immediate threats there, either.

Back at the farm, Kaitlyn spent most of her waking life immersed in social media, but even if she'd been in trouble, she had never yet leaned on me for help or support: she knew my name; she didn't know me as a person.

Wary, I said, 'Nobody's called.'

They will. And you need to see why. Without further warning, Crow jerked a nod at me. It was a long time since we had travelled to the lands of the living together. We did so now, raggedly, on the back of its angst, and came to rest on a beech tree in the Rookery that gave a distant view into Kaitlyn's bedroom.

It was springtime in Suffolk: damp and cold, nothing out of the ordinary. Kaitlyn was awake, lying on her bed, propped up on half a dozen pillows with a laptop balanced across her knees.

Crow's words were etched across my memory: *She's not ready.* So of course, I bent everything towards proving it wrong. I needed to be closer. I needed, in fact, to be with Kaitlyn. Abandoning the beech, I flew to, and then through, the window. Cold wrapped me as I passed inside and then I was perched on the headboard behind her, leaning over to read the screen.

Thus did I discover that it was just after six o'clock on the morning of Friday, 17 March 2023. Of the tabs currently open on Kaitlyn's browser, the live one was Twitter.

`@Green4Grrl: I wish someone would make`

```
some soft porn for the under 20s. You
know, where someone doesn't get choked
in the end?
Consensual  pain  is  fine,  but  this
isn't,  and  I  don't  think  it's  a  good
thing to be selling to screenagers.
Someone will get hurt for real.
#SafeScreenageSex
```

She hit send, then opened a DM to Niall.

```
@Green4Grrl: You awake?
@Niall9Lives: Yep. Seen it. Go girl.
I'm with you.
```

I was with her, too, obviously. But goodness, I wasn't sure this was the ditch we all wanted to die in. I positioned myself in front of her, eye to eye.

'Are you sure you're ready for this? Your mother is going to go batshit crazy. Your father . . .'

Maddie's rages were legendary. I had no idea what Eriq was like when he was genuinely angry, but I didn't think any of us needed to find out.

She couldn't hear me, and I couldn't reach her. I was endeavouring to write something on her screen when Hail's voice echoed in from the Between. *Let it go, Lan.* I couldn't argue with that kind of authority. I slid back through the window. To Hail and Crow, both, I said, 'You want me to go into the servers and delete the tweet?'

The fact that I could read the screen was nothing new: I'd been doing it for fifteen years. But entering a bank of giant servers on the other side of the planet and finding a single set of characters among the millions upon millions flowing through every minute? This kind of thing had been beyond me even when I was newly dead and I was sure it was not within my power now. Nonetheless, I was willing to give it everything I'd got.

You can't, said Crow.

'I'm sure I could at least—'

What our companion is trying to say, Hail offered, more kindly, *is that you shouldn't try. You have not been asked for help. Intervening on your own account is neither wise nor likely to lead to good outcomes.'*

'Then why—?'

You need to see how the impact of this moulds the lives of those we all care about.

We.

Hail cared about my family.

I was considering the implications of this when Crow said, *It would be good if you were to remain in there. You need to feel what's happening so you can act when the time is right.*

'What can I do?'

Whatever the situation requires. You will know when the moment arises. Crow tipped its head, encouragingly. *Like with Finn.*

From the Between, with the odd echo as if the wind had hollowed out his voice, Hail said, *You need to be more than a passive observer. You can only influence those things that have touched your heart.*

'I can see the colours around Kaitlyn in ways I couldn't before. Is that what you mean?' Caramel and lemon swirled hotly around her, with a penumbra of dawn-sky blue.

Crow's sigh was almost silent. *Don't overthink, Lan. You'll know when it's happening.*

Fuck. No pressure, then. I slid in through the cold-sharp window, settled again on the headboard and watched the swirl of feeling around Kaitlyn that I'd been ignoring as an artefact of the Crow-sense. With more attention, I could almost taste the tension in the air, the garish wash of pre-performance anxiety interleaved with more subtle layers of grief, and hope and a raw, unfocused rage. It hurt to look at it in real detail, so I drew back, until it was more like keeping a finger lightly on a pulse and less like staring at a firework at the moment of explosion.

I already knew that my granddaughter was no stranger to social media. She'd set up a vlog at the start of lockdown, and while it had been planned at first as a way for the group of village kids to keep learning together, it had soon become apparent that Stina, Prune and Nico were not overly keen on being seen on screen, which had left Kaitlyn as the sole presenter. She'd put a new plan together, talked it through with the family and, the next day, had turned the channel into a young-teen version of YouthxYouth, the educational channel created for young people by young people that had garnered a following around the globe.

With the family's help, she'd covered all the sciences, politics, renegade economics and cooking, with guest pieces from Jens and Matt on agro-ecological farming. She'd continued long after lockdown ended; her Twitter, Instagram and Snapchat follower numbers were all in strong six figures, while her TikTok and YouTube nudged into the early millions, all of them ready to amplify whatever she might offer them.

Thus, without any further action on her part, her early morning tweet had already been turned into a meme and redistributed on all platforms. In that first hour, the hashtag #SafeScreenageSex began to trend and her notifications leapt into the hundreds, thousands and tens of thousands. The overwhelming majority were urging her to shoot a TikTok video to amplify her reach with the younger generation, to free herself from 'the tyranny of 280 chars' and give herself a broader base from which to say more of the same.

Her core point was not new to them, evidently, it was just that nobody had got around to saying it aloud and now Kaitlyn had become their champion. She was also going to be the one to take the flak for speaking out, but nobody mentioned that.

She texted Niall:

@Green4Grrl: Making a vid for TT&T OK?
@Niall9Lives: Go grrl

Making a video required more preparation than I might have imagined. Kaitlyn took a shower and spent an astonishing length of time attending to her hair. It was darker than Finn's, a true raven blue-black, and she brushed it into an iridescent flag hanging over her left shoulder.

She selected makeup with the deftness of long practice and dressed in a cream linen shirt that made her skin look as black as her hair. She wore no jewellery, although the crow in me could feel it shine-lurking in a bedside drawer.

Sitting on the head of her bed was the very definition of passive observation and I could feel Crow and Hail growing tetchy. Launching up, I circled her room once and then flew through to the wider attic space next door.

Her room was a mirror image of Finn's, a smallish space with a walk-in bathroom at the southern end of the barn, the creation of which had triggered the Piggery renovations.

Now, the area between the two bedrooms, that had been a yoga/training studio, had become a video suite with a blue-screen backdrop, acoustic padding and professional kit.

The needs of the Grey Ghosts and Team Memory together meant that Finn had installed a private fibre broadband line which ensured broadcast-quality video capability. Also, the walls had been soundproofed so that she didn't have to listen to him playing Arena matches at three in the morning and he didn't have to listen to her making videos at six.

Finn was abed on the far side of his bedroom door. I eased through the pine planks and checked the logs on his computer. Team Memory was in the middle of a new tournament with the finals three weeks away. Accordingly, Nifty the Rogue had been playing until three thirty. The matches had gone well from the looks of things, and he was peaceful. His sleep felt deep and his dreams were beginning to evolve the punch and clarity of his mother's. I resisted the temptation to enter them.

Back in the attic video suite, Kaitlyn finished setting up the lights and took her seat. Speaking directly to camera against a blue-screen backdrop, she recorded a longer, more explicit version of her tweet.

I will spare you the details, partly because you can imagine them and partly because I couldn't and didn't want to try, which meant it was hard to hold onto the minutiae. The gist was that old, straight men routinely enjoyed watching videos of young girls being violently assaulted in a sexual context and because they had the money to pay for it, the internet was full of this, to the exclusion of pretty much anything else.

Thus, young people who were newly exploring the potential of intimate encounters and wanted to understand more of the available options (also, frankly, who were hunting for erotica, because lockdown had been long and lonely and they were still relearning how to negotiate actual human interactions), were being offered non-consensual violence as by far the largest and most accessible meal on the table, with staringly obvious impacts on their psyches.

This was, in Kaitlyn's opinion, the leitmotif of the older generation's wilful desecration of the young. She finished with a harangue that raised her ire to a new level.

'You've destroyed our planet, you've devastated our futures, you've broken our childhoods for your own gratification – and you don't *care*. All that matters is that you get what you want, when you want, at the cheapest possible price and to hell with the consequences for anyone else. That and shooting your rocks off whatever way you like, obviously. And just in case you think I'm exaggerating, watch this. I'll put a link in the notes.'

The passion in her voice, on her face, in the wild, synthetic music she laid over it in the first editing pass . . . she could have been reading the local bus timetable and it would have sounded electric.

She churned it through a video editing suite, adding an urban grunge background, and changed the colour saturation to create a truly eldritch feel. Given the flash of a triple-X-rated video she pasted on the end, the effect was finely tuned to stamp on every single raw nerve in the Twitter-sphere and beyond.

Predictably, the internet's collective head exploded, but it did so over time and in age-related stages, with the younger generations catching it on TikTok and Snapchat first and spreading it way beyond their home time zones in a massed viral ramp that reached Twitter and then Facebook last.

By the time anyone older than forty had woken up, the original #SafeScreenageSex hashtag had been reduced to #SSS, which was probably why it was as late as seven thirty before Maddie's phone rang.

I followed the sound across the yard to the farmhouse, leaving Kaitlyn on the phone to Kirsten, who had rung soon after the video hit Instagram. Finn was still asleep.

The house had changed again since I had last been there. Maddie was taking a shower in the wet room they'd built next to the bedroom with some of the money from the sales of Kate's sketches. Eriq flipped her phone to speaker and laid it on the sink. He kissed Maddie and wrapped her in a vast white bath sheet. I mention this because each act made its own set of sound effects, which later hit the airwaves.

She was leaning against him, teasing the knuckle of her thumb down his ribs when a woman's voice echoed off the tiles. 'Madeleine? Did you know your daughter was watching hardcore porn last night?'

So now I got to see what happened when Eriq lost his temper. Outwardly, very little changed. At the level where feeling roared, the air around him sparked scarlet and black with a deep and deadly attention.

'Who is this?' His tone was all friendly enquiry.

'Rebecca Watson. Madeleine and I shared a flat together in Glasgow.'

Maddie had frozen. At this, she shook her head slightly, frowning – and then remembered. 'Becky? Becky Childeran? You work for the BBC. Radio Two?'

'That was last year. Now I'm with the quality broadcaster.' A tinge of pride coloured the adjective.

'QBC?' Eriq's laugh was spiked with acid. 'Fox News for the Little Englanders.'

Becky-become-Rebecca heard him. Her voice frosted over. 'I was asking about Madeleine's daughter, Kaitlyn. And her porn habit.'

'*Our* daughter,' Maddie said.

'Right. And you got married for this one. I did have that in my notes. Sorry.' She managed to make both marriage and its absence sound like equal insults. 'But do you know what she does with her nights? And do you condone it?'

If she had been in the room, I think Eriq might have killed her for the tone of her voice alone. Maddie's hand on his chest was pale-knuckle-hard. 'I'm sorry, I don't understand what this is about?'

'It's about your daughter's tweet. You haven't seen it? Or her video? She's quite the internet sensation. She thinks—'

'We'll ask our daughter what she thinks, thank you.' Maddie's anger was the colour of the risen sun. She held it in long enough to switch off her phone, and say to Eriq, 'Can you see if Kaitlyn will join us for breakfast? I don't think I trust myself.'

With superhuman restraint, she did not look at her own social feeds while she dressed.

The family conversation took place downstairs at the long beech table in the main kitchen of the farmhouse. Long ago, Finn had installed a screen that could either function as a television or mirror the family's phones. At her mother's request, Kaitlyn projected the contents of her phone onto it, starting with the tweet, moving onto her video and ending, at length, with videos she had watched but not made.

Eriq was not a man prone to profanity: his upbringing had been strewn with words he had later expunged from his vocabulary as he began to move in different circles. Still, you can take the boy out of the suq, but . . . we all learned some new Moroccan phrases that morning.

Maddie sat with a stillness that would have cracked if she'd moved. Increasingly, she looked away from the screen. Long before they had mined the full depths of Kaitlyn's bookmarks, she called a halt.

'Show me the first tweet again,' she said. The usual sun-flare of life that was her signature had shifted to a screaming arterial scarlet that flared out so far around her it touched the edges of the room.

Kaitlyn knew the feel of this as well as I did and it pushed her over her own edge. '*Yous all dinnae—!*' Wide-eyed, she snapped her mouth shut.

In the crystalline silence that followed, two facts crashed to earth. First was that, of all Maddie's children, Kaitlyn had picked up by far the biggest dose of the acting gene and the emotional volatility that went with it: she and her mother were both capable of accelerating from zero to one hundred on the scale of any emotion you cared to mention without passing through any of the staging points in between. At this moment, both of them were hovering right up there at max range.

Second was that Kaitlyn, like most youngsters, was bilingual in her mother tongue. With her peers, she spoke an ever-evolving teenage patois that nobody more than eighteen months outside their age range could hope to decipher. With everyone else, she spoke as the rest of the family spoke: which is to say she sounded like her mother, who in turn, sounded like a hybrid between Kate and me.

If this had been all, nobody would have noticed. But Kaitlyn was in fact trilingual, having added to her repertoire the essence of her older siblings' Glaswegian. She may have spent less than two months of her entire life north of the border, but nonetheless, when heightened emotional tension drove her far from Family Speak, it was to the gutter vowels and glottal stops of the city's working class that she evidently reverted.

Maddie hated the sound of it. Few things were better guaranteed to trigger a meltdown in their mother than one or more of her children speaking the language of her youth.

Those three words had been pure, flat Gorbals.

Kaitlyn wasn't so far gone that she couldn't see the train wreck whistling down the track. She took a slow, controlling breath. In crisply enunciated Family, she said, 'None of you has any way of understanding the complexities of this.'

'I understand that.' Maddie matched her daughter's precision. 'Nevertheless, I would appreciate seeing your original tweet again now that I have some sense of what caused you to post it.'

Lips pressed tight, Kaitlyn brought it back up to the screen. Her followers had risen to one-and-a-half million and the tweet had been retweeted over five million times. As of the past half-hour, Eriq was one of the new followers. He began scrolling through the comments, stopped, and turned his phone facedown on the table.

Maddie said, 'Kaitlyn, we—'

'You don't have to be on my side. Just don't cut me down.'

She turned away and busied herself with her phone. Maddie reached over, snatched it out of her hand and set it down beside Eriq's. 'Why did you not say something months ago?'

'If I'd said anything at all, you'd have tried to lock me out of the net. It wouldn't have worked, and we'd have had rows about it. So let's not go there, OK?' Just a tinge of Glaswegian here, reined in tight.

Maddie was exerting self-control that was terrifying in its precarity. She didn't react at all to the flatness of Kaitlyn's vowels, but rather rose and, arms folded, began to pace the length of the kitchen.

On the second time back from the sink, she turned aside, opened the back door and stood on the threshold, letting the morning light fall on her up-tilted face.

I was in the old damson tree that grew in the front garden, watching through the windows. The moment the door opened, without thinking or asking permission, I hurled myself to ground level, becoming human as I went.

'Maddie?'

I tried to hug her as I had in the dream of her wedding night. My hands went straight through, but she shuddered, briskly, and the shimmering, blood-red fury shimmered less.

'Lan? Is that you?'

Oh, for a way to connect. 'YES! I'm here.'

'I wish you could speak to us, you know?' She leaned one shoulder on the door frame and let her gaze rest on the damson, and then sweep out past Ash Barn to the Rookery beyond. 'What would Lan do?' she asked aloud.

'You need to ground, Mads. Remember? We did this when you were small and it's always worked. Let the tree lend you roots. Let the earth take the rage. Nothing is worth breaking the family for and you're too bloody close to the edge just now.'

She closed her eyes. I had no idea if she'd heard, or felt, or even understood.

'Maddie?'

She half-turned, back to the room. 'If we do nothing, this might blow over.'

'It won't,' Kaitlyn said, flatly.

'Hear me out.' At last (*thank you*) Maddie opened the eyes in the soles of her feet in the way I'd taught her when she was seven and we both thought she was in danger of clawing the eyes out of Gail MacIntyre at school. I watched her push the rage down into the earth, saw the fire around her cool a bit. I wanted to crow with Crow, but it wasn't around and things were still too edgy for me to waste time trying to find it. I stayed in human form and eased into the kitchen.

Maddie was saying '. . . delete the tweet, lie low and say nothing to anyone for half a year, on- or offline. If I talk to Rebecca like she is a real human being—'

Eriq snorted.

'—we might put this to bed as an outburst of teenage angst.'

Kaitlyn's face was the picture that screamed a thousand words.

Her mother managed a smile. 'But we're not going to do that. You're right, this needed to be said and I am proud, in a way, that you had the courage to say it.' She shook her head. 'Not "in a way". Totally. I am totally proud of you Kaitlyn Karim Penhaligon. Truly.'

She stepped into the room, not quite touching her daughter. Kaitlyn frowned, against an ambush of tears. 'Really?'

'Really.'

Their hug was long, and the air far clearer when they eased apart. Eriq had kept his seat, but relief lit him up when they both skirted the table to wrap their arms around his shoulders.

Up and then down: that was always how it had been with Kate, too. I stayed in the room, but I wasn't really needed. Maddie made coffee and the three of them piled their phones under a cushion and sat back at the table.

'What now?' Kaitlyn said, and she was back speaking Family again.

Maddie shrugged. 'This is your call. We do what you need. Seriously. We should talk to the twins, obviously, but I'm not pushing—'

'Niall and Kirsten are already on board. I spoke with them earlier.'

But not with her mother and father. A generational chasm yawned across the table.

'Love . . .' Eriq started.

Maddie was faster. 'This is the young reclaiming the world. We get that. But if you're going to change things, I think it will go better if you let some of the older generations help, however much we got you into this mess. Can I ask one thing of you?'

'What?' Sharp again. Wary as a feral cat. I laid a hand on Kaitlyn's head, but it was Maddie who defused her.

83

'I'm asking, not demanding. Just . . . from now on, can you tell us what's happening as it happens? All of it. No holding back. No sweetening things or brushing them under carpets because we can't handle them. From our side—' Maddie laid a hand on Eriq's shoulder— 'we will not judge. We will do everything we can to help. But if we're going to work as a family, it has to be the whole family. Unless you want the two of us to step back and stonewall the calls and just get out of your way?'

It was an offer as huge as any made from a parent to their child. We waited, all of us, while Kaitlyn parsed it all through. 'I'd really like your help,' she said, and a bubble of relief rippled across the room. 'I will promise to tell you whatever's going on if you promise to see things through my eyes as best you can. Deal?'

'Deal.' They sealed it in the family way, bumping fist to fist to fist over the kitchen table.

After, wiping her eyes, Maddie said, 'At some point, I'm going to have to switch my phone back on. Before that, we'd better talk to Finn. He won't be happy to have missed out.'

Finn was not remotely happy to have been left sleeping through the crisis.

He wasn't thrilled, either, that his sister had chosen to, in his words, 'set the world ablaze' when he was three weeks from his defence of the European Arena Championship title, but he had his second degree black belt by now, and was de facto lieutenant to one of the world's most respected Shaolin teachers. Mo's mentorship had realigned his priorities. Raging at his family wasn't what the morning needed.

What it needed – what it got – was a family Zoom call that connected with Kirsten and Niall, in Glasgow, and Connor, who turned out not to be in Ireland but on the Berkshire Downs, where he'd been holding some kind of ceremony at the White Horse carved into the chalk on a hill outside Uffington. Tracking him down and getting him somewhere with a workable WiFi signal took long enough that Finn was awake and everyone else was on their third cup of coffee by the time he was ready.

The twins already knew as much as Kaitlyn did, a fact that would have been evident to everyone with half a brain given that Kaitlyn's video was pretty much a direct channelling of Niall on one of his angrier days. It began to occur to me that this particular rock thrown into the toxic cesspit of the body politic (thanks, Nye) may not have been as spontaneous as it seemed.

By the look on her face, Maddie was realising the same, but she had the sense not to ask about it: this, too, was not a priority for the moment.

The priorities were as follows:

1. Field the various 'legacy media', to wit: radio, television and newspapers – anything that had existed in the pre-broadband era.

Because the decision-makers in these establishments were on the far side of the generational dividing line, Maddie and Eriq were assigned to monitor them and suggest strategies, at least in the first instance. If possible, they were to identify allies and bring them on side, but that was a secondary priority: damage limitation came first, last and everywhere in between.

Kirsten voiced it most clearly: 'We've probably got three clear days before they really start to get nasty. We need to make the most of that time.'

The rest of the family were assigned to:

2. Raising an unstoppable following among the 'Living Media', which was anything requiring the internet, obviously.

Kaitlyn had already set the ball rolling, but she wanted more than a bunch of likes and heart emojis. 'Everyone under thirty-five needs to stand with us or we'll be crushed.'

Expanding on this, Niall said, 'We have Kaitlyn's generation on our side, most of them. Finn's probably, too. Ours – mine and K's – should come along if we get the messaging right. But the legacy generations – sorry Mum, Eriq, Grandad – are going to fight this all the way and we have to be ready with hard counters to whatever they do.'

Kirsten followed him seamlessly in the way they had of sharing thoughts and dividing the effort of speaking them. 'We're hitting every limbic trigger they've got. All those super-size amygdalas that have been pounded with the toxic mess of the tribal divisions . . . they'll be flashing red-hot and hard. Anyone who's been even vaguely culpable will feel ashamed and dirty and because they don't have the emotional literacy to cope with either, they'll want to shut it down as fast as they know how. The way to do that is to shoot the messenger.' She looked straight into the Zoom lens. 'Sis, are you sure you're ready for this?'

Flatly, Kaitlyn said, 'They found Shona-Beth last night. I'm ready for anything.'

Gazes sheared from screen to screen. Maddie looked a question at Niall, who pulled a face and nodded towards Kaitlyn.

Gently, Connor said, 'Can you tell us more?'

'We play Minecraft together. Played.'

'Is she dead?'

'According to her sister, her body was found at about one o'clock this morning our time: bound, gagged, raped and choked.' Kaitlyn flicked her fingers at the screen and her accent hit the centre of the Atlantic. 'Just like it shows in the movies, folks.'

Eriq swallowed down a noise that had no form.

Connor said, 'Do they know who did it?'

A shrug. 'Some rancid incel had been stalking her online for months. He called himself Graylock, but all we can be sure of is that's not his name. She'd reported him endlessly. Nobody did anything. All the betting's on him.' Kaitlyn wound her hands together, stared at her knuckles.

Connor mouthed 'Incel?' at Maddie.

Finn answered. 'Involuntarily celibate. A bunch of toxic losers from Reddit and 4chan who think every woman on the planet exists to serve them sex on a stick and the fact that they're not getting laid ten times a day is evidence of a vile conspiracy by womankind, not because they're unwashed, acne-ridden keyboard warriors with the charisma of a ten-day-old dog turd.'

Niall, who had been about to answer, shut his mouth and raised a respectful half-salute to Finn instead.

Eriq took a deep breath. 'Is he going down, this dog turd? He's been arrested and charged?'

Kaitlyn laughed. 'She was Black. He's white. What do you think?'

'I think the police should . . . Where was this?'

'Texas.'

'Oh.'

'Right.' Kaitlyn drew her thumb along the table's edge. 'Somebody has to do something, and I'm somebody. So . . .'

'So, when her murder hits the news,' Finn said, 'I'll get the Ghosts to link it to your video and start spreading it in the right channels. I don't want to make political capital out of your friend's death, but this is genuinely what triggered your post. That's a super-strong narrative.'

Kaitlyn favoured him with a withering glance. 'Nye, it's not even hit the county news. If it doesn't reach state TV, it's hardly going to make it to CNN, much less Reuters, and if it's not there, it won't reach the rest of the world. Nobody is going to hear about this beyond her family and friends.'

'Unless we tell them,' Finn said. He pushed out of his seat. 'I'll get the Ghosts onto it. And we'll find your Graylock.'

The door thudded shut behind him.

'And then there were six,' said Niall, tightly. 'Anyone else walking out?'

'He's trying to help,' Connor said.

Kirsten said, 'Working out some strategy first wouldn't have hurt.' To Kaitlyn, 'Who wants a bit of you this morning? The whole world? Can we triage?'

'Dozens. Sending them now.'

Phones pinged in the kitchen and the Zoom rooms.

Niall whistled. 'Four separate requests from Mum's friend—'

'She was *never* a friend.'

'—from Mum's former housemate who is now Grand High Toxic Pixie at the UK's hard-right mouthpiece for the Nat-Cs. Interview requests from the *Mail*, *Express*, Torygraph and Grauniad. A couple from local papers in Suffolk and three in Glasgow: I guess on some radar we're all still Scots. One from a women's safety blog. One from—'

'Nye?' Maddie muted him, but she'd used the short form of his name, which was a clear sign she wasn't about to erupt. 'We can read. What we can't do is lay out the hundred legal options and select which is best: that's what you're for. Just tell us what to *do*, please?'

Niall was a partner in Scotland's only cooperative law firm. The entire family had leaned on him for legal advice from the moment he'd started his degree, so it wasn't an unfair question. It was, in fact, the opening he'd been waiting for.

He pointed down to the mute button, and when he was clear to speak said, 'Sis and I can write a template reply that'll cover them all. Kait, you can check it, change the language if you want and email it. Whatever you do, don't talk to any of them directly without one of us being with you.'

'OK.' Kaitlyn's phone chimed as she slid it into her pocket. After a moment's hesitation, she pulled it back out and checked it. Her brows rose. 'BBC Radio Four's *Woman's Hour* wants an interview at ten thirty-five.' She checked the time. 'Just over two hours from now.' For the first time, panic strobed across her features. 'They want me to go to London. They're sending a car to pick me up from King's Cross.'

'No chance.' Niall made a swift throat-cutting gesture. 'Tell them you can set up professional quality sound and video from the farm and do it remotely. They don't need to drag you to London for the sake of it.'

Maddie shook her head. 'Even then, I don't think—'

Kirsten held up a hand. 'Who's doing the interview?'

'Frances Nolan.'

'Do it.' Kirsten pulled up a wiki page and threw the link into the chat. 'She's Mum's age, and half-decent. One of the old-school second-wave feminists, not the rat snakes they keep in the basement for targeted assaults on the unwary. She'll get her talking points from the right-wing tabloids, but it's possible she reads the *Guardian*, too.'

'Still a right-wing tabloid,' Niall murmured.

Kirsten waved him to silence. 'Only in the bizarre corners of your universe. Out here in the real world, the thing we have to remember is that the BBC isn't the wholly owned propaganda wing of the governing party, whatever it may seem like. As Frankie Boyle once said, it's more a federation of warring states, and some of them could be on our side. Frances Nolan might be the best we get, and on a quiet day, tomorrow's front pages lift their lines from the lunchtime news. If Kaitlyn can shine in one national broadcast, we can start the ball rolling in the right direction.'

'Which will give us time to prepare our lines of defence,' Eriq said. And, to the screen of blank stares, 'Niall said earlier we need to have our hard counters ready for when they attack. This gives us time to prepare them.'

'There is no preparing for this,' Connor said. 'Only minimising damage. I'll get in the car now. Mads, Eriq . . . if you don't have a spare bed, I'll sleep in front of the fire in the living room. I'll be with you by one o'clock.'

Maddie peered at him. 'We have two spare bedrooms. Why would there not be one for you?'

'Because we're coming too, obviously,' Kirsten said. 'We'll take a flight. Niall, shut up. We can offset the carbon with something you don't hate, but this is an emergency. And Grandad's forgotten there's space for us in the barn so he can have his pick upstairs. Eriq, I'll text you arrival times at Stansted. If you could pick us up, we can talk strategy on the way home.'

There was a pause. Goodbyes hung in the air. Niall said, softly, 'This is going to be ugly-dirty. We all know it, right?'

Maddie squeezed Eriq's hand on one side and reached an arm round Kaitlyn on the other. 'Right.'

The twins looked jointly at Kaitlyn, 'We're with you, Sis,' one said, and I couldn't tell you which for the blur of pain in my chest.

The other said, 'Just hang on till we get there.'

CHAPTER EIGHT

'Kaitlyn. One minute and we'll switch to you. Are you OK?'

Abigail, the BBC producer, was younger than the twins. She smiled a lot and treated Kaitlyn as if she were royalty, which is to say every sentence had to be repeated three times, but pronounced with extreme deference.

Now she was saying, 'Remember you'll be live, so please don't swear, but beyond that, just relax and speak your mind. It's what the listeners want. Speak as if you were talking to a friend.'

'Thanks. I got it the first time. I'm fine, really.' Kaitlyn leaned back in her chair, running her hands through her hair. More than any of the older generations, screens were her preferred environment. She looked as relaxed as she had done when she was making the first recording. All the colours around her were pastel shades of a quiet dawn, smooth and clear and clean.

Those weren't the colours she was showing the world. The Zoom screen showed the same urban grunge backdrop behind her she'd chosen for the video. In fact, the only difference was that she'd switched the pale shirt for a deep ochre shirt of Kirsten's design, with a hair clip the same colour. She looked like a supermodel: urbane, utterly at home and far older than her fourteen and a bit years. A red light glowed solidly just out of the camera's reach, ready to flash green when the feed went live.

Maddie and Eriq sat opposite her, well out of camera shot, clamped side by side, bolt upright on a long grass-coloured sofa that ran under the window. They looked as comfortable as you might expect.

Finn sat cross-legged on the floor halfway between. He had brought his laptop through and was connected to the whole distributed network that was the Grey Ghosts. So far, everyone involved was also a core member of Team Memory and most of them were veterans of the ReadyCheck days. From Hawck in Liverpool up to Vivacity in Canada, down to Charm the French-Algerian Healer-Priest in France and across to Juke in Israel, they were all logged in and ready to surf the net on Kaitlyn's behalf.

Their attempts to gain media interest in the death of a Black girl in the American red zone had been notably unsuccessful, but they'd stopped all their other work to focus on the interview so that if Kaitlyn was asked anything she couldn't answer, they'd have a response lifted from the net and relayed to her before anybody noticed a delay.

'Thirty seconds.' Abigail sounded as if she were standing by the desk. 'Tell your brother the sound's perfect. Any time he wants a job, just drop me a line.'

Finn laughed, silently. Kaitlyn pulled a face. 'Don't hold your breath.'

'No worries. OK, fifteen seconds . . . Ten . . . Five . . . You're live.'

'—And welcome to *Woman's Hour*, Kaitlyn Karim Penhaligon. You've created quite the stir this morning. Did you mean to?'

If you just heard Frances Nolan, you might think her sharp, but on the video feed, she looked casual and friendly, her smile disarming by design. She was an ash-blonde woman of Maddie's vintage, haggard-lean, dressed in pastel pink, with big statement glasses, lips and nails the same colour.

'I meant to draw attention to things that matter. The stir is a result of the facts, not my video, I think?' Kaitlyn let her voice rise at the end, which shaved about five years off her apparent age. It was either immensely clever or was going to make her seem naïve. On the sofa, Maddie and Eriq exchanged glances.

Frances Nolan's features softened a shade. 'I was going to ask you if all you said was really true, but when our lovely producer – thank you, Abigail – rang this morning with the news that I was going to be talking to you, I thought I'd ask my own daughter. She's nearly three years older than you are and, to my shame, we hadn't ever discussed this particular topic. I didn't know we needed to. The conversation was . . .'

'Painful?' Kaitlyn offered.

'You could say.' It was Frances's turn to sound younger. 'Educational, certainly.' She rolled her tongue round her teeth. 'It wasn't like this in my day. For the benefit of those listening who are anywhere north of forty, my daughter asked me this morning how on earth anyone was supposed to know how sex worked if they hadn't watched a video. I have never felt so old.'

'How *did* you know?' Kaitlyn asked. Maddie covered her face with her hands. Her shoulders shook. I was perched behind her on the back of the sofa and, even this close, I had no idea if she was weeping or laughing.

'I guess we kind of fumbled our way through it,' Frances said. 'The boys knew more than we did. They were reading the magazines, I imagine. We girls never got that far. Or at least, I didn't. I may have been uniquely ignorant among my age group, but I don't think so.'

Kaitlyn nodded, kindly. 'And we don't have magazines, either. We have an entire web full of snuff porn and we've been tapped into touchscreens since before we could walk, so no doors are barred to us. We've had the boys – some of them – demanding that we text them sexually explicit images of ourselves since we were eight years old, and they've been returning the favour whether we wanted it or not. All of which means, obviously, that we don't have to fumble. Instead, now that we have functioning hormonal systems, we have to work out how to get turned on in ways that don't involve non-consensual violence. I'm not sure I want to live in a world where the only route to orgasm is through pain I didn't ask for and can't escape.'

Don't swear, Abigail had said. So Kaitlyn hadn't, but still, in the frozen moment after she let drop this bombshell, you could feel its impact reverberating around the morning rooms and salons of middle England.

Finn stared at his sister with the startled look I remembered from the old days when someone had just done something truly daring in a battleground: the YOLO high-risk manoeuvre that would either see the team win spectacularly or wipe out so badly we'd never recover. He ghosted a fist bump. Kaitlyn nodded fractionally in return.

Eriq bit the knuckle of his forefinger till it bruised. Maddie, proving that our years of parenting had raised a woman of stellar courage, caught Kaitlyn's eye and raised a thumb.

Somewhere in London, Frances Nolan took a deep breath. 'I think very few of us wants this. Certainly not me. The situation is appalling. As a mother, as a woman, as a human being, I am genuinely horrified, both that this is where we've got to and that I didn't know before now that it was. I will not be alone, believe me. But I'm not clear exactly what you think we can do about it?'

Kaitlyn blinked, slowly. The resulting video – which went viral among her age group soon after – saw her quite clearly sorting through answers that didn't involve swearing, or egregious insults. 'You could stop it happening?' she offered, eventually.

'How, though?'

Kaitlyn was on a roll, channelling Niall so effortlessly that they must have had this conversation a dozen ways to Christmas. 'The way these things are always done, I expect: by using the levers of the state. Dig into the 96 per cent of internet traffic that is the Dark Web until you find the men who make this content and arrest them. Dig further until you find whoever funds them and freeze their offshore accounts in Panama or the Cayman Islands. Find the people who distribute the result and tax them for every frame they upload so it's not economically viable. You do this kind of thing all the time with things society doesn't like: drugs, political organisations, activists on the streets, immigrants. You can do it here if you all agree it's necessary.'

'So, you're advocating for censorship. Is that not problematic?'

'Why would it be?' Kaitlyn had learned *this* tone from her mother.

She'd learned, also, not to speak when nothing can usefully be said. When people are at an emotional edge, they will fill the gap and what they say may not be as considered as it could be.

Frances Nolan filled the gap. 'I mean, one man's – or woman's – pornography is another man's erotica. Where do we draw the line?'

Kaitlyn blinked again, for longer this time. Later, the spaces of her blink-time were drawn out and filled by other girls' voice-overs of her thought processes. The results ranged from scurrilous to libellous to outraged to hilarious.

In the event, she smiled her sweetest, youngest, most innocent smile. Niall would have run for the hills: he'd taught her debating and he could tell when he'd walked into a bear trap.

'Could we agree, do you think,' Kaitlyn suggested, 'that non-consensual violence has no place in sexual relationships – in any relationships, come to that?'

'Yes, of course. That's obvious.'

'Then, perhaps equally obviously, we could start by drawing the line at depictions of young girls – or anyone, really – being slaughtered for the sexual gratification of adult men.'

Kaitlyn's gaze hardened. It was difficult to remember she was not long past her fourteenth birthday. 'And if people are going to bitch – sorry, complain – about cutting off the incomes from the actors, then I think you could find them jobs making erotica that doesn't involve violence, and make sure it pays just as well. If they're being paid at all. I would be prepared to bet that a large number of the young people on these videos are not there out of choice. I would further bet that some of the girls we saw being abused are no longer alive.

'Even if I'm wrong, it's not beyond the wit of our society to find fulfilling employment for young women that doesn't involve false intimacy and faking excruciating death every night. The important thing is not to target the victims of abuse, which is what would have happened in the past: blame the women, disempower them, impoverish them and then you can haul them into new wage-slavery while an institutionally racist, misogynist, homophobic police force turns a blind eye.

'Just for a change, we need to target the abusers, which in this case is the funders, the makers, the distributors – and ultimately the end users. They come last, though. Maybe if they were offered something else, they'd find they preferred it. Worth a try, I'd suggest.'

Go, girl! I danced a Crow-jig on the back of the sofa.

In the land of the living, Frances Nolan nodded, briskly. 'I see. Yes. You've clearly thought this through. That's comprehensive and it would be . . . uncontroversial, I think. I hope. You and I couldn't make this happen, though. Governments pass laws, not people.'

Kaitlyn raised one brow. 'I think you'll find governments are people too?' Nolan had the grace to wince. 'But it's true that we elect

94

them based on tribal instincts. There's an election due sometime in the next couple of years, and this isn't something the tiny selectorate that actually has some agency in choosing our governments is likely to coalesce around. Is this what you're saying?'

It wasn't, but it was hard to argue with. Nolan didn't even try.

'What would you do?'

'Well, I won't be old enough to vote at the next election. Even if I could, my generation is facing voter suppression on a scale unseen in any democracy and I might not be *able* to vote. As with everything else that matters, therefore, I'll have to ask – to beg – people of your generation to make this important enough for the political parties to take it seriously.'

'You want it to be a key plank of any political party's election offer?'

'Why wait until the election? We know this government can change the law overnight if it wants to and I struggle to see any party pledging to return the "artistic" murder of young girls for pornographic purposes as part of their manifesto. This isn't like fox-hunting, or the cap on bankers' bonuses: once it's gone, it'll stay gone. My brother is a lawyer. He says the government drafting team could have a bill ready to publish by the end of the month if they put their minds to it. Then they just need to make time in the Commons for a vote. And nobody is going to vote against it, right?'

Right.

You'd think that would have to be right. Certainly, Frances Nolan seemed to think so, thanking her as they closed. And then Abigail-the-producer ('Kaitlyn! You were magnificent! Thank you!').

Maddie and Eriq definitely thought so. Finn and, more importantly, Kaitlyn, were less certain. 'I didn't nail it. I should have dug deeper into the inequities of the porn industry. That's where they'll hit us, I think. "Privileged teen hits at sex workers, depriving them of an honest living." That's the usual line.'

But it wasn't: not yet, at any rate. The lunchtime tickers on the BBC ran with 'TEEN CHALLENGES GOVERNMENT TO CLAMP DOWN ON VIOLENT INTERNET PORNOGRAPHY', and this set the agenda for a total of three solid hours, which at least was long enough for the rest of the family to arrive.

▼

Eriq headed off down the road to collect the twins from Stansted around one o'clock. He'd been gone less than a minute when his horn sounded a triple note that was audible only because Finn was frying onions for the lunchtime soup and he'd opened the kitchen door to let out the steam.

Maddie's head snapped up at the sound. She had time to wash her hands, dry them and hurl the tea towel at the table when there came a clatter of gears and bad mechanics, and a matt-black Citroën C5 nearly as old as the twins churned into the yard.

'*Dad!*' Hurtling down the steps, Maddie reached the car and wrenched open the door. 'Feck, am I glad to see you!' She went all Irish when Connor was around. The sound of it rolled through me, warm with the kinds of memories that didn't hurt.

'Maddie-girl, it's good to see you, too. Only sorry about the circumstances. And Kaitlyn. Finn. You're looking grand, both.'

His rolling old-oak voice emerged from the car well enough, but Connor himself followed far more slowly, shoving two solid-looking walking sticks out first, and then his false leg (he had lost the real one in his fifties to some African parasite I never learned the name of) and then, finally, his good leg and his big-boned rugby-farmer's frame.

My goodness, it was good to see him. His hair was shading towards a muddy pewter and his eyebrows had thickened, but these apart he'd barely changed at all from when we'd first met.

He wasn't a priest anymore – he'd long since ditched the Church in disgust at its politics and the god it had crafted – and taken himself off to parts of the world where he could make a difference to people who needed him. He'd never stayed anywhere long, but each place had seemed a bit more peaceful and a bit less destitute when he left. Letters and cards, and later emails and texts, had followed him in a great, wide comet trail as he traversed the planet.

He had retired around the time Kaitlyn had turned five and become something of an amateur archaeologist, pottering among the ancient earthworks and long barrows of these islands in ways nobody understood, but everyone assumed was useful.

And now here he was, the finest father Maddie could have had, half-leaning on his car and spreading his arms wide so the whole family could surge up against the rock of his being and he could enfold them in a vast, strong hug.

Which he did. And then as he held them close, Maddie in the middle, and her younger two children on either side, Connor lifted his head from his daughter's shoulder, looked directly up at where I was sitting in the old damson tree . . . and winked.

'CONNOR?' Shock made me loud. And again, louder, '*CONNOR?!*'

He blinked, slow and firm, but either he couldn't hear me or didn't want to speak aloud. He gave a nod that seemed also to be directed at me, then turned away and gathered everyone up and drew them all back into the kitchen and the making of lunch and the sharing of news and all the ordinary things families do when they haven't seen each other in a while.

I didn't follow them in, but sat in the tree, stunned into immobility, and only really got my act together again when Eriq's car drew up alongside Connor's and disgorged the twins so fast that Finn only just had time to pull the door open before they shouldered it down.

Niall strode in with both phones blazing. To Maddie: 'Did you explicitly say, "No Comment" to the *Daily Mail*?'

Maddie tried to hand him a bowl of soup and had to put it down on the kitchen counter nearby until he freed up a hand to hold it with. She said, 'I haven't spoken to the *Mail*, or anyone else. It may well be they've sent a text or an email but I'm having a mobile holiday today.'

'Nice. They'll have to retract and print an apology.' Into his left-hand phone, 'Rosh, can you start that ball rolling?'

Rosh was one of the senior legal minds in Niall's legal practice and one of the founding members of the Alba Rising community: on both counts, Niall trusted him as much as he did anyone in the family. From the phone a deep Glaswegian voice said, 'On it.'

And then Niall again, briskly, to Kaitlyn, 'Have you spoken to Ms Toxic Pixie at QBC?'

'Just came off the line. You said I should go for it.'

'I know. How was she?'

'Suspiciously softball.' Her eyes narrowed. 'Why?'

'Because that was the feint. They can claim to have given you a chance to put your side if we try to nail them for this. I'm sorry I didn't see it coming.' Niall pointed his phone at the widescreen on the back wall above the table, 'This is you, right?'

He was playing a split-screen video from the QBC Twitter feed. The left half showed a lesbian sex scene so soft that it wouldn't offend Twitter's standards enough to get the feed kicked. On the right, a partially dressed Kaitlyn was masturbating in front of her computer, a look of sensual abandon slurring her features.

In the kitchen, the silence became a fragile thing. Nobody looked at anybody else.

A commendably insouciant Kaitlyn took her brother's phone, pinched the sex video bigger, watched it all the way to the end and handed it back. 'It's not impossible.'

'Enough doubt we could say it's an AI fake?' asked Kirsten.

Kaitlyn drew breath to answer, but Finn talked over her. 'Not worth it. If they can show her IP address accessing the sites, and we can't show otherwise, the balance will go to their side and we'll have blown our integrity at the start.' He pulled her into a swift hug. 'Sorry, Sis. That one won't run.'

Kaitlyn grinned, faintly. 'Trust me, it could have been worse.'

'Trust me,' Niall said. 'It will be.'

▼

It got so very much worse.

The honeymoon time granted by the BBC interview died by a thousand cuts through the afternoon. Kaitlyn's followers rallied just as strongly, so that by four o'clock, two opposing narratives were coursing at full throttle around the net.

The first was Kaitlyn's from the tweet: the older generations were serially betraying the younger and the manipulation of young people's sexuality was just one plank in the wall of the Boomers' destruction of all that was good and whole and decent.

This was taken up wholeheartedly by Kaitlyn's supporters who kept #SSS trending on all the social media platforms. A fair few were emboldened or enraged enough to make their own videos for YouTube, TikTok and Twitter with the hashtag renamed as TripleS on the grounds that it sounded less like a stuttering snake. Facebook and Insta blocked them early, but the rest let them through and, given that the videos made the most impact, the movement soon became known as TripleS on both sides of the divide.

The divide was deep and clear. Kaitlyn's in-tray was flooded with DMs from people wanting her to give voice to their own stories of abuse, or just to hear them. Seeing his sister drowning in a flood of messages she couldn't process, Finn drew in Grey Ghosts from around the world as their time zones came online and set them to triage the incoming messages and sort out the ones everyone really needed to see. Everyone grew quieter and more haggard as the afternoon lengthened.

The counter-narrative arose just as fast on the feeds of the major newspapers and news stations and was reposted on Twitter and Facebook (this side of the argument wasn't blocked at all) by the legacy media ecosystem and its outriders.

With increasing ferocity, they presented Kaitlyn Karim Penhaligon as a sexually obsessed nonentity who was obviously using sexual notoriety as a means of self-promotion.

Her rising follower numbers were cited as proof that this was how the younger generations manipulated social media to their own ends. It wasn't like this in our day, obviously, when young people knew their place and the only way for them to keep in touch with each other was to hang around on street corners. At best, she was to be pitied. Possibly she could be offered help. Certainly nothing she said was to be given any credence. Also (whisper it), she wasn't white, which explained everything.

This was the kind version. It gave cover to a toxic voyeurism enthusiastically grasped by (mostly, but not exclusively) middle-aged, middle-class white men who obsessed over every single video uploaded to QBC's Twitter feed.

In the first few hours, nobody in the family gave credence to Niall's claim that bot farms were amplifying the 'old white dude' message, but Finn put the Ghosts onto it and they confirmed that, while Niall might well be a conspiracy theorist of the first order, in this particular instance he was right.

It wasn't clear where the orders were coming from, but tens of thousands of accounts tracing back to eastern Europe, South America and Singapore were selectively reposting those messages which commented only on Kaitlyn. These threads were nakedly racist, ageist, misogynist and homophobic and all of them were tagged with #SexStressedSnowflakes, until this, too, began to trend.

The intensity of it left even Kaitlyn weeping, and she was the last to crack, though her tears were hot vents of fury as much as anything.

'How are they getting this shite? They're going back fucking *years.*'

Maddie kept her head down and ignored the lapse out of Family.

Finn shrugged. 'You're not using the lens covers I gave you. Everything you do, they see.'

Wild-fast, she rounded on him. 'I'm not an idiot, Findley.' Everyone winced but Finn. 'I've used the covers since the day you gave them to me, which was years ago.' Kaitlyn waved at her laptop. 'Check for yourself.'

The whole family had set up temporary headquarters in the attic recording suite that bridged the thirty feet between the two bedrooms. Finn had set up a bank of monitors, magicked up some spare desks for the twins and a bigger sofa for the older generation.

It felt like a proper operations room, and meant it was easy for Finn to do exactly as his sister had suggested. Leaning back one long arm, he swivelled her laptop on its stand. A tiny black lens shield was stuck over the eye of the camera at the top of the screen, ready to be slid back if Kaitlyn needed to actually be visible, but a finger's length of Sellotape holding it in place said the webcam had never been used. He checked her phone and her iPad: both were similarly shut off from the world.

'I don't need the webcam. I've got the Canon Dad bought me last birthday.' Kaitlyn's gesture took in the rest of her recording equipment.

Finn looked as if he were seeing it for the first time, which he very likely was. Between Team Memory, Grey Ghosts and his increasingly responsible role as Mo Bakar's assistant, he hadn't had a huge amount of head space left over for the minutiae of his younger sister's life. Even setting up the link to the BBC earlier he'd been working to Niall's instruction, with most of his attention on his Twitch stream and Discord channels.

Now, he scooted Kaitlyn off the chair and stationed himself behind the recording desk. 'Passwords?'

'Your name and mine backwards, Grandad's forward, Lan's first dog with the first letter as a numeral. Uppercase on the names, underscores between each and an exclamation point at the end.'

Even if it was spelled 1sla, I was ridiculously happy with this, not least because it meant family lore was passing down the generations.

I realised, too, that Kaitlyn hadn't actually spelled the words out. Somewhere in her young life, one of her siblings had drilled good password safety into her and she was operating now as if all their mobile devices were open ears to whoever wanted to listen, which was probably a safe bet.

Finn grunted acknowledgement: he was already lost to the room. Everyone else watched, mesmerised, as he keyed his way into the guts of her operating system.

Presently, he lifted his head. 'Record something,' he said. 'Anything. Doesn't matter what.'

For someone usually so fluent in front of a camera, her recording of 'Hi, I'm Kaitlyn, this is a test for my brother, Finn', was remarkably wooden, but she was due a bit of stage fright after all she'd been through that day.

'Now show me how you shut everything down afterwards.'

She did. Finn danced with the keyboard a while longer, biting his lower lip ever harder. After a while, Connor levered himself out of his chair and hirpled across to look over his shoulder.

Nobody else moved until the maestro lifted his head. Even then he didn't speak but eased his way between the two desks to reach his sister.

'Kait, I'm so sorry I wasn't there when you needed me.' He lifted her into a hug. 'The fuckers got to your Canon the way they'd get to your phone or your webcam. They disabled the lights when they hijacked it so you wouldn't even have known it was on. I've blocked them so they'll not get any more, and if they try, we'll trace them back to whatever hole in the ground they live in and dissolve every bit of code they live by.'

That broke just about everyone. Kaitlyn clung to her brother, looking young for the first time that day. Eriq swore, softly, in the language of backstreet Marrakesh. Niall and Kirsten each wrote texts on their phones with matching viciousness until Finn spun to stop them.

'No texting. Don't send anything digital unless you're happy to see it on the front pages tomorrow morning.'

Niall's fingers flew on. ''S OK. We're using Telegram.'

'No.' Finn snatched his brother's phone away and turned it off. 'Seriously. Don't touch it.' And at their stricken faces, 'You can use Signal if you absolutely have to, but even then, I wouldn't write anything. We've been working up GhostTalk as a way for the GG team to text securely. I'll sort an app so you can share it with the people you need to talk to. Just give me a couple of hours.'

Kaitlyn said, 'I thought you were putting all your effort into getting Shona-Beth's death on the radar? You were going to find the incel who killed her?'

That could have been a low blow, but it was more of a plea. She believed Finn could achieve digital miracles and was waiting for evidence.

He dragged his fingers through his hair. 'We've tried our best. Graylock is almost certainly Graeme Matlock: he lives two blocks away from Shona-Beth and he was definitely harassing her on social media for months before she was murdered. We can't prove he killed her yet, but we're watching every digital move he makes and if he slips up, we'll send whatever we've got to the Feds. As far as her death goes—' he spread his hands— 'Twitter's alive with it. Facebook's letting it through the algorithms, at least for now, and it's all over Instagram, TikTok and Snapchat, but the legacy fossils don't want to touch it if it doesn't fit their narrative. Which it doesn't.

'They're treading old ground because it's comfortable and they know it works. Teens using porn: shock. Clutch pearls. Look horrified. Spend several hours watching videos of a kind you otherwise don't know how to access. Write long columns saying it all has to stop and the adults have to regain control of the internet. Advocate for toothless laws increasing parental controls so it looks as if you're Taking Things Seriously, and meanwhile continue to peddle the ultimate dopamine-soaked cocktail of sex and race-bait under cover of righteous indignation.

'In the attention economy, this is about as addictive a mix as you can get, and they'll keep the feeding frenzy going any way they can. A young girl's murder would only put the dampeners on their ratings and get people questioning their own motives.' His gaze softened. 'The Texas police have released some of the pathology report.'

'I know. I've read as much as I want to.'

'Figured. If we manage to get anyone to listen, though, they'll spread the details around; it's what they do.'

Kaitlyn knuckled her eyes. 'I've spoken to her sister. If we can stop it happening to someone else, the family'll bear just about anything. I can't promise them that, though, can I?'

'Not yet, but Hawck and Charm are on it full-time now. They both have skin in this game. We'll get there if we have to buy out the *Telegraph* and print it ourselves.'

Everyone took that as a joke, but I had some idea of what his Twitch account and the Grey Ghost hacking money were bringing in. Given that the *Telegraph* was in trouble and likely to be seriously undervalued, I thought he might be serious.

Whether the owners would have sold it to him was an entirely different question, and one that was never put to the test. Niall volunteered to make dinner and seconded Eriq to help. Their departure cleared the air enough for Maddie and Kirsten to head off downstairs to set up the beds so that, of the older generation, only Connor was left in the attic.

He glanced up at me once, to show he knew where I was (I still had no idea how. I still couldn't get him to hear me: I had tried), then eased himself onto the big sofa that ran under the window, leaning forward with both hands on his sticks. 'The question that comes to my mind,' he said in his beautiful rolling west coast lilt, 'is who are "they" who spied on a wee girl's private moments in the first place, and might try to do so again?'

Finn looked up from his phone. 'The government. If we're picking nits, we'd say the NSA spies on the UK population and GCHQ does it for the US and then they exchange the data so neither of them has technically broken the laws of their own country which say that the elected government can't put wire taps on their own population without a warrant.'

'For real?' Connor looked sceptical.

'For absolute certain. Snowden gave us the details, but it's been an open secret since about thirty seconds after the internet went global.'

'But why pick on Kaitlyn? What did she ever do to get onto their radar?'

'That's what I'm telling you: everyone's on their radar – you, me, Mo Bakar down the road who uses the internet once a decade. They're equal-opportunity data harvesters and their expressed intent is to collect everything about everyone and keep it forever. There's a US government databank in Ohio with at least a gigabyte of memory storage space for every human being on earth. They collect it in case they need it and presumably someone thought this was a good excuse to squirrel down into the files and see what they'd got. The real questions are, why they did they sell what they found to filth like QBC? And was this one operative working for money, or was it a policy decision from someone higher up the food chain?'

Connor rubbed the side of his nose with the knuckle of his thumb. 'Maybe we follow the money?'

'Possibly. It might be faster to make one more video, mark it and follow the trail. Like UV ink on bank notes passed out to kidnappers.'

'Could you do that?'

''S not trivial, but it's not that hard, either. You could do it if I told you how. The problem is we won't know who would notice and what they'd do in response. Which might not be fun.' Finn sat down beside his grandfather, elbows on knees, hands palming his face. 'Cancel that idea. Too risky. I think I'm good, but I'm not stupid enough to think I'm the best.'

'The bad guys are the best?'

'If this is GCHQ and the NSA working together, we have to assume they've bought the kinds of people who'd otherwise be serving time, and they're working them hard. Either way, it would take a lot of work to check in ways that don't trigger any warnings.'

Finn levered himself to his feet. To his sister, he said, 'I failed you today and I can't apologise enough. But this, we can fix. It's just going to take time.' He held his hands out for Connor and lifted him up, too. 'Tell Mum I'll forage as usual. Nothing personal—'

'No.' Kaitlyn body-blocked her brother even as she delivered Connor's walking sticks to her grandfather's hands. 'Eat with us. The bad guys aren't going to hide themselves any deeper while you spend an hour with the family. After that, you can become our heat-seeking missile, but I think we need some actual real-life solidarity now. And looking on the bright side,' she tapped her phone open and checked her feeds, 'I've got nearly a million more followers than I had this morning and they're all on fire.'

CHAPTER NINE

As dusk began to draw down on that first day, there was no possible doubt that the print and terrestrial media had taken their cue from QBC rather than the BBC.

The leading tabloid set the tone: 'PORN-ADDICTED GAY TEENAGER SLAMMED FOR SHARING X-RATED VIDEO ONLINE'.

The front pages showed several unflattering images of Kaitlyn, used to ensure everyone knew she wasn't white. A slew of articles and comment puffs followed, spreading over eight pages, padding out text with further heavy use of images pulled from the now-many videos of a semi-naked Kaitlyn and the sexual activities she was purported to have watched.

As Finn had pointed out, everything was covered in the spirit of 'Omigod! Did you look at this? Isn't it terrible? And this? Shocking! And *this*! My goodness, did you ever . . .?' Etc., etc., ad nauseam. The editors were clearly having the best day of their lives: free content, with sex better than Page 3, a Black girl to castigate who wasn't even royalty, so no risk of putting off their patriotic readership and none of it actionable.

This last had been stress-tested to extinction. Niall's legal team had done everything they could to find legal levers to pull, but the editors were cannier than they'd been in the days when hacking a royal phone was the height of their mendacity. They'd kept a hair's breadth on the safe side of any number of legal lines and nobody could touch them.

The opinion pieces made full use of standard tabloid invective. Kaitlyn was a gay (four times, and for the record, she identified as queer, which is entirely different), porn-sex-addicted (seven), woke (ten), snowflake (five), screenager in italics and inverted commas (three, plus an interview in the *Guardian* with Douglas Rushkoff, the

American academic who first coined the term) who had sullied the internet with her vile (five), depraved (three), orgiastic (only once, but really? Do they just pull out the thesaurus and run through it?) obsessions.

Running out of actual detail, the pundits moved seamlessly to an examination of the monstrous (three), perverted (seven), radical (only once? I resented that), activist (fourteen) family that had spawned this mentally unstable offspring.

They nailed Niall (activist lawyer), Kirsten ('unorthodox psychotherapist' was apparently enough of a slur) and Maddie ('"former" alcoholic', where the inverted commas were transparent in their intent, while remaining legally untouchable) but the bulk of their ire was reserved for Eriq, who was a corrupt foreign immigrant (tautology, sigh), who had 'seduced' (the implication was raped, but again, nothing was explicit, so there was no recourse to legal action) Maddie and foisted on her this not-white child out of wedlock.

The writing was ingenious if you analysed it dispassionately. They managed to link everything to colour so that Kaitlyn's depravity was self-evidently a product of her being half-Moroccan without their ever actually saying so out loud. And of course, much as the nice, white people of the UK were never racist, they did regretfully suggest that if she'd been properly Anglo-Saxon, this entire nasty business would never have happened. Still, everyone could agree it was all very sad. A sign of the times. Much shaking of heads.

The final blow fell when Frances Nolan made a guest appearance on a flagship Radio Four evening news programme, interviewing a celebrity child psychologist who explained how he would treat 'poor Kaitlyn's' sex addiction. There was no mention of the original tweet by either of them, presumably as part of a career-rescuing deal that let everyone pretend the *Woman's Hour* conversation had never happened.

Whatever the reason, it hit the family harder than all the rest put together. Only Niall remained sanguine: his opinion of the nation's broadcaster could not have fallen any lower. The rest took it as a near-fatal wound to their sense that the world had rules and those rules were fair.

▼

It was a bruised and battered family that gathered again in the attic near dusk.

In this, as in so much else just now, there was a clear generational divide.

Connor was by far the oldest, and the least perturbed, person in the room – in any room: the upright and breathing proof to the younger generations that not everyone over sixty was trying to destroy their future.

He didn't have to say he'd seen worse things daily in his younger years; just by his being there, it was clear. Too, he was tactile, and always had been. He dispensed passing hugs frequently and at random and everyone was softer when they came away.

Even a touch on a shoulder was enough for Maddie's mouth to relax from the clamped-tight line into which it had been pressed. I had never thought of her as particularly stiff upper-lipped, but on the day the fallout began she was its living embodiment, holding together by sheer force of will when everyone knew that if she let go once, the domino effect was going to topple the whole family. In word and walk, she trod with the care of someone crossing a minefield carrying the last child in all the world in her arms.

The rest of the family took her as their example. The laughter was too brittle and the smiles too thin, but when people wept, they did so silently and nobody hurled mugs at the wall, or trashed the computers, or vomited into the wastebins.

Instead, they all created Very Important Things to Do with no gaps to take stock. Finn, for instance, was running half a dozen Grey Ghost streams from his phone, plus one down to Mo Bakar's Shaolin house in the village.

Towards evening, reading from this, he said, 'Heads up, people. Candra says the paparazzi are on the hunt in the village. Pretty much everyone is stonewalling, but it's only a matter of time before they find the track up to the farm. We need to lock the gates and be ready to sue for trespass.'

Candra was Mo's most senior student after Finn, and wholly reliable: nobody was going to question the accuracy of this. 'How many?' Maddie asked, faintly. Her shoulders tightened, as if a new burden had draped itself across. Her fire was muddy and muted.

Finn shrugged. 'Assume the entire pack. Think Princess Diana being chased down a tunnel in Paris and multiply by two orders of magnitude because we're within reach of London. Also, we're not royalty so they have fewer constraints.'

'Nye?' Eriq asked, 'will the law hold them?'

'Not a chance.' Niall had pulled his hair back and tied it up with one of Kaitlyn's magenta phone cord hair ties. He looked older, more professional: angrier. 'The police never get between the press pack and its quarry. They might if it was Radical FM doorstepping a government minister, but short of that, it's not in their job description. If Grandad could magic up half a dozen hungry Rottweilers it might work.' He made big eyes at Connor. 'You're the dog-lover. How about it?'

Connor's grin was positively wicked. 'It would be my pleasure, now. Just say the word and—' His head snapped to the window. He scythed his arms out wide and flat. 'Down! Everyone! *Now!*'

This was a Connor none of us had heard. Without hesitation, the entire family flung themselves face to the floor. They were taking their second breaths, ready to ask what was happening, when a belly-deep thrum shook the building.

'Helicopter.' Connor's face was lean and lined, his gaze leaden. 'Lynx. They're old. Cheap to hire.'

He had lived through the Troubles. I watched the realisation of this ripple round the room and I don't think I was alone in wondering what he'd seen and done there.

Risking his grandfather's wrath, Finn rolled over and typed into his phone. A text chimed swiftly back. He nodded, 'Media', and held up the screen so that the rest of the family could see the newschannel logo on the helicopter's side. From the angle, the image had been taken from the village, down by Mo's place: Candra again. 'They'll guide the press pack in.'

'It's nearly dark,' Kirsten said. 'Maybe they won't come tonight?'

'They will,' Eriq said. 'There's a tow-chain in the shed I can use to lock the gates. It'll buy us some time.'

Maddie called after him, 'Switch on some music and a few lights in the house. At least they'll stand outside the wrong door for an extra thirty seconds.'

'OK.'

Eriq was already halfway to the stairs when Finn called, 'Dad, wait!' Eriq slammed to a stop.

I had never heard Finn call him 'Dad' before. Going by the shimmer of grief-shock-joy-wonder that flared around his heart, neither had Eriq. Maddie, too, gazed at her son as if seeing him anew.

Awkwardly, Finn said, 'The keypad for the burglar alarm inside the front door. If you key in Mum's birthday as six digits, it'll fire up a set of CCTV cameras set in the eaves around the house and hook them up to my servers.'

Eriq took this in with commendable clarity. 'Maddie's birthday. Six digits.'

'UK style, not US.'

'On it.' He resumed his run for the stairs. Down below, the barn's front door slammed open and shut.

In the silence after, Finn ducked into his bedroom and returned with a handful of boxes. 'The ones on the house will only really show us the yard and the Piggery,' he said. 'We'll need more out here. Kait? Time to run the protocol for real.'

''K.' Kaitlyn took up a particular position to the left of the attic window in a way that spoke of much practice. She opened the window and made a loop of her hands. Carrying two small cameras, Finn used her hands as a stirrup that let him vault up and out, turning to face inwards as he did so. The whole move was scarily reminiscent of the night of my death when he had climbed onto the roof, except this time he was clearly intending to live.

As soon as he was out, Kaitlyn braced both feet against the wall and gripped his right arm above the wrist, providing a secure hold against which he could lean widely out and round.

Maddie started to object, had a moment of sanity and snapped her mouth shut. She glanced a question at the twins, neither of whom had an answer. Moments later, when Finn returned, his hands were empty.

'One more at each end and we've got three-sixty coverage.' His grin faded as he caught sight of his mother. 'What?'

'Nothing.' She's a brazen liar, my daughter, but convincing. 'I was thinking we're going to need food in here unless we want to run the gauntlet of whatever's coming.'

'Good thought.' Finn pulled his phone from his pocket, flicked out a one-handed text and then nodded to Connor. 'You weren't in the papers: no head shots, no character assassinations. It's possible they haven't clocked you yet and the eye in the sky is going to be watching Eriq, so we have a window to get you out.'

He grabbed a sheet of A4 from the printer drawer and a pen from Kaitlyn's recording desk. 'If I draw you a map, could you head down the fire escape and take the back route across the fields to Mo's place so you can be our voice on the outside? It's a straight route to the mill. No styles and only one gate. I can walk it in just under six minutes.'

'Then I'll manage in ten.' The old man grabbed his sticks and levered himself to his feet. 'Your help with the fire door?'

Together, the two of them wrestled open the door and Connor clunked down the metal steps at something close to a run.

With him safely out of harm's way, the Finn–Kaitlyn climbing team assaulted the two ends of the attic through their respective bedroom windows. Finn tweaked the bank of monitors on the wall and new images of the farm replaced the rolling Tweets, TikTok videos and Instagram feeds.

At first, all they showed was Connor's awkward progress across the fields as he hirpled past the Rookery and down towards the mill at the edge of the village that was the centre of Mo Bakar's domain. From the opposite angle, a distant blur of movement appeared at the far end of the track leading up to the farm, while a camera above the front door of the main house showed Eriq shouldering in through the lower door of the barn, arms filled with a second kettle, packets of various teas, a loaf, a pat of Matt's butter and half a carrot cake.

'Emergency supplies.' For a man facing a siege, he looked remarkably cheerful as he laid his hoard out on the coffee table. 'I could do a second run for mugs and plates?'

Finn shook his head. 'We have plenty. Anyway,' he nodded to the monitors, 'too late.'

Shown from a dozen different angles, a handful of corpulent, camera-bedecked, bomber-jacket-clad men had gathered at the gates and were examining the solid iron links of Eriq's tow-chain. The padlock looked robustly unpickable, but each one tried it in turn, as if it might magically open for the sixth, when it hadn't for the second.

'We need a sound feed,' Finn said, but truly, they didn't. The incomers talked among themselves for a couple of minutes and then two of them pulled out their phones. It was easy enough to guess they were calling for reinforcements.

Kirsten said, 'Can they summon a tank, do you suppose?'

'Probably,' Finn said.

'Helicopter's leaving, though,' said Niall, who had positioned himself at a judicious angle to the long attic window. 'And it's not tracking Grandad.'

'You sure?' Unwary, Kaitlyn skipped over to take a look.

'Kaitlyn, no!' Eriq got to her, but not fast enough. Down on the ground, lenses jerked up like so many Viagra spasms. Even as Eriq spun his daughter away from the glass, victory howls sounded from below.

'Shit.' Finn cleared a screen and logged into a dozen news feeds. It took less than a minute for images of Kaitlyn and Eriq to appear: two Black faces full of alarm. Comments scrolled down soon after: triumphant celebrations, as if the white team had just scored a winning goal.

'Come to me.' Maddie gathered Kaitlyn into a solid embrace and sat down with both their backs to the wall beneath the window where they could neither see nor be seen. 'Finn, switch those feeds off, please. Or put them back to where we could see the photographers. At least that was useful.'

Finn shook his head. 'Denial's not the strategy here. We can't win a battleground if we don't know what players the other team is fielding.'

Maddie stayed where she was, holding Kaitlyn still. Everyone else gathered to stare at the output from the CCTV cameras as Finn began to manipulate the images. From these, it was clear that the size of the press pack gathered in front of the gates had already grown to nearly twenty men. All were studying their phones, raising thumbs to each other at each hit scored, but behind them, something big growled up the track, far louder than the helicopter had been.

'Range Rover.' Finn magnified one part of the screen. 'Cheaper than a tank, but it'll do the job. The gates will be gone within five minutes.'

Thirty seconds passed in grim waiting and then the Range Rover hit the gates, hard. In the attic, everyone but Finn flinched. On the ground, men shouted encouragement, advice or orders. The engine clashed into reverse, revved up and came in for a second strike.

'We can't let them get away with this.' Kaitlyn wrestled free of her mother and stood up, staring out of the window at the buckling gates. Furious tears leaked unattended down her face. 'Seriously. There has to be some way to fight back?'

She was looking at Niall, the brother for whom no emergency existed that wasn't simultaneously his one big chance to take down the system. He held Kaitlyn's gaze for a long, burning minute, then turned to his twin with a silent question.

Kirsten pressed her lips tight. 'Not the time for theory-crafting.'

The gate crashed to another impact that sent shock waves up into the room. Swallowing, Eriq said, 'Whatever you two have got, theoretical or otherwise, now would be a good time to share it.'

Niall said, 'We could jump to number three.'

Kirsten looked alarmed, and then surprised, and then gratified in swift order.

'Thank you.' She faced back to the room. 'OK, there's one really basic principle: no problem is solved from the mindset that created it. The old paradigm – what Niall would call the Death Cult – is based on scarcity, separation and powerlessness, on hijacking our limbic systems and keeping us in thrall to the dopamine drips of consumerism and outrage. We're like rats in a cage: we're depressed, stressed and isolated and we have nothing to do but fight each other. With me so far?'

Nod-shrugs all round.

Kirsten forged on. 'Right. We're not going to get anywhere if we fight by the old rules: this is our absolute baseline. We need to create a new system that renders the old system obsolete: Bucky Fuller said that decades ago; it's not new and it's not rocket science, it's just that nobody knows quite how we build a system that works while we're inside the one that's so clearly broken. It's like trying to change the sea while you're swimming in it, or trying to transform the bus as it hurtles towards the edge of the cliff. So much of what we do is just painting the wheels a new colour when fundamentally, we need not to be in a bus at all. . .

'This is where the theory-crafting has yet to be tested.' She looked across at Maddie. 'Lan was here earlier, right?'

What?

I'd been half-asleep on a high corner shelf, as worn down as everyone else, but without the ability to lose myself in Doing Important Things. I snapped awake as Maddie said, 'She's been around all day. I think she's still here with us now, but it's hard to tell.' She looked up at the wrong corner. 'Lan, we could use some help here. If you've worked out any way to talk to the living, this would be a good time to put it into practice.'

'I'm *trying*!' It came out as an undignified squawk, so it was a good thing none of them could hear me, and then I was burning under the scalding wash of my family's attention, all except Niall, who was constitutionally resistant to anything non-literal.

His cynicism was cool, not unkind, and it helped soothe over the sense of flayed skin that Crow-sense had brought. All day, I'd been see-feeling the power of human passion but I hadn't understood how wearing it was until Niall, all unwitting, offered his gift of unbelief.

It settled me, letting me think, until I could feel the textures of the ideas Kirsten was laying out, could map their routes back to old conversations we'd had when I was alive and forward to . . . I couldn't see where. But I could feel a dozen possibilities, all of them interesting.

After years in the Between where little had mattered beyond the flows of compassion, joy and grief, it was a delight to engage with things more prosaic. I may not have known what to do or how to communicate, but I was at least capable of thinking about it.

'This is why I'm here, right?' I asked, of the only two who could hear me.

Partly, said Hail.

And Crow said, *Pay attention.*

So I did.

'OK, I can live with that.' Kirsten looked lighter, happier for my presence. She spoke upwards, to where Maddie thought I was. 'Lan, I know you believe the only way forward is for us to find our place in the web of life, but Niall and I think there are some steps on the way. We can't expect a single mother with three kids under the age of ten living in a high rise in a concrete jungle to care about stuff like this. Most of them are just desperate for the government to sort out inflation, or the price of heating gas, or—'

'Affording food that isn't going to kill them,' Kaitlyn said, acidly.

'Exactly. And for sure, we can't go down to the yard and start talking about changing the narrative and how language shapes reality, we'd be as well talking Chinese. But we do have to communicate somehow. Really, actually communicate.'

She took a deep breath and flicked a glance at her brother. 'Niall doesn't agree with this, but I believe the only way through conflict is to *talk* to whoever's on the other side. Talk without an agenda. Talk as if we care about them and the things that matter to them. Human creativity, compassion, all that makes us good . . . these things only get a chance to come alive when we see the humanity in the people we would otherwise demonise. The only way out of our destructive cycles is to get everyone working towards a common goal. On a systemic scale, nothing else will work, which is why we—'

'No.' Kaitlyn said it, shortly, but was rendered almost inaudible as the gate took its third strike. Metal screamed on tortured metal. The Range Rover howled into reverse with the gate on its bull bars.

In the moment's silence after it wrenched itself free, Kirsten said, 'I know it's not what you want to hear.'

'You think?' Kaitlyn's voice burned like paint stripper. 'You want me to crawl out through what's left of the gates and tell that pack of rabid racists that I'm really sorry for existing, and I'll go to therapy, get myself bleached white and would they like to join us in a grand circle hug so they can talk through their traumatised childhoods and how hard it is being straight white men in a straight white world? Because you can fuck right off. Those *fuckers* – sorry Mum – are not the real world. Not anymore. They're the last fucking death throes of a dying order and I am going to fucking *destroy* them.'

Her rage rolled over everyone. I sank down under its pressure. Maddie held up her hands. 'Kaitlyn, we're not—'

Finn had picked up his laptop, where he and the Ghosts were working with the speed and fluency they usually reserved for battlegrounds.

To Kirsten, he said, 'Sis, you can't do this now. It might work in theory, but it doesn't in practice. Conversations with people who hate us are fine when they're not trying to destroy everything we care about. If – when – we fight back, it has to be on our own terms. To which end, the Ghosts have been doing some digging . . .' His fingers skimmed across his keyboard. The big screens cleared of their CCTV images and instead hosted still images of a dozen white, corpulent men with expensive lenses draped around their necks.

A further flicker and details racked up beneath each man: names, addresses, ages, employment details and National Insurance numbers, followed shortly by new images of wives, children, houses in suburban streets with hanging baskets and toys in the garden.

Satisfied, he turned back to the room. 'Not all fights need guns or tanks.'

Kaitlyn nodded, tightly. 'This is more like it. How do we—?'

Kirsten thrust herself to standing. 'We don't go after their kids. We can't do that.'

'Why not? They have.'

'That's the fucking *point*!'

Kirsten never swore. I mean, not just rarely, like Mads, or trying not to, like Eriq. I mean never, in all her years, had she once given voice to the f-word. She said it quietly, but still.

Everyone gaped at her. She sat down again, bone-slack. 'Please. I know this is not my place, and maybe I'm too old and too white and too . . . everything. But we have to stop thinking like this. It's not just that if we sink to their level, we will be crushed – actually physically crushed – and everyone who cares about decency and integrity will go down with us. It's that the whole foundation of this, the tribalism, the taking of sides . . . is what got us into this mess in the first place.

'Not just us' – she swept a hand to take in the room – 'but us—' Same hand: a wider arc encompassed the farm, the village, the county, the world. 'We're on the edge of extinction. There are a dozen ways we could wipe ourselves out and each of them boils down to this one infantile idea: that we are right and *they*, whoever they are, are not only wrong, but dangerously wrong and we have to crush them. This is the kind of thinking that's been destroying everything good and right and beautiful for the past ten thousand years, maybe longer, and we don't have time now to loop round it again. We have to do things differently: new paradigm, new thinking, new way of being. Please, *please*, can we at least try?'

That was another thing about Kirsten: she didn't beg. I watched the colours around her shift from the clear violet she shared with Niall (his had edges of a deep-water green that occasionally overwhelmed it), to something harder, shot through with gold, the colour of a too-harsh sun.

Down in the yard, the gate screamed a thin and ragged protest as the Range Rover returned for what was likely its final assault. It sounded weary, ready to give up the fight.

Over the sound of tortured metal, Maddie said, 'Kaitlyn? This is your call.'

Kaitlyn turned the fire of her gaze on Kirsten. 'You still don't get it.'

From across the room, Niall said, 'Kait, we—'

His younger sister raised her hand. Niall subsided, which was not a thing I'd ever thought to see.

Kaitlyn said, 'It's not that you're too old, or too white. Not even that you care too much. It's that you're too good.'

Silence. Maddie made a small 'keep going' motion with her hand.

Kaitlyn dragged her fingers through her hair, exactly as Finn did. 'You still think there's hope. You grew up in a world where there was still a possibility that you'd get to old age and everything you cared about' – she made the same sweeping motion with her hand that Kirsten had done – 'would still be there, still working. If Nye had his way, it would be working better, would be more equitable,

117

more sustainable, more just. You still believe this because it's what you've always believed. In your world, this is possible.'

She leaned back on the wall. For the first time, she looked tired. 'My world's not like that. I don't have hope that we'll all find our best selves and make everything alright. I *know* we're screwed. Everyone who can use Google for more than about five minutes knows we're screwed. The climate's in meltdown. The oceans are turning acid and the rain is full of forever toxins. Democracy is broken. As Niall never grows bored of reminding us, we've only ever had a kleptocracy calling itself democracy, but even that's being destroyed in real-time by the sociopaths who've stolen control. The economy is running out over a canyon like Wile E. Coyote, but gravity's going to bite soon and we'll all smash to tiny pieces when it hits the floor. Social media companies are feasting on the young and AI just went feral so you don't even have to know how to code to make bad stuff happen: any ten-year-old with a grudge can stitch together bio-weapons that could take us all out, and if the kid doesn't do it, the sentient AI will.' She paused to push a swathe of hair back from her face.

In the gap she left, Kirsten said, 'If there's no point, why are you fighting?'

'Because I'm *tired* of this. I'm tired of being gaslit. I'm tired of turning on the TV or walking into the village shop and seeing the papers lined up from a world that's *dying* and the headlines scream about total trivia because their whole world would collapse if they actually let themselves know the truth. Because when the bus that is humanity goes over the last edge of the last cliff, I don't want the old, white men who drove us here to have their fossilised fucking fingers still clamped on the wheel. I want some agency: just a fraction of time to feel like I can live my life outside the toxic, stinking shadow they've made. I want to breathe air that feels clean even if it's full of sulphur. I want to drink water they haven't poisoned and eat food that's not giving me diabetes. I just want the world to be sane for five minutes before the end.'

She was weeping real tears now, fat drops that slid down to stain her shirt. Deep in Crow-sense, I could smell the salt and feel the drops pool at her chin. More, I could see the despair that churned in her core and how only her rage kept it from overwhelming her. I had seen this all along. The difference now was that everyone else could see it too.

Maddie sank down the wall and lowered her head into her hands, slowly, as if sharp movements might cause something central to crack. Eriq looked like someone had just shot him and he didn't know how to die. The twins locked gazes. Something passed between them that I couldn't read.

Wearily, Kaitlyn said, 'I've been listening to you two all my life. "Old-paradigm thinking" is Niall's worst curse on anyone. Kirsten lives in a world of non-violent communication where everyone does their best to see both sides and reach consensus solutions. You're amazing, truly. I admire everything you do. But it's not what these people want . . .'

She held her phone up and flicked it into a rolling scroll. 'Between YouTube, TikTok and Twitter, that first video's had nearly *twenty million views*. Please tell me you know that's serious numbers? Shona-Beth's GoFundMe started at lunchtime and now it's at—' she thumbed to the site— '1.8 million dollars and rising, mostly in five-dollar increments. Just on its own, that's hundreds of thousands of people who care enough to do something. How do I explain to them, or to Shona-Beth's family, that we're going to kiss and make up?'

This last was lost to a terminal crash from the gate, and a drunken cheer from the press pack, overlaid by the scream-gouge of metal being dragged across gravel.

Doggedly, over the chaos, Kirsten said, 'Can we meet in the middle?'

Kaitlyn's laugh cut deep. She flicked a glare at Niall. '"Compromise: the last refuge of the feeble-minded." Niall Penhaligon, circa 2015.'

Niall closed his eyes. Sharply, Kirsten said, 'This is 2023. We've grown up since then. If you want something that isn't total surrender, we need at least to agree some ground rules: to know where we're coming from. You have to give your new model army some values to coalesce around or they'll start fighting among themselves inside a week.'

'Like us.'

'We're not fighting. We're finding reasons to go on. I still think there's hope. You don't. But the route forward doesn't have to be so different.' There was an edge to Kirsten now that only an attack on her brother could have brought out.

Maddie tensed to speak. Eriq moved his hand half an inch and stopped her.

Kaitlyn nodded, slowly. It didn't look like agreement. 'Go on, then, throw us some rules.'

Kirsten raised one hand, fingers curled, as if she kept rules in her pocket, that might, at any moment, break free. She listed three, straightening a finger for each.

'One: we don't hurt anyone physically. Not ever. We can point out their hypocrisies, hold them to account, demand different behaviour, but we never – not ever under any circumstances – resort to physical violence.

'Two: families are off-limits. Not just kids, we don't touch spouses or parents or siblings or cousins or anyone else who's caught up in something beyond their own control. For all we know, they're on our side, but even if they're not, we absolutely don't inflict "collateral damage".' She let her voice hook the quotations. 'We just don't go there.

'Three: we point out the hypocrisy of the system, but we make it clear that even those who are attacking us are victims as much as we are. The system is rotten and everyone's a victim. This is where the respect comes in. We're the Facebook whistle-blower asking the company to declare moral bankruptcy because then we can offer useful help, not because we want to wipe it off the face of the planet. We don't back down. We don't give up. We do what we must to survive. This is not pacifism. It's a way that leaves doors open for people to meet us in the middle if they want to.' She looked around. 'Does anyone disagree with any of this?'

Everyone waited for Kaitlyn to move. When she did, the left-right of her head was barely more than a tremor, but it was there, and after, she nodded towards Finn's screens and the scenes of riotous jubilation being danced around the Range Rover that now occupied the front yard, with the gate a twisted wreck in its wake.

'Nice theory-crafting. Out there in the real world, how do we win without risking their kids or actually running them over with a 4x4?'

Kirsten took a breath, but Finn got there first.

'We hit their pockets.' He and the Ghosts had been working while his sisters argued. 'Money is everything to these people and we have worldwide buying power. Or not-buying power. With Kaitlyn's viewing numbers, we can set up a global boycott on whoever is funding this.' He tilted Kirsten a look. 'Unless that counts as collateral damage?'

Niall said, 'If someone is funding these fuckers to break down our gates, they either stop funding them or they're implicated. Seems pretty simple to me.'

'Sis?' His gaze swung round. 'Both of you?' Kaitlyn and Kirsten both shrugged.

'Then we have a plan.' Finn scanned the room, bringing Maddie and Eriq into the conversation. 'I'll set each of you up with a list of the tabloids and TV stations that have hit us hardest. If you can gather the names of the top ten advertisers who prop them up, I'll get the Ghosts to build a campaign asking Kaitlyn's supporters to stop buying whatever they sell. If we get it right, we can crater their shares overnight.'

He was typing as he spoke, and hit Return as he ended the sentence. Everyone's phone pinged on an incoming list of names. 'Take one tabloid or media station each. We're looking for advertisers by company name and product. If you can rank them by frequency and size, we'll do the rest.'

His gaze drifted to Kirsten and then Niall. 'You've set the ground rules and we'll stick to them, but I have videos and stills of twenty men engaging in criminal damage. Also, the owner of the Range Rover is a local councillor. If she didn't report it stolen, then she's liable too. I get that in the eyes of the current government, it's only criminal damage if you're writing with chalk on the steps of the predatory banks, but at least we – actually, our legal team, which is Niall – can send the file to the police. If nothing else, we log online the fact that we've done so and then when they do nothing, we notch it up as evidence that the establishment is actively supporting pornographers.' He cocked his head at the twins. 'Deal?'

Kirsten said, 'Deal.'

The family set to work: having something to do was the best kind of defence against heartbreak. I only wished I could be more involved. I went to sit on the back of each chair in turn, and each time learned a little more of how to smooth out the knots in the textures around them, how to layer calm through the weave of feeling, so that each looked more peaceful when I left, even Niall.

Thus, faster than even the most pessimistic of my family had feared and far, far sooner than the optimists had hoped, began the siege phase of the assault on the farm.

CHAPTER TEN

Sunday, 19 March 2023

You may think that the dead have certain powers of retribution and coercion; that, given the right incentive, we can visit pain and wrath upon the living.

It's as well this is not true. If it were, Kirsten's ground rules notwithstanding, I would have done my best to destroy every single individual besieging the farmhouse that first weekend, called down fire and brimstone on their heads, their tents, their portable toilets, blasted them with lightning, machine-gun-sprayed them with hailstones as big as bullets and twice as fast.

I could even have said I'd been asked to do it. On that first Friday night, and then again whenever there was breathing space in the living hell of the weekend that followed, Maddie and Kaitlyn both spoke my name, pleading with me to intervene without defining the limits.

I tried: you don't need the sordid details, I am not proud of them now, and in any case, I failed to affect any material change beyond making the invaders feel slightly chilly. Impotent, I watched the cordon of the press pack grow tighter, the vitriol of the media grow more vicious. True to form, the Sunday papers were an exercise in character assassination that outdid everything that had come before, with the occasional concern-troll opinion piece that purported to offer 'balance' and instead sprayed petrol into the dumpster fire of tribalised social media.

The let-up came late on the Sunday night, when a storm gathered over the farmhouse. All day, I had felt the bones of my skull squeezed by the weight of the sky, until even the magpies had fled for cover and the air prickled with promise.

Somewhere near midnight, thunder finally cracked over the top of the farmhouse, and the heavens rolled back their floodgates. The living detritus (sorry, Kirsten) filling the yard could just about handle roughing it in the countryside, but not when the sky gods were dumping bathtubs of water on their suits and their precious tech. They fled for their rented rooms and all kinds of pressure lifted, so that I thought there might be a chance I could reach into the dreams of my family.

I tried Finn first. He wasn't asking for help, just thinking back to the games we'd played together, but his mind was on me and so I was drawn to his room.

I had been watching him all weekend, but only as one part in the family dynamic. Being close to him now offered a more visceral reunion. Some things had obviously changed: his height, his build, his Shaolin calm; and some things had not: the sharp edge where he stopped being able to handle real people and wanted to lose himself in the world of bits and bytes; the slow burn of his rage that took ages to reach boiling point, but was all-consuming when that threshold had been breached.

He wasn't there yet. Warcraft was the check valve it had always been, and tonight, he was partnered with Hawck, which was as good as it got.

They were in a pairs Arena match, playing low-level, under-geared characters to show the Twitch stream that you could win in the 1800 bracket while wearing armour basically made of tissue paper and wielding weapons with all the killing power of a balloon.

By definition, they were fighting low in the ranks, but each of them knew Arena dynamics well enough to have fun where others might sweat. Hawcklol was playing a Healer-Paladin, stunning a Hunter, while xNiftyx as a Balance Druid made life hell for the Healer-Monk, all the while offering a rap commentary on the action. He was surprisingly extrovert when the audience was invisible on the far side of a hundred thousand screens.

The Arena ended with Green team victory. On screen, for the benefit of his Twitch followers, Finn scrolled through the video replay, cheerfully slo-mo-ing Hawck's damage counts and his own crowd control on the enemy Healer.

His Twitch stream was alive with cheerful laughter – until it wasn't.

```
Do u f*ck your bl*ck b*tch sister like
yr dad does?
```

I saw Finn's mouth tighten, but not so that many would notice. On screen, he gave Hawck a virtual salute and then had his character lie down on a bench in the local inn. To the mic, he said, 'OK, people. It's well after midnight here and some of us need to recharge our batteries. See you tomorrow as usual and then at the weekend for the Championships.' In the Twitch stream, he wrote, **Team Memory FTW.** Aloud, he said 'For The Win.'

As before, the luck flowed, until it didn't.

```
ftw
ftw
luck
win good
I hope u dye IRL before you get in
arenas. And dye again their!!!!!
```

Finn cut the stream and leaned back, stripping the scrunchie away and dragging his fingers through his hair, leaving it a blurred halo around his head.

'You OK?' Hawck spoke for the first time. I'd forgotten the glow of his deep northern vowels, and the care he could put behind them.

'Still breathing.' Finn gathered his hair back behind his head again. His tone was the polar opposite of the light, careless laughter online. 'It's pissing down outside, which is good. The paparazzi have run for cover. I thought they'd break into Mum and Dad's house and sleep in the beds, but so far, they're letting themselves be ripped off for extortionate prices by the Half Moon and the Nag's Head. Apparently, there isn't a room to be had within ten miles of Blackthorn Rise for less than two fifty a night. Meals extra.'

'Nice one.' You could hear Hawck's grin. 'Got to love community when it works. How's the family?'

'OK so far. Connor's with Mo and a dozen students, not a single one ranked below second degree. He's probably safer than we are. The rest . . . we're coping. That's as good as it gets just now.' As he spoke, Finn scrolled back through the comments on his Twitch stream, wincing periodically. 'Twitch are going to stamp on our heads soon, though. Two warnings already for dangerous content.' He dragged his fingers through his hair. 'Fuckers.'

Hawck said, 'The text readers are too easy to con with asterisks and mis-spells: we need live moderation. The Ghosts'll do it. If we get the interns onto it in rotating tracks, it won't slow the stream down much. Most of them are watching already, it won't be any hardship.'

'I would just rather we didn't have to go there.' Finn came back to the keyboard, shifting his screen to a spreadsheet. 'On the flip side, the boycott's getting good traction.' He tabbed to a share tracker, with over half the entries in red. 'Eriq's spoken to Max and their company's announced public support for the #CompanyCooperativeClosedown. They've committed not to supply to or buy from any of the companies on the list.'

'I didn't know your dad was big enough to make a difference.'

'Big enough.' Briefly, Finn looked cheerful. 'They've moved into micro-finance since the pandemic, which means they can put pressure on the global south trackers, and that's dominoing to the Dow Jones and Shanghai. News went public a couple of hours ago. I thought things would be slow on a Sunday evening, but #CCC is trending here and in the US. I've put a link to the share indices in the GhostTalk channels. If you look down to Giant Flat Tomato and SportLynes—'

'Got them. Lead balloons, both of them. Reckon the rest will plummet with them?'

'Got to be good odds. Just because the mainstream media are plugging their fingers in their ears, doesn't mean the coke-bois in the City can't read trending hashtags. They're already staring at war, flood, famine and soaring inflation around the world. The markets are jittery anyway and nobody wants to be the last sap left holding a basket of worthless shares. Which means the likes of GFT can listen to us and withdraw their advertising or decide it's a blip and try to ride it out.'

'Do they piss off their main customer base in favour of their political puppets? Hard decision if you're the C-suite of a company that spends millions buying politicians and then suddenly your customer base turns radical in a way the politicos will hate.'

'Works for me. All we have to do is – wait . . .' Finn was scrolling on his phone. 'Juke says GFT will have pulled all promotions from legacy outlets by nine o'clock tomorrow morning, our time.'

'Riiight.' Hawk sounded newly uncertain. 'There are times when I worry about our Juke. He knows too much.' A ruffle of keys and he quit out of the game.

'I always assumed he was Mossad,' Finn said, absently. His hands strayed over the keyboard, seeking out other members of Team Memory who'd make good partners. 'Either working for them or hacking them.'

'You're avoiding the point. I think he bears checking out.'

'Can you do that? Given that you've been telling me for fifteen years that you're not still in our security services? If I'm right, and you trigger any alarms, you'll be in trouble with more than Juke.'

'I can have him checked and nobody will trace it back to us.' Hawck sounded uncommonly serious. 'I like him, you know I do. But sometimes he knows too much. I'll sleep better if we know he's not a back door to people we will never be able to trust.'

'OK.' Finn had found a Shadow Priest in Croatia who was up for a game and was about to queue them up.

Carefully, Hawck said, 'Let's call it for tonight, eh?' And, when Finn didn't respond, 'One of the things you learn in the army is that when the excrement hits the whirly thing, you have to take sleep when you can get it. You're currently in the fine spray of a fast spin. If I were you, I'd sleep now. You never know who'll turn up with another bucket.'

He sounded serious enough that Finn cancelled his play request, checked his in-game mailbox and quit. 'See you tomorrow. GG.'

'GG.' In the attic room, Finn's computer sighed to stillness. I was in the operating system, trying without success to get into the game. I did know Crow thought it was impossible, but I wanted to believe that, like lighting fire in the Between, if I focused enough will I could reclaim the skills I'd had when I'd first died.

I failed (memo to self: Crow is always right) and so, when Finn powered down, I moved into his phone, thinking I could at least try to send him a text, but he switched this off, too, dragged his clothes off and folded them (some things had changed a lot in the past fifteen years) and, against the weight of his own predictions, fell asleep within minutes.

He did not dream, and I couldn't reach him until he did. Nor could I reach Maddie, who was asleep on the sofa bed in the attic room: her sleep was too disturbed to hold the stability of a dream.

Soft voices murmured at the other end of the room. I blurred through Kaitlyn's door and found her sitting cross-legged on her bed, knee to knee with Kirsten. A desk light in the shape of a swan offered a puddle of illumination that picked out highlights in Kaitlyn's black hair and darkened them in Kirsten's blonde. Their hands were locked together, Kirsten's palm up, her fingers pointing to the ceiling, Kaitlyn's hooked over them, fingers to the floor. They were each leaning in, until their foreheads met in the middle. I could smell the meld of their breath, feel their joined pulses.

It was a stance Kirsten and Niall took often, but Niall was downstairs sitting with a cup of coffee, scrolling through the various social media threads, and that alone was odd enough to make it worth staying.

'. . . didn't mean to hurt you.'

This from Kaitlyn. At first, Kirsten didn't respond, but after a while, I saw her fingers tighten and then, 'When you take your belt gradings, do you hate the people who come against you?'

'No?' She didn't sound sure.

'Does Finn?'

Kaitlyn laughed 'Finn doesn't even hate the people he plays against in the Arenas.' A moment's thought. 'Except Klostrydium. He hates Klostrydium. He has a point, though: the guy is totally toxic.'

'What do you feel when you're facing someone on the mat?'

Kaitlyn shrugged. 'Respect, usually, if they're a worthy opponent. If you feel anything else it gets in the way.'

'And what makes an opponent worthy?'

128

'Mo says everyone is worthy.'

'Of course she does, she's Mo. What do you think?'

'The worthy ones are hard to beat.'

Kirsten was grey-pale, with shadows pooling beneath her eyes. She let the silence draw out.

At length, Kaitlyn nodded. 'OK,' she said. 'I get it. We could call this a match instead of a fight and treat the bad guys as if they were worthy. But you're still selling Hopium.'

'There's three kinds of hope, Kait.'

Kaitlyn raised a brow. 'Three ground rules, too. Everything comes in threes in your world?'

'It helps me remember.' Kirsten tapped her thumb on her sister's index finger. 'First is the hope without cause, pre-catastrophe hope. Hope that says everything's fine and we can carry on as we are forever. Niall calls it Stupid-hope. You can call it Hopium if you want. And yes, it's completely pointless. Also dangerous.'

Tap: second finger. 'Then there's the hope for a good death: hope in the face of certain defeat. That's the intra-catastrophe hope. In Niall-speak, Doomer-hope.'

'We're meditating so we can die a good death?'

'Got it.'

'I don't want to go there.'

'Neither do I.'

Tap: third finger. 'Last one's my hope, which does, yes, hinge on finding the best of ourselves so we can transcend the moment of total breakdown. That's post-catastrophe hope. Good-ancestor hope. Active hope that rolls its sleeves up and makes things happen. Hope that believes in emergence from complex systems.' Her thumb trailed across Kaitlyn's fingers. 'We lose nothing going for this, and I can't see any other way your generation gets to old age. This is literally the only chance and I don't want to throw it away because it doesn't sound cool.'

Slowly, Kirsten leaned back until Kaitlyn was taking all of her weight. It felt like an expression of trust, and, after a moment, Kaitlyn mirrored her, so that they balanced each other.

Kirsten said, 'If we stop now, I don't know how I'd get up in the morning.'

'I couldn't get up in the morning if I was trying to save the whole human race single-handed. I don't know how you do it.'

Kirsten's smile was painted in shades of exhaustion. She leaned forward until the tension in their arms was gone, then, with a nod to her sister, let go of the link and laid her hands flat on her knees. Sometime over the weekend, she had chewed her nails raw. 'I can't stop.'

Kaitlyn tipped in for a hug. 'If you're right and we make it through, I swear I'll be the one erecting a statue in your honour. Many, many statues.'

'Niall would rip them down on principle.'

Kaitlyn flashed a ferocious grin. 'He'll be welcome to try.' She shifted round to sit by Kirsten's side and pulled over her laptop. 'Let's see who's joined us in the last half-hour and find what they have to say.'

I left them scrolling through the media feeds.

It was hard to leave, but I badly wanted someone to talk to, and a tug in my solar plexus said Finn had begun to dream and was calling my name. When I found the thread, though, there was no power behind it, no passion; the link was gossamer-fine and broke as soon as I tried to follow its call.

I was struggling to reach him when a new, louder beckoning arose, a great, roaring road that positively howled for attention. I knew the feel of it as well as I knew Finn, and here, for sure, were words to be shared, ideas, thoughts, openings and understandings. I turned my back on the attic and hurtled down the hill to where Mo Bakar's converted water mill nestled in a crook of the river just outside the village.

▼

Blackthorn Mill was a tall place: four storeys of cold, grey stone, with the ground floor given over almost entirely to the mill wheel (newly restored to full working order), with reinforced glass floors looking down onto the foaming stream.

The room I needed was up two flights of stairs: a bedroom whose wide-planked floor was not level in either plane. It was joyfully old.

Just being there, I felt the age in the oak and the faint remembrances of other lives in other times: births and deaths, joys and griefs; of floods – at least two – and a fire that had left smoke stains on the walls beneath centuries of whitewash.

The bed had been manoeuvred until it occupied awkward angles to all the walls so that the occupant's head was pointing precisely west. And here was Connor McBride, deep in a wild and powerful sleep.

I came to rest on the edge of the bed, in the space left by his missing leg, and stroked his old, gnarled hand and remembered how much in awe of him I had been when I was alive. Feeling the power of his dream, this awe magnified.

'Who are you really, Connor McBride? I knew you were special when we first met. Now I'm thinking there're layers and depths I never imagined.'

He did not answer; his sleeping form did not stir, but I heard a high, fine chime and scented woodsmoke that had nothing to do with the mill's past, but drew me like iron to a lodestone, so that I couldn't have resisted if I'd tried. I didn't try.

It was sharply cold in the place Connor had built, with frost edging the air and stars incandescent in a spring sky. The man himself sat in a meadow with his back pressed against a giant megalith and his one good foot stretched towards a bonfire of truly epic proportions.

'Hello, Connor.' I came to rest sitting on a log on the opposite side of the fire and watched his face blur and sharpen through the flames.

'Lan. You made it.' He sounded tired. 'Thank you.'

'Have you been waiting long?'

'Fifteen years?' He made it a joke, when it clearly wasn't. 'This time around, only a wee while.' Connor squinted at me through the flames. 'How do I look to you?'

Old. Worn out. It didn't seem kind to say these things. Instead, 'Exactly the same as you did when I watched you leg-peg it down the hill from the barn.'

'I don't look like a hound?'

'Like a—? *Oh.*' I am a fool and a fool and a witless fool. A knowing struck my chest, solid as a lump hammer. 'Hail is yours? In the way that Crow is mine, I mean?'

'You call him Hail?' Surprise cheered him up. 'That's bold.'

'Why, thank you. I haven't had a compliment like that since I died.' I laughed and Connor beamed, and years melted away. His hair lost its pewter sheen and ripened back to the oaken dark of our joint youths. His eyebrows grew less bushy, his nose shorter and he shed the nostril-shrubbery of age. He even regained his lost leg. Here was someone with skill in the dream that even Pakak would have envied. And he could see me in the lands of the living.

'Connor?' I asked, thoughtfully. 'Did you make a promise too?'

He picked a stalk of grass and chewed on the end. 'Not in the way you did to Finn. And not in this lifetime. But, yes, long ago, something of the sort.'

'Are we talking centuries or millennia?'

'A bit of both.' He'd always been the master of the half-answer. Rising now, he stretched one hand across the fire as if the flames had no heat. 'I'll tell you about it when we have more leisure, but for now, we have work to do.' He frowned. 'Could you become a tad more . . . Lan?'

'Am I not?'

'More like a crow.' He said it sideways, in the way he might point out to a woman that she was naked: not that we don't like it, it's just not what we need right now. 'It's why I asked if I was a hound.'

I looked down, and in the looking, my clawed feet became legs, and I was clad in jeans and my old sweatshirt. Fully human, I reached through the fire to meet him, and we stood, hands clasped amid leaping flames that did not burn us.

'Better?'

'Better.' He nodded. Then, 'Did Crow show you how to step into the void?'

I shuddered. 'When I was newly dead.'

'Can you go there now? We need to see Kaitlyn's timelines.'

'Connor?' I snatched our hands apart. 'You're not serious? It's terrifying. Seriously. We could *die* in there. Not like this—' a sweep up my wholly human form— 'I mean actually gone. Not anywhere

132

or anywhen. Anyway, what good would going into the void do now?'

He looked uncomfortable. 'How else do we know what to do?'

'Fuck, Connor.' I felt my whole being shrivel. 'Look at me. I'm a child in this place. I don't have half the skill Crow has.'

'You have more skill than you think.' A pile of firewood was stacked at Connor's left side. Silent, he picked out three sticks as long as his forearm and set them slanting in a cone about the fire: elder and hawthorn and ash, the woods of my childhood, adulthood and elder years; the woods Uuri had burned in the yurt. Threads of their smoke wove round us both, pulling in memories of other stories and other people and other places, all of them more powerful than I had ever been.

'Why me?' I asked.

His gaze was on the smoke and the patterns it made. One thick brow lifted. 'Who else?'

'Connor, I don't understand quite where you stand on the spectrum of living to dead or humans to gods, but I am certain you could walk into the void better than me any day of the week. Crow definitely can. I would put good money on Hail and there have to be others I know nothing about. So let's try again. Why me?'

'I don't know, Lan.' He dragged his hand down his face. His knuckles were old-gnarled when the rest of him was thirty-something. 'I'm not omniscient.'

'Not a god?'

He laughed, surprised. 'Absolutely not a god.'

So many questions. Before I could ask any of them, he said, 'I know you don't want to hear it, but this is what you're here for. Everything hinges on what happens in the next few weeks, possibly the next few days. For Finn, for Kaitlyn, for all of them, you need to enter the void and split the timelines again. It's why you are who and what you are. It's why you have been who you have been and why you are here now. This moment now.'

I frowned at him. 'What's special about now?'

He laid three more sticks on the fire. Everything in threes. Smoke streamed past us, out and then up. Everything he did was urgent, when he was usually so languid. 'Do you remember what Pakak said about the day of perfect balance? It was the second or third time you went to stay there.'

'Of course.' An old memory, this one, slick with the stench of a seal-fat lamp and clamped tight in the marrow-freezing cold of an Arctic winter. Pakak had drummed himself far, far away, leaving me alone to watch over his body, which was an extraordinary honour. I kept the fire alive, kept the lamp topped up, watched the light drift on the curve of ice above us, on the white bear's pelt below, and tried not to think when we'd last eaten or might do so again.

Before he left, Pakak had told me to hold my mind 'full of emptiness' and I was at least half a day down the route towards internal stillness when he, or something that sounded somewhat like him, spoke from the ragged shadows beyond the lamp's reach.

'When the sun parts the sky on the day of perfect balance, the weave of time will part at your asking. The boy who holds your heart must be your anchor in sight of the blue mountain. The North Wind holds the key to the unblemished wall. Open time's rift and grasp the pearl you are offered there.'

Pakak's lips moved, but nothing else of him stirred; certainly, he wasn't awake. He didn't come back to his body and open his eyes for another three turns of the sun below the horizon, and when he did wake up he wouldn't talk about where he'd been or what he'd done there.

When pressed, he said he remembered nothing, and we argued, partly because I didn't believe him, but mainly because I was terrified by the weight and portent of what he'd said.

Now, I asked Connor, 'How do you know about that? I didn't tell anyone.'

'At your funeral, Pakak hunted me down just to tell me. He said when the wolves gathered at the door and the fire grew high, I'd need to remind you. He was . . . forceful.'

'That, I would have liked to see.'

Connor pulled a face. 'Better you didn't.'

'You'd think he'd have the good grace to come now, though. He must know we're here?' I thought maybe if I wished it hard enough, he'd step out of the fire, wrapped in sealskin, with his eyes black paper cuts in his blood-moon face. Unless . . . 'Is he still alive?'

'I haven't heard that he's not.'

'So, he could help us.'

'I think he's already done as much as he's able.'

'Right.' There was a time – a recent time, within the span of this dream – when I would have balked at any suggestion that I had this kind of responsibility.

Now . . . Pakak may not have joined us, but the scent of his seal-fat lamp was strong in my mind, just as real as the smoke of Connor's fire. His voice was a power in my head, all the words lining up to make a sense they had not before.

Now, if I let my attention rest on the world at my feet, I could feel a judder as it approached the balance of the equinox. I could hear the sun nearing the horizon. At a stretch, I could contemplate the void with equanimity. If nothing else, I knew without question the name of the boy who held my heart.

'What do I do?' I asked.

Connor's smile was packed with relief. 'Find Finn,' he said. 'The rest will unfold as you need.'

'When I get back, I'll be wanting answers, Connor McBride.'

'And you shall have them.'

I found Finn in a world where the ground was made of clouds. He was fighting a dozen Shaolin monks: real monks, not the modern ones that Mo taught. These had the essence of age about them, as if they existed in a time long since forgotten.

Finn alone felt young, though not as young as I knew him to be. He wore a navy-blue martial arts kit that flowed as he moved. His hair was wound up in an impossibly tall cone on the crown of his head, pinned with ebony rods that had animal faces carved into the ends.

The array of black-clad fighters came at him in ones, twos, threes, fives . . . a dozen came at once, throwing kicks and punches with equally impressive swiftness.

He blocked most of them, but not all. After a high kick to the head felled him, a tiny, heroically ancient woman swept in from the side and clapped her hands, once.

Thunder lived in that sound. Mountains rose at its call. The

135

fighters froze, mid-kick, mid-punch, mid-leap. Each one, Finn included, bowed so deeply from the waist that their noses touched their knees and then they knelt on the clouds. Thus did it become apparent that they had been sparring, not fighting in earnest; that I was witnessing a training exercise, and that Finn, in fact, had found a dream teacher of some significant power who now regarded him the way Kate used to when he'd done the washing-up without being asked.

Not that fondness made his teacher lax with him. Summoning Finn and one other to act as her opponents, she demonstrated the correct way to evade a kick to the head delivered from the left (by Finn), while also dodging a punch to the kidneys from the right thrown by a tall girl with dark hair and cat-green eyes who looked vaguely like Daisy Ju, one of Mo Bakar's more memorable students. When the old Shaolin clapped to signal resume, the sound sank into the haze and everyone went back to sparring again.

There was extraordinary peace here. The sky was a spring-washed blue. The scent of peach blossom flavoured the breeze. Somewhere, a turtle dove burbled in counterpoint to a small stream. I could have stayed here watching Finn work out for the rest of the night, but I could feel time slipping past and did not need Connor to remind me not to dawdle.

Finn. I spoke in his head the way Crow spoke to me. *Can we talk?*

He nodded to let me know he'd heard. At his teacher's next clap, he bowed to her, to the others and turned ninety degrees towards me. The rest lined up, took five steps back and knelt in a long row, watching.

'Lan.' My grandson bowed as low as he had done to the Shaolin. 'Want to spar?'

Later, maybe. If you can teach me how. I gave up being a crow and came to stand beside him in human form, capable of human speech. The clouds were softly yielding underfoot.

Finn said, 'You look younger than I remember.'

'Your mother said that.' Something close, anyway.

'Really?' He snapped a grin. 'She's not always wrong.' And then,

136

more soberly, 'I called you when I first started to dream, but you didn't come.' He glanced across at the eastern horizon, where a clear sun was rising. 'Is it the equinox that makes it easier now?'

Clever boy. 'So it would seem. Also, to be fair, you weren't calling as loudly as you did before.'

'Before?'

'When you broke up with the girl.'

'What gi—? Giullia? Did I call you then?' He palmed his face. 'Sorry.'

'You needed me. And now you need me again. I've watched what's happening with the family.'

'You can do something?' The hope that lit him then was painful.

'Don't get too excited. I'm going to try something I believe may give us some pointers. It's not trivial, though, and I need your help.' I looked past him, to the cumulus clouds stretching all ways to the horizon. 'Can you make a mountain here? Blue would be good.'

Crushed, he shook his head. 'I thought I was doing well to get here in the first place. Can't you do it?'

I'd had agency in Connor's dream, but Connor was a lot of things Finn was not. I glanced over at his teacher; she, too, was more than the sum of her age and skill. She was sitting under a peach tree that hadn't been there five seconds before, watching the petals spiral in the wind. At the prod of my attention, she gave five degrees of a nod, folded her hands together at chest height and ducked an equally marginal bow. It didn't help.

Except now I had a clear memory of Finn's room, and the photograph of Ben Nevis he kept above his bed, taken by Kate in the ice-chill of a spring morning about a decade before he was born.

Something like adrenaline smashed through me. 'Can you go back to your room without waking yourself up?'

'Let's find out.'

'Hello, Finn.' In human form, I stood at the foot of his bed. Holding the weave of his dream with a dexterity that made my heart sing, Finn sat cross-legged on the pillows with the mountain above him. The light he brought to the room was softer than in waking life, so that Nevis was washed in amber tones.

He grinned at me, proud of the clarity of his creation. 'What do we do?'

'Would you have to wake up to Google the exact time of dawn?'

He winced. 'We don't use Google anymore. Too busy commodifying our attention. See Niall for details. Anyway, we don't need it. The time will be on my calendar; I've got a rolling reminder of dawn, dusk, moonrise and moonset.' He looked chuffed again. 'You taught me well. Also, Mo says we should meditate at the half-light times.'

'Sounds good.' I looked around his walls and found no calendar. 'On your machine?'

'Yes. But I can't read yet while I'm dreaming. Can you?'

I could. I did. 'Dawn is five twenty-eight.' And, from the clock, 'It's currently five twenty-three.'

'Five minutes to go.' He tipped his head. 'Is that time enough to do what you need?'

'I'm not sure. Time isn't as nailed down when you step into the void.'

He frowned at me, Maddie-like. 'The void?'

I sat down on the edge of his bed. 'I'm going to try something I learned the night I died. Then, it let me . . . do what I did. You remember?'

'Lan, I'll never forget.'

Something like grief and more like joy swooped through us both. After, I said, 'It's not the same now, but I'm hoping I'll see some options of what you can do and where you might go.'

Finn did the family thing of lifting one brow high, only it was his right one that rose, where Maddie, Kirsten and Kaitlyn all lifted their left. 'Does this involve playing Warcraft? Because the game's not like it was in your day. Everything's faster now.'

'I'd noticed. But no. It involves me splitting the timelines in the void while trying not to disintegrate into an eternity of nothingness.' I whooshed my hands apart in a vaporising gesture.

'You're kidding?' Finn's gaze narrowed. 'You're not.' He shook his head. 'Don't do it, Lan. Too risky. There'll be something safer.'

'There isn't. And it has to be now, at dawn on the equinox, or not at all.'

'Can't you—?'

'It's already happening.' As with so many of these things, speaking the intent aloud had set it into action; I was halfway gone, streaming to the void, and not yet anchored.

Pegging myself to the image of Finn, and the blue mountain on the wall above, I said, 'Does Mo teach you how to ground?'

He waggled a brow. 'You taught me that.'

Well, yes. I taught a lot of people. Not all of them bothered to practise. 'I need you to ground like you are Nevis. Put down roots as deep and as strong as the mountain and hold them until I get back. If you wake up, stay grounded, but I don't think I'll be able to speak to you unless you can come back into the dream.'

I waited for him to ask how to do so, but he just nodded. 'OK. Good luck.' As they would have done waking, his dream-eyes closed. Three breaths later, they opened again, heavy-lidded. 'What if you don't come back?'

'If I'm not back by about five minutes after dawn, wake yourself up and call Connor. He'll know what to do.'

The void was a black hole, sucking me in. Finn was a mountain on the edge of my awareness, holding me steady against its pull.

Thin as old chewing gum, I was stretched between these two and neither Crow nor Hail answered my calls for help. Instead, a hint of peach blossom whispered a welcome and when I sought the source, I was led back to Finn's dream-garden: the place of blue sky and rippling cloud and the sounds of a foreign spring, where waited Finn's teacher, beneath a peach tree in full bloom.

She was dressed in black silk embroidered with ten thousand coloured threads in wild, rich patterns, among which I recognised a crane, a dragon entwined with a pheasant, ripe peaches, two cups. Uuri would have understood the symbology. I had no clue what any of it meant, except clearly this woman was older and wiser than I was, and perhaps more so than Crow.

I bowed as I had seen Finn do, nose to knees, and knelt as he had done. A press on my mind made me look up. *Let us go.* Her voice was a promise, and on its breath we were on our way through the void; her as a bolt of wind and me, a crow-black arrow, following.

We flew where before I had fallen, and I was navigating only loosely by my sense of up and down, north and south, yesterday and tomorrow, but in the land where Finn lived and breathed, I could feel the leading edge of the sun slice into the horizon. I was pregnant with the need to act.

The Shaolin woman was at my side. 'When we did this for Finn,' I said, 'I had to build his lifeline up to the present moment.'

Exactly so.

Right, then.

Because I remembered it clearly, I started at the moment of Kaitlyn's birth and walked forward, mapping out the fourteen years of her being. Through the soles of my feet, I felt the moments of choice and decision: *this* friendship, *this* night out, *this* tree climbed, game played, friendship ended; *this* cataclysmic tweet written and sent.

The last was hardly a cleft in the path: from the moment she had learned of Shona-Beth's death, Kaitlyn had been going to do something to shake up the world, and there it was, written and sent and sending shock waves out across time and space, palpable even here, in the void.

Another step and the present moment rose as a solid wall in front of me. Last time I had come, the laser power of Crow's will had burned on this one place to split open the boundaries of time-not-yet-passed. The old Shaolin had not moved from my side. To her, I said, 'Over to you.'

No. Everything now must come from you. Look inward. Stepping closer, she placed one hand on my heart, the other in the small of my back. *What do you feel?*

I had seen this woman sparring and so I had some warning of what she could do, but not enough. I don't think there could ever be enough warning for this. I felt the white-hot freeze of her hands, and then beneath it . . . power such as I had never known: the thrill of storms in high mountains, the blinding power of a tornado, rushing, rushing, rushing . . .

I felt the victory rush of a battleground, the exultation of topping out after a hard climb or the best sex, the feel of riding a horse in a rare moment of connection, the melding of minds, the heart-bursting joy of balance at speed.

The horse, said the Shaolin, thoughtfully. *Focus on the horse.*

I couldn't hold on to the sense of riding this fast, containing this much power. In my mind, I was a heartbeat from a broken neck and it made me skittish and the image kept falling apart. Better, or at least, more tenable, was the thought of riding a small cart. A chariot, maybe?

The thought made it real, if not remotely familiar. Connor would have known this, and all the heroes of old Ireland, but it was new to me, this gut-emptying acceleration, the centrifugal pressure of cornering hard and fast, the wind-whipped *speed* . . . so fast . . . too fast. Fast enough to rupture time if we . . .

Let it go.

I did.

Silence roiled like the aftermath of an explosion.

The smooth-black face of time rippled open.

'Hello, Lan.'

'Kate?'

Whatever I had expected, it was not to come back to the Between; me on the shoreline with the sea flat to my left, Kate just out of reach on the sun-bridge.

She was almost exactly as I had seen her last: a distant outline cast in silhouette by the blinding light behind. In the marrow of my soul I knew her shape, the tilt of her head, the sense of her closeness.

'What's happening? I thought you were . . . gone?' Dead, I had language for. For what came next, I didn't even have an idea to build images around, still less words that worked.

'I have. She has.' The figure took a step towards me and it became clear that she was neither cast in silhouette, nor lost in shadow, she was black: hair, skin, eyes . . . everything that had been red-gold was the colour of night. 'I'm not Kate.'

'Kaitlyn?' My gut became lead, falling. 'You can't be dead, I just saw you.'

'But this is not then.' She gazed at me as if it were obvious. Then, with a Crow-like huff of impatience, said, 'Lan, you just gathered enough will to blow planets apart and then used it to cut a rift through time. You are looking into the future. So, yes, in the future I am dead. Everyone dies, you do know this.'

141

'But you look so *young*.'

'So do you.'

Fair point. A shadow moved to my left: Finn's Shaolin teacher was standing on the shoreline in the Between as if she commuted there and back on a daily basis. Kaitlyn saw her and bowed as deeply as Finn had ever done.

'Is she your teacher, as well?' I asked.

'Bēi Fēng? Yes. She's the reason I'm able to talk to you, though when the sun moves another degree or two over the horizon, I think it won't be possible. Something to do with the balance between light and dark. Don't ask me for details, I have no idea why things happen, only that they do, and this won't last long.'

'What do you need me to do?'

'Watch.' Kaitlyn waved her hand and by its sweep created a window out over the water. It took a moment to clear, and there, almost within reach, the blue pearl of the earth spun slowly against the backdrop of space. I had always found this image captivating. This close, I felt I was being shown something private, and immensely precious.

'Keep watching,' Kaitlyn said, as if there were a danger I might look away.

At her words, a shadow began to edge across the ocean-brightness of the earth. I thought it was an eclipse, which was impressive in its way, but the feel was all wrong. This wasn't darkness etching itself over the earth, not merely the absence of light; it was the absence of, the eradication of, *life*.

A mould has life, or a fungus: cancer is life's exuberance unchecked. This was not that. Rather, it was a devastation so complete that neither life nor hope remained.

It wasn't even death, this blight: death is whole and beautiful. Death brings peace and, as I was discovering, complexity and joy. *They wrought a desolation and called it peace.* So wrote Tacitus of his Roman countrymen; old words from a dead age, but they rose up now, and echoed until I understood.

'Kaitlyn?' She was still here, watching through the same rent in time and space. 'Did we make this? Humanity, I mean?'

'Yes. It's what we've become.' She corrected herself. 'What we might become if nothing changes.' She reached out a hand. She seemed too far away to make contact, and certainly, I couldn't feel her the way I'd felt Connor in his dream, but when she squeezed my fingers, I knew it had happened.

'What comes next is going to be bad,' she said. 'But you have to see it all to understand. Try not to look away?'

I couldn't have endured it if she'd not asked. And even now, I defy anyone to watch the things we watched then and not be broken by the end. We know the evils of the world in theory, but Kaitlyn was right, it's different to see millions upon millions of small acts of unkindness stack up and up and up, to see them multiply and spread like a stain across the heart-mind of humanity.

In graphic form, we watched the poison of hypocrisy and avarice and the careless annihilation they evoked. We watched wilful sadism spread wide and the strident mob destruction that was so readily stoked in its defence. We watched war used as a weapon of power by small-minded men who cared nothing for its impact. We watched great, gaping holes eat away the hearts of otherwise good people who believed that they could consume their way to happiness. And we watched as the endless flow of discarded poison destroyed all life in the oceans and then on the land.

We watched the beauty of the world, its splendour and majesty, replaced by futility, misery, despondency, desperation, horror and a creeping, insidious terror that ground down hope, day after day after day until nothing was left to reach for the light, until—

—in the heart of darkness, a spark of green-sun-wild-possibility flared into life, a small chime of defiance set against the cataclysm.

Captivated, I wanted to nurture it, love it into existence and when it set down roots and began to grow, I dared not look away, in case my inattention undid it.

'Come on.' Kaitlyn pushed and we fell. Together, we swooped down until the chaos below resolved into people.

The life-spark looked up. 'Lan?'

'Kaitlyn? The spark is you!'

The jolt of my shock broke everything open. The earth shattered into ten thousand fragments, and we were back at the sun-bridge.

Panicked, I looked down at my feet. It was one of the first ways I had learned to get a grip on a dream. When I could see them clearly, I looked up. Kaitlyn was still there, a silhouette against the too-bright light of forever.

Tentatively, I said, 'When I came into the void last time, we kept coming back again and again to see as many possible futures as we could.'

'Yes, but this time there's not much variation on the overall theme. You'd struggle to catch the nuances of difference. We can try if you want, but I don't recommend it.'

Just the weight in her voice was enough to close off this avenue. I felt cold, and it had nothing to do with the void. 'You were right then,' I said. 'And Kirsten was wrong.'

'Eh?'

'On the bed, earlier this evening.' And when even that didn't ring bells, 'The night before the equinox. Kirsten talked about three kinds of hope. You told her there was no hope at all. You seemed quite cheerful about it.'

'I did, didn't I?' She pulled a face. 'But Kirsten was right. I was wrong. There is still a path through, though if we're honest, it's more of a tightrope strung across Niagara Falls and we'll all be riding monocycles and juggling flaming chainsaws.'

'That's pure Eriq.'

'Exactly!' Her grin was kind, like her mother's. 'The point is there is still hope, just that it won't be easy. I want to help, but the me-that-is-here has no way of reaching the me-that-lives or any of the family. You might be able to, though. That's our chance.'

'You know I can't talk to them? I can't tweak the operating systems like I did with Finn. That was a time-limited thing. The newly dead have licence and all that.'

'All I know is that you're the wildcard, Lan. Nobody knows what you can do, only that you're resourceful.'

Feck.

I must have wilted, because she nudged her shoulder to mine. 'I think it would be good if you could keep the me-that-lives from being afraid. Could you do that? I'm a lot more uncertain than I let on. When you get back, it would really help if you could connect somehow, let me know I'm not alone, give me the courage to stay true to the path I'm on. And then . . .' She looked teenaged, for a moment, and anxious. 'There'll be a time when the boys will need you, *really* need you: Niall and Finn and Dad. You'll know when.' She took my hand again, more firmly than before. 'I know you made one promise and it blew up in your face, but will you promise me you'll be there for them?'

'I can't say no, can I?'

'You can. I'm hoping you won't.' Time was moving. Kaitlyn was losing solidity and both of us knew it.

I said, 'I promise I'll do the best I can when you and the rest of the family need me.' It didn't have the weight of my promise to Finn, but it didn't have the naïveté, either. Further back on the shoreline, the old Shaolin woman bowed her head lower than before.

'Thank you.' Kaitlyn was far away, and going further, but I felt her dry kiss on my cheek. 'It'll be hard. I do know this. But it's got to be worth a try.'

'Kaitlyn . . .'

'I'm glad I met you. Look after the boys.'

When the rift in time smoothed over, I did not return to the endless void, but to Finn in the dream of his bedroom. The old Shaolin was not there, but I had her name. In places like this, a name counts for a lot.

CHAPTER ELEVEN

Monday, 20 March 2023

'Bēi Fēng? Sounds a bit anglicised, but I think it means North Wind. I can ask Mo.' Finn was still sitting beneath the image of Ben Nevis. His hold on the dream was more shaky than it had been, but I could still feel the solidity of his grounding, and was grateful. 'Did you get what you went for?'

'Yes. I have to talk to Kaitlyn. I think when you wake, you won't be able to hear me, so we should settle things now. Your sister needs all the support we can give her, from both sides of the boundary between life and death. Specifically, I must find a way to give her courage, to help her stay true to the path she's set herself on. If you could let her know I'm here, it will help.'

'OK. Are we done here?'

'We are.'

Without warning, my grandson leaned forward and wrapped both arms around my shoulders. 'I love you, Lan. I didn't say it enough when you were around.'

My heart puddled. For a moment, speech was beyond me. Then, 'Love you too, Finn. Let's wake you up, eh?'

He woke cleanly, with no dream-fog, and dressed as he left his room, knotting a rope belt around flapping trousers, dragging on a dark green sweatshirt. Years of Mo's training had made him almost silent on his feet.

In the attic room, Maddie and Eriq were still asleep. The wall screens showed muted feeds from the CCTV cameras set around the farm. A dozen different images showed that the storm had grown to the kind of magnitude you'd expect at the equinox: a screaming wind shredded the trees and spat rain with the power of a water cannon. The yard had become a lake. None of the press pack was in evidence, although the abandoned Range Rover still stood in the middle of the yard like a relic from a forgotten war.

Finn knocked lightly at Kaitlyn's door and she called him in. She was sitting on her bed, staring at her laptop, biting the knuckle of her thumb. She looked exhausted: quite unlike the Kaitlyn who had spoken to Kirsten earlier in the night. I wanted to hug her, to talk to her, to let her know that an older, wiser (deader) version of herself had things in hand. But I had no substance in the living world and couldn't find a way to reach her.

Finn heeled the door shut and sat on the edge of her bed with one ankle hooked over his knee. 'Ian's here. She's come to help.'

Kaitlyn took this as one more weight, pressing her down. Speaking to the air above his left shoulder, she said, 'They're attacking Dad. Can you help with that?'

'Who is?' I asked. 'Attacking how?'

They couldn't hear me, but a residue might have got through, because Finn said, 'Who's attacking him?'

'The banks are going to shut off credit to Cuidorado.'

'Eh?' Finn looked as clueless as I was.

Kaitlyn huffed frustration. As to a five-year-old, she said. 'Dad's company? The one he runs with Max?'

'I know.' Finn wasn't rising to the you-are-an-idiot bait. 'But Mum funded it with the cash from Kate's pictures and they haven't been in the red since day one. So . . . no banks?'

'But after Covid they wanted to move into off-patent pharmaceuticals, so they could make stuff at cost price, and that took more money than they had lying around, so . . . yes banks.'

Finn rocked back. 'Why didn't Dad ask me?'

'You're his son and it wouldn't feel right?' She gave a loose shrug. 'Also, you don't have enough.'

'How much?'

'You don't want to know.'

'Kaitlyn!'

'Two hundred million dollars.'

'Fuck. *Fuck*.'

147

Arms crossed, Kaitlyn said, 'In the world of Big Pharma, that's chicken feed.'

'Not in the real world, though.' Finn was crunching numbers in his head. Grey Ghosts and his Twitch stream were pulling in serious money, but not on this scale. Distracted, he asked, 'How do you know the banks are foreclosing?'

'A tweet. How else does anyone tell the world what's happening?' Kaitlyn held up her phone. 'He has forty-eight hours to stop supporting us or they'll wipe him out.'

She was jittery, scrolling social media too fast; all her colours were sharp and jagged. What was eating her wasn't all about money, and Finn could read her as easily as I could.

'What else, Kait? This isn't just about Dad, right?'

She shook her head. A tear leaked down her face. Slowly, she spun her laptop round into his eye-line. 'Ignore the vids. Look at who's in the other half of the screens.'

Finn glanced down and then snapped up, genuinely shocked. 'Is that—?'

'Prune, yes. And the next one is Nico. And the one after is Stina.' These were her group, her tribe, her core friends, the ones she'd played with since they'd been in nappies, the ones she'd gone through primary school with and then home-schooled with in lockdown. They were family.

Finn said, 'These aren't real. We can prove it.'

'That's not the *point*! The fuckers get to come after me; that's a given. They *do not* get to come after my friends.' Red-eyed, Kaitlyn spun her laptop back and slapped shut the lid. 'I know we have ground rules, but I want whoever's doing this to feel what it's like.' She turned a blistering gaze on her brother. 'Can you find whoever's pulling the money strings, and do this to them in return?'

'You mean, get videos of them watching porn and then spray them all over the net?' Finn gave a long, silent whistle. 'That's not trivial.'

'But is it possible?'

'Anything's possible.' He put an arm round her shoulders and pulled her close. 'The problem will be finding the guys at the top, the ones who pull the ultimate strings, who give orders to underlings who give orders to others down a cascade so long you can't trace back to the start. The guys who fly in this kind of stratosphere have been trying to get eyes on each other since they first poked their heads up out of the swamp. They'll have military-grade protection and they'll bite back if they think they're being compromised. It's not like spying on a fourteen-year-old.'

Kaitlyn glared.

'Nearly fifteen.' Finn gave a lopsided grin. 'Anyway, it might be easier to aim lower, go for the guys who are getting their hands dirty shit-posting this stuff, rather than the people at the top of their food chains. For sure, we can find the heads of the companies that are playing hardball, or the CEOs of the banks that are crushing Dad's company, or the politicians who are calling for control of the net rather than control of the porn, or the editors of the newspapers that are trashing you. They're the ones in the public eye and a dime to a dollar says they're watching far, far nastier stuff than anything we've seen so far. If we want to retake the moral high ground, they're the ones to target.'

'Can you do it?'

'Not on my phone. You OK if I go back to my room?'

'Whatever it takes.'

Standing, he leaned over to plant a kiss on the top of her head. 'Lan's here. Actually in the room.' He nodded near to where I sat on the bed. 'She'll look after you.'

As soon as Finn left, Kaitlyn swung her legs off the bed. Under her dressing gown, she was wearing sun-gold shorts and a T-shirt two shades lighter. She prowled the room. With her back to the window, she stopped, dark against the sky. 'You can hear me, right?'

Right. But I had no way of letting her know.

I moved to stand directly in front of her and thought it possible she felt some inkling of my presence. Aloud, I said, 'I'm here. I'll help as much as I can.'

Unseeing, she walked straight through me and sat again on the bed. 'I need your help, Lan. Everyone thinks I've got some kind of plan, but I don't.' She looked smaller than she had done, shrunk in on herself. 'Lan, please . . . can you at least send me a sign?'

I tried. I blew every blood vessel I didn't have, but nothing moved, not a breath of wind or a shift in the rain, not a lift of the tissue by her bed. All I did was to run us over the edge of Kaitlyn's patience.

'Never mind.' She hauled her T-shirt off and stormed towards the shower.

Edgy, I sent a thought out to Crow. 'What can I do?'

I don't know. The principle is the same as when you made your promise to Finn. Whatever happens has to come from you.

'Thanks.'

It may not have had any ideas, but in the talking I had stopped being human and become more crow. As always, there was a moment's dissonance as my senses settled into the sharpness of being, but when they had, I could feel further out. And then yet further out . . . seeking now, not just sensing. Nothing in the yard felt useful, nor did the trees around it. Nothing in the skies, either, which was not surprising given the power of the storm.

I pressed on, heading down the hill towards the river until my mind met a tangle-mesh of roots, and a whip of branches, smooth trunks spearing from earth to sky, a ruff of wet moss and sodden leaf mould: the Rookery.

At ground level, I nudged up against fur and fear: few things were enjoying the power of this storm. Questing higher, I found bright eyes and damp feather-mass huddled against the boles of the ash and oak and beech. Strictly speaking, they were not crows who met my touch, but rooks; the distinction seemed unimportant.

'Will you come with me?'

'Please come.'

'I am your kind. I have need of you.'

I was heard. My plea was considered. Around me occurred a many-faceted interrogation, a contemplation, a tasting of the skies, a pressing out and a drawing back. *The wind,* they inferred, *will kill us.*

I thought they were probably right.

I thought I could not ask them to risk their lives to fly past a window even if that was what it took for a young woman to believe in something intangible and give her the strength to strike the spark of her own soul. Even to save the world, I couldn't do it.

I thought there had to be another way and wondered what Crow would do. I thought that in its arrogance, it would beg a favour of the North Wind, who was almost certainly a god.

I was not Crow; I did not have its hubris. But as a crow, I rose up through the mesh-thorn of branches in the Rookery and out into the gale. Vast winds caught me as I emerged from shelter and hurled me at the sky. Rain pounded me. I couldn't fly; I could barely stay aloft. They were right: the wind would have killed any being of flesh and feather who tried to fly that night.

I was not Crow, but I knew now what it would do.

I arrested my spinning tumble and brought myself upright, then turning, I launched into the eye of the storm. I was already dead, there wasn't much harm it could do, but it gave it everything anyway: it punched and kicked and slammed – and in its pounding was a rhythm I recognised.

I had no training, but I'd watched Finn for long enough to understand the basics, particularly the set of moves that fended off a kick to the head from the left and a punch to the kidneys from the right.

I must have executed them with at least passable accuracy for within the storm grew a cushion of stillness. Cupped in its calm, I asked, 'Can you abate awhile, so that the rooks might show Kaitlyn she has not been abandoned? You were there in the void. You know this matters.'

No answer came, but the storm kicked me hard, and, as the rag of a crow, I tumbled tail over tongue into the branches below, and when I settled upright, a tall, blue-black rook sat on the bough in front of me.

Her eyes danced, bright as raindrops. Her head half-tilted to one side the better to look at me. I held still, and was examined, and not found wanting.

Others gathered around her, drawing in from the night: nine in all.

We shall come as you ask, they inferred. *Though we know not where we go, and you must show us the way.*

With me, we would have been ten, which has never been a mythic number. It seemed natural, therefore, to merge with the bright-eyed

151

rook who had met me first, so that she and I were one, and the total was nine once again.

Intelligence shone in Bright Rook's mind as it had in her eyes and the sensation of melding felt familiar and enthralling. The storm was abating, but there was still a good, brisk wind and we soared high, surfing a thermal that delivered us in one great, adrenaline-soaked swoop to the yard.

There was nothing on which to land that was close enough to Kaitlyn's window for her to see us. We came to rest instead in an inelegant row on the roof ridge of the barn. I stole a semblance of sovereignty within my rook, and, reaching into the living trees in the Rookery, felt-sensed their being. There, I discovered that not all woodlanders are made the same. Not even all ash or all beech or all hawthorn have the same feel when you really stretch into them.

Among the Rookery's population were trees old and young, wry and dolorous, impatient, hope-filled – and wryly resigned to death.

This last was a tall, spindly ash, infected with the dieback disease, but holding yet to life. Crushed between two midlife beeches that were stealing its light, it had sought survival in growing taller than the others around it, thinner, more pliant. Also, more likely to uproot in the storm: already it was shaking and loose. I liked its spirit.

'Would you like to become a Tree?'

It considered this a while. I believe it knew what was being asked. *How would I do that?*

'You join with me as we are joined now, but more closely. Come as if to stand in my shadow, *on* my shadow . . . Yes, like that. You will feel the sense of being More when we are one. Then we move out of this place where you are being strangled, to a better rooting where light is plentiful.'

There is no death rot in this new place?

'None that will be able to touch you.'

Then by all means, let us go there with all speed.

Moving as a tree was a strange, migratory process that felt a lot like ploughing through heavy mud. Part way to the farm, we paused.

I am no longer in the forest.

'You are not. I believe it is yet possible to go back if you desire

152

to return to your former state. But only now. Later, it will not be possible.'

You . . . believe? It laughed, huskily. *Let us not test this belief. My roots will find the roots of my kind wherever I set them down. We shall move at your direction.*

We migrated to the field outside the barn, to an open place where a healthy ash might grow to its full potential. There, we settled, and I set my mind to rooting it deep in the earth.

'In this new place we grow down . . . do you feel it? You need to kiss the stone beneath the earth; embrace it: reach down through the subsoil until your roots feel rock and then split it and sink deeper still.'

And yet, we are not a tree any longer. We have no physical form.

'Even so, you need to root. The dream of your being must be nourished by the dream of the earth. This is how you gain strength as a Tree. And it will allow the rooks yet in life to perch among your branches.'

Sharply, *This is your desire, Crow-woman?*

'It would be useful, yes. But I believe, too, that you will gain strength and purpose in this way.'

The young tree-become-Tree considered this a while, then, *As you say.*

Damp earth, solid earth, living earth full of other awarenesses held us, or moved at our push until we were rooted so deeply in the earth that not even a hurricane could have ripped us free. With that grounding established, we grew up and out.

'Stretch higher than you did before. Spread wider. Feel the air. Seek where the sun will shine most strongly. And if you will give me one thing before I leave you here, stretch a bough out across that window. We must make it more tangible. More—' I struggled for the word— 'more solid. Something a bird may sit on. A crow or a rook from the world that was. The world of rain and moss and fallen leaves.'

At your request. The tree that had become a Tree stretched forth a spirit branch and we pooled our shared memories of how wood might be, were it not only spirit. Together, we created a branch that ran parallel to the outer edge of Kaitlyn's window. Back in the Rookery, a young, weak ash gave up its fight to live and fell to earth.

We felt its loss, the new Tree and I. We did not mourn, but neither did we celebrate.

I said, 'I am more grateful than I have the capacity to express.'

I will call on you when I need you. Already, the Tree's voice was deeper and more certain.

'And I will come.'

Another promise freely made, and still I did not know the full extent of the binding to which I gave myself. But I had asked and it had offered and I owed it my oath.

I felt the new Tree stretch out tentative roots back towards the Rookery, to the great mass of underground life that had lately been its kin. It was met and embraced, and roots were sent out to join it: thus did the physical world merge with the dream.

Easing away, I found the bright-eyed rook waiting where I had left her on the roof ridge. I did not – would not – compel her to action.

'Will you come with me, and bring your kin?'

If this Tree you have made is to our liking.

'Perhaps you would care to test it?'

Perhaps.

When I launched up, the bright rook chose to join me. Soft as the dawn sun, we rose high and arced down. The long limb of the Tree was solid, and it held us, although I would be prepared to bet that no human eyes could have seen it.

We were nine, standing in a row on the branch in front of Kaitlyn's window when she stepped out of the shower room. She was wrapped in two towels: one struggling to constrain the great volcano of her hair, the other a cylinder of white fluff stretching from armpits to knees.

Melded as I was with Bright Rook, I had access to physical form for the first time since my death: I could tap on a window and be heard. I let the shape of this idea form in our head.

'May we do this?'

If it pleases you.

It pleased me a great deal. I spent a moment marshalling

154

old memories, marvelling at their clarity, and then, with a rush of exhilaration as great as the swoop to the roof, I tapped my granddaughter's initials in Morse on the glass. KKP: Dah dit dah, dah dit dah, dit dah dah dit.

From the look on her face as she turned, that may have been too much, but Bright Rook had given me almost complete control. I hopped sideways and bobbed my head in apology and Kaitlyn's recovery was as swift as her shock had been deep.

Scrubbing her hair half-dry, she hurled the towels on the bed and, naked, came to stand before the window. She met the eyes of every crow in the line, left to right, then right to left. Last, she came back to me.

'Lan?' A wary delight shone in her eyes, not yet believing.

'Yes.' I tapped twice on the glass. Just in case that wasn't clear, I bobbed my head.

She bit her lip. 'Wait. I'll get Finn.'

She was turning away, which was not the point. I didn't want this to be mediated through her brother. I tapped a triple run on the glass. When she turned back, I tapped up at the window latch.

She considered a moment, then walked across and opened the window. A sweep of warm air met us.

Spreading her awareness wide along the branch, Bright Rook asked, *You wish us all to step inside?*

'Interesting idea, but no, thank you, just you and me. The others may depart now if they wish.'

We will remain outside, except one young male, who hopped in with us, past an astonished Kaitlyn. I had no real way to prevent it and saw no need. In my defence, I would point out that I had limited experience of young rooks at this point.

Bright and I left the storm-still night and hopped into Kaitlyn's room.

She stretched out her arm, and I jumped onto her wrist, and from there to her shoulder, to press my head against her cheek as I had done in the void.

'Lan!' She bit her lip. Tears made diamonds of her eyes.

And me? Oh, the feel of physical contact! I cannot begin to tell you the wonder, the glory, the sheer undiluted joy of flesh against feather. Would that I could have been a cat, or a hound, to wind round her waist, weave through her legs, lounge across her shoulders.

But I was what I was and took such great delight from the feel-scent-heat of her skin.

I was not alone. 'Lan . . .' Tears dribbled off my granddaughter's chin. Bright took control of our safety, and so when Kaitlyn darted through to the shower room to grab a roll of toilet paper, we gripped her shoulder to keep from falling off.

Kaitlyn blew wetly into a fistful and then, easing back on her bed, said, 'Can you maybe not hold so hard?'

I cawed a laugh, and it felt so *good* to make actual noise that I did it again, and then hopped onto the bedhead and danced a little, up and down, tapping my beak in random rhythms on the wood before launching back up to her shoulder, gripping barely at all.

'That's better.' In wonder, Kaitlyn ran the back of a finger down my/Bright's back. I tapped a happy rhythm on her hand. She said, 'If that's Morse, I'll need to find an app to translate.'

It wasn't: my Morse was bad and slow, but it gave me an idea. I hopped from her shoulder to the duvet where her laptop lay abandoned after she had shown Finn the videos of her friends. A tap on the case, a quick meeting of eyes, and she spun it round, snapped the lid up and – yes! *Clever* girl! – opened a blank Word file.

She picked up her phone and then set it down again as if it had burned her. 'I'm guessing you don't want me to video this and stream it to the net?'

I do not! I cackled alarm. She laughed and sat back on her bed. 'Go on then. Write me something.'

When I was human and had two hands, I could type as fast as I could think, faster than I could speak and many times faster than I could write longhand, with the obvious advantage that the resulting text was legible. With only a beak to tap the keys, I was slower, and had to take care over what mattered most to say. Non-essential punctuation was ditched almost at once, and then capital letters. There was no way to hold the shift and type a letter and by the end of the third sentence, I decided that tapping the caps lock on and then off wasn't worth the effort when Return achieved much the same effect. The computer set a capital automatically after a full stop, and the auto-correct achieved some of the rest.

By way of introduction, I wrote, I am Lan. You asked me to help you.

'I did? When?'

in a time different to now a futureyou asked me to help u hold ur courage

Kaitlyn ran her tongue along the edge of her teeth. I saw her dig her thumbnail into the pad of her first finger.

In haste, I wrote, u r NOT asleep.

'Are you sure? You come to Mum and Finn in their dreams. Maybe I fell over in the shower and knocked myself out?'

But u can read this = not dream

Maddie had taught her well: she knew that reading things in a dream was hard. I saw her look away, and count to ten. Looking back, she stared hard at the screen, blinked once, and nodded. 'OK, so I'm awake. What help can you offer?'

What do u need

'Can you tell me why am I here? Everyone is born for a reason, right?' Abruptly, she got up and began pacing again. 'So then tell me. What am I here for?'

You are the heart-fire of the world.

On you depends the future of hope.

You are the spark that lights the fire that could, if we're all very lucky, push back misery and fear and unleash the glory of all humanity can be.

You are the seed of confidence humanity needs to thrive.

Each of these had seemed true when I was in the void. None of them really helped a young woman understand where her agency lay. Too, I had seen the weight that pressed down on her shoulders. Badly, I didn't want to add to that.

I considered a moment, then wrote, what matters most to u

'That's a question, right?'

I dipped a nod of Bright Rook's head. Kaitlyn paused in her pacing to stare out of the window at the night. 'Fairness matters. It's so fucking unfair. Not just this—' a swiping gesture at the laptop and the phone. 'Everything. The whole world is burning and there are still Boomers – sorry, Lan, I know it's not your fault – trying to pretend they can keep on buying stuff they don't need to impress people who don't care, and it doesn't matter, because Russia. Or because woke. Or because . . . random reasons that let them believe it's not their fault, their problem, their responsibility.' She spun round. 'It's just not *fair*.'

It was a passionate speech as far as it went, but she was channelling Niall and this was never going to light the fires I'd seen in the void-visions.

`what wld u die 2 defend`

Kaitlyn leaned over and put the question mark at the end. I hopped a little dance. She smiled, but didn't answer for a long, cool moment.

And then, slowly, she said, 'I would die to defend the family except I doubt if they'd let me. If my death would make the difference, I'd die to defend our beautiful blue planet: I'd die for the dormice and the voles and the hedgehogs and the beluga whales and the white tigers and the black rhinos and all the things too small for us to name or to notice that'll be gone before my kids are even born. I'd die to defend – or maybe to bring back? – love and life and decency and integrity and basic kindness. I would die to defend freedom if I thought we actually had it, but I am Niall's sounding board, so I know we don't. Still, I'd die if I thought it would buy us the freedom to be whole again, to unleash the best of ourselves on the world the way Kirsten wants.'

She came to sit beside me and ran her finger again, with great care and thought, all the way from the top of Bright's head to our tail. 'I would die to defend *you*, and you're a crow.'

`rook`

'Whatever.' She put her hand behind my legs, and I stepped back onto her hand, then up to her forearm. She lifted us up to eye height. 'That's a lot of dying, Lan. I am thinking that perhaps death is not so bad? Are you happy, now that you're dead?'

Many times in the past fifteen years, I would have said not. Now, I set Bright Rook's gaze to meet hers and nodded.

'Thought so.' Her smile grew wistful. 'Wouldn't the world be a different place if we stopped being afraid of death?' She leaned back against the bedhead, bracing her forearm on her bent knee. 'Is that what FutureMe asked you to tell me?'

Hopping back to the keyboard, I wrote, No. I was 2 remind u not to fear. 2 give u the courage to stay true to ur path. 2 keep going, in spite of the fear

Kaitlyn's tight, dry laugh sounded uncomfortably like the young ash that had become my special Tree. 'My instincts are what got us here. I threw out a tweet because I was angry. Look where we are now.'

U knew what u were doing. We are on the edge of change. world will change w u or w/out u

better w u

ur choice

'Oh, Lan . . . That looks so frustrating. We need to get a better way for you to type. But yes, of course, we're fucked if we keep on as we are. There's so much inertia, and so *much* needs to change. But I'm one person. I can't change an entire system single-handed.' She looked out of the window. 'You should be talking to Kirsten and Niall. They have theories of change that sound cool: emergence from complex adaptive systems, all kinds of things I don't understand. I just have rage to burn worlds.'

I was poised to write that one match could light a wildfire, but it wasn't the time for clichés.

Instead, I wrote, ur instincts are strong and right

u can b a beacon for others

She stared at this a long time, silent and still. 'If I believe you, do I become a megalomaniac? Is that not what the old white men all think?'

someone has to do something

u r someone

She laughed. 'That was corny even when I said it to Mum. Were you listening?'

I flapped my wings and hopped a bit of a dance. Still laughing, Kaitlyn cupped her hands around my body. In our shared being I felt Bright stiffen, and then relax. Together, we leaned into the sense of an embrace. Over our head, my granddaughter said, 'Lan, I am scared of this, it's too big. Will you stay so I can ask your advice? We'll find a better way to communicate.'

`Ill tr—`

Something metallic bounced lightly onto the floor behind us. We both spun to face it. Kaitlyn sprang to her feet. 'What the actual—? *Lan!* Is that a friend of yours?'

What could I say? I had entirely forgotten the young rook. Goodness knows he'd been patient enough all this long while, but now he was hopping along her dressing table, sorting through the tidy line of Kaitlyn's makeup containers.

I use the word 'sorting' loosely. The mess was considerable.

Kaitlyn was not impressed. 'Lan! Make it stop!' And then, because she was well brought up, 'Please.'

Easier said than done. Within Bright Rook's mind, I asked, 'Can you make him stop?'

She had retreated a long way, but even after her return, I felt her complete confusion. *How?* Also, *Why?*

'Tell him it's not good to destroy things?'

But he is enjoying it.

Oh, *bloody* hell.

As fast as I could, I wrote, `srry cant help`
`u carry him out`

And then, with caps lock on, `B KIND`

To Bright, I said, 'She's going to pick him up. Tell him she means no harm.'

And thus, we learned the limits of our communication. Bright had, evidently, no way to tell the youngster that Kaitlyn meant him no harm, or at least none that he believed when she endeavoured to lay hands on him.

The ensuing chaos brought the entire family to the room at a run, which did nothing to help, until Finn, who had trained in combat with the North Wind and had better reflexes in an emergency than anyone else, pushed the window to its widest and stood back to give the youngster a clear route out.

Bright had to follow him: a mixture of duty and care. I had the choice to flee into the wild night or abandon physical form and

160

remain with the family: no choice at all. At the window ledge, I bade her a regretful farewell and stepped clear as she soared back to the Rookery.

With them safe, the storm rose up again, howling, and the rain became once more a deluge.

CHAPTER TWELVE

Over the shattering rain, and the hum of a vacuum cleaner (thank you Kirsten), Kaitlyn said, 'That was Lan.'

'*Lan* was here?' Eriq, Niall and Kirsten asked.

'Lan was *here*?' Maddie glanced around the room. Inwardly, I heard her ask, *Lan, are you still with us?*

'Here. By the window.' I took human form to give the words more power. '*Here!*'

She couldn't hear me. Finn cocked his head more or less in my direction. 'I think she's still around?'

Maddie looked from her son to her daughter. 'She was the rook?'

'Not the messy one. The other one. Here—' In the half-minute or so of chaos, Kaitlyn had saved and cleaned up our text, added in her questions to make sense of my answers, and sent the whole thing to print. She lifted half a dozen sheets of A4 from the rack and passed them round. 'This will save a lot of explaining.'

Kirsten abandoned her efforts to clean up and sat on the bed, frowning. 'Are you sure it was Lan? She used to be fanatical about spelling and punctuation.'

'Sis, she was a crow! Beak. Keys. Tappy-tap.' Kaitlyn made nose-to-keyboard motions. 'Give her a break!'

'Wasn't she a rook—?'

'Sis . . .' I heard the warning in Finn's voice as clearly as anyone. To be honest, I should have felt the sudden flare in the room sooner.

I turned in time to see the last of the colour leach from Maddie's face.

Oh, *shite*.

I sat on the bed beside Kaitlyn. My weight made no dent in the duvet.

'Maddie . . .'

I thought she'd heard me. Aloud, she said, 'Alanna Penhaligon, what the actual *fuck* do you think you're doing?' Her vowels were flat, her glottals stopped. Never in my life or since had I heard my daughter revert so completely to the vernacular of her youth. The temperature in the room collapsed. The air grew teeth of ice and steel. Nobody moved, except me. I lurched sideways, desperate to get out of her line of fire, '*Maddie—!*'

There was no escape. Maddie's wrath filled the whole room. 'This is my *daughter* and you're asking her what she'd die for? You're encouraging her to take risks and we don't know where it'll end. You will undo this, or you are in deep, deep trouble.'

'Maddie, I don't think I can . . .'

Kaitlyn said, 'Mum, it's not what you think.'

'Oh, really?'

That tone would have sliced the balls off a charging bull.

I put myself in front of Finn so that our eyes were level. As clearly, as crisply, as loudly as I ever had, I said, 'Connor. Get Connor. Connor's really good when she loses it. GET CONNOR. NOW!'

His focus was on his mother, not me. His brow creased. He tilted his head as if chasing down a half-formed idea. 'In the dream, Lan said I should call Grandad if she didn't come back. Seemed like he'd know more of what's happening. The yard's clear, nobody's taking pictures. Might be safe to invite him up?'

'That's interesting.' Niall was braced against the window ledge, gazing at the storm. Of all my grandchildren, he had always shown the least interest in dreaming and been the most likely to remove himself from any conversation that was heading away from consensus reality.

He pointed down to the track where a torch light lurched unsteadily up towards the back gate in a rhythm that was unmistakably Connor's. 'Already on his way. Might be a good idea to put a kettle on and get him a towel or two. He's not looking dry.'

Five minutes later Connor, swathed in towels and hugging a mug of coffee to his chest, was shown the printed copy of my conversation with Kaitlyn. He read the paper and Maddie with equal fluency. Neither left him ruffled.

'Tell me what happened. Finn first, then Kaitlyn. All of it, dreams included.'

They spoke with clarity, precision and accuracy. Maddie listened with her arms folded and a murderous look on her face, but she didn't interrupt.

'And you can't hear her now?' Connor asked, when Kaitlyn reached the ending, where a young rook wreaked havoc in her room. 'Neither of you?'

'I can kind of feel her,' Finn said. 'But it's like a memory of a dream. I can't hear anything specific, but I'm sure she's still here.'

'Kaitlyn?'

'Nothing. I couldn't anyway. It was all just nods and taps and the crow, typing.'

'She did come as a crow, though. And the storm stopped for her.' Connor raised his big, shaggy head. 'That was well done, Lan. Bēi Fēng is a powerful ally.'

Finn's brows racked up. He hadn't mentioned his teacher's name. He was on the verge of asking how Connor knew it, but Maddie was there ahead of him. 'Alanna commands the North Wind, now?' There'd been a Chinese woman in the community for a while way back, between the twins and Finn. I'd forgotten. From the look on his face, so had Finn.

Connor, wise, wise Connor, took the question at face value. 'Nobody commands the winds,' he said, mildly. 'Just sometimes they choose to make an alliance. The storm calmed enough for Lan to reach Kaitlyn, and then it grew wild again after, so the press won't bother us: not the helicopters, not the drones, not the men with long lenses. We could dance naked in the yard and they'd get no photographs when it's like this.'

Nobody dared laugh. Connor shrugged. 'But it does mean we can go back down to the farmhouse, specifically to the Hall. I know it's not our favourite place, and, Maddie—' he held up one big hand— 'I know there are questions to be asked and answers to be had, but I do think that at a time like this, it would be good to light the big fire. You never know, it might open up our options.'

He wrestled himself upright, leaning on his sticks, looking older, lamer, more tired than he had done. At the door, speaking to nowhere in particular, he said, 'Lan, if the Hall's uncomfortable for you, let us know and we'll move back to the kitchen. I'll light the fire. Should make it easier.'

The Great Hall was old – and Great – centuries before this place became a farmhouse. It had long been host to a selection of angry and arrogant ghosts.

Not for them the kind of lingering grief that drifted up and down the stairs at Mo's Mill; rather, here were semi-sentient agglutinations of ancient malevolence gathered about the panelling and in the crevasses above the fire. Few things are more toxic than the bruised pride of old white men deprived of power to which they believe themselves entitled and the Hall had been home to more than its fair share of these.

Oak-panelled, with a fireplace big enough to roast a whole ox, this had been the central meeting place for the Templars in their heyday before the Tudor Reformation. Their fall from grace had been swift: folk memory in the village recalled the time when 'the men in brown robes jumped over the garden walls to escape the king's horses', but in the years of hubris before the end, they had found the time, gold and sheer mindless arrogance to build into the structure around them barbs against the establishment they loathed.

In the Hall, this resistance took the shape of a high plaster ceiling decorated with Katherine of Aragon's pomegranate insignia. The same motif was carved in relief over the fireplace and there was a rumour that the exiled and humiliated queen herself had slept here, warmed by the blaze, before she ran west for Ludlow, near the Welsh border, where her support had always been strongest.

Visiting historians were drawn here like filings to a magnet, but for the rest of us, the Hall had always been The Place Where Nobody Went: a room of bone-cracking cold that no amount of retrofitted insulation or painfully expensive, Grade-II-permitted double glazing had improved.

The only time it cheered up was when the whole family joined together. Then, for reasons not remotely explained by metabolic rates and thermal inertia, the room drew the warmth of the fire inward, rather than hosing it all straight up the chimney, transforming it into a bright, rosy place where grand ideas could ferment.

I fled Maddie, or I chose to go there ahead of the family to scout out the feel of the Hall, take your pick. Either way, I was already facing down the shadowshapes of old resentments when Connor brought in a basket of logs and hunkered down in front of the hearth.

He spoke towards the mantelpiece, near enough where I perched. 'On the grounds that this is far and away the safest place to be just now, I am guessing you are here. Also, it's warmer than I remember, which leads me to believe you may have had words with the residents. So I'm assuming you can hear me when I say that I think Maddie will come round, but I also think that in her place I'd be feeling pretty murderous towards you.'

'Connor, I've done nothing wrong!' Peevish, 'Anyway, what can she do? I'm already dead.'

'Of course, you're already dead, but there's still a risk she could banish you. Pray to the Wind or Crow or anyone else who might listen that she doesn't work out how to do that; or even try. She's mighty angry and she has righteous love on her side. That's a potent combination.'

'*Banish* me? Connor, you're not serious? I did what you told me to do: I went into the void and then I did what void-Kaitlyn asked me to do. This is not my fault. You *know* I wouldn't do anything to hurt the family!'

'Thing is, you're not trying to hurt Kaitlyn. You said what you said for a reason. Clearly something happened in the void, but I don't know what that is, and we don't have time to meet in the dream to find out . . . Feck, I wish I could actually hear you.'

'And I wish I could figure out a way to speak that wasn't just bursts of feeling. I don't know *how*.' I was losing coherence, in form as well as words. I struggled to hold together while Connor laid logs of ascending size over a heap of paper-thin kindling.

Rocking back on his heels, he said, 'We'll do what we can and hope it's enough. I haven't seen Maddie this mad in a while, though.' Connor was good with fires. The kindling beneath flared to his match. He leaned in to nurse the flame. 'I'm not at all sure of Kaitlyn's role in all this. I'm reading between the lines, but—' The fire leapt up. He jerked back. 'But Bēi Fēng helped you. That's big, Lan: huge. I've been around a while. The gods are more constrained than we like to think. It takes a lot for them to get involved and they don't do it unless there's big stuff hanging in the balance. I'm guessing here, and I'd really like confirmation of this, that Kaitlyn's at the heart of the big stuff and the rest of us are supporting cast.'

'I thought you knew all this? You called me to your dream. You sent me into the void, for goodness' sake. I was hoping for answers from you!'

In the great-hearth, the fire howled like a thing alive. The room grew no warmer, but Connor had laid the same fire here as he had in his dream and the three smokes raced together up the chimney: ash, elder, hawthorn, with all the power and wisdom they carried. I felt, if not safer, then less unsafe.

Connor said, 'Lan, we need to be canny here. You keep doing whatever you're doing and I'll keep putting the three woods on the fire, and we'll see if together we can't – ah, too late . . .'

We both heard the clamour of voices in the hallway. Connor snapped round to face the door. Low-voiced and urgent, he said, 'Lan, if Maddie tries to make you leave . . . I don't know what happens then, but I'll wait at the dream fire. If you can get back there, we can work out a new strategy.'

'Connor! For fuck's sake, you can't just throw that out and walk aw—'

He stood up, spreading his arms wide to the family. 'I got the fire going. Is that coffee? Well done.'

And that was it. The whole family here and me in a corner watching the ghosts and Maddie's anger and afraid of them both.

I'd had no idea it was possible for someone to make me leave. Where would they send me? Back to the Between with Crow and Hail? They'd bounce me straight back here again. I had a nauseating vision of shuttling back and forth for eternity like a laser between two mirrors. Ancient shadows leered and snickered.

I edged closer to the fire and was lost a moment in the spiralling smoke before I realised Kaitlyn was speaking.

'. . . trust my instincts, and not be afraid. If I can do that, I don't think it's unreasonable to ask it of the rest of the family.' When she jutted her jaw, my granddaughter was the image of Connor. 'I don't want this kind of responsibility. I never asked for it. But Lan said I asked her for this help. I am trying to believe I was wiser then. Also, that she'll let us know if I start doing something irretrievably stupid.'

This last was directed at her mother, who sat rigid and alone on the central sofa of the three, reading and rereading her copy of the Rook–Kaitlyn conversation.

Maddie wasn't looking mollified. To Connor she said, curtly, 'Is she here?' At least she was speaking more Family than Glasgow.

Connor tilted his head at Finn. 'I'd say so?'

Finn had been checking his GhostTalk threads. Hawck had messaged: **Juke = Clear**. He laid his phone facedown on the floor. 'I think she's over by the fire. On the mantelpiece, or close to it.'

Maddie nodded, as if this confirmed something she already knew. She crossed to the fire, and then, with deliberate slowness, crushed her copy of my text into a ball, wrapped it in old newspaper and hurled the combination into the flames.

Acrid smoke joined the blend that Connor had so carefully crafted. When it was at its harshest, she said, distinctly, 'Alanna Penhaligon, you can fuck off right to H—'

'Mum!'

'No!'

'*Madeleine!*' As if he had two good legs, Connor was up, one hand outstretched, his voice smashing down across the route to oblivion.

But still, her words had been a poleaxe and I the ox. I fell. The room faded. A bird called alarm that was both Crow and Bright Rook. Around me, frigidly radiant, the shadows laughed.

A crack opened in the firmament that was not to the void, or at least, not to any part I knew. There was an ache in it, a desperate, sucking desire to drag me in and suck out what was left of my being. If she'd finished that word, without question, I'd have been through, with no way back.

From a far, far distance I felt Connor marshal his control of the moment. 'Those would not be wise words.' His voice was rolling ease again. His gaze locked on his daughter.

Maddie did not flinch or look away. 'I am not a wise person.'

'You don't mean that.'

'What if I do?'

Each time she spoke, the gone-place grew stronger, its pull harder. I felt myself dissolving. Connor's features were my lifeline. I fixed on each crag and cleft of his face.

He said, 'Maddie, love, you need to grou—'

'*Fuck* that!' An octave up and all the power to reach the back of the auditorium. 'I'm not playing your dreaming games now, Connor McBride. Or hers.'

The room juddered with new layers of disquiet. Connor said, 'It's neither mine nor Alanna's. We picked up tools that have been around for the life of the planet, at least as long as humans have walked upright, and we picked them because they worked. Ground, Maddie. Open the eyes of your feet and set them to look down into the heart of the earth the way you were taught. You will regret this for the rest of your life and beyond if you don't.'

Mellow though it was, Connor's voice had all the power of his ten thousand lives. Even as Maddie took breath to answer back, her balance shifted and her roots went down. The room steadied enough that I stopped feeling sick.

Nodding, Connor said, 'Lan has been places none of us have ever seen, or could ever go. If you destroy her now, you destroy all the help we might otherwise get.'

'Would that be worse than what she was doing to Kaitlyn? This is my *daughter* we're talking about. She is not my mother's plaything. She's not a bit-part in her post-mortem dramas.'

'Mads, nobody is playing with anything or anyone. Lan is doing her best with what she is given. She is aware of the dangers, more than any of us. But she has said that this is a pivotal time and Kaitlyn is central in ways we don't yet understand. She wouldn't say so if it weren't true. She was not a liar in life and I really don't believe death will have turned her into one. Nor, I think, do you.'

Maddie did not put down her rage, but the touch of the earth diluted it a fraction. She slumped onto the sofa beside Eriq, who wrapped an arm around her waist. Earlier, she'd been afraid he would weaken her. Now . . . maybe she wanted a bit of that.

The sucking desolation loosened its hold. Not completely, but a bit.

'*Fuck . . .!*' I dribbled down onto the mantel.

Nobody heard me. Nobody knew I had moved. In the room, a tearful Maddie said to Connor, 'Dad, she's too *young*. You can't ask this of her.'

Connor said, 'Love, we're all too young by about a thousand years. Still, the time requires that we do our best. You must know that Lan cares deeply for all the family. She could have gone with Kate fifteen years ago and be long out of this, safe on the road to whatever comes next. That she chose to stay and fulfil her promise to Finn and then took on a new one to Kaitlyn is testament to the depth of her care. It's not been easy on her, either.'

'So my mother's the victim here? "Poor Lan"—' she hooked vicious finger-quotes— 'locked in the Between against her will by her needy family, is that it?'

'She's doing what she thinks is right. She always does.'

'You think?' Maddie tilted her head up. To the air above the fire, icily, she said, 'Alanna, I want to speak with you. Now.'

Fuck. Fuck. *Fuck*. I never did know how to handle Maddie's rages. Kate was the one who had grown up among redheads, her earliest reflexes honed to evade the terrifying combination of gunpowder and verbal cyanide. I was raised in the cold light of reason, amid ever-tight lips whose way of coping was to respond to everything in words of one syllable, as if to a child of limited capacity. In my opinion, it worked far better.

Stung, I said, 'You want me to show you what I saw? Trust me, you'd never sleep again.'

She couldn't hear a word. And I was too scared to think clearly.

Of us all, Kaitlyn was least freaked out by what was happening. She stepped into the gap between Maddie and me.

'Kaitlyn? Can you hear me?'

'Lan?' Her eyes lost focus, as if she were seeking answers far beyond the room. She couldn't hear me; none of them could. But I thought there was a chance she might feel me the way Finn could.

'Tell your mother that if she can't trust me, she can at least trust that we are not alone. I don't command the North Wind, not remotely, but Bēi Fēng helped us all the same and Maddie saw it. It wasn't a dream or a nightmare. It was real. That has to be worth something.'

This would have been a good time for Bēi Fēng to swirl in, to dance with the fire or rattle hail down the chimney the better to underline my point. None of this happened, but Kaitlyn's gaze came back into focus. 'Mum, we can't go back. There's only forward. And the crows *did* come. The storm *did* stop. We're not alone in all this.'

'Please don't tell me we're getting help from "elsewhere".'

Kaitlyn refused to deflate. 'We are.'

'So that you can be asked to choose which of half a dozen causes you'd die for? So she can tell you death's *not so bad*?'

'You'd rather I spent my life being afraid of it?'

'I'd rather it wasn't a topic of discussion for at least another half-century.'

'Mum, we're in the middle of the sixth mass extinction. Death is all around us.'

'Do not quote your brother at me, Kaitlyn Penhaligon. Do. *Not*.'

Scalded, Niall found something vital to study on his phone.

'Hey.' Kaitlyn crossed the gap and, before Maddie could stop her, nudged Eriq aside with her hip, squeezed into the space between them and folded her mother into a big, electric hug. She pressed kisses to her hair and stroked her hands down her back until we all felt the blur of true softening.

With no warning at all, the desolation loosed all its grip. I fell to my knees and vomited meals I had never eaten until I turned myself inside out.

Connor knelt again at the fire and blew it clear of all the paper-smoke. Careless of the heat, he cupped the three wood smokes and ladled them out into the air around me. I reached for their balm like a blanket.

On the far side of the room, Kaitlyn angled herself sideways, held her mother's face framed in both hands, balanced nose tip to nose tip, and said, 'Do you trust me?'

Tears gathered in the corners of Maddie's eyes. 'I want to. Honestly.'

'If you don't, then we need to stop while there's still time.' Kaitlyn pressed a kiss to her mother's brow. 'It's OK. I'll make the video that will put it all to bed. It'll take five minutes and it'll be out on the net within ten.'

'The one that says it was all a horrible mistake and you're heading for therapy and getting your skin bleached and the family would be grateful if the press would leave us in peace to process our responses to this difficult time?' Maddie tried for a smile.

Niall snorted, faintly. The room grew yet warmer; the shadows shrank to nothing. The fire sent tendrils of smoke into the room. Maddie dropped her face to her hands. 'I hate this.'

Eriq hugged her shoulders. 'We all do.'

Niall came to sit on the floor at her feet. 'If we don't bend,' he said. 'We'll break.'

Maddie's turn to snort. 'You sound like Kirsten.'

'I do listen occasionally.'

'You're our strategist. You're not meant to talk of bending.'

'No. I was the source of our rage, but I've been usurped by a crow and the North Wind, and my baby sister. Now, I'm the one waiting to be told what to do.'

Kaitlyn said, 'You're still Mr Strategy. I want good strategy. ASAP.'

'OK.' Niall lifted his own printout of the crow conversation. He tilted it at Kaitlyn first. 'Kait, I trust your instincts. Sis—' a tilt to Kirsten— 'has given us the ground rules: we're not assaulting people's families and we make sure they always have a way out. I trust her moral compass. I trust Finn—' third tilt— 'to give us our online strategy: we're using the power of our social media following against theirs. Mum will keep us grounded, so we don't do anything too wild, and Dad has two grandmothers who will skin him alive if he dishonours our ancestors, so he'll make sure we won't.'

He raised a brow at his mother. Maddie pulled a face but didn't interrupt. Beside her, Eriq was trying not to glow too brightly.

Niall dipped a quick nod and went on. 'For her part, Lan clearly wants to help, and she brings the wisdom Connor spoke about from the places we haven't seen and could never go. A clear route of

172

communication would be good, but in default of that, those of you who know how to meet her in your dreams had better do it as often as you can.'

'But?' Kirsten asked, who knew him as well as she knew herself. 'I can hear a but.'

'But . . .' Niall laid the paper flat on the floor. 'We still don't have our powerful why. We need a bigger reason for what we're doing than, "We want them to stop hurting us".'

'We want them to stop destroying everything that's good and decent and beautiful,' Kaitlyn said. 'How much more powerful can you get?'

Niall shook his head. 'First rule of activism: work for what you want, not what you don't want. We need to think hard about this, it's not something to bash together in the heat of the moment. In any case, the immediate problem is the threat to Dad's businesses. Whatever else we do, we have to kick that one into touch before their deadline.'

'You're Superman now?' Eriq asked. He was still too chuffed by the Dad thing to put any bite into the question.

'No, but I have some ideas. First line of thought is that Kirsten and I craft the most passive-aggressive press release the world has ever seen, along the lines that Cuidorado is caving to a bank whose board members have just pretty much outed themselves as purveyors, maybe even consumers, of child pornography. We'll have to run it through the legal mill, but if we get the wording right they're going to look really, really bad. If Finn's Ghosts can spread the message we'll have it running viral by lunchtime.

'That's a first emergency response. At the same time, we'll keep the TripleS boycott afloat, and then use Finn's hack-results to take the fight to the enemy as soon as we have data on exactly who we're engaging with and how best to get to them.' He raised one brow to Finn. 'Tomorrow?'

Finn spat back the mouthful of coffee he'd just taken. 'A week. If we're lucky.'

'So we're in a holding pattern for the next week.' Niall found a pen on the bureau in the corner and wrote himself a note on what was now clearly his operations list. 'We can do this – as long as everyone trusts everyone else. Trust is the glue that keeps us together. If one of us drops out, we're finished.' He surveyed the far corners of the room. 'That goes for Lan, too. I know I spent my life ignoring all the dream stuff, but I saw the rook in Kaitlyn's room, I've read the printout and . . .' He gave a strange half-shrug that might have been an apology. 'Lan's in this as much as the rest of us.'

'All for one and one for all?' From Maddie this, too, was an apology of sorts.

'That's the one.' Niall unfurled his mischief-smile in a way I hadn't seen since he was six. With a flourish, he lifted his phone aloft. 'All for one!'

Kaitlyn tapped it with her own. 'One for all.' Kirsten met them, and the others joined, all bar Eriq, who had not grown up with musketeers as part of his cultural milieu and had to have the whole concept explained.

Niall educated him and did it again, and they all laughed this time, even Maddie.

'Right.' Niall was Puck, a wild-haired trickster, awhirl in front of the fire. 'We'll generate an action list and get things going before the American continent wakes up. With luck, we can make the bad guys wish they'd stayed in bed for the rest of the week. And before all that—' a truly orchestral flourish here— 'Breakfast! We need bacon, eggs, toast. And about six litres of coffee.'

CHAPTER THIRTEEN

Monday, 20 to Friday, 31 March 2023

As predicted, Finn's Grey Ghosts unearthed potential dynamite from the hard drives of their targets. As also predicted, it took them over a week to do so: they didn't turn up the really radioactive stuff until the early hours of Monday, 27 March, ten days after Kaitlyn had posted her tweet.

In the days leading up to this, the family healed their differences and welded once more into a functional team. I had yet to find access into anyone's dreams – Pakak had been right about the tilt of the world being unique for us all – but I was in the room whenever decisions were made and Finn had taken to asking my opinion as a matter of course. I shouted responses. He felt . . . something, I had no idea what, and I was pretty sure he didn't change any actions on my account, but it felt good to be involved.

Working from Niall's priority list, the family's first success was that Eriq's bank did not foreclose on his business when the UK markets opened on the Wednesday morning as had been threatened.

Among the family, the ensuing celebration was tempered by a degree of shock at the realisation that Eriq had borrowed more money than anyone had ever seen. Niall, particularly, had opinions he was not afraid to air.

Niall: 'We're all pretty much embracing the Death Cult now.'

Kirsten: 'Yes, but if anyone's going to embrace it, it's good that it's Dad.'

Everyone's takeaway from this was that Eriq had become Dad to Kirsten as well as Niall. Of all the family, she was the one who still kept a channel open to Torvald, so this was huge.

Buoyed by his new status, and fortified by industrial volumes of coffee, Eriq spent the rest of the week in front of his Zoom account, surfacing on Friday evening with the news that he and Max had raised a bond issue on local South American markets and were paying off the loan anyway so the banks had no more leverage. 'Sorted.'

This was not the only win. At the start of the week, three different multinational banks had voiced their opposition to the #SSS boycott and had begun to put pressure on their own creditors in the way Eriq's banks had pressured Cuidorado.

Accordingly, all three were living through the PR nightmare that had been stoked by a supercharged combination of Niall's legal team in Glasgow, the Ghosts around the world and Kaitlyn's growing social media base, which had lately breached the ten million threshold worldwide. Over half her followers were under thirty, but a surprising 35 per cent were over fifty: she was drawing in the Boomers who had joined XR early and were now part of the newly formed Climate Majority Project, hunting for ways to make a difference and sharing the results across a solid network of agency.

The latter gave weight to the message that the banks were siding with a dying order, protecting old, white, male pornographers at the expense, not just of the under-thirties, but of everyone who wasn't actually an investment bankster, a politician or a media mogul. Given that everyone mistrusted banks anyway ('They make money out of nothing and sell it to us at a profit: what's not to hate?' © Niall, 2008), this wasn't a hard story to sell.

#BinTheBanks began trending worldwide late on the day of the equinox, Monday 20th. Niall promptly wrote and posted a series of Substacks and Medium blogs detailing alternative, regenerative ways to save and share money and these, too, began to pick up views in the low six figures, which was two orders of magnitude more than he'd ever seen (three if we were feeling unkind and looked at his average rather than his peak).

At roughly the same time, Juke, the scarily well-connected Israeli Mage on Finn's Arena team, forwarded an email allegedly from 'second deputy head honcho' at one of the major UK investment banks, alerting his team to a potential liquidity crisis. The meme-team did not reveal their source, but they weaponised the knowledge in a way that swiftly turned the potential into a reality.

#BuildBetterBanks (soon to be #BBB, or TripleB, running alongside the TripleS hashtag that had grown out of #SafeScreenageSex) began trending in all the G20 countries. As a natural consequence, the credit unions and ethical banks began a targeted push for customers, followed almost immediately by an emergency recruitment drive.

One of Finn's Ghosts was hired onto the IT team at one of the UK's oldest ethical banks, taking for herself the codename 'Jacinda' (yes, they wanted codenames; yes, they were chosen from the politicians they most admired. And no, it wasn't Juke's idea. This particular nudge came from Hawck, who was running strategy for the meme makers).

From day one, Jacinda reported a dizzying rate of account transfer applications, mostly from the under-fifties, but the bank itself was hampered by a top team divided on its support for the TripleS/B movements. While the winds of opinion blew in their bank's favour, they were happy to take in the new money. They were less happy to be seen to be in outright support of what one of them called 'the provisional wing of this week's disaffected youth'.

'Half of them think it'll blow over and don't want to be left exposed,' Jacinda said. 'The other half are afraid it won't blow over, and can't see where it's going. If we can find a way to bring at least one of those halves on board, we're a long way closer to broader credibility.'

Achieving this became Kirsten's priority.

She spent a day closeted with her laptop and came out having placed a series of articles in the legacy media, targeting the most-searched values of the board members who were most likely to shift in favour of #SSS.

She didn't publish under her own name. There were, it turned out, a number of established think tanks and independent media outlets happy to take articles from Kaitlyn's sister and feed them out under a pseudonym as if they were their own.

Finding press and TV stations willing to promote the same content took longer, but it seemed likely the movement had supporters in most of the outlets. Kirsten spent two days identifying who these were and persuading them to put her articles in front of their editors who, to the surprise of everyone except Kirsten, took them.

Nothing she had written was inflammatory; quite the reverse. Each article, blog and opinion piece was worded with a psychotherapist's insight and the full panoply of non-violent communication and restorative engagement theory designed to find commonality with readers anywhere on the spectrum.

They weren't going to change opinion overnight, but of the twins, Kirsten had always been better at the long, slow game. She had Finn write her a piece of software that trawled the social media feeds of her targets on the bank's board, weighting them on their tendency to support Kaitlyn or not, tested them with some hand-crafted memes, and then plotted a graph of their output, highlighting any changes in opinion. In the first hours after the early tranche of articles was released, she got a three-point move in Kaitlyn's favour. 'That's a win.'

Maddie: 'This can't be legal, surely?'

Kirsten: 'Mum, it's how the world works. The difference is that the people we're up against have been storing stats for years. I don't have their kind of depth, but I've got the Ghosts updating me in real-time on what our targets search for, what they click on and what they like most. We're just levelling the playing field a bit.'

▼

On the Friday evening, with the storm unabated, the press pack went home for the weekend. This was also the point when Eriq escaped from his Zoom purgatory. As the family's only real chef, he had celebrated by creating a multilayered dinner, for the occasion of which, family rules had been relaxed and digital devices had been allowed at the table: needs must and all that. Over five courses, Kaitlyn relayed the current sit-rep.

'Shona-Beth's GoFundMe is a squeak off three million dollars. They're giving most of it to BLM and money talks, so CNN ran a piece, and the *Washington Post* picked it up. They're not lifting any of our memes and they haven't linked her death expressly to the start of the TripleS hashtag, but they've noticed she died and one or two of the journo-Substacks are asking why the police did nothing when she first went missing. I've got people reposting these and we absolutely are making the link from her to us in ways they can't ignore. If the Ghosts can generate some new memes, that would be good.'

Finn nodded. 'On it.' Half a dozen Grey Ghost teams were working round the clock. Being a distributed network had its advantages; there was always someone for whom it was working hours, whatever the time in the UK.

Kaitlyn continued. 'SportLynes has issued a statement saying they won't cave in to, quote, "Attention-seeking youngsters who need to learn respect for their elders."'

'They actually said that?' Eriq's brows notched up.

'Their very words. They're playing to the Fox News and QBC crowd. Their share price is cratering, but they're claiming it's a blip and they'll wear it. On the other hand, Giant Flat Tomato—' she gave it the American pronunciation— 'have said they'll pull all advertising from, and again, I quote, "The unfortunate relics of the older generation who are clinging onto power long after their time and don't understand the way the world is shaping up."'

'Predictable on both counts.' Finn didn't lift his eyes from his phone. 'SportLynes HQ is in Minnesota with vulture capital underwriting every cent of their overdrafts. GFT is in a suburb of Berkeley. Their entire board is under forty and their consumer base is mostly software engineers. They'd be shooting themselves in both feet if they abandoned us now.'

Kirsten, too, was multitasking, reading out one set of quotes and scrolling through the comments on another. 'Business is splitting on generational lines,' she said. 'No surprise there. But we have more action on our side. Over the course of the past week, TripleS groups have set up all over the world and started taking independent action. There's one in Boston, made of graduates from the Stanford Persuasive Technology Lab who have decided they don't like manipulating people for The Man and they'd rather work for us.

'They're calling themselves Kaitlyn's Digital Army, which becomes KDA, because nothing's real if it can't be reduced to a three letter acronym. These guys are seriously good. They've identified eight more outlets on their side of the Atlantic who pay for significant advertising in the 'hostile legacy media', including a travel company that specialises in gap years – there are Gen Zs who still don't care about burning carbon, apparently – a fast food delivery company and one of the Uber-a-like zombie-platform ride services. Boycotts began two days ago and share prices of all the targets were looking shaky by the time the City markets closed this evening.'

'The even better news,' said Niall, who had trimmed his hair until it stuck up around his head and was looking more like Puck every day, 'is that they have taken it upon themselves to scale up and scale out. In the last twenty-four hours, Kaitlyn's Digital Army has set up mirror groups in Europe, Scandinavia, the Antipodes and Africa, particularly Ethiopia and Nigeria, all of whom are digging up targets in their own territories.'

He turned a beatific smile on Kaitlyn and raised his hand in a grand high five. 'You could actually change the world, sister mine. We just need to make sure the momentum keeps on rolling.'

On Sunday night, I met Finn in the cloud-dreams and he taught me to spar. We didn't talk, it wasn't that kind of dream, but we sat shoulder to shoulder under the peach tree at the end, before a tone on his phone pulled him back to waking, and I was as happy as I could ever remember having been.

The tone that woke Finn had come from the Ghosts, signalling the first concrete results of the 'bad guy porn-trawl'. It was five in the morning, way early for him to be up, but he spent the next few hours working flat out and then woke each member of his family with a printed note held at eye level.

Don't Ask. Get breakfast as normal and come up to Ash Barn. Leave your phone/tablet/whatever down there.

Alerted by an equally cryptic text, Connor walked up from the mill while the rest were gathering breakfast. He accepted a couple of rounds of toast and then dumped his phone in the pile on the table and followed everyone else up to the barn.

There, they found the attic turned into, as Kirsten said, 'an actual tin-foil pavilion'. Within the main room, Finn had hung a tent of something thicker than cooking foil but with the same matt reflectivity. Inside this were the bare bones of their essential work tools: the video suite, a handful of chairs, the big old sofa and a desk on which stood a single screen connected to Finn's laptop. A coffee machine burbled comfortingly in one corner.

'This is bad, right?' Kaitlyn sat on the floor with her back to the wall, fingers knotted together.

'It's certainly dangerous,' Finn said.

He was more of a showman than I'd realised, waiting until everyone was seated, before he laid out the gist: 'The Ghosts have excavated two separate seams of gold. Or they've fallen into two toxic vats, depending on how you frame your viewpoint.'

He passed round a printed list of names and occupations, divided into two categories. The first had well over a hundred names, the second, sixteen. 'These are the people for whom we've got videos, plus their respective positions. None of these is faked, I promise you, and I think we can prove it as and when we're accused of that. As we'd agreed, we looked mostly at the people who'd piled in on the dog fight against Kaitlyn: national political figures, or news editors or journalists who went ballistic in those first few days. A few are just the usual online trolls with huge followings and big mouths.

'The results are divided into two categories according to the danger level of what we found. The first, we're calling Grade B.' He turned on the screen. 'This is not actually illegal, but even so, Mum, Dad, Grandad, you might want to look the other way.'

He hit the play button on a set of videos that were constructed in the same way as the ones previously posted of Kaitlyn, except the individuals on the right-hand side of each screen were, for the most part, old, white men, and the sexual nature of what they were watching could never have been described as soft.

The family lasted a little under thirty seconds in silence before chaos hit the fan.

Kaitlyn: 'We can't publish this, we'll be insta-banned from every platform we touch.'

Kirsten: 'Kaitlyn, I don't think you should be watching—'

Kaitlyn: 'Do you seriously think I haven't seen this and far, far worse? That's. The. Whole. Point.'

Niall: 'But really, you don't have to—'

Kirsten: 'Niall's right. Mum, tell her she can't—'
Kaitlyn: 'Kirsten Penhaligon, you are not censoring—'
'*Enough!*'

It's a moot point whether it was Maddie's tone that ended the cacophony, or the fact that she'd just pulled the plug on Finn's five-thousand-pound system. Not just flipped the switch, but actually yanked the plug out of the wall by the flex.

That kind of thing is sacrilege to computeroids. Finn froze. 'Mum, you can't—'

'I just did.' Maddie took a steadying breath and surveyed the room. 'I am not losing it. Really. See? No raging. But we need some kind of coherence and watching this isn't helping.' She leaned back against the wall, blocking Finn's route to the plug. 'So, let me get this straight. Finn's bunch of delinquents—'

'Mum!'

'I didn't say they weren't competent.' She started again. 'My younger son's extremely professional group of entirely legal hackers has broken into the hard drives of a number of our elected and unelected leaders, and what they have found is not, Kaitlyn, something I want to know that you are watching.'

'But—'

'What you do in the privacy of your own room is up to you, but this—' She struggled for a word, defaulted to a sweeping hand gesture instead— 'is not fit for human eyes. I saw quite enough and absolutely never want to even imagine the rest. And reading this list . . .?' She slammed it on the table. 'Due thanks to whichever one of the Ghosts annotated this because most of these are names I barely know, but if these labels are right, we have the chair of the body designed to oversee our media, eight MPs – one of them a *woman*? Tell me I misunderstood that?'

Finn: 'You didn't.'

'. . . several parliamentary private secretaries and a former Treasury Secretary, a handful of current or former police and crime commissioners, and more journalists, pundits and general media people than I care to count. Each of these is watching things that should not, by any reasonable measure, exist.'

She lifted the list by one corner as if the paper itself was contaminated. 'And you think we should make this public. Are you out of your scrambled minds, the lot of you? They'll lock us up and throw away the keys.' She glared at each member of her family in turn. 'Tell me you understand this is a step too far?' Her gaze swooped up to the top of the window frame where she thought I was perched. 'All of you?'

Her children's glances wove across the room. Most of them looped back to Finn, which was manifestly unfair given that he'd done nothing more than had been asked of him.

He would have been well within his rights to point this out. Instead, he leaned back against the wall and hooked his fingers behind his head. 'What you've just seen,' he said, carefully, 'is the more decent end of what we found. I already told you to look away. And I'm not going to show you the Grade A, because while I've done everything I can to make this room inaccessible, if someone hacks us, guess who they'll stamp on for watching kid-flicks?'

Eriq jettisoned his heretofore dignified silence. 'You found those?'

'We found things you genuinely never want to go near. We found the illegal's illegal. This is seriously nasty stuff, and in a handful, the people involved not only watching, they're taking part. Some of these guys – so far they're all men – are in very high places. Not all are household names, but they will become so if this gets out. This is dangerous at every level. We knew it was possible, but the reality is fucking terrifying.' Finn was as serious as I'd ever seen him. 'I ran this past Niall before the rest of you woke up and he has a strategy. Nye—' he offered his truncated showman's flourish— 'the field is yours.'

Niall, too, was transformed from the spring-heeled Puck that had lately roamed the farm. Where Finn had become enlivened, Niall was more sober. 'As Finn said, we have two grades of dirt: the merely explosive, career-ending stuff, and the seriously radioactive, Epstein-grade, put-you-in-gaol-for-the-rest-of-your-life material.

'If we deal with the softer stuff first, you've just seen the kinds of videos the Ghosts have crafted. They're essentially mirrors to the ones that were made of Kaitlyn and her friends. There are one hundred and twenty-seven of these that we could launch now.'

Maddie, hoarsely: 'We can't!'

Kaitlyn: 'It is *exactly* what they did to me.'

Maddie: 'But some of these people are editors of major newspapers. They screwed us nine ways to Friday when all we did was tell them they were entitled racist fascists. If we do this, they'll mince us into fragments and flush us down the drain.'

'Mum's right.' Niall waved a hand and brought them all back to him. 'It's hard to know how they could escalate beyond what they've already done, but for sure they'll think of something we couldn't begin to imagine, and then we'll wish we hadn't bothered. Also, we have to decide if we want to be as vindictive as that? It's in the boundaries of our baselines, but I'm not sure that's the point?' He looked at Kaitlyn. 'Your call, but I think there's a better way.'

'Go on, then.' She looked mulish.

Kirsten took over: she hadn't been awake in the night, but they'd talked on the way up the stairs and what Niall knew, she knew. 'We leak the entire tranche to WikiLeaks. The Ghosts already have links in there. Then Wiki – not us – sends a fragment of what they've got to the people involved. Not the whole vids, just enough to make them realise they're neck-deep in shite. At that point, they have two choices. They can try to brazen it out and risk seeing themselves trawled through some pretty nasty muck, but by WikiLeaks, not us. Or they can shift their tone and start supporting TripleS. If they do the latter, and if they keep to it in private as well as in public, they're safe.'

Aghast, Eriq said, 'This is blackmail.'

'You could frame it like that.' Niall tilted his head. 'Or you could say we're giving them a way out before we destroy them. If you don't like this, and it's too dangerous or too unethical to publish ourselves, then Plan B is that we bin the lot and pretend we never saw it.'

Everyone considered this.

Kaitlyn broke the silence. 'If we send the vids to WikiLeaks,' she said, 'we need to blur out the sex workers first so there's no risk of them being identified. It's not their fight.'

Finn considered this, nodding slowly. 'It's more than they did for you, but we could blur out breasts and dicks too: anything and everything X-rated. It would get past the censors and the point would still be made.'

184

Maddie was still staring at the lists. 'What about the second tranche? The nuclear-grade illegal. You have a plan for it that won't see all of us in prison?'

'Kind of.' Niall rubbed his knuckle along his brow. 'The problem here is that the police are not neutral. This is the Downing Street Christmas parties, or the Sarah Everard vigil, or any amount of racist, misogynist, homophobic filth from their own ranks. They'll come down on people they don't like with all the force of some very nasty laws, but if you're a politician in power, or a rapist inside the force, they'll kick everything into the longest of long grass and suddenly there's insufficient evidence, or they don't investigate retrospectively, or whatever mealy-mouthed nonsense they dream up to explain why they're burying the evidence under three tonnes of concrete and then shredding the map.'

Eriq frowned. 'You're saying we can't just hand over all the evidence to the security services and expect the law to act.'

'I am saying that on previous evidence, if we hand it over, they'll prosecute whoever gave it to them and ignore as many of the bad guys as they can get away with. We can't risk it.'

'We can't touch them.' Maddie looked ill. 'There's a past Director General of MI5 on this list. He left years ago, but he must still be wired into the system. And a member of the current cabinet. Two members of the House of Lords. A TV news anchor.' Wide-eyed, she looked up. 'They'll actually kill us.'

'They might well try.' Niall offered a wan smile. He stepped back. 'Finn? What can we do?'

Everyone was patient while Finn ran his hands through his hair. He took a deep breath. 'Niall's right, if we give this to the police, they'll destroy us and ignore the bad guys. In some cases, they *are* the bad guys. So, we ditch that, at least in the UK. The FBI is more proactive. We can try them with some of the US names through routes that won't attach to us, mostly Juke and his team in Israel. They might bite and we lose nothing if they don't. But we asked the search teams to concentrate on the UK, which means that so far, all but four of our targets are in this country. I talked to Hawck about this last night. He does human better than me and he thinks—'

'Wait.' Kirsten held up a hand. 'You talked to him online?

I thought we were inside this tin-foil tent because nothing was secure?'

Finn nodded at a point well made. 'We used the updated version of GhostTalk. Charm says we're staying ahead of the game and she's the best we've got when it comes to crypto. Frankly, if it wasn't secure we'd have blue flashing lights in the yard by now; this conversation wouldn't be happening. And yes, you have the latest code: your phones update automatically.'

Everybody looked impressed. Connor asked, 'So what did your Hawk-man say?'

'He thinks these people spend their lives in fear of being exposed. We may believe the police will look the other way, but they're all waiting for their own personal Epstein moment. It's a life-defining terror, and chronically frightened people do stupid things.'

'Like turning themselves in?' Kaitlyn looked sceptical. 'Is that not asking a bit much?'

'Way too much. It's not impossible, but it's more likely at least one of them will panic and do something stupid enough to attract the kinds of super-public attention the authorities can't ignore. And when they do, they won't go down alone. They're all connected, either through the stuff they're watching, or their businesses, or they lend each other their holiday chateaus in the French alps, or they share private jets to cheer for Greta at Davos . . . it's one big incestuous nest and a lot of them have shockingly lax protection on their phones. It's like they think if they pretend they've got nothing to hide, nobody will cotton on.'

'If you're going to monitor their communications, we're adding espionage to blackmail,' Eriq said. 'If this goes the wrong way, we won't live long enough to see the outside of whatever hole they throw us into.'

'That's the risk.' Finn spread his hands. 'The pay-off is that we roll them all over. Contrary to what some of us believe – Niall, I'm looking at you – there are some decent, competent journalists in the world and a lot of people online who will take the threads and follow them wherever they go. We might not have to do anything except open the can of worms.'

Kirsten said, 'What if they work out who's doing this?' She scored her thumb under one of the names. 'However clever the Ghosts are, there has to be a risk and these people don't piss about. They won't wait for due legal process. They'll just have us wiped out.'

'Yeah.' After this one syllable, Finn was silent too long. And then a bit longer while he tried to find comforting words and failed. 'Hawck thinks we should sort out protection. It's not just that we're stirring up our own security services, big though that is. The more toxic incels are beginning to find each other, too; and by toxic we mean, likely to do something that'll grab headlines.'

'Like killing Shona-Beth,' Kaitlyn said, white-lipped.

Finn shook his head. 'We're watching the guy you said was harassing Shona-Beth.'

'Graylock.'

'Graeme Matlock, yes. He's definitely deep into incel territory, but he's a loner and, just now, he's doing everything he can to look squeaky clean. He's not the kind who brags ahead of time that his name's going to be added to the rollcall of idiots who run amok with a gun in a primary school or a mosque or a Black church or a gay bar. Those are the ones we need to watch.'

'They're all in the US, though, right?' said Niall.

'Sadly not. There are plenty over here and they're keeping oddly quiet, which means they're running under the radar and they're likely going to pop up with something nasty when we least expect it.' Finn was up, pacing, running his fingers through his hair so often I thought he might pull it all out. He stopped near his mother. 'What we'd like to do, me and Hawck – Juke in Israel agrees – is to organise some professional protection. We'll keep it as unobtrusive as we can. While we're here, you'll hardly notice anything. If we have to go out, then we'll have company, but it won't be like the press pack. And if it's overkill, then that's better than . . . the alternative.'

'Overkill?' Maddie glared at him. 'I don't believe you said that.'

Finn shrugged and pointedly didn't apologise. 'Hawck's found us a good team,' he said. 'They'll stay in the Piggery. Jens will help me sort the bedrooms before they get here. We'll tell people they're Ghosts come to help with the coding and they'll be on our payroll anyway, so it'll be true for a given definition of "help".' He leaned back against the wall. 'Unless you say no, in which case, we'll sort

187

the Piggery anyway, because we will need more people here one way or another; we're not going to keep GhostTalk ahead of the game forever, and before they crack us we want to have people on the ground, where we can hold actual real-world conversations in ways that can't be overheard.'

His gaze raked them all. 'I'll need a vote on this one. It has to be unanimous. Do we want security, people: yes or no?'

Maddie was crammed back into the sofa, hugging her knees to her chest. Tears stood proud in her eyes. 'Death's not so bad, right?'

She pushed herself upright. 'If you're asking me, we're too far down the road to stop now. This is what Kaitlyn wanted. If she still wants it, then I vote we give everything you've dug up to WikiLeaks and see what they can do with it. And we learn to live with guards watching our backs.' She looked across the room at her youngest daughter. 'You still want this?'

'Absolutely.' Kaitlyn's certainty was the one solid thing about this morning. 'We break the rotten fruit open and we might find we can plant a whole fresh garden.' She gave a short, fierce smile. 'It's what we all want. We may as well admit it.'

She was right: for all their fears, everyone wanted to act. And the early parts of the plan did seem to roll out with gratifying smoothness.

The Ghost's Grade B, not-quite-as-toxic-as-Grade-A revelations were passed to WikiLeaks, who duly sent out edited highlights to the one hundred and twenty-seven individuals on the initial list. This number increased steadily as the Ghosts spread their net more widely and delved more deeply.

The responses came in two forms. In some cases, individuals who had previously been vehemently opposed to Kaitlyn and the TripleS movement found themselves newly persuaded to support the younger generations, often, so they claimed, by their own children.

They were the greater number, just under 70 per cent of the total. The remaining third continued to shout online. In point of fact, several of them doubled down, becoming increasingly strident. Accordingly, when the first tranche of videos began to leak onto the web, these were among the early targets.

As Kaitlyn had requested, the identities of the sex workers were hidden. In addition, the branding on the revelatory videos was clever and new. Kirsten had created a lot of it and Maddie worried obsessively that the work was too obviously hers, and someone would trace it all back to the family, but nobody did: they were all too busy watching the fireworks of what, quite soon, and entirely predictably, became known as #PornGate.

There were, obviously, accusations that it had all been crafted by AI, but, as Finn had predicted, the weight of evidence was too great and quite quickly those who had tried to hide behind screams of falsehood were outed as liars on top of everything else.

For public figures, having been found to lie was not the career-destroying move it used to be, but in this case they were lying about something other than parties, alcohol and breaking lockdown regulations. #Hypocrisy began trending swiftly after, followed by #Resign.

And then the real-world impacts began.

Jobs were lost or notice given.

Marriages disintegrated.

Children were taken to grandparents, or, in one case, family friends, on the grounds that the grandparents couldn't be trusted either.

'Jacinda', the Ghost who had taken a job at the ethical bank (and had already been promoted), reported that two of the more anti-youth board members had resigned from the top team. Neither's name was on the lists, but absence of evidence is not evidence of absence and nobody was about to argue that they should stay.

With these gone, the remaining board members voted to begin an ad campaign explicitly supporting the TripleS boycott and stating that 'young people know what's right and what's wrong'. Account transfers rose by another 5 per cent.

At the farm, Finn's security detail took up residence in the Piggery: young, fit individuals of indeterminate gender who looked like they should be yomping up Snowdon carrying large parts of a Land Rover but had taken an easterly fork sometime after Watford Gap and never turned back.

They were led by Jan Westbrook, who joined the family in

the kitchen at breakfast time on the day after the team's arrival. Walking through the door, she didn't look dangerous: she was of average height, with averagely mouse-coloured hair and averagely brown eyes. In her trainers, jeans and grey tech-memed sweatshirt ('THERE ARE TWO KINDS OF PEOPLE: THOSE WHO CAN EXTRAPOLATE FROM BASE DATA'), she looked like the studious, slightly geeky kind of girl who read archaeology to post-doc and then took a job in a museum that involved a lot of cataloguing because being a librarian threatened to be too exciting.

Even so, in their own ways, each member of the family glanced at her once, looked again more carefully and then sat at a safe distance. All except Finn, who paused in cooking the bacon and offered the hand to elbow arm-clasp that he shared with Mo's students, and had taught me in the dream when we sparred, so it seemed possible she might have trained with him at some point in the past fifteen years.

'Jan's here to brief us,' he said, sliding bacon onto Eriq's plate. 'We'll keep it brief.' Nobody laughed, but Kaitlyn at least had the heart to give him a decent thumbs up.

Jan pulled out a chair and spun it round so she could sit astride it with her arms folded across the back. 'I apologise for intruding on your breakfast, but this seemed the best way to bring everyone together without alerting any watchers to a change in your patterns.' Her accent was as middle-England-forgettable as the rest of her. 'We've looked at the data and Finn's showed us the logs from the Ghosts. You have definitely poked various bears with various big sticks, so it's our job to make sure none of them turns on you in ways that might threaten your lives or even your livelihoods – yes?'

Eriq had raised a hand. 'Is either one of those really a risk?'

Jan ran her tongue round her teeth. 'Do you know what an OODA loop is?' And at the shaking of heads, 'Military-speak. Anyone who's spent more than five minutes in military company loves acronyms. In this case, Observe, Orient, Decide, Act.' Her smile was half-ironic as she ticked them off on her fingers. 'You have pissed off some quite serious people who actually live by these kinds of letters.' She glanced a question at Finn, who nodded permission. 'The Ghosts have access to what's being said deep in the bowels of places we don't normally see, so I can say with some certainty that they've observed and oriented and are in the decision phase. They may decide that no action is the best action: often it is. But they may not.'

'And if they don't, what kinds of actions are we expecting?' Niall this time, but he only voiced, thinly, what everyone was thinking.

'They won't go through official channels. The Hereford Gun Club – that's the SAS to ordinary mortals – is absolutely not going to turn up in the village with orders to wipe you out. Apart from anything else, the individual you've pissed off most is technically retired, and even if he wasn't, calling out the special forces would be a tacit admission that he's in trouble.

'That said, we've worked with him in the past and I can tell you from personal experience that he doesn't take well to people treading on his toes. He is, in the vernacular, a truly nasty piece of shit and has contacts among people like us, who work in the deniable zone, and who will do whatever he wants if he pays them enough.'

She paused. Her quiet gaze scanned the room. 'We think he'll pay enough. Plus, there are at least two others who are running the same loops, and who have access into the same corners of the Dark Net. I'd be really surprised if they're not talking to each other. As I said, they may do nothing: that would be the good option. Or they may decide to pool their money and pay for the really expensive teams. That would be the scary option.'

'Where do you rank on the scale of expenses?' Kirsten asked.

Jan looked at Finn, who said, 'Jan's team is near the top, but not all the way up. The ramp gets pretty steep in the higher echelons.' And before anyone could comment, 'The Ghosts are covering it, I already told you. Business expense. That's not up for discussion.'

Nobody asked questions after that. Jan said, 'We have three teams of four. We don't really have leaders. In fact, we've spent distressing amounts of time making sure that we have completely fluid dynamics and that leadership in any given moment passes to whoever is most suited to wield it. If the US Marines can do it, we can do it, but with more panache.' Her grin was bright, and fooled nobody. 'All that said, you need someone on point, so I'm your go-to on the daytime team and Nazir will be around on nights. The rest of the team floats as we need them.'

She tapped her phone. Nazir can't have been more than a few feet away because he pushed through the door almost immediately. His hair was matt-black, long and wiry, pulled away from his face in a way that made a chisel of his nose. He was taller and leaner than Jan, but otherwise he wore the same tech-memed clothes ('DEAR ALGEBRA, PLEASE STOP ASKING US TO FIND YOUR X. THEY'RE NEVER COMING BACK. AND DON'T ASK Y') and exuded the same vibe that messing with him would be insane.

'Hi.' Shyly, he lifted a hand. 'I'll be here from seven till seven, unless there's a flap on that needs all of us. I'll do my best not to intrude.'

'Who's feeding you?' Eriq asked.

When Jan grinned, she looked less like a librarian. 'Have you seen the kitchen in the Piggery? We could feed half a battalion from there. Honestly, you don't have to worry. In an ideal world, you'll forget we're here.'

'For the rest of our lives?' Kaitlyn asked.

Jan glanced at Finn again, who said, 'Or until we run out of money.' And then, seeing that everyone was taking this as if he meant it, 'Joking. The Ghosts have ramped up work so we have enough income to match the outgoings. And anyway, the threat's not going to last forever. We'll keep assessing. When it's safe, we'll ask Jan and the team to go back to the more exciting things they were doing before we called them up.'

He slapped a fresh round of toast on the table and slid plates to Jan and Nazir. 'Let's finish breakfast, keep life ticking over and see how we get on. If it's unbearable by a week from now, we can think again.'

Breakfast meetings for the rest of the week were subdued. Kaitlyn particularly was quiet. 'They were doing their best to destroy my life. It doesn't feel as good as I thought it might to see it happening to them, though.'

Eriq walked round the table to give her a hug. 'Good.'

As the Ghosts spread their net ever wider and the number of names on both lists mounted, Finn spent hours surveying CVs and conducting Zoom interviews helped by Hawck and Juke. In the first instance, they shortlisted people who had both the competence they needed and an innate understanding of and support for the values of the TripleS movement. Basically, as Finn said, the candidates needed to 'think like Niall'. When they'd narrowed down to a few dozen of these, they began the longer, slower, far more painstaking process of checking that they were safe. Slowly then, very slowly, those who passed were brought into the core team. I watched the costs mount, saw them absorbed as rounding errors into Finn's Grey Ghost company and began to realise just how much my grandson had grown.

I met him in his dreams nightly now. He was tight with responsibility, but I showed him how to become a crow and we played on the wind, and he was more relaxed when responsibility called him back to human form in the morning.

The fallout from the Grade A, highly toxic content was more subtle than that from the Grade B tranche, and considerably more profound.

A handful of days after Jan's teams arrived, the world woke to the news that a UK cabinet minister had locked himself in his garage and run his car's exhaust until he died.

Finn gathered the family in the tin-foil attic and said, 'This is the first of the Epstein dominoes. He was neck-deep in Grade A radioactive horror. Watch carefully.'

We all watched as the news unfolded on social media and, later, on the legacy media. Internet rumour posited two possible causes for his actions.

The first was that his wife had discovered the existence of the (obviously distraught) mistress/special adviser with whom he had continued sexting as he died.

The second potential cause was that a particularly corrupt lobbying deal was about to be disclosed by one of the tabloids. The tabloid in question denied that their journalists had contacted him about their upcoming exposé, which made them look particularly culpable.

A small fraction of the armchair investigators decided on no particular evidence that he'd been party to a drug deal gone wrong.

Nobody suggested hardcore porn, which was interesting given how much it had been in the news recently.

The prime minister offered muted condolences to the dead man's wife and family, sacked the SpAd and began a reshuffle which was derailed several times by MPs who not only turned down offers of positions at the top table, but resigned their seats.

Each claimed to be abandoning public life in favour of their families, thus triggering a number of by-elections to be held at a later date. Each was on the softer Grade B list, who had been contacted by WikiLeaks, with the result that in the ensuing days each gave interviews to those newspapers least hostile to Kaitlyn's cause to the effect that they had been listening to their children and it was 'time for the older generations to ease their hold on the reins of power in favour of those whose lives were most impacted by decisions made today'.

Niall had written this particular text, although it had been passed on by a series of different PR firms. The legacy media relayed the content verbatim and clips were played out on social media under the TripleS hashtags. A handful of those involved discovered the hard way what it was like to be on the wrong end of a flame war, but not all: two in particular managed to retain some dignity.

Kirsten began a series of blogs and Instagram memes to the effect that society had reached 'Peak Social Toxicity' and it was time to stop screaming at each other like infants and start finding a degree of common humanity to bring all sides together. She published these under her own name. The response was not as venomously hostile as it might have been.

The days flowed one into the other, with more names added to the two Grade lists, more blogs and memes posted, more money pouring into Shona-Beth's GoFundMe. The FBI had come under some pressure to investigate her death, but there was equal pressure not to. They were finding a middle ground where they appeared to be working hard but had not yet arrested anyone. They still weren't looking at 'Graylock' and the Ghosts had not yet dug up anything that might make them do so, much to Kaitlyn's consternation.

On the boycott front, Kaitlyn's Digital Army teams around the world were identifying plenty of new companies to target. By the time the Grade listers started to topple, one hundred and thirty nations had active boycotts running, covering eighty-three companies, most of them multinationals.

Of the early targets, GFT gained sales and its share price spiked. SportLynes' vulture capitalist funders collapsed when the FBI paid a visit to one member and another had an 'accident' cleaning his gun, having previously dumped his hard drive and all backups into a bath of concentrated nitric acid. Finn reckoned the FBI would still be able to recover the contents. Receiving news of his death, the rest of the board decided it was time to pull the plug. Ten days after the first boycott, SportLynes went into receivership with its share price effectively zero.

Buoyed by their early success, the Digital Army groups broadened their remit and began to target climate deniers/delayers, all of the major fossil fuel companies and any company that refused to divest from fossil fuels.

By the last day of March, #YouthInsurgency began to trend around the world, supplanting all the previous hashtags.

CHAPTER FOURTEEN

Monday, 3 April 2023

'You should be leading us. You're used to it.'

It was almost midnight on the first Monday in April. The older members of the family were asleep. Kaitlyn was sitting cross-legged on the end of Finn's bed with her laptop balanced on her knees. Five different windows were open on the screen, each with different scrolling text, videos, memes and comments. All the #YouthInsurgency metrics were rising along a steady curve.

'I lead battlegrounds,' Finn said, absently, 'not revolutions.' He was midway through quite a challenging Arena match with him on his Balance Druid, Charm playing a Healer-Monk and Juke on his Warlock. Like Kaitlyn's, his attention was mostly on his screen. The rest was listening to his team's commentary coming through the headset into his left ear.

Speaking to his right side, Kaitlyn said, 'This isn't a revolution. Revolutions just take us in circles. Ask Kirsten. We need systemic change which starts as a rebalancing of power in favour of people who aren't actual psychopaths. What's a battleground if not that?'

'It's a fictional landscape with ten not-real people on each side and it has really clear rules about who does what. Also, when you die, you come back to life twenty-five seconds later.'

'Nobody's going to die. That's Mum letting her paranoia run riot.'

'Please wait till I'm out of the country before you say so in her hearing. Also make sure Lan's safe somehow, if that's even possible. Anyway, Niall's your man for leading insurrections.'

'Did we just loop through a time warp? It's not an insurrection.'

'Tell that to a government that just lost another cabinet member and two more MPs in the past week. Or the tabloids, which are shedding editors, columnists and hacks like leaves in a gale. Or the TV stations, ditto. Or the Fortune 500, which is beginning to look like the Fortune 50. The entire FTSE and the Dow are both down to a two-year low and the Hang Seng's looking shaky. We could be heading for another global financial crash, but this time there's not a single fiat currency strong enough to get us through.'

'Hardly my fault.'

'I never said it was. I don't think even Niall believed it would go this hard or this deep, this fast. We thought—' NiftyDruid's health dropped below 10 per cent. Finn swore inventively, and for a moment nothing existed beyond the Arena. Charm shielded him with a Life Cocoon and slapped the bad guys away with a Ring of Peace. NiftyDruid stunned the Healer and hit him with a Cyclone. Juke Feared the Windwalker and they all killed the Warrior.

The victory chime sounded, and Finn logged out of his Druid and back to his Rogue. Queuing the new team, he flicked a swift look at his sister. 'Did you come here just to play semantics with the nature of the uprising you started?'

'No. I came to ask if you think I should accept the invitation to speak against the Toxic Pixie from QBC at the debate in Cambridge a week on Saturday?' And, at the arch of his brow, 'Fifteenth of April.'

'What time?'

'Three o'clock.'

'Sorry. Can't. I'll be—'

'Competing in the opening rounds of the Global Arena Championships, of which nothing, up to and including global war, will be allowed to get in the way. Noted.' He could have given his place to Yolo, the Windwalker Monk, but neither he nor Kaitlyn gave this serious thought. 'I wasn't asking if you would come hold my hand, I was asking if you thought I should go. Hard though this may be for you to believe, I can talk sense without you. If I get stuck, you can send me texts.'

'Multitasking is my middle name. What's the motion?'

Kaitlyn gave a broad and shameless grin. 'This house believes the youth insurgency should, and will, prevail.'

'Youth insurgency?' His attention skidded away from the screen. 'OK, strike the previous five minutes. I am right. Again. Still. Always.' He held up his hand. 'You must owe me something.'

Kaitlyn smacked him a five then hopped off the bed and spun an impressive air-kick. 'You want to ask me who's chairing?'

Finn rolled his eyes, but he was a kind brother. 'Who is chairing your debate, oh genius?'

'Leah Koresh.'

My ears pricked up. Leah Koresh read for her PhD at Bancroft Hall when I was warden there, opening up new avenues in the neuropsychology of language. Widely regarded as brilliant, her supervisor had high hopes that she'd pull in stellar grants for the department, but even before her viva she'd thrown it all in and gone to work for a media start-up, which had deflated almost everyone.

Finn was not deflated at all. '*The* Leah Koresh from Radical FM?' His attention was all on Kaitlyn. 'Kudos. She's seriously cool. Will it be public?'

'Live broadcast on YouTube and remote audience participation alongside Abbey Hall as full as it'll go, which, I'm told, is five hundred and eight, including the sound techs.'

'Cut it to four ninety-six and make sure there's space for all twelve of the security team. We'll need Jan and Nazir and all three squads on this.' Finn's gaze narrowed. 'Did you make this happen?'

Kaitlyn threw a couple of air punches. 'I might have mentioned it to Olivia.' And when no pennies dropped, 'Olivia Virani, eldest daughter of Oscar Virani, the mega-geek who—'

'—took Lan's place as warden of Bancroft Hall when she died.' Finn was still frowning. 'How do you know her?'

'She's going out with Nico.' One of Kaitlyn's home-schooled cohort from the village. 'So we play Minecraft together.'

'Of course you do.'

Kaitlyn flipped him a finger. 'It's the future, Findley. Gathering the creative genius of humanity in a field of radical invention. Your see-hunt-kill games are so old-paradigm.'

'I never said otherwise.' Finn glanced up towards where I sat. 'It's why I could play with Lan. Talking of . . . you should invite her.'

Kaitlyn's gaze softened. 'Lan, you're invited. Please come.' She sat back down on the bed again and cocked her head at Finn's screen. 'You just lost.'

'No shit.' Finn typed apologies into the chat and queued up again. The tone that announced a new Arena pinged loud into the room. Charm and Juke both snapped into his earpiece. He wrenched his attention back to the game. 'Kait, I have to—'

'Concentrate. I know. I'm going.'

She hopped off the bed and spun round to land on her feet facing the door, laptop still open and upright.

'Wait.' Finn dragged himself away one last time. 'What did the twins say?'

'Niall said to go for it but to check with you first.' Kaitlyn made a tick sign in the air. 'Kirsten said Ms Toxicity gets all her self-confidence from external reinforcement criteria, so we should put Dad in the front row, because she'll never cope with being eyeballed by a Black man who's obviously occupying the moral high ground.'

'Put Grandad beside him. She'll cope even less with his wild Irish Republican eyebrows. I'll make sure Jan's on the case and sort things with the college so they don't freak and try to turf out the security. Oscar's cool. He'll get that we need them.'

Finn turned back to his screen; they'd just lost the second game in a row. 'Charm, we're still not mitigating the Windwalker damage on the smaller maps. Can you . . .?'

Kaitlyn eased out of the door.

▼

On Saturday, 15 April the entire family (barring Finn), with every single member of Jan's eye-wateringly expensive security detail following discreetly behind, travelled to Bancroft Hall, Cambridge, the place that had been my second home for the latter third of my life.

Home.

Home was a field of snowdrops on the rewilded quad, the basketweave of winter-bare wisteria thick as pastry on the walls, the scent of old book bindings and new deodorant (less chemical than it

199

used to be, more mineral), the thrum of voices and scuff of trainers on stone flags that were old when the college was built.

Home was three storeys of Tudor architecture in the shape of a giant letter A (our earliest sponsor was Anne Boleyn and for a few scant years we were called Queen Anne's College, but that's a tale for another time), diaries written in complex mathematical ciphers at a time when plain text led to a grim death, blood on the flags that nobody had ever, or would ever, wash off, a coloured casement of stolen church glass so tall and narrow that the slivers of pigment were as shreds of torn fabric trapped in a thorn-work of lead.

Home was watching my successor, Oscar Virani, welcome my family as if they were his own, drawing them through to the senior common room where waited Leah Koresh and half a dozen of the senior staff, all of whom had been friends when I was alive. If you'd asked me ahead of time, I'd have said nothing could have drawn me away from the promise of sparky conversations laced with the scent of speciality coffee and the fluting interplay of colours and textures as my friends and family (including Jan and Nazir from the security detail who, as Finn had predicted, were accepted without question) got to know each other.

In reality, I felt like an interloper and couldn't stay. Even before the first coffees had been poured I eased through the door and back along the corridor towards the library.

When I'd been alive, this had been one of my favourite haunts, but the students shivered in my presence, which wasn't fun for any of us, and the junior common room was empty. Following years of ingrained habit, I turned left into my old office and tried not to feel unbalanced by the changes Oscar had made. There were new books on the shelves, new journals, a new computer. The desk had been turned through 90 degrees and I think there was new glass in the windows, with better insulation, which wouldn't have been hard.

In truth, it really wasn't very different to when I'd closed the door on a Friday evening fifteen years before, just that I'd always imagined I'd be back, and now I was here, I wanted to throw myself into the chair, tilt it back, hook my crossed heels on the desk. Any and all of which would have required a body. Pfft.

Disconsolate, I rose up and up again to the bedroom I'd slept in three nights a week for eleven years. Here, almost nothing had changed beyond yet more new windows and a darker shade of blue in the bed-linen – and the ghost who was waiting for me in the angle where walls and roof came together.

'Hello?'

This was neither a smudge of old grief such as lingered on the stairs of Mo's Mill, nor the toxic malevolence poisoning the shadows of the Great Hall back at the farm. Here was a spark of impossible sunlight in a room where the windows face north-east and north-west. Here was the scent of new-mown hay, a brush of shy laughter, the expanse of a frost-star sky, all achingly familiar.

'Ellen? Ellen Shreeve?'

Early in my tenure as warden, I'd decided it would be useful to decipher the diaries of our first warden, Silas Bancroft. The task and its fallout had consumed almost ten years of my life, but among the several things revealed were a number of priest holes in the fabric of the college. It was in the smallest of these, an upright, lead-lined box that was literally no bigger than a coffin secluded beneath the hearth of Abbey Hall, that we'd found a young woman's mummified remains. I had spent nine months of my life finding her name, and piecing together the facts that had ended her life.

The eldest daughter of a fairly prosperous mercantile family, Ellen had been three months pregnant at the time of her death, and the same mix of forensic pathology and genealogy that had let us name her had indicated the father of the child was either Silas Bancroft's successor as warden, Thomas Heatherington, or, more likely, his nineteen-year-old son, Richard.

Warden Heatherington had a reputation as a particularly pious supporter of the Protestant faith, but analysis of the DNA in the various priest holes – the most palatial of which filled the whole of the crossbar of the A above the entrance to Abbey Hall and was accessed through an almost invisible hatch in a stationery cupboard in the floor above – suggested he'd been hiding Catholics on an industrial scale at a time when the penalty for doing so was the stuff of nightmares.

It wasn't hard to imagine a young couple in love (or lust, but let's be generous), revealing the results of said passions to a man whose supposed quasi-Lutheran piety was the fiction that kept a whole world of catastrophe at bay. Panic was almost inevitable, and Heatherington's diaries reported that Richard was sent to Holland in July 1609, never to return.

Ellen, who was recorded as missing on the fifteenth of the same month, seems to have been dropped into the college's equivalent of an oubliette and left to die.

It may be that she was dead when she fell in. Certainly, there were no signs of violence on her body, and analysis of her stomach contents suggested she had consumed a large quantity of opium before her death, so it's possible Heatherington killed her with an overdose and then hid her body in the one place nobody would find it.

Those of us who felt closest to her let ourselves believe that her ending had been quiet, but we were left with the conundrum of how to bury her. It may not have mattered to us whether she was given Protestant or Catholic rites, but it likely meant a great deal to her and we had no clues.

In the end, in consultation with the theology departments of half a dozen other colleges, and two particularly flexible clerics, one of each faith, we created a rite that offended neither while fulfilling most of what had been considered essential to one or the other in the first decade of the seventeenth century.

In September 2007, in my last official act as warden before taking sick leave, I saw Ellen and her unborn son interred in the college orchard. I had thought about her, dreamed about her, talked to and about her, wept over her for the best part of the year. Then, in the last few months before my death, I have to confess I entirely forgot her existence.

Until now, when the scent-lift of mown hay flooded my old bedroom and sparks of light illuminated corners that had always been shadowed.

I dithered, uncertain. The malevolent hauntings of the farm's Great Hall were remnants of old unkindness, but true ghosts were a thing apart. According to Pakak, they arose when more than usually powerful emotions grabbed them around the time of death, but beyond this I had never understood what held them to the world, how long they could stay, what they could do – anything. I wasn't sure how we could communicate, only that we needed to.

As if I were talking to Crow, I said, 'Was it right, what we did? Did it heal the hurts?'

Ellen did not reply in a way I could hear, but sent an affirmation I could all but taste: a dip of lightness that did not come from a head but was a nod, and a feather of gratitude. Something else came too: an imperative? At the very least, a nudge.

At a gut level, I realised this must be how it was for my family when I was trying to talk to them. I had thought I understood their frustration, but I felt it now as a crabbing thickness in my core.

As clearly as I could, I asked, 'Is there something else I need to know?'

Her lightness beckoned. If I let myself be led, there was a direction to it, and an urgency. I was scooped up and swept through floors and walls back into Abbey Hall as the last few members of the audience filtered in to their seats for the debate.

The Chair and both speakers were already on the dais at the top end of the room. The hearth beneath which we'd found Ellen's body was behind them, screened off by a tapestry showing the college emblem of a five-fruited apple tree against a sky-blue background. The audience was arrayed in curved rows of twenty-five across. I couldn't pick out individual faces in the sweep and buzz of the crowd, but at the left-hand edge of the front row I felt the prickle of apprehension that was Maddie, and the deep river of Connor's equanimity. Eriq was sharp as an eagle, full of pride. To his left, I could feel the electric fizz of the twins, so bonded it was impossible to separate them.

Three rows back, I felt Frances Nolan from the BBC in a puzzlement of streaky violet beside a jagged shard of sun-fire fury that had to be her daughter. Many others were familiar from my college days, but I struggled to name them.

On the platform, it was easier to pick out features. Kaitlyn, on the Chair's right, was fizzing with potential. Rebecca Watson was calmer than I'd have expected, as if she'd taken too high a dose of beta blockers and they'd stamped on any edge that adrenaline might have given her.

Between these two sat the Chair, Leah Koresh, former star of the college. Leah wasn't beautiful and never had been, but her parents were Iranian and they'd blessed her with eyes as deep and dark as the loch, slanted cheekbones and perfectly straight black hair that flowed over one shoulder and down towards her left elbow. She wore black linen with gold at neck, ears and fingers, and, when she stood up, the way she gathered the authority in the room confirmed my estimation of her as future warden potential.

I listened with interest as she started to speak. At Niall's insistence, one of the later things I'd done in my time as warden was to allocate a small fortune to the creation of a new sound system, and, like so many things, I had died before I'd heard the result.

'No phones. If I see a screen, if I hear a tone, this debate is over. Not just the panel, but the audience. For once in our lives, we can live for an hour free of digital interference.'

Perfect: her and the technology, both. Movement rippled through the hall as phones were retrieved and switched off.

Leah turned her attention to Kaitlyn and then Rebecca Watson. 'No ad hominem attacks from the stage or the floor. If either one of you attacks your opponent personally, you will lose by default. We're arguing points of principle here, not resorting to social media toxicity.'

Kaitlyn was in the process of switching her phone off. She nodded, distracted. Rebecca Watson smirked in a way that left me twitching.

Leah caught it too. She half-checked and then turned back to the audience. 'Rules are standard: each speaker will have two minutes to state their case, then a minute to respond to their opponent. After that, we'll take questions from the floor, both live and online. Please keep them to the point and please make them questions, not statements of fact or belief with an Antipodean uplift at the end of a six-paragraph sentence. Anybody unclear about this?'

Not unclear, but I was itchy, edgy, spooking at motes of dust dancing in the light from the coloured casements. I felt woozily nauseous and couldn't pinpoint the cause.

Ellen was drifting higher. I moved up towards her.

'I don't understand. What are you trying to show me?'

Senses came of the apple trees, and damp soil, the lilt of two clerics joined for a girl nearly half a millennium dead, mown hay again, and a wash of gratitude so powerful it brought me to my knees.

Where my perspective shifted.

I was no longer Lan, languishing in nostalgia. I was raised up to the ceiling, looking down with exquisitely sharp Crow-sense on the living patterns woven in word and thought and feeling beneath me.

I am a creature of pattern and these were captivating in the truest sense. I lost myself in the wave forms and their periodicities, in the shift and slide of passion, as the debate kicked off with Kaitlyn speaking for two minutes, and then Rebecca Watson. I never truly heard what they said, only saw the impact flare and dip in different sections of the audience, saw colour and pitch amplified, or tamped down, echoed or scorned.

Kaitlyn was as I had seen her in the void, weaving magic with words that opened doors to the futures she and Kirsten and Niall had been building these past few weeks: futures where decent, thoughtful people were empowered to bring the whole weight of humanity's creativity to bear on the wicked problems of the moment.

All the narratives of the recent past were recharged here, coined afresh and bright and true: no problem is solved from the mindset that created it; we live in a complex adaptive system and we need total systemic change; the way to change a system is not to fight it, but to create a new system that renders the old one obsolete; when a system is far from equilibrium, small islands of coherence in a sea of chaos can (maybe) bring it to a new order.

This was as close as I could imagine to the living embodiment of the void-vision: she wasn't crushing dissent, or flattening hate, rather she spoke to those who wanted to orient towards life, and in her presence they flourished.

Rebecca Watson remained strangely muted; something was clearly amiss that had nothing to do with being on a platform in front of a largely hostile audience, but nonetheless her words curdled old hurts and new ones, bundled together in a kind of limbic rage that had its own power and found resonance with about a third of those listening.

Kaitlyn's supporters took up most of the rest, but Jan's security team were threaded among them, shifting their attention from the stage to the Hall and back again in wide, rhythmic arcs.

At first, I thought that was it. But as I sifted the patterns, I saw four gaps of almost-nothing that were spread out as evenly as Jan's team. They paid as little attention to the rhetoric and each was studiously avoiding the others, although they all checked in periodically with a single figure in the middle of the back row.

I was just making sense of this when Ellen sent a suffocating nudge that wrenched my attention back to the stage.

On the Chair's far side, Rebecca Watson had sharpened. Like a hound on point, all her attention, too, was on the centre of the back row. Nazir noticed at the same time I did. Under cover of stifling a non-existent sneeze, he murmured a word or two into the cuff of his sweatshirt. Jan was sitting at the end of a row on the right. She lifted a hand to her ear, nodded, counted out half a minute, then quietly got up to leave.

I drifted, uncertain.

A nudge brought my attention back to Ellen. She hovered higher with each breath of the crowd, dissipating through the roof tiles, into the spring sun. Her leaving was a chill on the back of my neck, as of a door opening behind me. It did nothing to make me feel safer.

I sank down towards the family at the front row and came to rest in front of Connor.

'Connor? CONNOR! CAN YOU HEAR ME?'

He frowned and looked at least halfway in the right direction. 'Lan?'

'Something's wrong. You need to talk to—'

'Lan, I need you. Lan. *Lan, now!*' The voice was Finn's and the image of us flying together, buffeted by a sudden storm. Never had he called me with such urgency.

I fled back to the farm, swept along a whistle of tension up to the attic and into his room.

Which was empty.

'Finn? *Finn!*'

On his computer – his *abandoned but not put to sleep* computer – the tone sang out for the start of a new game. A glance showed that the teams were halfway through the opening rounds of the Global Arena Championships. Team Memory was playing and Nifty the Rogue was not there to take part.

World War Three could have broken out and Finn wouldn't have missed a game, but he was not here. I poured myself into his operating system, into the game, into the match. Yolo, Charm and Hawck faced the Deadline team they all feared most.

Hawck? Playing in the Global Championships? *Hawck?* Playing a Damage-Dealer? Leaving aside that he was too old and his reflexes too slow for this level of play, he was a Healer: all his instincts were wrong for dealing damage. This was a guaranteed loss. Why him? Why not Juke?

I lost a couple more seconds trying to make text flow out across Hawck's screen, but if I could have done that, all kinds of things would have been different. With time ticking and Finn still nowhere, I gave up.

I could still read text, though, if I couldn't write it. I ran back through the hallways of the game: Finn had been there at the start and they'd won the first three matches in a best-of-five knockout, clearing the first round without losing a match.

The teams had had a thirty-minute break between rounds. They'd been about to come back to the game again when Juke had sent a Whisper to Finn:

```
Juke: Where's ur sister?
Finn: Which one?
Finn: Nvm. Both @ Debate: Bancroft
Hall in Cambridge.
Juke: Get them out. Everyl
Finn: WTF?
Juke: Yr Grade-A Bad Bird just pinged
a go-signal and went off-air. Bad
news. Get yr family out. I'll sort
game. Go.
```

A frantic set of texts to the team, and then Finn messaged Hawck.

```
Finn: You sure Juke's good?
Hawck: Totally
Finn: Look
```

He forwarded the conversation.

```
Hawck. Ditch the debate. Get the
family safe.
Finn: Where's safe?
Hawck: Public. Out where they'll be
exposed. Lots of people.
Finn: 500 people and live TV in Abbey
Hall. K'll kill me if I embarrass her
in front of all that.
Hawck: Better embarrassed than dead.
Get them out ASAFP.
```

That was the last of it. I shattered out of the machine.

'FINN!'

Nowhere. I spread out thin across the whole farm: still nowhere.

Thinner. Further. I bumped up against Bright Rook and sent a feel-taste of Finn.

We have seen this one. It came as a buzz from the younger rooks. An image arose of Finn sprinting down the back route towards the village.

He'd gone for Mo's car. Of course he had: he'd been her second driver since he was old enough to pass his test and he kept the spare keys in the drawer of his desk. 'Thank you. *Thank you!*'

Join with me? Bright Rook offered, and I did.

Together we soared over the Suffolk countryside, on up to the roundabout with the A45 where Mo's old Volvo was stationary for just long enough that Bright Rook could land on the bonnet.

'Lan!' Hope bloomed in Finn's eyes. He gunned the engine and pulled out into the Saturday traffic. '*Thank you.*'

I let Bright Rook go and pushed through the windscreen to sit beside him. With Ellen's example of how communication worked across the boundaries of life and death, I crafted a simple query, put all my focus on the feel of it and gave it the scent of hawthorn smoke, spring mornings and the loch. 'How can I help?'

'Wow.' His brows jumped. 'OK, I still can't hear you, but that was clear. Kaitlyn's in danger. We have to get her out of the Hall. I can't get anyone on their phone. Not Mum or Dad or the twins.'

'Leah made them turn all the phones off. Call the porters. THE PORTERS!' I made images of college, the scent of mown grass, the special old-leather and book-binding smell of the porter's lodge.

'Yes, exactly. I figured they must have switched them off, so I tried the porters. They're not answering either.'

That can't be right. The porters take their duty as a sacred responsibility. They wouldn't abandon their posts unless the college was actually on fire. Or there was an accident – Oh, *fuck*. 'FINN. I'LL GO BACK!' River scent. A pull towards town. A flood of urgency.

'Right. Yes. Go back and tell them. I don't know how you'll do it. Get a crow to crash-dive through the casements or something. Just get them out of there. I'll break every speed limit, but you can still travel faster than I can. Fly fast, Lan. This isn't good.'

Twenty miles as the crow flies. But I wasn't a crow, I was a . . . me, faster by far, and I could find Kaitlyn, I knew how she felt and where she sat.

I was there almost before he'd finished speaking and Kaitlyn was fine. Fine. *Fine*. Happy. Proud, even. The debate was over. This house believes . . . carried by an overwhelming majority.

Rebecca Watson and her dwindling pack of supporters apart, this house was euphoric. The air around Kaitlyn flared like fireworks with the sheer bloody joy of doors beginning to open, of hope in the face of hopelessness.

She was all the promise of the void, and more. Her smile was the sun, and down in the audience it was reflected everywhere, no brighter than where Maddie sat next to Eriq, her fingers clamped on his wrist, making pride-blossom bruises all the way around.

Elsewhere, all the colours looked the same as they had been, only far more intense: same textures of hope and fear, outrage and optimism. The empty-waiting-whorls had gone.

Fuck.

I ricocheted down to the porter's lodge by the river. Chris Eglington was on duty, who traced direct lineage on his mother's side back to Silas Bancroft's sister. He'd been an industrial chemist until he just couldn't carry on being part of the problem anymore and applied to come back to college. He was the kind of porter a warden would give their right arm for; apart from anything else, he never abandoned his post.

Except for accidents. Particularly, for water-accidents. As a postgrad, Chris had seen a student drown after the May Balls. He wouldn't see another if there was anything he could do to prevent it.

A flicker of movement caught my eye and – *fuck* – down by the river's edge was a flurry of chaos. Chris knelt there, giving CPR to a body in a sky-blue sweatshirt with five green apples on the left breast. A figure stood on the water, wreathed in puzzlement.

'Hello?' I took human form, and she gained shape as I did, becoming far easier to see: a girl, small, round-ish, still with the hum and sizzle of recent life. She'd not been at the debates, I'd have known the feel of her.

She tilted her head. 'Who are you?'

'Alanna Penhaligon. I was warden here before your time. Who are you?'

Puzzlement again. 'I don't know. I think . . . Ruth? Am I Ruth? Something's happened.' She looked down at her own corpse, and Chris, who was still fruitlessly pumping, counting, tilting her head back and doing his best to expand waterlogged lungs. Blood began to gel beneath her head, showing the real cause of death. 'Did someone drown?'

'I think they were hit first, then fell in. Where were you going?'

'To the library. Essay . . . hand in Monday morning. Oh crap, I haven't even got the arguments straight, how am I going to—?'

'Ruth, stop. You might not have heard of me, but—'

'Of course I've heard of you. You broke the Bancroft cipher. I'm citing you in the essay. But I haven't—'

'Ruth, you need to listen to me carefully. Don't worry about the essay. Right now, it's important that you not get lost. There's a young woman called Ellen Shreeve up ahead. Look where I'm pointing. What can you see?'

'The river? What's it doing over there?' And then, because she wasn't stupid. 'Ellen Shreeve's the girl you found in the—'

'—priest hole. Yes, but she's moving on now, I think. I might be wrong, so don't worry if you can't find her, the river's what you need. Walk along by the water's edge until you find a bridge made of light. Bright, bright light. You need to cross over that bridge. People you know will be there to meet you and take you over: friends. A kind of induction committee, like Freshers' Week, but – Jan? What are you doing here when . . .? Oh, *shit*.'

As clear-edged and three-dimensional as Ruth, Jan was standing on the other side of the chaos doing the whole OODA-loop thing: Observe, Orient, Decide, Act. It had sounded amusing when she'd described it on her first day with the family and was much less so now that I was the focus. She was Orienting on me, and not happy with the deductions thereby arising.

'Did you just say you were Alanna Penhaligon?' Her voice sounded far more northern than it had done when she was alive: Newcastle, or thereabouts. She took an impossible step right over Ruth's body and came to stand directly in front of me.

On old instinct, I held out my hand. She shook it and I felt her; I clearly felt the pressure of her skin, the calluses on her palm. I said, 'Finn's grandmother, yes.'

Her eyes flared wider. 'So, I really am—?'

'You are.' For Ruth's sake, I cut in. 'It's not as bad as you think, especially if you can navigate the next bit cleanly and fast.' I caught Ruth by the elbow and pulled her into our huddle. 'This is Ruth. She's not quite up to speed yet. The shock can take a while to settle, but it really matters that you keep moving. Could you take her with you?' I put a plea behind this, a feel of a favour asked, with an offer of something in return.

'Will do.' Jan gave Ruth a cheerful smile, but her gaze switched keenly to mine. 'If you'll give a message to Nazir for me.'

'I can try. I've probably had more practice at this kind of communication than you.'

'He's in charge now. Tell him the shooter's one-sixty-two,

Caucasian, brown eyes and dyed blond hair. Black sweatshirt with a skull on the left sleeve. He's got a silenced pistol, but also something much bigger.'

'I'll do my best, I swear.' I gave Ruth a small shove in the right direction. To Jan, I said, 'You two need to be going. There's an edge place up ahead.' I nodded to what I saw as the shoreline of the Between. 'Might look like a seashore, or a riverbank?'

Jan shook her head. 'Snowline. Tundra and snow. Like where we trained in up in Norway.' Wonder filled her.

'Nice. Keep to the edge and head for the light. There's a young woman ahead called Ellen Shreeve: mediaeval dress. Tell her I sent you, she knows who I am. I think she's more familiar with the route. At the very least, she's more familiar with the state you're all in. Ruth, you can go with Jan. She'll see you right.'

Jan took her arm. A pace or two on, Ruth twisted round. 'You'll sort my essay?'

'It'll be fine, really. But the two of you need to go now, or you'll be late. You mustn't be late.'

Ruth was a good student, the kind for whom lateness was unacceptable. She let Jan march her to what still looked to me like the shoreline of the Between superimposed on the River Cam.

I was not a good warden. I did not stay to sort out Ruth's essay. I laid a brief hand on Chris Eglington's head and sent a pulse of what compassion I could muster, then rose swiftly up, seeking the ugly vortices that had drowned a young woman and used the distraction to murder the head of Finn's security team.

I didn't immediately find the bad guys, but Nazir and his half of the squad were huddled round Jan's body outside Abbey Hall, speaking into their earpieces. They didn't need me to tell them about the pistol, it was lying by her head.

Nazir looked as if someone had just blown his world apart. I went in close. 'Jan says you're looking for a white kid with a black sweatshirt and skull on the sleeve. He has another gun.' With the benefit of Ellen's example, I put a scent of gun oil behind the words, a half-ironic smile, the vowels of Newcastle.

Nazir's head cracked up. 'Jan?'

'FIND THE SHOOTER!' The scent of fresh blood, a skull, horror.

Nazir's head jerked round and he snapped at his squad, 'Danny, you're with me. Back to the principals and get them out of there. Anything out of the ordinary, call it in. No more subtlety. *Go!*'

I sent a pulse of hope to Jan then fled on towards the Hall, where word of at least one death had percolated through to a crowd that was well on the way to panic.

Leah Koresh was striving to hold authority, and in large part succeeding. She was still on stage, organising everyone to exit calmly through the extra-wide double doors at the opposite end of the Hall.

Two worried men in dark suits with security-style earpieces huddled in conference just inside the far smaller side door. I had to assume they were college security, though I struggled to imagine us having such a thing. At any rate, when Nazir took over and started giving orders, neither of them argued.

One of the worried pair was despatched to the stage to stop Kaitlyn jumping down to join the family. At her side, Rebecca was no longer calm. She flared an ugly yellowing grey, like the tail end of a summer migraine. She tapped the spare worried guard on the elbow and signalled down to where her daughter waved from the crowd. He let her go.

'NO! TELL HER TO STAY. SHE'S UP TO SOMETHING. OR SHE KNOWS SOMETHING. DON'T LET HER—'

Shit.

She was gone and everyone except me was happy to see the back of her. At Kaitlyn's request, worried-guard number one jumped down into the crowd to collect the rest of our family.

Maddie ran ahead of him and hopped up onto the platform. 'What's happening?' She put an arm round Kaitlyn. 'Why's Nazir here alone? Where's Jan?'

Worried-Two looked ever more flustered. 'We don't have much detail, but one of the students has drowned, and your head of security is in trouble. You're our first concern. We'll get you out and connect you with the rest of your team. They're . . .' Pride evidently lost a brief internal tussle. 'They're better trained than us.'

'Who are you?'

'College security.'

When did Bancroft start paying for security?

Kaitlyn wasn't impressed. 'If we're going, we go as a family. All of us.' She jumped down to where Eric, Niall, Kirsten and Connor were gathered at the foot of the dais, Maddie a little behind.

'Fine then. All together. Door's this way.' Worried-One was more confident now they were in control of the geography. He nodded to Nazir. 'We'll get them out. It's a solid stone corridor. No hidey-holes for bad guys.'

'He's right.' Worried-Two stepped up behind, gabbling with nerves. 'There's a door at the side here, under the arch. The corridor goes through the wall. It's the fastest route out, and secure. Narrow, though. One at a time. When you're out the door, you'll be on the lawns. We mowed that bit. Nothing can hide there that's bigger than a centipede. The rest of your security team's there.' He ushered them all along, a duck with his brood. 'Ladies, if you'd like to go first, I'll bring the gentlemen up behind.'

That's not right.

'Nazir! DON'T GO!'

Nazir was well trained. He had already grabbed Connor, Eriq and Niall, pulling them to a halt. Physically, he held them back. Danny, his ginger-haired, blunt-faced colleague, pushed forward into the tunnel to get Maddie and the girls. Which was when the Worried pair became competent.

One jabbed rigid fingers into Danny's solar plexus. Two hacked a stiff hand to the side of his neck and folded him to the floor, by which time One had already kicked shut and locked the door on which Nazir was now pounding.

Neither of them moved up the corridor. One called, 'Ladies, bit of a problem back here. If you'll keep moving on smartly, we'll sort it all out.'

He sounded so utterly plausible. Maddie, Kirsten and Kaitlyn kept on walking, pushing fast for the daylight, the green, the lawns: safety.

'Maddie! *No!* Don't go out! *MADDIE!*

'KAITLYN! STOP!'

'Lan? Is that you? Mum, can you hear Lan?'

'I thought I just did. Keep going. This place is creepily dark. We'll

214

stop when we get to the lawns. Lan knows her way around, she'll help us find a way – who's that?'

'That' was a pseudo-blond youth in a black sweatshirt with a skull on the left sleeve who stood about twenty feet back from the doorway that Kaitlyn and then Kirsten and then Maddie stepped through. They weren't in the open part of the college: they'd come out of the back, sheltered from the rest.

The door shut behind them, two inches of solid oak.

Skull-Boy had not been in the audience: there's no way I'd have missed the colour of his hate. But he was backed up by the empty-vortices: four of them made a semicircle behind him. Two of Finn's security detail lay on the ground between him and them. No puzzled souls hovered near them, though; they were still alive.

Skull-Boy screamed something. I didn't hear what, and it didn't matter. All that mattered was the gun in his hand, the big gun: US-schoolyard-massacre big.

I grabbed hold of time, what else could I do? I wrestled it, crushed it, powered it into glue-like slowness.

But I could not stop it.

The bullets moved like slugs on a leaf. I put myself between them and my family. They drilled through as if I was just more air, leaving me in fragments.

They spun me round, threw me down, ripped time from my fingers so that it sped out of control.

And when I could look again, and see, they were dead.

Kaitlyn.

Kirsten.

Maddie.

Our family. Just ours. And only the women.

▼

No.

No!

I knelt on the gravel pathway between Maddie and Kaitlyn and tried to . . . wanted to . . . pleaded with all the gods for something I could do.

215

Nothing. I could do nothing. I could not stop the blood from flowing, or the shock of impact from breaking the bonds that kept them living. At the last, I could not push their essences back into the blood and the flesh and the bones of who they had been. They rose around me, fresh with the confusion of death.

In fifteen years, I had not been in the presence of anyone at the exact moment they stepped out of life and had not expected to be; not yet; maybe not ever.

I saw them now.

Maddie.

Kirsten.

Kaitlyn.

One after the other, they took leave of the physicality of their bodies. To me, they lost the swirling-felt-heard textures that had blurred them in life and became sharply clear, as Ruth and Jan had done at the riverside, but with a searing hurt I had not felt there.

'Lan?' Maddie was first to see me: she'd had practice in her dreams. 'What are you doing here?'

'Failing to keep you alive.'

'Lan?' Kirsten was next. 'I had a headache and it's gone. Did you make that hap—' She spun towards the back wall. 'What's that?'

It was the suppressed stammer of silenced handguns: four shots so close together it was only because time was still syrupy that I heard each one distinctly.

In the shadow of the wall, the armed boy toppled, and was still. Three men and one woman who had been vortices in the audience walked steadily, one might even have said slowly, towards the gate on the far side of the orchard.

Just as Maddie, Kirsten and Kaitlyn had done, the boy rose up from the flesh he had been.

Just as they had done, he looked confused.

He showed no sign of recognising the women he had just murdered. He fastened onto me. I had most solidity. 'Who . . .?'

'Leave. Now. *Go.*' Words were my weapons and I hurled them without care or caution. Everything I had once thrown into the void, I threw at him. For one shocked moment, he stared at me, then, as smoke in a storm, he dissipated and was gone.

'Lan?' Kaitlyn stood in front of me, claiming my attention. 'The boys are coming. They'll need you more than we do.' She looked a bit older, but not by much, except for her eyes; they looked ancient, older than Connor, older even than Bēi Fēng, and I'd thought she was older than time itself.

This was the Kaitlyn I'd met in the void, the one who'd told me – no, the one who had let me believe – that her death was decades away.

'You knew?' I grabbed her shoulders. 'Did you know this was coming?'

'Lan.' She lifted my hands and clasped them between hers. 'Later, we can talk. For now you need to—'

'*Kirsten!*' Nazir may have led the way out of the main doors and round the side, but Niall had run fastest and now he fell between us, his pain a vivid slash of lightning that seared the air.

Devastation poured from him with a power that pushed us back and up, and then others were with him: Nazir, Eriq, Connor more slowly; Danny and two others from the security team; the warden, Oscar Virani. They were talking, but I couldn't hear them over the clamour of Niall's grief.

'Lan?' Hands pulled me round, dead hands: my daughter's hands. I said, 'Maddie, I'm so sorry.'

'We're dead?' Certainty was settling on her and it wasn't pretty. 'All three of us?'

'I'm so sorry.'

'How could you let this happen?' She wasn't raging now, at the end, just confused and hurt and heartbreakingly stricken. And I should have known. I *should*.

'Maddie, I had no idea. I swear I didn't. I'd have done anything—'

'Niall. What's he doing? Niall, will you look at me? Niall. Niall*Niall*Niall . . . !' Kirsten threw herself on top of her own corpse and cast arms around Niall, shaking him, screaming his name over and over and over until it chained into one long moan that wrenched Niall further into danger zones I could feel but not quantify. Death lay at the end of this, or insanity.

'Kirsten.' I caught her arm. Now that it didn't matter, I could hold her. 'He can't hear you. He can't see you. Kirsten, stop. Please stop. You have to let go. It's over now. Kaitlyn, can you make her stop? This is how ghosts are formed.' Out of rage and shock and the unwillingness to let go of the ones we loved in the life just departed: I understood this now. 'We have to—'

Rubber screamed on the road as Finn hurled Mo's Volvo through the college gates and nobody stopped him. That is, Nazir sprinted forward, but he wasn't actually suicidal, he jumped clear just in time.

I couldn't watch Finn do what Niall had already done. I hauled Kirsten bodily from her twin and shoved her into Kaitlyn's embrace. Of all of us, my youngest granddaughter seemed most together. Our eyes clashed over her head. She looked so . . . unbothered. I was still eye-burstingly furious. 'Kaitlyn Karim Penhaligon, I want answers. Fast.'

Something shadowy crossed her features and was gone. 'Lan . . .' With one arm, she held Kirsten and drew her back. With the other, she gripped my shoulder so that I had to look into her eyes. She was so *old*. 'Please don't give up on us now.'

'What is that supposed to mean? I can't—'

'*Lan*.' Quite a different voice, this: a command, no turning away. It came from behind me.

Finn was on his knees beside the bodies of his family. He was ruining forensics, but he was hardly the first and nobody stopped him. He had both arms round Niall, who was clearly about to hurl himself into the river if somebody didn't stop him. The air around him was black with a rage the power of which I'd never seen before.

He might have been holding his brother to life, but his gaze was fixed on us: on me. 'Did you know?'

'Of course not. Ask your sister. If one of us knew, it wasn't me.' With all of Ellen's teaching, I pushed remorse into the words, a sense of betrayal, horror, shock.

'Fuck that.' He shook his head. His lips were pencil straight and white. He wasn't raging: he'd never had that gene and, even if he had, nearly two decades of study under Mo would have balanced it out. This was worse, a frigid lucidity that joined the same dots I'd joined with Kaitlyn: what's the point of heading into the void if it doesn't help you see what's coming.

Which is exactly where he got to. 'If you didn't, you should have done. If you did, and you chose not to stop it . . .' His eyes closed against the possibility. He prised them open again. 'Either way, we're done. You can go—'

He didn't define where I might go to, but still, I felt the terrifying suck of the desolation, like a tidal current, dragging me out into an eternity of nothing. Kaitlyn grabbed me and was an anchor. I didn't feel any safer.

Frantic, I said, 'Finn, don't. I didn't know. I should have done. I don't know why I didn't. But I. Did. Not. Know.'

Finn snapped his fingers at me. He hadn't done that since he was ten. 'I'm not going to tell you to go to hell, but we are finished, you and me. Whatever you promised, you're free of it now. Connor said you stayed behind when you could have gone with Kate. So, now you can go. Be free. Do whatever you would have been doing if I hadn't made you promise to stay. I was young and selfish and I should have let you go years ago. So now I am.'

He stood up, pulling Niall with him. Over his brother's shoulder, he said, 'Alanna Penhaligon, I renounce you.'

I had trained him well, my grandson. He knew how these things worked. He fixed his gaze on the shattered parts of my soul and repeated it twice more.

'I renounce you. For the rest of this life and any beyond, I renounce you. Begone.'

INTERLOGUE 2

I clung to the shoreline of the Between as if my being depended on it. The shingle, the salt air, the Tree: these were the tangible things that kept me whole as Finn's words smashed through ties I had not recognised until they were gone.

In the moments of blinding panic I clung to Kaitlyn too, and was held.

And then, I wasn't.

Her form dissolved even as the sea and the shingle took shape. Regret washed over me, hers, not mine, and a swell of hope that felt as unreal as it was fleeting. For a handful of heartbeats, she was the spring-green spark from the void that had held all the promise of a connected world, and then she was gone, her and Maddie and Kirsten sweeping along all together in a breeze of love and loss that flowed to the sun-bridge so very much faster than I had ever done.

I felt Kate come to gather them in. The care of her grand, wide heart and all the brilliant contours of her mind were as clear as if I could see her. More bluntly, I felt those who came for Ellen, for Jan and Ruth, for the killer boy, who was here, however briefly: evidently I had not banished him to somewhere irretrievable in the anguish of the moment. I thought this was probably a good thing, but I was not a good enough person to be glad.

I felt them all step onto the sun-bridge, felt the sense of a wild, gods-filled landscape on the far side, felt the impossibility of passing as if it were a tangible thing. I found Crow's apple tree and sat beneath it, and felt an emptiness fill me that was not unlike the void.

Lan.

'*Crow!*' It was there among the apple boughs. 'Did you know this was coming?' I wanted to be angry and didn't have the energy even for this.

Crow came down onto my shoulder, and pushed its head against my cheek. In all the time we'd known each other, I'd perhaps stroked my finger down its back once. I couldn't remember a time when it had returned the gesture.

Look, it gave a small shove to turn my head the right way, towards the bridge.

Kate was still there. I could still feel the shape of her care, still smell the mix of scorched metal and Danish oil and planed wood that was her signature as much as mown hay and apples had been Ellen's.

If nothing else had come of this, I understood at a visceral level more of how a yearning to communicate on one side of a divide could be felt on the other side. To Kate, I said, 'If you can hear me, please tell the girls I love them, that I'm sorry, that I truly didn't know.'

So much else to say and I couldn't bear it. I turned away, seeking the loch and the sense of quiet it brought.

Lan . . . Crow's feet gripped my shoulder, tugging me back. *She's come for you.*

I stopped. I did not turn. I felt the shore teeter beneath me. Something thick wadded my chest. 'I can't leave. You said so. You *said* so.'

That was then. This once, Crow was patience personified. *Your promise to Kaitlyn died when she did, and Finn has just released you. We are free, both of us.*

I did turn then, and Crow lifted into flight. Kate was not yet solid, but it landed on the mist of her shoulder and did not sink through. I saw a host of other Crows, high on the arch of the bridge, and felt their pull as strongly as anything I'd ever experienced since I'd died.

Gently, Crow said, *It's all over. You did your best, and it was more than we expected or even hoped. Nobody can see the future, but you have made a difference to the trajectory of the world. We'll understand more when we reach the far side of – Lan?* Louder, *Lan! Where are you going?*

'Somewhere I can think. This isn't right.' I was a crow, flying as

221

fast as I knew how and already halfway to the loch. 'Wait if you can. I'll be back.'

Perched in the hawthorn by the loch, I felt oddly alive. The water was choppy, dancing in the early-morning light. A family of coots swam out of the reeds and cut arrowheads across the surface. The osprey hunted, and the otter. I dropped down to the rock and took human form. 'Hail, are you there?'

A broad nose bumped my palm. 'Hail!' I knelt to embrace him. 'I missed you.'

Lan. He leaned into me, his voice as deeply rich as it ever had been. *I wasn't sure you would come back.*

'This is home. Where else would I be?'

That's disingenuous.

True.

I sat on the rock, dangling my legs towards the water. 'There's a decision to be made.' And not one I wanted to make alone. 'Can you still speak with Connor?'

That might be difficult. He is . . . not who he was. Hail's voice cracked in a way that made my heart lurch.

'He's not dying? He's ten thousand years old. He *can't* die.'

He can; he does, often. He is just reborn without a rest between and with a knowing that leaves him old from childhood.

'He can't go now, though. Finn needs him. And Niall.' And me. I needed him. I didn't say this, but Hail was as good at reading between my lines as anyone.

He will stay as long as he can.

Bloody hell. Bloody, *bloody* hell.

In a world newly blurred, I walked the few paces down to the loch's edge and peered out across the water, waiting for things to settle. Hail rose and offered himself as a steady weight against my hip. After a while, I rested a hand on his shoulder and kneaded the corded muscles of his neck.

When I could see clearly again, I bent to scoop up a cupped palm of water and let it run out between my fingers, watching the patterns ripple and dot across the surface as it splashed back to the greater whole. I could draw metaphors out of anything if I tried, but this was easier than most: me the water; Crow – a whole murmuration of Crows – the drops and ripples spreading out to craft a route through to the wild lands Beyond. There was a great deal to be said for leaving now.

And yet . . . Several of the unfocused bits inside me joined up and made sense. 'I need to go into the void,' I said. Even to myself, I sounded uncertain. I put more backbone into it. 'If there's a timeline where I'm still here, still useful, still doing something that helps Finn and sees Kaitlyn's vision brought closer to reality, then I have to stay whether they want me or not.' I felt naked, and cold and in need of support. To the hound at my side, I said, 'Will you be my anchor if I go on my own?'

Hail blinked at me. *It would be my honour.*

I could have wept. But the intention was set; already the un-wind of the void whistled past, blurring the loch and all that held me there. I dug my fingers deep into Hail's thick ruff. 'Let's go.'

This was my third time in the void, and threes have their own power.

I came first as an ingénue, innocent and ignorant in equal measure. Second time around, I was dragged here barely willing and given precious little freedom of movement, though I learned a lot. Now, I was here because I chose to be. All decisions were mine and, freed from the pressure of others' expectations, all agency was mine. This time around, success or failure was all down to me. It felt better than I might have imagined.

We came to rest on the edge of nowhere, me and Hail. He cocked an ear in my direction. *Why are we here?*

'I need to see what happens with the family and whether there's a timeline in which I still have an active role to play.'

My intent was clear and clean. In the time it took to say it, we were at the broad, flat plain that marked the edge of time. Hail was more a tree than a mountain: his roots were thick rivers that ran to the heart of the earth.

'Right then.'

As I had twice before, I stamped my foot and spread forward the timelines.

As I had once before, I walked the line of Finn's life to the present moment.

As I had never done before, I drew on the depth and power of Hail's grounding and speared roots of my own deep, deep, *deep* into the firmament of the void . . .

. . . and rode the surging speed, the flesh-bending G-force of a turn tighter than physics should have allowed, the ramp and ramp and ramp and all the power of all the worlds poured into one focal point, and that focal point was me.

I held it one moment longer and then . . .

Let go!

Time sundered, sharply. Caught off balance, I lurched forward and tumbled, as a Crow, then human, then Crow again, spinning rump over beak across a newly mown meadow, where the grass smelled of vehicle fumes and the salt tears of gathered mourners, and both were mixed thinly through the old, familiar scents of the farm.

And then my Crow-senses caught up, and I was crushed thin as feathers under the slamming weight of my family's grief.

INTERLOGUE 2.1

Saturday, 13 May 2023 – first time around

I couldn't move. I couldn't think.

The farm was lost in a miasma of grief, dense as a thundercloud, and as grey, cut through with hatred the sickly green of old pus and raw, red arterial rage.

I was a puddle of regret smeared across the lawn, caught between the need to find safety – the void seemed a safe place, in comparison – and Kaitlyn's voice, deep in my bones, *There'll be a time when the boys will need you: Niall and Finn and Dad. You'll know when.*

Now. They need me now, damn you, and what am I supposed to do?

And did you know, Kaitlyn Karim Penhaligon? *Did you know* this was coming and not tell me?

Two things kept me from bailing out: Hail was anchored so deep in the heart of the earth that my own heart was held firm and I could not have wrenched free even if I'd wanted to; and here in this dream of the farm, a voice called from Rookery Wood.

Greetings, Crow-woman. Will you fly with us?

Bold as a lover turning back a sheet, Bright Rook unfolded the core of herself in invitation and I had not the wit nor the will to turn her down. I felt like a child, skipping school, but I grabbed the offer and fled to the blood-warm stability of her being.

'I didn't know you could be here, in the dream of this place.'

Perhaps we are not. She was amused again; always. *Even so, clean air flows here between land and sky, untainted by that which assails you.* She pulled our attention upwards. *Shall we fly?*

I didn't know how much I needed it until we were airborne,

knifing into thermals that spiralled lazily over the wood in perfect counterpoint to the horror that hunkered over the farm.

Bright swooped a couple of long arcs and then launched us into a particularly tricky set of counter-currents with a grace and skill I couldn't have hoped to match.

Abandoning all semblance of control, I relaxed into the thrill of each giddying turn, and the side-sliding speed-soars aslant the top of the wood. I don't know how long we played, but others from the Rookery joined us, one by one until we were thirteen in all, looping fast and fierce across the sky, our mind full only of the wind and its currents, of our place in the dance . . . except somewhere in the whirl I was aware of a hunger, gnawing below my heart.

Hesitant, I asked, 'Could we feed?'

Surely.

I'd had in mind a scuttle of woodlice that I could hear-feel under the bark of the young ash that had died to make the dream-Tree outside Kaitlyn's window. Bright had other ideas. She and her cohort slipped down the wind and, before I could protest, we'd passed through the thunderous pain to land on the roof of Ash Barn.

The fog had neither lifted nor been dispelled, but Bright was evidently immune to its horror and, as her passenger, I had passed through without incident.

Viewed from the inside, it was no less ugly, the colours were as discordant and the feel as grim, but it was easier to look away, particularly when Bright teased a fat squirmy thing from beneath the old weathervane and swallowed it whole.

We savoured it equally, but the flickering pang of revulsion was enough to kick me out of her, so that I saw the last spasm of her swallowing from the outside.

Still in Crow form, I ducked my head. 'My thanks. I should go.'

Bright regarded me, sharply. *You do not wish us to enter the white house?*

She nodded back over her shoulder towards the field behind the farmhouse. Looking down, I saw with a visceral lurch that the pavilion was up again. Of course it was. We'd used it first for Kate's funeral and then the family had put it up for mine, then again for Maddie's wedding, Finn's twenty-first, Matt and Jens's civil partnership, and a couple of random village events. Now, a familiar black carpet stretched to it from the farm's back door, with clots of mourners walking slowly along.

Finn wasn't among them, but the pressure of his pain was at least part of the passion that fogged the farm. Grief was there and the blood-red rage and, layered not far beneath, an implacable sense of *rightness*, possibly even righteousness, that wrapped his memories of banishing me.

I had no idea what would happen if I were to be banished from a void-dream, but inviting an entire parliament of rooks into the pavilion was as fast a way as any to find out. Even Bright Rook alone was guaranteed to be seen: there aren't many places to hide a black bird in a white tent.

To her, I said, 'Thank you, I will go alone.'

She blinked down at the thronging crowd. *You are wise. We might not enjoy the company of so many. We shall go. Return to us if you have need. You are always welcome.*

What signal she gave to the others I did not see, but I felt the lift and crack of their wings and, soon, was a Crow alone, facing a sea of grieving people.

I recognised a surprising number of the faces, but there were only a few I really cared about. Connor was one, obviously. It took me a while to find him, because half of Team Memory were on his one side and the entire Shaolin student body were on the other.

The man himself was exactly as broken as Hail had suggested. Before-Connor had been fit and bounced around on his prosthetic leg like the original bionic man. Today-Connor was a hollowed wraith who looked one step away from a Zimmer frame, or a coffin of his own.

Inching painfully along the black carpet leading from farm to pavilion, he was supported by Hawck and Mo Bakar, with everyone else clustered around, talking, moving, making patterns that looked random unless you watched from crow height, where they were clearly designed to screen Connor from anyone and everyone else.

Or perhaps from specific people. Scanning the crowd, I had the same sense I'd had in the debate: the majority of those here were decent people who cared, while about 10 per cent were there out of morbid curiosity or to leech off the passions of the rest. The remaining handful were empty shells, who might have turned up simply to record the proceedings or might have had their own assault rifles tucked away somewhere, ready to spray the whole place with death.

Among all of these was threaded Finn's security detail led by a vengefully watchful Nazir, who positively radiated the need to kill someone, preferably several someones. If the shell-people could sense anything, they'd take him out first or else change their plans. Either one seemed better than their targeting Connor.

Inside the pavilion, three handwoven wicker coffins rested on a long trestle at the back of a dais. A dark-blue velvet curtain hanging from ceiling to floor made a sober backdrop. In front of the stage, a hundred and fifty chairs had been set out in rows, thirty to a row with an aisle in the middle. The tech systems were professional: lights, microphones, cameras were hung from the roof structures and a dozen vast screens took up the walls: four set along either side and two at either end.

Each had a time and date stamp at the bottom right-hand corner, from which I learned that it was Saturday, 13 May, four weeks to the day since the shootings. I thought the inquest must have been held with merciful swiftness, and then thought, less kindly, that perhaps a panicked government had pushed things along to avoid the tidal wave of Kaitlyn's movement from becoming a tsunami. Perhaps it had worked.

As Connor and his protectors entered, the wall screens came to life, rolling through stills and videos of Maddie, Kirsten, Kaitlyn, up to and including, their deaths.

I had no desire to watch the shooting played over and again in slow motion, and I definitely didn't want to watch people I barely knew weeping over those I still loved, so I escaped into the operating system controlling the video feed. The laptop was Finn's and while I still couldn't manipulate text I could drift through his GhostTalk threads, Twitch and Discord streams, and his recent forays into World of Warcraft.

He hadn't been playing as much as I would have expected: hardly at all, in fact.

The Global Championship Finals had been halted when news of the shootings had come through. Knightmayr, one of the three commentators, had broken into the middle of a match between DredLok and Retail Pandemic to pass it on. 'People, we've learned why Nifty left the team fights: his mother and his two sisters have just been shot.'

The news hadn't reached any of the feeds, so this was the first public announcement. The chat boxes erupted, but more strikingly all six competitors stopped fighting and their characters sat down *in the middle of a match*, and every single team refused to play on.

There followed a scramble of texts and calls with the sponsors before LadyTrieu, the Vietnamese-Canadian Gladiator girl on the commentary team, announced that the Championships would be refought at 'a better time' and that they were calling for a minute's silence now, to 'honour our fallen sisters'.

Since then, a number of in-game communities had set up with the initials KKM somewhere in the title and the wider global WoW community had spontaneously organised an hour's play-free time to coincide with the funeral.

Not everyone was on board, of course. On every server, a rough 12 per cent of the player base had celebrated the killings and made a hero of Carl Thomson, the incel who had pulled the trigger.

In recent days, these groups had coalesced into a couple of huge trans-server communities who had arranged massed in-game World PVP events coinciding with the funeral to prove ... whatever they thought this was going to prove. I checked in on one of the North American servers, where Horde and Alliance were facing off in Orgrimmar for a major battle.

Numbers are patterns. I knew most of the Grey Ghosts' IP addresses and it didn't take long to work out that a significant number of those flying into the mountains just outside the Horde capital were infiltrating Ghosts, fighting in the newly cohesive incel communities, finding names, talking in private DMs and generally gathering data. It wasn't quite Northern Ireland in the late 90s when seven out of ten members of the IRA arrested by the Royal Ulster

Constabulary turned out to be agents of the British state, but it wasn't far off. I'd have told Finn, but if talking to him was an option, there were any number of other things that would have had a higher priority.

Frustrated, I eased out of the laptop and back up to the roof struts to watch for other mourners I might recognise, and was rewarded by the sight of Torvald – the twins' father-by-blood if not anything else – glowering his way into the pavilion. He, too, had lost a daughter: I shouldn't have been as surprised to see him as I was.

He was dressed in a suit, which was a first, and looked sober. Glancing round, he saw nobody else he recognised, squared his shoulders and marched over to the huddle of gamers around Connor. The conversation promised to be interesting and I was sidling cautiously along the spar to listen in when a bustle at the entrance diverted my attention and Frances Nolan marched in, half a step ahead of the angry young woman she'd been with at the debate.

Frances was one of the few mourners dressed in black. The invitations in Finn's laptop had said, 'Dress however you feel most comfortable' and almost nobody felt comfortable in black. Frances certainly didn't: she looked frumpy, which was quite an achievement for someone who appeared perpetually to be on the verge of an eating disorder, but there was an air of hair-shirted martyrdom about her, as if colour might atone for all she'd done in the past few weeks.

By contrast, Leah Koresh, lead reporter on the UK's sharpest political broadcaster, Chair of the fatal debate and survivor of the shooting, wore black and looked stunning. She didn't have Kaitlyn's beauty, but she had the height and poise to draw attention.

Entering a dozen people behind, she scanned the crowd and then carved a path through it.

'Frances? Frances Nolan?'

Nolan cringed behind her daughter until she saw who it was. 'Leah!' The two women clasped a double handshake, Frances introduced the angry young woman as her daughter, Jodie, and the two fell into industry gossip. Leah was halfway through an anecdote about the Health Secretary's latest feud with the prime minister when their phones buzzed on an incoming text.

They weren't alone: every single phone in the room vibrated in sync; a digital seating plan moved into action and people followed the directions on their screens. A second, milder tone marked the correct seat. A third reminded them to turn their phones off.

The background music dimmed. Until this moment, I had been deliberately tuning out Kaitlyn's teenage taste in cat torture, but as the last person sat, it sighed to silence (*thank you*) and the lights dimmed and now it was clear why the backdrop to the coffins was such a dark blue, why the lighting was set thus, why there were so many cameras hanging from so many roof struts.

The big screens were blank for a lingering moment, and then they all cut to images of the coffins, and the dais beside them, where a single spotlight spilled a puddle of waiting.

One at a time, Eriq, then Niall, then Finn stepped up from the soft shadows beyond the light. Niall looked broken, but then they all did. If they'd had any sleep in the month since the shootings it didn't show, and if they had stopped weeping, it hadn't been for long. They were angry, too. Even Eriq looked as if Maddie's volcanic rage had seeped under his skin and he was struggling not to let it spill over the waiting mourners.

After that first flickering check, though, it was Finn who drew all my attention. Outwardly the calmest of the three, inside, his grief and rage had the same lucid, bone-deep power that his roots had done when I had asked him to ground like Ben Nevis so that I could void-walk to Kaitlyn.

And yet he was not grounded. Searching for a sense of his roots, their thickness and depth, I found instead a barrier set deliberately across, like inch-thick slates laid across the source of a spring.

So now I knew the origins of the sick headache-fog around the farm. Almost two decades of Mo's patient teaching and at least six months with Bēi Fēng and this was the result. What I didn't know was why he was doing something so contrary to all he'd ever been taught.

Whatever the reason, he was well aware of his own power, and was holding it on a viciously tight rein. When his gaze roamed the pavilion, I hid down behind the central roof stays, reaching for Hail in case I needed to bail out early, but my grandson was not looking

231

for me, only checking that everyone was seated and the ceremony could start.

Heart-sore, I hunkered down to watch and listen as Eriq and then Finn spoke of the women they had lost – as wife, mother, sister – with a power and poignancy that left everyone present blowing into their handkerchiefs and scrubbing their eyes.

It was beautiful and moving and none of it gave me any clue as to whether my remaining family had any use of, or need for, my continued presence in their lives. Somewhat disconsolately, I was thinking of Crow and Kate, imagining how it might feel to cross the sun-bridge, when Niall started to speak.

He sounded a lot calmer than Crow-sight made him look. Jagged reds and greens, both deep enough to be almost black, surged around him in a mirror of the greater cloud assailing the farm, but you wouldn't have known it by his tone. He sounded almost professorial, in the old sense, when white-haired neurodivergents warmed to their latest obsession and didn't really care who was listening.

'Before I, too, talk about our family, we wish to acknowledge that we are not unique. Across the world, people lose their families – whole communities – to the ravages of psychopaths, not all of whom wield a gun: some are more distant killers, programming drones or mines. Others are heads of corporations who can claim to know nothing of the poisons they throw out, or the militias they fund. Even in this country, this safe place where bad things don't happen to good people,' his voice etched every word with quiet violence, 'whole families are lost to drugs or gangs, to cultural altercations, to house fires, to the horrors of domestic violence.' A glass of water stood on the lectern. He took a brief drink. 'So please know we are not claiming any kind of privilege. We're suffering what others suffer. We're only making headlines because we were already in the headlines.

'More of that later. We also need to recognise the names of others lost in what was clearly a linked sequence. The first is Shona-Beth: you have all heard of her by now. She was Kaitlyn's friend, and her murder – I am not going to sully her memory by suggesting it was anything else – was the kick that started Kaitlyn on this path. Her funeral took place two weeks ago and I know many of you joined online, as we did, to honour her. But today I wish us all once again to remember this young woman and all the horror of a life cut short.

He bowed his head, fingers laced, and everyone followed his lead. Half the screens cut to images of Shona-Beth, a smiling young Black woman caught in various poses amid the hellish facade of twenty-first-century US deprivation.

Sixty seconds later, the screens faded to black and then back to Niall, who went on, 'And then there is Ruth Butterfield, another young woman who had a life of promise ahead of her, this time as a student at the college where my family died. Her drowning was not accidental. It seems likely she was murdered simply to cause a distraction: a life destroyed because she was in the wrong place at the wrong time.'

There followed another minute's silence, in which to view Ruth, who looked a lot more vibrant in life than she had done when newly dead. Her hair had purple highlights, her smile was pure mischief, though when she played cello, which she apparently did well enough to be in the college orchestra, she looked as if her soul was dancing in her eyes.

'Finally, we want to honour Captain Jan Westbrook, who gave her life trying to protect my mother and my sisters. Jan was valued during her military service, and when she left the army and set up her own personal protection squad, she was accounted one of the best in the business. We hired her because of her reputation, and she was murdered for it, too.'

From all the images, Jan was sharp in all the ways you'd expect. We saw her as a young woman, a young soldier, climber, race-runner, sharpshooter. She looked uncomfortable in a dress when she had to pick up her various awards, and most at home on the wild hills of Northumberland, which had been her home.

Niall waited several seconds after the last image faded, then said, 'Our final additional death, of course, is Carl Thomson himself: a young man from Canvey Island, not far from here.'

The screen showed a video of a youth in a skateboard park. In slow motion, he performed a creditable kickflip and pumped a cheer for the camera. This was all we saw of Carl. The screens cut back fast to Niall, as he picked up again. And now his stepping forward to the microphone woke wild, ugly things that gnawed at my innards and grew progressively more frantic as he began to speak.

I wasn't alone: in the pavilion, a hundred and fifty mourners who had been almost hypnotised into stillness began to shuffle and squirm and roll their shoulders as if the temperature had just dropped by ten degrees.

Niall sailed on, uncaring. 'As we know, Carl was shot dead in the minutes after he murdered my mother and sisters, which in turn was not long after he shot Jan Westbrook. He may have pushed Ruth in the river, though that would require him to have moved very fast, so we think it's unlikely: he had help setting this up and help making it happen, and we think Ruth was murdered by others, less open.

'Because Carl was completely open: he posted his manifesto on Reddit as he left the house on that Saturday morning. The detail has been picked apart in the media for long enough, we don't need to rehash it here, except to reiterate what we all know: Carl was a regular inhabitant of what we might call the incel web. The TikTok channels, Reddit threads and 4chan forums to which he was a regular visitor all stoked his belief in his own white male supremacy and his sense of victimhood at the hands of women worldwide. There was nothing in particular to single him out, except that he lived within reasonable reach of Cambridge, and when the so-subtle request went out, for someone to "do something" to combat the surge in unconscionable support for a young Black woman, he answered the call.

'Let's be clear: Carl was not a "lone wolf", whatever the press and his online cheerleaders would have you think. In a country where such things are still illegal, Carl did not acquire an assault rifle and the rounds to load it by accident or luck. He didn't even have a driving licence, and yet there is no record of him taking public transport to get to Bancroft Hall, and no taxi service delivered him; he's not even recorded on CCTV. In this most-monitored corner of the world's most-monitored island, there is no sign of him anywhere in Cambridge. We know, we've checked the video feeds.'

Niall what the absolute fuck are you doing?

Nothing he said was wrong, and yet the words screeched as if they were fingernails drawn down a chalkboard and out there in the listening world, certain people sat up and took sharper notice with every passing sentence.

Niall had to know what he was saying was incendiary, but he pushed on, smiling a little. The fog above the farm became denser and nastier and it dawned on me slowly that, while Finn may be holding it steady, Niall was at least his equal in spawning the wrath from which it was formed. It followed therefrom that Finn was perhaps not deliberately crafting a pressure cooker that might explode at any moment, rather, he was doing all he knew to keep his brother's rage contained.

Oh Finn.

Oh, my beautiful, brave and wonderful boy.

What have you taken on? And how on earth can I help you?

I sat frozen up near the white canvas roof and only slowly understood that Niall was still hurling out his verbal grenades.

'. . . Carl was primed, provisioned and pushed by people who haunt the shadows, who think they are forever hidden.

'But they are not, and we'll make sure they know it. Starting now, today, we are going to shine the brightest spotlight we can find into their swamp. We are lucky to have many friends who can delve into the hidden chasms of the internet. Working round the clock since the murder of our family, these friends have unearthed credible online fingerprints which show how Carl was groomed to take the actions he took.

'We might ask why, but the answer is obvious: we threatened the establishment. Specifically, Kaitlyn threatened the Death Cult that is the establishment, and heaven forfend that a queer, Black, fourteen-year-old girl should go up against the old, straight, white men and show signs of winning.'

The audience murmured a brittle laugh; it didn't last long.

Niall's smile was arctic. 'She wouldn't like me to say this, because she believed fiercely that we are all heroes in our own way, but still, as her brother, I am entitled to believe that Kaitlyn was unique: the kind of role model who turns up once in a generation. She had absolute integrity and absolute courage. And shining with those, she had the charisma to speak to millions. I don't have any of these. None of us—' a wave of his hands to Eriq and Finn— 'left in our family does. But we do have determination, and we will not be found wanting of courage. We literally have nothing left to lose.'

Niall, please! You know that's not true.

He believed it, though. And others were listening who believed it, too. On the private networks they inhabited, messages were spinning back and forth, weaving plans that tasted of cyanide.

Niall bowed a little to the cameras, and surrendered his place to Finn, who took the microphone with a confidence that he'd previously only shown online. He was pale, but he gave no sign that he disagreed with anything his brother had just said, either the words or their implications; quite the reverse.

'Obviously, we are not making these allegations out of nowhere. If you check your feeds under #LiftingTheLid and follow the links there, you'll find the entire digital trail that leads directly back to the security forces of this nation, showing in disturbing detail how Carl Thomson was led to believe he had joined an incel group, all eight members of whom were planning acts of terror against women who "got above themselves".

'In fact, Carl was the only real person in this group. The rest all trace back to a single IP address that links to Cheltenham, specifically to GCHQ. We don't know exactly who gave the orders, but we have the names of three men we had not yet linked to the #PornGate exposés but whom we believe were implicated. All three are now or have been members of the government or the security forces at the highest levels. All three had been in regular communication with each other since the scandals first broke. And all three checked in with the team that armed and supported Carl Thomson.

'Of course, the Powers That Be will claim we have made this up, but there are facts among the text threads that cannot be faked, and which, in themselves, give fascinating insight into how our government works behind the scenes, from the war against Russia, to the escalation of our inflation rates, to bribes paid to ministers by the fossil fuel companies that are wilfully destroying our world.

'Our government is corrupt to the core. We all know this. Most of the time, we choose to ignore it. We are not going to ignore this anymore. Because this isn't just about the tragedy of murder. This is about our future. It's about my children and yours, and their children's children. While we're mired in corruption, nothing is going to change. And *we need change*. We're all caught in a bus accelerating towards the edge of a cliff and those who have taken control of the wheel are never willingly going to change course or hand over control. To be fair, they don't know how. It's not their fault that we have a system designed to push narcissistic sociopaths to the top, they just take advantage of what they're given.

'So, as Kirsten so often said, imagine a world where the best of us get to make the decisions, not the venal dregs of a bankrupt system. Actually, she was much kinder than I am. She never used a word like "venal" in her life. But she's dead and we're left and we're saying that now is the time for change.

'Urgently, we need new, wise, decent people – individuals of integrity, creativity and emotional literacy – to steer the governance of our nations and our world. We need not just to turn the bus, we need to dismantle it, and find a different way of moving ourselves forward. We—' a gesture that took in Niall, Eriq and most of the first four rows of those listening— 'will do whatever it takes to make this happen. If you want to join us, make yourselves known. Because this is the last chance. It may be too late, but we're going to give it everything we've got.'

Abruptly, Finn stopped. A breathless gap followed. Nobody knew what was coming next. Nobody knew what was *supposed* to come next, only that there must be something. The tension was a cheesewire at head height: barely visible and utterly lethal.

Until it snapped.

'Well said!' White-faced, Frances Nolan rose to standing, a monochrome figure stranded in a sea of parrot-bright uncertainty. 'Bravo!' Raggedly, she began to clap.

At her side, Jodie shrivelled with shame, hands wrapping her face. But Leah Koresh was in the row behind and she, too, stood to applaud. She was less tentative. The sound bounced off the tented walls.

The Ghosts sat tight; Mo, too, and Nazir, and Torvald. Anyone with half a brain could tell who was in on this by clocking who was so carefully not catching anyone's eye, not contributing, not letting it be seen on the inevitable videos that they'd fed this.

Finn's face was fixed with a bland look as if it didn't really matter, but I could feel the sledgehammer of his heart from the roof beams, amazed that it wasn't rocking the stage.

And then a man lurched to his feet. I had no idea who he was, but his hands were big and meaty. 'You tell those fuckers!'

Someone laughed and someone else whistled and – at last! – the dominoes fell in one long ripple until the Ghosts and Connor and Mo and Torvald were free to stand and applaud with the rest without looking as if they had started it all.

The cameras captured everything, and sent it live within seconds, hashtagged to the hilt: #ChangeMustHappen and #KKMForChange ranked up there with #LiftingTheLid, though the one that took off most was #WeNeedChange.

It took a long time for the noise to fade. When it did, Finn bowed to the audience and people dropped their heads in return.

He stepped back. Niall stepped up, changing the gear.

'As Finn has said, we need real change. Not a general election that elevates a different bunch of blokes in suits with a slightly different-coloured tie, and a slavish media cheering them on. That's not going to put the carbon back in the ground, fix the ecosystem crisis, create social equity out of a system designed on the back of exploitation . . . or bring the dead back to life.

'We need nothing less than revolution. But it *must* be peaceful and we must bring everyone with us: if my twin taught me anything in our nearly four decades of time on this earth, it was that we can only make the changes we need if we all walk together willingly, and nobody walks anywhere willingly if they're staring down the barrel of a gun. Nonetheless, let there be no mistake: change is coming, and we will make it happen.

'We are going to create a whole new system of governance, a new way of configuring our democracy, a new way of electing the brightest and the best, not the kleptomaniac psychopaths. We'll create deliberative democracies where citizens come together in new ways to gather consensus so that everyone knows they have been heard and understood.

'We will create ways to harness the astonishing power of everyone working together, not to enrich ourselves, but to help all of us weave new communities, or revive old ones; regenerate our countryside so that everything thrives and we can feed ourselves; generate power in ways that don't destroy our futures; educate our children for the world they're growing into, which will be so, so different from the one we thought we were building.

'None of this is rocket science. The answers are already out there, we just keep on sticking our fingers in our ears because it's better for the guys at the top to keep racing to the bottoms of our brainstems. Triggered people are easy to control. So we're going to put a stop to the limbic hijacks. No more nudging people into toxic tribalism with carefully targeted triggers. What we do from now on, we do openly, with full disclosure at every step and we do it for ourselves, and the living planet.'

This time, the applause began before he'd finished speaking. On the net, #HellYesKKM surged. In the big pavilion, someone set up a cheer and the sound system gathered it in, amplified it, and fed it back until it sounded as if the whole world cheered with them. On the dais, Finn withdrew his focus from the world around him, and instead focused on the rage he had held so carefully contained, for so long. A thought, a breath, a small shift of his intent and he let it all loose on the people whose attention he had gathered.

Finn, *no*! You shouldn't even know how to *do* this.

But he did. With his rage he fed . . . things that should never have been fed. And in the pavilion and across the world, the massed ranks of mourners cheered and cheered and *cheered*, and the tone was poisonously exultant.

Except me: I wasn't cheering anything. The screaming mess in my chest had expanded until there was no space for anything but panic.

The pressure was too much. I could not stay. My hold on the moment cut loose and I was a flat stone skimming across the surface of time, setting down briefly, haphazardly, catching glimpses of the future that spooled out from that one surging moment.

It was much as you might expect: rage was met with rage, hate with hate, threatened destruction with actual annihilation. In a world where governments start wars to hold on to power, you can't declare open rebellion and expect to get away with it.

In small bites, I saw cars converge on the village. Not Range Rovers come to break down the gates this time, but high-end vehicles nonetheless, that could move fast if they needed to, all in navy or black, the better to remain hidden after dusk. They came at night, when the East Anglian mist lay heavy as felt, but the drivers all knew the way up the farm track without having to ask.

They stopped just shy of the newly mended gates and shoved open their doors. Time juddered and, a skip later, I saw a dozen figures in dark clothing stealth up the drive to the farm and into each of the occupied bedrooms. No hesitation: they knew where to go here, too. I heard the punch of silenced weapons, heard heartbeats stutter and stop: Connor, Eriq, Niall, Finn; elsewhere Mo and her students, Torvald, Leah Koresh, Nazir and three of his team. I saw them rise from their bodies, confused. I could not interfere. I mourned, but did not try to reach them.

Another skip. A drift of petrol fumes hung in the air after the cars left. The explosion was portrayed on the BBC as a 'freak accident with the on-farm fuel tank'. Nobody believed this, but that was the point. 'See what we can do, and you have to pretend to believe our lies or you, too, will lose all you love.'

A skip and skip and skip and at each touch-down, I saw others die: Hawck, Charm, Juke – *Juke!* Who had to be something big in Mossad – nobody was immune. The top ranks of the Grey Ghosts across the world were removed all in the same night, even in St Petersburg, Vladivostok, Archangel: Russia was quite happy to work with the West if it had to, and never mind what was happening in Ukraine.

The US worked with China, Korea, with Germany, Nigeria, Kosovo, Hungary . . . there was not a nation on earth where the Ghosts were safe. Their homes were destroyed, saving only their hard drives, which were carried into vehicles and thence into warehouses where teams of young men (and a few women) set to breaking them open.

Half a day later, when the drives had given up their secrets, another wave of people across the globe fell under cars, or off buildings, or caught a particularly pathogenic virus and died without regaining consciousness.

By morning in America, all the KKM hashtags were gone. In under twenty-four hours, the insurrection had been destroyed.

Heart-sick, I sank back into the void.

I steadied myself.

I gripped onto Hail's anchor, speared my own roots down into the heart of the void – and stepped back into the flow of time.

INTERLOGUE 2.2

Saturday, 13 May 2023 – variations on a theme

Navigating the vortex over the farm was easier now that I knew its nature.

With regret, I turned down Bright Rook's offer to merge, though the lure of aerial acrobatics and a meal of crunchy beetles whispered promises at the edges of my awareness.

Seeing Connor was also less of a shock second time around. Frances Nolan looked just as frumpy, just as lost, her daughter just as angry.

Feeling just as exposed as I had done, I retreated to the heights of the pavilion, seeking small sparks of difference that would set this time-thread apart from the last iteration. If I found nothing early, I wasn't sure I had the heart to sit through it all again.

I was watching everyone take their seats, when Torvald swerved late through the crowd, radiating irritation. This was new. He sat next to Frances Nolan, displacing someone else who had been about to sit next to her. Seeing a woman he didn't know, he switched on his thousand-watt grin and shuffled his chair a little closer. She didn't shuffle hers away.

Definitely different. Hope blinded me, and when it cleared, Eriq, Finn and Niall were on stage, nearing the end of their orations.

Finn was reaching the crescendo of his speech: '. . . want to join us, make yourselves known. Because this is the last chance. It may be too late, but we're going to give it everything we've got.'

It was the same call to action as I'd witnessed before, the same delivery, the same power, the same sense of a breath held as the last word landed and nobody was quite sure what was happening, or what they should do.

Because I knew what came next, all my attention stayed on Frances Nolan. I saw the moment she drew in her courage and began to rise, saw her take a breath, choose the word and—

Torvald Magnusson laid his big Viking hand on her thigh.

Shock froze her in place. Her breath hissed. She grabbed his index finger and was about to bend it back to breaking point when he tilted his head to hers. His clipped Swedish consonants were a murmur just above a breath, but I was a Crow: I heard them.

'Stop. Think. If they start a revolution, what do you imagine will happen? Five women were just murdered for less and one of them was my daughter. I do not wish to lose my only son.'

Frances Nolan swallowed back her courage and let his finger go. When she might have drawn her hand back, instead, she left it lying over his. Behind them, I saw Leah Koresh think about getting to her feet, but she had heard the gist of Torvald's warning and she, too, remained seated. Fat-hand-man in the back rows didn't even think about getting up.

Nobody stood. Nobody applauded. Nobody cheered. Online, a few hashtags appeared from Ghosts who had been primed: a thousand maybe, or two. Faithful fans picked them up and the numbers stumbled upwards, but they were hardly going viral.

On the stage, Finn took a breath, slid his phone from his pocket and, with a wry look at the audience, held it up. 'Ten thousand already. That'll do nicely.' To the cameras, as if this were the plan all along, he said, 'We are a digital world; one great nation. Borders don't matter anymore. Wherever a dozen can get a decent signal, we are there. And trust me, we are the 99 per cent. We shall make the world the kind of place Kaitlyn would have wanted to grow up in.'

Niall stepped in swiftly, but his was a closing speech, not a call to rebellion, and the atmosphere in the tent was hollow and erratic, lurching from mild amusement, to confusion, to the ache of something missed. Finn took on the same distant, meditative look, but already the pressure of the vortex was less, and all he had to do was open up his grounding and it sank away.

Relieved, I left the pavilion and skimmed along the timelines, thinking they might be safe. But no: I saw the quiet work in

Cheltenham that ensured Finn's internet connection was cut, and that of each Ghost, so their digital insurrection died unborn.

They were not shot, and the farm did not burn, nothing so dramatic, but over the next eighteen months, the grinding power of the state found 'irregularities' in their tax returns that led to endless court wrangles and soaring costs while their credit ratings plummeted and their bank accounts were hacked so often it was impossible to know which expenditures were real and which were money they didn't really have being siphoned off to scammers on the other side of the world.

In Brazil, the banks that had previously bent to the force of the TripleS hashtags now foreclosed on Eriq's businesses and there was no youth insurgency to stop them. Kaitlyn's Digital Army disbanded and its members returned to their previous jobs. Eriq sold his shares in Cuidorado to Max before they became worthless, but the money went into legal actions and wildly implausible tax bills. Eriq himself was stripped of his UK citizenship and deported to Morocco, which wouldn't have him. He ended up with Max in Brazil and even that was contentious. They emigrated to Mexico and hid in an off-grid community that still thought they were heroes.

Frances Nolan married Torvald and divorced him ten months later. In a joint ceremony witnessed only by the family and the village, Finn married Leah Koresh and Niall entered into a civil partnership with one of Mo's students whose name I didn't recognise.

Two years after the funeral, with Leah a month away from bearing a daughter, the farm was sold and the entire family spent the last of their money to pay for a flight to join Eriq in Mexico. He met them at the airport, haggard, bearded, drained of his joy.

They never made it to the community. When I saw them last, they were dead in a van at the side of the road, victims of a truck that had 'run out of control'. I watched them rise into the afterlife and felt from them only relief.

Heart-sick, I returned to the void, steadied myself and started mapping the parameters of possibility in as coherent a fashion as I could.

*

Focusing power in this place of the everwhere and the neverwhen was, I discovered, a lot like any other skill: the more I practised, the more accurate I became. I visited a lot of funerals after those first two, put a lot of effort into teasing out different threads that led onto different paths, with different outcomes.

Overall, two distinct patterns became clear.

The first was that if Finn and Niall so much as mentioned the digital trails connecting the shooter to the security services, the entire family and their immediate friends died within three years; the only variables were the time and method of their executions.

Through uncounted iterations of the funeral, I learned the feel of the more overtly confrontational paths that led to immediate death, and the softer ones where destitution and despair came first.

Some were more plausible than others. I chose not to go far along the tracks where the entire funeral was the subject of a 'terrorist attack' that left the farm in smouldering ruins. At the other end of the spectrum, I avoided also the versions where the family invited only close friends, and all the conversation was blandly apolitical: if nothing else, these ones struck me as so fantastically improbable that I didn't hang around to see where they led.

In the end, the state of the passion-cloud over the farm became such a reliable indicator that I could predict what was coming by the pressure I met when I first approached, and the colours threaded through it. In some futures Niall and Finn built their combined rage to boiling point and used it intentionally as a weapon, while in others their grief held sway and everything was softer.

In the former they invariably died, but I also began to understand that this was not accidental: Finn clearly knew what he was doing, but so, too, did Niall. The cloud was a conscious creation and, in those futures where they succeeded in building it with clear intention, they loosed it on themselves as much as the world; their deaths were a wholly predictable consequence.

In the softer futures, where they either failed to gain the skill, or simply didn't try, they wanted to die every bit as badly just didn't pull everything together to make it happen.

*

Somewhere between the two extremes, I tracked one of the softer variants in which the funeral was as big as the first one I had seen, and the emotions as ragged, but no threats were made to expose state actions and the demands were limited to a 'Kaitlyn's Law' banning all pornography from servers accessible by children under the age of consent in any given nation. This was not welcomed with cries of delight by the establishment, but neither did it cause them to destroy the family, and the law did eventually pass through parliament, at least in the UK.

Niall came away feeling he had done enough to keep his pride intact. He stood as a Green MP and failed to be elected but gained a position as a local councillor and was able to join a coalition of progressive councils. He didn't achieve much, consoled himself that Kirsten would have been proud (we both knew he was lying). It was Niall, not Finn, who married Leah in this particular future and their daughter was called Madeleine Kathryn. The entire family went back up to Scotland and joined a satellite community to the Alba Rising one that Niall and Kirsten had formed. This was tamer, more acceptable, less inclined to polyamory, more focused on nationalist politics. Niall and Leah divorced, but kept joint custody of their three children.

It felt like a nauseating UK version of the Waltons, but it wasn't a night attack and a bullet in the brain or a lingering descent into destitution ending in a faked road accident: nauseating was better than grimly fatal, right?

Wrong.

This was the second thing I learned as I combed the void: however far along the timelines I roamed, however widely I spread my net, when I looked a decade or so beyond the placid versions of the funeral, what I saw wasn't Penhaligon-Waltons skipping lightly into the sunset: I saw them all die.

And, yes, of course everyone dies.

But these were not timely deaths, entered into fully after a life well lived. These were not even a succession of 'accidents' wrought by power-stained individuals caught in the death throes of a predatory system.

The deaths of my family – and those of their children, when they

246

lived long enough to have any – were the grim, violent, terrified results of cultural breakdown that happens in every place at every time when resource flows fail and nobody has laid the groundwork for a viable alternative.

The exact details varied: climate apocalypse vied with rogue AI and half a dozen man-child wars to see which could most swiftly break the back of civilisation. In some futures, the six-continent, just-in-time supply chains collapsed as fossil fuels became too expensive and economically illiterate governments wholly owned by the fossil fuel companies watched people starve and freeze rather than push against their paymasters.

Or the mineral supply chains ground to a halt as copper and then lithium and then a host of minor-but-essential rare earths ran out and the capacity to build batteries, or solar panels, or wind turbines failed at the same time as fossil fuels became impossible to shunt around the planet.

Infrastructure that could have been built decades before wasn't there and nobody could organise priorities to make sure everyone was fed, warm, sheltered and had access to clean water.

In all the futures I saw, the end result was the same. Power grids failed, water mains collapsed, and industrial agriculture poisoned the land, rivers, air and oceans.

A desperate population burned the last trees for heat, light and cooking fuel in the name of survival and thus the world's forests became net carbon emitters instead of net carbon sinks, which tipped the whole living biosphere off the edge into extinction.

In a few hair-thin timelines, indigenous peoples in the deeper jungles and the highest mountains survived as they always had, pushed to the margins of a burning planet, but they were adaptable enough to keep going so that eight, ten, a hundred, a thousand generations down the line, they could teach their children about the weird white people who had tried to poison the soul of the earth and had poisoned themselves instead.

Mostly, though, the infantile tantrums of the world's leaders saw them dump glyphosate on the jungles and blow up the mountains on the basis that if they were dying, they were going to take everyone with them.

I saw more variations on the way humanity failed to transcend the adolescent phase of its evolution than I could ever have imagined. This was the desolation I'd seen in my second void-journey made real over and over and over again. If I hadn't also seen Kaitlyn as the flare of life amid the darkness with at least the possibility that there was a larger meaning behind her living and her dying, I would have stopped after the first dozen heartbreaking iterations.

But I had seen exactly this and eventually, when I had enough data points to map out the full spectrum of possibility, I stopped hurling power at the planes of time and let everything settle. The void was becoming a new second home: I understood its parameters and possibilities and could navigate them with remarkably little effort. But it was not a place from which to plan the intervention that I needed. With a twist of new intent, therefore, I gathered up Hail and returned both of us to the Between.

Welcome back, said Hail, from my right. 'That was well done.'

'Thank you.' I sat on the rock, revelling in its solidity. 'I'm going to propose some theories and you are going to help me find the holes in them. This is basic science: propose theory, test theory, propose new theory, repeat ad infinitum until no more holes. Fair?'

Hail nodded. *Fair.*

I took a while to order my thoughts. 'If I do nothing, Finn and Niall and Eriq and a whole host of people who have been kind to them, are going to die. If they persist in naming names and lifting the lid on what happened at Bancroft, they'll die fast. If they go for absolute passivity – and frankly Niall would have to be lobotomised for this actually to happen – they'll die in the kind of horror I saw when I came into the void with Bēi Fēng and we met Kaitlyn: the creeping desolation that annihilates all life.' I slanted a glance at Hail. 'Still fair?'

He nodded. There wasn't much to say.

'Kaitlyn believed there was a chance for change. When I saw her in the void, I saw the possibility of a generous, decent, flourishing life not just for our immediate descendants but for the whole living planet.

'This is a future I'd give anything to bring into being, but I didn't see it in any of the void-walks, which means it must happen in some version of the future in which I play a part. My question – the one I don't know how to test – is whether the future-Kaitlyn showed me a timeline that could genuinely happen.'

Hail lay in his usual place by the loch. He looked out across the water for a while, and then back at me. *The void cannot lie*, he said. *There are an infinite number of possible futures, but if you saw something when you were with Kaitlyn, that option may happen.*

'When I first went into the void for Finn, Crow told me I could never see the futures in which I played a part.'

You can't. That is, you shouldn't be able to. Kaitlyn . . . He paused to worry some burrs from the coarse hairs under his left foreleg. *I don't know what Kaitlyn did. She commandeered the rift that you had made and used it to show you . . . generalities. I don't think you saw exactly what you could do, am I right?* He looked pained that universal rules had been so easily broken, and unhappy with where that breaking led. *Did you see how to bring about this future Kaitlyn lived for?*

'No.' I knotted my fingers around my knees. 'No details.'

Well then.

'Still, it's not hard to imagine a middle way between the assault of that first funeral and the lobotomised passivity of the last ones. The boys abandoned Kirsten's core values, this was the first obvious mistake. They took their rage and fashioned of it a weapon of the worst kind. Kirsten would have been beyond horrified: she'd have done whatever it took to stop them.'

She would.

'But it's not just about stopping them from abusing power, it's about helping them to transcend the instinct to do so in the first place. If we can't all evolve beyond this one core bug in humanity's collective operating system, there's no hope. Kirsten understood this. Kaitlyn, too.'

Agreed.

'So if we take this as our baseline – that we need to step out of predictable responses – then I can feel a route through to things that might work. The problem is that I'd need to talk to someone who'd both listen to me and have the leverage to make things happen. Connor would be perfect, but I didn't see a single timeline where he wasn't broken.'

I said this uncertainly, waiting to be told I was wrong, but Hail laid his chin on his paws, every line of his body unstrung. *You will not find one. He cannot be what you need.*

We held a moment of grief together. The loch lost some of its lustre, and peace.

Presently, I said, 'If not Connor, then I need to find someone who will listen to me long enough to understand the possibilities, and who also has enough standing with Finn and Niall that they'll be listened to in their turn.' It took me a while to wrestle the next idea into words. 'I could ask Bēi Fēng. She stopped the storm when I was with Bright Rook and she showed me what to do in the void. She seemed to have a vested interest in Kaitlyn's future being the one that actually happened and I can't believe she wants to see Finn destroy himself?'

I didn't often frame statements as questions. In fact, most of my students knew it as a quick way to fail whatever they were trying to pass. So, we'll put this instance down to my fear of all the futures I'd seen and the idea that if I couldn't do something useful – maybe even if I did – one of them was going to happen.

Hail raised his head and studied me, carefully. At length, he said, *Lan, I can't tell you what to do, I can only offer support in decisions you make. But that sounds like a good idea. I think if you ask in the right way, Bēi Fēng may well be able to help.*

'Thank you.' I stood up. A certainty settled in my gut. 'I need to go back to the farm.'

Just don't try to wind time backwards, Hail said. *It won't work.*

My laugh sounded like Crow's. 'If I believed there was the slightest chance I'd succeed, I'd have done it already.'

Good. He nudged my arm with his nose. *Go, then.*

I thought of the farm in spring, of the ash tree that stood outside Finn's window, and set the time for the first hour of the first day of the first week after the shootings.

INTERLOGUE 2.3

Monday, 17 April 2023

I arrived in the ash tree outside Finn's bedroom.

No rage-cloud swirled over the farm yet: if I'd got anything right, I was a good four weeks from the funerals.

Over in the east, the first haze of grey tinted the night, and the buildings were all shrouded in early-morning mist. The air smelled cleanly of almost-frost and the start of spring. A pair of wood pigeons burbled to each other from the lime tree above the Piggery. A blackbird chucked at the vixen trotting purposefully down the hill towards the Dairy.

Moving onto the roof ridge of the farmhouse, I could feel the family sleeping beneath: Connor, Eriq, someone else ... Leah Koresh? It seemed likely. She had figured strongly in every one of the futures I'd seen; her role had changed from timeline to timeline, but her presence had not. When I checked the barn, Niall was sleeping downstairs in the room he always took. Kirsten's room next door to it was empty, as was Kaitlyn's room upstairs. The whole place felt hollow.

I reached for Finn with great care, and found him deep in a dream. I did consider joining him – the threads were easy enough to see, and he had not yet blocked his link to the earth, nor built the pressure cooker for his brother's rage – but we were less than seventy-two hours from his banishing of me and the rawness of it still curdled cold around his heart. I did not have the courage.

Instead, I retreated back up and out onto the roof of the farmhouse. The chimney was cold: Connor wasn't burning any more wood to keep the hungry ghosts at bay, but it was a stable place to sit.

Taking human form, I folded down cross-legged and began to construct images of a peach orchard, with a lake on its southern side covered in waterlilies; somewhere quite different from the cloud garden where I'd met Finn, yet with flavours the same.

Bēi Fēng arrived slowly, a sublimation of flowery scent and shimmering pastel colours that hardened into a woman as old as time, sharp of edge and mind, whose gaze asked a question of needs and wants and the difference between them.

I knew the answer, but tested it in my head before speaking aloud. 'I need to step into the dream of someone who can – and will – listen to me and who will be listened to in their turn. I think Eriq or Leah seem most likely, but if you have a better idea, I will listen to you.'

Until it didn't happen, I didn't know how much I wanted Bēi Fēng to let me know that Finn hadn't meant what he said, that I could safely enter his dreams and he'd greet me with joy and we could plan a way forward together.

No sense of this crossed between us. Instead, she tilted her head in thought and I sensed that she, too, was testing ideas. In time she stood, and cupped her palms together and raised them to waist height. Her hands were full of night. As a farmer sows grain, she cast it wide between us.

The ground ceased to be.

I fell through.

I came to rest in a desert at night: a monochrome landscape of undulating stillness that smelled of scorched silica. In the black sky, constellations wheeled above my head. They were moving too fast, just one step short of dizzying, but with an odd stop-start motion, as if time stuttered while I stood still. There was no pattern to their motion that I could find.

A light breeze patted my cheek. *Remember what you have been taught.*

Among the many things I had been taught in life and in death, first and last and all the way through, like letters in a stick of seaside rock, was the need to set a clear, clean intent.

Aloud, I said, 'I am here to ask permission to enter the dreaming of one who will listen and understand what is needful, and whose advice my family will heed.' Seeking the power of three, I repeated it twice more.

The stars slowed. When they came to rest, a lion was picked out on the horizon. Not the hazy, half-guessed and frankly imaginary shape of Leo that astrologers were so fond of. This was something more obviously leonine, also more obviously feminine.

It stepped down out of the sky and padded across the sand towards me. Leagues were eaten with each stride. The land shuddered with portents of earthquakes. A mile or two before it reached me, the beast stopped and sank down to its haunches. It lay alert, head up, forepaws stretched out. I could not see its face, but in the set of its ears was an invitation.

When I put my mind to it, I could move step-leagues across this desert, too. Arriving, I fell to my knees at its feet and crashed my brow to the sand. This was not an act of volition, more something that was drawn from the air and the sky and the sheer, incomprehensible *size* of this thing. Its paws were big as double-decker buses. Its head was bigger than the sun. It smelled of sky and stars and cat-breath.

With my face to the hot sand, I said, 'I wish to speak in the dream with the one you protect. Is this possible?'

Why do you wish this? The voice was the root-song of a mountain. My ears throbbed. I looked up into the face of a she-lion and saw also the face of a woman, long of nose and cheeks, high of brow. She looked like the busts of Nefertiti.

Of course she did; this was Egypt. And I had never been good at riddles.

Answers tied knots in my head. The Lion huffed a sound that could have been a laugh or the prelude to a roar that would bring the sky crashing down. The mountainous voice said, *There is no trick to this. All we require is absolute clarity.*

We.

I could have lost a lot of time wondering who was held in the circle of this plural.

Not now, though.

Now I needed to set the clearest intent I could muster. This, at least, I knew how to do. My words chose themselves.

'I stepped into the void and split open the futures. Each timeline led to terror and hatred, to the destruction of humanity, of all life. I believe there is at least one path leading to something worthwhile, to a future where all that is good and right and beautiful can flourish. I am here to find such a path and bring it into being.' If I can. If I have not succumbed to the most appalling hubris in history and completely overestimated my role in all this.

The silence stretched. Eventually, I looked up. As if she had been waiting for me, the Lion-woman tilted her head. Her eyes flickered through a range of greens and settled on a blood-tinged amber. *You will find the one you seek amid the roses.*

Roses? In the middle of the Egyptian desert? What's that if not a riddle, and I swear, I'm really bad at—

A breeze whispered past, carrying the deep, roiling meatiness of cat-breath – and the pale sunrise scent of roses.

I followed my nose and walked clockwise around the Lion. The end of its tail was unsettlingly fluffy. I trailed my fingers along and it felt as it looked: like catkins in spring. It twitched out from under my fingertips, testily. I moved on, faster.

Ahead of me was a high wall, in the rightmost third of which, a vast wrought-iron gate cast ornate star-shadows across the sand. In my hand, newly, was a key, also of iron, also of a scale to open the sky.

The lock turned with a silvered chime. The gate swung open of its own accord, and I was knocked back a pace by the gathered scent of all the world's roses.

The gate snicked shut, leaving me caught in a walled rose garden at sunset, on Midsummer's Eve. A low, late sun flowed gold along the horizon. The evening star made a single polished point.

'Hello?' My voice took a turn around the inner parts of the walls and came back alone. I stepped through an opening in a small box hedge and found a labyrinth laid out in roses, the kind with a single route that a toddler could navigate in and out of and be neither lost nor scared. I entered.

The roses at the entrance were pink, boringly ordinary. As the path curved round, they shaded down to colours deeper than old blood or burgundy and then in stages grew pale again, so that as I approached the disc of mown grass at the centre, they were white.

When I reached it, as is the way of dreams, the tiny patch of lawn expanded to become a wildflower meadow stretching to the horizon, with an ornamental lake in the centre.

Which was where I found the dreamer whose place this was, sitting on a wooden bench, facing the water.

Whoever it was did not have a clear hold on their dream. Even as I walked towards the bench, they faded away so I had no chance to guess a name. In the labyrinth, the roses became brown dust.

I stopped, and, after a while, like a slow breath, the dream-figure returned to almost-solidity, bringing back the roses and their scent.

And then, sometime later, they left.

And later still, returned.

I knew the rhythm of insomnia as well as I knew the farm. The next time the figure left, I sat in front of the bench directly in their eye-line.

On a count of twenty, they began to gain form. Around us, roses budded and bloomed, releasing a wash of scent. At the peak of their presence, I said, softly, 'If you look at me, I can help you stay here.'

For a heart-squeezing moment, I thought I had scared them away. I lost my nerve and turned aside, looking into the water rather than directly at their face. Perhaps this was enough. The faint reflection grew stronger on the mirrored surface of the lake until I could make out features and, at last, a name.

'Hello Leah.'

With barely a glance in my direction, Leah Koresh walked to the lake's edge and checked her reflection. Her gaze met mine on the water's flat surface, in the cagey way hairdressers make eye contact with their clients.

'Do I know you?'

Careful now. She had to go back into the lands of life and wakefulness and speak the absolute truth to my family, specifically to Finn, who would be on highest of high alerts as soon as she mentioned the word *dream*. So yes, Leah Koresh and I had met half a dozen times during her postgraduate studies, but I had looked much older then; I didn't think there was any great risk of her recognising me now.

'The Lion who guards the gates to this place let me through,' I said, truthfully. 'This wouldn't happen unless I were safe to be here, and you were safe in my presence.'

She was dressed in black again; a long linen suit with wide-hemmed trousers that flowed as she walked. Seen in the lake, the water swirled the fabric around her. I was shorter, but not by much, and older, but again, not by much. She still didn't look at me directly. 'You haven't answered my question.'

And had no intention of so doing. I asked, 'Do you have a date for the funeral?'

She didn't ask whose funeral, which was a good start. Her eyes narrowed, thoughtfully. 'They said they'd release the bodies by the end of the month. We have to miss the coronation, so we're going for the thirteenth.'

We, not *they*. So already she was involved in the planning. This hadn't been the case in every future I'd seen.

'What's today?'

'Last time I looked at my phone it was one in the morning on the seventeenth of April.'

Good. *Good.* I sank onto the grass.

When I looked up, she was studying me. 'If I offered to take you to the place where all dreams begin,' I said, 'would you come?'

Her face didn't change, but the scent of roses became softer and more penetrating, and I could see the evening star more clearly.

Rolling her tongue across her teeth, she said, 'Why does that sound like an offer I can't refuse?'

'I can't make you. You have to come of your own free will.'

'And still, it doesn't sound as if I have a choice.'

Fuck. I wasn't good at this. 'Leah, I'm not sure how long I can hold us both here. You trust the Lion and it let me through. I need you to trust me.'

'Then you'll have to be a lot less opaque. If the Lion let you get away with that kind of rubbish, it's not the right Lion.'

A huff of hot laughter reached us both. Leah smiled, which was a start.

'Let me show you.' The grass here was long, and in full-summer seed. I plucked a stalk and bent it into a V, then picked another and laid it at the tip, so the two together made a Y, which I laid on the bench behind us. When I looked up, she was studying the result with notable scepticism, but at least she was still there.

I spoke fast. 'Most of the time history rolls on day after day with its own momentum; people are born, they live, they die, the sum total of human life brings us a fraction along the path of our progress. But once in a while something happens that has the potential to change the course of everything, a fork in the greater road.'

I tapped the grass. Leah Koresh snorted in a way that asked if I really thought she needed a visual metaphor to explain the branching of time.

I needed it. I forged on. 'We have to take one way or the other; it's not an option to go on as we were. The events of the past few weeks have been the catalyst to a really major fork, maybe the last chance humanity has to make things right before climate chaos tips us over the edge. We are here.' I tapped the junction. 'If we turn one way—' a gesture left— 'humanity and the rest of life on the planet thrives. Your children's children could grow up in a world where life is actually worth living. If we take the other path—' a tilt to the right— 'this is . . . not the case.'

Her eyes searched my face. 'Bad?'

'Worse than you have the capacity to imagine. Worse than anything anyone has ever imagined.'

I watched her mind skitter over millennia of colonialism, of black holes and concentration camps, the living hell of simply being poor in a world where the price of everything topped the values of humanity. I saw her try to frame things worse than these, and shy away from the result.

'And you are telling me this, because . . .?'

'The funeral of the Penhaligon women is the fulcrum. What is said there in front of the world's screens, how it is said, the intent that flows into it and from it . . . all of this makes or breaks the future.' I swept the grass off the bench. By happy chance, the two strands separated, future and past, to fall either side of her feet. 'Finn and Niall respect you. They listen to you. They have asked you to help them plan the structure. I believe you have the capacity to nudge events in the right direction. You may be the only one who can.'

She picked up my good-future stalk and twirled it between thumb and forefinger. 'The entire future of humanity turns on me. Is this a joke?'

'Not just humanity. There's a lot of life that isn't human.'

Bad move. She lost solidity. Fast, I said, 'Leah, it's not a joke. I wish it were. If it makes you feel better, everything actually hangs on my persuading you to come with me to the place where you can see the possibilities. When you have seen how things go wrong – when you have *felt* it in the core of yourself – you and I can work out what might work instead.'

I stopped, breath held. I could see straight through the young woman sitting in front of me. The roses were scentless dust. But her eyes still gleamed, and they were focused on my face. I said, 'So really, the pressure is all on me, and I'm afraid I'm screwing it up, even as we speak.'

She laughed, thinly. 'Is it fair, that so much should turn on someone so obviously . . .' a flip of a hand that already had more detail, 'fallible?'

'I don't make the rules, I'm just trying to explain them.' Heaven help me, I was channelling Crow. Not that this was necessarily bad, but this place needed – demanded – total integrity.

I thought about truth and need and honesty, and when I spoke, even I could hear the difference. 'Leah, what we are doing here is not an exact science and I'm a novice. I don't know why it's down to me or to you, and we'd both be better if we had guides with more experience, but we are where we are, and we do the best we can do, and if it's not enough at least we tried. Is that not why you became a journalist when you could have been powering on up the academic ladder on a post-doc at MIT?'

She had been staring at the water. Her head snapped up. 'I *do* know you!'

I ignored her. 'The place where the futures thread out from is in total emptiness. It's not a fun place to be. Frankly, it's terrifying. But your Lion let me through to you.'

She pondered this for a long time. Her eyes were big and smoky. She had the same grace and power as the god outside. Just when I thought I had failed, she gave a smile that made my heart sing. 'At least I'm asleep. For that, I'll face a lot of things. And I can always have it out with Herself at the gate when we come back if I don't like it.'

That I would like to see.

I didn't say so aloud, but whatever Leah read in my face was enough to make her laugh. She swept her hair back from her face, and looked like the media professional she'd become. 'I have to be up and sane by seven, so if we're going somewhere, we'd better go soon.'

She grinned. I felt lighter by the second and just this lightness started us moving. The wind began to whistle around us. Paradoxically, the roses snapped into full bloom.

I grabbed Leah's hand. 'More than anything, please remember that all you have to do is watch what unfolds. We must not interfere. It would be very, very bad if we got caught in the place we are going and were unable to return. You'll understand quite how bad when we're there. Please hold on to the absolute fact that you *must not move*, else we'll be stuck. Don't speak. Don't let go of my hand. Got it?'

'I have to not move, not do anything, and not panic in any way, or we get trapped in a place that clearly scares you rigid.' Her big eyes burned into mine. 'You have to trust me as much as I'm trusting you.'

'Really.'

She squeezed my hand. 'I'm ready if you are.'

Until this moment, I'd had no idea whether I could take a living, breathing human into the void. I hadn't known it would be necessary, or even useful. But intent is a beast of its own volition and once set on a trail, it doesn't give up.

I laced my fingers through Leah Koresh's longer ones and the rose garden faded around us.

'Fuck. Fuck. Fuckfuck*fuck*!'

There are a large number of intonations an intelligent, creative – and deeply shocked – human mind can bring to this one word. On our return from the void, Leah Koresh cycled through most of them.

I held her hand while she did so, standing by her dream-lake in her dream-rose garden. Everything was insubstantial at first, but the scent grew stronger as she stabilised, followed by a wash of pastel pinks, and then the ground took on a familiar solidity.

Last, the lake became liquid instead of just an empty space. The low sun and the evening star punched motes of fire onto the water. Our reflections became visible. Abruptly, the swearing stopped.

Leah and I were still holding hands. I unhooked my fingers from the talon that her grip had become and guided her to the bench at the water's edge. She folded into a sit, as if her bones knew how to do this, and the rest of her was newly catching on.

In several of the alternative futures I had witnessed, both alone and just now in her company, Leah had drunk coffee. This was not my dream, but I gave it the right kind of attention, and two big, fat-bellied, stoneware mugs appeared on the bench: milk in both, no sugar. I passed one over, handle first. 'It's hot. Don't drink it fast or you'll burn your tongue.'

She stared at me without recognition.

'Leah?' I tapped her knee. We knew each other now, as well as anyone can who has seen a fellow being's soul stripped to the bone. I waited a while and tapped again.

On the third tap, she shook herself like a dog out of water, and scooted back on the bench. Her eyes flared wide.

'Fuck.'

'Might be time to expand our repertoire a little?'

I used my tutorial tone, and it worked. She looked at me with some of the old sentience. 'Is it always like that?'

'Generally. With luck you won't ever have to go there again. Drink your coffee, it'll help ground you back to the here and now.'

She looked down at her mug, back up at me. 'I'm still dreaming?'

'As far as I can tell.'

'Dream-coffee, huh? Who knew?' She drank, though, and became more stable, and presently her gaze drifted across the lake towards the evening star.

'I didn't see what to do to make things come out right.'

'No. We never do. If we were shown how to act, we'd be puppets and there'd be no point. Instead, we are shown what to avoid. You saw this in some detail: the things we'd give our lives to keep from happening, yes?'

'Fuck, yes! Sorry. Repetition. But absolutely, yes, I could spend the next year telling everyone what *not* to do, starting with, it's a really, really bad idea for Finn and Niall to weaponise every scintilla of rage and pain they can dredge up and then power it out to the world. Which may be obvious, but it's unlikely to get much traction if I can't suggest something better.'

She looked at me over the top of her mug. 'You didn't enjoy that any more than I did and you clearly knew what we were heading for, which puts you way ahead of me on the curve. You want to throw me some ideas?'

Would that I could. Leaning back against the bench, I looked out across the quiet water of the lake. Venus was still balanced on the horizon, reflected as a single sharp point. A wasp came to visit, but only briefly. A skylark roused up out of the meadow and turned gyres in the evening air.

And in all of this was the first thread of an answer. 'Your actions have to arise from the core of who you are, that's the single most important thing. There's a particular feeling when things are right: a clarity, an integrity, a sense of flow. For you, it'll probably have some of the same textures as this place.' I gestured to the vibrant life of the flower meadow, at the roses in their tangled labyrinth. 'If you were to distil your sense of this place into a few words, what would they be?'

Leah nodded, absently. I watched her attention slide inwards and, because scrutiny was likely as uncomfortable for her as it was for me, I held most of my attention on the water.

'The Lion's Grace.' She was still inward when she spoke, her eyes still closed, her words slow, as if they were forming anew from the soil at our feet. 'From the beginning I've always felt this particular grace that the Lion embodies that feels . . . right. It's got exactly the sense of clarity and flow and integrity you described. When I was at college, it helped me find the best questions to ask for my thesis. Now, I try to remember it in my interviews; a willingness to listen in good faith, and not bring all my stuff to the conversation.'

'That must be hard to maintain in a world where everyone brings bad faith to the table.'

She gave a wry smile. 'I try. I don't always succeed.'

'But you know the feeling. If you can help the others to embody the Lion's Grace, that'll be a good baseline. Eriq won't be a problem, he'll understand a Lion in the desert and he'll be wholly respectful. Niall will be sceptical, but Kirsten would have got the idea of the Lion's Grace in a heartbeat and he'll hear you through the memory of her if you can do it without pushing him deeper into grief. Finn'll be easier. He has the grounding of the Shaolin when he chooses to use it. His teacher is Běi Fēng, the North Wind, who brought me here. She knows your Lion. Together, the two of them will help, I think.'

Blast.

Alanna Penhaligon, you irredeemable idiot.

When the silence had stretched thin enough to see through, Leah said, 'Findley Penhaligon not only lost his living family on the day of the shooting, he lost a connection that stretched beyond the boundaries of life and death; one that had sustained him more than he realised till it was gone. He cut it because he believed his grandmother was at least in part responsible for the deaths of his mother and his sisters. Sins of omission, I think, rather than commission, but still . . . was he right?'

It turned out there was catharsis in speaking to someone who was willing to listen. 'Finn's grandmother loved her family enough to remain in the place between life and death, in honour of a promise. Two promises, actually. The first was to Finn, to be here for him when he needed it. The second was made to Kaitlyn, to support her in fulfilling her life's purpose.'

Leah glanced at me, sideways. 'Maybe drop the third person?'

And this, too, was like shedding a load I hadn't realised I was carrying. 'I gave that second promise, having seen the tweet and the early repercussions,' I said, and Leah's smile faded. 'I had been taken into the void. You've seen what that's like. We're shown a lot of things we never want to see again and given precious little idea of where to go instead. Kaitlyn met me there – an older, wiser version of Kaitlyn that existed outside time – with nothing to suggest her death was imminent. She showed me a glimpse of a future worth having and I believed her when she told me it was possible. Even so, if I'd known the shooting was going to happen, I'd have risked everything to prevent it.' I was speaking too fast and with too much feeling. I stopped.

'Even the future of humanity? Would you have risked that?'

'To save my family? Probably.'

Leah nodded. Her smile was quite different.

Bees droned themselves to sleep in the quiet. The sun had sliced down into the horizon. She said, 'When I can't sleep, I try telling myself the bastards would have found another day, another way, that the debate was just a convenient time and place. Even so, I'll spend the rest of my life wondering whether they'd still be alive if I'd turned Oscar down when he asked me to Chair.'

'That's a lot to carry, Leah.'

'And it's mine to deal with.' She plucked a stem of grass, twisted it into a ring, threw it into the breeze. We both watched it fall. 'I came to your tenth anniversary seminar series in 07,' she said. 'Do you remember?'

'Do I remember your being there? Sorry, no.' Abbey Hall was full; the audience was a blur. 'Do I remember the words? Definitely.' It was the closest I ever came to speaking aloud what I really believed. '*Weaving the New Mythology: The role of language, frame and metaphor in shaping a core narrative for the twenty-first century.*' Incongruously for an English rose garden, a scarab beetle half an inch long strolled across the ground between my feet. I watched its progress. 'Not the catchiest of titles. I'm amazed anyone came.'

'Then dying's scrambled your brains. Word had got out that this was Warden Penhaligon really going for it and we'd have swum through starving sharks to be there.' Leah eyed me aslant. 'When I met Kaitlyn, I did already know where she got her radicalism from.'

'She was channelling Niall.'

'Who was – is – channelling you.'

I blushed, which is not a thing I knew I could still do. 'Thank you.'

Her dream-laugh was warm and sunned more roses into bloom. Their scent wrapped us together.

She said, 'I didn't understand half of what you were saying, but I got the bit about needing to change the narrative: that as long as the money-men were peddling a reality predicated on scarcity, separation and powerlessness, we'd never get to a future worth living. I applied to Radical FM the next morning.'

'Wait, what? *I'm* the reason you left college?' I grabbed the bench behind me for stability. 'Felicity Zhao will *kill* me.'

'Again?'

'Yes! I mean, no, obviously. I mean, if she'd known this while I was still alive, she'd have ripped my guts out and strung them round the orchard like fairy lights. You were her next big thing. You were going to transform the entire field of neurolinguistics. You were—'

'I was a question looking for an answer and Prof Zhao didn't have it.' Leah picked up the scarab and set it marching in the other direction. 'What I've learned since, though, is that pushing against the mainstream is a mug's game. Even before the debate, I'd started thinking again about what you said.'

'Which bit of what I said?' I'd given five one-hour seminars spread over a week. 'There was quite a lot in there.'

'Right at the end. When you went ad-lib.' She looped her hands above her head and leaned back, looking up through the lace of her fingers. In tones more clipped than I had heard so far, she quoted me back to myself. 'The divisions in our society are not there by accident, nor are they a given. Humanity is a prosocial species. For three hundred thousand years, our forager-hunter ancestors lived as an integral part of the web of life. Humanity, if you like, was the part of the web that gained self-consciousness and could work with clear intention. But about ten thousand years ago we took a wrong turn and we've marched ourselves down a cul-de-sac where all we know is that buying more stuff is never going to fill the great, gaping hollow inside.'

I had been skating close to so many edges, I hadn't thought anyone had understood, never mind they'd remember all this time later.

Heartened, I took over, the words clean and whole and sharp. 'We need a circuit-breaker. A fresh start. The contained encounter with death that every whole and healthy culture has ever given its young people so they can find the courage to set down the insecurities of childhood and step with confidence into the commonwealth of adults. Imagine what we could be if we brought the best of our technology together with the best of our humanity in service to life instead of endlessly destroying it.' I'd been quoting Pakak pretty much verbatim. I did reference him. I'm not sure many people noticed.

Leah rolled over to rest on one elbow. 'Could this be the circuit-breaker? For everyone, I mean, not just your family.'

A light breeze ruffled the surface of the lake. I saw a steppe eagle skull in the sculpted water; it turned to face me, blank eyes filled with smoke and possibility.

Prickle-skinned, I said, 'These kind of things only work if they're embraced consciously.'

'Right. Everyone has to be on board. They have to jump at it.' She thought about it. 'Maybe not everyone, but enough.'

'That's still a big number, Leah. How would you make it happen?'

'I don't know.' She shrugged, sharply. 'I don't even know if I'm right. I could just be grabbing at an idea, trying to turn it into something good, all the while wading into the mire of cultural appropriation. That's perfectly possible.'

The eagle flew over the water. Uuri's breath sang warm in my ear. 'Or you could be thinking at the scale we need. We both saw the horror in the void. Nothing small will work now.'

The textures around us wove more tightly. The margins of the lake became more distinct. A dragonfly hovered over reeds and then darted towards us. Leah said, 'I don't want to dishonour Kaitlyn, Kirsten, Maddie. Their deaths weren't . . . they were more than a momentary meme.'

'They would want a fitting memorial, though.' The dragonfly sped a jerky zigzag to the centre of the lake and back. 'I am imagining a world where eight billion people start behaving like adults. Actual adults.' Big-hearted, strong-hearted, clear-hearted, full-hearted adults like Pakak and Uuri. 'What could be a more fitting remembrance?'

'You're being kind.'

'I think I am being rather brutal. You are the one who has to make it happen. I'm just throwing out ideas. The key is going to be bringing the boys on board.'

'Without mentioning you, obviously.'

'Please.'

'That'll be interesting.' She stood and, Niall-like, began to pace along the edge of the lake. 'The boycotts are still going, and

265

the whole #PornGate thing. Kaitlyn's Digital Army dialled back a bit after the shootings, but we don't control them. Re-orienting the whole movement towards something bigger is not going to be easy.'

'You'll have help, though. The Lion isn't just a source of grace. You can ask for its advice when you need it, and there may be things it can do in the wider dream that will help shift people to something constructive instead of destructive. Also . . .' The dragonfly came to hover directly in front of us, and then sped away again. The edges of the lake were becoming less distinct.

Rising, I touched Leah's shoulder. 'How often do you dream the dragonfly?'

'I've never seen it before.' She frowned. 'Does it matter?'

'Maybe not, but we've been here a long time. If we go on much longer, you'll wake feeling as if you've run a marathon, which might not be ideal.'

'Fuck, no.' She dragged her hands down her face. 'Interview with the Health Minister in the morning, to see if I can get him to say why he hates the prime minister. Proper sleep would be good.' She stood up. 'What happens if I forget all this?'

'We wouldn't be here if you were likely to forget.'

'OK. Thank you.' She held out her hand. We shook, and then, disconcertingly, she raised my palm and kissed it, folding my fingers over.

'It's been an honour to meet you.' Behind her, the lake hummed with the green-gold life I had seen in Kaitlyn's future. 'I don't know how, but I will do whatever I can to make this work, to bring the Lion's Grace to the funeral, and to create a circuit-breaker that will work. And I won't tell the guys that I met you. On all of these, I give you my word.'

A promise, freely given. A blast of hot breath welded it in place. Beyond the entrance to the labyrinth, the gate through which I had entered blinked back into being. The dragonfly flickered there and back, then settled just in front of us.

Leah regarded it, soberly. 'How do I sleep more deeply? Always when I dream like this, I wake up straight away.' The prospect crushed her where the void had not.

266

This was not my dream, but I had made coffee, which was no small feat: I had some agency. 'Would you let me make a place for you to sleep?'

'You can do that?'

'I have a place that works for me. I think I can bring it here.'

Fervently, 'Please.'

Closing my eyes, I walked the paths of my own dreams and, so doing, brought them into being. At a particular turn on a particular track, I felt the world around me shift and slide into a new, hybrid shape.

Encouraged, I said, 'If you follow the dragonfly to the south-west of the lake you'll find a wooden gate.' I pointed back over her left shoulder. 'Go through that and down the spiral path that takes you from there to the river. There's a place to sleep there, shaded by hazel boughs in full nut. You'll know it when you get there. If you lie with your head pointing upstream, you'll sleep well.'

She frowned into the distance. 'I don't see a gate.'

'You will when you get there.' I offered a quick embrace. 'Go quickly, while the dream still holds. You'll sleep until just before your alarm rings and feel better when you wake.'

She was already halfway there. Her voice floated back on a lift of roses and autumn grasses. 'Give my love to the Lion on the way out.'

The Lion waited for me at the far side of the gate, on the edge of sunrise. The desert sand was cooler. Skeins of migrating birds flew high overhead in a sky that was already painfully blue.

'Leah sends her love.'

Indeed. The beast was all feline now, no woman to it at all. I edged round it, clockwise. It moved a paw to block my path. I looked up. It curled a lip. Its canines were the circumference of my torso and three times the length of my body.

'What?' I asked. And then, tetchily, 'I have done everything I can.'

Whence go you now?

This had enough of the cadence of a riddle that my guts curled in on themselves. Even when I teased out the strange grammar, I still had no answer and I was too tired to think. Maybe I could just lie down and sleep? Images of Leah lying somnolent beside the river flooded my mind. Sleep would be grand. A century or two might do the trick.

Sleep? the Lion asked, and the word crashed at my feet, freighted with duty and guilt.

Blindingly, I remembered Kate, the sun-bridge, the invisible barrier I had not been able to cross. Except Crow had said I could cross now, that *we* could cross, the two of us, and, actually, now that there was nothing binding me, I might have to, thereby leaving the weight of all the worlds on the shoulders of the young woman I had left sleeping under the hazel boughs. '*I will do whatever I can to make this work . . .*'

Leah Koresh had not asked for my help. I had not offered it.

Yet.

Tilting my head back, the better to look straight into the green-gold eyes, I said, 'Can I offer you a promise?'

One brow peaked up. The Lion did not say no. I took time to line up words that would work, and only those.

'I offer to you, Lion of Koresh, this promise: that I will do whatever I can to assist the young woman whose dream is the rose garden to fulfil the task she has undertaken. Specifically, I will do whatever I can to help humanity cleave to the path in which all life on this planet flourishes in perpetuity.' I stopped. Something else nudged forward. I added, 'I give this freely. It is the third such promise I have made.'

She did nod, then, and an ache lifted away from my soul. I stood a little taller.

I accept your oath, Alanna Penhaligon. Freely offered. Freely taken.

With terrifying delicacy, the Lion extended a claw and, reaching out, pricked the underside of my arm. I bled a single drop of bright, arterial blood. Where it fell, a rose pushed up out of the sand, and unfurled a single bud. The colour was so darkly blue as to be black. It shimmered, as Crow did, newly preened, like a wash of early light on an oil spill.

When I looked up, the Lion had gone. New constellations wheeled steadily overhead. A mountainous voice said, *You are free to go.*

*

At the sun-bridge, I made sure I was in human form as I walked the last few strides along the shoreline.

The light was less blinding. The mist had gone. Crow had moved back to the apple tree. At the sun-bridge, the scent of scorched iron and oiled wood was so tangible I could have spun it into coloured threads and woven the history of our lives therefrom.

But not of our deaths. To whoever was listening, I said, 'Did everyone except me know I had a choice to make?'

The weft of Kate's scent was touched with autumn smoke and the rain in Glasgow, with love and regret, both. Behind her a murmuration of crows bled across the sky.

In the tree beside me, the one Crow that I knew said, *Only those of us that love you. Are you angry?* Its feet cramped on the apple bough.

'No.' Tired, I leaned against the trunk. 'You couldn't have said anything. A promise – this promise above all the others – had to be freely given.'

Indeed.

'This one feels more open-ended than the other two.'

You knew this when you made it.

Which was the point, but still . . . 'Can I come back here?' I didn't want to end up like Connor, trapped in a thousand lifetimes with no rest between.

When the time is right, I believe so. I hope so.

Parts of me that were holding together shook loose a little. A little certainty would have been nice.

Once again, Crow flew forward and landed amid the kaleidoscope of regret and pride and love that was Kate. Something shifted and – perhaps a last gift? – I could see them both clearly. Crow sat on Kate's shoulder. They nudged cheek to cheek in a way that spoke of long familiarity, and of love.

'Crow, are you leaving, too?' I tried not to sound panicked, and failed. 'Do you have to?'

Do I have to? No. Am I going to? A long, stretching wait. *I am tired, Lan. And it is time. I am free to cross the boundary now, when before I was not. You could hold me here, I think. Will you do so?*

Of course not. I was weeping. It was a long time since I had done so. 'I'll miss you.'

And I you. Truly. But you will not grow if I am here, and you need to grow. I need to let you grow. Just remember that each cycle round is new. Take nothing for granted. Everything flows from this.

'You know I don't understand a word you just said, right?'

Crow croaked a laugh that was halfway to a sob. *But it will not always be so. All things will become clear. I swear this is true.* It bobbed a deep bow. *Farewell, Lan. When you are ready, I will be here, I promise.*

'Truly?' The weight of it was as solid as any of the oaths I had offered, the gods heard as clearly.

Truly. Crow did not move, but the scent of skin and passion saturated all that I was in an embrace as real as any Kate and I had ever shared, and as transient.

'Goodbye,' I said, but they had already gone.

Book Three

— THE POSSIBLE PATH —

You never change things by fighting the existing reality.
To change something, build a new model that makes the
existing model obsolete.

— Buckminster Fuller (attrib.)

When we are dreaming alone, it is only a dream.
When we are dreaming with others, it is the beginning
of a reality.

— Dom Helder Camara (quoted in *Post Capitalist*
Philanthropy by Alnoor Ladha and Lynn Murphy)

CHAPTER FIFTEEN

'So, a Gen Z and a Boomer walk into a bar . . .'

No toxic cloud hung over the farm. In this, the live, happening-in-the-flow-of-time, Lion's Graced iteration of the funeral, a brisk breeze soughed through the Rookery. If I stretched my senses wider than the world of my family, I could catch on its wings the scent of burned sand, hot breath and roses.

In the land of the living, grief filled the pavilion, and not a little rage, but it was a relatively clear and peaceful Finn who stood at a lectern on the dais and finished his speech with Kaitlyn's favourite joke. Or at least, he told the one joke among her recent repertoire that was least likely to offend any of the people packing the pavilion, or the millions watching live around the world.

'And they order coffees: oat milk latte for one and double espresso for the other – and if I need to tell you which is which, you need to tell me which colony of Mars you've been locked away in for the past thirty years. Anyway, they start talking about all the things wrong with the world because, with things as they are, what else would you do, right?'

He checked out the audience, live and online: his gaze bright across the room. This was the Finn I had known, the true, clear inheritor of Mo's teaching and Bēi Fēng's wisdom, a soul capable of embodying the resilience Leah's dream required.

Whether he was doing so or would continue so to do was another question entirely, but I had paid enough attention to the preparations that I was prepared to hope.

He said, 'This is Kaitlyn's joke, and those of you who have only come to know her in the past month might think they'd be talking about pornography and the industrial abuse of young women by the purveyors of late-stage predatory capitalism.

'But actually, because this is Kaitlyn's joke, they start with climate chaos and ecosystem collapse and dead zones in the oceans and the runoff from industrial agriculture and the toxic rain, full of Forever Chemicals and the downhill slide to the sixth mass extinction with side orders of rogue AI and nuclear war. Because these, too, were the things my younger sister cared about. And, obviously the Gen Z—' he said it 'Zee' in the American way— 'thinks every last part of this is the Boomer's fault and the Boomer is super-defensive and says it's just the way the world is and what could they have done differently and young people today don't realise how hard it was to get a university degree even when you got a full grant and didn't have to hold down three jobs so your loan stayed under six figures; or how risky it was to buy a house when a five-figure mortgage felt like a lot; or how important it was to keep going with the holiday flights to the sun even when they were so obviously wreaking climate havoc, because hey, how else do we have fun? And anyway, don't you know it's easier to imagine the extinction of the entire human race than the end of economic growth?'

Finn stepped away from the lectern, pulled a chair from the shadows in the back of the dais, flipped it back to front and straddled it, with his arms across the back, the way Jan Westbrook had done on her first morning's briefing at the farm.

Nobody outside the family knew the resonance of this, but I could sense the gathering of Jan's attention, the newness of it, just as I could feel that Maddie, Kirsten and Kaitlyn had been here from the start.

The encounter with Ellen had taught me a great deal about the nature of the veils that both joined and separated the lands of life from the Between, and the Between from the Beyond. I was fairly sure Maddie, Kirsten and Kaitlyn could not engage with the living any more than I could but there was nonetheless a sense of distant holding that felt kind and clean and this, like so much else, was encouragingly different from anything I'd seen in the void.

The pavilion was the same, the layout of the seating and the giant screens on the side and back walls were the same, but otherwise

. . . the drapes on the back wall were no longer navy blue, but a pale dawn-sun yellow; the coffins were silver-grey felt, petalled with blackthorn and elder; a scent of roses drifted past, pushed by a small fan hidden below the dais; the music at the start was no longer Kaitlyn's favourite strain of strangled cats, but a recording of Eriq playing his Brazilian cavaquinho in a melody that managed to be at once hauntingly mournful and light.

Leah had changed the order of seating, too. Torvald was in the middle near the front, but Frances Nolan had been shunted far back on the left. For obvious reasons Leah herself was now in the front row with Connor on one side and Matt and Jens on the other. A remarkably quiet, un-vengeful Nazir kept watch from the row's end.

By mutual agreement, the rest of Jan's team had departed as soon as the inquest was over, but Nazir had asked to stay for the day and nobody'd had the heart to turn him down.

Exactly what this entailed had not, as far as I could tell, been worked out, but he wore a pale green GG-branded sweatshirt now, and his hair hung loose around his shoulders, which made his nose look less like a beak. Above all, like Finn, he looked more peaceful than he'd done in any of the void-visions. At this stage, it was all that mattered.

Taking the seat, Finn had paused a moment, to let the silence settle. Now, more quietly than before, he said, 'These are old arguments. We don't have to rehash them here, and anyway, the point is that they're friends, these two, and they don't want to chew over old stuff forever, either. So in the end, the Gen Z says, "This is hopeless. What we need is someone who can see both sides: a Millennial with a degree in neuropsychology and a PhD in behavioural economics and a few years of post-doc in a climate lab. But where are we ever going to find one of those?"

'And the Boomer throws up her arm and yells, "Waiter! We need you over here!"'

The pavilion billowed to the laughter of eighty or so mourners (fewer than before, more carefully chosen: warmer). Finn tipped a glance at the huge screens on the walls where some showed images of Maddie, Kirsten and Kaitlyn at their best, but over half hosted incoming streams from audiences around the world: live feeds of rooms packed with raised faces all caught on wide-angle video, or Zoom galleries, forty to a page, with a dozen pages at a time.

Each was identified by location, prefixed by the Kaitlyn, Kirsten and Maddie Will Live Forever hashtag: #KKMWLF-Stuttgart, -Ocotal, -Kampala, -Adelaide, -Ottawa, -Limerick, -Budapest, -Cochabamba . . .

Many of these were local groups of Kaitlyn's Digital Army, the autonomous, self-organising chapters that had formed to push the #SSS boycotts. These were still organising new boycotts, but since the shootings they'd joined in a loose confederacy and had agreed to co-ordinate with Charm and the Ghosts.

Renamed for the funeral, they represented the bulk of the new hashtags, but not all, by any means: there was a steady trickle of new groups nobody had seen before.

Loudspeakers spread around the pavilion imported waves of laughter from every one of these. Even if they'd heard this one before, Finn's delivery made it fresh, and earned him a ripple of applause. Already, this was not a funeral where shades of English decorum held everything constrained.

Rising from the chair, Finn gave a kind of salute to the image of his mother and sisters at the back of the pavilion, and then stepped back, making way for his brother.

Niall was dressed in the same style as Finn: washed-out jeans with a pale, smoky grey shirt of Kirsten's design, that had a world tree printed on the back. He looked relaxed, which was a testament to how utterly deceptive looks can be.

In the first days after the shootings he had been a dead man walking, a shadow whose only animation had been the ceaseless flow of tears. That they had been silent by the second morning had not made their flow less fierce, or the pain that wrought them less keen.

A week later, when Juke, Hawck, Charm and the others had presented their findings on the motives behind the shooting, he had wrapped a deep, volcanic rage around himself exactly as I'd seen him do in the void.

*

But Leah had seen it, too, and was prepared, or so we'd both thought, and she'd had nearly a month to lay the groundwork of a new path.

She had been honest about the dream: her task would have been impossible had she not spelled out in detail the hell she'd seen in the many versions of the void. She had spoken, too, of the Lion and its Grace and I had been right about Eriq: the mention of the desert and a beast that stepped down out of the night sky had steadied him as little else could have done.

About the other two, I had been wholly wrong.

At first, Finn had refused to listen to anything Leah said. He was still white-hot furious with me and any mention of dreams or dreaming drove him from the room. If Eriq hadn't so clearly wanted to keep Leah as part of the team, he'd have told her to get lost.

Then, at two o'clock in the morning on the Saturday after our joint dream, Leah had gone up to his room to interrupt his Arena match.

'You dream with the North Wind?' she asked.

He ended the game before it was over, which was not a thing I'd ever seen. 'How do you know?'

'I *dreamed* it, Finn. I've been telling you for days.'

'The Lion's Grace. Right.' He shoved his chair back from his desk, one step short of bolting from the room.

Arms crossed, Leah stood in the doorway, trapping him in. 'I want you to dream to Běi Fēng and ask what she thinks we should do.'

'She doesn't . . .' At least he sat down again. 'I can't just summon her.'

'If you want me to stay, then you'll try.' It was the first time any of us had seen Leah angry. Leaving, she slammed his bedroom door behind her and I was the only one who saw the fear on her face as she leaned back against it.

Me? I was terrified.

It worked, though. The Finn who joined the others for breakfast the next day was at least open to listening, and on the day after he brought his laptop with connection to Charm and the Ghosts, to offer digital help.

That left Niall, and while citing Kirsten's understanding of grace might have helped, not even Leah dared go there.

Niall wasn't eating much and was sleeping less. He sat in on the strategy meetings, but the family's chief strategist offered nothing beyond the occasional nod and these only when he was explicitly addressed.

Even on the night before the funerals, nobody had known if he'd do what he'd been asked, or drag them all down one of the many paths that led straight to destruction.

That night, both Leah and Finn asked for help in the dreams. I have no idea if their requests were answered, but Niall at least got some sleep, and when he woke I saw him reach for the gaping hole where Kirsten had been and begin to freeze himself off from it.

Watching this happen was like watching someone pour ice across a lake so deep and dark that even to look into it was to drown. When I gave it the right focus, I could feel the frigid air of his new creation, could taste its tension and map in nauseating detail the disintegration that must attend its breaking.

I didn't like it, but it wasn't my call: the rest of the family had embraced the change without remark or consternation or any of the other things that might have cracked what he had wrought, and it was this ice-bound, walled-off Niall who took his place at the lectern now, and blinked amiably out across the mourners.

'Well, that was fun. Kaitlyn, if you're watching, I hope you felt we did it justice.' He pulled a smile and it looked real. 'Finn and Eriq have spoken of those we love, of the loss to us and the world. But now is the time to speak of their legacy. We can't watch our family shot in front of us and just plant rose bushes on their graves and walk away. They were not like this and we're not like this and I don't think the world wants us to be. They deserve something bigger: something future generations will thank us for.'

He paused and the silence prickled. Anyone who knew anything about Niall knew he wasn't into half-measures. With a nod to their waiting, he leaned one elbow on the lectern as if he were leaning on a bar in the west end of Glasgow, talking activism and politics through the night.

'In our case, this means letting go of our rage against those who destroyed our family for no better reason than that they wanted to keep the fossil-fuelled bonanza of the Death Cult going for a few more years.'

Fuck. This hadn't been in any of the rehearsals. In the front row, Leah's head snapped up. In all the realities to which I had access, time and possibility stalled.

Niall smiled, faintly. 'Letting go is hard,' he said. 'Perhaps the hardest thing we've been asked to do. The urge to go on the rampage in an orgy of righteous anger is overwhelming and I'm not sure many of you would stand in our way.' Niall lowered his gaze to Leah's and held it a moment, before looking out once more to the wider world.

'But we're not going there. My mother would not want it. My younger sister would not want it. My twin ... Kirsten would be beyond horrified. Honestly, I doubt she'd ever speak to me again.'

And ... breathe. Leah's shoulders lost some of their woodenness. I unclamped my Crow's feet from the roof strut. From the immediate audience came a murmur that was part understanding and part support and mostly just a release of tension they'd not known they were holding.

Niall pushed on, still off-script, but not completely off-piste. 'We have been told—' a fractional nod that gathered in Eriq and Finn and ended on Leah— 'that we could view this moment, this whole ghastly, cataclysmic, soul-wrenching, devastating horror – as a rite of passage, an initiation, if you will. That sometimes – maybe, perhaps – we could use it as a circuit-breaker so complete that we leave behind all that we've known and become all we could be. In short, we – and now I mean all of us here, perhaps all of us in the wider world – could make of this a turning point away from our race to self-destruction.'

He grabbed the seat that Finn had carefully left on the dais, flipped it round to face the front and sat down, pulling one knee up onto the other thigh. I'd never seen any rehearsals with this, either, but he'd been brought up around the stage far more than Finn had; he knew how to use a prop.

'To say I was resistant to this idea would be a grievous understatement. It's too big. It's pretentious. It takes a private, devastating grief and expects the impact to spread to people we don't know, who don't know us and who didn't, to be brutally honest, know our mother or our sisters as anything other than pixels on a screen. Each of these things is true.'

He looked down at his hands. 'And yet we *are* in the middle of the sixth mass extinction. We *are* in the dying days of the old order. Everything *is* going to be different from here on in. It's quite possible we might look back on this time now as the good old days and if that doesn't terrify you, please let me have some of whatever you're smoking.'

A rustle of laughter came from the pavilion and was echoed on the speakers and Niall forced another smile. 'If we – all of us – don't do *something* new, none of us are to make it through.'

He brought his gaze up again. 'Kaitlyn and I used to talk about what it would mean to be a good ancestor. She wasn't planning on having kids, particularly, but good ancestors are the ones you look back on, the people who inspired you, the people who, with a hundred thousand small acts, paved the way for the generations who come after them to live decent lives. We all need to be the good ancestors now, which means trying new things, even things that make us curl up inside.'

Standing, he squared his shoulders and this one gesture said more about how much he was curling up inside than all the words in the world. 'So we're going to try this, however weird it feels. We're going to see if we can make this be our circuit-breaker and step forward from this moment with the best grace we can muster. We're going to experiment not just with different ideas, but with a different way of being. We're going to step out into the world as if people matter, as if the chaos we face is not insurmountable, as if we're already living in the world we'd be proud to leave to the children Kaitlyn never had and now never will have.

'We are going to put every fibre of our beings and every moment of our lives into creating a world where all of your great-great-great-too-many-greats-to-count-grandkids hold ceremonies to celebrate the changes we made that let them flourish on a planet where all life thrives.'

His gaze was scalding now, but it was met by each of those it crossed. 'This is one massive experiment. We will make mistakes, that's a given. We'll likely feel we're drowning in quicksand most of the time, certainly we'll be ploughing our way through mud in a blizzard at midnight. I am not sugar-coating this, because the one thing we know for sure is that we can't do it alone. It's too late for a handful of people to be the change, to experiment at the edges of inter-becoming, all the stuff we've talked about for half our lives. This has to be a massed – and massive – movement across the world or it won't work.

'So, you're all invited to join us. If you want to be a good ancestor, if you want to be part of a real and lasting change, if you want to dance at the emergent edge of inter-becoming where nothing is ever predictable except that we have to abandon all we've been told about the way things are, there's a big, friendly join-up button on the front page of Changemakers.life . . .' A swift glance sideways to catch Finn's nod. '*Now!*'

Both brothers stepped back, creating a natural break in the proceedings. This was another new feature, but, I'd stopped counting each deviation from the darker paths: by this point, the only similarity to the void-vision funerals was the speed with which people signed up on the website.

Sliding into the OS of Finn's laptop, I watched the first few thousand hurtle in and I can tell you without question that the Ghosts were not creating this avalanche. Eighty-three sign-ups came from the pavilion. The rest came in their hundreds of thousands – by the end of the first minute, millions – from Aalborg to Zumpango, and the entire alphabet in between.

As soon as they breached the first million, scrolling counters appeared on the screens with graphs underneath showing uptake by continent and age group. Quite soon after, Finn GhostTalked with his core team:

```
Finn: Need more space?
Juke: Nope. We got extra servers.
We're good
Hawck: Best bring them up to speed
Charm: Already on it
```

281

The last two responses came from inside the pavilion. Juke had not travelled over from Israel, but Charm and Hawck had come in person, and were somewhere down below.

I'd been too focused on the family to seek them out before, but the most likely landmines were behind us and I had the time to look for people I knew intimately but had never seen.

Hawck was a middle-aged white man and there were too many of those to narrow the field, but Charm was a French-Berber woman and I found her almost at once, sitting in the front row next to Matt and Jens.

I would have known her sooner, except that I'd thought her a relative of Eriq's: they shared the same high cheekbones and desert-dark skin. Eriq was small, though, and Charm was almost as tall as Torvald, with a poise that looked positively regal. Dressed in a deep maroon dashiki with silver embroidery at cuffs and hem, she could have been the empress of a lineage that traced back to the time of the earliest Pharaohs.

And all of this was a sideshow, because the first thing everyone saw was the fact that she had shaved off her hair. The shimmering roof lights wrought a crown that added to her height. Jens couldn't look away. Matt kept elbowing him and it made no difference. Charm was charmed and said so in the molten chocolate voice I remembered from that first night when she'd taken my place in the battlegrounds: sheer magic.

Leah sat quietly two seats to Charm's left, and I read relief in the spirals of lilac and amber that were her resting textures. We had not met in the dream since that first long night and I had not yet found a way to speak with her in any other way, but she recognised my presence, sometimes, and now she smiled and nodded and said, softly, 'OK, so far,' which was as good as it was ever going to get.

Five minutes later, when it looked as if people might stand up and start moving around, a chime sounded from the shadows behind the dais. The high, fine note shimmered in the air and, by the time it died away, the pavilion had fallen silent once again.

From the dais, Finn said, 'If our enthusiasm serves to tide Mum and Kirsten and Kaitlyn on their way, I don't think we could have asked for anything better. Please keep signing up. But while that's happening, we wanted to let you know the ideas we're starting with. Dad will go first.'

Eriq was thinner and more stooped than he had been in any of the void-visions of the funerals, but he was still as much a showman.

Springing up to the dais, he kept his back straight and his eyes bright and said, 'If you've listened to anything Kaitlyn, Kirsten and Maddie said, then you'll know we think business is a core driver of the current crisis. As a family, we've tried to make our work serve the needs of humanity, but in this last month we've realised we didn't go far enough.

'So we've started talking to the pathfinders, the people who live in this liminal space where real transformation happens. One of these is Riversimple Movement, a company in Wales that makes hydrogen-fuel cell cars. Just for this they're interesting, and there's a link on the website if you want to explore, but what interests us most is their Future Guardian Governance model: it's genuinely outstanding. We believe that if every business in the world took this on today, by tomorrow we'd be halfway to a solution.

'The idea is simple: the company has investors like any other business. But unlike any other, investors *don't* have voting shares. Instead, one person speaks in their interests, but they're balanced by five other 'custodians' who speak for—' Eriq ticked them off on his fingers— 'the workers, the local community, the customers, the suppliers and the environment.'

He dropped his hand. 'With the investor custodian, that's six in all. We want to include a seventh for future generations, and while we haven't sorted out who that will be quite yet, we have allocated the other six, and yes, we have taken the best jobs for ourselves, you can vote us out in a year if it doesn't work.' The grin he flashed rendered him younger, stronger, more like the magician Maddie had married.

Just as fast, he sobered. 'But there are only three of us up here, so you can see where this is going, I'm sure. We lost three women and without ever suggesting we could replace or supplant them, we have invited Mo Bakar, Leah Koresh and Hawa Taleb to join us on the board.'

And this was when I learned Charm's real name. Seeing her leap onto the dais, I thought maybe she and Finn might get together. Not yet, obviously, but in a while, when some of the raw hurt was less.

It was good to imagine him happy and I let myself drift in a sea of possibility where the words of the living floated past, light as dandelion seeds on summer thermals. I hadn't relaxed like this since I'd died. I loved it.

Niall drew me back with his too-bland voice, the one that had always said he was stirring trouble.

'. . . could campaign for a Kaitlyn's Law, of course. We're lawyers, we could draft the bill. It might even get through parliament. But it's not going to give power to those with wisdom, or wisdom to those with power and nothing less is good enough now.

'On the same basis, we could call for revolution, but, as Kirsten used to say, revolution just takes you in a circle back to where you started and that's not an option any more, either. So while Dad and Finn—' he nodded to Eriq when he said 'Dad' and here was another sketchy moment when Torvald could have gone off the deep end, but Leah had been thorough and the twins' father had been warned this was coming: he gave a wry wave towards the dais and that was it, no drama.

Niall made sure everyone had seen and then carried on. 'While Cuidorado and the Grey Ghosts are busy changing the way the entire world does business, I've been figuring out how we can drag the mediaeval nightmare of our political system into the twenty-first century.

'Which is hard. We don't have the power to make demands and, anyway, they take too long. What we're doing then is making suggestions: we are *recommending* three changes to the way things are done, and three is obviously not a random number.'

His smile fell away. He pulled up the chair and sat again. 'Our first recommendation is made in my mother's name. Most of you know she struggled with alcohol when Kirsten and I were young. She gave up before Finn came along and never went back, but not everyone has the support she did, and we can all imagine how it feels

284

to lose hope and take solace in a bottle, or a can, or a needle, or a nose full of cocaine, or a bag of glue, or any of the thousand ways we blunt our experience of a world that is designed to crush our spirits and remove all hope.

'Let's be totally clear. None of us ever has, or ever will, blame people who turn to drink or drugs as ways of escape. But we absolutely blame people who hold positions of trust and power who don't get the help they need and decide it's OK to sit in our Houses of Parliament making laws that destroy people and planet while they're neither clean nor sober.

'This has to end. Our legislature must have the clarity that comes from sobriety. If we—' a sweep that took in the room— 'are not allowed to pilot a plane when we're under the influence of alcohol, cocaine or heroin, then others should not be allowed to pilot a bill through parliament unless they are clear of these things, too.

'We recommend, therefore, that a transparent and incorruptible unit should conduct random drug and alcohol tests in both Houses of Parliament. There should be a graded system of sanctions – three strikes.

'The first time a test is failed, the individual involved has a week out of parliament and the offer of help; the second time, they're banned for a month and the help is mandatory; third time around, if they're a lord, they're expelled. If they're an MP at any level, up to and including the prime minister, they lose their job, which is to say their seat in parliament, and there is an automatic by-election in their constituency in which they are not allowed to stand. Nor will they receive the huge pay-off that is normally given to MPs who lose their seats. They will be dismissed as any one of us would be dismissed if we turned up to work in a state that wasn't compatible with what we were being paid to do.

'None of this is unreasonable. In the business world, it's too obvious to need stating. In our government, it should be basic common sense and we ask it in our mother's name. Clarity was Maddie's guiding light. It will be ours.'

Brilliant, beautiful (and only lightly Photoshopped) images of Maddie at her best flashed onto all the big screens. Niall lifted a hand and, in a voice that cracked towards the end, said, 'Mum, I hope you're proud of us, wherever you are. We are so proud of you and all you stood for.'

Nobody applauded: it wasn't called for and, in any case, too many people were wiping their cheeks. But the net lit up and the hashtag #Clarity rose swiftly, nudging up against #ChangeIsComing and all the myriad #KKMWLFs.

When Niall resumed, the quality of the silence was noticeably more alert: everyone had come expecting something radical; nobody had expected anything this concrete.

'Our next suggestion is in my twin's name and for her we want to address corruption. Kirsten knew that while we might all disagree about which party is the most corrupt, the one thing we all agree on is that they *are* all corrupt. I could list the ways, but we'd be here too long.

'Our second suggestion, therefore, calls for fiscal transparency: specifically, that we put all government spending on the blockchain which may be a climate-destroying disaster in its bitcoin incarnation, but the basic concept of a distributed and incorruptible ledger is sound. We'll create a way to track every single government payment in real-time, and if the code is open source – which it will be – then anyone can check it. They say change happens at the speed of trust and, with transparent spending, we will build real trust.

'Finn assures me the technology exists to do this cheaply with minimal energy input, and if the government can't do it the Ghosts will be happy to help in ways that can themselves be audited. We won't charge. We have as much interest in achieving transparency as anyone else.

'This, then, is our second suggestion: full transparency of government finances, and we ask it in Kirsten's name.'

#Transparency began to trend. Bursts of enthusiasm arose in places I wouldn't have expected, either because they seemed politically unaligned with the rest of the movement (red states in the US, for instance), or just a long way off in terms of geography and time zones (Makassar, Kununurra). From my point of view, though, the response from the UK government and its many overt and covert agencies was becoming a priority. I slid again into the threads of the net and followed the cold places, the emptinesses, until I found the conversations that were not remotely in support of what was happening in a field in Suffolk.

Consternation met me. Whatever the hidden observers had been expecting, it wasn't this. They had coped with the idea of drugs tests just about, but the idea of shining a light into the fiscal shadows was hurling grenades into their equanimity. When I slid into the wider web and followed the threads and WhatsApp channels, I found chaos bordering on panic – and no clear strategy.

Niall, who might have guessed this, but couldn't yet know the detail, moved on to his third point.

'And so we come to Kaitlyn, who started us all down this particular path. She was the most radical of our family and our testament to her is no less.' Niall folded his arms.

'Sometime in the next year and a half, this country will go to the polls in a general election, in which, if she were still alive, Kaitlyn would be too young to vote. This is insane, frankly. If you want to argue that she wasn't politically aware, I will give you full access to all her emails, videos and WhatsApps detailing her political thinking – she thought more deeply and broadly than most of our commentariat seem able to.

'In her name, then, we're asking for Fairness. The minimum voting age for the Scottish and Welsh legislatures is sixteen. But you have to be eighteen – *eighteen* – to cast a vote for the UK parliament. Kaitlyn would have had no voice for nearly another four years, which is wholly unfair.

'In her name, therefore, we recommend the whole of the UK moves to fifteen as a minimum voting age. This will be lower by one year than anywhere in the world, but young people have most to lose; without question they should be given a say in what's happening.

'By the same reasoning, we also think there should be a *maximum* voting age beyond which someone's investment in a generative future is recognised to be too limited, the tendency to vote purely on the basis of narrow self-interest too great.

'Specifically, we suggest that between the ages of fifteen and seventy-five, everyone can vote, but that between the ages of ten and fifteen, or seventy-five to eighty-five, if you want to vote, you should pair up with someone at the other end of the age range and talk with them online for at least three hours to find out how they see the world.

'Clearly there are dangers with this, we'd need to provide trained facilitators to offer emotionally literate moderation and to guarantee safety, but we can do this. We'll create safe spaces where people can say what they need. Then, if both sides agree that the other has at least listened and they've been heard – note, they absolutely *do not* both have to agree on any of the issues, they just have to have listened and understood – then both can vote. If either says the other hasn't listened, then neither can vote.

'Over eighty-five, I'm sorry, you got us to here and here is not good and you're not going to be around long enough to live through the consequences of bad decisions. Age and wisdom are not coterminous. I'm sure there are wise people over eighty-five with the capacity to set aside their personal interests for the greater good, just as there are thirteen-year-olds with postgraduate degrees in astrophysics, but these are not in the majority. So, sorry, but you've had your day. You can still be an activist, knock on doors, make phone calls, make videos, talk to family and community, you just don't get to vote when you're unlikely to have to live for decades with the results.'

Finished at last, Niall bowed to the cameras. 'Kaitlyn, Kirsten, Mum. We are doing this because we think it's what each of you would have asked for. We hope you're as proud of us as we are of you.'

A moment's silence followed, and then a cheer so sudden and so loud that it spun Bright Rook and her family out of the spinney.

With the sound surging over them, Niall, Finn and Eriq came to stand at the front of the dais. Above them, a digital banner proclaimed Change is Coming. Rise up Strong. #Clarity, #Transparency and #Fairness scrolled on continuous loop underneath.

Online, the #KKMWLF communities were already spinning out ideas that took the three suggestions and repurposed them for their own nations. #FairVotesForYouth trended far above everything else.

Only one section of the internet was different. On the hidden WhatsApp groups where members of the establishment talked to each other, what had been confusion and consternation had morphed into a kind of disbelieving euphoria.

```
Did they just say what I think they
said?
Are they completely mad?
```

And most cheerful of all,

```
Doesn't matter. We've got them.
```

CHAPTER SIXTEEN

Monday, 15 May 2023

'First rule of engagement: never interrupt your enemy when they're making a mistake.'

Niall started quoting Napoleon when he was eleven years old, playing Go by daily email with a girl in Helsinki. She won the game five weeks later.

These days, he was less inclined to hubris, but even so, I heard him say it three times in the first week after the funeral, tentatively at first, then with savage satisfaction and finally in breathless disbelief.

The first of the three was on Monday, 15 May, two days after the funeral that had set everything in motion. The surviving menfolk of my family had wrapped themselves in whichever coping mechanisms seemed currently to be working, brewed themselves the strongest coffee they could stand without kicking off fibrillations, and gathered upstairs in Ash Barn, where Finn's giant display hosted the live feed of Leah Koresh facing off against Frances Nolan on BBC Radio Four's *Woman's Hour*.

You might have thought recent events would have softened Nolan, but she was as passively aggressive as ever.

'Would you seriously have stood in front of our late queen and told her she was too old to vote?'

This was hardly an original line. The Sunday papers, whose editors had planned to lead on some of the softer edges of the funeral (early editions: 'A NATION MOURNS'), had instead reverted to type in time to garnish the front pages with righteous outrage.

The broadsheets had led with the original of Nolan's question: 'FAMILY OF MURDERED ACTIVISTS CLAIMS LATE QUEEN WAS TOO

OLD TO VOTE', complete with images of the sovereign looking radiant in white silk and diamonds and not a day over eighty.

The tabloids, oddly, but perhaps cannily, had leaned towards the iconic image of Elizabeth II sitting hunched and alone at her husband's Covid-impacted funeral below headlines, the kindest of which suggested anarchists were planning armed revolution to evict her son from his throne.

Just in case the readers were in any doubt as to the varied racial origins of the anarchists in question, double portraits of Eriq and Charm (aka Hawa Taleb but, at her own request, nobody at all called her this), Niall and Leah, Finn and Mo were set in a semicircle below Elizabeth II. Never let it be said their photo editors missed their chance to race straight to the bottom of the brainstem in their quest for sales.

If the shootings had initiated an amnesty in the legacy media's treatment of the family, the unveiling of Changemakers as a – what? Political party? Charity? Social movement? Radical anarchist commune? They weren't sure but despised them all equally – had shredded the goodwill and buried the remains in a bog.

With no sense of irony, they subjected Mo, Leah and Charm to the same quality and degree of racially fuelled character assassination as they had Maddie, Kirsten and Kaitlyn in the weeks before they had been shot.

The women weathered this with a kind of forewarned and forearmed stoicism, strengthened by their various roles in holding the men together.

Charm's role was in many ways the simplest: she was managing the Ghosts' day-to-day operations, keeping track of the money, allocating tasks, bringing in new members to fill the fast-evolving round-the-clock teams who were monitoring the burgeoning social media feeds of friends and foe. And she still played Arena with Juke and Finn at levels ordinary mortals (and me) could only dream of.

Finn therefore had two women watching over his equanimity, three if you counted Bēi Fēng, which I did: she met him nightly in the dream of the peach-tree garden, and, though he wept while he sparred, he woke more able to cope than he'd been when he went to bed.

He wept while he sparred with Mo in the daytime, too, and, while he was finding meditation almost impossible, she kept bringing him back to the cushion with such unconditional compassion that he learned swiftly he could lean on her when he needed; and did. I was not jealous of her place in his life. Not. At. All.

Leah and Mo both watched over Eriq, though most of his care came from elsewhere. He spent hours in Zoom calls with Max and I thought he came away from these worse, not better. What bolstered him best were the long calls with his two grandmothers, conducted in a language I couldn't parse, whose words tasted of desert wind and old dust and a regret so profound I could not remain long in its presence. Eriq was stronger after, but I had no idea what it cost him.

Niall appeared immune to support. He didn't reject anyone's care, yet it was clear to all of us that it didn't touch him. His only concession to vulnerability was a habit he'd developed early on, of looking up into the high corners of whichever room he was in and holding what appeared to be a moment's conversation: a question and its answer, at least.

The obvious implication was that he saw Kirsten there, and I put a significant amount of time into testing for her actual presence. I neither saw nor felt anything, but Niall was her twin and I wasn't ruling anything out.

For my part, I did what I could to soften the more ragged passions roiling through the farm without ever doing anything so overt that I would be noticed.

In case Leah needed me, I had returned to the Lion of Koresh on both nights since the funeral. Thus far, she had not.

She was, in fact, doing a remarkable job of fielding the pressure the funeral had unleashed. On *Woman's Hour*, she answered the 'You're dissing the queen' question with the same languid calm she had brought to all her public appearances. 'I think you'll find the royal family does not exercise the right to vote. Certainly, Her Majesty never did.'

Before Frances could intervene, Leah asked, 'We are suggesting that clarity, transparency and fairness should be built into our political system. Do you disagree? Or perhaps you think we have these already and nothing needs to change?'

Waspish, Nolan said, 'I don't think you should stop our senior citizens from voting.'

'Senior citizens?' In the barn, Finn snorted. 'What, are we Americans now?'

Eriq was more thoughtful. 'We need to work on our pushback. This is getting out of hand.'

'No. We're good. Leah's got a PhD in neurolinguistics. She can handle anything Nolan throws at her.' Niall was doing the *Guardian* sudoku. If the world needed proof that some cog deep inside Kirsten's twin had turned to a new ratchet, this was it. The Niall of old took Noam Chomsky as his philosophical lodestone and had read *Manufacturing Consent* until it fell apart in his hands. Accordingly, he despised the *Guardian* as an agent of the Death Cult and held to the view (entirely off his own bat; nothing to do with American academics) that doing numerical puzzles was the first sign of a disintegrating intellect. It was one of the few aspects of life on which he and Kirsten had consistently disagreed.

Now, he folded the paper and looked at the air beyond Finn's left shoulder. 'Four minutes. Getting there,' he said, then turned his attention back to the Koresh v Nolan match on the screen.

'. . . that you genuinely believe the people running our government are the brightest and the best?' Leah was leaning across the table, drawing Frances Nolan out of herself by sheer force of character.

A little desperately, Nolan replied, 'We have the oldest democracy in the world. We destabilise it at our peril.'

'Oh, *Frances*!' Leah's laugh rocked the room. 'We don't have a democracy. We have a kleptocracy run by psychopaths and clowns bought and paid for by the corporate lobby. You are welcome to give me one instance of a government minister in the past decade who was honest, decent and competent. I'll wait . . .'

Nolan didn't even try. Leah pressed on. 'When our parliament first sat, only land-owning men over the age of twenty-one could vote. This was not reasonable, fair or good. When women first got the vote, they had to be over thirty and, even so, the establishment fought it all the way. You have a PPE from Oxford. I am sure they remembered to mention the suffragettes and suffragists? Emmeline Pankhurst and the king's horse? The force-feedings and beatings and lives destroyed? That was only a little over a century ago. The men in charge then said if women could vote it would cause anarchy and resisted with all they had. Do you think they were right?'

It was a rhetorical question, and she didn't give time for an answer.

'We're not destabilising democracy, Frances, we're trying to find a way to reform a desperately broken system so that we bring the best possible people together in the best possible way to create a future we'd be proud to leave behind. A system that elects sexual predators, liars and second-job grifters and then pays them three times the median wage even if they don't bother to turn up in parliament is no longer fit for purpose. If it ever was.'

'But you can't just dismantle it! That's the very definition of anarchy.'

'We're not *dismantling* it. We're dragging it into the twenty-first century by the scruff of the neck. If you want to argue that our members of parliament should be drunk, drugged and corrupt, I'm all ears, but you can't seriously tell me that if young people from the age of sixteen are old enough to pay tax, they're not old enough to have a say in how our money is spent.'

'Of course not, but—'

Leah ran over the top of her. 'Sixteen-year-olds can vote for the Scottish and Welsh Parliaments, just not in the Westminster elections. That's either blatant vote-rigging or discrimination or both.'

'Leah!' Frances Nolan hissed a sigh that left me feeling sorry for her daughter. As if to a slow undergraduate she said, 'If you give fifteen-year-olds – even sixteen-year-olds – the vote in UK parliamentary elections and take it away from everyone over eighty-five, you will fundamentally change the political configuration of this nation. You will never be allowed to do that.'

'*Stop!*' Half out of his seat, Niall clawed at the screen. 'Don't say anything. Never interrupt your enemy . . . *Please*, Leah. Just . . . don't speak.'

Leah showed no sign of saying anything. The silence grew second by second: aeon by aeon in radio time where a gap of more than two heartbeats has the continuity announcer checking the feed. Plenty of time for the world to watch Frances Nolan realise what she'd said live, on the nation's biggest and most trusted broadcaster.

Her producer joined much the same dots at much the same time and the gap lengthened as Nolan's consternation faded to the almost-not-there look of a woman trying to appear attentive to the room while someone further up the food chain was threatening retribution in a voice that only she could hear.

Fetching up a smile that didn't even attempt authenticity, she said, 'Well, this has been an enlightening conversation all round and I'm sure we'll come back to your three "suggestions" in the days and weeks to come.

'In the meantime, thank you to Leah Koresh of Radical FM, here in her role as an adviser to the newly formed Changemakers Future Guardian Group. We're going to move now to the southern hemisphere where a young Chilean woman has set up an app to help growers and farmers measure the carbon sequestration potential of their land . . .'

The producers cut to a recorded package but in the fractional lag before the live feed ended, the studio cameras held their focus on a surprisingly calm Frances Nolan.

Finn clipped a screenshot and zoomed in on her face, frowning. 'She knows what she's done and she's not worried.'

'Maybe she's got another job lined up for when they sack her.' Sharply, Niall tilted his chair back, hooked his heels up on the table and laced his fingers behind his head. 'Anything hit the channels yet?'

'Give it another twenty seconds. Charm's pulling the video of that last sentence.'

Charm had moved into the Piggery, taking one of the bedrooms upstairs and organising the lecture theatre downstairs into an expansive open-plan office, ready for the expected influx of Ghosts.

She was in charge of ironing out the wrinkles between the Ghosts' standard operating procedures and the horizontal work structure Changemakers was evolving. (Niall: 'No hierarchy. We're doing this the new way. Trust me, I can make it work.' Finn: 'Ghosts can be a special case, though, right? Because you may not like hierarchies, but we know how we work, and it can be pretty fucking linear at times.')

Finn cast a thoughtful look at his brother. 'Did you tell Leah what to say?'

'Findley Karim Penhaligon, that's an unutterably sexist question and you should be ashamed even to think it. If anyone's calling the shots, it's our new strategist.' Niall threw a savage grin up at the ceiling. 'Bait them with the queen and switch to taxes. I wouldn't want to be the press officer given the job of explaining why sixteen-year-olds can pay income tax but are not trusted to vote. And that's after they've had to argue that drink, drugs and corruption are integral to the process of government, and the entire country will fall apart if we root them out, thank you.'

'We're still aiming for fifteen as our lower cut-off, though, right?'

'Ideally. But there's a margin for compromise if we need it: we'll shift to sixteen if we have to. But before that, we'll roll over and give them eighty instead of seventy-five as the lower limit of "you have to talk to a young person" bracket, so they feel they've had a win. One way or another, we'll get the changes we need.'

Eriq passed Niall a fresh mug of semi-liquid tar masquerading as coffee. 'According to Leah, we're supposed to be holding to the things we want, not counting the ways we can destroy the system.'

'Dad, trust me, I am holding so hard to what we want I am in grave danger of choking it to death before it sees the light of day. But I do want to point out that the entire establishment has just walked straight into Leah's bear pit. Or, as Kirsten told Prune when Matt's collie had a litter, "If you want a puppy, start by asking for a pony and they'll—"' Too late, Niall heard what he'd said. His teeth cracked together.

Shit. . .

Niall. I reached out and pulled back and hated myself, even as a part of me thought Niall's ice might break here and now, and it wouldn't be a bad thing.

It didn't.

Exhaling softly, Finn asked, 'So we're going to scale down the original ask and let them keep the over-eighty-fives?'

Niall's nod was thanks and agreement, both. 'That's the obvious concession. Get rid of the drink and drugs, tag all the money with digital markers so we can see exactly where it goes and give votes at the very least to sixteen-year-olds across the board: local, regional and national elections in all four nations of the UK. If you do all this, we won't push for you to take the votes away from some of the grey-haired loons who started voting for you before Thatcher took power and aren't going to change now. It's not what you'd call total systemic change, but as Frances Nolan pointed out it has the potential to significantly rearrange the political map.'

'Did she mean to say that? Did Leah put her up to it?'

'Honestly? I don't know. The most likely answer is that Leah's staggering intellect hypnotised her into saying what she actually thought for once, but the result's the same. Everyone under forty knows now that the system is deliberately rigged against them and everyone over forty knows they know. The cat is totally out of the bag. The emperor is shown to be naked. You can't undo these things. The Number Ten press office are going to have to dance very, very carefully round this. I can't wait to see what they dream up. Do we have anything?'

'Not yet.' Finn had his hand over his earpiece and briefly took on the same half-not-there look that Frances Nolan had in the studio. 'Charm says #YouthVote is rising and we didn't kick it off.'

'Good.'

'And the Ghosts have put the video of Nolan's last sentence out through all our channels. If you just play the audio, she sounds monstrously patronising: the ultimate Boomer put-down of the young. They're mapping it onto video montages. Thatcher and Churchill are getting the most reposts. Generational irony for the win.'

'Better.'

'Hashtag KKMWLF-Madrid has clipped Leah with her bit about drink and drugs being part of the system. They've put it on TikTok and it's already huge. This didn't come from us; not the Ghosts or the Digital Army: we have a whole new nexus of useful support and we don't know who it is or where it's based. Charm's got people trying to reverse-engineer it to see who did it and where they are. Seems to be narrowing down to South America but there's a lot of digging still to do.'

'Best!' Niall, recovered, was almost enjoying himself.

'Yep. No . . . wait . . .' Finn paused mid-nod. His eyes flared wide. Disbelieving, he said, 'Recalibrate. The BBC just tweeted that their journalists do not speak for the Corporation and they don't believe that preventing young people from voting is deliberate government policy.' His voice broke on a bubble of laughter. 'Never believe anything until it's officially denied, right?'

There was a brief, implosive silence.

Eriq broke it. 'Nobody is that stupid. We must have friends on the inside.'

'It's possible the BBC occasionally employs someone under forty,' Niall suggested.

'Yes, but . . .'

'But interns don't get to put out communiqués.'

'Exactly.'

'Someone does, though,' Finn said, uncertainly. 'Whoever it is, they've just posted a link to a Professor Anne Charringford's paper on the new constituency boundaries with a clip from a commentary she wrote three months ago. Is she someone we listen to?'

'Absolutely.' Niall sat up, fast. 'She's the best statistician in the country and she understands whereof she speaks. That paper, if I remember correctly, says that if you specifically delineate voting areas to corral all the poor, not-white people into one place, you'll also end up with a lot of young people inside the same boundaries. So you'll have concentrated people who are never, ever going to vote for the incumbent party in one place. Which conveniently loads their votes onto people who were already going to win. Current predictions are that the young, female Opposition MPs will increase their vote share by 17 per cent.'

'But that just means their seats become ultra-safe instead of super-safe,' Finn said.

'Give that boy a gold star. Exactly. You've created ghettoes of people who hate you. But here's the clever thing: you herd them all into one place and then you *make it really hard for them to vote*. Specifically, you demand ID and make it almost impossible for anyone under sixty to get hold of it: bus passes count for pensioners, but not for students . . . that kind of thing. And then you draw the boundaries based on *registered voters*, not the actual people living in any given place.'

Niall was warming to his theme. 'So you've got all the people who hate you in the one place, you don't let all of them show how much they hate you, and then everywhere else, the cis, straight, white Boomers are still voting the way they did when Thatcher was selling them council houses on the cheap. If Charringford's right, the government will increase its majority by another twenty seats. Even if they give fifteen-year-olds the vote.'

'Wait. What?' Finn's face was painted in confusion. 'They win anyway? We're doing all this and it won't change anything?'

'Exactly.' Niall polished his archest smile. 'So, they have Nothing. To. Worry. About.'

'Niall . . . Crazy man . . . If it does nothing, why are we partying like no one's watching?'

Partying might have been overstating it somewhat. Niall didn't do more than tilt his chair back, hook his heels on the desk and direct his cold-bright smile up at the ceiling again. It was becoming a favourite stance.

'Patience, Grasshopper. We party because we are happy people. Though we are keeping our party so far below the radar that nobody at all will see us. We're small. We're insignificant. We are definitely not a threat. And in our unthreatening way, we will wait and see what answering move the other side makes. And we absolutely will not, under any circumstances, interrupt them.'

CHAPTER SEVENTEEN

Uninterrupted, the day unfolded.

The government press office remained resolutely silent, while TikTok went wild. #GerrymanderedToExtinction began to trend with videos of young people being harassed by police around the world. Lyrics to the tune of 'Imagine'.

Niall looked impressed. 'Generational irony on steroids. Did we do this?'

They were in the kitchen. Finn had just finished training the senior students and was wet from the shower. He towelled his hair with one hand and checked his phone with the other. 'Not us directly: the new nexus. They're in Brazil and they're locking in with the Digital Army. Max kicked them off, apparently.'

'Nice. Can we move the vid to Twitter?' Niall asked. 'Nobody over thirty knows where TikTok is, or cares.'

'Charm's on it.'

Charm was, indeed, on it. Her section of the Ghosts – their numbers were growing daily, vetted by Juke and Hawck – had been working in shifts around the clock, transporting all the relevant videos to Twitter and garnishing them with hashtags that the establishment trolls couldn't possibly miss.

Finn's cadre of Ghosts, meanwhile, kept 24/7 eyes on the government coms, though, in truth, there wasn't much to report when, as Finn pointed out, 'everyone is waiting for someone else to say something they can disagree with'.

'Good discipline, though,' he said, several hours later, when not a single member of parliament had put out a single comment. 'When was the last time the Culture Secretary took a whole afternoon off Twitter?'

Niall said, 'The men in suits confiscated all the phones and locked them in the Downing Street safe.'

'Seriously?'

'Not seriously. They don't have to. Whatever you think about the infant-level IQs of Our Beloved Leaders, they all know if they say the wrong thing now, they're finished. It's just that nobody knows what's right, that's the beauty of it.'

'The other guys could say something, though,' Finn said. 'Her Majesty's loyal Opposition? They don't have to wait?'

'They're running focus groups to find out what to say.'

'Seriously?'

'Seriously.'

'Wow.' Finn's forehead thunked dramatically on the table. 'I guess we'd better have a look at what they're finding. I'll get someone onto it.'

Niall grimaced. 'Wake me if it's something we don't already know.'

Few things were secret when the Ghosts put their minds to unearthing data, and the Opposition party's focus group results certainly weren't. As predicted, they showed that the over-sixties (I refuse to refer to my own generation as Boomers) believed the young were frivolous, woke peacocks, too occupied with glitter and 'like-aholism' to be given the serious responsibility of voting.

The young pointed out that the existing voting record of the old had been anything but responsible and had, in fact, seen a series of kleptomaniac sociopaths elected to high office, none of whom was 'fit to be dog-catcher in Trumpton' (this particular line came from one of the white-haired commentators who specialised in taking a contrarian view, but was circulated so widely that its origins were soon lost), and perhaps it was time to let the people whose futures were being stolen in real-time actually have a say in how the present was being run.

Of particular interest to the political advisers of all parties was the central bracket: people born after 1980 but before the turn of the millennium. These appeared to be divided into three camps: those with children over five years old, who sided mostly with the young; those with no children, who sided with the old by a sliver; and those with children under the age of five, who were too sleep-deprived to respond to surveys.

By general agreement, nobody else from Changemakers made themselves available for comment so there was no risk of the core message being sullied. In the absence of anything else, Leah's conversation with Frances Nolan was picked over until the bones fell apart.

Various pundits set themselves up as unofficial speakers for either side, but without more information there wasn't much to say beyond, 'Changemakers has three suggestions and you either think they're essential to rebuilding a decent government or you think they're the straw that's going to destroy our democracy, and there isn't much common ground to be found.'

Stalemate.

Everything progressed smoothly until around three o'clock, when Eriq called Finn and Niall over to the main house for what was either an improbably late (but welcome) lunch or an early dinner.

They wandered over slowly, their heads full of the latest non-updates from a government in paralysis. Eyes on his phone, Finn said, 'Twitter just denied rumours that they've banned the entire roster of the UK's MPs. They're trolling, obviously, but the BBC's political correspondent is reporting it as serious.'

'The BBC's packed with stenographers who copy whatever the SpAds feed them. Got rid of proper journalists years ago.' Niall dropped into his old chair at the table. 'Lunch smells amazing.

'Suffolk–Morocco fusion,' Finn said, sliding his phone into his jeans pocket. 'Dad, you're a wonder.'

Eriq turned round, a dish of steaming casserole in his hands. Finn was the only one looking his way. He made a small noise.

Niall spun. 'Dad?'

Eriq faltered halfway across the gap. It wasn't that he didn't like being called Dad, it was that he liked it too much. I watched a decision waver and harden and still had no idea what it was: not good, though.

He set the dish on the table and sat down.

'You're leaving,' Niall said flatly.

Eriq stared at him a long moment before he nodded. 'I can't stay. That is, I could . . . of course I could. But you don't need me.'

'And Max does?' Finn asked. Eriq looked more ill than ever, and now we knew why. Absently, he picked up the salt and pepper mills and juggled them, the way other people might fiddle with a knife when they needed some calm. It had none of the fluidity of which we all knew he was capable.

'I need Max,' he said. 'Which is a whole different thing. More than that, I need to be useful. Here . . . you're doing all the work and I'm making coffee when I'm not having Zoom meetings that would be better done in person. And the Immigration Office is already piling in with the whole hostile environment thing, trying to tell me I don't have residency status—'

'That's ridiculous. You and Mum got married fifteen years ago. We can stop them,' Niall said. 'The government may be ripping up the rule book as it goes along, but we still have a notionally independent judiciary and—'

'And people are waiting four years on remand before their case comes to court. I'm not losing sleep for the next four years while they dream up ever nastier ways to harass us. Finn, I need you to know this isn't about you. I was here when Kaitlyn was born and I'm going back home now she's gone and it's easy for that to look as if I only care about her.' He pulled a fork into the juggling mix. 'It *feels* like that.'

'And that feeling is wrong, because . . .?'

'I love you more deeply than I ever knew was possible. I stayed for Kaitlyn when I realised I should have been here when you were born and been your father through all your childhood and I didn't want to repeat the mistake. Also, I realised how deeply I loved you and your mother. But Maddie's dead and you're nearly thirty and . . . you don't *need* me.'

'Dad . . .' Finn sounded small, and young and dangerously hollow. I watched him reach for Bēi Fēng and felt the whisper of her reaching back and was sliding into self-pity until I snagged on a memory of Maddie's voice (*It's not all about you, Lan*). Then I really did lose the place for a while, and when I came back, Finn had snatched the salt out of the air and brought a knife and a spoon into the mix.

Juggling together had been one of the first ways he'd bonded with his father when Eriq came back to stay. 'What can you do with Max that you can't do here?'

'Build Changemakers in the global south? Keep a finger on the pulse of the half of the world that isn't on the verge of being eaten by AI, but might still be invaded for its lithium? I don't know. But I know staying here and waking at four every morning thinking I've just heard the Immigration Land Rovers pull up in the yard is not healthy. It's not like we'll be cut off. We have email. We have GhostTalk. As long as you think it's safe, I'll log in to all the meetings. I'll still be core to Changemakers in any way you want.'

Home. Home was with Max now. Perhaps it always had been. The thought ricocheted off the walls and, more than anything, this sealed the conversation.

'Dad, it's OK.' Niall laid a hand over Eriq's. 'When are you leaving?'

'Now. Taxi'll be here in five.'

'A taxi?' Finn looked appalled. 'I can drive you.' Not Niall: nobody was so tired of life they'd let Niall behind a wheel even when he was in the best frame of mind.

Eriq shook his head. 'What will we say that won't hurt? Drawn-out goodbyes are never good.' He pulled an envelope from his pocket and slid it across the table. 'Car's yours.' Besides his clothes, his wedding ring and a handful of devices, the car was Eriq's only possession.

'Dad . . . I can't.'

'Well, I can't take it as cabin luggage, so just keep it running till I come back. Deal?'

'Deal.' Finn's voice broke on the word.

CHAPTER EIGHTEEN

Eriq had never been loud, but in his absence the farm became a place of strange shadows and clattering disquiet.

Five minutes after the taxi left, Niall decided he couldn't keep sleeping in the downstairs room of the barn any longer. He abandoned his lunch uneaten and poured himself into moving all his things from the barn to one of the spare rooms in the farmhouse, one door along from where Leah now slept. Like everything else he'd done recently, there was a frozen polish to his movement. Nobody got in his way.

Finn headed straight for the smaller of the two training gyms upstairs in the Piggery and spent an hour throwing himself through Shaolin forms that looked like they dissolved every joint in his body. He didn't weep in the way he'd done first thing, but he raged the air blue with every not-approved word he'd ever heard.

A brutally hot shower later, he leapt into the Arenas, lost three games in a row, logged off and took to his many social threads instead. His first message was on GhostTalk, to Leah:

```
Finn: Dad's gone to Brazil.
Leah: Gone? As in . . . left? Really?
Finn: Really. Heading for Heathrow as
we speak. Tell me that wasn't in the
dire-dreams?
Leah: It wasn't. If we're looking for
breaks from the super-bad stuff, it's
definitely a break. Brutal, though.
Let's talk more when I'm back. Train's
on time. I'll be with you by 7.
Finn: K. I'll get Charm over and we
```

```
can hold a meeting when you get in.
Dad cooked us lunch and we didn't eat
much. It'll reheat.
Leah: Deal.
```

Leah was on the train up from King's Cross, sitting at a table triaging emails on her laptop.

After he signed off, she powered down, leaned back and closed her eyes. *Alanna?*

She was not my flesh and blood, but something had shifted in our shared dream so that when she focused hard on my name, I could hear her, more or less. Communication was as frustrating as ever, which is to say she couldn't hear me, but she could feel the bigger ideas if I pushed them hard.

'Eriq was so alive,' she said. 'I can't imagine him not there. Who's going to play the cavaquinho in the evenings, or juggle kitchen knives while he's stacking the dishwasher?'

I pushed a thought of Finn tossing knives high in the air: he wasn't Eriq, but he was the second-best juggler I'd ever seen.

'Finn's OK at the juggling,' I said. 'And he's not bad on the drums. Useless on strings, though. Charm, maybe?' I remembered hearing Charm play her guitar between Arena matches.

Leah nodded, thoughtfully. 'I need to connect better with Charm. She's holding everything together like a boss, but we don't want to overload her. Finn's right, though. We are a big step off the timelines, and every step we take away from the old patterns has to be good. Or at least, not guaranteed to be bad. I wish I knew where to go from here. I was hoping to run everything past Connor, but he's not . . . His thinking's not where we need it. Can you talk to him?'

Worth a try. I pushed a half-assent, and left.

'Not where we need it' was the polite version of Connor's current state.

The more accurate, infinitely more devastating, version was that Connor was a husk of flesh and bones with very little autonomous animation. He was still staying with Mo Bakar, but he'd moved from the mill to the big Georgian house a hundred yards further along the river, which had once been a country house hotel and was now the residential unit where her international students stayed, and where they currently rotated shifts, caring for Connor round the clock.

I had tried without success to slide into his dreams most nights since the shootings, but it occurred to me now that he might not be sleeping and so might not be dreaming in the truest sense.

On a hunch, I went back to the loch, to where Hail was lying by the water's edge. 'How do I find him?' And then, panicked, 'Hail?'

He was old and grey about the muzzle and, when I ran to him, he rose unsteadily onto legs that looked too old to hold him.

'Hail, I can't lose you, too!' I knelt at his side and let him rest his muzzle in the crook of my elbow. I'd sat with dying dogs over the years and this was too close. 'Hail, we're in a *dream*. You don't have to let yourself grow old.'

He huffed a bit of a laugh. *Some things are not entirely my choice.*

'If Connor's doing this to you, I'll kill him. Is he here? Can I talk to him?'

Ha! One shaggy brow crooked up. *Go up beyond the waterfall and set your mind to when the world was young. I can't guarantee you'll find him, but it's your best chance.*

I'd take any chance over more nights of frustrated un-dreaming. I flew north of the loch to places I had never explored, and here, past the edge of what I had made, I hunted for Connor among the tangled briars and bogs of a place that was old when Connor McBride was young.

This was old, old Ireland, a place of mythic landscapes, where a half-human crow was the least remarkable thing to fly the skies or pace the edge places where field met forest and mountains sent rivers cascading down to the sea.

I flew low across the land, hunting by Crow-sense and the feel of Connor's heart, following clues hidden in the patterns of lichen on the rocks above the waterfall, on old carvings on a triad of standing stones, in the numbers of berries on the hawthorn trees until I came, in time, to a lough, not unlike the loch by which I had left Hail, except that this one had the waterfall at the south-eastern end, and stretched out in a long finger to the north-west, in a mirror-image of the one I knew.

I dropped down over a long, fissured rock at the waterfall's edge to a sandy ledge that led in behind the curtain of tumbling water. It was wide enough that I could fly in without getting wet, and it led to a vast, dry cave, lit by the evening sun filtered through water, so that the light was always moving, and always a different shade of sandstone-gold. It was a beautiful place to sleep, to rest, perhaps to die. I did not plan to let him do any of these things.

'Hey, big man.'

Connor was curled in foetal position beneath an overhang of rock. Stalactites and stalagmites made a shark's-tooth barrier further in, but here, a dozen paces in from the cave's wide mouth, the floor was smooth, with a faint dusting of sandy grit, the walls were rounded, the ceiling high enough that he could have stood on his own shoulders three times and not reached it.

As a Crow, I stood on the floor, a distance away. He opened bleary eyes and struggled to focus.

'Lan?'

He wasn't sure. I hopped closer and then, because he was still confused, took human form. My voice was the same. 'You planning to hide here forever?'

'Lan.' He made it sound like a curse, but he lifted his big, gnarled hands to rub his face and rolled out from under the overhang. Moving looked like it hurt and none of his joints had a full range of movement, but, in time, he managed to sit, with his knees crooked up and his elbows balanced on his kneecaps. He propped his chin on his hands and I saw him teeter on the edge of forgetting.

'They're dead,' I said. 'It wasn't your fault.'

I am not kind. I have never pretended to be. But, in this, I thought a fast remembering was significantly kinder for all concerned than losing him again in the thickets of amnesia.

His eyes flared. His face grew tighter, harder. I thought that, for the first time in my life, I might see Connor angry.

The moment ebbed. He pushed himself to his feet and fitted his shoulders to the wall, arms crossed. He looked younger. He looked, in fact, a lot like Finn used to, when he wanted something he couldn't have.

'Why are you here?' he asked.

'You're needed.'

'I'm not. No more than Eriq was.'

'You saw him leave?'

'Dreamed it.' When I didn't follow up, he walked to the cave's edge and cupped his hands under the backspray from the waterfall. I felt the damp, watched him scrub his face clean, felt the sharp, icy edge of it.

I thought about all the soft, conciliatory things I could say, and abandoned them. 'Eriq was a good man. He wasn't the son of a god.'

Connor had his back to me, but I saw his shoulders shudder and when he turned he was laughing. 'Is that who you think I am?'

'The clue's in the name, at least if we take "god" in its gender-neutral sense.' McBride. Son of Bride, also known as Brigid, Briga, Brid, god of fire, of war and poetry and blacksmiths. Among other things. 'Am I wrong?'

He stared out at the water for a long time. I wasn't certain that I had more patience than he did, but I was prepared to wait a long time to find out.

I have no idea how much time passed before he turned round, only that he did. 'I was her lover, not her son.'

I frowned. 'Then you're not Ruadán?'

'Lan, you won't find me in the myths, I've had plenty of time to make sure of that.'

I would do the same, I think, given the time, but I couldn't tamp down the curiosity. 'Can you tell me what happened?'

He sat down with his back to the rock. 'I didn't know she was a god. There was . . . danger. This was in the time when people were still connected to the land, to the life of it, but some were breaking away, learning to enjoy violence, and the power that came with it. I thought she was going to be hurt. I promised . . .' His gaze turned inward. 'I promised I'd not rest until she was safe and nobody could hurt her.' His face was raw. His laugh had layers I'd never unpick.

'Later, a long, long time later, when I realised who – what – she was, she offered to let me off. I was young, though, compared to now, and I still thought I could make everything right.' He spread his hands. 'I said no.'

Ten thousand years since the start of agriculture, since the breaking of humanity's link with the web of life. Ten thousand years at least. And Connor had wedded himself to a god.

Uuri taught me early that all gods, in the end, are the soul of the earth. Bride is Gaia as much as she is anyone else. The question, I suppose, is whether the god dies when the biosphere dies, or is bound to the rock and dust and magma that is the planet, which will keep going at the very least until the sun melts down.

Connor watched me think this through, eyes crinkling.

I said, 'Do you think you can make things right for her now?'

'Not on my own. And not in this life. Fifty years ago, in my hubris, I thought it might still be possible, but not now. Kaitlyn might have started something that will. I would very much like for that to be so.'

Which explained, I suppose, why he was here, in this family, at this time. Why, against all kinds of likelihood, and without contravening any vows concerning fidelity that he might have given to the god he loved, he was Kaitlyn's grandfather. Still so many questions to ask.

One pushed the rest aside. 'Do you know what comes next?' I asked. 'For you, I mean.'

'I do not. That is, I'll be born after I die, with not much of a gap in between. And then I'll take up where I left off. If I can.'

His gaze was distant and I could see the years on him then, and the countless lives. Never again will I complain about the void. I would not have the fortitude for this. 'How do you find the strength to go on?'

'I love her. That never changes.' Connor gave a faint smile and then, bending, gathered some dust from the floor. He opened his fingers, sifted it through, as if the grains were an oracle and he could read futures in the way they clustered. When all was gone, he lifted his head. 'The boys are on their own?'

'They have Charm,' I said. 'And Leah. And Mo. Matt and Jens are still around, obviously, and they've always been a stabilising influence. But the oldest of these is half your age. There's a wisdom that is lacking.' I didn't say, ten thousand years is a wisdom beyond price; we were long beyond platitudes. But not beyond asking for favours. 'If you can hold on a bit longer, the stability would help set their course straight.'

He thought a long time. I did not interrupt. At the end, he said, 'Go back to the farm. I'll join you there. I'll be awake and aware, I promise.'

▼

The pale fingernail moon was ducking under the horizon by the time Leah's taxi pulled up outside the farm. Finn had the coffee ready. Charm was already there. Niall was sprucing up the leftovers from lunch.

I thought Leah might have plans to turn this into a working meal, but Finn barely waited for her to sit down before he said, 'What are we trying to create?'

Niall had pounced on the papers as Leah dropped them on the table: digital headlines were all very well, but even when things were normal he'd preferred the security blanket of the real thing.

His answer, then, came without much thought. 'A movement,' he said, turning over *The Times* ('RADICALS THREATEN FRAGILE NATIONAL STABILITY'). 'An unstoppable wave of people holding to a vision of a future we'd be proud to leave behind.' He turned over the *Telegraph* ('IS NEW YOUTH MOVEMENT TERRORIST?'). 'We're not restricting to the young, either. Anyone who gets what we're doing is welcome to swell the numbers.'

'But we're also building community.' Finn put bowls in front of everyone. 'We need communities of place, purpose and passion linked by common values.' And when they looked at him, 'What? Niall isn't the only one who gets to channel Big Sis.'

Niall's laugh was all surprise. 'Yes, but do you even know what it means?'

There was a time when a question like that would have seen Finn pick up his phone and leave. In a more recent time, Eriq would have done something to soften the atmosphere.

Finn, to his credit, lifted nothing more than one angled brow. 'Bro, I've been playing Warcraft since before you left school. I live in a community that has my back every night in the battlegrounds and

311

they pitched in actual dollars to the Twitch stream by their millions even before the funeral. You're cool on the theory. I am—' he paused for effect— 'the lived experience.'

Ouch.

Among the many, many things Niall cited as evidence of a limp intellect, this phrase ranked near the top. Granted, I may have used it once, but not in his hearing.

Charm laughed. 'With respect,' she said, and it was either stellar timing or she had got to grips with Niall's foibles in a remarkably short time span, 'we play because we enjoy it. It's not a chore.'

Finn gleamed at her. 'My point exactly. If we're going to create a movement that can power through to a future that works, it has to be built on people wanting it so badly they get up in the morning and race for it with open arms, not because they've been bribed or coerced or bullied or herded at the point of a gun. They have to want it as much as Charm and I want to play.

'But it needs to be more than just online. We need to embody the thing we're trying to create in our actual reality. Which means we need to build something here.' He made an expansive gesture that took in the whole farm.

'So, if the bad guys want to nuke us, they only have to take out one small patch of Suffolk?' Niall at his most acid looked painfully like his mother.

'Doesn't matter.' Leah shook her head. 'You can create the most distributed network the world has ever seen and if they want you dead, you'll be dead. In the dream, I saw Juke go down. If they can get to him, they can get to anyone.'

'Which,' Finn said stolidly, 'is why we need to start building community now.' He thumbed his phone one last time and set it down with a weighty click. On this cue, there came a tap on the door and a young voice said, 'It's Prune. I'm with Nico and Stina. May we come in?'

Niall's gaze nailed Finn to the wall. 'Sure, door's open.' Nothing about his face matched his voice.

They trooped in bearing gifts: three wise youths. Nico, tall, dark-haired, bespectacled, was the most assured, partly because he was seventeen and already had a place to read law at St Andrews, latest in a legal dynasty that had been running in unbroken lineage since the civil war. His mother was a QC. His father had played oboe in the National Philharmonic before heading back to teach at Clare College, but Nico didn't have a musical bone in his body, so law it was. Nico's parents were good people, they must have asked their only son if it was what he wanted, but what kind of kid decides at seventeen that he's going to break four hundred years of family tradition?

When he wasn't studying, he wrote half-decent poetry and helped his dad smoke hams. Accordingly, he had brought a joint of home-cured ham and laid it now on the table. A rolling, meaty scent overpowered the bite of evening coffee.

Stina was sandy-haired, verging towards straw-gold where the ends brushed her shoulders, and had a lot of shiny metal nudging her teeth into the places her orthodontist said they should be. She smiled with her mouth shut.

Thirteen months younger than Nico, she wasn't ever going to compete with him in academic terms, but she was streets ahead on the climbing wall, and the racetrack, and just about anything that involved athletic capacity or physical dexterity. She brought a basket of eggs and a bouquet of hawthorn and hazel that shimmered spring-green and brought the kitchen alive.

Prune was the youngest, only six months older than Kaitlyn. Clearly his parents had not named him Prune at birth, but his mother had died when he was four and his father, who had never planned for single parenthood, had called him an 'absolute prune' once when the others were within earshot. His dad wasn't being unkind and his peers were not the bullying sort, but it had stuck nonetheless, to the point where nobody seemed to remember his original name.

Shorter and stockier, he had neither Nico's sharpness nor Stina's athleticism. He spent most of his free time down at the Dairy with Matt and Jens, honing an instinctive feeling for growing things. I hadn't worked out if this was natural or just mined out of sheer determination to do something useful (also, he had a crush on Jens, but then so did half the village, so that's barely worth mentioning), but the end result was the same.

Prune didn't carry anything. He stayed just inside the door, looked to Finn for confirmation and, at the briefest nod, said, 'We want to help.'

Wary, Leah asked, 'What kind of help?'

Niall spoke over her. 'You can't. It's too dangerous.' With Eriq gone, Niall was feeling into his role as the adult in the room.

Nico opened his mouth, shut it again and waited. Stina didn't speak if she could avoid it.

Prune gave a short sigh that wasn't really aimed at anyone else and said, 'We're the people you're fighting for. If they call an election tomorrow, not a single one of us will be old enough to vote. It's our future that's being spaffed up against the wall and we don't have a say in how to change it.'

He watched all levels of this sink in, then gave a small smile when he saw them re-evaluate him in real-time. He didn't sigh again, but the space where he might have done was loud.

'If you ask us what our parents think,' he said, 'you'll undermine everything you're building, so please don't. In any case, they'll be along in the morning, offering the same. We've been sent to soften you up, which is almost as patronising as it sounds. Bottom line: just as Finn said, Kirsten's vision was of communities of place, purpose and passion. You've made purpose and passion happen online, or you're trying to. We're your oven-ready community of place, and if you don't let us play our part there's no point in anything else you do.'

In the hush that followed, Charm got up and began to lay out places for the incomers. Finn kept his attention on his phone, which fooled no one.

'You knew about this?' Niall asked.

Finn shrugged. 'Nico's got 180K on his Minecraft stream.'

'Sorry, what?'

Patiently: 'He's the one who taught Kaitlyn to play Minecraft. He's an international superstar with a huge following in his own right. He's been coding for the Ghosts in his spare time since the first lockdown. So yes, I knew.'

'We'd be here anyway,' Prune said, crossly. 'This is about more than computer games. Kaitlyn's been our friend since we were old enough to crawl across the carpet. Maddie was a second mother to all of us. Kirsten inspired us to believe the world could be better. They may not have been our blood family, but we loved them. Kaitlyn wanted change. Kirsten wanted to build community. Maddie wanted us all to grow into a future that was worth having. This is how we get all three. Also, you need a Custodian for Future Generations on your board. We think it should be one of us. Specifically, we've voted Nico. He'll pass it to Stina when he goes to university and she'll pass it to me unless you have someone better by then.'

His gaze was benign, but not remotely flexible. 'We are by far the youngest people you know.'

'But . . .' For once, Niall struggled with words. 'School?' And then, when Prune frowned in genuine confusion, 'Even if you're all still home-schooling, you still have to learn stuff, right? When are you going to find the time to do . . . everything else?'

'Guys, with the greatest respect, we've been teaching ourselves on our own for the past three weeks while everyone else was busy planning the funeral.' Prune had a way of saying difficult things with an ease that smoothed them safely. 'We're way ahead on syllabus. If you want us just to learn for the exams, we could do it in three mornings a week. But at some point we have to say out loud what we all know: that the whole curriculum is one giant exercise in gaslighting and it's not preparing us for anything we're ever going to need. Unless you seriously believe we have futures that include mortgages and jobs and payments on the car, it's a total waste of time. We'd learn a lot more that was useful if we learned how to build a community with you.'

Kirsten might have been saying this for the best part of a decade, but to hear it from a teenager who looked as if he *should* have a future with a mortgage and a job and a car left them queasy, even Niall, who said, tentatively, 'So . . .?'

'So, if we're building community, it needs to be around the things we already do here. We have the Ghosts and the coding, but we also have a farm, which means land, which means we can grow our own food: for ourselves and anyone within reach.

'Kirsten taught us to gather our information from the people who are closest to the things on the ground, in all senses. I think we

315

should get Matt and Jens to tell us how we can build up the farm so it'll feed as many people as we need. Within reason.'

'Within reason,' Niall echoed. And then, 'They ... you have plans for this?'

'Matt and Jens have had plans for years: they've been at the cutting edge of the regenerative farming movement since Lan died and lockdown only ramped it all up. The difference now is that we can see a way to make it happen. They want to shift to more agro-forestry so they can combine carbon sequestration with feeding local people. If we can get twelve more growers to work on the land, we think we can feed up to a hundred. After that, it scales pretty much by the same ratios. Beyond two hundred mouths to feed, we'd need to rent more land.'

'We.' Already, Prune was an integral part of the making.

'Which means,' Stina explained, because nobody's lights had gone on yet, 'more of the Ghosts can come to live here. Juke thinks we've got about six months before the security services hack GhostTalk and we need to have a good solid group who can talk face to face before then.'

'Also,' Nico said, 'communities of place that combine passion and purpose are going to work better than anything else.'

And from Prune, 'Plus, Matt and Jens say the future of food is in localism. Ergo, we need as many people actually living within walking distance as we can get.'

'What about immigration?' Finn asked. 'Dad was already getting hassle.'

Nico shrugged. 'Jess says she can sort the work visas, but a lot of the Ghosts are from the US and Europe so it's not so much of a problem.'

This sounded rehearsed, particularly the bit where he called his mother by her first name. Everyone looked at Finn, except Niall, who studied the three youngsters thoughtfully. 'Where are all these extra people going to live?'

Stina flashed him her rare, shy smile. 'The Piggery has eight rooms. Charm's in one, but that still leaves seven. Nico's parents have a garden office they've turned into an Airbnb. It sleeps six.'

'Some garden office.'

'Prune's dad says he'll give us sole use of the Half Moon, which will take fourteen; twice that if they don't mind sharing a room: single beds, though they'll push together to make doubles if we need.'

Charm said, 'That's twenty-seven assuming nobody shares. We have fifty-three Ghosts already cleared and Hawck has more on the list. If—'

'You really want to talk to Matt and Jens before you get too carried away.' Connor's voice shouldered through the open door to the yard, startling them all. The rest of him stomped in behind. He'd followed Prune and the others up the hill, but he'd been slow and they'd all been too busy talking to notice him.

Guilt flared around the room, but he grinned at them, and pulled up a chair at the head of the table, which had been Eriq's place and nobody else had wanted to sit there. I watched everyone's shoulders relax.

Finn got up and poured him coffee. 'Grandad.'

Hugging the mug to his chest, Connor said, 'There's a flat acre along the back of the Rookery that would be perfect for a dozen or more shepherd's huts or glamping pods or whatever you want to call the wee houses that'll get past the planners. As long as people aren't fussy about composting toilets and getting water from the standpipe, they'll be grand.'

His tone suggested that anyone interested in building community shouldn't be fussy about hot and cold running water. He swept his hands through his hair, leaving it wilder than before. At the end of which he glanced up at me and away again. It was the closest we dared go to connection when Finn was watching him so closely.

'Would Matt and Jens want to do that?' Leah asked, cautiously. 'Build cabins on the hay fields?'

'They'd bite your hands off,' Prune said, without hesitation.

Connor, leaning forward, said, 'This is the world they've been wanting since they first came to help Lan. They're just seeing a way to make it happen now.' He leaned back. 'They're not wrong, either.'

The questions dried up. Finn looked thoughtful. Nico, Stina and Prune looked hopeful.

Only Niall didn't share the common cheer. 'So, we're building an actual, living intentional community.' Something newly caustic lined his voice. 'And it's all Finn's Ghosts plus the people who live here in the village. No offence. I love you all, but we already have a community. Alba Rising has nineteen members with pretty much a zero loss rate. We could expand tomorrow given the resources we have now.'

Finn palmed his face. He'd never lived in the twins' community in Glasgow, but he'd stayed there for weeks at a time in the school holidays: he knew as well as anyone what it was like and who the key players were. He laid his hands flat on the table. 'You can invite everyone down, Nye. They'd all be welcome. You must know that.'

'They wouldn't move south of the border if you paid them. You must know that, too.'

'Then you can set up a satellite in Glasgow.'

'Finn, you're not listening. We already have a fucki— a community. It's not a satellite of anything. It's. A. Community. It's been up and running for seventeen years. People live there, love there, have jobs and family . . . roots. Their future is there. It's *Scotland*. It's my home. It was yours once. We're heading for Independence and we already have the kind of government you're begging people to create down south.'

Finn began turning coins over between his fingers, the way Eriq used to. 'Nye, I don't know what you want. We need to build a critical mass of Changemakers into a community and we can do this here. What we can't do is uproot everyone and drag them to the frozen north to join in the glorious revolution. Also, last time I looked, the Crescent had twenty-four bedrooms. It's nowhere near big enough. Unless you want to sell the farm?' His gaze was clear and direct and carefully held no challenge. 'We own half each. You could force a sale.'

I thought the Ghosts probably had enough money to buy a fair-sized country estate in Scotland, but it wasn't, after all, about the money.

'You know that's not going to happen.' Glacier-calm, Niall forced his gaze up to the space in the top left corner of the room where he had decided Kirsten was located today. I eased out of the way to let the silent communion take place.

Moments later, flatly, he said, 'For now, then. But we keep the

318

whole lot of them in the loop as members, not as a "satellite". And when we win the next Indy Ref, I'm going up the road, whatever's happening down here.'

'And by then we might join you.'

'You'll be welcome.' Niall looped his fingers and stretched them together over his head, popping the joints. 'In that case, do we have an agreement that we can – what the *actual* . . .?'

Loud in the quiet, Finn's, Charm's and Nico's phones had all pinged together.

Finn's eyes flared wide. 'PM's put out a video.' To Niall, cautiously, 'You OK if we pause the conversation to watch?'

'Sure.' Niall managed to shrug and toss him the TV remote at the same time. They all shuffled their chairs round to face the big screen as Finn thumbed to the right channel in time to catch the last few sentences.

'. . . a proud nation, and secure, held safe by the traditions that have always made us great. This I promise, with all the gravity of this office and the ancient democracy that we uphold: we shall ensure that the menfolk of this country know how to keep their women safe in their own homes. Thank you, and good night.'

The Prime Minister of the United Kingdom stepped back from the blond-wood podium and paused between the flanking pair of oversized polyester Union Jacks. A brassy orchestral cover of the national anthem surged as the screen faded to black.

In the kitchen, a shocked hush ate at the air. Niall began to stack the dishwasher. Finn began to rinse pans. Each was waiting for the other to break the silence. Someone else beat them both to it, loudly.

'*Fuck* that.'

Niall, nerve-shot, dropped the plate he was holding. Finn engaged his Arena reflexes and caught it before it hit the ground.

Everyone else's attention was on Stina. Her colour was high, but she stood her ground. 'What? Someone had to say it. "Our menfolk keeping *their* women safe?" I can't believe anyone even thinks this garbage anymore.'

'You don't have to believe it. You're not the target audience.' Niall took the plate back from Finn, then the pan he was holding, leaving both his brother's hands free for his phone. 'How's it playing?'

Finn folded back into his chair. '#YouthVoteNow is already being shunted down the trends by #PrideInTheUK and #LittleWomen across all the media.'

'Bots,' Nico said. 'Has to be. Nobody under eighty would go there and nobody over eighty knows how to use a hashtag.'

'It's not an age thing, it's geographic.' Finn hit a couple of keys and the big screen on the wall above the table glowed with a handful of graphs and a map of the UK on which towns were marked with scarlet dots whose size was proportional to the population.

His phone doubled as a laser pointer sweeping from one to the other. 'If you live anywhere with a population density over thirty per square hectare, which is pretty much any town over the size of Derby, then you think what we just heard was jingoistic, misogynist bullshit. If you're rural or small town, upwards of 60 per cent think it's just about spot on. And that's the population the new constituency boundaries are designed to amplify; the government needs to reach them and hold on to them.'

'So they're playing to the crowd and to hell with the damage it'll do to actual women.' Stina looked as if she might spit on the floor. 'Nothing new there, eh?'

Finn frowned. 'Why, though, when Prof Charringford estimated they'd have a hundred-seat majority? That was the whole point of them pushing through the boundary changes and all the voter suppression. All they have to do is sit tight and they win? They know this. We know this. Why are they winding people up for the sake of it?'

'Because, Grasshopper,' Niall had rediscovered his equilibrium, 'they win by the aforementioned and much-vaunted landslide *only* if their core vote doesn't split. That's the sting in the statistical tail that we've been sitting on all along.'

'And their vote'll split because . . .?'

Niall shrugged. 'People like new blood, mostly. The current lot have been in for a decade and a half and everyone's tired of them, and the other two parties are doing their best to make sure you couldn't slip a worn credit card between them on policy, so it basically comes down to which colour of rosette you want pinned onto your mindless neoliberal suits. In practical terms, half the country could vote red, yellow or blue and, absent some kind of sane proportional representation, nobody's going to notice the difference.'

Stina said, 'So you're telling me they're using *the deaths of your family* as a political football to appease their core vote?'

Niall nodded, tightly. 'Nothing new there, eh? But yes, exactly this. They'll have focus-tested every adjective and noun. That's why it took them till now to get something together.'

'What do we do?' Finn asked.

'Practise our patience. Play Go, or mah-jong, or chess. Kick bricks. Go murder some harmless Orc in Warcraft, if you really must.' Abruptly, Niall checked his watch. 'For the rest of us, sleep's likely the best option. Anything that doesn't interrupt them while they're making their mistake.'

Everyone recognised an instruction to head for bed when they heard it. The youngsters left with a promise to return. Charm went back to the Piggery. Leah headed upstairs to the spare room that had become hers the night after she woke from the Lion's Grace dream. Only the family remained.

Niall and Finn were clearing the last remnants of dinner when Connor asked, 'What would their mistake be?' 'I'm not sure,' Niall said. 'All I can tell you is that nervous politicians make really bad strategists.' He set the dishwasher running and leaned back on the wall, then cocked a brow at Finn. 'What has the Health Secretary said?'

'Nothing. Why?'

'I had an idea but I might be wrong, in which case there's no point in bringing the theory-crafting out to play.' Yawning, Niall made for the stairs. 'Go to bed, people. A night is a long time in politics. Something will have shifted by morning. Connor, do you want to stay upstairs? We can put clean sheets on Mum and Dad's bed in half a minute.'

CHAPTER NINETEEN

Tuesday, 16 May 2023

'Ms Toxic Pixie from QBC's interviewing the Health Secretary at the top of the hour.'

Finn shook Niall awake with the news. His brother sat up, thumbing sleep from his eyes. There was a moment of un-knowing when he mentally searched for Kirsten and found her gone.

'Nye . . .'

'I'm fine.' Niall rubbed his face free of sleep. He still held himself too tightly, still glittered too brightly. He was still not eating enough, nor was his sleep restful and I could hear the distant groan of rotting ice whenever I got close enough. He was functioning, though, and I was beginning to think this was as good as we were going to get.

Rising, he threw a glance to the upper left corner of the ceiling. As I had before, I dodged out of the way and let him connect with whatever he found there.

Finn, who had already spent half an hour kicking ten bells out of a padded bolster, nudged his brother's arm with a freshly made coffee.

Niall blew across the top of the mug. Bursts of bitter flavour lifted into the spring morning. 'Which hour?' he asked.

'This one.'

'Finn!'

'Sorry. Seven. In the morning. Five minutes and eighteen seconds from now.' And then, because there was no response. 'Today's Tuesday.'

Niall withered him with a look that found new focus even as he hurled himself across the room to the dressing table and started hunting for clean underwear. 'Have you slept at all?'

Finn, who rarely showed his face before ten thirty at the best of times, looked briefly scared, as if staying awake all night were a family felony. Niall dragged a clean sweatshirt out of a drawer, flipping the question away. 'Forget I asked. Thank you for waking me. We'll need the team.'

'Leah's already in the barn, watching the preambles so we don't miss anything vital. Charm is in the Piggery with Nico, firing up the shifts around the world to watch it so we can craft a response; she'll head up to the barn as soon as she's done. Stina's on the way up from the village, she'll listen on her phone if she's not here in time. Connor's going down to the Dairy where they're having trouble calving a cow. Prune's been there since crack of sparrow-blink, mopping a fevered bovine brow and murmuring encouraging things to Matt who's doing the obstetrics. It's fine.'

Niall hopped round to face his brother, one leg in his jeans. 'And I'm last to know, because . . .?'

Finn regarded him flatly. 'I know because Charm called me. Charm called me because Juke called her. Don't ask me how he knew: he knows everything, including the fact that I was in the gym and Charm was at her desk.

'I told Connor ahead of you because he slept in the room at the top of the stairs, where you put him last night. I didn't have to tell Leah because the Lion woke her up and sent her to find out what we were talking about. Connor called Prune who was already up, because cow with mini-cow stuck in pelvic girdle, see previous conversation. Is this really the question you want to ask?'

Finn checked his phone. 'You can head down paranoid alley, or you can hear Ms NutJob do her thing with *the guy you name-checked last night*. Your choice, but if you go for the paranoid option, next time I'll let you sleep in. And you'll have left Charm to decide which bits of video to push out. You have three minutes. Bye!' He bolted, his feet a stutter on the stairs.

Niall made it to the barn with his hair brushed and his mug ready for a refill as Rebecca Watson, recently promoted to political editor at QBC, finished her introductions. '. . . Secretary, we certainly live in interesting times. Welcome to QBC.'

323

The producers panned to a wide shot of them both, and then pulled in on the talent: mid-fifties, almost-white hair cropped short, framing a ferrety face not remotely enhanced by a pair of ludicrously large Harry Potter glasses.

For obvious reasons his name among all the lobby journalists was Specs. One of the tabloids had put it on the front page in the first months of his parliamentary career and since then nobody had ever bothered with his real name. Niall had said long ago that he must have paid through the nose for it, given that his real name was Brian Arthur Doidge, which didn't come out well even if you reduced it to an acronym and put 'Doctor' at the front; especially then.

The 'Doctor' bit was not a scam. Specs had been an honest-to-goodness GP before he'd discovered politics, and there had been a giddy moment after he was promoted to Health Secretary when everyone had thought he might buck the trend of NHS destruction-by-starvation. This hope had died a merciless death, but even so the press accorded him unusual respect, and he behaved as if it were earned. Among other things, he usually turned up in a pinstripe with his tie as the only flicker of colour. Today, he was notably out of character.

'Jeans and an open-necked shirt?' Niall flopped into a chair. 'Going for the Yoof vote. I'm offering ten to one on that he says the PM's a useless waste of space who isn't fit to run an egg and spoon race, never mind the nation.'

Nobody took him up on it: nobody ever took up Niall's bets on the grounds that he never offered odds unless he was guaranteed to win.

Whatever he planned to say, Specs was not looking impressive. He ran his hand twice through his hair, tried on a smile then discarded it in favour of statesmanlike and thereby displayed himself as both insincere and lightweight. He caught sight of himself in a monitor feed and smoothed his hair flat.

'Could do with more media training,' Finn said, airing quotes round the words.

'Look harder.' Leah leaned forward. 'He's had more media training than you've played Arena matches. Not a single muscle shift is unrehearsed. The early part of that sequence was designed to make you realise he's human, see his vulnerability, feel sorry for him. The final twitch was because he wanted more preamble and Watson hasn't the wit to offer it. Whatever you think of the BBC, their anchors are better than this.'

Finn said, 'First-generation large language models would be better than this.'

'Hush.'

Even so, we missed the first few words: '. . . time to step back from the front bench to make it clear that the PM's jingoistic misogyny is unacceptable. To be honest, I should have done it months ago when he was first elected, but one keeps believing that the office will make the man. There are times when it really does – we can all list former prime ministers who surprised us with their statesmanship – but we have to accept that, in this particular instance, the man has not risen to the office and it's time for change.'

Rebecca Watson asked, 'So do I understand you are planning to resign?' The shine in her eyes lit up a scoop in the making.

Specs favoured her with a rueful smile and handed it to her on a plate tied up with ribbons.

'I am resigning my position now. Here. Live on QBC. I am not about to abandon my party, but as of this moment the prime minister will need to find a new Health Secretary. I suspect I may not be alone. We have seen many low points in this administration, but using the death of three women to make cheap political capital inflicts a whole new level of damage on our body politic.'

Credit where it's due, Watson did not get up and dance a jig on the table. Soberly, she nodded. 'What, then, would have been your response to the Changemakers' demands?'

'They're not demands, they're suggestions, issued by the surviving members of a family who saw a wife, mother, twin and sister murdered in front of them by a young man who should have had help long before he got his hands on a gun.

'And to be honest, I would struggle to argue with any of their list except withdrawing suffrage from those older than eighty.' He lifted one shoulder. 'I'm not so far off myself and I like the illusion of having power once every five years.'

Rebecca Watson had the sense to follow the bigger lead. 'Are you suggesting your government – the government of which until a moment ago you were a member, and which is still the government of your party – is drunk, drugged and corrupt?'

Niall lifted his hand, palm out. Finn met him in a high five. Neither took their eyes from the screen.

Specs' sigh stormed down every single corridor of power. 'Rebecca, you've been a lobby correspondent in your past. Let's drop the pretence. We both know that banning alcohol and drugs would transform the way our administration functions. This is an open secret. And I have to say that shining the light of new technology into the murky world of government contracts would be a blessing to all concerned.'

He paused. Watson said nothing, though her hand on her earpiece suggested things were vocal in the production office.

After a moment, Specs took the silence as an offer. 'People think most politicians are corrupt. Most of us are not, but we move in circles of immensely wealthy, powerful individuals who think it's normal to ask for favours in return for services rendered, and by the time someone's been ground through the mill that makes them an MP they often don't know how to refuse.

'What Changemakers is suggesting is a gift to everyone ever caught in a difficult bind. If we do this, then, when the next oligarch turns up and says they'll . . . I don't know—' warming to his theme, a flourish of hands— 'build a new hospital at knockdown rates, but only if the government gives them the right to run the ambulance service at a profit . . .

'If the new rules are in place, then my successor as Health Secretary can simply point out that this will require their entire oligarch business structure to be visible on the blockchain and turn their business into a not-for-profit venture along Future Guardian lines. I promise you, they'll leave without another word. It means the Secretary can still maintain the fiction that he's their kind of man. Or woman, obviously. They might even still be able to secure donations for their party from their billionaire friends. I doubt that, to be honest, but the next obvious step is that we ban private funding and each of the parties gets public funds in proportion to their share of the vote, which is what happens in most of the saner nations of earth. I think it's brilliant and, frankly, I wish I'd thought of it. This is going to transform our politics.'

'That's . . . a remarkable level of candour.' Watson's too-rapid blinks semaphored a producer on speed, but she managed the segue between earpiece and room far better than Frances Nolan had done. 'Do you think your party will approve of your lifting the lid off the political machine in this way?'

'I sincerely hope so,' said the now-former Health Secretary. 'If it doesn't, it's not the party I joined thirty years ago.'

'Wow.' Niall was round-eyed with awe. 'I thought he'd fire off a salvo. I wasn't expecting an entire ship-sinking broadside.' Thoughtful, he stared up at the ceiling.

Finn said, 'How did you know Specs was going to do this?'

Niall shrugged. 'Politics is a blood sport. There's blood in the water and sharks will do what sharks will do. Specs was just the biggest Great White in the feeding frenzy. He *loathes* the PM. He's been waiting for a chance to break him since he lost out in the last leadership contest. We've given him the chance.'

Finn took a wild stab in the dark. 'And we're not planning to interrupt him?'

Niall snorted a laugh. 'Definitely not, but it wouldn't hurt to fan the fires a bit. The more they arm the circular firing squads, the easier it will be to pick through the pieces afterwards.' Niall rubbed his thumbs across his eyes. 'Please don't pull the sense of that apart, I've only just woken up.'

'Noted.' Finn rose and began to make coffee for Charm and Stina, who were racing each other up the stairs.

Charm won. 'Strategy?' She folded into the seat beside Leah and fixed Niall with her battleground stare. 'His and ours, in that order.'

Blinking, Niall said, 'Specs needs to get his party on side which is a horrible job. There are three factions: the ones who hate the PM but have no spine, so they're a lost cause. There are the ones who despise him but didn't have a good alternative: now that Specs has shown his colours, he has to persuade them he's the best option. At a guess, he's got strong double figures on that one, maybe more.

'The third group is the most interesting. They loathe the PM, but they don't really like Specs. They have to decide if they're going to mount a separate campaign. I'd lay a bet that one of the women is going to raise her standard ASAFP. My money's on Jo Mattieson. She's made a reasonable job of the Business brief, and she's aligned pretty much in the centre. The press already love her. She's been on quiet manoeuvres for years.'

Niall rose and began pacing the room. He looked thinner, and more angular than he had done before the shootings, his actions more rangy.

'We need as much data as we can possibly collect. Can we set the Ghosts to watching the output of all the MPs? Maybe not the SNP or the Welsh nationalists, they don't really have a horse in this race, but the three main English parties.' At heart, Niall was always a Scot; England was always a foreign place.

'On it.' Already, Charm was opening new GhostTalk threads.

Finn moved over to sit beside her and abandoned his phone in favour of his laptop, the faster to type. To Niall, he said, 'Are we looking for anything in particular?'

'Just identifying who leans to which faction. The Opposition parties will start playing their own musical chairs. It's a reflex. They don't know how not to react. So, we make sure we know their angles and if we need to amplify one slightly to make it seem stronger, it'll push the others to more extremes.'

'And extremes are good?' Leah was looking a little ahead of him, the line of her gaze predicting where he'd go next.

'They are if you're trying to unwind a system. Watch what Russia did with Brexit. We're doing the same, only we're trying to heal the nation, not rip it apart.'

'OK.'

Niall may have been the family strategist, but he'd always had Kirsten to act as a buffer between himself and the rest of the world. He stared at Leah now, as if her lack of resistance had felled him.

On a new breath, slowly, he said, 'Feels to me that we're still on track with the dream. But I'm relying on you to tell us if we step off it.'

Leah offered her fist for a bump and, when he met it, said, 'I'll do my best. In the meantime, we have a system to heal.'

*

The entire team decamped to the Piggery, where the office had both enough space and, thanks to Charm's latest efforts, the best broadband connectivity on the farm.

There was also an amount of new technology, including a (quite impressive, I thought) 100-inch cinema screen on the end wall to the left of the door.

Niall hated it on principle. To be fair, Niall had slept badly and was more walled-off than usual, but it's also true that Niall hated any obvious shows of consumerism, and, even on his better days, was quite keen to point out the destruction of lives and habitats that went into the creation of anything shiny and new.

He was outvoted, though, and pacified with more coffee and the rest of the morning passed in relative peace until, not long before lunch, when Finn said, 'Houston, we have a problem.'

Heads raised around him. 'Rocket not on the right trajectory?' Niall asked.

'Rocket takes too much carbon dioxide,' Finn said. And, when this evidently didn't clarify anything, 'We're trying to get the Ghosts here, but we can't fly them. That is, we don't want to because there is no way to offset the carbon that isn't greenwashing bullshit and none of them would come if we pretended otherwise. We can get people to their respective coasts without burning a shit-tonne of carbon, but crossing oceans is a whole different level of hard.'

'You have an answer, though,' Charm said, without looking round from her screen.

'Might do.' Finn nodded. 'What do we all know about Raye Kameransky?'

Everyone shrugged except Leah, who closed her eyes and read off some internal Rolodex where all her celeb-facts were kept. 'Gen Z scion of Russian expat oil money whose family emigrated to the US about thirty years ago. "Oil money" is a cover for laundering all kinds of bad stuff, mostly arms to whichever militias the US wants to arm without being seen to do it, but also everything from slavery to bad coke.

'Raye came out as enby about a year ago. Daddy rocks several degrees to the right of Fox and didn't like having a non-binary heir so there was a dramatic and highly public disinheritance and they dropped off the radar. This was all six years ago. I'd heard they went back to Russia, but that's hardly a friendly place for anyone playing with gender norms, so I'd guessed it was a feint.'

'Might have been for a while,' Finn said, 'but they've been in Vladivostok for the past year. Nice view of the Koreas and Japan and a shipbuilding yard that's not averse to trying out new ideas, particularly if there's serious money involved.'

Stina raised a brow. 'How do you have serious money when your alt-right father has disinherited you?'

Leah grinned. 'You wait till the day after your twenty-first birthday to come out and, by that time, the patriarch had already handed his one and only heir a monster-chunk of shares. Strangely, given that the US has the world's second most corrupt legal system, he still hasn't found a way to grab it all back. Also, Raye's a crypto-genius which means it's mostly in fancy digital currencies by now, so it's not like Oil-Daddy can lean on the banks to turn it over.'

'Even if he did,' Nico said, reading off the web, 'Raye's been creative with the crypto-investing. They could lose their seed capital and barely notice.'

'Great.' Niall had evidently not recovered from the morning's altercation. 'Capitalism on steroids. Why do we want to know this person?'

Finn was at his most patient. 'Because crypto-genius doesn't even get close. Raye Kameransky is Vitalik 2.0, twice as smart and with more of an interest in prosocial, regenerative Web3 stuff that you'd be really into if you knew what it was. They're leveraging quadratic funding to flow money to the likes of Digital Gaia and GreenPill and TreeGens: the whole GitCoin thing and – what?'

'Word salad much?'

'Nye? I know it's a bad day, but this is twenty-first-century 101.'

'And I am a twentieth-century boy,' Niall said, flatly. 'Humour me.'

Finn leaned his chair right back and hooked his hands behind his head to look up at the ceiling. 'Vitalik Buterin is the mega-brain who created Ethereum which is the thinking person's blockchain: the "Look-it's-not-Bitcoin!" on which everything good and right and beautiful in the crypto-universe grows and thrives.' He hooked a careful glance sideways to Niall. 'Making sense?'

'I'm hearing capitalism for the uber-libertarian tech-bros who want to create white supremacist tax-free nirvanas in which to consume themselves to a standstill.'

Finn closed his eyes. 'Nye, that was ten years ago. There's a whole universe out there now of really smart people engaging with really smart tech they think will really solve the meta-crisis. It's more than currencies, blockchain is all kinds of useful. We're talking Regenerative Finance, Regenerative AI – trust me, it's a thing – Regenerative Living: all the things you love.'

Niall's shrug was as close as you could get to a middle finger without actually lifting a hand. 'So we just switched from steroids to ayahuasca. Let me sit in the forest and commune with the plants and then I'll design an app to make the rich richer and keep the poor in servitude and sell it to my friends for imaginary money so I can *keep on buying stuff* to bandage over my damaged ego. It's still breaking the planet, Finn. It's still not good.'

Finn had picked up a handful of pens and started juggling. 'Cryptocurrencies are here to stay. Hating them won't make them go away.'

'So you keep telling me. Personally, I was planning on a whole new way of sharing value that's not hitched to the dollar, but still—'

'Guys . . .' Leah's arm arced down between them. 'Time out.' She nodded a 'shut up now' look to Finn and to Niall said, 'Raye Kameransky is at the cutting edge of the cutting edge of all the new stuff, doing things nobody else can even imagine, never mind understand. They're on our side in this, I swear.'

Now it was Niall's turn to put on the exaggerated patience. 'In which case, leaving aside the fact that my baby brother is easily seduced by anyone with an IQ in triple digits, why *exactly* are we discussing this super-genius, not-really-a-capitalist in the context of getting the worldwide Ghosts over here to craft the perfect techno-utopia?'

With an air of discovery, Charm said, 'Shipbuilders in Vladivostok. With money.'

331

'Thank you.' Finn threw her the winning-in-Arena look. 'Where they have spent the past nine months prototyping this.'

Swivelling his chair to face the end wall, Finn hit a key and pushed the image up onto the big, wide, super-fine-resolution screen Niall had hated so passionately.

It was met with stunned silence, except from Niall, who – mostly unconsciously, I thought – whispered, *'Fuck!'*

On the screen had blossomed a sleekly beautiful three-masted catamaran, its hull glistening silver under a wide summer sky.

Whoever had taken the picture had known exactly what they were doing. You could smell salt and seaweed, taste the cocktails on deck of an evening. It was more than beautiful. It was a paean to all the possibility Finn and Leah had promised, shaped by a sharp mind with new ideas ready to break old moulds and to do so in ways that were genuinely breath-taking.

'Whatever they want,' Nico said, 'they can have it.'

'See the detail first,' Finn said, and split the screen in two and threw up diagrams on the right-hand side and grid form models, demonstrating a pair of wings that extended out on either side, increasing the surface area for solar panels. The stats rolling down the farthest edge claimed numbers for power generation that were either grossly exaggerated or a significant improvement on comparable technology.

Finn leaned back on the wall and deployed his laser pointer. 'Raye says this is the fastest sailing ship ever built. It's designed to have a genuine zero carbon footprint: it draws in energy and dumps it into sea-water batteries that are ballast and a power source for the tech at the same time, though the actual motors are driven by hydrogen-fuel cells. Excess power goes into splitting the water to create the hydrogen in a loop that'd let it sail forever if it needed to.

'And it leaves the oceans cleaner than when it started. This—' the red dot circled a scoop set between the hulls— 'gathers surface plastic and renders the junk into bricks that go into the ballast and can be used on shore in the building trade: they have better load stats and insulation parameters that blow actual bricks out of the water. The sails are some kind of new aerodynamic creation of Raye's, designed to generate more thrust than even racing yachts, with the excess also splitting hydrogen or topping up the batteries. The prototype can carry eighty people including crew, which is enough for what we need. They're designing a cargo version so that if we could replace every container ship on the planet, they'd clean up the oceans inside a decade and drop our global emissions by 20 per cent.' Finn turned to the room. 'It's done two successful deep water trials, can carry all the Ghosts on the current list and Raye's offering it to us free of charge. And they'll give Changemakers a share in the IP of the tech when they get here.'

Niall said, 'There has to be a catch.'

'They want Changemakers to name them the Custodian for Future Generations. They're really interested in building—'

'Nico's doing that!' Finn had been braced for an explosion from Niall, but in the event it was Leah who slammed her hands on the desk. 'You can't kick him off the board just because someone with more money than Musk wants to muscle in!'

'And a triple-digit IQ,' Stina said. 'Don't forget that.'

Finn sliced a glance at Nico, who said, 'We could share it, though? Nobody said a custodian had to be just one person.'

Everyone looked at Niall, whose frown deepened from merely thoughtful to calculating. 'You trust Raye?' he asked Finn.

'As much as I do anyone else I've exchanged messages with for less than an hour. Which is to say, not with my life, but if they can get everyone here, it'll count for a lot.'

Leah said, 'And a big ocean-crossing in a smallish boat is a grand way to get to know people. Nothing like facing twenty-foot waves for team-building.'

'Indeed.' Niall gave a sharp smile. 'Guess we get to convene our first full custodians' meeting to find out if there's a job-share option. I'll call Dad and see if he's somewhere he can log in.'

By three o'clock, the full board of Changemakers Custodians had been consulted, six of them in person plus Eriq, who was still in transit to São Paulo, chipping in on GhostTalk.

The proposition was easy and the decision unanimous, with the result that, by three twenty, Nico and Raye were officially job-sharing as Custodians for the Future Generations, with a guarantee to review from both sides when the swiftly renamed *Ocean Ghost* made landfall.

For their part, Raye had agreed to pick up the rest of the Ghosts from the various ports en route and deliver them to whichever port in the UK seemed most useful and/or accessible at the time when that call had to be made: Liverpool was their default. Niall was arguing for Glasgow. As the call wound down, Raye asked for permission to bring two friends, because Vladivostok was 'becoming unsafe'.

Nobody demurred.

CHAPTER TWENTY

Wednesday, 17 May 2023

'It's not Jo Mattieson.'

'Really?' Being woken early by his younger brother was losing its novelty for Niall, and he slid over the moment of returning memory more smoothly than he had done the previous day.

Throwing a passing glance up to the corner of the ceiling (right front this time. I needed to learn to predict better so I wasn't forever in the way), he levered himself out of bed with every sign of being fully awake. 'Who then?'

'Melanie Urquhart. Apparently she got the Defence brief a year or two back when Specs was moved to Health. She's live on Sky just now saying she thinks the PM is being soft on the "youth anarchists" who want to tear up our constitution. Apparently, "when" she's elected, she'll enforce the ten-year prison sentence for anyone deemed to be causing a nuisance, whatever age they are. When I came to find you, she was holding forth about the desirability of prison ships in the North Atlantic as suitable holding pens for young offenders.'

Finn was white about the eyes, like a spooked horse. 'You said Mattieson would go for the centre between the PM and Specs. Urquhart is so far to the right she's off the map. She's come out of nowhere, but Sky seems to think she's in the running.'

'Could be.' Niall had not slept any better than the night before, but he seemed more peaceful than on the previous day. He scrubbed his hands through his hair. 'She's the headbanger's headbanger, out there with the alt-right American wing-nuts who think Hitler had all the right ideas, just lacked strong enough conviction to carry through. She's fully on board with the vision of a white supremacist patriarchal theocracy stretching from Dublin to Vladivostok and ruled along mediaeval lines, because the last time things were done right, the Inquisition was calling the shots.'

'Is this an actual thing or are you sailing off into Conspiracy City again?'

'I can send you the references and you can decide.' Niall pinched granules of sleep from the inside corners of his eyes. 'She's probably being paid by the same mad Russian monk who pulls Putin's strings, though doubtless she thinks it's coming from some oil-funded Atlanticist think tank with twenty layers of offshore accounts to give her plausible deniability. She hasn't got two functioning brain cells to rub together, but she's viciously partisan and she speaks the language of the tabloid comment threads filtered through the worst of Twitter's twist-nets. The PM fobbed her off with Defence because the Chiefs of Staff weren't going to listen to a word she said. Nobody took her that seriously.'

'Sky just gave her ten minutes at the top of the hour.'

'Which—?'

'Seven.'

Niall yawned. 'Why do you not need sleep, Grasshopper? Are you undead and I didn't notice?'

'I slept till half-six.'

'When from, though?'

'One? Ish.'

'Definitely undead.' Niall lifted a T-shirt, sniffed it, and hefted it neatly into the laundry bag near the door. 'I need a shower. Clip me the Urquhart highlights, will you? And scour the channels for Specs' response. This is about to get interesting.'

In the end, it wasn't Specs who garnered all the attention. Having been scooped by QBC and Sky, the BBC took proactive steps to get back into the lead on the biggest political story of the week, month and year.

By the time the top of the next hour rolled round, the *Today* programme on Radio Four had secured an interview with the individual whose task it was to gather the letters of no confidence in the prime minister.

Lady Catherine Westaway, Chair of the relevant committee,

announced live on air that she was three letters short of the minimum required to trigger a vote and had been promised at least a dozen more by the end of the day.

She was discussing the implications of this with the BBC's political editor when they were interrupted by the senior correspondent, a man in his late sixties with an affected Mancunian accent that vaporised when he was under stress. Just now, he was speaking perfect home counties RP.

'So sorry, we have to cut you off there. The PM is on the line from Downing Street and has asked to speak to the nation.'

'Fuck!' Niall, who had been cruising the newspaper sites, dropped his phone and spun his chair round with almost old-Niall animation. '*Fuck!*'

There was no video on the feed of the prime minister, only a lean, pepper-haired BBC veteran pressing his headphones to his ear with the frantic look of someone who thinks they may have just won the lottery but the ticket's in the washing machine and they can't stop the spin cycle.

'. . . believe you have an announcement to make?'

'I do.' The Prime Minister of the United Kingdom had spent years trying to develop a voice suited to the gravity of the role. He gave it his best shot. 'I have considered the comments arising from both sides of my party and am deeply sorrowed by the divisions they are creating. I have devoted my political career to healing the wounds of the past—' Niall snorted an entire mouthful of coffee down his nose— 'and it is deeply upsetting to watch the party I love being torn apart and all that good work undone. Far worse is the damage to our proud nation. This behaviour lacks the dignity that our people expect and deserve—'

'Twenty-second of June.' Niall stood rock-still in the middle of the room. 'He has to give a minimum of twenty-five working days. And the boundary changes aren't in place yet. He's going to be so *fucking* unpopular!'

'—are in a period of global and national turmoil. Our health service is on its knees. Our supply chains are broken. Oil prices are rising, inflation is at an unprecedented high and our crops are failing.' His voice cracked with the enormity of it all. 'People are *starving* while my colleagues play petty party politics. I have decided, therefore, to call a general election. We will conduct ourselves in an orderly fashion, finish our parliamentary business and spend the full five weeks campaigning. Accordingly, the general election will take place on Thursday the twenty-second of June. And may the best—'

'*Yes!*' Whatever else the PM had to say was inaudible over Niall's incredulous, 'This is it, Bro. Whatever happens now, we have at least some chance to mould the outcome. And we do not – abso-fucking-lutely *not* – interrupt our enemy when he has just made the single most spectacular mistake of his life.'

The airwaves detonated.

Every journalist called every number they had on their contact lists. Every politician who could form a coherent sentence was invited to offer an opinion and used the opportunity to start staking out territory. Most of those in the governing party also used it to express 'surprise and disquiet' at the PM having called an election without at the very least waiting for the new constituency boundaries to come into force. They were, to coin Niall's phrase, 'going ape-shit'.

'Can the party get rid of him before the election?' Finn asked.

'Technically. But there is no universe in which any party dumps its leader five weeks before going to the polls.'

'Even if he's a liability?'

Niall did that odd thing where he both nodded and shook his head at the same time. 'The sight of Specs and Ms Batshit Crazy screaming insults at each other in a hyperfactional leadership war is more of a liability than being led by a man who's already compromised with the electorate. They'll do the metrics and decide to get rid of him afterwards.'

'He must know.'

'Of course, and he's just bought himself five weeks' breathing space which is an eternity in politics. It's almost clever.' Niall tilted his chair all the way back to the horizontal. 'He could win.'

'You said he was making a mistake,' Finn said, patiently. 'The whole not-interrupting thing?'

'Because he's not looking further than saving his skin today. We are in the business of mapping the paths beyond tomorrow.' Niall hooked one ankle over the other and stared at a blank patch of wall. 'They're running by the old rules. We'll be running with the new ones, just as soon as we've decided what they are.' Blinking, he looked around. 'Where are the others? Leah, Charm, Nico and friends . . .?'

'Charm and Nico are already in the Piggery. The rest are on their way.'

'OK. Let's invite them all to a working breakfast, eh? One way or another, we need to craft a response to this.'

CHAPTER TWENTY-ONE

The first day of the general election campaign kicked off with deceptive decency.

Under normal circumstances, sitting MPs would recycle themselves. As Niall was never shy of pointing out, only the Scottish National Party realised it might be useful for every MP to undergo primaries for reselection at each new parliament rather than simply sailing through regardless of alternative candidates who might have more skill. 'Or, indeed, any skill at all.'

These, however, were not normal circumstances. The election had not been expected until December and many parties had used the relative downtime of the coronation to begin – and in many cases complete – the process of selecting candidates based on the proposed boundary changes.

Except, as Niall was also happy to point out, the process of selecting candidates in a UK election was, 'The usual constitutional catastrophe that layers mediaeval practice over imperial time-wasting and sprinkles on a shedload of partisan manoeuvring, and it's *slow*, children. Very, very slow. And now they're going to have to undo it all. Which means, in saving his skin, our boy has missed the boat that was supposed to save the party, and upset large numbers of his own team.' He raised his phone in the now-familiar musketeers stance. 'Let the nasty, vicious, partisan, take-no-prisoners battles commence!'

A multitude of battles did, indeed, commence, but, as with so many of the internal conflicts of UK politics, the worst of the eye-gouging, skin-tearing, poison-spitting horror slid under most of the media's radar.

Most, but not all.

Leah was still technically a presenter with Radical FM, and as

340

such had privileged access to the airwaves. Her contact list was no different to anyone else's, but she had Niall as her core strategist, suggesting who to call, in what order and what questions to ask.

'You live next door to Specs' constituency,' he said on their first phone call of the day. 'Have you got people in his party hierarchy who would talk to you if they were planning a shake-up?'

Leah laughed, dryly. 'You're kidding. He's won every election there since 1997. It's one of the safest seats in the country. Who in their right minds would shake that up?'

'Just rattle the tree and see what falls out, eh? And if you get something, you might want to hawk it round to some of the bigger fish in the pond. Wear gloves – they'll bite your hand off.'

Thus it was that Leah Koresh scooped a ninety-second news clip for the BBC, reporting from outside the glass-fronted constituency offices in Godalming, Surrey, where the party Chair had just resigned. She had called in the story, she was on the spot and, fair play to them, the Beeb let her run with it. They credited Radical FM, so everyone was happy, with the possible exception of the newly deposed constituency Chair.

Back at the farm, Niall was directing operations, with Finn fielding the tech through Charm to the Grey Ghosts. 'Outgoing Chair is Gerald Blackwood. Did we have anything on him from the GhostFiles that would have been compromising enough to see him kicked?'

'Nope.' Finn shook his head. 'Not in the A or B tranche.'

'I know. I checked those. Dig a bit deeper, eh?'

Nico found a file deep in a selection of folders marked, 'Ignore because not useful'. He ran up from the Piggery to deliver the news in person. 'He was having an affair with an aide.'

'Consensual?'

'Looks like it. Stacks of WhatsApps from both sides. Many protestations of undying love.'

Niall frowned. 'That's hardly a resigning issue. If it were, the PM would be gone long since.'

'You're making assumptions and all of them are wrong.' Nico looked smug. 'The aide's Black, male and younger than the old man's grandson, though still a good five years over the age of consent. The

Chair's in his late seventies and plays to the ultra-old-school side of the fence. Also, his wife is second cousin to some minor royal.'

'So he was pushed over a very small cliff. Assuming that they have the same data we have and there isn't something more incriminating. Who's replacing him?'

'Jen Tarrant and Heidi Morrison seem to come up most often in the chats.'

'Unless there are two Tarrants at the top of the party, that'll be Ms Tarantula who was the PM's special adviser when he was at the Home Office. She's a seriously nasty piece of work and she still dances to the PM's fiddle. Specs is out of a job.'

Niall thumbed his phone. Leah, still in Surrey, picked up on the first ring. 'Specs is going down. They'll decide they want someone "more electable" to run in his place. If there's a young Asian woman in the local party, it'll be her. If there's more than one, they'll pick the one with the most pronounceable name. Find the most likely and make sure the predator class at the BBC knows what you're thinking.'

'Pronounceable.' Leah's voice poured scorn down the line. 'I loathe these people. I'm on it.'

Leah was granted a slot on a hastily convened mid-morning news show, where she floated the idea that Baruni Gupta, a second-generation Bengali with a law degree from Durham, was likely to be the governing party's candidate for Specs' safe seat.

Various pundits and government MPs laughed openly and mansplained all the reasons she was wrong. Several suggested she was projecting her own political ambitions and had gone for someone who looked a lot like her. She offered them small wagers Niall-style, winner to pay a paltry amount to the charity of the loser's choice. None of them took her up on it.

At one o'clock that afternoon Jennifer Tarrant, the newly selected Chair of Specs' constituency, announced Ms Baruni Gupta as the prospective parliamentary candidate, on the basis that she was 'more representative of our party as it moves into the twenty-first century'.

Specs was gracious in defeat.

Leah's stock among the commentariat soared.

Niall raised his brows in a minor victory wiggle and then looked a question at the Kirsten-space high in the left corner of the room.

'He'll not give up,' he said, eventually. 'He'll be looking for another safe-ish seat that hasn't yet named a candidate.' To Finn, 'Can Charm get us a list?'

'Way ahead of you.' Finn pinged a file to the screen. 'Of the constituencies yet to declare their candidate, least likely is Barnsley in North Yorkshire. The constituency Chair is a woman who is rumoured to have had an affair with the PM, so Specs won't be welcome there. There's another in Dumfries and Galloway, but—'

'—you don't parachute an English candidate into a Scottish constituency and expect anyone except your agent to vote for you.'

'You stole my line. The only other one is in Berkshire and it's not what you'd call safe. The party Chair went to Trinity, though. Dublin. Same as Specs.'

'Specs studied medicine in Ireland?' Niall's brows touched his hairline. 'Why did I not know?'

'Didn't ask?'

'Fuck you.' It was said without rancour and Niall looked vacant for a moment, scoring the probabilities. 'Seat's not safe enough. I don't think he'll go for it. But still might be worth Leah getting some vox pops from the constituents, just in case.'

'On it.' Finn sent a series of texts. Wheels turned. Leah got the vox pops and they went straight to file because Niall was right, Specs didn't even try for the Berkshire seat. He retired to his estate on the Devil's Punch Bowl in Surrey and dropped out of sight and mind.

Shortly after two o'clock, Leah was offered a spot on the following evening's BBC *Question Time* panel.

Niall rang as soon as he heard. 'Don't touch it.'

'Niall, you're an amazing strategist and I'm in awe of your predictive capacities, but *Question Time* is the top of the tree. Hell hath no fury like a QT producer spurned. I'm saying yes.'

'Leah, it's a festering pit of alt-right trolls dressed up in the flayed skins of their human victims and they're starving for blood. You can't go there.'

'Not even to announce I'm standing as an Independent candidate in the neighbouring constituency to Ms Gupta?'

'Why there?' Niall sounded genuinely confused.

'It's where I live. Except when I'm staying for prolonged periods at your farm, obviously.'

'Right.' The gap where Niall processed this swirled thick with possibility. At length, 'We need to talk.'

'I know. I'm on my way back. I'll be with you just back of five. Don't blow any blood vessels before I get there.'

▼

Niall said, 'You can't turn Changemakers into a political party, there isn't time.'

He and Finn were upstairs at the barn. Leah stood on the threshold. She had brought a bottle of wine with her. 'Peace offering?'

Niall's mother had been an alcoholic in his early years. He turned down the offer and ran water for himself and Finn instead. Leah left the bottle outside and matched him.

'I'm not turning anything into anything until we've all agreed on it,' she said. 'But no, we can't become a party. Even if there was time, they'd find some kind of technicality to stop us. We can't let this pass, though, it's the chance of a lifetime.' She tilted her glass at him. 'What do we have to lose?'

'Are you kidding?' This was Niall at his most rebarbative. 'You could *die*, Leah.' He spaced the words out, one, by one, by one.

Leah looked down at her hands. The silence stretched thin and tight until she said, quietly, 'It's my call, though, don't you think?' And, as Niall took a breath, 'If you accuse me of planning wilful martyrdom, I'm out of here, Niall Penhaligon.'

He let the breath out. Turning pointedly to Finn, Leah said, 'Would Nazir and his team come back? Could we afford them?'

Finn had been making a fair stab at invisibility. Forced into the limelight, he said, 'Would they come? Pass. Can we afford them?' He shrugged. 'Yes.'

'Because they were so very effective first time round,' Niall said.

Finn snapped, 'Nye, that's why—'

Leah tapped his ankle and there followed another long silence.

This time it was Niall who spoke first. 'Do you really want to do this?' His voice was no warmer, but it felt less like a scalpel. He was still way too contained, constrained. Before-Niall would have been up by now, pacing the room, throwing out ideas like a sparkler in a gale.

Leah was wise enough to match a question with a question. 'What do you think?'

He huffed a laugh. 'I think you're batshit fucking crazy. But . . . personal safety issues aside – and I don't think we *should* put them aside – it's not a terrible idea.'

Finn's gaze ricocheted between them and came to rest on his brother. 'You seriously think you could stand?'

'I seriously think *Leah* could stand. Maybe others with her. Not me. I'm a shadows man.'

'Spooky,' Finn said. 'Also true. How, though? Standing, I mean.'

'We go the Flat Pack Democracy route from Frome.'

Finn raised a hand. 'Can I say "word salad" and survive till morning?'

'Ha!' Niall croaked a laugh. 'Flat Pack's as close as we get to emotionally literate politics without designing a whole new system from the ground up. Frome *was* an averagely collapsing town in the Somerset hinterlands with an averagely dysfunctional council riven by toxic tribalism. Think the US Congress with West Country accents.

'Gridlock ate them from the inside out until a bunch of the local Transition Town people got together in a pub one night and decided they could hardly do worse, so they might as well stand. Politically, they were all over the spectrum, but they put themselves forward promising to ditch the old style of power-over rather than power-with, and focus instead on listening to the townspeople.

'It worked. They've had a majority since 2015 and now Frome is a pretty good place to live. The old council had a ten-year waiting list for allotments. The new one realised they could just buy a field and that was the ten-year list gone overnight. They do this kind of thing across the board and now the model's been exported wholesale to other councils. It's just waiting to be scaled up to national level.'

'You think we can do it?' Leah was trying not to look hopeful.

Niall was trying not to look as if he were standing on the edge of a precipice. Both were failing.

'If the boycotts are anything to go by, we certainly have the momentum,' Niall said, cautiously. 'It's not impossible.'

'Except, personal safety is the deal breaker,' Finn said. 'And even if we spend all the money the Ghosts have got, we can't guarantee it.'

'None of us are safe, though, are we?' Leah turned wide eyes on him. 'We are never going to be safe anywhere at any time. This is what the dreams showed and just because we got onto a different path, doesn't mean we're *safe*.'

She rose and went to lean against the far wall so she could face them both at once. 'I'm here with you now instead of Netflixing in a flat on Godalming High Street because I've dreamed things I never want to see again. We talked about the Lion's Grace. We talked about a circuit-breaker. We said we were going to be good ancestors, whatever it took, and this is a chance we'll never see again.'

She sat down on the sofa next to Finn. 'It's my risk; you can't stop me. But I'll do better, so much better, with you—' this to Niall— 'helping on strategy, and you and the Ghosts—' to Finn— 'working the tech. We might even win.'

'One seat won't make enough of a difference, though, will it?' Niall asked, and anyone could see he'd jumped, and was in free fall, and not entirely hating it. 'Or do you think you can find six hundred and forty-nine other candidates?'

'Won't need that many,' Leah said. 'We'll only stand in the seats the government is likely to win. No point in splitting the vote in seats they're guaranteed to lose.'

'Even so, that's at least three hundred. Closer to four if we're still on the old boundaries.'

'Which we are. But if I announce it on *Question Time*, we'll get others.' She caught Finn's gaze again, and then Niall's. 'I lied. You can stop me. Here and now, if you say no, I'll forget it. I won't even mention it again. I think we'd be making a terrible mistake, but if we go, we're a team all the way, with whatever that entails. Lion's Grace, no in-fighting. We have each other's backs all the way down the line.' She held her fist out for a bump. 'Deal?'

Finn met her. 'Deal.'

Niall crossed the room to do the same. They met, all three in the middle, and a bump became a tentative embrace.

Niall stepped back first. 'What's your platform?'

'We keep our core values: decency, integrity, honesty. We tell the truth always. We speak in good faith and believe everyone else will, too. We can't talk about the Lion's Grace in public, but we absolutely embody it in all we do.'

'Woolly.' Niall met her glare. 'You'll need solid policies or you'll never make it off the *Question Time* panel alive.' He spun away, turned back, changed his voice and sounded remarkably like a masculine version of Rebecca Watson.

'If miracles happen and you and four hundred others win your seats, what will you do in your first hundred days? We're in the middle of a power crisis, a cost of living crisis, climate and ecological breakdown, and the collapse of the entire predatory capital model. You can be honest all you like, but that won't suck the carbon out of the air or find ways to feed people, heat their homes and sort the inflation rate. We'll still be in the middle of the sixth mass extinction. What will you *do*?'

Leah opened her mouth and shut it again. 'I can't do this on the fly. Or on my own. I need help from you and everyone else. This has to be all of us.'

'Good.' Niall gripped her shoulder, as if she'd passed a test. 'Let's convene our first full global meeting of the Changemakers and see if the theory even begins to work in the real world.' To Finn, 'How fast can you get us a decently representative sample of the membership who'll commit to staying online for at least two hours?'

'Give me an hour and I'll have you ten thousand.'

Niall beamed him a savage smile. 'Make it happen, Tech-Bro.'

In the event, it took closer to two hours to bring everyone together, but when they had done so, the numbers were closer to five hundred thousand, which meant Finn had to play interesting games with the GhostTalk servers to manage so many two-way video feeds.

He'd also spent a significant proportion of the time designing software on the fly with Raye in ways that seemed to stretch him to the edge of his comfort zone.

At nineteen hundred hours UK time, an uncommonly nervous Finn hit the button to open the GhostTalk equivalent of a Zoom call. The edits he and Raye had 'knocked together' managed to make it seem as if all the participants were sitting in a series of concentric circles, where everyone was visible to everyone else.

Kirsten had said often that 'Real change can only happen in circles. It's the best way to cull the hierarchies of power,' and Finn was doing his best to make it happen online.

For their part, the team in the Piggery had moved all the desks so they actually were sitting in a circle. Screens made an unbroken circumference around them, so the half million Changemakers from around the world were projected in a ripple of growing rings around the seven Custodians who held the centre, each with a label on the screen that denoted their area of responsibility: Niall spoke for staff and workers; Mo: local community; Eriq (who had landed, and looked more rested, and whose office in São Paulo was a beauty of dark wood and packed bookshelves) spoke for the commercial partners; Finn: clients and customers; Charm: environment (local and global); Leah: investors. Given that Changemakers was a cooperative where the members were also customers, local and global community and often the suppliers, the separation of powers was not quite as neat as the original Riversimple Movement design, but thus far it was working.

These core six were grouped in pairs: Eriq with Charm, Niall with Leah, Finn with Mo.

Nico, Custodian for Future Generations, was the odd one out, sitting alone against a blue-screen background. He looked different and it took a while for me to realise he had taken off his glasses and was wearing the Ghosts' shirt; he looked more relaxed than usual.

For a moment, he drew all eyes, and then he leaned slightly to his left and someone (Finn?) made technical magic and Nico was on a yacht, in the high-summer Atlantic, and there was Raye Kameransky, leaning into him; light to Nico's dark, but otherwise they were two tall, slim, young people, both slightly serious, blinking as if they weren't used to a world seen without spectacles: shy, but going for it. Examined more closely, Raye exuded the elegance that only extraordinary amounts of money can induce, though often doesn't.

They were fair-headed and fair-skinned with a sea-burned tan, and, if Nico had dressed up, Raye was dressed down in weathered, cut-off jeans below an open-necked shirt that had either been ragged-cuffed and sun-bleached by years of wear, or else had been keel-hauled often enough to make it look as if it had.

To top it off, they held a mug of coffee with Future Generations Custodian printed on it, which was quite impressive given that the *Ocean Ghost* was currently three hundred miles out from Haiti, heading on a course for Caracas, weaving elaborate patterns around the kinds of ocean currents that were best avoided.

They were also watching for submarines, which seemed a touch paranoid to me, but then I had never knowingly encountered anyone related to a Russian gangster. If Raye thought their father could commandeer a nation's navy and order it to sink their piece of floating genius-tech, nobody was inclined to argue.

Their appearance signalled the start of the meeting. Finn was still on edge, but Niall had the chair and he was as controlled as ever. As was his habit now, he looked up into the corner of the ceiling that held this morning's Kirsten-projection.

This time I stayed where I was, right in his line of sight. Since the last close shave, I'd conducted a fairly detailed examination of the risks versus the benefits, and decided I didn't need to keep edging out of the way when Niall sought communion with his sister.

I was in Crow form, but not distinctly so. I was more vapour than anything: an idea of a memory of what a Crow might be. Other than Connor, none of my family had shown any sign of having seen me and, of them all, Niall had always been the least interested in the dreaming, which made him the least likely to clock my existence.

Also, his chosen corner was the one place Finn never looked, as if even glancing here was an intrusion on his brother's privacy, so really, the risk of exposure was so vanishingly small that I could see no harm in letting the brush of connection warm me, even if I was thieving it by proxy from my own granddaughter.

I held my ground when Niall glanced up and we were eye to eye for the first time at least since I'd died; longer. Which was when we learned (again) that dying had not made me any wiser. Without really thinking, I sent him a pulse of hope and care. His eyes sprung wide and he swallowed thickly, and for a moment I could hear the groan of rotting ice so loudly I thought the whole world would hear it.

Niall! Fuck, I'm so sorry. I—

But he was Niall, who was remarkable in many ways; his balance didn't waver. He nodded once, firmed his shoulders, and brought his gaze down to the group.

'OK, people. Welcome to Changemakers' first global meeting – all five hundred and twelve thousand, eight hundred and seventy-nine of you. We're closing the doors now, so you're our first test group, for which thank you, *thank* you. We're really grateful. We're going to live by our ideals which means we're experimenting with deliberative democracy and this might all crash around our ears. Please be kind to us and each other if it does. Be kind anyway: that's what Changemakers is about. Anyway, here's what we're going to do . . .'

He spoke for just over three minutes. The GhostTalk translation software kept up with him, running closed captions across the foot of every screen, with moderators tweaking the phrasing in real-time if they felt it wasn't offering an accurate interpretation. When, in closing, he asked for questions, there were none.

Brows raised, Niall waited for a long count of five, then finished what he'd planned. 'Please keep things workable. Anyone advocating thorium molten salt reactors or nuclear fusion or anything of similar ilk needs to explain how they're going to get their tech up and running on a national scale by this time next week. I don't care how "just around the corner" it is, if you don't have a working model you can demo tonight, don't go there. Equally, we don't want you just to say "we will fix the climate emergency". Unless you have a detailed proposal for how you're going to bring about total systemic change overnight at a global level, that's not going to fly. Think big or think small, just make sure whatever you suggest is going to edge us to a future we'd be proud to leave to the generations that come after us. Tell me this makes sense?'

The GhostTalk system had the same facilities as any other video call. Nobody broke the hush, but a forest of thumbs rose across the screens and Niall's fingers relaxed their grip on the arms of his chair.

'Thanks.' Finger poised over Return, Niall looked out at the throng. 'Questions? No? Right then, people. Let's make the world a better place.'

He hit the key. Nearly fifty-seven thousand breakout rooms opened and over half a million members of Changemakers set out to change the world.

To say I did not understand how this meeting was managed would be a gross understatement. I knew the world had changed in the decade and a half since my death. I knew my family had changed with it. This evening was my first detailed introduction to the places they had explored that I had never imagined.

Finn had long inhabited technical realms far outwith my experience: that he had ranged so far and with such skill was not surprising. But great sheets of sky blue and citrus had flared nervously around him when Niall had hit the key to open the GhostTalk rooms and a nervous Finn was worth exploring.

I flickered back through his texts with Raye Kameransky and found, amidst pages of tech-speak I could never hope to understand, a brief conversation that I did.

```
Finn: Wld be nice to have RNG rly
random, not pseudo - we'll have enough
ppl who'll know the difference
Raye: Lava lamps?
Finn: Not original. Waves maybe?
Raye: Periodicity too predictable.
Finn: Spray patterns?
Raye: Perfect. Brb
```

And five minutes later –

```
Raye: Coming to you now
```

The Random Number Generator was required to sort out the half million members into breakout rooms of nine (or ten, to soak up the extra), in which there was a statistically negligible chance that any of these people had ever met, talked to or otherwise engaged with any of their new room-mates.

After the first brief flurry where slow connections left people hanging in mid-ether, Finn said, 'You've got the capacity to raise a star, colour is your choice. Please hoist it now if you know anyone else in your room.'

A few moments passed while the translation software expressed this in fifty-seven different languages, and then another, longer, moment while everyone waited to see what happened. Not a single star appeared. Finn's smile was ragged, but bright. 'Back to you, Nye.'

From here, Niall continued to manage the meeting as planned. It wasn't entirely an experiment, just that he'd based it on a system he and Kirsten had evolved over the past decade at their Alba Rising community in Glasgow, where the maximum number of members had peaked at twenty-three. Half a million was a whole new venture.

Nonetheless, the principle was the same: the nine or ten people in each breakout room were given ten minutes in which to complete two tasks beyond making basic introductions of who and where they were: first was to decide on three topic headings that at least half-plus-one of their number could agree were useful and interesting enough that they'd be prepared to explore at least one of them more deeply.

In doing this, they had to reserve enough time for the second task, which was to choose one of their number to be their speaker – someone who could outline their three topics clearly, and advocate on their behalf.

At the end of ten minutes the original breakout rooms closed and the speakers were sent forward into a new group of nine/ten in which each presented their three topics. This new group then had time either to combine several policies into one (so, for instance, 'degrowth economics' was combined with 'doughnut economics' in at least half of the groups I dropped in on), or simply voted some down, until they had a three *they* could send – with one of their members as speaker – forward into the next tier of conversation.

The smart feature was that, at each level, the broader groups were able to watch the discussions as their speakers progressed up the line and, in turn, chose new speakers. Any group had the right of recall at any point in the process if the members decided their elected speaker was not adequately representing their interests.

Those recalling were given thirty seconds to select a new champion. If they failed, one was chosen at random by Finn's wave-spray-generated RNG. I saw eight or nine recalls in the first round of speakers and only one in which a random member was sent forward. This one poor individual so obviously hated the entire process that nobody tried this route thereafter. In any case, everyone learned fast: by the second round, the groups were better at defining their criteria and the speakers at upholding them: there were no more delays. Sometime in the middle of the fourth round, Finn texted Niall.

```
Finn: 90% of speakers are target
callers on WoW. Do we need to change?
Niall: ?????
Finn: The ppl elected as speakers are
mostly the ones who call targets in
a battleground for everyone else to
hit.
Niall: So they're good at thinking on
the fly & expressing clearly?
Finn: Y
Niall: Fine
```

Almost exactly an hour later, the final group of speakers presented three primary topics to the combined meeting, together with the nine closest 'also rans', to make a total of a dozen policy areas for consideration.

New 'Core Topic Groups' formed to address Economics, Politics and Power Use. These were open to people dropping in or out, except for twelve core moderators who had to stay in the same topic for the duration. They were given forty-five minutes to create a skeleton policy proposal of no more than a thousand words, working by consent, not consensus, which meant it wasn't necessary for everyone to agree with any given proposal, only that everyone not *dis*agree. Anyone withholding their consent had to give concrete reasons why the relevant proposal wasn't good enough to pass.

A fifteen-minute slot was allocated at the end for presentations, collation and editing of a final policy document (Niall: 'Definitely not a manifesto').

Which was when things began to fall apart.

Five minutes into the final quarter hour, Grok, the nominated 'speakers of speakers', dropped back into the main room and asked Finn to close the breakouts.

'We can't do what you want in the time you've given us,' she said. 'We're still learning how to talk to people we've never met, in languages that don't match, with assumptions that often aren't valid in the context of a UK election. Crafting policy is a whole new skill set and it's going to take longer than tonight to learn it.'

She was small, neatly made, probably Hungarian, I thought, though her English was unaccented. Her hair was bubble gum pink, gelled into hedgehog spikes. She'd come through all the speaker selection rounds which meant she'd had a lot of practice at putting things clearly, but most importantly she had the guts to face Niall at his most blank-faced.

Until then, I hadn't realised quite how wary everyone was, as if even on the far side of the world, the ice that held him was tangible, and they were tiptoeing across, praying it wouldn't break.

Given the circumstances, Niall was commendably calm. 'What can you give us?'

'We have the three core topics and we've worked up a couple of Day One Actions for each that will probably blow everyone's fuses for long enough to divert them from picking holes in the rest.'

'Like?'

'Like for Economics, you set a maximum wage that's a defined factor of the minimum. We're still arguing the figures. Consent mostly goes with the max topping out at thirty times the minimum, which is what you guys already use in Cuidorado, but there's a strong case for Plato's five.'

'Fifty-two pounds an hour maximum salary?' Niall cracked a sour smile. 'Heads really would explode. We'll stick with thirty;

nobody can possibly argue they need more than three hundred an hour. What else?'

'Politics: we disband the House of Lords on Day One and replace it with rolling Citizens' Assemblies some of which put time into working out the details of a Constitutional Convention: who to invite and what questions to ask. We're stuck on whether the CA places should be allocated on a demographic basis or purely random jury-style.'

'We could do both and run them in parallel and see if the results are different,' Leah said.

Grok pulled a face. 'This is why we need you guys in the rooms. We should have thought of that inside the first thirty seconds.'

'You'll get there,' Leah said. 'We're learning. It's why we're here. Give me my Day One talking points for Power and then we should call it a night. We can flesh out the rest later.'

'Power's easy. You sign the Fossil Fuel Non-Proliferation Treaty the day you get into Number Ten. You can make it clear we know it's not all about the carbon, but if we don't stop the CO_2 rising, we're fucked, so that's a no-brainer. If you want to go deeper, you nationalise all UK power sources and distribute the profits as a citizens' dividend like they do in Norway. Pay it monthly and make sure there are rent caps so it doesn't just get sucked up by the 1 per cent. Deeper still and you get every fossil fuel company in the world under global management and have a global citizens' dividend weighted so people in the countries that have been resource-gouged hardest and longest get the top rates. All of this is pretty obvious. Harder is working out how we get from nineteen terawatts rolling global power use down to five within ten years, which is what the smart money says we'll have to do if we're going to stay this side of the cliff edge.'

'Got it.' Leah was making notes for herself. 'This'll keep us going for the first few days, but we'll need a talking points document on the GhostTalk open edits where you guys can top it up and candidates can access it in real-time.' She leaned back. 'This is good, people. I think we're done. Thank you all for— Grok?'

Grok's hand had gone up. 'We have a slogan,' she said. 'You need to see the slogan.'

'And you wait till now to tell us?' Leah pulled a face and earned herself a few heart emojis in the chat.

Grok shrugged half a smile. 'The Design Team hasn't settled on font or colourway. I have my own idea, obviously.' With a theatrical flourish, she hit Return and the slogan unfurled across the screen. The font was Comic Sans. The colour was the same pink as Grok's hair.

Power To Those With Wisdom,
And Wisdom To Those With Power

For half a second, nobody breathed. Then, dryly, Niall said, 'If this ends up being the final design, I will resign and go live in a tent on the side of a mountain. With no WiFi.'

Clever boy. Grok's laugh was all relief, but it was real, and it rolled around the world until it became one big tsunami of relief.

The noise was overwhelming: nobody could speak and expect to be heard. Leah made a tent shape with her hands and then flipped it to a heart. Finn found a mountain emoji and loaded it up and the chat filled with tents and campfires and mountains and the sense of a slow motion car crash happening in real-time eased away.

Eventually, when the volume had begun to fade, Leah raised her hand to speak. 'This is good. Far better than I'd have got to alone,' she said. 'I can go out into the world and make this work, but I'm depending on you guys to get me something with more heft as fast as you can. Because we might get away with this to begin with, but they'll be coming for my jugular as soon as they've had time to think.'

The chat function ground to a halt as half a million people wrote their promises and sealed them with hearts.

Niall leaned in to the lens. 'We'll close now. You all know how to set up your subgroups. Anyone who wants to keep talking, contact your group tech hub and have them set up a new GhostTalk room. You have as long as you need, but make sure you get some sleep. Go to it. And people—' He tapped his index finger to his brow in salute— 'Thank you for being here. You're amazing. We'll get this done.'

*

The Piggery emptied slowly over the next minutes until only Leah, Niall and Finn were left. The three sat together in the half-dark, lit by the soft grey spark of stars. Nobody moved for a while until Finn went to the kitchen, and brought back a jug of Jens's homebrew and three glasses.

He tilted a look at Niall. 'It's basically green tea with sugar. Jens swears you get more alcohol eating an apple off the tree. But if you don't want it there'll be some actual apple juice over in the farmhouse.'

'It's fine. Thank you. We need something.'

Finn poured. Bubbles spun columns of muted effervescence.

Silence held them a while longer, until Niall said, softly, 'I'm so sorry.'

'Not your fault,' Leah said. Her voice was level. I couldn't see her face.

Niall tipped his chair back and hooked his heels on the desk. 'Half a million people took two hours to come up with something I could have done in ten minutes. Five. While doing the sudoku. Blindfold. And I'd—'

'Niall . . .' A warning in Leah's voice. 'Trust the process. Did you see their faces? Nobody thought this was OK, but they're on fire now. We'll get to the good stuff.'

'In time?'

'I haven't declared yet. We have breathing space. I can riff on what we've got if I have to.'

Niall was quiet for a while, thinking, then, 'You're going to need an agent.'

Leah watched the bubbles swirl in her glass. 'I guess.'

'Not me.'

'No.'

Words soft in the dark and nothing around them. Tentative, Finn asked, 'A what? And why?'

'Consigliere,' said Niall.

Leah said, 'Someone to take the fall if I fuck up.' And then, more kindly, 'A political minder. Someone who'll stick to me like glue and field the—'

'Nazir?' offered Finn. 'I texted him already. If we want him and the team, he'll come. We could—'

Niall shook his head, a blur in the dark. 'Not that kind of minder. Someone who has the names of every politician, pundit and SpAd right at their fingertips where they can be moved about on the fly in a giant game of quantum chess.'

'Not Nazir,' Finn agreed.

They sank back into the drifting quiet.

'Donella Lloyd,' Leah said, eventually. 'Kiwi. Sharp as tacks. We were at college together. She's working for Piers Henderson, and he's in the pocket of the nuclear fuel lobby; he pays big bucks. We might have to offer a few arms and legs to get her on side.'

Finn said, 'The Ghosts can match whatever—'

'It's not about the money,' Niall said. 'She has to get what we're about.'

'She'll get it. If she's up for moving, can I make her an offer?'

Niall opened his mouth, but Finn was there first. 'All expenses go through Charm. Clear it with her and we're good.' He checked with his brother. 'Nye? You OK?'

'I am if you are.' In the dark, Niall raised his glass and tilted it at an almost-musketeer angle. 'Power to Wisdom and Wisdom to Power.'

All three glasses clinked. All three finished their drinks, said their goodnights, and, in various degrees of trepidation, went their separate ways to bed.

CHAPTER TWENTY-TWO

Thursday, 18 May 2023

Unpeaceful, my family went to bed and, unpeaceful, I followed at their heels.

Finn didn't even try to sleep, but then it was barely midnight, why would he? He logged Nifty and played a few desultory Arenas with Juke and Charm, though most of his attention was on a GhostTalk chat thread with Raye Kameransky.

Raye was heading up the tech policy group which had already divided into a dozen different subgroups. They talked tech for a while, but the conversation soon blurred back into a continuation of a thread from the previous night, talking about themselves, life histories, ideas, hopes and regrets.

Watching both sides of this conversation, I could see that among all the many threads Raye was juggling was one with Niall. This was fair: Raye was the new Joint-Custodian for Future Generations, they were also deeply interested in alternate democracies: the two had a lot to talk about. Almost as much as Raye had to talk about with Finn.

I stayed in the flows of text longer than polite behaviour might dictate, trying to sort through the many, many layers of meaning and likely missing most. By the time I left, it seemed that neither conversation had crossed the lines to text-intimacy yet, and that Niall's side seemed to be heading less directly in that direction.

Nonetheless, I feared for Finn. Niall and Kirsten had always subscribed to the ideas of free love, but Finn's relationships had mostly been online, mostly involved playing Warcraft or talking tech and, the eminently forgettable Giullia apart, they had mostly been asexual: in-person connection wasn't really his thing.

Given what I'd seen in old channel threads (yes, an invasion of privacy and no I'm not sorry), I thought IRL might not really be Raye's thing, either, which promised a degree of plain sailing all along until the *Ocean Ghost* made landfall in late June. At least there was time, I thought (hoped, believed), for things to settle.

I'd intruded enough for one night. I moved on, heading for the desert outside the walls of Leah's rose garden.

A Lion the size of a mountain stepped down out of the night sky. We met under the stars, with the scent of roses soft around us. I bowed, face to the sand.

She does not request your help, the Lion said.

'She didn't request it before,' I said, sitting up. 'I still went to her. This is huge and I could . . .' I didn't know what I could do, but there had to be something. I could feel Leah's presence like cool water in high summer, and I was parched.

Rising, I took one step to the side and another forward. A claw the size of a pylon speared the sand a step ahead.

Implacable, the gusting voice said, *Else she calls you, you cannot go.*

'Where then?' I was desperate.

The realms of fire and air are not yours this night. Go to the water. Speak to it your need in the company of those who already aid you.

Its words were a command. Stars wheeled and me with them, and when I could hold myself upright again, I was in the Between, standing at the lochside on an early summer morning, with Hail dozing in a shaft of sunlight near my feet.

Lan? Blearily, he raised his head. His muzzle was a dirty off-white. His eyes were yellow with cataracts.

'Hail!' I fell to my knees on the shingle and wrapped my fingers in his ruff. 'I'm a bad friend. I should have been back to see you long since.'

I'm fine, so. He grunted, pushing his neck up into the knead of my fingers. *What's the matter?*

'Too much time in the company of the living.' I tried to smile. 'Or perhaps not enough.'

He turned his big head to study me. *You're missing Finn.*

'Not just Finn, the whole family. They've hit the rocks and I want to be *useful*.' The whine in my voice was pathetic. 'Never mind. How's Connor?'

Better than he was since you went up to the cave. That was well done.

'Not dying?'

Hail curled a bit of a smile. *Everyone's dying, Lan. But not today, no.*

'If he's dreaming, could I go to him? We could maybe sort a way for me to help?' Still pathetic. I was sliding fast into self-pity and the route from there to self-loathing was well travelled. I thought I'd grown out of this decades ago. Crisply, I said, 'Never mind. I'll find—'

Hey. Hail nudged my hip. *Lan, he'd always be happy to talk to you. But he's not dreaming just now and pulling him in would be hard.* He rose and came to my other side, to lean against me, tilting his head so I could scratch under his ear. *In any case, I think it's not him you really want to talk to.*

Who then? He was right, obviously, but when I combed through all the extended family, I found no answers.

Matt and Jens? I liked them a lot, admired them, even, but I hadn't spoken to them in fifteen years – tonight seemed a bit late to start.

Hawck? What would I say besides 'Look after Finn'? Which he was already doing.

Raye Kameransky was clearly interesting, but turning up in their dreams as Finn's dead and banished grandmother was unlikely to scatter fairy dust on whatever was or was not growing there. And the thought of what Finn would say when he heard about it was enough to shrivel me to crow-spit on the floor.

Hail said, *Lan?* and we both knew I was prevaricating. For days now, I'd been listening to the undertone of shifting ice. Even in the meeting, the grind of great tectonic floes warping past each other had been deafening at times.

'Niall,' I said. 'He's the lynchpin holding everything together. For him and everyone, it'll be a disaster if – when – he falls apart.'

That seems ... not unlikely. Hail shifted. With him standing and me sitting, his head was level with mine. In the rising sunlight, the cataracts were less obvious, his eyes the colour of peat in a river.

I said, 'He doesn't dream, though. I mean, everyone dreams, so obviously he must do, but he doesn't remember anything and he's certainly never tried to do the kinds of things Maddie and Finn learned.'

Hail said, *He was there often enough when you spoke of these things. It's not that he doesn't know, just that he never tried while you were alive. You could call to him now. See what happens.* When I did nothing, *What have you to lose?*

All kinds of things, none of them tangible, most of them fantasies of my own making. Still, it took time to gather my courage, or any sense of what I could do.

When I had threads of both, I walked the few steps down to the water's edge, well aware that this was where the Lion had bade me go. Looking out across the loch, I dropped the childish whining and set my intent as clearly as Crow had ever taught me – and Uuri and Pakak and all of the others: it does no harm when setting intent to recall the memory of one's teachers. I listed all thirteen, name by name, and invoked my memory of each in aiding me to connect with Niall in whatever way would be most useful to him in this time of great need.

My grandson, Niall Penhaligon, whose twin is dead.

To meet Niall, the strategist, whose strategies had – at least tangentially – sparked disaster.

To see Niall whom I loved; to speak with him.

Niall.

I built his shape and the feel of him, both the rotten ice and the lift of his smile; the sense of burgeoning panic as he'd realised the meeting was producing a clutter of nonsense; the edge to his voice when he'd snapped at Finn and the way his eyes had flared wide when I'd sent him the pulse of compassion – let's name it properly: of love – before he opened the Changemakers meeting.

I had his shape, the sound of his laughter, the ache at the core of his soul. And the ice. I had the ice in all its ugly, dangerous precarity.

I sent him love again, and a plea.

Lan, Hail said in warning, and when I opened my eyes, a long, sinuous shape was powering through the loch towards me.

A big, fierce shape with knives for fins. I thought it a shark, a conger eel; a frantic and hysterical part of me thought it was the Loch Ness Monster made real at last.

The water stilled with the beast right at my feet. It was a salmon – a Salmon – at least six feet long, barrel-bodied, clear-eyed: ancient.

Crow-woman, why do you call?

It spoke into the marrow of my being, as Crow had done when I first stepped into the Between, but far more deeply, and in a voice so very much older.

It wasn't speaking English in any form I knew: this was the language of prehistory, the oldest tongue of these lands, a song of unkent syllables that hushed deep into the rigid parts of my core.

Furred in lichens and etched with broken promises, the sound made flutes of my long-bones and reeds of my ribs. I felt impossibly young in its presence.

Feeling the way its words changed the patterns of my being, I thought it might be older even than Connor, who was the oldest thing I'd ever met.

'Are you a god?' I asked.

Its twin-bladed tail sliced wounds in the water. *What is a god*, it asked, dryly, *but an ambitious child who grows fat on the devotions of fireflies?*

I thought of Bēi Fēng and what she would say were she here, and turned the imaginings away. Ancient eyes watched me do it. I read scorn in them, I read distaste, I read boredom; I read every iota of self-reproach I'd entertained since the day I was born.

The Salmon's tail flicked again, impatient with the human weakness. *You wish to meet your grandson. He is in the place of his birth. Will you swim with me, Crow-woman?*

Niall was born at the Southern General on Glasgow's Southside. As far as I knew, it had long since been subsumed into some private financed giant that sucked money into the US mega-corps.

I was trying to figure out why my grown-up grandson would be in a hospital that didn't exist anymore and how I would find him when Hail bumped his shoulder hard against my hip, and hissed, *Lan!* in a tone that meant 'Get a grip!' and 'This is the *Salmon*, what are you doing?' and 'In the name of all that's good, just go!'

'How though? Can I fly over it all the way to Glasgow?'

It's a dream, *Lan. Swim, why don't you?*

Point. It didn't feel right to take the shape of a salmon, but a trout was doable and, because it was indeed a dream, I could keep up with something that swam at the speed of an intercontinental ballistic missile, though I felt thrawn doing so. I never liked swimming much. I definitely never liked having my head under water.

Newly, I discovered I hated the feel of it hissing over my gills, and the thick sense of breathing liquid. I did not whine.

My loch was not a sea loch. Nonetheless, we reached the sea in the time it might have taken me to walk up to Connor's cave behind the waterfall. I tasted salt, and knew we were in open water. Soon after, I tasted raw sewage.

Foul, the Salmon said, and shame gnawed at my guts.

'I'm so sorry.'

Beasts who foul their own nests do not live long.

'We can clean it up.'

I will watch with interest your endeavours. Let us go deeper.

We went deeper, further, faster. I tasted the sweeter water, the notes of heather, bracken and bog myrtle, the high mountains calling me home. I could have leapt up waterfalls then, and spawned a thousand, thousand offspring at the top.

We left the sea, swerving into a river's open mouth and I knew the Clyde as clearly as I would know the farm or the loch. Familiar scents assailed me, and names, and aged histories of blood and restitution and conflict, and then back past the flashing swords and the scaled armour, to the builders who used stones and shaped brochs therefrom. I was free in the water; fast.

At Clydebank, we turned south into the Black Cart that became the White Cart and so I knew where we were going.

'He's at the Crescent!'

The Alba Rising community occupied the entire half-circle of Tantallon Crescent, tucked away in the jumble of clashing styles where Battlefield met Langside.

To my sure and certain knowledge, no tributary of the Clyde flowed into the fifteen-foot diameter pond that Niall and Kirsten and Rosh and a dozen others had dug one long summer in the place that had once been a tennis court and was now a permaculture forest garden filling almost all the Crescent's arc.

Such a tributary existed now, called into being at the Salmon's behest. It deposited us abruptly in the pond, to the consternation of the resident frogs.

In the dream of this place, it was night time, in the latter half of the year. The air tasted of dying leaves, and autumn bonfires. A full moon hung high in a clear sky. The Salmon finned itself steady. *He is here, the one you seek.*

I was a fish. With some effort, I summoned the will to become a bird again. The Salmon remained in the pond. 'Will you come in with me?' I asked.

My presence is not required.

'Aren't you to Niall what Crow was to me? What Hail is to Connor?' Bēi Fēng to Finn, but that didn't seem politic given the Salmon's scorn of gods; Lion to Leah even less so.

Flat eyes glared. Forcibly, I was reminded of Taliesin who had become a salmon, and of Mungo, saint of Glasgow, who had sought a salmon's wisdom. In the hinterlands of my mind, a dry voice I didn't recognise said, 'The Salmon *is* Wisdom,' and I had the sense to turn away.

I had asked for help. I had been given a gift beyond price. In all the myths, only the most reckless idiot asked for more. I was trying not to be this.

I bobbed my thanks to the Being that had brought me here, spread my crow's wings and remembered how to fly.

Tantallon Crescent was (still is) an architectural anachronism. Built in the closing decades of the nineteenth century, it had been conceived as a dozen discreet dwellings, wrought in pale sandstone with Rennie Mackintosh glass in the doors, both outer and inner; a talking point of the time.

The stained glass roses were still there, and the intricate ceramic tiles that lined the hallways and landings, but by the time the people

365

of Alba Rising were looking for somewhere to start their experiment in communal living, it had fallen out of favour and was a derelict, rat-filled mess. The mortgage companies didn't want to touch it and only some fancy sleight of hand on Niall's part had got them the loans they'd needed.

The day he and Kirsten had picked up the keys, the whole community had set to with sledgehammers, knocking down most of the interior walls and making free use of rolled steel joists, so that twelve had become one and, while every member of the community had a room of their own, the kitchens and living rooms were shared, and doors were rarely locked.

This was the place Niall and Kirsten had called home since before I'd died. It was filled with the people they had loved and who had loved them. Like their mother's community in the Trossachs north of the city, fluid relationships were part of the deal.

Many people came to test out communal living, and those who stayed were the ones who could cope with polyamory, poly-sexuality, poly-anything you could imagine. They'd all known Kirsten as well as anyone who wasn't her twin, with the result that their home was as deep in mourning as was the farm.

It seemed to me that if Niall was going to find solace in dreams at all, coming home was an obvious place to begin. And yes, when I slid through the fanlight over the door to his bedroom, Rosh was there, holding him, rocking him, saying his name over and over and over as Niall stared dry-eyed at the ceiling.

I didn't want to intrude. I backed up into a corner, but Niall's gaze tracked my movement and I pushed swiftly out through the wall before he could see me.

A new conundrum: in the world of the living I was the breath of a memory. Connor apart, my family couldn't see me even when I wanted them to.

In the dream, though, I couldn't *stop* them from seeing me however much I needed to. I was a being of the dreamtime, I was its essence: disappearing was not an option. If I wanted to remain incognito the best thing was to change shape. Which left me a universe of options. I roamed the Crescent, imagining possibilities: I could be wind (if Bēi Fēng didn't take it as a mortal insult), I could be

366

a feather, a dried leaf, a mote of dust. I could be anything I wanted, when what mattered was what *Niall* wanted, what he could embrace in his dream that would let us connect without shocking him awake.

And then, quite literally, I tripped over Brillo.

Brillo had been a five-week-old black kitten roughly the size and shape of the eponymous pan scrub when some arse had dumped him behind the bins in the old tennis court before it had become a permaculture masterpiece.

Kirsten had found him huddled among the dead bodies of his siblings, and had loved him better, feeding him goat's milk round the clock until he was old enough to take solids, and then moving onto tinned sardines which she'd decided was perfect cat food, and which had gone down a storm in a community that was, at that point – we're talking 2006 or thereabouts – mostly hardcore vegan. (They're not anymore, but that's another story.)

Brillo had become a central member of the community and another of its touchstones: however poly-everything someone was, if they weren't into cats they didn't stay long.

I nearly stepped on him, lying fast asleep at the place in the hallway where three sets of heating pipes crossed under the floors; it had always been one of his favourite haunts.

Never tell the kids, but I was always more of a dog person than a cat person. Still, I was here for Niall, who loved Brillo like a brother.

In Crow form, I sat in front of him. 'Brill?' He was dead to the world. On third repetition, each one louder, he levered open one muddy yellow eye. Even then, it took a while for him to focus. Eventually, laconically, *Lan. Good to see you.*

Well that's one question answered, several, actually, and only one still outstanding. 'Is this Niall's dream?'

The one eye closed again momentarily, then both opened together. They were like faded autumn leaves, yellow, with streaks of walnut. *It would seem so.*

'May I use your shape?' I could have taken it without asking, but Pakak had taught me long ago of the need for absolute integrity in dreams. ('Don't take without asking, Lan. Don't do anything you're not happy having done to you.')

My . . .? He was a wise cat. *Ah. Be my guest.*

His invitation was more sinuous than Bright Rook's, the routes in more complex and his body felt less solid. It was a dream, though, and he was a part of the living world. I stretched through all of him, flexed his claws, twitched his ears, flicked his tail.

As Bright had done, he settled back into the recesses of our shared being. *Niall's not sleeping long. Best not tarry.*

Niall was alone when I walked through the door, lying on his bed, staring up at the ceiling, fretting.

This being his dream, the room had lost its contours and become smoother, more shell-like. Ice was everywhere, not wet and dripping frozen water, but the *idea* of ice, the protection it gave, the things it kept contained.

Oh, Niall. This is not sustainable, can you not see?

I was standing on the threshold, not intending to think aloud, not even really shaping the thoughts, but Niall rolled over, slowly, frowning. 'Brill?' Surprised and then, startled. '*Brill!* What are you doing here?'

'Just strolling through.' Cautious, I hopped onto the foot of his bed. 'You OK if I join you?'

He croaked a laugh. 'When did you ever need to ask?'

'I wasn't sure you'd want company.'

'Your company? Always.' He edged over and stretched out an arm and there I was, snagged in the crook of his elbow, feeling his heartbeat, and it might have been a dream but my goodness it was good to feel flesh and blood again.

I shoved my head against his cheek. He stroked his thumb along the length of my chin and I squirmed up to lie on his chest. I wanted to talk to him about the waking world, but one really fast way to wake up a beginner is to tell them they're dreaming.

Carefully, I said, 'I miss her too. All of them.'

'Yeah.' A catch in his voice. No cracks in the ice. 'Thanks.'

'I was thinking you're keeping her legacy going. It's a good thing.'

'Am I though?' He raked his knuckle along my spine. 'It's scary, Brill. Tonight was a mess. The ideas are all there, but corralling them into coherence is going to be like herding cats. Sorry.' He nudged his chin on my head. 'Like herding unherdable things.'

For a beginner, he had a startlingly firm grasp of the waking world. 'But you'll get there,' I said. 'So many people. And they all have new ideas.'

'They do. It's good. But I don't think they understand that we're all about to jump into a tank of piranhas. Politics is as toxic as it gets.'

'Can you de-toxify it?'

'Not without completely changing the way things are done. It's *designed* to be toxic. We're in the whole chicken and egg thing. To get to the point where we can change things, we need to win, but how do you win a death match if you're trying to spread decency and integrity and all the things she cared about? We don't even have a clear set of policies. It's horrible, Brill.'

Anxiety was tipping him back towards waking. Urgently, I said, 'Leah's dream—'

'That's the thing. Leah has the Lion. Finn has the North Wind. I have—'

'*Me!*' A head-butt, right on the point of his chin.

He sat up, suddenly, drawing me with him so I was balanced on his raised knees, my nose touching his. 'That's kind, Brill, but—'

'I know I'm not a Lion or the Wind, but I'm—'

'You're fucking brilliant.' He winced. 'Sorry. K would hate me saying that. But you are. You're brilliant, Brill. I love you, you know this. But how do I talk to you?'

'You are talking to me now.' Remarkably well, in fact.

'Yes, but Leah—'

'Talks to the Lion in her dreams, just as Finn talks to. . .' Careful, Lan. Outing yourself now would not be clever. 'To his teacher, I'm sure. You can talk to me like they do. Just come back here and we'll meet.'

'I don't know how I got here, though. I was awake and then I was here. It just happened.'

That would be the Salmon and this kind of help doesn't happen often, or without big strings attached. I said, 'Try to think of here when you fall asleep. I'll do what I can from my end. Now we've met, I think I'll be able to find you again.'

'Really?' His eyes were big and brown and serious. 'OK. I'll have a lot of questions, though. I truly don't know how we're going to do what needs to be done and everyone expects me to have the answers.'

'Kirsten always said that not-knowing was the point of the emergent edge. If you knew what to do, you'd be recycling the old paradigm.'

Ah fuck. Alanna Penhaligon, you are a fool. The mention of her name caught him somewhere soft and unprotected. I felt the whisper of melting ice and, on the back of it, a fast-clamped surge of freezing repair, of ice layered on ice, topped with more ice, and he was a beginner dreamer and it was too much; panic cast him out of the dream, and me with him.

I landed back in the Between, on the shores of the loch: a spring morning: raining. Beneath the scent of wet shingle, three smokes tinged the air.

'Connor!' I threw myself at him, still more than half cat.

'Hey.' He was still old and still lined, but strong and upright. He hugged me close and by the time he let go I was human again.

He scooted along on the log and gave me room to sit beside him. 'It went well?'

'It went . . . I fucked up, Conn. He's as closed-up in the ice as ever, maybe worse. Did you see what happened?'

'Hail saw the important parts.' He leaned his elbows on his knees, gaze on the flames. 'You didn't fuck up. You called the Salmon. That's huge.'

The enormity of this was still fresh. I wasn't sure what to do with it. 'It was so *old*, Connor. But it said it wasn't a god.'

'Of course. Gods need people to give them strength. They need people to care about them, to love them, or at least, to give them a lot of focused attention. The Salmon doesn't need anyone. It just is.'

'It said the same thing, more or less.'

'Then believe it. It's older than the gods. And wiser than anything I know.'

'So why did it come to me?'

'I don't know. We've crossed paths, Salmon and me, but never had what you'd call a conversation. Certainly never swum together. Go canny and don't treat it lightly.'

He leaned in to lay a bough on the fire. Flames spun high and fresh smoked caressed us.

I thought about Niall and all he was carrying and the extra weight of refurbished, repolished, refrozen ice. I thought about melting and breaking, and when one might become the other and the risks and the benefits and the time pressure he was working under.

'Could you find a kitten?' I asked, slowly. 'A black one?'

Connor's face fell blank. 'Are you thinking what I think you're thinking?'

'But can you do it?'

His nod was heavy and full of thought. 'Matt's Mabel had a litter in the hay barn down at the Dairy about February time. There's one they were going to keep, but for Niall they'd maybe let him go, I think. Kind of black-on-black tabby. Looks quite smart when the light hits him the right way.'

'There are kittens at the Dairy?' How did I not know?

'For a Crow, you're way out of touch.' Connor patted my shoulder. 'There's all kinds of wee animals there: kittens, calves, lambs. You should come down and visit sometime. Gus is having a fine time feeding them all.'

'Gus?'

'The others all call him Prune. He hates it. His name's Angus.'

'If he hates it, why doesn't he say something?'

'You've been dead too long, Lan. Imagine you're the chubby kid in a group where everyone else is shaping up to be a super-sharp lawyer or an Olympic medallist or is already an overnight video sensation, and they all decide it's cool to change your name. What do you think happens when you say you don't like what they're calling you?'

Sinkingly, 'They're not bad people, though.' This was Nico and Stina and *Kaitlyn* we were talking about.

''Course not. They're kids being kids and if you're a smart kid, which Gus is, you know there's nothing you can say that won't make it worse, so you shut up, and three years down the line you're still Prune and it's too late. Except the lads can see through that kind of crap in about two seconds flat, so down at the Dairy he's Gus.'

371

Connor rose, cracking his hands above his head. 'I'll be woken up soon, but it was good to see you. I meant what I said about coming to visit. Honestly. You'd love it.'

'I don't like leaving the family. I know they don't—what?' I knew that look. 'Connor McBride, stop squinching your eyes at me. Did I just say something totally stupid?'

'No. Except last time you were in the void you were dancing along the timelines like a pro. D'you not think you could be in more than one place at once by now?'

'Eh? How?'

'I don't know, Lan. I can't cruise the void the way you do. I certainly can't call the Salmon. But I'm thinking if you tried you could put yourself in more than one place at once. Can't be that hard and—' Abruptly, Connor's outline began to fade and the strength of his voice. 'Finn's here to wake me up. I'll see about a ki—'

Hail went with him. Left alone, I watched the loch a while, thinking about time and space and how ice might safely be broken, and when I returned to the land of the living it was dawn and Connor was just waking up.

Around mid-morning, I was in my usual haunt in the top left corner of the Piggery when Connor peg-legged in with both sticks in one hand leaving the other free to hold a cardboard box that made scrabbling noises.

Niall was at the desk furthest from the door, chewing the end of a pen, surrounded by the printouts from the night's subgroups. The ice that bound him was as solid as I'd ever seen it.

Connor hirpled past everyone else and thrust the box into his arms. 'Here you go.'

'Grandad?' The scrabbling became more marked.

'Wait while we shut the windows.' Connor did that thing where he planted his peg leg and spun around it, one arm spread wide, like a unilateral propeller. 'Windows, people. Close them all. Now.'

The Piggery was all windows and Suffolk was in the early days of a heatwave, so they were all open. With commendable coordination, Charm, Leah and Stina each ran to a different wall and began shutting the large windows. Nico shut the door through to the kitchen. Finn put himself at the foot of the stairs up to the training gym.

Prune (Gus!) edged in through the outer door and butt-shoved it shut. He was carrying a bin bag in either hand, one small and heavy, one larger and lighter. He was way too wise to grin, but I could feel the effort he was making to keep bland.

Niall had not moved. The box mewled.

'*Grandad!*' He jerked back as if it had snapped him ten thousand volts, then ripped open the lid.

The kitten that launched itself onto his shoulder was at least four times the size Brillo had been when Kirsten first found him. As Connor had said, he was tabby-striped, black on deeper black. His eyes were a grubby green, like mud smeared over spring leaves.

'Fuck, fuck, *fuck* . . .' Each of these quieter than the last, until at the end, a haggard whisper.

Niall sank to the floor.

With a sound like the crack of midnight, the ice that bound him shattered.

For a heartbeat longer, he kept his teeth clamped shut, the noise all inside so that only he and I could hear it. Then the first raw edge of a howl broke through and the noises that followed were humanity stretched to its furthest edge.

Carried on the wave, I joined him and was not alone. Everyone broke but the kitten, who clung to Niall's shoulder and watched with interest as first Connor, then, at a flick of his hand, Finn and Leah, Charm and Stina, Nico and finally Gus, came in to hug him and then, when there was no more space, to kneel or sit or crouch or lean around him, with a hand somewhere on a shoulder, an elbow, a knee.

Finn squeezed in between his brother and the wall so he could cradle Niall's back to his own chest, both arms locked around his body. The kitten took it all with remarkable panache, stepping delicately across shoulders, past bowed heads, over a haphazard clutter of angled joints. He ended again on Niall's arm, pushing his head against his cheek over and over and over again.

No outward work got done for the rest of the morning, but when they all walked over to the farmhouse for lunch it was as a family.

Niall named the kitten Brilliant, and set to altering the house to make it safe. Windows were closed throughout and to hell with the heatwave. Gus turned out to have brought one bag of cat litter and half a dozen litter trays. Matt had sent with them a promise to come and fit cat flaps in all the doors, but not until they'd kept everything shut for six weeks. 'Unless you want to keep coming back to the farm to pick him up,' which wasn't the worst thing that could happen, but nobody planned to let him out.

Connor cooked. Everyone ate, even Niall, who found his voice enough to tell them about Kirsten and Brillo and the early days of the community at Tantallon Crescent.

There was no ice to be seen or heard and I never saw any near him thereafter. It didn't fix the policy vacuum, but it gave him an energy that lit up everyone who came into contact with him, and there were thousands of these – many, many thousands. The Talking Point documents began to take shape.

CHAPTER TWENTY-THREE

That evening's edition of the BBC *Question Time* political panel show saw the shift to the more normal, mutually assured destruction phase of the election campaign.

Early on the morning after the Changemakers inconclusive meeting – an hour or two before Brilliant-kitten had made his debut – Leah had called the *Question Time* production assistant to see if the offer to take part was still valid and had her arm chewed off, so that was one question out of the way. The assistant had been kind enough to fill her in on the identity of the other guests.

With an eye for the highest possible ratings, the producer had found it useful also to invite Specs and his former cabinet colleague Melanie Urquhart, plus Ceinwen Williams, a recently selected contender for the main opposing party, who was widely tipped to take the leadership from the incumbent in the unlikely event that Her Majesty's Opposition crashed and burned.

Nobody believed this was really on the cards, but only because the governing party was so bad, not because the Opposition had proposed a single new, useful or interesting policy, so there was a background fear that they might yet 'lick defeat from the sweaty handshake of victory' (credit: Nico, to widespread horror).

The fifth member of the panel was Jacob Miller, a makeweight from the minor Opposition party, which survived, rather like an orphan lamb, by stealing protest votes from the bigger parties without ever making such a nuisance of itself that either was minded to kick its head in. It did well in by-elections, but its main function so far had been to split the anti-government vote in enough constituencies that there was little chance of the Opposition gaining a foothold for long.

Miller was hardly the sort to raise anyone's pulse, but it didn't matter: the evening's entertainment was more than amply provided by Leah, in her role as political commentator, plus two panel members each of whom had to pretend to support their own party, while each was, in fact, desperate for their side to lose, and then Specs, who was guaranteed to say something incendiary even if nobody knew what it might be. In televisual terms, it promised dynamite.

'Yes, but the audience is still a hand-picked horde of rabid fascists.' Leah was in a taxi from King's Cross to Broadcasting House getting a final pep talk from Niall, who, for obvious kitten-related reasons, had stayed behind at the farm.

The traffic moved slightly slower than walking pace, but the heatwave was turning London into dust-city and Leah's hair had been polished to a shimmering obsidian gloss; she wasn't about to walk in the open if she could avoid it.

'You'll manage. Go hard on Power to Wisdom and Wisdom to Power. Calling out the inadequacies of the current system is a solid starting point and they won't give you time to do more than mention the Day One platforms. Just remember you're talking to the millions watching, not just the front row.'

Back in the kitchen, Niall waved across the room to Connor, who was chopping onions on the other side of the table.

Leah was not impressed. 'Niall Penhaligon! Don't you dare hand me over!'

Shocked, Niall glanced around the room. 'Have you got a webcam on somewhere I don't know about?'

'No. But you're completely predictable. I don't need Connor to tell me I'm grand, I need strategy from you.'

'No, you don't. Just don't call anyone Gammon and you'll be fine.'

'Niall!'

Niall laughed. All wide-eyed innocence, he held the phone away from his ear then leaned in and said, 'Don't tell me it wouldn't cross your mind.'

'Leaving aside that it's a good eighteen months past its sell-by date, I guarantee you that word does not figure anywhere in my vocabulary. Or, it didn't until you just said it and now it's the virus that's going to keep on giving. Give me decent advice, for fuck's sake. Or else put your Brilliant-kitten on and I'll listen to him purr for the next five minutes.'

'Be my guest. He's really sharp on policy detail . . .' The kitten was batting bits of papery onion skin across the table. Niall made a ramp with his arm, and Brilliant clawed his way up to his shoulder from where he offered a shrill and tinny purr.

'OK.' Leah sank back and closed her eyes. 'I'm good. Economics: degrowth. I can talk about 100 per cent taxation over a ceiling of £300 per hour. Politics: abolish the Lords, and set up a People's Assembly to work out the best way to configure a Citizens' Assembly to pull together the questions to be answered in a Constitutional Convention to report within six months.' This had been Raye's idea from the text chats. 'On power, we'll sign the Fossil Fuel Non-Proliferation Treaty but emphasise that it's not all about the carbon. If there's time, I can talk about a citizen's dividend and throw out numbers from Norway. I can do this.'

'You can.' Niall was at his driest, which was better, really, than layering on false encouragement. 'You know your stuff without advice from me. Announce that you're standing as soon as you can, and the rest is window dressing and firefighting, in that order. Talk common sense, it'll set you apart from the rest. In fact, you can say exactly what you've been saying to your Radical FM audience for the past three years, only now there'll be more than eight people listening.'

'Fuck you!' Her laugh was half a tone too high. 'We have three hundred thousand followers on YouTube.'

'Right. And Big Brother holds an internal inquiry to figure out who to sack if *Question Time*'s numbers drop below fifteen million. They're pushing tonight like it's *Bake Off* meets *Strictly* but with real blood on the walls: half the country will be watching. Say what you believe to be true. You'll be the only authentic individual in the whole room and everyone's bullshit detector will irradiate the rest. If it helps, imagine your three hundred thousand followers on the other side of the camera lens.'

'You mean the couple of dozen that bother to turn up at any given time?'

'That was more or less my earlier point.'

'I know.' Brakes hissed. A heavy door clunked. 'We're here. Well done: you and the small furry beast kept me sane. See you on the other side.'

'Leah?'

Her thumb was on the button. She lifted it off. 'Yep?'

'We have more than the Beeb's highest-ever viewing figures in Changemakers now and the only ones not watching are in time zones where it's four in the morning. Even then, there's a few thousand who've got out of bed. If you need to speak to anyone, speak to them.'

'Love you, Niall.'

'You too. Break a leg.'

▼

'With the greatest respect, I'm not sure the former Health Secretary's opinion is relevant to this discussion. He will not, after all, be a member of the next parliament.'

If Melanie Urquhart was a natural blonde, I'd eat several hats. I'm pretty sure the blue eyes, too, were fake: nudged into the startling zone by coloured contacts. Even her voice was manufactured. Heavy elocution coaching had removed the ghastly nails-on-a-chalkboard edge that had been a hallmark of her ascent up the political ladder back when I was alive.

The only thing that hadn't changed in the past fifteen years was her politics. The difference now was that, even as recently as five years ago, she had been the crazy one that only the Murdoch media would talk to, and even then, only when they needed a fresh touch of crazy to remind everyone else how much safer they were with the status quo.

By the time Leah sat on her left at *Question Time*, 'Hardcore Mel' was the single most invited guest on the national broadcaster's flagship talk programme. Her capacity to knife her opponents with poison on the blade was legendary in the world of political entertainment.

Specs beamed at her as if she'd just made a slightly risqué joke.

Leaning one elbow on the table, he cupped his chin in his hands, and more to the camera than to the woman on his left, said, 'Last time I checked, people who were not MPs were still permitted to hold opinions and some of them were considered useful. I think taxing the fossil fuel companies till the pips squeak is an essential step in tackling the climate emergency.'

'Seriously?' Melanie's snort hovered halfway between a laugh and a stab in the eye. 'They're the wealth creators. You'll destroy our entire economy. And Green Gas is the fuel of the future. We can't power our way to a recovery on sunlight in a country where the sun hardly shines.'

Specs stifled a sigh. 'With respect, filling the post-fossil energy gap wasn't the question.'

Deliberately, he turned his attention away from Urquhart and towards the audience. 'Roderick in the front row asked if it was a better idea to levy a windfall tax on the energy companies or to go down the French route of capping price rises. As I said, I would do both. Mr Miller thinks neither are a priority while Ms Williams has reminded us that her party's policy is to let the market find its own balance, which, as far as I can see, is indistinguishable from the policy promoted by my right honourable friend, the member for prison ships. I'd be interested to know what Dr Koresh would do?'

Asking the questions wasn't strictly Specs' job and he flash-shrugged an apology at the host. Harry Collins was a clean-cut, bland-suited executive who had previously hosted the lunchtime news and was still finding his feet in the world of political blood sports. Collins took his cue a beat too late, which, in turn, meant that Leah had to hold her answer in for an extra half-breath.

This gave her thinking time, which was a life-saver, because, buried though it had been in all that flowed after, #MinisterforPrisonShips was the critical outtake from what Specs had just said. He knew it, Melanie Urquhart knew it, and by the time she opened her mouth for the second time, Leah knew it too.

Her years in front of a camera had taught her how to speak to the lens, without looking as if she were cutting out the rest of the room.

'I don't think Ms Urquhart is entirely in charge of the prison ships yet? There's still a chance sanity might prevail.'

'We can certainly hope so.' To all intents and purposes, Specs was now running the panel. He gave Leah an encouraging nod. 'And you? Where do your political instincts lead you?'

Back in the kitchen, Niall went white. Brilliant-kitten, roused by his sudden stillness, nudged his arm and he offered a finger for a chin-rub, but all his attention was on the screen, and the kitten, miffed, went off to find someone more fun. Niall said nothing, too afraid that he might somehow shake her concentration.

In the studio, I felt a matching shiver in the audience, and a small near-silent huff of laughter whose textures I knew, but could not place. It felt like Connor, but he was peeling potatoes in the kitchen. The feeling was there, though; someone I trusted.

Leah favoured Specs with her most audacious smile. 'I couldn't have asked for a better question, thank you.' She turned her attention back to the camera. 'Since I have the opportunity and it might not come again, this feels like a good time to announce that my political instincts lead me to stand as an Independent candidate in my home constituency of Surrey West. Adjacent, in fact, to the one currently held by the good doctor.'

The good doctor broadened his smile. 'Will you be alone?' he asked, helpfully. Niall caught his breath.

Leah's smile broadened to match Specs'. 'I hope not. We're hoping I will be joined by four hundred Independent candidates aligned with Changemaker values in England.'

'Four hundred. And none in Scotland, Wales or Northern Ireland.' Specs tilted his head, thoughtfully. 'So, you're only targeting the seats my party holds, or might conceivably take.'

Leah's nod left an opening. Specs took it. 'Suppose you get fifty seats. That would be enough to produce a hung parliament. Who will you go into coalition with? I mean, which party?'

'We'll put all we have into securing the four hundred. Anything over three twenty-six and we won't need a coalition.'

'But in the real world?'

Leah shrugged, conceding the point. 'We'll talk to whoever is open to genuine change. If they share our values, if they sign up to our three recommendations, if they'll agree to listen to people and work towards finding ways we can get ourselves out of the current mess, not just talking points that their friends in the media can parrot, then we'll work with them.'

Specs laughed, softly. 'Given the nature of our political establishment, in and out of government, that's a tall order.'

'Doctor, we're on the edge of extinction and, with all due respect, we're run by a bunch of public schoolboys who thought it was funny to party while people were left to die alone without their families at their bedsides. We need urgently to bring power to those with wisdom and wisdom to those with power or we're not going to make it through.'

'Interesting idea. Care to tell us how you plan to do this? Assuming nobody already in power has the kind of wisdom you believe we need?'

The audience was breath-held silent. The producer had been smart enough to call for a talking-head shot on a bifurcated screen so that out in the world the panel-game, gladiatorial pit was gone. For this moment, Leah and Specs were the only two people in the room.

Leah said, 'Let's spell this out. Our entire culture is addicted to fossil fuels and it's destroying not just us, but the entire planet. We've burned more oil since 1995 than the whole of the rest of human history, and the whole "net zero" thing is the most monumental greenwash.

'But it's not all about the carbon. There are Forever Chemicals in the rain, and microplastics in the clouds, dead zones in the oceans and mines you can see from space that are polluting whole continents as we try to dig up enough minerals to keep the wheels of consumption turning.

'Our politicians tell us we live in a democracy when what we have is a kleptocracy devoted to finding ever-better ways to monetise the apocalypse. Thank you, Jacob, let me finish—'

Jacob Miller subsided.

Leah used the break for a change of tone. 'We all know things are bad. There is not a single person on the planet who thinks that we're on our way to a better world. What we argue about are the ways to fix it. You'd think it was obvious, but let me spell this out, too: cutting taxes on the ultra-rich—' a nod to Melanie

Urquhart— 'isn't going to help anyone heat their homes, or pay for good, nutritious food in a world where the seasons are beginning to break down.

'Rounding up everyone whose skin isn't white—' her gesture swept from herself to the few in the audience who fitted this— 'and weaponising infantile culture wars isn't going to suck the carbon out of the air or make the water safe to drink. Did you know there are now dozens of toxic chemicals in women's breast milk? It's still the best possible food for new-born infants, but we have *no idea* what this is doing to them. Nobody does.

'Locking up protestors while you drill for more oil isn't going to stop the epidemic of depression and suicide or heal a health service that has become a sickness service because we live in a system designed to make the rich richer and keep the poor running like hamsters to do work that's never going to pay the bills. We were not born to pay bills and then die. You know this. I know this. So why do we let the system keep us running on a treadmill that everyone hates?

'I'll tell you: we do it because nobody's ever asked us what we really want.' She raised her head to stare straight into the big lens of the central camera. 'What *do* you want?'

She answered her own question. 'I think at heart, everyone – even the Minister for Prison Ships – wants to wake up in the morning and feel safe. We want to look forward to the day without having to worry about whether there's enough to eat, or our job's just been axed, or the cost of heating has just tripled again, or some dictator with abandonment issues is about to nuke another dictator to prove their virility and tip us over the edge into a global war nobody can win.

'We want to wake up and feel that we're useful, that we're leaving the world a better place for our children and their children. I *hate* feeling that I'm making everything worse because I'm locked in a system I can't change, that's destroying the world I love. I want to feel that I can do what I'm good at and be valued for it. We all do. Human creativity is absolutely f-ing amazing. There are people all round this country – the whole world – with ideas that could make things better if we could just agree that we all want to be safe, to be respected, to be loved, and then work out how to get from where we are to where we want to be.

'Now is the time and we are the people. We're being pushed over the edge of extinction by people who don't get it and don't care and we—' she surged to her feet— 'we are better than this.' A hand slammed hard with each word. 'So let's bring the best of ourselves to the table, agree where we want to go and find ways to make it happen. Thank you.' Abruptly, she sat down.

The studio exploded.

Harry Collins was locked in a silent conversation with his producer. Melanie Urquhart was all but standing on the desk in her effort to be first to speak next with Jacob Miller a terrier yelping at her heels. Ceinwen Williams was glancing left and right with the trapped look of someone who's lost their talking points and doesn't know who's hidden them. Only Specs was unruffled.

In the kitchen, Niall said, thoughtfully, 'He knew she was going to stand.'

'Or he guessed,' Finn said.

He and the others had come over from the Piggery and caught the last five minutes. They were competing to see who could build the most enticing mini-obstacle course for Brilliant with copies of the day's newspapers, luring him over fences and through tunnels with dangly feathers and wisps of braided grass.

Niall watched them with the kind of restraint his mother used to show when someone else wanted to hold one of the twins.

'So either he has a mole inside one of our breakout rooms,' he said, 'or he's thinking three moves ahead at least.'

'Five hundred thousand people in those rooms, Nye. We can start building communities where everyone knows at least one other person, but it'll take time. If there are infiltrators, we might not catch them.'

'We're not even going to try.' A flick of Niall's head. 'No witch-hunts. We make this work by having the ideas that work or we fail at the first fence. Watch now, Urquhart's going to try to drag us back to her own talking points.'

In the *Question Time* bear pit, Harry Collins was finally

able to speak and be heard. 'Melanie Urquhart, you wanted to comment?'

'Is she—' a slashing sideways nod at Leah— 'seriously suggesting that she'll ask other *candidates* to sign up to her "Three Suggestions"?'

Leah was kind enough to wait for Harry's nod.

'Of course. I helped draft them. And it means that, if we're elected, we can guarantee all our MPs will be sober and clean and our government's spending will be transparent. We'll upgrade our democracy so that it's fit for purpose, which definitely means introducing a form of proportional representation that gives everyone a voice. It's functionally insane that Ms Urquhart's party can poll considerably fewer than half the votes but still end up with eighty more seats than everyone else put together. That's not democracy. That's a tiny elite clinging on to power so they can carry on trashing people and planet.'

'Here, here!' This from Jacob Miller whose party's only chance of any power rested on PR.

Harry Collins ignored him and nodded instead to the end of the row. 'Ms Williams?'

'No, wait!' Melanie Urquhart surged to her feet and Ceinwen Williams didn't have the strength of character to intervene. Urquhart rounded on Leah. 'You said you were going to listen to everyone?'

'We will.'

'By blocking the over-eighties from voting? That's screaming hypocrisy.' The chalkboard nails were slanting back into Urquhart's every sentence. Somewhere, a voice coach cringed.

Leah's vowels, by contrast, were rolled in velvet. 'Pensioners can vote if they pair up with someone at the other end of the age scale to listen and talk and, at the end of a defined process, each thinks the other has heard their point of view. Seems perfectly reasonable to me.'

'Not when they're over eighty-five.'

'That's under the current system, which is skewed so that their votes count for far more than anyone else's. This is what got us into the current crisis and the absolute definition of insanity is doing the same thing time after time and expecting a different result.

When we have a sane and equitable voting system, we'll open the franchise to fourteen with no upper limit. We're contemplating ways to weight votes by age so younger people have more of a say. We'll let you know when we have the system worked out fairly.'

This wasn't on the Talking Point documents yet: the 'youth democracy' group had floated it in the early hours of the morning. I wasn't sure Niall had even seen it, but he gave a brisk, impressed nod, while on the panel Urquhart, Williams and Miller all laughed with varying degrees of disbelief. Not Specs, though: he was frowning, thoughtfully.

Again, Melanie Urquhart got her response in fastest. 'You need a referendum to change the voting system.'

'You really don't. Voting for us is voting for a new and better system. It's that simple.'

'That's anti-democratic,' Ceinwen Williams said.

'No, it's not.' Specs leaned over, cutting in. 'It's just like the idea of the two main Opposition parties forming a coalition, which, for the record—' he nodded to Williams and Miller— 'you should do. Both of these are perfectly legal options, and are, frankly, the only intelligent way to wrest democracy back from the government. Trust me,' his smile was cheery, 'I was still in the cabinet when we held the crisis talks about what to do to counter the prospect of an anti-government coalition and I promise you the conversations were a lot more animated than any of the ones about funding the health service or ways to reduce inflation. They'll be having the same discussions now about Dr Koresh's three suggestions and, if you throw PR into the mix, they'll have apoplexy. When you threaten their jobs, the people with the power pay attention. It's the only time they do.' He took off his glasses and turned his naked gaze on Urquhart, who was doing a fair impression of a landed cod.

'Right. Thank you.' Harry Collins muscled into the gap she'd left. 'We have more questions from the audience. Lady in the red top on the second row . . .'

The evening flowed on with the usual barbed indecencies but no actual surprises. Nobody examined Leah's points in any detail, in fact, at one point, she was labelled a climate alarmist, but Urquhart, who had thrown it out, was outnumbered four to one, so it felt more like a desperate swing than a real left hook.

Specs was reminded that he had resigned from government, but not from the governing party, and asked if he'd run on their ticket if they offered him a safe seat. Professional to the tips of his fingers, he managed a masterful non-answer that didn't leave any openings for speculation.

Ceinwen Williams got heated on the subject of price caps on heating fuel, which was one of the few areas where her party differed from Melanie Urquhart's (they were probably for them, but only within a specific price range, and they reserved the right to change their minds without notice), while Jacob Miller said something about relaxing planning laws while preserving the green belt.

The last question went to 'the gentleman with the grey hair in the middle of the back row'. I felt the Connor-like thrum in the air again and saw Leah sit up straighter as a mellow Merseyside accent said, 'Perhaps Dr Koresh can tell us how her Independent candidates are selected? Is there a process or can anyone stand, and does that leave the voters to decide whether they're in alignment with your core principles?'

Hawck? *Hawck!* How did I not know you were here? I found him as the first words came out of his mouth: mid-height, stocky but not yet stout, with a greying fringe to a bald head and a weathered face that spoke of experiences best not spoken aloud.

He wasn't what I'd imagined, but as soon as I saw him, all my imaginings evaporated. He was Hawck and he was perfect. Hawck . . . hell, but I have missed you.

And—

Did Niall get Finn to prime you with that question? Because it's a gift, wrapped in gold and drizzled with voter-honey. Leah's going to be so happy.

He was at the end of the row. I brought myself down to floor level, a harder manoeuvre than I'd have imagined, and viewed the panel from his perspective. I wanted to hug him, and settled for leaning close, the way Hail leaned in to me. I thought I felt him lean back in return, but I was probably making it up. He wasn't another Connor. Just a really, really sorted bloke. I made myself Crow and sat on the back of his chair and felt like I'd done when Connor brought the kitten to the Piggery, but without the worry.

As predicted, Leah was happy, though she covered it by tilting her head to look at him quizzically, as if the question was unexpected. In the kitchen, Niall whispered, '*Don't over-egg it now.*' It was definitely a plant.

Hawck must have lied sequentially through about eight sets of interviews to get into the audience, and from the look on Harry Collins' face, this wasn't the question he'd thought was coming.

Before anyone else could intervene, Leah said, 'Anyone has the right to stand as an Independent candidate as long as they have their name down before nominations close. We can't lay down a veto. What we can do is offer support and community to anyone who clearly shares our values. We want people who value listening above speaking, who value inclusivity over tribalism and who care about collaborating with everyone, regardless of their place on the political spectrum.'

Once again, she directed her gaze to the lens, and the wider audience. 'The deadline for nominations is 4pm on the twenty-fifth of May, so time is tight. If you feel you'd like to join us, please contact the Changemakers team through the website. We'll do whatever we can to support you.'

Specs said, 'Do I gather you already have other candidates?'

Leah graced him with her brightest smile. 'We have one hundred names already pledged, including mine.' They'd started flowing in as soon as Niall had closed the Changemakers' meeting the night before. 'The names of the candidates and the constituencies where they'll be standing will be up on our website by the end of the programme.'

'Right.' Harry Collins managed a reasonable smile. 'Well, that was interesting. Thank—'

Specs said, 'One hundred and one.'

Everyone stared at him.

Collins said, 'What?'

The audience froze, halfway to applause.

Slowly, Leah turned her head. She cocked a brow and this time it wasn't a show for the public. She didn't speak; she didn't have to.

Specs stood up, straightened his tie, then, as if on a further thought, pulled it off, stared at it ruefully, and dropped it. With his shirt top open, and the tie pooled at his feet, he turned his most authentic gaze straight to the camera.

'I hereby renounce my membership of the party I have loved for over thirty years. I gave it my best shot, but it's time to admit that my former political home is toxic beyond repair. Worse, it's incapable of fresh thought and Dr Koresh is right, if we're going to face the crisis of our times, we need radical new ideas, radical new ways of doing things.'

Turning to face Leah, he offered his profile to the camera. 'If Changemakers will have me, I would like to offer myself as an Independent candidate in the constituency that is my home. I will bring all of my experience and, I swear, none of my tribalism. Without hesitation, I will sign up to your three suggestions and the values that underpin them. Power to those with wisdom and wisdom to those with power sounds a good foundation to me.'

He thrust his hand past Melanie Urquhart's nose. 'Will you take me?'

What could she say? If he'd gone down on one knee and offered a ring and cloud-castles in the sky it would have been no more surprising, nor less binding.

Rising, she took his hand. Camera four zoomed in to see them both grip tightly. 'We are a collective,' she said. 'It's not my call, but speaking personally I think you would be a credit and an asset to our movement, and I cannot imagine anyone suggesting otherwise.'

CHAPTER TWENTY-FOUR

'Are you kidding? Running on the same ticket as this guy is like the frog offering the scorpion a ride across the loch. When he stings you halfway, he won't even drown, he's Teflon-coated and he floats like he's full of helium.'

It was midnight, after the debate, and those still awake were gathered in the living room at the farmhouse. Connor had lit the fire and then gone to bed. The room was hardly warm, but it didn't need to be: Niall was steaming enough to raise the whole house to boiling point.

Of the rest, Leah had curled on the sofa, too worn out to argue. Hawck, who had driven her up from London, was hovering nearby, watching the two of them as if one might need to be hauled off the other at any moment. Finn sat on the floor with his back to the sofa, GhostTalking with Raye Kameransky, although, he, too, seemed ready to intervene if he had to.

He didn't. Niall's rant ran down. He looked straight up at my corner for a long moment's silent communion in which I carefully took no part, and then picked up his worn-out kitten and draped its unresisting form along his arm.

Hawck sat opposite and leaned forward, elbows on his knees. 'You couldn't have stopped him, and you would have looked bad if you'd turned him down. Niall, we're going to have to run with it.' Back to Leah. 'The rest was grand. You made our manifesto on the spot. It was a miracle.'

Everyone caught the 'we' and the 'our'. I saw Finn open a new chat thread with Charm about spare rooms in the Piggery.

Niall gave a deflated shrug. 'It's infiltration. He's the establishment embodied. He'll wait until he has leverage and then derail everything we're trying to do.' A careful glance to Finn. 'He must have someone on the inside. Several someones.'

'And we're still not going to start a witch hunt.' Finn made it almost a question.

'Definitely not. It'll break us. Which might be the point.'

'Then we make sure he never gets leverage,' Finn said with finality, and then, 'Hawck, you'll stay? We have room in the Piggery.'

Hawck nodded. 'For a while, yes.'

Radiant, Finn dragged Hawck away, leaving Leah and Niall alone, which was, I'm pretty sure, not an accident.

Certainly Leah was happy with it. As soon as the door had closed behind them she said, 'I'm sorry. I didn't mean to screw up.'

'You kidding? You were a walking, talking miracle.'

They were on opposite sides of the room. Niall picked up Brilliant, carried him over to set him on Leah's knees, then sat down alongside. 'Peace offering?'

'You don't need to.'

'I know. But still.' They contemplated the kitten's sleeping form for a while, then Leah said, 'Donella Lloyd's agreed to be my agent. You'll like her. She's quarter Māori. She gets everything.'

'Good. Great.' Niall considered the angles, then, 'Dare I ask what she cost?'

'Best not. Half what I thought, but I was thinking big.'

'We don't want to cripple the Ghosts.'

Leah snorted a quiet laugh. 'Charm showed me the accounts. They won't notice it's gone. And if it gets us a win, it'll be worth it.' Brilliant was waking up. Leah pulled a bit of paper from her pocket and tore off a strip, so she could dangle it just above kitten head height.

Niall watched her a while, then, 'I'm sorry I snapped. The day's been . . . weird. The *week's* been—'

'This whole time is weird, Nye. But it's good to have you back.' Only family used the short version of his name: only family were allowed to. I felt the hitch of her uncertainty.

Niall felt it, too. He bumped his shoulder against hers. 'Thanks.'

A boundary passed. On the back of it, I watched him gather his courage. 'I had a dream last night.' He waited, awkward and vulnerable.

Leah kept her focus firmly on the kitten. 'Want to tell me?'

'I met Brillo.' He lifted Brilliant. 'Brill's predecessor back at the Crescent. He spoke to me.'

'Did he say anything useful?'

'That I should be myself, mostly.' Niall let that hang, and then, when she didn't respond, 'Which is word for word what your Lion-dream said to you.'

Actually, it was me who'd said that, but Niall didn't know. Leah did, though. She sat very still. 'So we have cats at either end of the size scale who are comparing notes behind the scenes.'

'Or it's true.'

'I'm not sure these two are mutually incompatible.'

Gathering the kitten, Niall stood up. 'You were great. Please believe me. I'm not given to pointless platitudes.'

'I'd noticed.'

'Are we still on track with all you dreamed?'

'I don't know.' Leah put up the fire guard and followed him. At the foot of the stairs she said, 'We're doing our best, which is all we can ever do. If I hear anything different from the Lion I promise I'll tell you. But you have to tell me if Brilliant says anything likewise. Deal?'

She held up her hand. They bumped fists, softly. 'Deal.' Niall followed her upstairs to bed.

Even before the debate, I'd been experimenting with dividing myself in the way Connor had suggested. It wasn't trivial: I had to find the same kind of focus I'd had in the void and then split myself in the way I had split the time lines, leaving part of myself to become Brillo and dream with Niall, while another, equal, part followed a fizzing-with-potential Finn . . . got lost in the scatter of his energy, doubled back, followed the sparkling trail . . . lost it, round again, he's so happy Hawck is here, so look for Hawck as well: he's more grounded, slightly worried: happy but cautious, because caution is what animates him and . . . *there!* in the kitchen at the Piggery, with Finn showing off – and Hawck duly admiring – the shiny steel and polished worktops.

I arrived in the midst of an animated three-way conversation with Charm. '. . . not just in here. We've got eight rooms upstairs.

Charm's in one, and Nico said he might move in. He's Minecraft, but he's cool. You'd be among friends.'

'And the rest are coming,' Charm said. 'Grok and Zerg will get here in the morning.' In Hawck's presence, she brought out her battleground voice, that was noticeably deeper and less compromising than her daytime tones.

'That's the Grok the Arms Warrior target-caller from the Amber battleground team, right?'

'Yep. Zerg's their Fire Mage. Good in 2s Arena, too. The rest of the team's on their way. Eight of them are in the UK; they'll be here by the end of the week. The others are catching a lift with Raye. They'll be here by the end of next month, as long as the *Ocean Ghost* doesn't get knocked off course.'

'*Ocean Ghost*? Is that not like naming it *Mary Celeste II*?'

'Not our call,' Finn said, and perhaps I was imagining a defensive note there, though if Raye needed protection from Hawck, we were all sunk.

'You're crazy, the lot of you.' Hawck shook his head, but he was grinning. 'Who else?'

'All four Warcraft teams plus their backups and a dozen or so others we know well enough to trust,' Finn said. 'Not Juke, but everyone else. We'll have places to put them by then, but not all of them in here. So if you want to stay here, best to nab a room now. And before you say anything, we do need you.'

Hawck tilted his head.

'You know how to cook.'

Hawck gave a strained laugh. 'You want me to cater for a bunch of Warcrafters?'

'You told me you were a chef after you left the army.' Definitely defensive.

'I did what I had to do to survive. I'm not doing it now.'

'Fine.' Finn paced across the room and back. 'I thought you liked cooking, but if you want to pole dance to the tune of "Eleanor Rigby" in the middle of the coding room, that's your call.'

This was delivered so deadpan it sounded serious. 'I don't care what you do. I just want you to be here, and be part of what we're building. Be in the meetings in person. Be ... you: good, solid, no-one-fucks-with-me you.' A big breath. 'And we need a backup leader. Who else can do that?'

Hawck cracked his knuckles, slowly. 'Finn, I'm not your dad and I'm not going to stand in for him. Not for Connor, either. Don't look at me like that. He's clearly dying. Denial's not your style. I know what he is to all of you and I'm not stepping into his shoes when he goes.'

The silence that followed was less fraught than I might have expected.

Even so, it was a while before Finn turned and slid boneless and, for once, graceless, into a chair.

'Nobody can fill Connor's shoes,' he said, tightly. 'And I swear I'm not looking for a father-figure: credit me with at least that much self-awareness. I'm trying to craft a team that'll survive all we have coming down the track. Charm's amazing and she's saved us a dozen times already—' a quick salute offered and accepted— 'but it's too much to ask of one person. Charm, don't argue, it is.' Charm let out the breath she'd taken. 'I'm getting back into the driving seat, but I'm not a people person and there's no point pretending otherwise.'

Hawck gave him the no-shit-Sherlock look.

Finn shrugged a grin back. 'Exactly. We need someone the entire team trusts enough that they'll take orders, because charming though my brother's ideas of horizontal management might be, we know these people and there are times when someone needs to tell them to shut the fuck up and get on with the work.'

'And your battleground leader is standing in front of you,' Hawck said. 'She does exactly this three nights a week.'

Finn dragged in a sigh. 'Yes, but Charm doesn't *like* managing people. She only leads the battlegrounds because you said you didn't want to do it anymore and, even now, you're the one who spends half the night calming the 'Lock on Zerg's team who rage-quit because he got one-shot by a Hunter, or helping Writ through his latest marital crisis, or getting a #GoFundMe off the ground to help Daphyd on the Cerulean team when they were kicked out by their family. I'm crap at that kind of thing, Niall's worse and Leah might be good, but she's just parachuted into the political warzone for the foreseeable, we can't load more admin onto her before the election.'

Finn couldn't sit still for long. He filled a kettle and clicked it on. Over the beginning hiss of the boil, he said, 'You can always leave if you hate it.'

Hawck made a circuit of the room checking equipment, cleanliness, order. Matt and Jens had built this place: he was never going to find any fault.

His capitulation, when it came, was straightforward. 'Ground rules: no drink, no drugs. I won't come otherwise.'

'Fine.'

'I mean none. Not a glass of red on a Friday night or a swift pint after work or a quick spliff behind the bike sheds, or whatever is the Piggery's equivalent.'

'Spliff?'

'Roll-up. Grass. Weed. Skunk. Whatever you call it these days.'

Finn flashed his first real smile. 'You nearly said "you young people" then . . .' Hawck pulled a face, and Finn's smile stretched broader. 'It's fine. And we're way ahead of you. One of Kirsten's founding tenets was that drink and drugs bring down more intentional communities than anything else. So that's already etched into the walls.'

'And I want the freedom to make things less . . . techno-sharp.' Hawck pointed back through the door to the vast open-plan office. 'It's like a barn in there.'

Aggrieved, 'It *is* a barn.'

'And it'd be better if it was less . . . techno-industrial. It needs to feel like home.'

'Charm has charge of the accounts,' Finn said, his last ditch to defend.

'It's good.' Charm smiled, charmingly. 'As long as I can join in.'

They both looked at Finn, who raised both hands. 'Just don't run us into the red, deal?'

'Deal.'

▼

'Nye, are you up here in—What the *actual* fuck? It's like a sauna in here! What are you doing?'

Thus did Finn find Niall on the morning after Leah's *Question Time* appearance, after Specs had so publicly joined them; after Hawck had joined too, much less publicly.

It was eight o'clock and already the heatwave was beginning to bite. Niall had all the windows shut. Now, he waved a warning hand at Finn. 'Door, Bro.'

'You're going to suffocate. You and the furry beast, both. Wait—' Finn backed out of the door leaving Niall alone in what was, admittedly, a fairly warm space.

Niall's armpits were already black with sweat, but that might have been as much work as anything. He'd been up for three hours already and was surrounded by a sea of scribbled paper. If I'd not spent half the night easing him back to the dream of the Crescent so he could tell me-as-Brillo about Brilliant and then recount the day's events, I'd have been seriously worried.

But he had, so I wasn't, and soon Finn came back with a carpenter's bag and a fat roll of chicken wire.

'Bro?'

'Kitten-proofing the windows. Seriously, you're going to die in here.'

'Hyperbole, much?'

Finn was assaulting the windows with a speed and efficiency that shouldn't have surprised me as much as it did; he had, after all, helped convert the Piggery and he'd done all the wiring in his own and Kaitlyn's rooms in this very attic.

Presently, he stepped back from the newly meshed – and open – windows. The room sighed to the swish of fresh air. Everyone relaxed a notch.

'Right. Let's start again.' Finn sat cross-legged on the arm of the sofa and produced a new string-toy from his pocket to play with Brilliant. He cocked a wary eye at Niall, who had turned back to his calculations. 'What happens to Grasshopper when He Who Has All the Answers burns himself out?'

'Grasshopper finds new answers. Better ones, probably.' Niall pushed his chair back from his desk and hooked his heels up. 'Is Hawck staying, or is this a temporary miracle?'

'Staying until or unless he gets bored. Which isn't going to happen.' Finn wasn't so easily diverted. 'Finding better answers would require Grasshopper to know the question in the first place, which he doesn't. What answer do you have, oh Wise One?'

'We're going to hold a parallel election.'

Finn stayed frozen for a long, silent moment. Eventually, 'How, Nye? *Why?*'

'Why: because it's something Specs can't hijack. We'll do it properly, securely, with twenty-first-century online tech created by our resident genius coder, and show who'd have been elected if we had the sane voting system we're proposing. We need proof of concept: this'll be it.'

He held up one fist, the arm slightly angled to his left. 'Then when we have elected our hypothetical MPs, we can bring them all together and set up a parallel parliament backed by a suite of regional Citizens' Assemblies, feeding in the things the local areas need.'

He angled his other arm so the two made a V. 'It's called forking the government and it worked in Taiwan. Audrey Tang is the world's youngest Digital Minister on the back of it and they're proving that real democracy works. They had deaths in low double figures in the pandemic and they're managing to create social media that isn't a race to the bottom of the brainstem. It's Changemakers in action on the other side of the world. We're going to make it happen here.'

'Right.' Abandoning his cat toy, Finn crossed the room to lay his palm along Niall's forehead, deftly dodging the hand that batted him away. 'Nye, you have any idea *how* we're going to make this happen?'

'Tech is not my problem. I'm just the lowly strategist. You're the genius coder. Murmur something confident about blockchain at me. I'll feel so much better.'

'Something confident about blockchain.' Finn delivered this straight and then picked the kitten up again and sprawled back on the sofa, blinking up at his brother. 'You're not looking any better.'

'It did lack a certain conviction.'

'Because I genuinely have no clue what you're trying to do and I doubt very much if a distributed ledger system is the answer.'

Niall sat down on the floor and gave all his attention to Brilliant, who was growing cross at being moved around.

When Finn said nothing, he sighed and tipped his head back to thunk gently on the wall. 'I want you and the Ghosts to set up a voting app which allows every British citizen between the ages of ten and eighty-five to vote securely, once only and with the same privacy as we have when we put a cross in a box on a piece of paper. I had the idea this was a blockchain-y sort of thing, but if you can find another way to do it, that's fine by me.'

Finn opened a GhostTalk thread to Charm, Juke, Hawck and Raye. After some thought, he brought in Nico, too. 'Parameters?'

'We'll need one tranche that starts with sixteen as the lower cut-off so nobody can say we're gaming the system. That's the first tranche, they should be easy. Harder will be sorting out the two age groups at the margins we've already identified, which is to say ten to sixteen at the lower margin and eighty to eighty-five at the upper, giving them the option to talk to the other end of the age scale, so we can include those who choose to engage and exclude the ones who don't. Everything needs to be 100 per cent secure and safe and unhackable by any bad actors up to and including governments, ours and others.

'On top of this, we need to undo the voter suppression so that everyone who wants to vote, can vote, but everyone can only vote once. We don't want to ask for voter ID but I think – please correct me if I'm wrong – that we'll need iris recognition like they have in Uganda, or fingerprints, or something equally secure. We'll also need people to be able to vote offline if they don't have a smartphone.' At Finn's look: 'There are people without. Trust me, I met them all the time in the day job. Some of them didn't even use email.'

'You live in the weirdest alternate realities.' Finn didn't lift his head. 'Can these hypothetical technophobes vote on someone else's phone?'

'As long as we can guarantee it's them voting, not the phone's owner or half a dozen random others. Maybe they can go to a library or church or village hall and vote online there?'

A pause followed in which Niall let Brilliant bat his fingers and watched Finn thinking it through. 'Doable?'

'We have four-and-a-half weeks to get it right and no chance to run a dry test?'

'Pretty much.'

'Then the best I can offer is that it's not impossible.'

Niall laughed, weakly. 'That'll do. I have faith in miracles. You sort the logistics. I'll sort the politics. And somewhere between us, we'll build the community that'll see us through.'

'OK.' At the door, Finn paused. 'If I can mesh the windows in the Piggery, will you come down and join us?' He didn't say, this place is too redolent of Before. He did say, 'The others are beginning to come in. We're trying to weld a team of strangers and you're our strategist. We need you.'

Niall looked up from his paperwork. 'Text me when it's cat-safe and I'll be there.'

CHAPTER TWENTY-FIVE

Monday, 22 to Friday, 26 May 2023

The days took on a routine.

The growing team (currently numbering eighteen, but more were arriving daily) showed up for work between half-five and six, partly because there was a lot to do, but mainly because the heatwave hadn't let up and mornings were by far the most pleasant time of the day, even in the Piggery, where the giant windows along the back wall had all been flung wide. Finn had meshed them soon after he'd done the attic, so everything was kitten-safe. Everyone coming in knocked first before opening the door.

Hawck was *definitely not* the group's chef – this was still Connor, but Connor was spending his days among burgeoning spring life down at the Dairy, and thus everyone got to enjoy Hawck's coffee and agreed that his pancakes were to die for, so he caved and made breakfast. ('I'm not doing lunch or dinner, OK?')

Long before then, Finn had already cycled down to the village, picked up copies of all the morning's papers and spread them out on the desks in order of priority based on the size of the headline type and its content.

On this, the first Monday of the campaign, the headlines were mostly devoted to the fact that the two Opposition parties had taken Specs' advice and agreed a mutual non-aggression pact that saw them each standing aside in seats the other was likely to win against the government.

This new venture, officially named the Combined Opposition Party, had been abbreviated to COP within minutes of the announcement late on the Sunday night.

Niall had been gobsmacked. 'That acronym alone is going to lose them 1 per cent of their potential vote and that's their margin in at least a dozen seats.'

None of the headlines agreed with him (yet), but various COP-related puns made the lead in all the papers except the one tabloid that was backing Urquhart to the hilt ('WE'LL MAKE BRITAIN BEST AGAIN! SAYS MINISTER FOR PRISON SHIPS').

None of them mentioned Changemakers Independent Concordium (now universally CIC) in their opening pages, but, as Niall was never shy to point out, the legacy media wasn't about to give Leah and her radical ideas the oxygen of publicity by choice.

The vast bulk of her support was online, though so far, even the power of Kaitlyn's Digital Army wasn't enough to keep #PrisonShipsRGo from trending above both #Changemakers and #CICFTW.

'Got them scared.' Niall made a check mark in the air. 'First, they laugh at us, then they curse at us, then they throw the entire online, round-the-clock toxic heat of Russia's bot farms at us. Looking at this purely objectively, their capacity to push hashtags up the charts is quite impressive.'

Finn had finished stacking the dishwasher and was juggling his phone, a stapler and an empty coffee mug. Niall tossed in a block of Post-its and one of the cat toys with which the Piggery was now cluttered.

Finn caught both and spun them on without losing rhythm. 'There are more of us, though,' he said. 'And our algorithms are better. We'll be back at number one by the end of the day.'

Nico was cleaning out the litter tray, a task which was being tackled on rotation by the team. From the door, he said, 'Still 1.6 million, though?'

'So far.' Finn did something slick so that phone, mug and stapler landed in a neat row on top of the *Mirror*'s headline ('COPs PROMISE GREEN GROWTH!'). The catnip mouse spun towards Nico.

'You shouldn't be fixated on numbers, Nic. They'll break your head.'

'Like I'm alone?' Nico snatched the mouse out of the air and tossed it to Brilliant, who caught it more neatly.

Finn shrugged. Everyone was watching numbers obsessively by now, checking anew when they updated at noon and midnight.

The overkill video screen on the back wall of the Piggery had been breeding quietly overnight (or Charm had bought in a lot of new screens. I prefer the breeding option, myself), turning the wall to the left of the door into one vast, twelve-by-twenty-foot screen-of-screens.

Here, the left-hand side listed in a column:

- the name of each candidate standing for CIC;
- the name of the constituency in which they were standing;
- the name of the agent representing them;
- the name(s) of the strongest opposing candidate(s).

Underneath – and the place everyone looked first – was the current total number of CIC candidates: 374. And then the number of hours left before nominations closed: 80.

The number of candidates was rising at every refresh. Niall reckoned they both wanted and could get 390 by the deadline at four o'clock on Thursday afternoon. He mentioned this roughly twice a day.

The figure 390 was fewer than the total of UK constituencies because, as Specs had predicted, no candidates for CIC were standing in Scotland or Wales. Both the Scottish National Party and Plaid Cymru had accepted the three suggestions and outline policies across the board, and required their own candidates each to give a public oath that, if elected, they would enter into a coalition with the CIC. They had asked to put people into the policy groups. A meeting of the existing groups had voted to accept.

The Green Party of England and Wales had done the same, and discovered a surge of supporters on the ground happy to deliver their leaflets as long as they mentioned their affiliation to the CIC in the text. On the back of this, they had raised their number of target seats from three to five.

Northern Ireland was more complicated, but Niall was hopeful that at least the non-sectarian Social Democratic and Labour Party would come on side if there was a hung parliament. The polls suggested this might well be the case, but the polls were so obviously failing to keep up with the volatility of the electoral landscape that nobody was taking them seriously yet.

The question that occupied most attention among Changemakers' supporters – and the one Nico had referenced – was the difference between the number of voters registered under the old system, and the number estimated as eligible to vote under the CIC 'recommendations'.

Charm kept the relevant data displayed in red at the top of the wall screen in order of priority:

Total population of UK: 67,736,802
Total registered to vote: 49,328,046
POTENTIAL CIC POLL: 50,938,677
Difference their vote/ours: 1,610,631

'Our vote' was in-house shorthand, not to be repeated elsewhere. Shortly after they'd been informed of Niall's plan, the legal team at Alba Rising had decided that while they absolutely could *not* be seen to be holding a parallel election, CIC could legitimately conduct an 'exit poll' on a CIC Exit Poll App, with a wider remit that could include the hypothetical votes of those excluded under the current system either by virtue of age or voter suppression. The app was still under construction, still under the 'not impossible' tab.

Thus the 'Exit Poll' became the official fiction for Niall's strategy, though nobody was in any doubt as to the reality, or its reasons, or what conclusions might be drawn from the results.

Everything thereafter hinged on the reliability of the data.

Finn's core Ghosts – it goes without saying that Raye was now counted among their number – had found a way to estimate the total number of additional voters who would be allowed to vote under the Changemakers' rules and had come up with a number of just over 1.6 million.

Nobody questioned their arithmetic. Everyone acknowledged the total as a gamechanger of seismic proportions in a system where recent elections had been won or lost by a couple of thousand votes either way in swing constituencies.

Everyone put a lot of time, effort and bandwidth into imagining where these hypothetical votes might go.

Niall (in collusion with Raye) began to write a series of Substacks and opinion pieces outlining the creation and function of what he took to calling the People's Parliament – as opposed to the Boomers' Last Gasp.

The terminology took off in the policy groups, who spread it online. Requests to write for the legacy press dried up a bit, but not completely: the editors of the *Guardian*, the *Mirror* and, surprisingly, *The Times* were all still keen to hear from him, though each reliably ran at least three pieces offering opposing views whenever they printed his offering.

One thing everyone agreed on was that the young were unlikely to side with a government that was busy trashing their futures in real-time. With everything else in chaos, this became a favourite point of conversation among the pundits and those whose opinions they sought.

Specs in particular was vocal on the unfairness of 'destroying the hopes of the young'. He was vocal on many things that sounded entirely in alignment with all that Changemakers was endeavouring to achieve. I still didn't trust him, but that's mostly because I took my lead from Niall.

'The fucker is just too clean.' He was staring moodily at the *Guardian*, whose central pages sported images of a chirpily insouciant Specs out on the campaign trail. 'He's either been lying for the entirety of his political life, or he's lying now.'

'He's a politician,' Hawck said. 'Lying is coded in his DNA.'

'So long as we never need to trust him.' Niall went back to writing his latest blog. Everyone else went back to their coding, unless they were playing with the kitten, in which case, they went back to this; some managed both.

Thus did the days roll over.

The CIC's ratings racked up and down, sometimes, depending on what order you read the polls, up *and* down at the same time.

Ghosts continued to converge on the Piggery and were allocated to teams depending on their skills.

Charm had control of logistics and was still controlling the videos for social media.

Finn and Hawck were leading the app-building team. Halfway through the week, Hawck assessed the work so far and nudged it a hair's breadth up from 'not impossible' to 'possible'.

Nico had charge of shooting any videos that needed actual people in them: the upstairs space in Ash Barn was turned into a complete blue-screen room, though memories of Kaitlyn made everyone reluctant to spend a lot of time there.

Stina had a flair for design and was heading the meme-teams.

In the outer world, terminology continued to evolve. The COPs tried to change their acronym and found they were too late. Changemaker groups online began to parse CIC as Change Is Coming, and this took off.

The Changemakers policy forums continued to refine and extend the existing policies and create new ones to be put to a general vote. Niall dipped in and out and offered comments pretty much at random and then monitored the resulting Talking Point docs and continued to churn out blogs that spun everything into a useable narrative.

Leah and the other candidates read everything nightly and had the new ideas at their fingertips in case anyone asked the right questions.

Frances Nolan, who had been promoted (or demoted? Nobody seemed sure) to the BBC's political desk, asked the right questions with increasing regularity. 'You're talking about replacing the Lords with a Constitutional Convention. Can you tell us more about what this is and how it might work?'

Leah: 'We will set up People's Assemblies – self-selecting groups who are interested enough to come together – who will create the questions to put to a randomly selected, demographically weighted Citizens' Assembly, which will then craft the agenda for a Constitutional Convention, where experts and members of the public will get together in a curated format to work out how best to create democratic structures that are fit for purpose in the twenty-first century.'

One screen on the long back wall of the Piggery was always on whatever channel hosted Leah or one of the other candidates. There were twenty-three Ghosts in the Piggery now. A ripple of thumbs were raised when Leah came to the end of this particular interview. Nobody applauded: loud noises in a room full of neurodivergents who were likely to be deep in their coding was universally acknowledged as unwise.

Niall and Finn were sitting together at this particular point. Niall ran his tongue around his teeth. 'You think we have someone else who's infiltrating the policy groups?'

'Could be,' Finn said. 'But Jodie Nolan's a moderator in the Politics group, so her mother probably doesn't need anyone else.'

Niall jerked round. 'And I am learning this now, because . . .?'

'You have enough to worry about. Let it go. Leah's handling it.'

Leah was handling most things. Becoming more adept at splitting myself across space and time, I was able to leave one part with Niall and Finn (sometimes, this part was too divided to keep an eye on each individually) while another part followed Leah around the country.

Given the heatwave, most of the meetings were outdoors and I could be in Crow form, or, pleasingly often, could borrow a corvid of some sort in the way I'd borrowed Bright Rook, and perch nearby. I watched her speak to crowds of ten and others that topped three thousand. She joined with new CIC candidates by the dozen, who ranged across every possible demographic you could imagine. Mostly, they were welcomed, rarely ignored; I didn't once see them spurned and there were no threats of violence that anyone could detect.

Juke had oversight on the Ghost group tasked with monitoring the incel threads, and so far nothing had turned up. Raye helped. Raye helped with almost everything. They were said to be levelling a character in Warcraft. Finn walked lighter through the days and spent less time beating harmless dummies in the gym above the office. He still wasn't meditating, but I could see a time when it wasn't far off.

Throughout, Hawck and Charm found time to plan their refurbishment of the Piggery. They did it in stages and always overnight, changing the bulbs to create areas of softer shadows without crippling the screen-work, or painting the stark white walls a pastel yellow with Roman blinds for the south-facing windows, or hanging artwork including Kate's ethereal, almost mystical, *Sunrise at Holkham Beach*, which was one of the images they'd found in the camera after Maddie's wedding, and which they'd kept back when everything else had been sold.

The changes were never flagged in advance and the challenge for everyone else was to see who first noticed the new stuff: winner got the first of Hawck's morning pancakes with their choice of topping.

The biggest change came on the night of 24 May, the day before the deadline for nominations closed, when a large van drove up and parked outside the Piggery. Nico, Stina and Pr—Gus all turned up to help unload. Everyone else was bought off with a curry in the farmhouse, and laid under oath not to come and disturb the work.

Niall was last in on Thursday morning. He carried Brilliant in a wicker basket that looked more like a birdcage, but Harry Pearce in the village had made it for him and Harry had flown the last Spitfire before it had been decommissioned, so nobody was inclined to argue.

'OK, people.' Niall set it down on the floor and crouched to unwind the spiral of cane from the staple that made the lock. 'We are now microchipped and fully registered so if we do a runner, we—' He stood, slowly, leaving Brilliant to saunter off. 'What the ever-living fuck is *that*?'

'That' was a sinuous glass tank set on top of a moulded wooden base. It rose to three feet off the floor and was eighteen inches wide, and the whole thing wove in a long, low sine wave from about six paces inside the main door, angling back and down towards the door to the kitchen. The tank was filled with water, with a bed of pea gravel, from which grew a selection of aquatic plants, their fronds waving lazily in shades of red and green.

'Cat TV,' Hawck said, with the pride of a new parent. 'Let us get the plants acclimatised and it'll have about a thousand neon tetras in there. Then, when they're settled, we'll add some gouramis. It'll be pure magic, trust me."

'Right?' Niall's eyes swivelled nervously. Stina took pity first. 'It's a planted aquarium,' she said, from the room's far side. 'They're good for offices. All kinds of neurophys says so. We'd have left it without a lid, but kitten-safety says no, so it's completely safe. And we've sorted the power for the pumps and lights: it's all coming from the solar panels and, failing that, the wind turbines.'

'We have wind turbines?' Niall asked faintly. The solar panels had been up a while.

'Keep up, Nye,' Finn said. 'They've been up for a week, out the back above Five Acre Deep. Raye's design. They're 3-D printed in Portugal at a place that runs on Mondragon lines; you'd love it. They're vertical axis and small, partly to make them easy to ship around the planet but mostly so they won't freak out the local birdlife. Allegedly. Any excess power goes into the salt batteries round the back. If it doesn't work, we'll think of something else. We have to power this place, and fossil fuels are not the answer so this is our first shot. See the "Power Reduction" policy group for details.'

'Riiiiight.' Niall settled at his desk and ostentatiously perused the day's new data.

All was peaceful until the last fifteen minutes before the four o'clock deadline for candidate nominations. The CIC candidate count was up to 379. Predictably, one of the Ghosts had started a book on whether they'd get past 380 before the deadline. It was ten short of Niall's original target, but an order of magnitude more than anyone else had dared to hope for.

Everyone was pretending to work. Everyone was watching the timer count down the minutes, except Hawck, who was *definitely not* the chef, but was nonetheless baking brownies for a celebratory tea break and kept slipping out of the kitchen to check on progress.

With seven minutes to go, Nico gave a stifled squeak as two people registered, taking the total to 381. He was in charge of updating the table on the wall screen. He began typing, fast.

Around the room, bets were called in and settled. Most of them involved something virtual, but Grok walked across the room and handed a five pound note to Zerg (tall, Jamaican, hair like black treacle).

The two shared a high five and Grok was about to say something appreciative about the plants in the aquarium when Niall hurled his pen so hard against the wall that it bounced back six feet.

'*Fuckers!* They can't. They fucking *can't!*'

Brilliant bolted, leaving claw marks where he'd been. Niall was wearing shorts. Beads of blood welled on his thighs. Consternation streaked across the room until Finn caught the kitten and cradled it close.

Connor was nearest to Niall. He'd 'dropped in to say hello', which happened quite often when Hawck had brownies on the go.

Bending, he picked up the pen and laid it on Niall's desk close enough that their hands touched. 'Nye?'

'Nominations,' Niall said, hoarsely. 'I think they can't go any lower and then they fucking blow the baselines out of the fucking water.'

All attention turned to Nico, who read fast from his spreadsheet. 'The last two sign-ups were Charles Naismith and Estrella Cunningham. She's the green-haired one with all the piercings who got done last autumn for breaking windows at a bank. Trial was last week and the jury said not-guilty, plus she just turned eighteen, so she's cleared to stand. She's standing for Norwich South.

'Naismith's an old, straight, white dude who used to be MP in the Home Counties with politics on the far edge of Urquhart's head-bangers. He reckons he's had an epiphany because of the sewage in the rivers and he's come out of retirement to go for Norwich North. Those two are polar opposites, but they must have sorted something out between them because they're due on a platform in the city with Leah this evening. Potential for big fireworks.' Nico fanned his fingers up and out. 'And maybe old white dude's a plant?'

'No.' Woodenly, Niall shook his head. 'I mean yes, probably right on all counts, but that's not the problem.'

Grok said, 'Cassandra Cartwright registered to stand for the government against Leah about an hour ago. She does something fancy with horses when she's not being a management consultant on a thousand an hour. Tall, blonde and jodhpurs. The Surrey set are going to love her.'

'Leah knows.' Niall's gaze tracked blindly to Stina, where it sharpened. 'We need a colour and a logo that works,' he said. 'Urgently.'

'Vote's tonight.' Stina's team had been working on a logo for days. 'We've taken the Cs of CIC and thought about Sea, so Sea-Change, so we're working up variations with Hokusai's *Great Wave off Kanagawa*. They'll all be ready for the meeting, plus a World Tree if nobody likes the wave. Colour's harder. All the primaries are taken. We're thinking rainbow because—'

'Teal,' Niall said. 'Or lilac.'

'But—'

'*Teal.*'

'Nye, what's the sudden hurry?' Connor was the soul of calm, but even so the gaze Niall cast him was ruinous.

'Deadline's up,' he said.

There were four minutes still to go but nobody was going to get picky with Niall in this mood. A faint ping said someone else had squeezed in under the line. Nobody looked.

'And?'

'And a minute ago, Melanie Urquhart's friends in Capitalist Running Dogs plc registered three hundred and seventy-nine "Independent" candidates with names close enough to ours that you'd have to squint really hard to see the difference, each new name designed to be on the line above our candidates on the ballot paper.'

'*What?*' The entire room asked the same thing, if not all in the same language.

Niall bared his teeth in a bloodless smile. 'Exactly. So when random Surrey voter is confronted with Ms Lena Karoshi (Independent) ahead of Dr Leah Koresh (Independent), a significant number of them are going to put their cross in the first box they come to.'

'Enough for us to lose?' Hawck asked.

Niall took a breath to explain the hurtling volatility of the polls, but Hawck knew the details as well as anyone; he let it out again, unused. 'They clearly think so, therefore we have to think so, too. We're going to have to make CIC candidates as distinct as we can. Ergo, we need a logo by close of play tonight.'

He shoved his chair back from his desk and was at the door before anyone thought to ask where he was going. It slammed hard behind him.

Finn was already up. He planted Brilliant on Charm's lap and waggled his fingers at his eyes, then the kitten, then the room. 'Eyes on the furry one, people. If we lose him before Nye gets back, every single one of us'll have to emigrate.' He left at a run.

Even so, he was still a pace or two behind Niall as they stepped through the gate onto the blackthorn-lined track that wound up the hill. It was cooler here, but the crow part of me was sharply aware they were following the path I'd seen Finn take in my first void-walk: the one that led up the hill to Five Acre Deep, which was plenty deep enough to drown in. I couldn't see Niall doing anything daft: Iced-Niall maybe, but not now. Still, I was nervous.

Finn, too, but the path was too narrow to walk alongside. He padded soft-footed behind till they broke out on the meadow above the reservoir. The day was scorching.

'Going for a swim, maybe?' I asked it half-aloud: they couldn't hear me anyway, but no, Niall turned left and headed uphill to the open moor where a couple of dozen vertical wind turbines spun sluggishly in the barely moving air.

A post and rails fence guarded the area: this, too, was new. Niall leaned on the top bar, looking over the site of construction.

Finn caught up and came to lean alongside. 'We should have told you about these. Sorry. There was too much else going on and I didn't want to distract you.'

Niall pulled a strand of tall grass and chewed on it. 'Raye's idea?'

'And Charm's. She's hot on alternative power.'

'Raye, though. They a thing?'

Finn raised one shoulder. 'Maybe. Don't know.'

'Do you want them to be?'

'Maybe. Landfall's not till last week of June. Might be put back if they have to make a detour to Lisbon, which is looking likely. We're trying to get some of the Regen Finance people on board. They have skills we could need.'

'You know we've been talking?'

'You and Raye? Yeah. They said. People's Parliament stuff. Sounds good.' A pause. 'Unless it's all virtual, you're going to need an actual physical place to hold your new government.'

'Maybe.'

'And that means buying somewhere.'

'Maybe.'

'Did Raye talk to you about Kilbrechan?'

'Yep.' Niall had spun this to me-as-Brillo the night before. Kilbrechan was an island off the west coast of Scotland. Bigger than Iona, not as big as Mull. Big enough for the kind of size a parliament might need. There was a ruined hotel in the middle, and derelict crofts. It was a project and a half, by any measure and the asking price was in eight figures which was one of several reasons why it had been on the market since before the pandemic. Also, it had a good deep water berth on the landward side and Raye thought it would make a good shipbuilding site.

Niall said, 'I don't like rich people throwing their money about, however cool they are.'

'You'd rather they threw it at rockets to Mars?'

'Raye asked that.'

Finn turned round to hook his elbows over the fence and look out across the valley. 'You keep telling us that money won't be worth anything soon. Spending it on a place that might change the whole world seems not a bad idea.'

'They said that, too.'

'And?'

'And I don't know, Finn. I love the Crescent. I don't really want to live on a rainswept bit of rock that's cold and dark for half the year and the midges will eat you alive for the other half.'

'Raye'd buy somewhere in Glasgow if you—'

'I don't *want* Raye to buy me anywhere. I want . . .' Niall bounced a fist off the fence's top rail. 'I don't know what I want. I don't know what's possible. Everything might all fall apart on election night anyway. Can we just wait? I can't stop Raye buying an island. They could probably buy the whole of Scotland from the petty cash. But not to give it to me. Anyway,' Niall, too, turned to look down at the village, 'I thought you'd want them here.'

411

'Kind of like things the way they are.'

'You're weird, Bro.'

'Love you, too.'

They lapsed back into quiet. Finn's phone chimed the tone for a family text. We both heard the catch in his breath as he checked his texts.

Sharply, Niall asked, '*Ocean Ghost* OK?'

'Fine.' A breath, for courage, I thought. Finn looked out to the far horizon. 'Grandad thinks you should go to Norwich.'

Niall laughed, a little weakly. 'No.'

'Leah's going there.'

'And yesterday she was in Saffron Walden and tomorrow she'll be in Peterborough. I do read the sit-reps. The only new bit is the two new candidates are in Norwich and she'll have her work cut out stopping them from assaulting each other.'

'It'll be exciting?' Finn offered.

'It'll be carnage, but she'll manage it. She doesn't need me.'

'Hawk's been training the volunteers who set out the tables and chairs and sorting the talking point groups. He's going up to see how they get on. It's an hour away. You could catch a lift.'

'Still no.'

'Nye, please?' Finn tried his most persuasive look. 'You've been inside too long. You need to get out more. I'm getting worried. Leah's worried. *Grandad's* getting worried enough that he asked me to get you to go. Bottom line: you go listen to Leah and the others explaining how Universal Basic Services will transform the NHS or he'll have you down on the Dairy wrestling piglets and feeding lambs.'

Niall gave a horrified shudder. 'Cats, Bro. I'm a city boy. I do cats. I don't do small squirmy things that shit all over you and scream in your ears.'

'So you'd better give in graciously. Because when Grandad kidnaps you, I'm not going to stand in the way. He got you the rescue-kitten. You'll never be able to say no to him again.'

Niall grudgingly accepted Hawck's offer of a ride up the A11 to Norwich and spent the early evening making life hell for the sound tech who was trying to manage an open-air stage and loudspeakers of a quality to reach several thousand.

Leah didn't say anything she hadn't said a dozen times already, though the combination of her looking as striking as ever in black and gold, and on stage with a white-haired old man who insisted on wearing a tweed suit in 30-degree heat and an eighteen-year-old with fluorescent green hair and a lot of facial metal, was deemed picturesque enough that it made several front pages the following day.

Niall came home that night with sunburn, and a smile and, by the time he opened the back door to the farmhouse, the Changemakers' logo was a teal wave with three small crimson tear drops falling from the crest.

In the next twenty-four hours, almost everyone found a scarf, or a tie, or a belt: anything in the right colour. Almost everyone looked good in it. Specs had turned up to speak on the evening news sporting a new pair of teal-framed glasses with crimson flashes. These, too, made several front pages.

CHAPTER TWENTY-SIX

June 2023

With the deadline for nominations closed, the gloves came off and the campaign descended into a naked cage fight of the kind previously seen only on the western side of the Atlantic.

The online fight for hashtag supremacy became ever more heated and the memes ever more strident.

Live television broadcasts began to take on the atmosphere of a World Cup final and every sentence uttered by any candidate was dissected for sense and nonsense.

Newspaper headlines paradoxically became more bland as editors tried to gauge the mood of their readerships in a world where chaos in the polls had rendered all predictions moot, sowing panic in the ranks of the established parties and their media supporters.

Changemakers had cracked the old structure apart, exposing new fault lines in the voting pool that hurled all the old number-crunching out of the window. The three hundred and eighty-two candidates standing under the CIC umbrella were drawn from across the old, obsolete left–right spectrum, with Charles Naismith (tweed-bloke) and Specs at one end, and Estrella Cunningham (lime hair and piercings) at the other.

The final person to sign up had been Zerg (real name Josiah Jeremiah Jamieson), who swore it wasn't just a ruse to win the fiver from Grok, and that he really did want to stand in his home constituency of Barking in East London where his Jamaican origin was a guaranteed plus. As the last sign-up, he had nobody with a scarily similar name just above him on the ballot paper, which was definitely A Good Thing. He was released from coding and sent off with the full CIC Independent Support Pack, which by then ran to fifty pages.

The majority of the candidates were evenly arrayed among the myriad potential identities of age, race, gender, sexuality, ability and neurodiversity. Of these, only age remained a reliable predictor of voting behaviour. Changemakers was polling 87 per cent of the under thirty-fives, with steadily diminishing returns in the decades above this until the over-eighty-five bracket where, not surprisingly, their support was too low to measure.

For sure there were men and women in their late eighties and nineties – vocal and connected ones who called in to radio phone-ins and praised CIC to the heavens whenever they had the opportunity – but they were so few that the team back in the Piggery knew all of them by name.

You would think all of this made the calculations straightforward, and, up to a point, you'd be right. Everyone was agreed that if every registered voter between the ages of eighteen and sixty put a cross in a box, then Leah and her cohort would be forming the next government.

Similarly, if this group decided not to bother voting (or the voter suppression worked and they were not allowed to), but instead everyone of pensionable age put their cross in a box, then Melanie Urquhart would get her hundred-seat majority and prison ships would become a reality, along with unbridled contamination of the land and seas, and a swift public execution of the NHS with the carcass sold off to the vampire vultures of US health firms.

Nobody believed either extreme was likely, but equally nobody had any clue what was actually going to happen, nor any way to find out.

In the Piggery, Brilliant continued to grow sleek and confident, the various policy teams continued to refine or invent policy, Niall continued to write blogs explaining how a People's Parliament might work and Finn's development team working on the Exit Poll App continued to wrestle with the parameters they had been set.

Halfway through the morning of the second Monday in June, Finn upgraded the potential delivery of the app to 'quite possible'.

Hawck, who had taken to visiting Matt and Jens in the early mornings and had come back this time with a basket full of soft fruit and cream, made old-fashioned strawberry sundaes to celebrate.

Handed his, Niall sank down the wall, pressing the cold glass to his brow. With his characteristic inclination to go against the majority, he was becoming increasingly sanguine about the voting numbers, but had begun losing sleep over the quality of CIC's candidates, particularly those who had jumped ship from either of the two main parties.

'What happens if we actually win? Or even hold the balance of power?' he asked, lowering his glass so that Brilliant stopped trying to walk up his face to get to it. 'Specs'll be throwing spanners in the works from the get-go. He's the Biden and Blair of the Changemakers. He'll make all the right noises and do nothing.'

This question was not new, and previous iterations had been generally understood to be rhetorical. This time, Finn answered with unusual sharpness. 'Nye, can we park that for later? Right now, we have a bigger problem. QBC is setting up its own version of our intergenerational conversations in their lunchtime news programme. The producer's niece, Ceri, aged ten, is being hauled into a live TV studio, to have "a conversation on values" with Robert, eighty-nine years of spittle-flecked, unreconstructed white dude.'

'*What?*' Niall smacked his sundae on the floor and strode across to look over Finn's shoulder. 'That's insane. Who's facilitating?'

'Toxic Pixie.' Finn's voice was ironed flat. He never had liked his mother's former flatmate, but this was a new level of loathing.

'Seriously? They're throwing a ten-year-old child into a bear pit with an angry old man and the only adult in the room has the emotional literacy of a gerbil on crack? They can't do this. It's child abuse.'

'And yet it's going live two minutes from now.'

'You got Ms Toxic's number?'

Finn scrolled through his contacts. 'Coming to you.'

The call took less than ninety seconds. Niall hung up chalky-white, his hair a wreck. 'Bloody hell. Bloody, *bloody* hell.' He managed a credible imitation of Rebecca Watson's estuary drawl. '"We're only doing what you're doing thousands of times a day in hidden online spaces. But we're doing it in the open." She's not just clueless, she's fucking lethal. This is going to be carnage. She'll destroy this kid and they're cueing it now, there's no stopping them.' He stood up and began to pace. 'We need to start the pushback. Our take on this has to surge before theirs ever starts.'

'OK, people.' Finn spun his chair to face the room. 'Drop everything else. We're all on this.'

The Ghosts mounted a creditable defence.

In real-time, they uploaded a live video narrated by Charm which critiqued the horror show of a child being bullied by an angry old man and pointed out the differences between this and the intergenerational conversations they were holding. To wit: Changemakers would never leave young girls alone with anyone: there was always at least one trained facilitator in the room who made sure the conversation was respectful on both sides, and if anyone showed signs of losing control, they stepped in long before any damage could be inflicted.

Leah was diverted on her way to talk to a sixth form college in Surrey to a video room her agent managed to locate and persuade the owners to open.

Her thirty second take to camera was solid gold, but gold wasn't the currency now. The other side, frankly, had won this particular race to the bottom of the brainstem before the starting gun had ever popped, and a sober video expounding intellectual arguments was never going to have much traction against the sight of a ten-year-old girl sobbing uncontrollably until her mother broke onto the set and physically carried her to safety.

Within minutes of the programme's end, the net went wild. For a blink or two, it was filled with old, white men crowing over the woke snowflake girl who had been owned by one of their own, until Melanie Urquhart's rebuke elicited the necessary handbrake turn, so that the narrative instead became one of righteous outrage at the woke adults' abuse of vulnerable children.

Riding this hard, the bot farms patched #CICAbuseKids all over the net and soon new videos appeared in which dozens of angry old men with scarily high blood pressure screamed into their phones the message that angry old men with evident hypertension should never be allowed to scream at a ten-year-old.

'Fuck it ten times sideways. This is a firestorm, and we're the straw men set up for burning.'

Niall was multitasking: pacing the Piggery and eating his nails at the same time. Everyone else was glued to their desks watching the Ghosts' running polls document trickle, then flow, and then flood of evaporating Changemaker support.

Grok said, 'It's not that they hate us, it's just they won't bother to turn out to vote for us.'

'Of course.' Niall had his head in his hands. 'Suppressing the vote is their only option now. And lo, they have suppressed it. We're going to need a team meeting. Where's Leah?'

Leah was talking to the sixth-formers, who at least understood the dynamics of what was happening. This was more than could be said for most of the commentariat. Half an hour later, she called Niall from the train.

'Frances Nolan's asking if I'll go on the six o'clock news.'

Niall hissed a breath in through his teeth. 'She's not a friend, Leah. She'll mince you into tiny pieces and dance on your rotting remains if it pushes her career. Owning you on TV is just what she needs. Tell her to jump.'

'If I do that, they'll empty-chair me. Sorry, but this is my call and I'm going. What I need from you guys is every single sentient Ghost picking up the soundbites and getting them out there. If we ever needed to amplify something, it's now.'

Niall looked up into his Kirsten-corner and this time I did send him a blast of all the support I could muster. I pushed Brilliant, too (he was always more amenable to suggestion) and the kitten made his shoulder from a standing start. Tears sprang bright in Niall's eyes, but didn't spill over. 'OK,' he said. 'Give it hell. We're with you.'

The evening was warm, the pavements still hot, dry and dusty. Specs fell into step with Leah as she walked the last few hundred yards to the studio.

'Mind if I join you?'

418

Tight-shouldered, she matched her stride to his. 'Did Niall send you to babysit?'

'I haven't spoken to Niall once since this campaign started, and nobody in their right mind thinks you need a babysitter. I do, however, have moles in the production team who told me you were coming and I thought you'd like some moral support.' He stepped ahead of her to open the door and then held it for her to go through. 'After you.'

A brief hesitation, and she stepped inside, turning back when she was through. 'That kind of sexism died in the nineties.'

'But I was born in the sixties, last of the good-time Boomers. I'd apologise, but neither of us would believe it. The lift is to your right and we need the third floor as soon as we've signed our way through security. Don't trust the guard to your left, he's a paid-up member of Melanie's proto-thugs.'

All of this delivered in an undertone while he smiled cheerfully at the thug-guard and greeted the desk staff by name, ignoring the mesh of glances that threaded the room as soon as Leah signed in. Whispers tracked them as the lift doors closed.

'Notoriety sticks harder than fame,' Specs said, before Leah could comment.

'Then I need to become notorious for something other than not bullying ten-year-old girls.' Leah leaned back on the wall of the lift. 'Why are you really here?'

He regarded her for a moment. 'Do you know what a dead cat is?'

'It's the noxious thing you throw on the table to distract people from something you don't want them to see. The former leader of your former party was something of an expert in the art.'

Specs inclined his head. 'Technically, he's still party leader until the election. Don't underestimate him.'

'I wasn't planning to. The problem is that his dead cats often came to life and we ended up with zombie policies whose only value was to placate the comment threads of the tabloids. I'm sure yours stay dead, but all the same, please save them for a greater emergency than this.'

'You have this covered?'

Leah shone him her biggest, broadest smile. In the far distance, a lion coughed a laugh. Specs found himself studying his shoes. Frowning, he looked up again. 'Mind if I watch?'

'You and five million others? Be my guest.'

In the event, the live viewing figures were just shy of eight million and the numbers soared far beyond this when the clips went viral.

They cut in at the point when Frances Nolan said, 'My daughter is seventeen and I wouldn't subject her to that kind of abuse. So why do you?'

'We *don't*! We never would! That's the —ing point!' Leah managed to swear without actually giving them a word to bleep out. She also managed to lose her temper in a way that was both captivating and terrifying.

Nolan winced back in her seat. Leah leaned in, elbows on her knees, a giant praying mantis on the cusp of a meal. Her voice was sharp with fresh angles. 'No human being with a functioning heart would do this to any other human being, least of all a vulnerable child. So you have to ask yourself why the producer of QBC thought it would be fun to throw her ten-year-old niece at a lump of Gammon. Why has nobody asked *her*?' One fist slammed into the other for emphasis. 'Why?!'

'Gammon?' Back in the Piggery, Niall froze mid-pace. All expression bleached from his face. 'Oh, *girl* . . .'

'Gammon?' Nolan swallowed, twice. From the way her hand twitched to her headpiece, her own producer was melting down. 'You can't say "Gammon". That's racist.'

'What else would you like me to call an obese, pink, entitled *monster* who can't regulate themselves around a child? What else do you want me to say to a woman who throws an unprotected child to someone *she knows is incapable of self-control*?'

'But—'

'But *nothing*, Frances Nolan! This is abuse, deliberately conducted for political ends. This . . . *this*, is exactly what's wrong with politics in this country. You people aren't trying to win the arguments. You're certainly not working together to find solutions to the climate crisis, the extinction crisis, the energy crisis, the cost of living crisis, the billionaires raking in money crisis, the surging destruction of women crisis, the whole rotten systemic crisis that is at the root of all of these ... instead of trying to fix these, you're pandering to people who pull stunts with *their own —ing children* to divert attention away from their utter lack of ideas. And you, the pliant, complicit media, are parroting whatever they tell you. You're as rotten as they are. Worse, you're too stupid to see when you're being used. I'm *done* with this.'

Surging to her feet, Leah ripped off her microphone and hurled it onto the table. 'Call me back when you're ready to actually solve things. If you're going to break children for public entertainment, count me out!'

The whole rant came in at just under fifty-five seconds. Stina's team ran it on Twitter unbroken. On Insta, they cut it into segments and ran them sequentially. On TikTok, they put the fragments to music and, within an hour, someone was rapping the entire tirade against a backdrop of Leah's best outtakes. In part or in whole, #LeahLosingIt or #LeahOwnsTheGammon, depending on who was sending it on, was trending within ten minutes and nothing knocked them off the plinth.

The Ghosts threw high fives around the Piggery. Finn, Charm and Hawck were seen to dance. Niall gave Brilliant into Nico's care and went out, alone, and nobody knew where.

At eight forty-five that night, not long before dusk, Niall arrived at Cambridge station, holding tight to a bouquet of honey-coloured roses.

Leah was one of the first off the London train, a head taller than the rest, buzzing with a predatory vibe that left a penumbra around her clear of both friends and foe.

Niall, who was virtually invisible, had to fight through the swarming mass of people desperate to get home to eat, drink, sleep and wake to an alarm that would throw them back onto the train.

He kept one protective arm around his roses, until he met and entered Leah's forcefield.

Suddenly shy, he said, 'I know they're probably grown by child labourers in Kenya using enough water to supply a whole village, but I needed to make a statement.'

Leah looked at the flowers, at Niall, and back at the flowers. 'And that statement is . . .?'

Puzzled, he took a half-step back. 'You're a strategic genius and anyone who argues differently is an idiot. Isn't that obvious? I think you just rescued the entire campaign.'

She bit her lip. 'I thought I was about to be sacked and you were being kind.'

'What?' Now he was really thrown. 'Why? Either one?'

'You're being kind, because under the take-no-prisoners exterior, you're actually quite humane. And my being sacked because you explicitly told me not to say the word Gammon or to lose my temper in public, and I did both.'

'*And* you said "you people". To the Beeb.'

'That, too.' She grimaced. 'I think I just broke all of Kirsten's rules of communication. And my own.'

Niall swayed round a cluster of Japanese foreign language students who were debating how best to call a taxi. He caught the gaze of the nearest and said, 'The rank is outside. Just tell the first driver where you want to go.'

Leah was waiting for him, despondent. He said, 'Sometimes we have to do what works and until we have those with wisdom in power and those with power understanding what healthy human culture looks and feels like, you have to start where they are.'

'I wasn't modelling healthy human culture, though, was I?'

'Leah, we were being destroyed. If you hadn't stepped into the breach, we'd be finished. As it is, you didn't actually lose your temper, but you acted it well enough to be convincing, with the result that the Gammon-net's collective head is exploding over the fact that a not-even-white, not-male said That Word and they've completely forgotten everything that went before, while the rest of the world has seen QBC for exactly what they are. On the genius scale of nought to five, this rates a ten, easily. So: flowers. Because a rose or two says it all faster.'

'Thank you.' She took the bouquet. The scent furled past, thickly.

Together, they threaded past the bike-commuters and on towards the car park. Leah said, 'I was thinking we should offer the girl – Amy – some counselling. Also probably her mother. And we should see if any of our actual intergenerational pairs would be happy for us to put their videos up online as long as we can make them non-identifiable.'

Niall's stride hitched. 'We think very alike.'

'You'll do it?'

'Already done. Amy and her mother accepted the offer of counselling paid for by us. And there's a thirteen-year-old in Dundee called Rosie who had a pretty decent conversation with Petra and Daniel, a retired couple in Okehampton. All three, plus Rosie's parents, plus Matt, who was facilitating, are happy for it to go public. Charm's video team is busy sorting outtakes as we speak, to ensure anonymity.'

They had reached the car park. Niall stopped, searching through his pockets. He nodded down to the grey e-Golf beside them. 'This is it.'

'Your car?'

'Eriq's.'

'I thought he left it to Finn?'

'I borrowed it.' Niall's thoughts on cars had not changed in the years I'd known him. So, until about an hour previously, Eriq having spent money on an electric vehicle, even a second-hand one, was an astronomical waste of carbon and the only thing it sustained was the obscene profits of the vehicle manufacturers. 'What?'

Leah was clearly sorting through a number of possible comments before settling cautiously on, 'Would you like me to drive?'

He contrived to look wounded. 'You don't like my driving?'

'I've never experienced it. Finn has suggested I'll sleep better – and live longer – if this remains the case.'

With a sigh, Niall flipped the key hand to hand, then tossed it to Leah. 'Knock yourself out.'

Surprised, she snatched it from the air. 'Niall? It doesn't actually need the key in the ignition to make it go, it just needs to be in the car.'

Niall's brows met in the middle. 'Metaphor. Who holds the key drives the car.'

Leah got in and slid the driver's seat back a touch. They settled in edgily, as if a line had been crossed. 'Home?' she asked.

'That was the plan. There is likely to be a degree of celebration. Cake was mentioned. I imagine music may arise. There may even be dancing and most of it will be in circles around you. You pulled off quite a coup.'

Leah leaned at an angle against the door. 'Might you be open to other ideas?'

'Such as?'

Tentatively: 'We could make a detour via The Wild Oak at Cottenham.'

Niall laughed. 'Leah, I know you're a cultural icon, but the Oak's got a Michelin star. It's booked out for months in advance. Years. You won't get a table this side of 2025.'

'Unless you know the owner. In which case there may be a couple of spare covers in a quiet corner.'

'Rosie Arden? You'd have to know her very . . .' His brain caught up with his mouth. His gaze narrowed. 'How well?'

Leah's shrug fooled neither of them. 'We split up just before Christmas. Amicably. I have a standing invitation. We'll get a table if we want one and she won't assault you with a carving knife.'

Whatever else he'd expected, it wasn't this. In the silence, the car seats creaked as his weight shifted forward, then back.

Leah's sigh was barely audible. 'This isn't a prelude to sexual assault, Niall.'

'Obviously.' This was his 'I'm not an idiot', tone.

Leah stared, pursed her lips on the beginning of a word, abandoned it, and started again. 'Are you getting locked in old-paradigm thinking, Niall Penhaligon? Because last time I heard, Alba Rising wasn't overly fixated on monogamy, or weird ideas about sexual monotony?'

'We're not.' Niall's flush pinked the ends of his ears.

'But you assume I am?'

'Absolutely not!'

'Is this about Kirsten, then? Is she going to object to you having dinner with me?'

Niall looked down at the knot of his knuckles, cramped on his knees, and then to the car's upper corner. Presently, he nodded. 'The Oak, then.' He sounded as if he were surprising even himself.

The Oak lived up to its promise and the drive home was considerably more relaxed than the drive there had been.

They slept apart that night, but when I took my Niall-dream part to the Crescent and joined with Brillo, calling Niall into the dream was almost effortless. Maddie had always dreamed more fluently when she was courting Eriq.

He didn't mention Leah and so Brillo-me couldn't ask. I held to my customary role of listening and asking questions and letting Niall sort out his own answers. It's been the pedagogy of the grandmother since time was young and works, evidently, even if the grandmother is the dream of a cat.

We worked together and Niall woke warmer and softer, I thought, and the team in the Piggery was wound a bit less tight as they ran down to the election day wire.

CHAPTER TWENTY-SEVEN

Wednesday, 21 to Thursday, 22 June 2023

'Get out the vote. Nothing else matters now but that we get the people who've said they're going to vote for us, actually to put their mark in our box.'

Leah was addressing the final collective GhostTalk call on the night before the polls opened. Logging in were the policy groups, the gathered candidates of the Changemakers Independent Concordium, plus their agents and as many of the ground teams as could be persuaded to stop knocking on doors before it was completely dark. All in, the numbers came to just shy of one hundred and twenty thousand.

'I'm not saying anything that isn't being said in constituency and party offices across the country. Anyone who knows anything about elections will tell you that the single most important thing on election day is to get out the vote.'

This once, Leah was in the attic, sitting at a carefully curated desk with the long blank wall behind her. Nico and Stina had worked for two days to create a backdrop image based on a picture Eriq had taken of Maddie, Kirsten and Kaitlyn playing volleyball; one of those chance shots where all three were in the air, free of care, full of laughter, joyous: happy.

Life glowed from them in a way that triggered mirror neurons across the board. That's the thing about human physiology: it's enormously complex, but also quite predictable, and images of beautiful women looking genuinely joyful raise the oxytocin levels in pretty much anyone who isn't an actual psychopath.

It helps, though, if they're not framed by a ramshackle Piggery with the front left headlight of an old car poking past the waist of the oldest player, so careful Photoshopping saw them overlaid on the ethereal silver-gold layers of Kate's *Sunrise at Holkham Beach*, the same image that now graced a wall in the updated Piggery.

It wasn't a tsunami wave, or even something you could usefully surf, but the layers of mist over a North Sea swell with the sun gilding the waves matched the wave of the CIC logo in ways designed to resonate without being ostentatious.

Leah had prepared a script, but she wasn't reading it: she never did. Leaning closer to the camera, she said, 'OK, people. We win this if our vote comes out and theirs doesn't. This might sound obvious, but by this stage it's the gamechanger. What none of the other parties will say in public, but are definitely saying in private is, "Anything you can do to stop the other guys' votes coming out, do it."'

She leaned back.

Charm flicked a few switches and Leah was shunted to the left half of the screen while social media feeds flared and flowed on the right. Leah flicked her thumb in their direction. 'You need to know what we're up against, so these are what we've scraped off the feeds. Most of them are from Urquhart's campaign, but at least a third are from the COPs; they fight really dirty, it's just they have less money. Everything you see will have been tested throughout the campaign and refined down to what will work.

'So, if you're a white male over sixty who reads the tabloids and lives in the urban constituencies in the north of England you are being hit with a spray of videos saying your grandkids are being indoctrinated into Islam at school and Changemakers all look like me and therefore, obviously, will bring in Sharia law.

'If you're white, over sixty and read the broadsheets instead of the tabloids, then whatever your gender and wherever you live, you're being told that only Melanie Urquhart will save your pension and the entire monetary edifice will collapse if she doesn't get at least a hundred-seat majority.

'If you're a woman of any demographic in any area, you're also being told Changemakers encourages the showing of pornography to ten-year-olds, that we'll remove the lower age of consent and legalise polygamy.

'If you're in one of the county towns, you're being shown videos

427

of the raw sewage being pumped into the rivers with me opening the tap. Or a still of a fracking well with "Supported by Changemakers!" across the top.' And in response to a question in the chat. 'Yes, there are people who will believe this. No, they have no facts to back it up, but they don't need them: the image goes in under the level of conscious thought: it's how this stuff works.

'In rural areas, farmers are being told we'll cut off their funding, take their land and turn it over to rewilding projects, while young vegans in cities are being told we'll cut all social services and pour subsidies into industrial meat production: concentration camps for chickens and thousand-acre fields growing biofuels that will suck the water tables dry while polluting what's left of the rivers.

'Scotland and Wales are being told that only Melanie Urquhart will give them Independence, while the 10 per cent who still want to remain in the Union – plus most of England – are being told that Urquhart's their only chance of keeping the United Kingdom intact.'

        In the chat: True, though?

Leah laughed aloud. 'We have to win first. And, people ... winning is not a given. We're not going to match their lies. We're just not going there. We need to win because people believe in us, not because their brains have been hijacked by Cambridge Analytica's evil younger cousin. So we have to undo their damage in real-time, which is where you come in.

'Our priorities are this: if you're in the UK, get out and vote and make sure all of your friends vote too, even if you have to drag them to the polling station. Make sure you have the right ID. But we *also* need you to call up your parents, grandparents, aunts, uncles, cousins, walk down the street to your neighbours and *talk to them*. Tell them there's no indoctrination at school. Let them see your vegan TikTok feed that shows something opposite to the one that red-meat Grandpa just got. Whatever it takes to get through, do it.

'And while you're at it, beg them to give Changemakers a chance: tell them why *you* think we need change. The time for talking points is over. Build your own visions of the way the world could be better for all of us. If they don't buy into this, then beg them to give your generation a chance of a future. If they can't vote for us, at least they can stay home and not vote for the other guy.'

Leah stood. Nico, who was working the camera from the far side of the room, panned back so that she was standing on the edge of a mist-glimmered beach at dawn.

'Finally, remember, we have two polls: the one that will see us elected, and Niall's "Exit Poll" on the app that will give us the People's Parliament. We need everyone to vote in both so we can change the system from the inside and build the better system on the outside.

'Right, that's it.'

She crossed her hands on her chest and gave a bow from the waist. 'Everything we've done hinges on tomorrow. Give it your best shot. Now is the time. We are the people. Go for it.'

Nico cut the feed to a prepared sequence showing Leah, Specs, Estrella Cunningham, Charles Naismith, Zerg and dozens of others at market squares and shopping malls and sports grounds all around the country.

The music was the rap of Leah's 'whole rotten systemic crisis' rant at the BBC; not the original, but a cover done by one of Raye's Ocean Ghosts. It was softer, more melodic, with gulls mewling in the distance. It had reached the charts in a dozen nations and had become Changemakers' default anthem.

One by one, the video feeds dropped. Leah waited for the call to cut and then looped her hands over her head, cracking out stiff joints. Nico and Charm shared a quick glance and quietly, unobtrusively, made themselves scarce.

'OK?' Leah asked.

'Perfect.' Niall was still shy of her, even in private. Especially in private.

When she brought her arms down to rest her forearms on his shoulders, he froze, staring at the door. She pressed a dry kiss to his temple. 'Touching's not illegal, Nye.'

'I know.'

'And you said Kirsten's OK.'

His gaze flicked up to the corner. 'Yes.'

She lifted his hand, threading her fingers through his. 'Will you chill when we've won?'

He smiled, thinly. 'We'd have to define winning. I'd say it involves a complete change of political, economic, social and structural systems and, while I swear I would chill if we got there, I'm not holding my breath. But if we get our MPs elected in double figures, I swear I'll be happy.'

She raised his hand up into a high five. 'I'm holding you to that.'

They still hadn't shared a bed, and they didn't now, but the air crackled with the promise of it.

I met Niall in the dream that night, but he was too tired to talk and there was no point. I nudged him off into deeper sleep and the night passed faster than any of us expected.

▼

Leah left before the polls opened at six the next morning.

Niall stayed behind, pale and fidgety. He paced the width of the Piggery, alternately staring at the super-array of screens on the end wall and leaning over the shoulders of any Ghosts who let him. Once in a while he stopped and sat on the floor and played with Brilliant, but not as often as he usually did and, after a while, the kitten abandoned him to go and stalk fish along the length of the aquarium.

Everyone else played online games, or worked on a new version of the Exit Poll App, or GhostTalked with their friends.

Finn kicked his heels up and spent the entire time texting with Raye, who was negotiating a storm somewhere just south of Caracas. Nobody at all looked at the giant screen-of-screens on the end wall. Except when they did.

This had been cleared of all running totals and in their place was a giant map of the UK with all the constituencies marked out and spaces ready for app-data.

The first tranche of this was due at noon. Niall had wanted it to be continuous from the moment the polls opened but he'd been voted down by twenty-eight to one on the grounds that nobody's blood pressure could take the see-saw of shifts that were undoubtedly going to come in. Six hours of data was worth having, nothing less. After that, it was due to refresh at three hourly intervals until the polls closed at ten, after which there was an enforced gap until the actual results started to come in. The first were expected soon after midnight.

On the map, someone had colour-coded the headers: teal for Changemakers, blue-black for the outgoing party of government, orange for the Combined Opposition parties, unless it mattered to differentiate them, in which case they were red and citrus-yellow respectively. In Scotland the SNP were amber and in Wales Plaid Cymru were a different shade of green to the actual Green party.

Northern Ireland's more sectarian parties had been coded orange if they were Unionist and likely to side with Urquhart, and pale green if they were Republican or the non-sectarian SDLP. Niall still thought these last might align with Changemakers. They hadn't made any comment, but just after midnight Leah had been sent a good luck text by an SDLP candidate, which had to mean something. Nobody knew what.

Other screens on other walls displayed comparison graphs in a mind-bending array: nobody but Niall understood them all. Nonetheless, every Ghost was poised to collate any numbers he asked for, compare them with existing data, create statistics for the social media teams to feed out to the world and, most important of all, do whatever it took to bring about the biggest turnout among the under-sixties the nation had ever seen.

Niall continued to pace.

At eleven fifty-five, Finn caught him as he passed a chair, toppled him into it and sprang up to sit on the adjacent table, folding his legs up neatly.

'OK, people. This is it.' He nodded at the sudden flurry of jazz hands and raised thumbs. 'We need to go silent, though,' he said. 'If anyone hacks us, we're finished. Niall will tell you polls are designed to bend opinion, not reflect it, and the one poll that will definitely shape anyone's opinion is a running total of how their friends and neighbours are already voting. Leaving aside that it's immoral, it's also illegal.

'This is the point where the scary monster music starts because if the bad guys get hold of one single sparkly data point, they'll leak it. Then we go down and take Changemakers with us and there ends our chance of a better future. This is why your phones are heading offsite and won't be back until after ten tonight. And no, I don't know where they're going, so no point in asking.'

Hawck had begun to circulate while he was talking, holding open a bag that was quite evidently lined with lead, collecting phones from people who hadn't been without them for months, if not years – in a few cases, decades.

Finn could have grinned here to take the sting out of it, but this was the Finn who could sit immobile for hours on a meditation cushion and dreamed with Shaolin monks. He looked as serious as I'd ever seen him.

'You're all here because we trust you. Even so everyone is open to pressure, so we're making sure that if someone kidnaps your favourite pet stick insect and threatens to grill it with ginger and turmeric, you genuinely can't reach them.

'Obviously, you're all online and obviously we have incoming data, but the routes out are locked. I wrote the code, so it's fool-resistant, not totally foolproof, and if you spent the entire day trying, you might squirrel past without Charm or me noticing. But I am asking you – begging you – not to. This is our chance to change the world, and we really don't want to fuck it up.'

Finn let his gaze sweep the room. Nobody looked especially surprised or upset at being separated from their phones. Satisfied, he glanced up to the clock on the wall. 'Here we go. If anyone needs a bio break, now is probably the time. It's going to be a long day and a longer night.' Softly, 'Good luck, everyone. Break a leg.'

Forty-eight seconds of rising tension later, the app's first data points hit them with a surge that stretched the Ghosts beyond anything they had practised in the run-throughs.

The numbers were good. Some of them very good. Some of them (Cornwall, West Midlands, places where people went to work early and didn't vote till the evening) were terrible. Niall crunched them nine ways to midnight, but there wasn't much he could actually do.

At three and six, he pounced on the new influx, marked them out, juggled them a bit . . . and went back to pacing.

At six-thirty, Finn, rightly judging that he was staring mutiny in the face, caught his brother's wrist and drew him down into a chair.

'You need to go to Surrey.' He held up the key to Eriq's car. 'I've programmed the sat-nav. It'll take you straight to Leah. Just don't turn off the route and you'll be fine.'

'Right. Thanks. We . . .' Niall drifted off, his gaze drawn back to the graphs and bar charts and pie charts and raw data flows. With an effort he wrenched back to face Finn. 'We're doing OK.'

'Unless every single person is lying on their inputs to the app, we're doing fine. We just have no way of gauging the accuracy. We knew it would be like this. So, go to Leah. Be at her side when her results come in. If you leave now, you'll get there before the polls close.'

'But—'

'Nye . . . There is nothing else you can do. We will look after the little furry fish-botherer. If you get home really late – or not at all – he'll sleep with Grandad. It's all sorted. Stop fighting the inevitable.' Finn knuckled his brother's bicep. 'Go south, young man. And don't come back without a smile. Whatever happens with the polls, young hearts are more important.'

Niall made big, round owl's eyes. 'Fuck off, Grasshopper.'

'Love you too.'

In Niall's absence, the Piggery relaxed. Everyone breathed out. Shoulders softened. Keyboards tapped in a smoother rhythm and, although correlation is not causation and nobody tried to pretend otherwise, the figures flowing in from the app became distinctly more encouraging: until then, they'd been reasonable, but no more. Now they were good. Hawck brought out pizza, and, briefly, work was abandoned.

While everyone else was distracted, Charm leaned over Finn's shoulder, and, in exactly the same drama-free tone in which she'd say 'rogue in the flag room' in a battleground, said, 'Data mismatch.'

Finn lifted the seat beside her, spun it round and straddled it, laying his forearms across the back. 'Show me.'

On her screen, Charm pulled up a map identical to the one on the wall on which she highlighted five constituencies and then isolated them, so the confusing clutter of ever-changing numbers and graphs disappeared.

All five were in England, two around Leeds in what used to be called the 'red wall' and was now as contested as anywhere else, one in Norfolk, another just south of London and the last in the southwest, halfway down the Cornish peninsula.

Finn pointed to the one in Norfolk. 'That's Estrella Cunningham's constituency.'

'Yes. And the one just south of London is Leah's. According to the polls, all five of these should have been in play for our people.'

Finn said, 'You just used the past tense.' English was Charm's fourth language. She was never careless with her tenses.

She chewed her lower lip. 'At the moment, the numbers we're getting from the app are 4.8 per cent different from the ones in the pre-polls, and the disparity is all coming from the twenty-three- to twenty-five-year-olds. No other common features. We're getting a spread across gender identity, sexuality, race and previous stated voting habits.'

'And they're all shifting away from us? Where are they going?'

'To whoever's least likely to win. That's the COPs in Leah's constituency. In all the others it's Urquhart's candidate.'

Finn pulled his hair free of its tie, shook it out and tied it up again, thereby buying himself eight seconds of thinking time. 'So either we had bad data before, or we're getting bad data now, or someone is managing to hijack some votes, and then the question is whether they're real votes on bits of paper in the polling booths or someone messing with the app.'

'Messing with the app would be hard.' There was an edge to Charm's poured-chocolate voice: she hadn't been on the main team, but even so she had written significant sections of the code. 'We'd notice.'

Finn chewed his lip. 'OK. But we still need to see if there's a vulnerability that someone's exploited.' He looked around without making it obvious what he was doing. 'Is Grok free?'

'Could be.'

434

'Unless you know someone else who can read tokens better and faster, get her on it. We don't want block explorers, we need someone who can read the actual hashes.'

'Grok, then.'

Finn waited while Charm typed out a request to Grok, who was just the other side of the fish tank, but text was faster and private. It didn't take long for a raised thumb to show through the glass.

'Next?' Charm asked.

'We can't identify the voters, but we can see what wards they were in. Maybe narrow down to the polling station?'

'Maybe. Probably.'

'Get Nico's team checking to see if there's anything on the social media threads of the people who might have voted there. We don't want to frighten any horses, but we need to know ASAP if someone's been pushed into voting a way they didn't intend.'

Charm sucked in a slow breath. 'We're talking tens of thousands of data points – votes. Might need more people.'

'Right.' Finn lifted his hand to his hair and dropped it again. Charm was patient. 'OK, we don't need tens of thousands, we just need a hundred to know which way the data's being skewed. I can write some search code, but we'll still need more hands on deck. Stina busy?'

'She's on meme creation. We can pull her off that. And Gus is at the Dairy, but he said he'd come up if we needed him.'

'Gus?' Finn looked genuinely confused.

'Prune.'

'Right.' It took a moment to process this and then, 'He's not what you'd call tech literate?'

'He's people literate, though, which is what we need. And he knows his way around a keyboard. If you write search code, make it easy to use.'

Finn gripped her shoulder. 'On it.'

435

CHAPTER TWENTY-EIGHT

Thursday, 22 June 2023

Niall reached Surrey with thirteen minutes to spare before the polls closed at ten.

The car took him straight to the concrete-brutalist secondary school in whose sports hall the count was being held. Already the car park was full, and he had to park behind a Mini on the entrance drive, angling up onto the pavement.

Paper arrows printed out on A4 and taped to the walls prodded him along corridors that smelled of old linoleum and young hormones. He hunched his shoulders and jogged. School had not been kind to Niall; one of the reasons Maddie had pulled the twins out and taught them at home in the community.

The swing doors to the sports hall were plastered with notices reminding him that the count was an essential cog in the wheels of democracy and please could he not interrupt the counters without *exceptional* cause.

He shouldered through into the bright lights and echo of a space that had room for a full-sized basketball court with a netball court set at right angles to its long side. It stretched all three storeys up: he could see the patches of sky through the roof lights, pale behind the electric dazzle. Around three sides, at the height of the second storey, was a balcony, almost empty.

But not quite. 'Niall! Here!' Leah was up there with her agent, Donella Lloyd, who was leaning on the balcony rail so close to Leah that their forearms touched. All the shudders from the corridors came back, more fiercely. He froze. Leah leaned over further. 'Door's in the middle, under there.' She pointed down and to his left. 'Take the stairs that hook right up to here.'

Niall was never short of courage, just that it sometimes took him a moment to gather it. He ran up the stairs and was just past the second landing when he met Leah, coming down. Pouncing, she yanked him into an embrace.

Six steps up, on the second floor, a glass fire door hissed shut. Half a dozen people sat at a white desk in the room beyond, holding an animated conversation that involved much waving of coloured marker pens and scribbles on a whiteboard. On the balcony behind them, Donella speared Niall with a hard look and pointedly turned away.

Leah crushed him so close he squawked.

'What?' Her voice was fuzzed by his hair.

'I can't breathe. Also – thank you – what did I do to deserve this?'

'You didn't tell me you were coming.' Letting go, Leah thrust him at arm's length, a stunned happiness lighting her eyes. Her linen suit was picked out here and there with teal highlights that matched her rosette: the buttonholes, the edging around the sleeves of the jacket, a spark on the buttons; her makeup and fingernails the same, but so subtle he wouldn't have noticed if he hadn't been looking. He looked for so long the silence baked crisp.

Swallowing, he said, 'Finn confiscated my phone and I forgot to pick it up on the way out. And then the sat-nav wouldn't let me stop.'

'The . . .? OK. Remind me never, ever to let you drive, but I kind of get it; stopping on the M25 is horrible. Finn stealing your phone, though. Is that not a tiny bit paranoid? If anyone's going to leak stuff to the bad guys, it's not going to be you.'

'Apparently there are ways of digitally hijacking other people's phones and making them send stuff under the radar.'

'If Finn says this, it must be true.' Her smile grew flatter. 'How was it looking?'

'I haven't seen anything since I left, but it was OK then.'

She prodded him. 'As in, we're not going to look complete idiots? That kind of OK?'

'Too close to call.' He took her shoulders and turned her bodily to face the glass fire door. 'If we're going to talk about this, it needs to be somewhere nobody *at all* can listen. How much do you trust your laser-eyed thugette?'

'Dell?' Her laugh had edges. 'We shared a room in college in first year, then we were an item for half of the Michaelmas term in second year.' Gently, 'It was a long time ago and I'm not planning a reprise.'

'She, of course, wouldn't have you back in a heartbeat even if you begged. And if you believe that, I have a bridge to sell you. Is she safe?'

Leah shrugged. 'As safe as anyone who isn't you and me. I trust her. You don't have to.'

She ran back up the stairs and poked her head through the door. To anyone and everyone inside, she said, 'We're going out. Back in five.' And then to Niall, 'The fire escape at the end of the corridor's the fastest way out. Race you!'

Along, through, down, away from the smell of school. Niall gave breathless directions to the car and thereby lost the race. He'd have lost anyway; she could have been ten times as far in front if she'd tried.

Leah tagged the bonnet and then turned to lean on the passenger door, slowing her breathing. The night was still warm. It hadn't rained for weeks, though the forecast kept promising it would soon: tomorrow or tomorrow or tomorrow; and today maybe they were right because the evening sky was a wash of bruised clouds, limned in scarlet.

Niall fished about in the glove compartment and pulled out a notepad and pen. Shielded by her body, he wrote:

England: Gov: 22%, COPs: 40%, Us: 38%.

Leah's fingers pressed white against the roof of the car. She didn't speak. Niall continued to write.

Scotland: SNP: 83%, COPs: 10%, Gov: 7%.

Aloud, he murmured, 'The Liberals always do well in the Hebrides and Outer Isles. I think they'll get five or six seats. Gov has four seats all concentrated together in Edinburgh and surround, where the English live. The "we get more seats for fewer votes" magic doesn't work in Scotland. They'll get all four, but no more. To be honest, it's not so different from the 2019 election: no CIC Independents stood there, but the SNP has signed up to everything we want.'

He was writing as he spoke.

Wales: Plaid: 64%, COPs: 19%, Gov: 17%.

'Again, all Gov votes will be from English immigrants in the north. Plaid is *way* up on 2019.'

NI: 6-way split. SDLP: maybe 4 seats, APNI: 1, Sinn Féin: 7, Unionist parties: 6.

'That's majority Catholic for the first time ever. Whatever else happens, Ireland'll be united again by this time next year.'

Leah took a long breath. She didn't ask about the numbers for her own constituency. There's a point where not-knowing is probably better than bad news, and definitely better than good news that might be wrong.

Instead, she asked, 'How does this translate into seats here?'

650 total of which 533 are Engl—

'Niall!' She grabbed his pen. 'Talk to me? Please.'

Frowning, Niall nodded at the phone in her pocket. 'Finn says they can listen in on our—'

Her glare blasted him back a pace. She dialled it down. 'Sorry. Key?' He laid it into her cupped hands. She unlocked the car, pulled out her phone and dropped it into the glovebox, relocking the car over her shoulder and heading long-paced for the road.

'Let's go for a walk. There's a gun shop down the road. You can tell me all about how murdering pheasants for fun is the epitome of neo-predatory capitalism.'

'Predatory neo-liberalism.'

'Whatever.'

The gun shop was locked and barred. Niall leaned his back to the iron mesh covering the window. 'Caveats,' he said. 'One: our app might be wrong, or at least might be gamed. Finn swears there's no way to hack the input, but that doesn't stop people lying to us. Second: I left just as people were getting home from work and that's when most of the voting happens. On the other hand, the vote and the predictions match, so I'm inclined to believe it.'

'Seats, Niall. Just tell me how it translates into seats.'

He ignored her. 'Caveat three: the government always gets way more seats than their percentage of the vote would suggest. That's how they end up with an eighty-seat majority on less than 40 per cent of the vote and 23 per cent of the actual population. The COPs have the same effect but about 20 per cent less. We have no way at all of knowing how that applies to us. Seats are guesswork.'

'*Niall . . .*'

'At current figures, over the whole country, I'd put the government on about one ten, maybe one twenty if they're lucky, COPs about two twenty-five, SNP on fifty-ish, Plaid on early twenties.'

'And us?'

'When I left we were on target for two hundred and two. If the SNP and Plaid support us, we go to two seventy-five-ish. If the SDLP and APNI from Northern Ireland join in, then we're at two eighty-two. I'd like to say we'd get Sinn Féin, but they won't take seats in parliament while they have to swear allegiance to the crown and if we can overturn that we don't need them.' Niall was trying really hard not to grin like a Cheshire cat. 'Whichever way you bake it, we're looking at a hung parliament. Nobody gets to the three twenty-six needed to form a majority government, but we're the biggest group in the biggest block.'

Leah kept her eyes fixed on the rooftops opposite. Thoughtfully, she asked, 'Would the SNP and Plaid throw their hand in with the COPs? If they have the most votes, there's an argument—'

'The two Opposition parties are both Unionist. They've explicitly ruled out any deals on Independence.'

'Will they keep to it, though?'

'I think there are elements in each who would want to, but I don't think they'd be trusted. They have form for saying one thing and doing something completely different.'

'And we're clean.'

'Exactly. So you go into the negotiations with full Independence as your first bid: we'll give them referenda in the first year of the parliament if they'll back us on proportional representation, replacing the House of Lords and moving to a degrowth economy. Heck, we'll let Northumberland and Cornwall become nation states if they want. What?'

Laughing, she nudged her shoulder to his. 'Referendums, idiot. Everyone says that now. Referenda is the grammar-nerd in you.' She sobered, biting her lip. 'You're not joking, are you?'

'Not about this.'

Leah stared down at old chewing gum flattened on the pavement. 'What gets in the way?'

'The largest party gets to try first, which would be the COPs. When they fail, we get to try, but they could argue that we're not a real party, in which case the government gets a shot ahead of us. Or we might get a chance but then enough of our candidates turn out to be Trojan horses and our bargaining power evaporates.'

'Trojan horses?' She was studying him more closely now.

'A Changemakers candidate who wins under our name and then decides it's fun to join forces with the COPs. Or Urquhart. They're all independent. They can do what they want.'

Her eyes were lamps in the gloom. 'Who would do that?'

'Specs.' And at her look, 'We've had this conversation. He's been making all the right noises, but he's spent his entire political life supporting the Death Cult. You can't be in government for all that time without one of the banks, or the fossil fuel companies, or the weapons freaks or Big Pharma, or Big Ag, or *someone* having their hooks in you. He could easily join with the COPs. He might join with Urquhart if she offers him something big: Chancellor might be enough. He could claim he was bringing Changemakers thinking into the heart of power.'

'You really think we should have thrown him out.'

'If I could have seen a way to do it with grace, I'd have said so. But then again, if we get to the point where one man can derail us, we're doing something wrong.'

They stood in uneasy silence. Niall gave a small, tight smile. 'I think the phrase you're looking for is bloody, bloody, utterly exsanguinated hell. My grandmother used to say that. The one we don't mention in front of Finn.'

'Really?' Her laugh was strained. 'No, I'll settle for fuck.' She pressed the heels of her hands to her eyes. 'Fuck, fuck, fuck, fuck, *fuck*!'

'We'll know soon . . . On all fronts.'

Leah pushed herself away from the store front. 'We'd better go back. Dell's harmless. Be nice to her. Jealousy doesn't become you.'

Niall said, 'I don't see that'll be much of an issue if I'm down on the floor while she's collating numbers up in the balcony room?'

She frowned at him. He lifted his wrist. 'It's ten o'clock. Count's about to start. We need to be watching it happen. I thought I'd volunteer.'

Leah fumbled for her phone, realised she didn't have it and spun instead to check the church clock, two streets away, on a spire that stabbed the sky. 'Right.' She drew in a big, big breath. 'Let's go stare at the counters, then. I'm sure they'll enjoy being watched.'

From the outside, it seemed to me that the electoral count was the single most tedious event Niall had ever experienced, worse than sports day at school.

He lost patience inside ten minutes. As soon as he thought Finn would have sent the data, I could feel him yearning for his laptop, desperate to drill down into the latest results from the app.

Leah had it, though, up in the ops room, and this in front of him was the real thing, however slow: it mattered that they get it right. So he stayed, watching the pink-rinsed counter he'd been assigned to, counting as she counted, and checking where she put each ballot slip. It wasn't hard to work out which pile belonged to which candidate when he'd worked out the order they'd been on the ballot paper.

If he caught a glimpse of a ballot paper with a cross in the government box (and, to be fair, the counter made it really easy to do so), and tracked that paper to its pile, then did the same for the Combined Opposition and again for Changemakers, the rest were broadly irrelevant. After that, as long as she hadn't switched the piles when he looked away for a moment, it was all fairly easy.

That was the interesting bit over. From then on, it was just a matter of counting the papers that went onto each pile and marking four verticals and a slash for every five in the right box on the counting sheet, as if this were not mind-numbingly stupid eighteenth-century technology dragged into the new millennium because nobody with a functioning brain had ever been near the entire process.

Niall checked the clock for the fifth time and it still said twenty past ten. He wanted to know what the BBC exit poll said and didn't know who to ask: all the people nearby were watchers for the other parties, marked by rosettes, and in the case of Urquhart's squad, by their matching navy-blue sweatshirts. They regarded him with disdain at best and outright loathing at worst; certainly they weren't about to engage in conversation.

He had just decided he could take his attention from the count long enough to grab Leah's phone and text Finn at least for the headline data, when an energetic teen with a short fuzz of red hair bounded across the sports hall floor.

'Sam. Hi.' He thrust out a hot hand. Niall shook it. Sam said, 'Leah says can you go upstairs to the ops room?' Redundantly, he nodded up to the balcony on the second floor. 'She says you know the way. I've to take over.' He looked at the table, the counter, the piles of papers and squared his shoulders. 'I've done the training.'

Niall didn't quite say, 'They *train* people for this?' but it was a close call. He gave a wan smile instead, and passed over his notes, nodding down to the table. 'The piles are in party by alphabetic order right to left from our perspective. They're making it easy for us.'

Sam pulled a face. Niall laughed. ''Luck.'

'Snore.'

Niall was still laughing when he reached the ops room upstairs.

Leah was with Donella and a dozen of the local Changemaker co-ordinators in the room behind the fire doors. Niall caught her eye. 'Problem?' She didn't look like she was celebrating.

She didn't even nod. Just said, tersely, 'No BBC exit poll.'

'It's late?'

'No. They're not putting one out. Nothing official, but Terry Zakander, who used to be their political editor, has tweeted that there's a decision from the high-ups not to publish what they've got.'

'Yes, but have you . . .?'

'We got Finn to verify the tweet. It's real. And Zakander's not been wrong yet.'

Niall's knees wouldn't brace. He slid down the nearest seat like a sack. 'They did this in Scotland at the Independence referendum. That was the only time they refused to release an exit poll.'

'I know.'

'And then the postal votes got the Union over the line with a 90 per cent turnout rate, all for staying with England.'

'I know.'

'The voting company was owned by an ex-government minister. Dead people voted. Lots of them.'

'Niall, I *know*. You've told me too many times to count. I thought you were a crazy conspiracy theorist. I still think so. But this . . . Why are they doing it and what do we do?'

Niall held out his hand. 'I need to talk to Finn.'

All brittle edges, Leah smacked her phone into his palm.

Finn was waiting for him on the other end. 'Nye? That you?'

'Yep. We need to—'

'Are you safe to talk?'

Niall blanched. 'What kind of safe?'

'Get somewhere without microphones.'

Grabbing his laptop, Niall sprinted down to the landing, where he could lean his back to the wall and see anyone coming from below or above. 'Right. Talk.'

Finn took a bracing breath. 'We may have lost five key seats to a new scam: not the name-a-like thing; this was more targeted against people they really, really don't want to win. Leah got the brunt of it, but Estrella Cunningham was pretty high on their hit list, along with three others whose names I don't know, but probably should.'

'You can send me details later, Bro. What happened?'

'Across all five, around a thousand CIC supporters in their constituencies were targeted by DMs or texts purporting to come from you, me or Leah. The message pinged to their phones when they were within a minute's walk of the polling station.'

'Telling them to vote for someone else.' Niall's voice was wire-tight.

'Exactly. The messages were identical: "Hi *Name*, this is *Name of whichever of us you've liked most often*. We know you're one of our strongest supporters and are about to vote for us, but we desperately need some tactical votes in your ward. If we've caught you in time, would you be prepared to vote for *Name of irrelevant candidate not remotely likely to beat Changemakers*? Just reply Y or N and we'll know. No worries if not! And thank you for being there, we really appreciate all you're doing for us. *Signed off by name as per above*".'

'Fuck. Why would anyone believe we'd— Wait. They're young and vulnerable and pre-tested as prone to taking direction?'

'Nailed it.'

'*Bloody* hell.' Niall took a breath, and looked up and left for Kirsten. In a while, he said, 'So we're down 1K across five constituencies, and it's enough to swing things?'

'They didn't all fall for it, so more like five hundred, but yes, it could be enough to skew the result. These are all really tight seats: margins in any one of them could be double figures either way.'

'Fuck. *Fuck.*' Niall cracked his open palm against the wall. In the room above, Leah looked down, and made to open the door. Niall shook his head, curtly, and she backed away.

To Finn, he said, 'OK, first priority is pastoral care of the people who were targeted. We need to contact them and let them know it's not their fault, and ask if they'll put the DMs out on their various threads. Then the Ghosts can pick them up—'

'Gus is already on it.'

'Gus?'

'Prune. His real name's Angus, but he's happier with Gus.'

'Is this a joke, Finn? Because I'm really not in the mood for—'

'We owe *Gus* the most massive . . . something. Whatever it is he wants, we'll get it for him when the dust has settled, because he found this needle in the haystack of data points. He also found the key determinant that decided who to target.'

'Vulnerable,' Niall said. 'Obvious.'

'Yes, but Gus found the conditions just by studying the feeds, which let us reverse-engineer and then track down every single one of the people who'd been targeted. The boy's a genius.'

'OK, we'll buy him a cow. Give him half the farm. Whatever. What. Did. He. Find?'

'A bunch of our most ardent supporters, each of whom has between zero and negative numbers of friends. They never post about their family, have no partners and either no job or the kind of job designed to annihilate your self-respect. And – this was the key that Gus found – they'd all Googled ways to kill themselves within the past six months. They're not just vulnerable, Nye, they're super-fragile: the very definition of unsupported, unresilient, unresourced.'

'And we've been their lifeline.'

'Exactly. For each of them, Changemakers has been their reason

445

to hope. They've each put out dozens of posts per day: hundreds. They're lost and lonely individuals whose highly unstable sense of self currently hinges on Changemakers winning so the world will change. If we lose, and they think it's their fault . . .'

Niall sank to the concrete. 'We should've seen this coming.'

'Don't, Nye. We need you strong, and blaming yourself for something this off-the-wall isn't useful. Stina's mum's a psychotherapist. She and Gus—'

'I thought Caro was an Olympic pole vaulter? Silver medal? Big cheers? Bunting round the village?'

'You're getting old, Nye. That was twenty years ago. Long jump. Commonwealth Games, Manchester 2002. Then she had Stina and now she's a therapist and everyone says she's good, so she and Gus are working out ways to keep our super-vulnerables from jumping under a train. In the meantime, we need a political strategy. So strategise. Please. Maybe deal with the easy stuff first: anything that doesn't involve body parts and blood.'

Niall nailed his elbows to his knees and bunched his fists against his temples. A minute later, slowly, he said, 'Exit polls are usually accurate to within 1 per cent of the final tally: all you're doing is asking people how they voted as they walk out of the polling station and then extrapolating up; it's not rocket science.'

'So if the Beeb is keeping quiet on this one, it's because they don't like what it says?' Finn said.

'Right. And they have reason to believe the final result will be more in the government's favour. Which means they know about one of the scams or they've stacked the postal vote, or both. Either way, if we can get out our own poll now, we can build a narrative that might give us grounds for challenging the result if we have to. Depends how close it is, but we've got nothing to lose. How clean is the rest of our data?'

Finn said, 'As a whistle, so far as we know. We've got everyone combing through it now. After the polls closed we opened comms again and all the Ghosts on land and sea are on it. So far, we haven't found anything and, if the app is right, then we got 98 per cent of our predicted turnout of 89 per cent, which means an 87.22 per cent turnout; 48 per cent of that—'

'Wait, *87 per cent* of eligible voters turned out in a general election?' Niall's face lit up. 'That's more than 1950. Show me the data, Grasshopper.'

'On its way.' Finn was typing as he spoke. 'Tranche One first: hardcore Changemakers' Recommendations: everyone from sixteen to eighty, nobody over eighty-five and the tens and up are in if they co-agreed with the oldsters between eighty and eighty-five. This is your full-on People's Parliament. You're going to be super-happy.'

'I'm only going to be happy if—*Finn*!' Niall crashed to his feet, crushing Leah's phone in his fist. '*Fuck . . .!*'

'Amazing, eh?' You could hear the size of Finn's smile down the line. 'You get this lot into Westminster and that's your People's Parliament right there. Boomers' Last Stand just slides as a footnote in the history books. Second tranche is almost as good.' He hit another key. 'This is where we strip out the under-sixteens and let the over-eighty-fives keep their votes so it's one step closer to the actual result. Even now Changemakers are running the country with no need to offer deals to anyone.

'Tranche Three is the actual exit poll under current voting rules: eighteen and up only with no upper limits. I'm sending you the constituency breakdown coloured by likely win. There are at least thirty too close to call, including all five in the text-switch scam.'

'Leah's too close to call?'

'Sorry, Nye.'

'*Fuck.*' There followed a pause as Niall closed his eyes and took a few breaths, then opened them and checked the rest of the results. 'This isn't too far off what I showed Leah earlier. CIC's down on the earlier predictions, but if we can make a deal with the national parties in all three Celtic nations, we might still get across the line.'

'So do we release this now?'

Niall contemplated his inner chess board again, shifting pieces a hundred moves ahead.

Slowly, he said, 'No exit poll means the election night newsrooms have nothing to talk about. We can fill that void. Release the People's Parliament data first. Go for Tranche Two, where there's no upper age limit so nobody's got a chance to whinge that we're stifling the geriatrics, but the sixteen-year-olds have had a chance to vote. Show the world what parliament would look like if the younger generation had been given a real say in their future.'

'There are templates in the election night drive to build the hypothetical parliaments, right?' Finn asked.

'Yep. Data transfer is automatic. Nico's on it. Just tell him Tranche Two and the names will slot into the relevant constituencies, all we have to do is pick our perfect cabinet. Under the circumstances, we should highlight the ones who've been scammed. Put Leah in as PM, Estrella Cunningham in the Treasury, that'll freak them out, but she has a degree in applied maths, she can talk circles round anyone who tries to troll her.'

Niall glanced down at his screen, thinking on the fly. 'Adam Holdsworth in St Albans is a trades unionist, so put him in the Home Office. Danni Raines is an agriculture student, and we're bringing Environment and Food up to be the sixth Big Office, so announce that and give DEFRA to Danni. Sally Austin in Cornwall was a fossil fuel exec until she blew the whistle on backhanders to government ministers; she can have the Foreign Office. That leaves Health.'

'Specs?'

'Too obvious. Make him Deputy PM in charge of constitutional change: abolishing Lords is his Day One and then set up a Constitutional Convention. He can speak to that for hours without pausing for breath. Give Health to—' A pause to look at the candidates. 'Meredith Jones. She's a gastroenterologist in Cardiff, but she was leading the junior doctors' strike for the whole of the south-west. She can talk about links between food, health and NHS funding.'

'I'm only taking names, Nye, not details.'

''S'fine. You got the app running, that was your bit. We did the forward planning. Nico and Stina between them have templates all set for memes and videos of how the cabinet is shaping up, with sparkly Day One Actions sprinkled like confetti. They just need the names.

'Let that run for half an hour and then start with the new videos of how the world might look five, ten and fifty years down the line when we've really got into gear with degrowth, minimum power use, Future Guardian Governance across the board, full UBI and

UBS in place, and Citizens' Assemblies at all tiers of government; regenerative food systems, reparative justice: the works.'

Finn was thumbing through the election night drive. 'Nye, some of these videos are running up to five minutes. You think people will watch something this long?'

'They will if there's nothing else to do. Get the Ghosts to pump them hard on all channels. The newsrooms will have to pick them up and, if they don't, we can trend the fact that they haven't. As long as we can outpace Urquhart's bots, we're good.'

'I have news on that,' Finn said. 'Raye's parked the *Ocean Ghost* on top of a transatlantic data cable. They think they can choke the bore of the transfers from the US to the EU.'

Niall's eyes flew wide. 'Is that a thing?'

Finn's shrug folded down the line. 'If Raye says it is, then it is. They won't shut it off completely, just pare off 10 per cent, so the impact is less, but not so big that someone goes hunting for a cause. It'll take the edge off the US bot farms which is where most of Urquhart's messaging comes from.'

'OK. It either works or it doesn't. So we—'

'Hang on, let me get all that started.' Finn muffled his phone over what sounded like a ten-way conversation.

Leah was at the glass door again. Niall threw a thumbs up that fooled neither of them. She pulled away.

Finn returned to the call. 'We're rolling. Hawck's managing your release timetable.'

Niall checked his watch. 'Keep that going till eleven thirty. By then, I'll have written a press release to say we're tired of waiting for the BBC, there's obviously something fishy going on. We send that out, and then release the Tranche Three data: our version of the exit poll where eighteen and up vote. Let's see them try to argue round that.'

''K.' Finn was taking notes. 'What about the text scams? Do we go big on those?'

'Fuck, I don't know.' Niall pinched the bridge of his nose. 'In an ideal world, yes, we want to blow it wide open before the results come out so it doesn't look like bad blood if the five who were targeted lose. But . . . we absolutely can't do that until we know everyone involved is safe. It's not just about giving them counselling – not saying we shouldn't, only that it's not enough. We have to turn them from victims into heroes; not just so the rest of the world believes it, but so *they* believe it, so that when this comes out, we can say they acted in good faith, but they were manipulated by a political movement so shorn of integrity and ideas they had to resort to this.'

'Nobody's going to claim this, surely? That would be admitting to election theft. Even Urquhart's not that mad.'

'I don't think they care, to be honest. A win is a win and they'll brazen it out. What will anyone do? They hold the reins of power and they'll do whatever it takes not to let them go.'

'They can't—'

'Finn, they absolutely can. But even if they don't, we're going to feel pretty sick when they flood the net with rants that look like they come from us, screaming at a bunch of vulnerable people for making us lose.

'And then while we're occupied trying to shut that down, we have a hundred youngsters throwing themselves off Beachy Head. The tabloids'll laugh at the woke snowflakes while anyone with a nanogram of empathy will despise us forever for hounding innocent kids to their deaths, and the more we say we didn't the less anyone will believe us. We'll end up where we were with Toxic Pixie's stunt on QBC, but actual people will have actually died and the world will think we killed them.'

A shocked silence followed, while Finn thought through the angles. 'Gus and Caro are by far the most human-literate entities in the room right now,' he said. 'I'll get them on it ASAP.'

Niall rolled his eyes. 'Just make sure they feel needed, wanted and respected. Maybe invite them to the counts and get them involved in things on the ground so they have actual living people around them when the shit hits the fan. People's lives matter more than politics. If we can hold them together through what's coming, they'll all be stronger at the end of it.'

'Nice.' Relief soaked Finn's voice. 'You're good on strats. Remind me to teach you how to play battlegrounds sometime.'

'Get lost.'

'Love you, too. Be nice to Leah. She should've won.'

'She might still.'

'Right. I'm here when you need me.'

'Likewise.' Niall hung up and leaned back on the wall. Leah wasn't watching him anymore. He took a step up towards her, and then changed his mind and ran lightly down to the second floor and along the most obvious corridor to the toilets.

He was washing his hands when a shadow moved in the mirror.

'Leah, we need—' Not Leah. Donella Lloyd leaned her long frame against the door, blocking the exit. She wasn't beautiful by conventional standards, but her features were strong and there was flint at her core.

Half-rinsed soap dripped from his hands to the tiles. 'I . . . we haven't—'

'If you hurt her, I will find you.' Her voice barely rose above a whisper.

Niall snapped his mouth shut. 'Right.' His skin was grey.

She favoured him with a look that would have curdled water, kicked the door open and left.

He went back into the cubicle and emptied the rest of his gut contents into the pan. Then, gathering the frayed ends of his courage, he followed her back up the stairs to find Leah and break the news of the scam that might have cost her the seat.

CHAPTER TWENTY-NINE

From ten forty-five until nearly midnight, Niall's timetable played to the letter.

Changemakers released the People's Parliament data, and then released the videos of what the country would look like in the years ahead with Leah as PM leading a cabinet of fellow Changemakers.

Short versions of these had been an integral part of the campaign, but there had never been time for detail, and the focus had always been on the immediate actions required to kick-start a genuine democracy.

Given the luxury of more space and time, the video teams had gone to town with AI-crafted future visions of car-free cities where Guerrilla Gardening had become mainstream and aerial views saw grey replaced with green, public transport was electric and cargo-bikes moved things around hubs where people spent more time connecting and less – or no – time locked to the nine-to-five. Water was conserved, human waste was recycled and the rivers were clean.

They'd crafted a countryside full of grazing livestock where the fields were smaller, the hedges thicker, the woods more plentiful and the soil was alive, growing back topsoil at a rate that shocked everyone who hadn't actually looked at what was possible. Biodiversity was increasing and the number of species on the 'endling' list of those heading for extinction was shrinking. All fishing was halted in the entirety of UK waters and marine biodiversity increased. Mussel beds started filtering out the microplastics and the outflow of nitrogen and phosphorus from industrial agriculture ceased, returning the oceans to stability in time to avert the Gulf Stream's collapse. Carbon dioxide output stabilised and began to fall.

In both town and country, people worked fewer hours for fewer days in jobs that gave them a sense of being and belonging: an entire video series mapped out a future without the 'bullshit jobs', showing how the economy worked when it was designed to meet the needs of people and a living planet, instead of the whole living biosphere being destroyed in service to growth.

Industrial output fell when fewer people consumed fewer things and the core of manufacturing that remained was powered by multiple different sources. Niall's original objections to molten thorium salts had been overturned (the technology was far more advanced than anyone had realised) and community-owned small-scale reactors provided a safe nuclear baseline for the traditional rebuildable technologies of sun, wind, wave and biodigester power.

By fifty years out, the independent nations of the former United Kingdom were shown leading the world in regenerative technologies, distributed democracy and transparent governance. Across the board, people spent more time with their communities, creativity soared, toxic tribalism vanished and all the well-being indices rose. Yes, the world was hotter and ecosystems were still collapsing, but regeneration was happening and everyone took it seriously.

The vision was unashamedly utopian, but there was a clear path through that made sense. CIC supporters were already organising ad-hoc Citizens' Assemblies in their communities, inviting them to start considering how and where they'd implement change in their local areas. They were given organising templates and support, with the only request being that they video all proceedings and upload them to the Changemakers' servers to act as a global resource.

Within half an hour, files began to trickle in. The Ghosts identified the best outtakes and created montage clips which spread out under #ChangemakersFutureVision.

The idea took hold beyond the borders of the UK. Across the world, hundreds of thousands of videos were uploaded to TikTok and Instagram, Facebook, YouTube and Twitter until the digital world sang with the potential for a regenerative, degrowth future.

Unsurprisingly, #RiseUpStrong and #ChangeIsComing joined #ChangemakersFutureVision at the top of the trend charts, but beneath them were a whole host of others: #FutureGuardian was top of the list, closely followed by #RegenerativeFoodSystems, #ReFi, #CommunityTemplates #GreenPill, #DigitalGaia, #GlobalNation, #BikesNotPlanes, #LivingDemocracy.

The atmosphere of hope was contagious enough to infect the election night newsrooms, where the roving microphones stopped asking random voters what they thought about the 'immigration problem' and asked instead how they'd feel if they were invited to join a Citizens' Assembly, or were given a basic income and had access to basic services.

In studios, the anchors began to wonder aloud how their life would change if they worked for a company that gave workers, the local/global community and future generations as much of an input into decision-making as the money-men. Or (some nervous laughter here) what they'd do in a world where the maximum wage was thirty times the minimum. Or less.

The conversation evolved rapidly from arguments about who needed more than three hundred pounds an hour to how a community might start fixing the energy crisis, to cleaning the rivers, to ending corruption in politics, to ways of making a four-day week standard, to transforming the transport system, to bio-regional boundaries and bio-mimicry cities, to an entire nation of Future Guardian companies. 'What would happen if we made it compulsory? Companies have to pay tax. You could offer tax breaks to the Future Guardians or big, big tax hikes to those who won't do it. What's not to like?'

According to Finn, few of those whose answers were streamed live to the TV studios had ever been affiliated to the Changemakers, but now their ideas were being dissected as if they were real policy, and new suggestions were being thrown in by pundits for whom the concept of a Changemakers parliament had been anathema less than an hour before.

The atmosphere of potential was electric until even Urquhart lost her habitual scowl and in one unguarded moment agreed that it would be wise for the government to reconfigure the health service so that it actually worked.

*

All of which meant that, at ten minutes to midnight, when Niall released the app's actual exit poll – the one where the seats were chosen only by those aged eighteen and upwards – the whole country felt as if it had just slammed head-first into a brick wall.

Sparky online chatter died away as the words 'hung parliament' and 'balance of power' began to percolate back into the newly liberated electoral lexicon. Nobody welcomed them. TV pundits visibly shrank, pulled up their spreadsheets and began doing exactly the arithmetic Leah had done hours before, standing on a pavement outside a sporting gun shop in Surrey.

'We could still hold the balance of power, though.' Niall and Leah sat with the rest of her team in the balcony room. The screen on one wall was split vertically: on the left, it showed CCTV images of the count happening in the sports hall below; on the right was the BBC's election coverage.

Leah had Channel 4 on her laptop and Niall was surfing through four different social media streams. Their knees were touching under the table, and once every few minutes Niall nudged his against hers, to show he was still there.

Until this time, Leah had smiled on each occasion, and laid a hand on his shoulder, or his arm. Now, without looking up, she said, 'Hertsmere got their count in ahead of Stirling. They're returning now.'

'It's going to Urquhart. Massively reduced majority, but still . . .'

'I know.'

'But we'll find out if our app is accurate.'

'Niall . . .'

'Sorry. Statement of the Bleeding Obvious is my second name.'

'That's . . . OK. Good. You got me to think of something else. Now will you shut the fuck up and let's hear the actual numbers? You can practise vivisection on them afterwards.'

Faux-wounded, Niall made a zipper sign across his mouth. Leah leaned over and kissed the back of his neck.

The returning officer for the constituency of Hertsmere took her time over the announcement, but yes, Melanie Urquhart's stand-in had won by just over a thousand votes. The Changemakers

Independent Concordium candidate came second, beating the Combined Opposition by another eight hundred votes.

It was lost on nobody that if either the Changemaker or the Combined Opposition candidate had withdrawn, and if all their votes had shifted to whoever was left, the remaining candidate would have stepped over the line with an unassailable majority.

The Changemaker, a medical student, acknowledged as much in their concession speech. Leah turned the sound down as the Opposition candidate opened her mouth.

Niall cocked his head. 'You don't want to hear it?'

'They hate us.'

'They do. And Stirling's already announcing.'

'SNP.'

'Of course. Cheltenham's ahead of them, though, and it's is too close to call. Our flurry of People's Parliament support notwithstanding, the Beeb's going to stick with a government win as long as they can but the other channels are showing real-time updates, even QBC.' He eyed Leah with care. 'We could be about to see our first win.'

The CIC candidate won the constituency in Cheltenham, Gloucestershire, by six hundred and eighty-nine votes.

Elated, Leah said 'GCHQ is there. Do you think they'll move it somewhere else if we do end up in government?'

'We won't give them the money to move anywhere. So: no. Stirling's gone to the SNP. Dudley North has a result, but the government candidate's demanding a recount.'

Sam had handed over to another counter and was slumped in a corner, struggling to stay awake. He propped his chin on his fist. 'Can they do that?'

Leah said, 'Yep. Usually the returning officer won't allow it unless the vote's close. They can keep doing it. Amber Rudd got in on the third recount in 2017.'

Niall said, 'Three more to the SNP in Scotland. Outer Hebrides has gone to the Lib-Dem flavour of the COPs. Wales is going hard to Plaid.' He looked up. 'So far, our app is 100 per cent accurate. If we keep with our hit rate then Dudley North is going to Labour for the

COPs, but Dudley South and Solihull are coming to us.' He looked up, to check that everyone was listening. 'The red wall's crumbling.' Someone in the back of a room gave a small cheer and snapped open a can of Red Bull.

Leah's results were called at one thirty in the morning, when everyone's cortisol levels had sunk six miles deep into the lowest points of their metabolic trenches. Sam was asleep, lying in a corner with his head pillowed on someone's laptop cooler. Donella was arguing policy, sharply, with one of the other assistants. Everyone else was watching the wall screen or their own laptops, mainlining instant coffee and digestive biscuits; except Niall, who had spurned the coffee on the first sip and was surviving on cans of Red Bull 'borrowed' from Sam.

Tones pinged around the room as results came in. Donella said, 'Specs has increased his majority. He's in by the best margin of anyone so far', just as Niall, gaze locked on his laptop, said, 'Zerg sailed through with 10K to spare. Estrella Cunningham squeaked in by three hundred and eight votes.'

Leah was the only one not staring at her laptop. Wearily, she abandoned the crossword and did the arithmetic. 'It would have been another four hundred if two hundred scammed vulnerables hadn't voted for someone else.'

'It's still a win. We can bank it against—' A shuffle outside the door. Niall's head snapped round. Faintly, 'Oh.'

The returning officer was at the door, a tired man, prematurely grey. His glance took in Leah and Donella as if they were the only two in the room. 'A private word, ladies?'

They were gone less than a minute. Returning, Leah sat down, heavily. The whole room balanced on the edge of hope. She shook her head, 'Cassandra Cartwright's agent has asked for a recount.'

'On what grounds?'

'I'm up by eighty-six votes and that doesn't accord with their counters.'

Niall lifted one shoulder. It didn't accord with Leah's counters either and everyone knew it.

Leah said, 'The RO has ordered the counters back into place.'

From behind her chair, Donella hooked a thumb at the rest of the room. 'We need to watch them.'

Leah started to stand. From either side, Niall and Donella pressed her down. 'Not you.' The others filed past, all except Sam, who was still asleep.

Leah caught Niall's elbow before he could step past. 'Lena Karoshi got two hundred and thirty-one votes. Without her on the ticket . . .'

'I know. Everyone knows. Nobody is going to be able to pretend that anyone who won like this is legitimate, but they're still the ones elected. We can't change the rules until we're in power.'

'I keep thinking there must have been something else we could have done.'

'It's late, and you're tired. Please let it go. We did everything we could short of leading people into the voting booths and holding their hands while they marked their cross. We made videos showing a pencil skipping her name to yours underneath it. There is nothing else we could have done. I'm so sorry.'

'She isn't even here.'

'If we can prove she doesn't exist, we have twenty-one days to appeal. But they wouldn't be that lax. She might have changed her name by deed poll just before the registration window closed, but she will be a living, breathing human being. Let me watch the recount. If you win by one vote, it's still a win.'

Her hand dropped away. 'How many times can they . . .?'

'The record is seven. But nobody sane goes beyond three.'

Leah's count went to four, because, after the third one came out in Cassandra Cartwright's favour, Donella demanded the final one. Even before it was done, counters were falling asleep over their ballot papers, and when the results of the third and fourth counts were identical, Leah physically blocked Donella from raising her hand.

She lost by thirteen votes. Her concession speech was brief and gracious, and she managed to shake the necessary hands – candidates, returning officer, agents – and walk back to the foot of the stairs before she broke.

Niall caught her as she fell, hooking his hand under her armpit, braced against a weight that was less than he'd been ready for.

Donella was on the other side. 'The car,' he said. 'Now, before anyone sees.'

Sam, newly awake, ashen, walked tight behind them. He was joined within seconds by others who had spent all night in the room on the balcony, working numbers and spreadsheets and eating data and figuring potentials. They made a tight shield around Leah and nobody got in their way.

At the car, she was aware enough to fumble in her bag for the key. Niall took it from her, ducking his head to look her in the eye. 'I'm driving. This is not negotiable. I'll get us home safely, I promise.'

She frowned at him, slowly parsing out what he'd said. Then, 'It's two streets away. Can't I walk?'

'We're going to the farm. Not your flat: the press'll be camped on the doorstep. This is not over. We need to be among friends, and we can—'

His phone rang: Finn's tone. Through Niall's loudspeaker, he said, 'You're booked into the Albury. It's seven-and-a-half minutes by car. I'm sending the What3Words to your phone.'

Niall looked briefly panicked. Donella caught his eye. 'May I?'

Wordless, he passed her his phone. To Finn she said, 'This is Leah's agent. Actually, as of five minutes ago, I'm unemployed. But I can work a map and a car. I'm not on the insurance, though.'

'Third party cover,' said Finn, relieved. 'It's four in the morning, you'll be fine. Just drive. Sleep. I'll join you there. Grok's giving me a lift down so she can go celebrate with Zerg. I'll wake you with coffee at eight.'

Donella drove. The hotel sported five stars and the duty manager still had her teal pin in her lapel. There was a moment's consternation when they had to decide who went in the double room and who in the adjacent twin, but Niall solved it by leading an unresisting Leah into the twin, where he and Donella helped her undress before Donella retired next door.

He fell onto the bed semi-clothed. He didn't dream. None of them did: there are some planes of exhaustion too deep for dreaming.

CHAPTER THIRTY

As promised, Finn woke them at eight o'clock. He brought coffee and promised a full English breakfast was on its way. He did not bring the morning papers, but then he didn't need to: the results were plastered all over any and every website they cared to open.

The double room had a meeting-suite attached. Finn had brought fresh clothes for Leah and Niall and a pale grey Ghosts sweatshirt for Donella that was at least one size too big, but wrapped her like a comfort blanket. She drew her hands up inside the sleeves and hugged her coffee to her sternum. She looked terrible: they all did.

'Priorities?' Niall asked, gravel-voiced, when they were all seated. 'What's happening with the scam-vulnerables? Are we firefighting a blame war?'

'Not yet,' Finn said bleakly. His skin was slack for lack of sleep. He had dozed in the car, and arrived at the hotel an hour after Niall and Leah. Still, he looked better than they did.

'Four hundred and thirty-two CIC supporters fell for the scam, so we lost that many votes.'

'Seats?' Donella asked. 'Besides Leah?'

'Four out of the five seats went down. Everyone except Estrella lost to the nearest rival. You could say there is a degree of unhappiness in the Changemakers' camp, but nobody on our side is blaming anyone else on our side, which is down to some serious work by Gus and Caro overnight. The meme-teams have been on it solidly and so far, everyone's holding up. Of the people involved, we tracked down all but three before the polls closed. The entire facilitation team were there with one-to-one counselling for whoever needed it, plus they're being hailed as heroes online: everyone gets it.'

'Mainstream?' Niall asked.

Finn pulled a face. 'News broke around an hour ago and shit hit various fans at speed. A surprising number of people are calling foul on this one: we lost these four, plus another fifteen to the identical-name scam, and it's hard to spin any of that to look good. There's a lot of noise but so far no pushback against the voters, even from Urquhart. Might be she's too decent to go there—' Niall and Donella both snorted— 'Or else they got wind of Raye planting the *Ocean Ghost* on the US cables and pulled it. A trickle of sparks isn't a flame war, it's an embarrassment.'

'What about the missing three?' Leah asked. 'Have you found them? Are they OK?' She had her eyes closed, her chin resting on her fist to keep her head up.

'We found two and, yes, they're fine.' This, evidently, was one reason Finn was so grey. 'The last one is Sigi Kostinen, nineteen-year-old bicycle courier from Derby. She dropped off all media at six o'clock last night, about two hours after she cast her ballot. We've got people on the ground checking all known addresses and we won't stop till we find her.'

Finn tilted his chair back on two legs and pointedly turned the conversation elsewhere. 'Donella, are you still getting Leah's media invitations and, if so, are there any she should take?'

Donella stared into her coffee. 'Leah? You want to smile at lenses?' Her accent was all South Island, far stronger than it had been.

Leah bit her lip. 'I'd rather poke my eyes out with a blunt pencil, but I'll do whatever you think is best. Just let me have a shower.' She shoved back from the table. Niall and Donella both half-rose, and then each saw the other and stopped. Leah gave a ghost of a smile. 'I can get there and back on my own, I swear.' They both sat down again.

With the door closed behind her, Finn caught Donella's eye. 'You said you weren't her agent any more?'

'Not as of her concession speech last night.'

'Want to stay on the team?'

'Doing what?'

'Whatever you want. Name a job title and Charm will make it real.' Neither of them was looking at Niall.

'Political adviser?' Donella hazarded. 'To the whole CIC? Subordinate to Niall, obviously.'

Now they did look at Niall, who shrugged.

'Welcome to the team.' Finn tapped a key or two.

Grim-faced, Niall pulled his own laptop open at last. 'Guess we'd better get our heads round the results. Can't advise if we don't know the numbers.'

The final result, as displayed on the BBC website, was:

Government: 206 (-138 from 2019)
Combined Opposition: 178 seats (+28)
Changemakers Independent Concordium: 173 (+173)
Scottish National Party: 51 (+3)
Plaid Cymru: 24 (+20)
Democratic Unionist Party: 4 (-4)
Ulster Unionist Party: 1 (+1)
Alliance Party of Northern Ireland: 3 (+2)
Sinn Féin: 6 (-1)
Social Democratic and Labour Party: 4 (+1)

Niall studied the list, chewing the inside of his cheek. To Donella, absently, he said, 'BBC will be wanting an interview, for sure.'

Donella nodded. 'Frances Nolan. Ten. Go for that?'

'Your call.'

She threw him a sideways look. 'I'll set it up.'

Breakfast arrived. Finn took the trolley from the door and started passing plates around.

Niall ate absently, deep in the results. Donella was speed-reading her emails, WhatsApps and DMs. Without looking up from her screen, she said, 'The PM's taken back control of his party saying Urquhart's extremism is what lost them the election.'

'Is she letting him?' Niall asked.

Donella made a wobbling gesture with her flattened hand. 'She's

462

not started a leadership bid yet. He says he's leader of the party with the most votes and he's going to form a government.'

Niall's laugh was hollow. 'Who's going to join him but the Ulster Bible-belters? Five more seats does not a majority make.'

'But he can spin out the talks for weeks if he tries. More important to us, Specs is holding talks on behalf of the CIC with the Scottish and Welsh national parties'

'Fuck that!' Niall half-rose. 'He doesn't have the *fucking* authority!'

'But he's on the ground and we aren't. We have to get on top of things before he starts making promises we can't undo. We're going to have to go to London.' Donella flicked a look at Finn. 'We also need a base to work from. Technically the elected MPs will all have offices in the House of Commons, but we don't want them in there, it's a psychopaths' hunting ground. So we need somewhere within easy transport reach with good WiFi, safe to talk, but mainly it's going to need to have rooms for one hundred and seventy-three people who all thought they'd be back at the day job on Monday, plus their mothers, lovers, agents and anyone else they bring along as moral support.'

'You want room for five hundred?' Finn looked dubious.

'Call it two. The hangers-on won't stay long. We'll give them tea and biscuits and send them on their way.'

'OK.' Finn was already typing. Leah returned looking damp, if not refreshed. She read the results over Niall's shoulder. 'Where am I and when?' was all she said.

'BBC. Ten o'clock,' Donella said.

'You've got time to eat before we go,' said Niall.

Leah looked from one to the other and relaxed slightly. 'They'll want to know our strategy.'

'We'll have it worked out by the time we get there,' said Donella.

'And in the meantime,' Niall said, standing, 'we need to fill you in on Specs. He's gone on manoeuvres and we need to head him off at the pass. Several passes.'

Specs' 'manoeuvres' continued as Finn drove them into London.

Donella, in the front seat, kept the lines of communication open while Niall and Leah worked through strategy in the back. Or dozed. Mostly they dozed; there wasn't a huge amount of strategy to discuss: Leah hadn't been elected and even if she had been, she wasn't likely to lay out their negotiating tactics on live television.

Niall wanted her to talk about the People's Parliament, explaining how it could work and what it could do to change democracy, but the BBC wasn't likely to give this airtime while there was a hung parliament still to sort out.

'Heads up, people,' Donella said, quietly, as they neared the studio. 'Specs has offers of a full coalition from the Scots and Welsh. He wants to talk to us before he accepts.' She held up her phone to show the text. 'He says he'll meet us at the Beeb so we can "find somewhere quiet without the rest of the world listening in."'

Leah cut her a disbelieving glance. 'Broadcasting House has more microphones per square metre than anywhere else in Europe. It's the very definition of the rest of the world listening in.'

'Apparently there are a handful of soundproofed recording rooms and if you know the right people, they'll remove the microphones.'

'And Specs knows the right people.' Leah ground the heels of her hands into her eyes. 'I hate how much he knows that we don't even know needs to be known.'

Donella said, 'We won't get there in time for him to catch you before the interview. He wants to meet us when you come off-air.'

Finn was searching for a space to park outside Broadcasting House when Donella growled at her phone, making them all jump.

To the general alarm, she said, 'The *fuckers* have invited Cassandra Cartwright to join you.'

'They can't—'

'The PM has just made her Housing Minister.'

A moment's shocked silence, and then Leah laughed, loosely and too high. 'Now they're just trolling. He doesn't have the seats to form a government. He can't just pick random new MPs and make them ministers.'

'You guys have no written constitution,' Donella said, acidly. 'He can do what the fuck he likes and dare the rest of us to stop him.'

'But—'

'You're already late.' Finn slid into a slot in a taxi rank. 'Go. I'll park and come back.' He turned to the back seat and held his fist out for Leah to bump. 'Break an arm.'

They were distinctly late. Security guards grabbed Leah as she pushed in through the doors and all but dragged her into the studio. Cassandra Cartwright was already there, blonde hair haloed by dazzling lights.

'Hello Cassandra.'

'*Ah!*' A wordless in-breath, hands to mouth. She looked as if she might vomit.

Leah sat down. 'Nobody told you I was coming?' And then, because clearly they hadn't, 'They're soulless, inhuman bastards. I'm sorry. We don't have to make good television for them. Just say what you think. I'll do the same. We'll sort our differences when we're off-air.'

Cartwright's knife-frown deepened. Leah might have said more, but Frances Nolan eased into the chair between them and swiped her gaze left and right. 'If we're comparing sleep, I've had none. And no, this was not my idea. Let's make the best of it, shall we?'

She twitched a finger to her earpiece. 'Live in fifteen. Congratulations to Leah for getting here. Next time, a bit of leeway would be good.' She directed a saccharine smile at the camera as the green light flicked on.

And then they were live.

'Good morning. Welcome to the first hung parliament we've had since 2010. To help us sort through last night's chaos, we have Leah Koresh, one of the founders of the Changemakers Independent Concordium and Cassandra Cartwright, her opponent in a previously safe government seat of South-West Surrey, now the one with the tightest margin of the night.'

Both of her guests stared at her. This was not the usual introduction to a newly elected MP and her defeated opponent.

Frances's smile tightened. 'We are all aware by now, obviously, of the two alleged frauds perpetrated against Changemakers candidates. First, and most obvious, was the standing of candidates with near-identical names. Dr Leah Koresh lost two hundred and thirty-one votes to Ms Lena Karoshi who, because the candidates are organised in alphabetical order of surnames, was immediately above her on the ballot paper. Ms Karoshi had no discernable policies and had not campaigned. She was clearly not a serious candidate.

'Second, and more contentious, is the claim that several hundred individuals in five key seats were fraudulently contacted by texts purporting to come from Changemakers, asking them to switch their votes to rival candidates.

'In the seat of South-West Surrey, this switch was made to the COPs which enabled Cassandra Cartwright to take the seat. So, Ms Cartwright—' Frances turned in her chair— 'do you feel you earned your win? Do you deserve to be the elected MP?'

Cassandra Cartwright opened her mouth. No real sound came out. Before she had time to collect more of an answer, Leah said, 'That's entirely unfair. Nobody *deserves* to be an MP. It's not a prize for good behaviour, it's an election in which the people of our constituencies make decisions as to who they believe will best represent their interests in our parliament. Cassandra was elected. She—'

'If I might say so, for someone endeavouring to modernise our politics, that's a particularly old-fashioned view. Elections are a slug-fest. We all know this. And you've run on a ticket whose entire point is that the current system is corrupt. We've just seen this corruption in action. Are you seriously saying that Changemakers is not going to lodge an objection? You won't try to overturn the result?'

'What?' It was Leah's turn to look confused. Nothing she and Niall had talked over in the car had gone anywhere near this. 'Of course not. The rules are clear. The votes cast are the votes that are counted. And in our case, counted and counted and counted. Cassandra won more votes than any other candidate, therefore she has been elected to represent the people of South-West Surrey in parliament. You're right, the system is dangerously broken and we urgently need to bring it up to speed for the twenty-first century. But to do that we have to work within the rules. There will be no legal challenges.'

'Leah, there's one already. Adam Holdsworth has challenged in Blyth Valley. He lost by fifty-seven votes to the Combined Opposition and claims that two hundred and seventy-one votes were switched to the governing party in the fake DM scam. He's launched a legal objection on this basis.'

Leah closed her eyes for a moment longer than a blink. Her lack of sleep was etched across her face. 'I didn't know. I can't comment. We are an affiliation of Independent candidates. People are free to do what they feel is best.'

'Well, that's very gracious of you. Ms Cartwright, of course, is similarly free to resign her seat if she feels she won it unfairly.'

Frances raised a brow. Cassandra Cartwright found a smile. 'You're not getting a live television resignation, Frances. That's not how these things work. I am with Leah on this. The system may be broken, but we fix it by creating a government that works.'

'You can't seriously think you're going to be Housing Minister, though? Your party hasn't got anywhere near enough seats to command a majority.'

'We have more than anyone else. Unless we put forward our plan for government, how will we know if anyone wants to join us? The Liberal Democrats have formed a coalition with us before. They may do so again. The entire Combined Opposition might decide to join us in a "government of national unity". We don't know. All options are open and the prime minister remains the leader of our party. I am proud to have been offered a place—'

Frances laughed. 'Please. We're in the real world. You can say what you really think.'

'This is what I think.'

'Leah? If you were invited to form a government of national unity with the sitting prime minister, would you join?'

'If I truly believed the prime minister was aligned with our values, I would.' Never had we seen Leah reach so obviously for the Lion's Grace. She managed a smile that looked almost real.

Frances Nolan grinned back. 'And what are the chances of that?'

'Zero to none, but I might be wrong and speculating won't help. We need to be talking with the newly elected MPs, which we can't do when we're sitting here talking to you.'

'Indeed. Well, this has been fascinating. We'll let you go and get some sleep and move to Monica Chang, our political correspondent in Westminster, who has the latest news on the PM's attempt to form a government of all the talents. So far, he has failed to appoint anyone outside his own wing of the party, so the talent pool is more of a puddle, but it'll be fascinating to see what he comes up with.' Frances Nolan bared her teeth in a not-smile. 'Monica. Over to you.'

The green light flared off. Frances Nolan held her focus for a long five seconds and then turned away from the lenses.

'Thanks, both of you. If you want a recommendation from someone who's been around for the past five elections, I'd point out that it's going to be a long, long week, possibly month. Getting some sleep needs to be your overriding priority or you'll lose the capacity to function.'

Specs was leaning on the wall outside the studio, ready to greet them as they came out. His smile was complex, full of things that could not be said aloud in a BBC corridor. He nodded to Cassandra Cartwright, 'Well done,' and looked elsewhere when she flushed. Catching Leah's eye, he gestured towards the left-hand lift. 'The others are downstairs. Shall we?'

Niall, Finn and Donella were waiting in a tiny basement studio which sported dimpled black foam on walls and ceiling and a soft, yielding floor. The air smelled of stale coffee and electronics. The atmosphere was tense and fogged and over-air-conditioned.

By way of welcome, Finn said, 'It scans clean, but we can't assume it is.'

Leah nodded, too tired to be clever. 'So we don't say anything we don't want to see on the front page of the tabloids.'

'Or hear broadcast on the six o'clock news. Got it.'

'Leah, you need to sit down.' Specs pulled out a chair for her and then took the seat opposite, his hands clasped on the sound-desk in front of him. For a moment, he was clearly sorting through prospective headlines for whatever would be least damaging, then, equally clearly, he screwed up his caution and threw it over his shoulder.

'I've had messages this morning from three of the MPs who won their seats in the fake text scam, including Adam Holdsworth's opponent in Blyth Valley. They all want to join Changemakers. They are promising to align with our values.'

Donella's question, 'Is this a way of avoiding legal action?' clashed with Leah's, 'Is Cassandra Cartwright one of the three?'

'Yes and yes.' Specs flicked his gaze from one to the other. 'Cassandra's text came through while we were in the lift. She'll resign as Housing Minister.'

'She can't *be* the fucking Housing Minister!' They were all way too jumpy for the force with which Niall smacked his hand flat on the table. He raised it slowly. 'Sorry, but this is a farce and we have to stop it. They don't have the numbers. It's never going to work.'

'It's not impossible, though,' said Specs. 'If the COPs join with the government and you throw in the Ulster Unionists, then they'd have a working majority to form a government of national unity.'

Leah's eyes took on a hollow, lightless cast. 'Would the COPs do that? Join with a party they despise just to keep us out?'

'Pass,' Specs said. 'In the old world, there's no way: they've spent their political lives hating the other guys and being hated in return. But I'm not sure the old rules apply any more. There's an old adage that two parliamentarians, one of whom is a socialist, will forever have more in common than two socialists, one of whom is a parliamentarian.'

Niall snorted. 'Not just socialists.'

'Of course not, that's my point. The establishment is one big public school debating society. They may scream at each other across the chamber, but in the end, they're all the same class. At the point when they realise that the one thing they all have in common is that they *like* the way things have been done and don't want anyone to change anything beyond the colour of their ties, then all bets are off.'

Donella had been studying him through all this. 'You have a strategy.' She didn't sound as if it were likely to be a good one.

'Move fast and break things.' He gave a dry laugh. 'We have to move swiftly enough that they don't have a chance to start talking to each other in shady corners. Or to tell us we're not a real party so we don't get to even try.' He eyed them all. 'That's the biggest risk, because it's true. If we're going to counter it, we have to stake our claim as the biggest coalition as fast as we can.'

'We get the numbers if we join with the Celts, right?' Finn said.

'Precisely.' Specs was noticeably less inclined to meet anyone's eyes. 'As I'm sure you know, I've had formally informal conversations with Kirsty McLeod who looks like she'll lead the SNP at Westminster. She kept Stirling last night and she's sharp: she has the full backing of the administration in Scotland. Gareth Wynne-Jones held on to Ceredigion for Plaid Cymru and they're happy he speaks for them; he called me at nine this morning. Northern Ireland's a bit more complicated but Aoife Fitzgerald took Belfast East by the skin of her teeth and she's speaking for the SDLP, at least until the dust settles.

'They all want Independence referendums ASAP, but if we can guarantee that's the first legislation we'll bring forward, and they join us in a formal coalition, that'll get us to two hundred and eighty-two MPs.'

'Why did they call you instead of Leah?' Finn asked. Somebody had to.

'Because he was elected and I wasn't,' Leah said, wearily. 'I stopped being relevant the moment I conceded.'

'She's right.' Specs pulled a grimace. 'It's horrible. Most of the way Westminster works is horrible. But we can change things.' He eyed Donella, who subsided. 'Hear me out. If you hate what I've got in mind, we can think of something else.' He took in the whole table now and nobody was pushing back. 'Two eighty-two isn't a majority but it *is* enough to get the first crack at forming a government. If we add Cassandra Cartwright and the other two who wrote to me this morning, that's two eighty-five.'

Working his phone, Niall said, 'There will be other defectors. I could name four of the old left from Labour and at least as many Lib Dems who would come over if we gave them the right incentives. That would take us within reach of three hundred and when we get close to that, people will see which way the wind is blowing. I'm just not sure there are many others we'd actually trust.'

Specs pulled off his glasses and gazed at them with naked eyes, a move that reminded them all he'd had no sleep, either. 'Niall,' he said, wearily, 'I know it doesn't look like it from the outside, but not all of my current and former colleagues are venal, self-serving idiots. Some of them are genuinely trying to make things better, and if they see the way the wind is blowing I think we'd see others joining us, at least on a confidence and supply basis. We don't need trust for that, just numbers walking through the lobbies.'

'Not good enough.' Niall shook his head. 'There's a point where it all becomes window dressing. We won't be able to pass anything that actually makes a difference.'

'We won't be able to pass the really radical stuff at first,' Specs agreed. 'But we'd get the ban on drink and drugs through straight away: that was popular with every single voter polled. Anyone who stood against it would basically be declaring themselves an alcoholic junkie, so they won't. We don't even have to put a bill before parliament to start random testing and anyone who tests positive will have to follow the three strikes rule. If we get that in place, I promise you, we'll lose at least two dozen of the legacy MPs within the first six months.'

'Two *dozen*?' This from Donella, laughing. Sort of.

Specs grinned back. 'At least. *Some* of my former colleagues are decent people who want to make the world a better place. Significant numbers of the rest – and, actually, there's a small but significant overlap – have no idea how to function without industrial quantities of alcohol, and nose-related frostings. Trust me, all we need to do is set up blanket testing so there's no way to escape it, and they'll be on their third and final warning by September and out by the end of the year.

'My suggestion is that we put key people in the Lords – Leah would be first, obviously – and then bring her into government so the world can see them in action: Communications Minister, maybe? Or Education: there's so much to transform there. Maybe Deputy Leader, though I think we'll need to give that to Kirsty McLeod for the ScotNats. Anyway, when the first of the drunks drops out, we pull Leah back to stand in the by-election. By then people will have seen what we can do, and she'll sail through.'

In the thickening silence, Specs kept all his attention locked on Leah.

For her part, after the first mention of the House of Lords, she had shifted all her attention to Niall, who looked like he'd just stepped barefoot on a dog turd.

471

Now, frigidly, he said, 'Getting rid of the House of Lords is top of our Day One Action list. You are not pulling it. You *can't.*'

'Not pulling it, just tweaking the timetable. We'll say we'll do it in the first year, which will give them all time to find other jobs.'

By accident, maybe by design, Specs turned to Finn as he spoke.

And so Finn responded. 'It could work if we get the narrative right. Everyone knows Leah's seat was stolen. They'd be with us a hundred per cent to get her into parliament. We could even say what we were doing: if the junkies are as bad as Specs says, they'll still be out by Christmas.'

'Bro?' Niall laughed, and then didn't. 'No,' he said flatly. Then, looking from face to face, '*No!*'

A painful silence crabbed around the room.

More desperately, Niall said, 'Leah, I know last night was horrible, but you can't seriously think this will work? It's the very definition of incrementalism. This week you're deciding to keep the Lords. Next, you'll be all cool with privatising the NHS, banning unions and throwing anyone who disagrees with you into a prison ship. The week after that, you'll be back to bunging billions to the fossil fuel companies and arranging tax breaks for billionaires. You cannot do this. It destroys everything we've worked for.'

Specs raised one brow. To him, avoiding Niall, Leah said, 'We'd need a timetable we could all believe in: non-negotiable dates for the Independence for Scotland and Wales and a unity vote in Northern Ireland, bringing the voting age down to sixteen in England and a really clear timetable for abolition of the House of Lords and transformation of the voting system: the whole Constitutional Convention. Could we get all that through?'

Specs shoved his glasses back on. 'I was in the whips office for ten years,' he said. 'I know where the bodies are buried on both sides of the aisle. Yes, we can get it all through.'

'Leah, stop.' Donella had held quiet until now, but her fingers knotted on the table. 'Niall's right. This is how they suck you in: endless promises of power tomorrow, never power today. You can make all the deadlines you like, but they'll sing past and sing past and you'll be glued up in parliamentary business for the rest of your natural, and somewhere down the line you'll decide to stop testing for drink and drugs because the only way you can live with yourself is through the reflection in the bottom of a bottle. Don't do it, Leah. Come away and let us build the People's Parliament and make it work. We can do better than this.'

'Can we, though?' Leah looked more awake than she'd done all morning. Slowly, she stood up. 'Do we really just walk away, let them form their Coalition of Boomer Mediocrity, watch society tear itself apart in artificial culture wars and then collapse into extinction as they keep on burning fossil fuels to the end of days?'

'We do what we planned for all along when we thought we'd get votes from the under-thirties and nobody else.' Donella, too, was on her feet and they squared off across the room. It had the feel of an old pattern, both of them locking horns as if nobody else was around.

As to a ten-year-old, Donella said, 'We have the app-data that will shape the People's Parliament: a true vote of the people whose futures are at stake. We'll boycott the Boomers' Last Stand – like we planned – bring together everyone who would have been elected under our system and build an alternative parliament based on everything Niall and Raye have been developing: distributed democracy, quadratic voting, participatory budgeting – the works. Within a month, we'll be the functional option throwing out new policies that will shape a better future while the dinosaurs in Westminster scream themselves into irrelevancy. We'll be the living demonstration of how a democracy works that's fit for the twenty-first century so people understand what the real options are.' Donella's gaze narrowed. 'We did talk about this. A lot.'

'That was before, when we thought the app result was going to be completely different to the real thing. Dell, *one hundred and seventy-three* CIC candidates were elected last night. You can't pull them all out to take part in a fantasy parliament when they just won seats in the real thing!'

'I don't see why not. If the IRA can boycott Westminster for decades, our MPs can do it for the couple of years it'll take to make the whole place redundant. Fuck their dysfunctional polity: we can make something that works.'

Leah's brows moved so close together they were in danger of making a vertical stack. 'You wouldn't be saying this if I'd won.'

'I so would.'

'*Why?* You just spent five weeks of your life trying to get me elected to the "dysfunctional polity". Why did you do that if it's not worth our time?'

'You asked me to. Why do I ever do anything?' Donella sat down, heavily, hooked a knee up to her chest and clamped her arms around her shin. 'We needed to see how it would play out. Now we know. They'll suck you in, soften you up and stop anything from actually changing. It's *obvious*, Leah.'

'Not to me.' Leah closed her eyes, searching inside for roses and desert sand, but they were too far away, lost on the other side of the night. Sighing, she said, 'We need to sort this out somewhere private that doesn't have hidden microphones recording everything in stereo.'

She leaned back against the wall. 'Specs, you have an office in the House of Commons?'

'I do.'

'OK, I think you should hang out there and see who else makes advances. Don't offer any promises on our behalf until we've brought all of the Changemakers into this. Can we trust you to do that? No nods. No winks. No hidden understandings and political credit to be paid off later. Nothing until or unless we've gone through our own democratic process.' She held out her hand. 'Deal?'

Specs shook it. 'Deal.'

CHAPTER THIRTY-ONE

The walk back to Finn's car was . . . tense.

The dividing lines were clear. Niall and Donella in unlikely partnership on one side and Leah on the other. Finn was endeavouring to straddle the line between. He wasn't really succeeding but it didn't matter much: he was the tech-geek, not the policy-nerd.

He was, however, the one who knew where they were going. He typed a new destination into the sat-nav. 'Caterwaul Loft,' he said, to nobody in particular. 'It's fully connected, with WiFi almost as good as the Piggery, and there's room for five hundred as long as they don't all expect desks.

'That's the Pirate rave place?' Donella asked, which proved someone was listening.

'Best I could do,' Finn said, apologetically. 'They're great supporters of CIC and they're offering us the whole place until we can find somewhere better. And it has places to sleep which has to be our first priority.' He turned round to Niall and Leah who were in the back seat, knees no longer touching, arms folded, each looking out of the windows on their own side, emphatically not looking at each other. 'Any objections?'

None. Finn pulled out into the traffic. 'Might need to brace for the music,' he said, but by then the others really were not listening.

The music. Dear gods and little fishes, the music . . . Finn hauled aside the big sliding door at the front of the Caterwaul Loft and everyone stepped forward, then rocked back, flattened.

'What the *fuck*?' Niall hissed, through tight teeth. Finn, a step or two ahead, and leaning into the pressure, said, 'Mouth shut, eyes open, Nye.'

Inside, the loft was bigger than the sports hall where Leah's count had been held; tall, cathedral-airy, full of carefully curated light, and it smelled of new paint. The walls were no longer the white-and-steel of Finn's pictures, but – wetly fresh – the teal of Changemakers' branding. The carpets were yellow and lime-green in bold 60s zigzags. The music was ultra ... something. Techno? Garage? Something newer? And very, very loud.

Leah shuddered. Donella muttered something in a language that was definitely not English. Under his breath, Finn said, 'Smile. This is your home for the foreseeable.'

Leah swallowed and smiled. She was the recognisable one, the face of the campaign. She was, therefore, the one on whom a dozen or so Gen Zs converged, wanting to shake her hands. And shake them. And shake them.

They wanted to commiserate, too, which was when Niall stepped in. He was upset and angry, but he wasn't a total idiot. Detaching himself from an athletic redhead, he said, 'Leah's had almost no sleep. Is there anywhere quiet we can bunk her down? Or just maybe ... quiet?'

'Ohmy*god*, of course.' The redhead swept an arm through the air and the music cut out so suddenly that Leah staggered as if punched.

'Sorry. I'm Lucy. Really sorry for Leah. But it's exciting too. This is the real thing? Real change?' She turned and waved an arm the other way. Whale-song meditation music murmured from the speakers. 'Better?'

'I think actually ...' Niall struggled. 'Maybe nothing for a while?'

Lucy's face was a landscape of confusion. 'Silence?'

'Would that work for you?'

Hesitantly, 'We can try.'

'Please. It's been a difficult night. Sometimes we just need to process stuff without music curating the feelings.'

'Right. Yes! You must feel terrible. Whatever you want.' One of the others waved an arm slightly differently and the music faded to nothing. They were all wearing yellow wristbands.

'Motion sensors?' Niall asked.

Lucy grinned. 'Well done.'

Having seen them through the door, Finn had set off to walk the perimeter, holding his phone out. Periodically it emitted a short, soft tone. Lucy said, 'He thinks we're bugged?'

Leah said, 'He's checking we're not.'

A lean youth, whose rust-orange sweatshirt proclaimed *Call me Ash*, said, 'Tell him we sweep it daily.'

'It won't make any difference,' said Niall. 'He always does it himself.'

'Due diligence.' Ash nodded, cheerily. 'Like it.' The group huddled and, after a conference of nods and shakes and hand-clasps, Lucy said, 'We'll leave you to it. Everything's obvious. Food. Drink. Music. Or not, obviously. Computers. Finn knows. You can make yourselves at home. Really at home. We'll be down the street at The Pirate Place. It's like this, but bigger.'

'Really?' Niall looked scared, but, to the outside world, a scared Niall wasn't too different from an impressed Niall. 'We're immensely grateful,' he said, and the group surged away to a big double door diagonally opposite the one by which they had entered.

Finn completed his circuit and then guided the others to the centre of the room to big squishy sofas in iridescent colours grouped like psychedelic hippos around a wavy-contoured coffee table in bottle-green glass.

'Sit.' He pressed them down. 'We can talk safely here. I'll make something to drink. Try not to rip each other's heads off while I'm gone.'

A big ask. They sank into the sofas as into clouds. Leah may have fallen asleep or she just kept her eyes shut so the other two couldn't gang up on her. Even so, by the time Finn came back with some decent coffee, the air had become dagger-sharp and the temperature hovered not far above absolute zero.

Finn passed out the mugs. Niall nodded thanks, but wouldn't meet his eye. Leah didn't even look up. Donella was texting a contact in New Zealand (Henry: he seemed quite nice) with a savagery that threatened to demolish her phone.

Finn set her mug on the table, and settled into the one place left where he could see each of them.

He set his attention clearly on Niall.

Quite deliberately and with all the care he could muster, he asked, 'What would Kirsten do, Nye?'

'*Finn!*' This was Leah, appalled. Niall's head jerked up. He didn't speak.

Doggedly, Finn continued. 'I don't think she'd tell us to make war among ourselves just when things got tricky. How do we build a healthy human culture if it's not working on micro-repairs between ourselves until we get back into balance?'

This was pure, unadulterated Kirsten. Leah looked pained, but held silent. Even Donella knew enough not to wade in. Niall's lips had gone grey, the rest of him dirty-chalk.

Finn took on the kind of poise he brought to the mat when he faced a worthy opponent. Outwardly, he was calm. Inwardly, he was doing everything he could to ask Bēi Fēng for help.

Silent, waiting, he hooked his ankles up underneath him until he was sitting cross-legged, then set his elbows on his knees and rested his chin on the hammock of his fingers.

'We are Changemakers,' he said. 'We do things differently here. Though up until now, if we're honest, we've not strayed far out of our comfort zones. Now we have our first real challenge.' He let his gaze swing past Niall and the two sat up straighter, more awake, wary. 'How does this fit with your dream, Leah? With all you told us before the funeral? Are we still on track with the Lion's Grace?'

Until now, it hadn't been clear whether Donella knew about the Lion-dream, but she didn't look puzzled enough for it to be news. Rather, she clamped her fingers to her mouth and said, thinly, 'I hadn't thought to ask that.'

'We hadn't either and we've been living it for weeks. Trying to. We're all beyond exhausted. We haven't stopped running since the funerals—' a glance at Niall— 'you and me since Kaitlyn's post. And then the campaign sucked us into the kind of toxic soup people don't usually crawl out of with their souls intact. We're raw and vulnerable and we need sleep more than anything. But I think we need to go to sleep as friends or we're finished.'

He made a clear effort to soften his gaze as he turned it on Leah. 'Over to you. Am I right?'

'Of course.'

'The dream?'

'Wait. . .' She closed her eyes.

We waited. A whisper of roses gentled the cathedral space of the loft.

At length, Leah opened her eyes, saying, 'The void-visions never got this far. We're in uncharted territory, but Finn's right, we need to get back to working as a team or we're sunk.' She raised her mug and tilted it towards the space between them all. 'Power to Wisdom. Wisdom to Power. We know this. It's just hard to live it.'

'But we're doing our best.' Finn tapped his mug to hers, balancing it on the outstretched tips of his fingers in a way that made Donella wince.

Turning to Niall, he said, 'You're going to build the People's Parliament.' It wasn't really a question, but Niall nodded anyway. 'Where's it going to be and who's going with you?'

Niall cast his first clear glance at Leah. 'For real we're getting Independence in Scotland?'

'Nye, you're the policy wonk, but it sounds like it to me. The votes are clear and a rump parliament in England is not going to hold an entire nation to a union it doesn't want. So yes, in Scotland, Wales and Northern Ireland, we need to make clear what's on the table and let people vote. I don't know how long it takes to set this up, though. Maybe a year?'

'Then I have to be there.' Niall cast a haggard look at Finn. 'I love the farm, Bro, but—'

'Nye, it's fine. Everyone knows Scotland's your home. Go where you need to. Who's going with you?'

A big shrug. 'Plenty of people said they were up for it when it was all hypothetical, but whether that translates into reality, is anyone's guess. It might end up being just me and Brilliant back at the Crescent firing off blogs. Or maybe everyone who stood but didn't get elected comes on up. Tranche One gave us three hundred and eighty-one out of three hundred and eighty-two elected, and we only missed Danni Raines because of the text scam; they should've got in. If everyone wants to come, that's a couple of hundred people which is a lot to get together in one place. We could create a virtual parliament, though. Maybe this is the time to experiment with digital democracy, and then when we get Independence, we can replicate it in each of the three nations. Four if Ireland wants to play.'

'Raye says—'

'Tell me they haven't spent eleven million on a parking place for the fancy boat?'

'Not yet. But they want to set up a Scottish arm of the Changemakers to work on digital democracy with you. Did they mention?'

Warily, 'No.'

'I think they were waiting to see the results, but they were thinking we could jointly buy somewhere in Glasgow to be an office. Near the Crescent, maybe?'

'You're becoming such a capitalist, Bro.' Niall rolled wild eyes at him. 'Can we talk about this later? After we sleep?'

'Sec.' Finn turned to Leah. 'If Changemakers are heading up the Boomers' Last Stand, are you going to stay?'

Leah was red about the eyes. Wordless, she accepted the tissue Donella passed over and she blew her nose. To Niall, she said, 'Can you give me a year? Even six months to see if Specs is leading us all on? If he is, I swear I'll be up the M6 faster than you can blink.'

Niall, too, looked raw. 'There's always space at the Crescent. Or wherever we end up.' He held his fist out for a bump. 'Deal?'

Leah met it, relief in her every line. 'Deal,' she agreed, then, yawning, stood. 'And now we sleep. Perchance to dream, though I think—'

'Wait.' Donella took a breath. 'If Niall will have me,' she said, 'I'd like to help build the People's Parliament, too. Wherever it is.'

Leah took a sharp breath. I felt the Lion stir. Niall caught her hand. 'Still a team.' And to his left, cautiously, 'Scotland's cold. And I have a legal requirement to warn you about the midges.'

Donella grinned. 'Grandad's family came from Skye. Midges are part of family lore. And the rain. And the dark winters.' She held out her hand, palm flat, and they clasped, hand to wrist, like some of the Warcrafters did, both wary, both surprised. Both, I thought, hopeful. Then Niall reached for Leah, and Donella gathered Finn and for a while there weren't enough tissues, and nobody cared.

At last, wiping her nose on her sleeve, Leah said, 'Can we sleep now? We're going to need to be bright for the new intake when they get here.'

'This way.' Finn drew them all up with him towards the back of the room. 'The sleeping pods are out here.'

'Pods . . .?' Leah asked, faintly.

Finn bit his lip. 'Set into the far wall. Like a spaceship.'

He led them through a door in the back wall to a space behind. No teal paint here ('Thank fuck,' said Donella, quietly). It was all steel, bulging out in a gigantic blister pack of brushed aluminium.

Metallic buttons promised/threatened electronics. Finn pressed something near the door and one of the metallic shells rolled upwards revealing a reasonable-sized cavity behind, sporting what would have been brilliant-white duvets and plump pillows, only someone had thought to filter the light to teal.

Niall took a step back. 'You're not serious?'

Finn shrugged. 'It's that or the floor.' The floor was poured concrete, quite chilly. 'You'll be fine. Just don't sit up too fast. The ceiling's about six inches above your face and you'll give yourselves concussion. In theory, you can reset the temperature and humidity when you get in, but I wouldn't play with the dials if I were you. There's music, but I'll figure out how to turn it off and you'll—' His phone pinged the family chime. He read it once, twice, his gaze suddenly fixed.

'Bro?'

Finn pulled a smile that was more of a grimace. 'Sigi Kostinen's still not been found. I should go back up the road. I'm fine, Nye. Chill. I slept in the car while Grok drove. You guys need to be bright for the new MPs. Go in and lie down. You'll be asleep in minutes.'

'Not in a million years,' Niall said. But they crawled in, Niall and Leah and Dell, each to a pod, and when the doors sighed shut and the electric lights muted to a dull amber, they all slept.

And dreamed . . .

▼

Today, the Crescent drew me in rather than the other way around; no divisions or separations, all of myself came to the one

481

place. I arrived in the hallway and found Brillo in his usual spot between the living room and the kitchen doors, where the heating pipes crossed.

In crow form, I stood in front of him and said his name, once, twice . . . it always took three times. 'Bri—'

'Hello Lan.' Quietly. Behind me.

I sprang back, but I was still a crow, not yet remotely Brillo. I had nowhere to hide, nowhere to go, except back to the Between, where I'd started and—

'Niall?' He was in the living room, on the old green sofa that was all they could afford when they first moved in to the Crescent. Brillo was sick on it once. Probably more than once.

'Come and talk to me? I'm not going to banish you. Or tell Finn you're around.'

His dream-edges were more distinct than I'd ever seen them. I hopped forward, keeping to the floor, sending tendrils of awareness to the Between, ready to fly and to flee.

'Were you waiting for me?'

He grinned. 'Seemed only polite. You've come for me every night for weeks now. I thought I'd see if I could get here before you.' Sliding off the sofa, he sat on the floor. He looked younger, the age he was when Brillo was a kitten, though just as tired as when he'd crawled into the space-pod. He stretched out his hand in invitation.

I hopped onto his wrist. I'm better as a Crow than a Brillo, though there was something nice about the whole purring-on-his-chest thing. I looked back through the door towards the hallway. Brillo was gone.

'He died three years ago,' Niall said, a little sadly. 'It's how I knew it was you. One of the ways.'

Fuck. *Fuck!* 'You knew all along?'

'Sorry.' Not sorry. 'I kept looking up into the corner where you were, and asking you questions. At first you kept running away, then you stayed and—' an uneasy shrug— 'you did seem to help sometimes.'

Oh, I am such an idiot. 'I thought none of you could see me. Even when you wanted to.'

'We can't. But there's a feeling that's all you and once I knew

482

what to look for, it was obvious. That day in Kaitlyn's bedroom was a gamechanger.' And, because I was not keeping up. 'The day Mum freaked out. You'd been writing to Kaitlyn and it was so clearly from you. Really you: not Little Sis making it up.'

He stroked a tentative finger down my back. 'I may be pathologically logical, but that cuts both ways: it's difficult to not-believe something when you've seen hard evidence. Then, when I started paying attention, you were everywhere. Literally never more than about six feet away the whole time.'

'Thank you for not telling Finn.'

'Might be he knows, but it's a bit of a no-go zone. You can't un-ask that question. I don't think he would banish you all over again if he knew you were there, but it's not my call. If he wants to talk to you, he'll say. If he doesn't . . . best left, d'you think?'

'Absolutely.'

'Good. I'd miss you. There were times these past few months when knowing you were there was all that kept me sane.' He smiled, his young boy smile that jabbed under my breastbone and stole my voice. 'Can you look like a person?' he asked. 'Or are you stuck as a crow forever?'

I could. It wasn't easy, but it wasn't impossible, either. 'Better?'

'Wow.' He rocked back. 'You're so *young*.'

His mother used to say just the same. The memory made me plaintive. 'I look older than you do, Niall Penhaligon!'

'Well, yes. Just . . . Never mind.' Solemn, suddenly, 'I never said goodbye properly.' Rising, he grabbed me in a fierce, tight embrace and I felt the thud of his heart and the wet of his tears and the weight, the terrifying weight of everything he was trying to carry and all I could do was hold him, and let him hold me.

When, at last, we let each other go, he gripped me by the elbows, an arm's length away. 'I didn't know ghosts could cry.'

I croaked a laugh. 'All the time.'

We sat down again. Niall held my hand in his and traced the lines of my not-old fingers. A sadness clouded him in textures I knew well.

'Ask, Nye.'

'Do you see them, ever?'

'I'm sorry.' I shook my head. 'They moved on so fast after . . .

483

After. It's better, honestly. It's the way things are meant to be. I'm only still here because I made promises.'

'To Finn.'

'And Kaitlyn. And then Leah's Lion. And a Tree.' I gave a shy shrug. 'In for a penny . . .'

Niall eyed me sideways and I watched him join some dots. Nobody ever suggested he wasn't smart, just that often his thinking took him places nobody else had ever been. 'Did you send the dream to Leah?' he asked. 'The one that got us to Changemakers and all the rest?'

'I stepped into her dream. More accurately, I was *permitted* to step into her dream, which is a different thing. But then, yes, I took her into the void where all the futures fan out and we saw all the ones that were going to be horrible. After that, it was up to her to work out what might be good. She's doing well, I think.'

'She is.' He rolled his shoulders forward and back, a little like Finn before a training bout. 'Can you take me into the void, too?'

'*What?* No! Seriously, Nye, you don't want to go there. I've never been so scared of anything, and I'm already dead. It's not safe, I promise you.'

'Leah managed it.'

'Leah had the Lion.'

'And I have you.' He blinked, all boyish innocence. 'You said so when you were Brillo. Or is a Cat who's also a Crow not as good as a Lion?'

'Nice try, but let's not get diverted, eh? It's not the void you need to visit now, and you know it.' Standing, I held out my hands. 'Shall we go?'

It was dusk when we reached the desert, and winter. In the west, the sun's last light hacked a bleeding wound across the horizon. Elsewhere, frost and night held the sky between them, with stars marked out as claw-pricks of perfect brightness. When the Lion stepped down from the frigid dark, I held Niall's hand as much for my own comfort as his.

We walked towards the beast, half a league per stride. When we were close enough to feel the scorch of its breath, to smell the meat on it, I said, 'Kneel. *Now.*'

He did. We did, and then lay prone on the cold sand, with the point of a single claw driving down between our shoulder blades.

We said nothing, were asked nothing, offered nothing and promised nothing, but the claws lifted, and the voice of a god said, *You know the way.*

'Thank you. I do.'

Still holding his hand, I drew Niall up and forward to Leah's rose garden. Newly, the gate was wooden, carved with sinuous spirals like you might see on the standing stones of Scotland.

Niall balked at the wildness of them, eyes wide, features pinched. 'Maybe not such a good idea?'

'We're fine.' I had hold of his hand, and here, this was as good as ownership. I led him through into the garden and this, too, was wilder. The roses here grew with abandon, the paths of the labyrinth little more than clefts in the exuberant growth. The lions that guarded the entrance were warm sandstone, not bronze, and they sat upright, watching us with living eyes.

I started forward between them, but Niall dug his heels in, dragging me back. Turning, I caught both of his hands. 'Niall, you wanted this. We're going to walk the labyrinth. Leah will be in the centre.'

'I can't.' He was anchored to the ground in ways I could not move. 'What if she doesn't want me here?'

The Lion let us through, I thought. Aloud, I said, 'She loves you.'

'Lan?' Even scared, he could manage withering scorn. 'What's love but projection and lust? Leah's not that shallow.'

Which is why, obviously, Donella worried him so much. I thought this, I didn't say it.

Instead, 'Why do you think I'm here and not wherever we end up after this?'

'You made a promise to Finn.'

'And why might I have done that?'

He looked down at the path. It was thick with the shed fur of a lion god. He dug his toe in a little. 'Family love is different.'

'Ah.'

'What?'

Gently, 'Niall, you can love someone, and it doesn't have to dilute what you felt – still feel – for Kirsten. Twin-love is different. We all know that.'

'Lan . . .' His certainty crumbled. His whole being blurred. 'You *don't* know. You think you do, but you don't. And I can't explain.'

'Try.'

He stooped and picked up a couple of bits of gravel and juggled them far better than he could ever have done in life. 'Kirsten was the other half of my soul. Without her I am not whole. Not ever going to be whole. Even when she was alive, I never knew how to love anyone else. I never needed to.'

'But you . . .'

'I could have sex with people. I could be nice to them and kind; we both could. But loving them?' He hurled the gravel between the stone lions. 'I don't think either of us knew how to do that.'

At last, he looked at me. 'If I was going to love anyone, it would be Leah, but she doesn't deserve the hurt I'd bring. Also,' he smiled thinly, 'if I hurt her, Donella is going to put my balls in a liquidiser and feed them to me through a nasogastric tube.'

Ha! If I hadn't been there when she didn't quite say this, it would probably have been graphic enough to distract me. Even as it was, I nearly got hooked on the fine thread of admiration weaving through.

But we had things to do, places to be. I leaned into his shoulder the way Hail did with me when I needed support.

'We're in Leah's dream,' I said, firmly. 'Do you want to meet her, or do we go tell the Lion you chickened out?'

'I don't know what to say.'

'You could start with what you just said to me about Kirsten and love and then actually listen to what she actually says when she's heard you. The rest will be whatever both of you make it. Come on.' I turned and pushed into the labyrinth. Wild roses swayed back on either side, letting me through.

Three strides in, when I thought I'd screwed up and lost him, I heard Niall follow behind.

The centre of the labyrinth was as wild as ever. Leah was not there. Endeavouring not to panic, I led Niall through what was now a plain wrought-iron gate in the south-westerly corner, and down a spiral path.

'This is different,' he said. 'It feels more like you.'

'It was mine once.' Not anymore, though: now it was wild, almost alien. The river was wider, running white, so you could kayak down it and feel lucky to be alive when you reached the end.

Willow and alder grew thick along the bank. A hammock was slung between two trunks, woven through with lion hair and strewn with rose petals. The scent coming from it should have been cadaverous, but was more earthen, as if the whole great, living globe of the earth had come alive and reached out to this place and found it good.

Leah was not here.

We found her a dozen paces on, round a bend in the river, sitting cross-legged beneath a broad-trunked hazel, dressed in shorts and a T-shirt in wildly shifting colours that spoke of deserts and stars and power. She was not alone.

Knee to knee and hand to hand, Donella Lloyd sat opposite dressed in . . . very little. Fine tattoos spiralled over every part of her body. Fire attended her, too: a crisp scent of burning iron and the crackle of flames on the edge of vision.

'Nye!' Leah stood, patently delighted. 'We were waiting for you.' She spread a hand out and the riverbank grew a carpet of rose petals and lion fur. Donella spread over it fire that did not burn. Her smile was no less broad, no less fierce, no less real.

I felt Niall falter, and then gather himself. He took half a step forward. 'I don't know where we're at,' he said. 'Any of us.'

Niall, Niall. Logic is going to drown you one of these days.

Not my place to say so, though. Leah said, 'I don't either, but I want to find out.'

And from her side, Donella said, 'I can go if you want.'

'No,' Leah said.

And Niall, more fiercely, 'No!'

I became a crow, and barely there. In the distance, a hound howled once, with a sharpness that called my name. I backed away slowly, trying not to shock any of them into wakefulness. I thought of the loch. Hail howled again, more urgently. I left.

I was between Leah's dream and the loch, fading to nothing in the first, becoming more established in the second, when a hand fastened on my shoulder and hauled me round.

'Bēi Fēng!' If I had ever thought her benign . . . she was furious. The realities around me, Leah's river and my loch, began to lose coherence. I was all here, too: whether I liked it or not, there was no hope of shredding parts of myself and sending them away to safety.

Sharply, the North Wind said, *Finn needs you.*

Finn. I remembered the swirl of panic as he'd read the text in the loft. 'You want me to go into the Between and see if Sigi Kostinen is there?' It made a kind of sense.

Bēi Fēng sighed. Somewhere in the living world a hurricane spun across the land, and died away. *Sigi was found hours ago. She'd gone caving.*

'Caving?'

The Wind spelled it out. *Sigi Kostinen is alive. Uninjured. Safe.*

'Then why . . .?'

Just come!

Finn was at his desk in the Piggery. His laptop told me it was two forty-five in the afternoon of Friday, 23 June, a little under three hours since he'd tucked Niall, Leah and Donella into the space-pods, telling them lies about coming back for Sigi Kostinen. Finn was not a habitual liar.

The rest of the Piggery was empty. Even Brilliant wasn't around. Newly, there were fish in the aquarium: a living kaleidoscope of neon blue life.

I was pulled towards them, but not. I couldn't move. Bēi Fēng held my shoulder in a punishing grip and the pair of us were wrapped in a cocoon of wind that was ours alone: nothing in the room moved.

I said, 'Finn.'

He was busy, fingers skittering across the keyboard, attention skittering across dozens of open GhostTalk threads.

'FINN.'

He lifted his head and looked directly at the corner of the room where the wind held me trapped. He looked like the living dead. He looked, in fact, like he'd done on the day of the shooting. This wasn't just the exhaustion of a night with no sleep. I didn't know what it was. 'Lan.'

He pushed his chair from his desk and came closer. Bēi Fēng did not release her grip on my shoulder so I couldn't shift to crow form, but I shrank as far away as I could.

My terror must have filtered out, because Finn stopped in the middle of the room. 'Lan, I'm not going to banish you.'

The words were right. The tone was not. I shrank back further. Aloud, I said, 'Bēi Fēng, tell him Sigi's been found.'

Finn frowned. A breath of air rattled the trees outside. His brow cleared. 'Sigi? Yes. She's fine. Caver-girl. Hates social media and holes in the ground have no signal, so they're a good place to be if you realise you've done something unutterably stupid and want to go off-radar. Quite clever, really.' A note of admiration flared and died. 'It's not that. It's Connor. Nobody's seen him since lunchtime yesterday.'

'*What?*'

He felt that, alright. Ugly-sharp, he said, 'Yesterday was busy. You might have noticed. Nobody thought to look for him until the new batch of fish for the tank arrived halfway through this morning and Hawck realised Brilliant wasn't here to see the great release and then everyone went looking for Connor and . . . He's gone, Lan. We can't find him.'

He drove back knowing this? We're lucky he didn't pile the car into a bollard. Not my problem. Finding Connor is my problem.

'Where have you looked? FINN! Where. Have. You. Looked? Oh, for fuck's sake.' I spun, fast. 'Bēi Fēng, if you're going to hold me here like a fucking prison guard, the least you can do is help us communicate.'

I heard no more breeze, but Finn was still again, and then, 'We need you to tell us if he's dead.' And for clarity, 'Bēi Fēng says you'll know.'

'How does she think—? Fuck. Yes, of course.' I had been right that they wanted me to look in the Between, only wrong about who I was looking for. 'Let me check.' I writhed free of Bēi Fēng's grip, and found myself still caught behind the wall of wind she'd built around us. I slammed my palms against it, uselessly. 'I need to go to the Between. I can't tell from here.'

'But you'll come back,' Finn said. Bluntly, not a question.

'I can shout the answer into the wind.'

Exasperated: 'Lan, for heaven's sake, if I wanted you gone – really gone – I'd have done it long ago. It's not like I didn't know you were still around.' With unpleasant crispness, Finn planted himself, legs wide, arms folded, right in front of the corner in which I was trapped.

'Lan . . .' His face was a hand's breadth from mine. I could feel the heat of his body, smell his sweat and the desperation that prickled through it. Distinctly, all the syllables clipped, he said, 'I'm sorry. I was angry. Threatening you was a mistake. I should have said so ages ago. I'm really sorry. Please, we need your help to find Connor. Bēi Fēng says you're the only one who can.'

Even in the days when his mother had stood behind him with a face like thunder, he'd pulled off the 'I'm being made to apologise' less woodenly than this.

Nonetheless, Bēi Fēng must have thought it was fine. She let me go, and it felt as if someone had snapped a bear trap off my leg.

I fled. At the edges of the shift, I paused. 'I'll come back as soon as I know what's happening,' I said. It was a promise as binding as any I'd made. Finn may not have heard the words, but we both felt them land.

Far away, Hail howled for the third time.

Hail was waiting for me at the edge of the loch, aquiver with urgency.

Where is he? Here, now, I was a Crow and speaking only with my mind.

Follow.

I had never run with Hail before. I had never run like this with anyone; fast, fast, fast as if the Wild Hunt itself was after us. Or we were the wild ones, and we were hunting.

We were the wind, slick and silent and faster than sound, passing through and around and over things that had seemed like obstacles

490

before: the loch was far behind us, and the shoreline; after them followed a cold wilderness, an Irish bog, a city, blinking too many lights too fast; all of it blurred.

I recognised the scents of the stopping place before we fell still: wood and water and a particular balance of gorse and blackthorn that said we were back in the lands of the living. 'He's up at Five Acre Deep?'

He was. We flew-ran a hundred paces on and Hail slid to a halt, and stood on point, foreleg raised. Ahead of him, Connor's big, strong form lay by the water's edge, one arm submerged, his face planted in leaf mould and mud.

'*Connor!*' Hail sank down with me as I fell to my knees at his side.

'Hello, Lan.'

I lurched round to my left. Connor-in-spirit was sitting a dozen paces away with his back to one of the old black poplars that fringed the water, its trunk as thick as his waist. His legs were drawn up to his chest. Both of them. Whole.

Out loud, I asked, 'Are you dead?' Inside, I thought, *Finn will kill me.*

'Not quite yet. If I were, I'd be moving on already.'

Moving into another life with no gap to rest in between, and all because of a promise made unwitting to a god.

Turning back to his body, I tried to pull him over and couldn't, but I could feel his heat, see his chest still moving, just. 'You're still breathing.' I stood up. 'I'll get Finn.'

'Good idea.'

That big, broad grin: I knew it so well. 'Connor McBride, did you set this up?'

'Me?' Positively angelic.

I scowled. 'You and the North Wind? That's scandalous. We don't need—'

'Not you, maybe, but Finn needs something to get over his pride.' He looped his hands behind his head and lounged back, daring me to argue. When I didn't, he said, 'You don't have to leave me. Just send part of yourself to get him.'

'Part of . . .?' Oh. Right.

491

I was human and then crow and then human again. 'I'm safer being a crow in his company, right?'

Connor snorted, hard. 'You need to mend this, both of you. I'm not wasting a perfectly good death with you two playing silly beggars. You love each other. It's OK to say so. And you're older, which means wiser. Give the lad a break.' He smiled again, but there was pain in it, and grief.

'Oh, Connor. I hate this.'

'You get used to it. No, actually, you don't. I hate it too, but it's the way things are.'

'I'm here, at least. Thank you for calling me.' I had no doubt that he had done. 'Let's make the most of what's left.' I kissed him lightly on the crown of his head and sat down at his side. He slipped his hand into mine and laced our fingers and we both watched the crow part of me (which still felt safer) head off back to the lands of life to be wise in Finn's company.

Finn ran so fast he didn't have time to send texts on the way, though he'd flung out a voice memo to Niall before he left and a part of me caught the subtle vibrations in the sleeping pods of the Caterwaul Loft that nudged Niall and the others awake. New threads looped between the three of them, stronger than before.

Just as I had done, Finn fell to his knees by Connor's body. He phoned for help, noted the time and moved into CPR with a speed that spoke of hours of training. I stayed where I was with my back to the tree, alongside Connor-in-spirit.

By luck, instinct or the intercession of Bēi Fēng, Finn looked over at us. At me. 'Thank you. I'm sorry I didn't call you sooner.' He sounded like he meant it.

'I'm sorry I wasn't more use when the girls died.'

Now, when it mattered, Bēi Fēng's translation was seamless. Finn shook his head. 'You were with me. I'd called you. If you'd been there, maybe you could have—'

'Finn, no . . .' I left Connor then, or a bit of me did. 'Finn, I *was* there. I tried everything I could think of but I don't have any traction in the land of the living. You know I can't even pick up a pen. I certainly couldn't stop a bullet. I'm so sorry.'

'Not my fault?' A shadow lifted that I hadn't seen he carried.

'Definitely not.' A thought. 'Bēi Fēng could have told you.'

'I thought she was being kind. And I was too angry to listen. I'm sorry. I'm really, really sorry.' He fell apart then, almost as Niall had done when Connor had brought Brilliant, but more contained. 'I can't lose you both.'

'You won't. You can't lose me when I'm already dead. Finn . . .' Hell, but it felt good to be nearby. I wanted to hug him. I tried: a triumph of hope over experience. My arms made no contact. '*Fuck this. Just once, I want to—*'

At the poplar, Connor stood. 'You're doing good, Lan. I'm proud of you.'

My heart crashed to my feet. 'You're going?'

'You don't need me anymore.'

He was moving, fast; him and Hail. I clung to the slipstream. 'You can't just *go*.'

On the floor of the clearing, Finn screamed his name.

Can't stop, Lan. Tell Finn he did his best.

'You can stop if you want to, Connor McBride! You're like me. Just think yourself into the Between. Think of the Loch, and the waterfall and the moorhens. You can at least slow down a bit, surely?'

I focused all my will on the loch, every part of honed intent Crow had taught me all that time ago, when I was new and raw and naïve.

The loch became real, the trees, the waterfall. A moorhen made a V across the water.

We slowed. Both of us. Connor was with me, young, oak-haired, vibrant; a joy to see.

See? Not that hard.

I'm impressed. Connor reached out a hand to my hawthorn tree and steadied himself. *We truly can't stay long.*

'You're taking Hail with you?' Another hole in my heart.

Connor looked down. Hail looked up. They both looked at me. Connor said, *I'm sorry. We have to.* He reached his other hand to pat my shoulder, then drew me into a fierce embrace. Pushing me back, he held me at arm's length. *You're not trapped, you know. Not in the way I am.*

493

'I am, though. Kate was clear. I can't go on.'

But you did see Crow leave. His gaze was tight on mine.

'What difference does that make?'

Time and space are what we make of them. You know this. He thought a moment. *Can you be a crow for me?*

I did. He held out his arm and I stepped onto his wrist. He walked us to the edge of the loch. The water was glass. Our reflections were as vivid as anything in life. Connor was his youthful self. I was . . . Crow. I'd never looked at my own reflection. I was exactly the Crow who had kept me safe, taught me to navigate the void, taught me everything.

Oh, hell. Oh, bloody, bloody, totally exsanguinated hell. So many pieces fell into place. 'Connor, I am such an idiot.'

Hardly. It's a lot to get your head round. Time and space, Lan. Time and space. You can split yourself across all of them now. You have that skill. Connor thrust his fist up, launching me high in the air. *I can't stay. Go well. Remember each time round is new, Lan. Nothing is predictable, but there will always be help when you need it. Trust, and you'll be fine.*

He began to blur. I could fly fast, but not that fast. 'At least tell me where you're going? Who you'll be next? Will you be in the family? Tell me a continent at least? A language group? Anything!'

He paused, half a shape of shadow and memory. *I can't tell you that. I'll try to send Hail back to you, see if he can help you find me. We'll need each other, I think.* He raised a hand. *Fare thee well, Crow-Lan. You are wiser than you think.*

EPILOGUE

Nine days later

Alanna.

I don't recognise this voice. It's been a while – a long, long while – since anyone called me by my full name.

I am in fragments, not all of them broken. I sense through the disparate parts of myself, seeking which one has heard this.

Not the part with Finn. He is at Conwy on the Welsh coast which has, apparently, a nicer harbour than Liverpool, certainly quieter and there are no press photographers (yet) waiting to greet the *Ocean Ghost* when she makes landfall in about an hour.

Finn's videoing the shaded swell of the Irish Sea, where a speck in the distance might conceivably be a tall-masted catamaran.

On the boat, Raye Kameransky is similarly taking videos of the sea off the port bow where a darkening of the horizon might conceivably be the north Welsh coast. They are sharing their near-identical videos of grey sky and greyer sea, sharing too ideas of what they'll do when Raye gets to the farm. They are coming to the farm, though for how long remains an open question: certainly till after Connor's funeral, which will take place next Saturday. Matt and Jens and Gus are putting the pavilion up again.

Finn feels me near and he looks around for any sight of a crow. I haven't taken physical form. I could probably borrow a kittiwake for a while, and remember what it is to breathe and feed, but it's a seductive thing, breathing, and I'm not sure I want to get to like it too much.

Finn's presence though, the touch of his awareness, the nights dreaming in the Shaolin training grounds . . . these are an addiction I could cheerfully indulge in for a very long time.

He's still sad about Connor, obviously, and the greater underlying grief for lives ended before their time is not gone, either; I don't think it ever will. But he is meditating again, teaching again, laughing again, and when Raye comes I think he will know now how to take pleasure in the first brush of a half-known hand, first embrace, first dry-lipped and fleeting kiss. Raye's going to be good for him. I hope.

Neither of them just called my full name, though.

Niall, maybe?

He's at the farm, deep in strategy meetings with Dell. Leah sleeps here when she can, and when she's here . . . Brilliant is more jealous of sharing Niall than anyone expected, but the easy fix for cat-jealousy is a trip to the Piggery to watch murmurations of tetras in the aquarium.

In between, they are sorting out the logistics of the People's Parliament and the Boomers' Last Gasp and how both can be turned towards something useful. They want to work in tandem, not at odds, but the devil is in the detail and there are many, many, many moving parts. Too many for one person to hold, or even three.

Specs is helping. He has moved in to Caterwaul Loft which is proving not to be as weird as you might imagine. As predicted, the outgoing PM blocked the CIC from setting up a coalition on the grounds that they were not a real party, but the Scottish National Party were there as the next biggest party after the Government and Opposition both failed to form a government and there was no blocking them.

So now the four nations of the UK are in discussion about the way forward. Leah has the numbers, the rest have the power and, frankly, the experience. They all want the same thing, but none of them would accept a parachute in a burning plane from any of the others if they thought there might be a price attached, so it's teeth-achingly slow.

I don't know how Leah bears it, but she'll become Lady Leah Koresh of Blackthorn Rise if they can all just get onto the same page for long enough to make something happen. Which they will do. They have to; nobody wants to call another election before they've recovered from this one.

There are fragments of me at the Dairy, milking the cows with

Gus and watching Matt train a young collie and a final part sits near Connor's freshly dug grave in the heart of the Rookery, waiting for a sense of who he might be next and how I might find him.

I miss him more than I would have thought possible and it's driving me crazy to think he's going to be born soon – maybe already has been – and I can't find him.

Alanna!

'*Yes!*' The final fragment of my being is in the Between. It's been a lonely place since Hail left. I don't put my attention here often.

I do so now, landing in the hawthorn tree.

'You.'

Bēi Fēng is as I first saw her, a small, heroically ancient woman sitting with her back to a fruit tree that was not here before. I am not entirely comfortable with this.

'I didn't know you could visit uninvited.'

She tilts her head. *You could dispel me.*

Because dispelling a god would be a really clever thing to do. 'Why are you here?'

Listen. She stands, cocking her head to the north-west, where the waterfall plunges, long and white, from almost-sky to almost-sea.

If I bring all my attention to this, I can hear the roar of water, the whistle of a red kite far in the distance, the creak of the old hawthorn . . . and then, faintly, the high, silver note of a cry.

'Is that a *child*?' I am a-shiver with hope.

Bēi Fēng shrugs, helpfully unhelpful. *It's behind the waterfall.*

She is the wind. I am the Crow, and we are each as fast as the other.

Crossing the distance together, we land on the outcrop of waterworn granite on the edge of the cliff. A curtain of water thunders down, drenching us in fine spray. The ledge leads in towards a mirror of the cave where I found Connor after the shootings.

The cry comes again, more strongly. My heart is a salmon, leaping.

Without waiting for the wind, I walk in behind the water, and I am human, I am Lan, and here is a big, sandy-floored cavern, with a gap in the roof letting in green-tinged light from the bracken fronds high, high above.

And here, where the pale green wash of sun meets the rainbowed light from the tumbling water is—

'Hail! Oh, Hail . . .' It's not Connor, but this is good. It's *good*. It's so very good.

I fall to my knees on the sanded stone, then lie flat, my chin cushioned on my fists. The pup is eight weeks old or thereabouts, enough to be away from his mother, just. He is brindle, in the way of pups, where the colours are a blur of dark within gold, not yet defined. He has a white flash between his eyes and his left foreleg is white to the carpus, as if he's stepped in cream and not yet lapped it off.

'Hail?' At the sound of my voice, he pushes himself up on unsteady legs and waddles over to press his nose to mine. I crook a knuckle under his chin, and when he presses into it, I run my whole hand along his back. He nips my nose and gives a high snip of a bark and leaps up to curl against my arm.

Dizzy with delight, I sit there for a long time before a puff of wind lifts the sand around my knees in drifting spirals. I stand, holding the pup in the crook of my arm.

'Thank you.' Mere words are not enough. Nose to knees, I bow to the god of the North Wind, who, for the first time in my knowing of her, smiles back.

You are most welcome, Crow-woman. A stiffer breeze tugs at the curtain of water, and she is gone.

Hail grows as I carry him down from the high cave.

By the time I reach the hawthorn, his head is level with my hip bone. He has a fair bit of growing yet to do, but he seems to pause here.

'Does this mean Connor's been born already?' I ask.

He rolls over, tongue lolling, waiting for me to scratch his sternum. *He has.* Turning upright, he grows serious. *The early years are never easy. He has the body and the mind of a child, and the memories of many, many lifetimes. It can be hard for him to make sense of it all.*

'I can help.'

Lan, my friend. Always kind. It is good to be back. He laughs again. He laughs more than the old Hail did, and I wonder at the way he is different-the-same even as I bask in the coppery glow of his humour. I scratch behind his ears. He writhes happily for a while, then gets up and throws himself down again on my lap, pressing me onto the rock.

He is serious again. His big eyes meet mine. *Do you not have other things to do, Lan? Another place to be? A part of you, obviously, not all.*

Ah. Yes. That. Connor's last command, even if he did wrap it up as a suggestion.

I wait a while.

I wait a long while, taking time to check on the parts of me that are with the rest of the family. It's evening in the lands of life. Raye has landed, Leah is back up from London, Hawck is sharing a quiet dinner with Charm. Nothing has changed: everything has changed. It depends how you look at it. And I am not leaving them. I tell myself this. Only one part of me is shifting through space and time and I will, at least for a while, know all that it knows.

Connor's words roll like tidal waves in my mind. *Nothing is predictable. Each time round is new.* It terrified me when he said it and it terrifies me now. I remember another voice, a long, long time ago. *I would like for you to have at least a semblance of choice.*

I have had choices. I am content with those I have made. And this one, too, I make freely. I want that made clear.

When I come back to the Between, Hail is lying on my feet, tongue a-lol, as if I've been gone less than the course of a breath. As if he has never been gone at all.

I say, 'I should go.'

He nods. *I will be your anchor. If you'll let me?*

I need an anchor for this? I suppose I do. 'Thank you.'

In human form, I press my back against the trunk of the hawthorn, keep my gaze on the dazzle of the loch. A part of me becomes a crow, and that crow, launching up, flies in looping spirals, always with the sun at the centre.

Time is what we make of it and I have learned to spin the thread back and forth. Crow taught me this. I just didn't know what I was learning. Relearning.

I circle back to when Connor was alive, and beyond.

I circle back to when Maddie, Kirsten and Kaitlyn were alive, and beyond.

I circle back to when I was alive, and a little bit beyond.

I circle back to a late February afternoon, the light grey-silver rain sluicing the windows of an old stone building with brick and concrete added on in ugly lumps. In one of these, a window faces west, towards a setting sun that is itself hidden behind a ramp of clouds.

I circle one last time and land high in an ash tree. None of its branches grow near the right window, but it is not hard to shape one in that does. Presently, I slip-slide down to a branch of perfect diameter that stretches parallel to the glass.

I edge closer to the trunk of the tree and settle in to wait. Nine nights and nine days. Thrice three, the number of Bridge, and nine, the number of Odin. I am patience embodied.

And then a young boy with a breaking heart leans over the white sheets to tap on the arm of his grandmother.

'When you come home,' he says, 'can we—'

AUTHOR'S NOTE

This novel arose out of my own dreaming. I've blogged about the process in more depth,[1] but in essence the narrative arc arose after a week of sitting out on the hill at dusk, watching the crows go to bed.

This gave the opening scene and the central premise, plus a sense of Lan's character. More, it also brought the visceral understanding that Ursula K. Le Guin is right (of course; always), and Amitav Ghosh,[2] and Rob Hopkins.[3]

To paraphrase all three: we live in a disimagination machine designed to persuade us there is no alternative to a system that commodifies grief, destruction and death. Those in power are not going to craft a way out, and to be fair we shouldn't expect them to: they wouldn't *be* in power if they wanted to, or knew how. These are the modern equivalent of the mediaeval monarchs who claimed divine right to project their insecurities onto the outer world and make life hell for whoever got in the way.

Dieu et mon droit: it wasn't true then any more than it is now, but the change came when enough of us stopped believing.

Any human power can by human agency be changed.

All it takes is enough of us to stop believing in the old order. I don't know how many is 'enough', but in a world where tipping points are galloping past like so many runaway horses, this is one I would like to see coming, and what is clear from all those whose inspiration fed my week on the hill is that the time for writing stories of the past, or even iterations of the present, is over.

Now is the time when we who weave ideas into words, possibilities

---

[1] https://mandascott.co.uk/mandas-new-novel/

[2] *The Great Derangement* by Amitav Ghosh (University of Chicago Press, 2016)

[3] *From What Is to What If* by Rob Hopkins (Chelsea Green Publishing, 2019)

into stories, ideas into future actions, must urgently map out routes from where we are towards a future we'd be proud to leave behind.

This book is such a route map. The first vision of its need and shape arose at the summer solstice of 2021 and I am writing this last note within touching distance of the winter solstice, 2023.

The world has changed since I wrote the first lines. The aforementioned biophysical, democratic, geopolitical, technological and cultural tipping points are hurtling past faster than I'd ever imagined.

And yet there are also more people working at the emergent edges of possibility than I had ever dared hope for: more people learning what it is to build communities of place, purpose and passion predicated on the values of being and belonging, more acts of radical courage at the edge of what Indy Johar has called 'Inter-Becoming'[4] where we can't yet see the new system, but are an integral part of its emergence.

This is what gives me hope and, because it matters that these ideas are explored as widely as possible, and that you, too, can map out routes to a future you would be proud to bequeath to the generations yet unborn, I'll keep an updated list of references on the website[5] for as long as seems useful.

As far as the structure of *Any Human Power* is concerned, the key tweet (it was still Twitter when I wrote the scenes in question) is an almost-verbatim replica of one posted in the summer of 2021 by the then twelve-year-old daughter of someone squarely in the public eye.

It caused a certain amount of consternation and was swiftly deleted. I was shocked by the content, but nonetheless awed by the young woman's courage and entirely unimpressed by the actions of those who silenced her. And I wondered how things might have been different if her family had offered their wholehearted support.

One of the great privileges of a novelist's life is the ability to ask

[4] https://accidentalgods.life/becoming-intentional-gods-claiming-the-future-with-indy-johar-of-the-dark-matter-labs/

[5] https://mandascott.co.uk/any-human-power-resources/

'What if . . .?' and then explore and share the answers. I would like to believe the world would have risen and the establishment would have stepped back with more grace and less violence than depicted here, but that would have made for quite a different story.

On a broader scale, everything I have written – the dreaming, the social technologies, the potential for change – is based on my understanding of how our reality functions. I am aware this is not everyone's view, but the parts that are verifiable within consensus reality are (mostly[6]) already in practice: the Flatpack Democracy[7] model that arose in Frome, for instance, is now gaining far wider traction; agroecology[8] is one key route forward to feeding ourselves with nutrient-dense food that isn't actually poisoning us;[9] a quadratic voting app[10] has been built and is in use for local decision-making and could easily be scaled up; a national government has already been 'forked' with good effect.[11]

In the area of business, Riversimple Movement Ltd[12] is blazing trails with their concept of the Future Guardian™ model of governance,[13] which seems to me to be a genuine game changer. Imagine a world where every single worker knew that they had the right to nominate one person to a six (or in our case, seven) member board which defined the company's trajectory: with the right of recall if that individual is not representing them fairly. I'd imagine in any case it would be a rolling position, held for a few months

---

[6] For those who want to take things apart, I did pull together the design of the *Ocean Ghost* from a number of other sources, though I can't see why it wouldn't work. Finn's app might take rather longer to code than I allowed, but it, too, is possible in theory.

[7] https://citizen-network.org/news/the-launch-of-flatpack-democracy-2021

[8] https://www.agroecology-europe.org/the-13-principles-of-agroecology/

[9] https://www.theguardian.com/commentisfree/2023/nov/18/cocktail-toxins-poisoning-fields-humans-sewage-sludge-fighting-dirty

[10] https://accidentalgods.life/cultures-of-commoning/, https://www.furtherfield.org/culturestake-2/

[11] https://www.wired.co.uk/article/taiwan-sunflower-revolution-audrey-tang-g0v, https://80000hours.org/podcast/episodes/audrey-tang-what-we-can-learn-from-taiwan/, https://www.brookings.edu/articles/taiwans-unlikely-path-to-public-trust-provides-lessons-for-the-us

[12] https://www.riversimple.com/

[13] https://www.riversimple.com/governance/

and passed on. Elsewhere in business, the B Corps[14] and companies committed to the Economy for the Common Good[15] are making changes to outlook and practice. Dark Matter Labs[16] are pushing the frontier of practice with their Net Zero Cities[17] and Life Ennobling Economics.[18]

In the areas of social technologies, Sophy Banks hosts the amazing 'Healthy Human Culture' course online where she teaches the skill of crafting micro-returns in the healing/prevention of trauma[19] the Doughnut Economics Action Lab[20] is spreading networks across the world establishing routes to an economy predicated on the needs of the living planet; Trust the People run free online courses[21] to educate and encourage local activism; Parents for Future[22] are exploring ways for people to hold the difficult conversations with those we encounter in our daily lives, and, of course, the Climate Majority Project[23] co-founded by Rupert Read, progenitor of the concept of Thrutopian[24] writing, continues to grow and thrive.

The list is growing so fast that I could update it daily and this book would never make it to print – which is the point. *Nothing here is new or particularly radical*, all I have done is weave together threads of other people's endeavours to craft a tapestry of possibility. You would take the same threads and weave something different. Please do: we are all creators. We all step into the futures we have imagined for ourselves. The system isn't working. We all know this. If we want something that feels good – if *you* want it – then we can work together to craft the routes forward. We can be better than this. And we start now. Today. Tomorrow is too late.

14 https://bcorporation.uk/b-corp-certification/what-is-a-b-corp/

15 https://www.ecogood.org/

16 https://darkmatterlabs.org/

17 https://darkmatterlabs.org/7GenCities

18 https://drive.google.com/file/d/1EiU8MQ3JKtuCJIUTrxkl2Fzx0xWBiWDu/view

19 https://healthyhumanculture.com/

20 https://doughnuteconomics.org/

21 https://www.trustthepeople.earth/

22 https://parentsforfuture.org.uk/

23 https://climatemajorityproject.com/

24 https://www.huffingtonpost.co.uk/rupert-read/thrutopia-why-neither-dys_b_18372090.html

ACKNOWLEDGEMENTS

It takes a village to craft a book and this is the place where I have a chance to celebrate the astonishing grace, creativity, compassion, patience and good humour brought by our village to this endeavour.

Boundless gratitude is due to many, many people, but in particular:

Robert Caskie, my fabulous agent, held the space for a new novel to grow with good humour and great patience – thank you

Hannah MacDonald is, quite literally, the publisher and editor of my dreams. I had given up hope that there existed someone with the insight, stamina, patience, grace and enthusiasm to engage with a manuscript at all its many levels. I am ever in awe of the process, but this felt more than usually magical – thank you

Helen Bleck stepped into the later drafts with a grasp of language and the nuances of plot that made my heart sing, and Clare Hubbard brought clarity and sense to the later proofs – thank you both

Alexandra Allden designed the cover I had dreamed but not been able to articulate. I am beyond grateful – thank you

Charlotte Cole directed editing, kept all the copy in line and combed out my Word-related tangles – thank you

Amie Jones, Tabitha Pelly and Katy Loftus have all polished the ideas to bring them shiny and bright to the wider world with panache and clear intent and – again – the depth of attention every author dreams of – thank you

Lou Mayor, dreaming apprentice, teacher and friend, holds the dreaming with grace and wisdom and infinite patience – and read the many drafts – thank you

Hannah Schafer also read more drafts than any bar the author ever should, and offered insight into Shaolin Kung Fu, peaceful activism and politics – thank you

Grace Rachmany offered detailed, thoughtful and thought-provoking commentary on many of the technical aspects of economics, cryptocurrencies, citizens' assemblies and more – thank you

Rose, heroic Disc Priest and outstanding battleground leader, checked my WoW facts – thank you

Gill Coombs, Amy Weatherup and Roz Savage all read and offered encouraging and insightful comments on drafts along the way – thank you

Too many to name are the dreamers who have shared our circles through the years, but you know who you are and I'm grateful to you all for sharing the journey, the learning and the ever-deepening spirals of our dreaming.

In a similar vein, I am beyond grateful to the guests and listeners of the *Accidental Gods* podcast for their generosity of spirit and endless willingness to engage at the emergent edge of a different future.

Thanks also to those who have and are engaging with the Thrutopia Masterclass[25] and the Thrutopian Writers' Association that is arising therefrom.

And first, last and everywhere in between, my love and deep, deep gratitude to Faith, who shares the journey strong-hearted, open-hearted, clear-hearted and full-hearted. My love, you brighten my days and my dreams, thank you.

---

[25] https://thrutopia.life